W9-AMZ-692

NIGHT ANGEL NEMESIS

By Brent Weeks

THE KA'KARI CODEX

THE NIGHT ANGEL TRILOGY
The Way of Shadows

Shadow's Edge

Beyond the Shadows

Perfect Shadow (novella)

THE KYLAR CHRONICLES
Night Angel Nemesis

OTHER SERIES BY BRENT WEEKS

LIGHTBRINGER
The Black Prism

The Blinding Knife

The Broken Eye

The Blood Mirror

The Burning White

BRENT WEEKS

NIGHT ANGEL NEMESIS

The Kylar Chronicles: Book One

DELRAY BEACH PUBLIC LIBRARY
100 WEST ATLANTIC AVENUE
DELRAY BEACH, FL 33444
561-266-0194

orbit

orbitbooks.net

This book is a work of fiction. Names, characters, places, and incidents are the product of the author's imagination or are used fictitiously. Any resemblance to actual events, locales, or persons, living or dead, is coincidental.

Copyright © 2023 by Brent Weeks

Cover design by Unusual Co.
Cover copyright © 2023 by Hachette Book Group, Inc.
Maps by Tim Paul

Hachette Book Group supports the right to free expression and the value of copyright. The purpose of copyright is to encourage writers and artists to produce the creative works that enrich our culture.

The scanning, uploading, and distribution of this book without permission is a theft of the author's intellectual property. If you would like permission to use material from the book (other than for review purposes), please contact permissions@hbgusa.com. Thank you for your support of the author's rights.

Orbit
Hachette Book Group
1290 Avenue of the Americas
New York, NY 10104
orbitbooks.net

First Edition: April 2023
Simultaneously published in Great Britain by Orbit

Orbit is an imprint of Hachette Book Group.
The Orbit name and logo are trademarks of Little, Brown Book Group Limited.

The publisher is not responsible for websites (or their content) that are not owned by the publisher.

The Hachette Speakers Bureau provides a wide range of authors for speaking events. To find out more, go to hachettespeakersbureau.com or email HachetteSpeakers@hbgusa.com.

Orbit books may be purchased in bulk for business, educational, or promotional use. For information, please contact your local bookseller or the Hachette Book Group Special Markets Department at special.markets@hbgusa.com.

Library of Congress Cataloging-in-Publication Data
Names: Weeks, Brent, author.
Title: Night angel nemesis / Brent Weeks.
Description: First Edition. | New York, NY : Orbit, 2023. |
    Series: The Kylar Chronicles ; book 1
Identifiers: LCCN 2022057396 | ISBN 9780316554909 (hardcover) |
    ISBN 9780316554916 (ebook)
Classification: LCC PS3623.E4223 N54 2023 | DDC 813/.6—dc23/eng/20221202
LC record available at https://lccn.loc.gov/2022057396

ISBNs: 9780316554909 (hardcover), 9780316554916 (ebook), 9780316566728 (signed edition), 9780316566735 (BarnesAndNoble.com signed edition)

Printed in the United States of America

LSC-C

Printing 1, 2023

For those who answered the call—and still pay the price.

&

For Kristi, who surprises me still with her grit and grace.

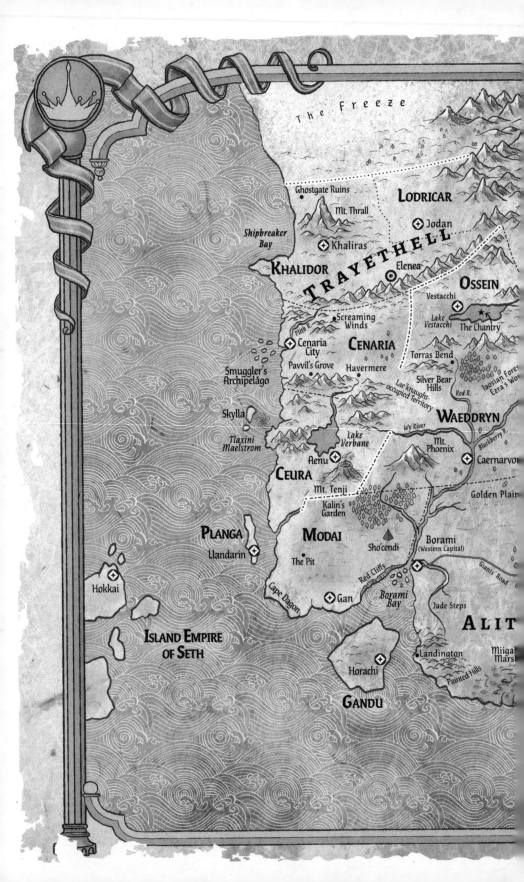

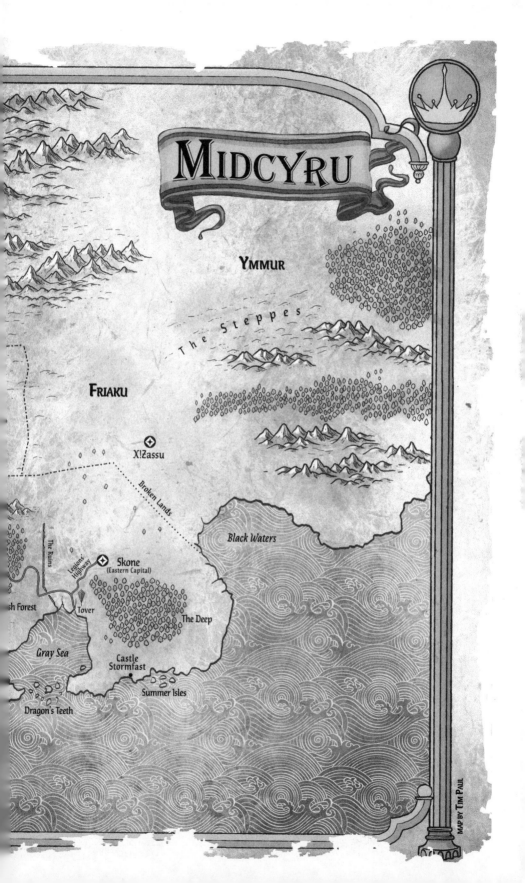

NIGHT ANGEL NEMESIS

Chapter One

An Innocent Kill

$\mathcal{H}$e's young and likely innocent and I wish it made a difference. If he doesn't move in the next three minutes, this kid has to die.

Most people don't understand my work: They think murder is the hard part.

In the beginning, maybe—when you're fourteen years old, hiding under a bed, breath loud, knuckles white on the steel, eyes hot with tomorrow's tears, footsteps approaching.

But even then the hard part wasn't the destined dead; the hard part was the living. They never follow the plan. The living always crowd forward, treading on the heels of those fated to die, as if when *they* meet Death, they'll nod a greeting and pass on by.

My first time, it was a castle maid, coming to check on her worthless lover I'd been sent to kill. He was leaving her; instead she joined him in eternity. My first murder of an innocent.

Now it's this kid.

What's a kid doing out playing ball at this hour? Why's he got to be *here*?

From my perch I feel as if he's a thousand paces away, tiny across the chasm of experience, and I alone atop a cliff—though he's merely on the ground, and I on a rooftop across the alley.

He has a few rocks set out to show the width of the goal. As I watch, he spins around an imaginary defender, bounces the ball once, then kicks it against the compound's wall.

ka-tunk, ka-tunk, ker-chunk

Over and over. He puts his hands up and makes a sound like a crowd roaring its approval. Young kid, twelve maybe, all stupidity and big dreams. Maybe he thinks he's found his one way out of these slums.

~Remind you of anyone?~

I ignore the ka'kari speaking in my head. If it weren't so helpful when it wants to be, I'd throw the damned thing as far away from me as I could.

Twilight is a burning fuse, and soon the sun will explode merciless on the horizon, revealing all I've done or left undone. But still I wait, hoping I'll find some third way.

ka-tunk, ka-tunk, ker-chunk

He's just a kid.

But he's *not* giving up his practicing.

Knowing what it may mean, am I really going to do this?

Yes, yes I am. She's worth it. They deserve justice.

All right, that's it. Morning's coming. Time's up for both of us.

I move, dropping silently from the roof into the deeper shadows of the alley.

ka-tunk, ka-tunk, ker-

Streaking in from nowhere, I snag the ball out of the air. Left-handed, no less. Maybe I missed my calling. I could've been a streetball great.

The kid's jaw drops and his eyes go ridiculously wide at the sight of me. It's a bit satisfying, in that I-feel-proud-that-I-can-scare-children sort of way. Is this one of those dark pleasures of power Count Drake tried to warn me about? I haven't dressed to impress. Tonight—this morning technically—I'm in my mottled black-and-grays with a hood and face mask, an unstrung bow tucked away and a black short sword in a tension-release back scabbard.

~There's something interesting about the ball.~

I look at it. It's leather over a goat-belly air bladder, stitched into nearly a perfect sphere. Kids in this neighborhood usually make do with a wad of rags and twine.

"I'm gonna ask you a favor, kid," I growl. "My business isn't with you. So I'm asking you to leave. Quietly. Please. You understand? There's a man out tonight who'd kill a child."

I pause long enough for him to wonder whether I mean myself or the dirtbag noble who lives in the compound beyond this wall.

Lives, but maybe I'll remedy that.

"He give you this?" I ask, spinning the ball on one finger, then another. "Lord Repha'im?"

The kid can't even nod yes, frozen, but I know I'm right. Such gifts are a cheap way for a man to buy loyalty in a slum like this.

"You're the Night Angel," the kid chokes out. "You're Kylar Stern."

The ball's spinning slows, stops, but it stays poised on my fingertip.

They know I'm back in the city. Lord Repha'im knows I'm coming. That explains the magical traps twisting in the air above his walls, keeping me from simply climbing over them. And if this kid knows about me . . .

"You work for him," I say, taking the ball in hand. "*That's* why you're out here at this hour. You're a lookout."

~Ah. This makes things more complicated.~

I thought by showing myself, I might scare him away, that I could give myself an excuse to spare him. But as a lookout, he's too dangerous for that, isn't he?

He gulps again, but then his eyes dart greedily back to his ball. He should be running away right now, but I have his treasure, and he can't bear to leave it behind. His life, for a stupid ball.

"Kid, what do you call an innocent who helps bad people, even if only a little? What do you call an innocent who gets other innocent people killed?"

He doesn't answer. And still doesn't run.

~I have a better question. What do *you* call that innocent, Kylar?~

Today? Today I call him an acceptable loss.

The lines get blurry. But that's what this work is. It's why I hate it, almost as much as I love it.

"They've given you some sort of signal," I say. "A flare or something, if you see me? I'll be straight with you. You give them that signal, you die."

He blanches, but his eyes flick to his ball again. His treasure.

If I have to kill him, the world won't be losing one of its great minds.

"Kid, I have so much power that it scares me. Power so big it needs bounds. I could become worse than the men I've killed. Maybe I already have. But I'm trying here. Trying to be good, you understand? So I've been working on some rules for myself. Trying them out, anyway. Here's one: Never let anyone see my face, or they have to die."

If I let him walk, he'll think my attention has shifted away from him and onto infiltrating the estate. Then he might come back and warn them. But if he runs away, I can draw my blade and chase. He'll have no idea how long I keep coming after him. He probably won't stop running until noon.

I pull my mask off. "What do you think?" I say.

He squeaks but doesn't break. Tough kid. Or maybe just that dumb.

"I know what it's like, kid, working for these kinds of people. I've been there. Here, actually. I grew up not far from here, in a part of the Warrens that makes this place look soft. The streets don't give most kids a chance. I know that. Hate it. So with me everyone gets a chance. One. One chance. Then my judgment is final. I offer mercy first, if I can, then I bring justice, ruthless and red."

He's not running away, not taking the out I'm trying to offer him. Which means I'm going to have to send another body bobbing white down the sour sludge-brown river.

Unless...

A glimmer of it comes to me. My third way. Maybe.

I turn and kick the ball at the goal. I narrowly miss. Dammit. I'm not my master yet. But it does bounce back to the kid, who scoops up his little treasure convulsively.

Facing the wall and the brightening sky, as I put my mask back on against the stench of the river and slums, I ask quietly, "So tell me, what do you choose?"

There's no response but the quiet scritch of fleeing feet on cobblestones. The kid is gone. *Finally.*

I draw blades, snarl, and run after him. He throws a look back as he rounds a corner, his face blanched, eyes wide, stumbling on trash spilling out of an alley. With him in full flight, I stow my weapons, pull the shadows about me, and pursue him on the silent feet of a nightmare.

I have a poison. Knocks out a grown man. I could use it on the kid, scaling the dose down for his weight. But there's a chance it'll kill him. You just can't tell.

In wet work, a mistake can mean a dead kid. If you can't deal with that, you're in the wrong line of work.

After a couple of quick turns, the kid heads down a street parallel to the estate, and I start to think he's wised up and is running home. Then he slips into a space between a dilapidated shop and the compound's pristine wall. There, amid rotting wood and crumbling mortar, he disappears.

My chest tightens.

I find the hole only by the sound of his trousers scuffing along the ground as he crawls. I follow.

The tunnel stinks of dander and cat piss. Unpleasant as it is, it's a good sign. If it were clean, I'd know adults had built and maintained it. Nonetheless, here

I take it slow. Not from claustrophobia. Tight spaces only terrify if they also make you feel powerless, and when I was little, tight spaces kept me safe from the older kids. Nor does a fear of the oppressive dark slow me. Since I bonded the black ka'kari, darkness welcomes my eyes.

No, here is where I'd set the real trap, if I were hunting me.

The big trap I'm currently avoiding by entering the estate this way is directly in and above the walls of the compound. Hanging invisible in the air is some kind of magical snare that appears to be the work of at least three different magi. Two of them were subtle. The third is a fire mage.

Fire mages don't tend to be good at *subtle*.

I don't know what the invisible hooks and bars and switches above the walls do—I'm no mage myself—but I know when you see a bear trap, you don't test it by sticking your foot in.

The *ball*, I realize.

There was magic on the ball, wasn't there? I ask the ka'kari. *Why didn't you tell me?*

~You're a big boy now, Kylar. I'm not going to spell everything out for you.~

That's what was strange about the ball, not only that it was too expensive for a street kid—the ball itself was the lookout's warning flare. He was probably supposed to throw it over the wall if he saw me.

I push through the tight tunnel as fast as I dare. Then I pause at its exit in the lee of a large rock that leans against an outbuilding, the hole itself overgrown with long grasses. The exit's too small for an adult to pass. Even the kid had barely made it through.

That's the good news. It means this isn't the manor's emergency exit. It means Lord Repha'im may not know it exists.

The bad news is that the estate's dogs aren't ignorant about this hole, and every last one of them seems to have used this corner to mark its territory and empty its bowels.

I hear a distant pounding on a door, and the kid's voice raised, shouting.

I need to hurry.

I scrape at the hard earth with my bare hands, widening the exit. The ka'kari *could* help me with this, but it doesn't, and I don't beg it to. The ka'kari's magic could also blunt the smell of the fresh dog crap the kid stepped in and smeared everywhere as he scrambled out of the tunnel—but again, it doesn't.

Why is it always sewers and bare rock walls with a thousand-pace drop in this line of work? Why don't my jobs take me on pleasure cruises with beautiful women and expensive alcohol and chamber music?

I make it out and step gingerly past all the dog excrement. It doesn't matter if your own body doesn't have any scent—as mine doesn't—if you reek of what you stepped in. My master always told me that it's the little things that'll get you killed.

He worried about the big things, too. And the medium things. And half the time, a bunch of things I'm pretty sure were imaginary.

The bitter business is hell for paranoia.

I flit from shadow to shadow, getting away from the tunnel entrance. I consider climbing to the roof of a low outbuilding but instead stay on the ground to avoid silhouetting myself, quickly pulling the unstrung bow from my pack. I brace the lower limb of the bow on the ground, set the string in its lower notch, step through, bend the bow, and set the upper string. I check my arrows by feel, then nock a swallowtail broadhead.

The boy's not a difficult target. He's twenty paces away, and he's left off pounding on the door as yelling mercenaries charge toward him with their weapons drawn. His precious ball awkwardly tucked under one elbow, he raises his hands in surrender.

The time is now, before they surround him. The reason I chose a broad-edged swallowtail head on this arrow is because if you shoot someone in the torso, the arrow itself points back toward your location.

My intended shot is more difficult by far. If I clip his scrawny neck with the fat swallowtail head, the arrow will keep flying, disappearing into the darkness. There will be the whisper of an arrow in flight, the alarming spray of arterial blood, and he'll go down, silenced before he can make my work too difficult, with little hint what direction his death came from.

I told him the price. I gave him the choice. He chose death, not me.

I draw the string to my lips. There's no wind. Frozen with fear of the approaching mercenaries, the boy's holding very still. I've got this.

I don't know if you've ever shot a recurve bow, but they're not made to be held fully drawn. Yet I hold.

He's a child.

A child protecting a monster. An acceptable loss.

I think of Count Drake. I'm recording this for him, narrating everything to the ka'kari. He'd never have asked me to do this job. He'd tell me I'm imperiling my soul. He'd ask if I was certain I'm doing this for justice.

I am.

But how can I look him in the eye and tell him I killed a child?

I can say kids die in wars, that our war's not really over yet, that it *can't* be over until justice is done.

A huge brute of a guard is moving forward. He'll obscure my shot in about two heartbeats.

One.

I slowly release the tension on the arrow. Lower the bow unshot. Cursing silently, I unstring it, tuck it away.

The door opens, and a man in fine clothes comes out. I lose sight of him as I start moving once more. I hear only snippets of the conversation, questions flying back and forth. I catch glimpses of wild gesticulations as the man in charge interrogates the others.

No, the guards hadn't seen the agreed-upon alarm, so what's the problem?

No, they don't know the kid, but they're new, they don't know plenty of people here.

Then, as I come close enough to hear his words clearly, the tenor of the leader's voice changes. With one hand, he's got the kid by the front of his tunic; the other hand is holding the ball. "Are you telling me the Night Angel *talked* to you? And you didn't give us the signal?!"

The guards exchange glances, some filled with disbelief, others with sudden fear.

As the man drops the kid, I see red sigils on the man's bare scalp lighting up.

Ah, a red mage. Probably the same one whose work I'd seen above the compound's walls.

"I didn't want to lose my ball," the kid says plaintively.

With a roar, the mage hurls the kid's ball over the wall and into the slums beyond.

As the ball flies through the weaves above the walls, a deep red light pulses over the whole of the compound. Tendrils of red light burn as if along oil trails to every window and door of the mansion, which then pulse with the same red. The *snick* of mundane locks slapping shut joins the hum of magics activating, sealing the entire estate.

"My ball!" the kid yells.

Up in the air there's a blur of blue magics and a meaty crunch. The nearest guards flinch, thinking it's an attack. Everyone turns to see a bat drop to the ground in several bloody pieces, its predawn hunt cut short.

The red mage snarls at the kid, "*You* didn't come over the wall. And you didn't come through the gate. How'd you get in?"

"I, I—"

"Never mind." The red mage abruptly turns to search the darkness. "You little fool, you led him right inside. The Night Angel's already here."

Chapter Two

The Book of the Dead

*P*ulling her eyes away from the page, Vi slouched in her chair, measuring her breaths so as not to betray the manic smithy in her chest. The handwriting certainly looked like Kylar's, but having been raised among the Cenarian Sa'kagé, Vi knew a forgery was always possible. She wasn't an expert. She could be fooled. And the more important the document, the more skeptical you should be.

The Sisters were treating this book as if it were very, very important.

They'd summoned her from her lessons. She'd been expecting that. Her friend Gwaen wished her luck with a tense smile. Vi knew she was going to be punished sooner or later, but the stern, silent Sister hadn't taken her to stand before some tribunal. Instead, she'd led her to this cozy library with half a dozen scarred black walnut study tables and a few hundred tomes and scrolls, high in the White Seraph. Refusing to answer any of Vi's questions, she'd seated Viridiana at a table with a single unimpressive codex on it. Common goat leather from the look of it, worn, dyed black. It was blind tooled with a few paltry geometric designs rather than embossed with gold, the edges not gilt or gauffered. And yet it rested here on a platform with gold contact points under a gold-framed glass dome.

Chanting some spell below Vi's hearing, the Sister had pulled a lever to one side of the dome. Air hissed and a violet pulse shimmered inside it. The Sister carefully lifted off the dome.

"The book stays in this library. So do you. Don't touch it with magic. All you do is read." Then the Sister had left.

The book didn't look worthy of precautions. It looked like a traveling merchant's account book or diary, sized to fit in a large pocket and plain so as not to tempt thieves. Vi'd opened it with some trepidation, but there had been no explosion of magics.

Nor had there been so much as an inscription to say who it belonged to or what it was. She'd read a few paragraphs before she realized why the handwriting looked familiar. Then she'd become immediately skeptical. A journal? Kylar?

But as she'd read on, her doubts had faded. It was definitely Kylar's voice through the text. She recognized his way of speaking as clearly as if she were seeing his face. But what was this book? How had the Sisterhood gotten it?

Attempting to mimic the detached interest of her tutors, she looked at one of her least favorite people in the world, the Special Problems and Tactics Team leader Sister Ayayah Meganah. "What is this supposed to be?"

"So you can read it?" the Sister asked, her chin up, her tone suggesting Vi were something repulsive.

"Of course I can!" Vi snapped. "You think I can't read? You think I've been spending all these hours in the library since we got back just to see how long it takes the chairs to flatten my a—my butt?" So much for calm.

She closed her eyes. In her old life, she would have used a lot more profanity and at least a few insults, but Sister Ayayah didn't seem disposed to praise her.

Dripping condescension like bloodrot venom from her white teeth, her old team leader said, "Not 'can you read,' *little sister...*"

Before she'd come to the Chantry, Viridiana had never appreciated how many ways one could be called 'little sister.' Her teachers had explained that the term was intended to be a friendly reminder for full Sisters to be generous with the shortcomings of the less-experienced women training here.

From the sinewy older woman, it had not been anything so kind for a while. Not to Vi. Not since Castle Stormfast, and even less since they'd returned from the debacle on the storm ship. Slowly, as if Vi were stupid, the Sister said, "I asked, 'Can you read *it?*' Watch."

Sister Ayayah kept her dark hair trimmed close to her skull and wore large hoops in her ears, but she moved with such stately deliberation that her earrings didn't bob and swing when she moved. She might as well have been an idol of hungry Oyuna carved of ebon wood.

With irritating grace, the Sister glided toward Viridiana's table, where the solid little tome lay open on a table in the tiny library high in the Chantry.

Vi had wondered why the Sister had stood so far away as Vi had read the first pages. Now she saw why. As the Sister came closer, the words on the page scrambled.

Vi couldn't even tell if the letters still made actual words. But Sister Ayayah's tightening lips made her guess they didn't. "What...what is this?" Vi asked quietly, her rancor forgotten.

"I assume even you aren't so stupid as to be asking whether it's a magical book. So I assume, *little sister*, that you're asking, 'What is this magical book I'm reading? Why does it let *me* read it, but not my betters?' And, in contradistinction to your first question, *that* is a very good one indeed."

Vi snapped her mouth shut. She'd taken greater abuse in her former life, but Sister Ayayah had figured out early that being called stupid cut Vi deeper than other attacks. The Sister delighted to stab at that place, claiming always that it was for Viridiana's own good, that she was helping Vi build up mental scar tissue on a soft spot.

"*This* book," Sister Ayayah said, clipping her words, "is offal. It's trash. It probably has nothing to do with Kylar at all. He certainly didn't have the expertise to craft such magic. But now, I am happy to say, this book will wreck your career as it has nearly wrecked mine."

"What?"

Sister Ayayah went on as if Vi hadn't spoken. "Because for some reason, despite or because of your gormless lack of sophistication, this book allows *you* to read it and so far as we can tell no one else. Thus, it falls to me to let you know that the Council for Peace is giving you three days to read it all, finding whatever clues you can, and then to make a report thereon."

It felt like the bad old days, when the twist who'd been her master would sometimes start a training session by punching Vi in the nose, then attack ferociously, making her defend herself while dazed, her eyes streaming blinding tears and her nose fountaining blood.

"Why is the war council meeting?" Vi managed. "And clues? Clues to what?"

"We need to find—pardon me. *You*..." Sister Ayayah smiled cruelly, as if in having failed a thankless task, she was now discovering the joys of handing it to someone else. "*You* need to figure out where Kylar's body is."

"From this book? But you said you don't even know what's in it, so how do we know that it will—?"

"From the book. Yes. Don't make me repeat myself. It makes you sound stupider than usual."

Breathe. Slowly.

Blinking, gaze averted, it took Vi only one breath to master herself.

"But...why? Why do we care? Kylar didn't exactly make many friends here. There's no way the Council cares enough to send an expedition back to Alitaera merely to give him a proper burial. Not with how we left things, certainly."

The Sister's mouth thinned. "You used to be an assassin. Isn't it obvious? When one hears that someone as powerful as Kylar Stern is dead, it always pays to see the body yourself."

"There's not going to be a body! I already told you. There's no way he made it to—"

"We have reason to believe he did. At least a short ways."

"But, but I thought the Seer's magic had already confirmed he was dead. Is dead."

With Kylar, there was a yawning gap between those two phrases, but Vi hoped Sister Ayayah had missed it.

Ayayah Meganah suddenly broke eye contact. "Fine. He carried something, allegedly an artifact with potent magics. We have reason to believe he kept it on himself secretly at all times. Did you know about this?"

"No. So you want the artifact. You don't actually care about his body."

Vi could see it was true, but Sister Ayayah wasn't going to give her the satisfaction of admitting it. "But you care, don't you?" the Sister shot back. "You can tell the others whatever you want, and maybe they'll believe you. But I saw how you looked at him."

This time, for Vi to find the flat, expressionless face of Sisterly hatred was no effort at all. "If I find him, will I be allowed to bury him?"

"Oh, little Viridiana. You've seen the Sisters arriving from all over the world. A full Convocation has been called to discuss the Alitaeran mess. We'll vote what to do in three days. As your superior, it will be my strong recommendation that you not be allowed to go on that or any other expedition, not for years. So your job begins and ends with your *ass* flat in that chair. Given your disastrous performance at the storm ship, if you fail us in this, there will be consequences for your position in this Sisterhood. You have three days, Viridiana," Sister Ayayah said, smiling unpleasantly. "And today counts as day one."

DAY ONE

Chapter Three

Outracing an Amnesty

I'm clinging to the side of Lord Repha'im's highest tower under a bank of barred windows, waiting for a guard to move.

I've already botched the job. I should've abandoned it the instant the words 'Night Angel' came out of that kid's mouth. Definitely as soon as he called me Kylar Stern. There's no good reason I can't wait and take up the job in a month, or six months, or two years.

Well, no good reason other than the high king's decree.

The black ka'kari is covering my skin and blinding any magic-users to my presence. It's told me I can choose invisibility to mundane sight or invisibility to magical sight, but not both at the same time. Then again, the ka'kari may have lied to make my life harder.

~Me? Lie?~

Given the mages here, I made my choice. So now I'm pressing myself into dark corners, glancing periodically at the guard inside the window and the sky.

The rosy fingers of dawn are scratching the horizon's back even now.

If I said I was here killing someone for my friend the high king, you'd think you know what I mean. But it's more complicated than that. Harder. I'm hoping to kill someone without his orders, maybe even against his orders, and yet keep the king my friend.

If I leave only the one monster inside this building dead, Logan might forgive me. If I butcher a dozen men—regardless of how much they deserve it— he'll be done with me. In fact, he'd probably send his own people to arrest me, and then he'd execute me.

Would he order the execution of his best friend?

Let's just say I have good reason to believe he would.

I can still abort the job. In some ways, I have all the time in the world.

Terrible people always have lots of enemies, and no one can live on high alert forever. Deaders get impatient. They hole up for a while, but eventually they get bored, decide the danger has passed, and come back out.

That is when my master kills them. It's the smart approach. It's what I *should* do.

But if I can finish this tonight, the high king might still forgive me. If I do it tonight, it'll still be plausible that I hadn't heard about his big amnesty. I did outrun the messengers to get here first. But the heralds will be announcing the amnesty first thing in the morning.

But that's not the real reason I'm here, and we both know it, huh, Count Drake?

Truth is, I can't let it go. It's too late to save my foster sisters. But it's not too late for vengeance.

Justice, I mean.

I rub my eyes with one hand. I haven't slept well in the months since the last battle at Black Barrow, and not at all in the last day or so. That's not good. My Talent can't compensate for slow reflexes and dulled judgment.

Finally, the guard walks away. I look at the bars on the window. The ka'kari can devour small slices of steel to cut through the bars, but it's full of power already. It would be like trying to fill an oil lamp with a full reservoir. More oil will only splash outside the lamp, which isn't wise when you're dealing with fire. In the same way, cutting the bars with the ka'kari now will be like lighting a flare up here in both the magical and the visible spectrums.

I shoot a glance down to the courtyard. A mage, this one helpfully dressed in blue robes, is patrolling there. I can use magic for internal things like strengthening my muscles for a leap without being seen, but anything external I do will be like waving a torch in the darkness. He might not see it if I'm fast enough. If I time it to when he turns away . . .

No, not worth the risk. Some other pair of eyes might see me.

I pull myself up to peek through the window. The guard is still walking away, heading to the opposite window to join another man there. If the other one turns to greet him while I climb past the window, I'm in it deep.

There are simply too many eyes that might be turned toward me, and too many ways for me to reveal myself through plain bad luck.

Gotta risk it. Here we go.

I feel the tingle of the ka'kari at my fingertips as it soaks up moisture and oils to help my grip. As I said, very helpful when it wants to be.

Decorated corbels support the overhanging flat roof of the tower above me. No magic, plus windows, plus the overhang mean that my best bet is going to be a quick series of dynamic movements. Once more I'm thankful for the years I spent with no Talent. In trying to keep up with my master, I had to learn good climbing technique.

However, I also fell to the ends of lots of ropes in those years—and I never tried anything this stupid. And this time I've got no rope to catch me.

I visualize the moves quickly: a quick run up the wall, leap out from the wall with a half-twist, snag the gargoyle below the overhang, spin around it to backflip onto the roof.

No problem, right? I got this.

I am gonna die.

Peeking inside, I see one of the guards hike his thumb toward my window. The other glances over, nods. One of them's gonna come this way any second.

Now!

I mantle the windowsill with a Talent-assisted heave and run my hands up the bars outside the windows like they're a ladder. My feet follow, racing up the bars. I twist to face away from the wall and leap up and out into space.

For a brief instant, my body twists, disconnected, touching only air. Then my hands slap onto the bulbous round stone eyes of the gargoyle carved on the corbels above me. I spin around it like an acrobat spins his body around a bar to throw me back in toward the building.

But as I pull myself, hard, one of the stone eyes tears away in my hand, throwing my trajectory off.

My body is heading up, but not quite high enough and not far enough back *in* onto the rooftop.

As I complete my flip, my knees hit stone instead of my feet, barely on the edge of the roof. Too soon, my momentum fades and my body reaches that sickening moment at the apogee of a jump where you stop rising.

My center of mass is still off the edge of the roof.

I throw my hands back to snag the crenels on either side of the gap, but they're too far apart. There's no way I'm not falling.

But I stab my legs out to either side, doing the splits, and catch a crenel with one foot—and land a great deal of my weight directly on my groin.

Then, with nothing to grab, I slip off.

I only keep from falling by snagging the edge of the roof with one hand and one extended foot tucked into the gargoyle's open mouth, where it barely protrudes beyond the overhang.

I can barely move for several long moments, struggling even to breathe. There's something mystical about testicular pain. But you can be trained to endure it and still do what you must.

You want to guess how my master trained me to ignore that kind of pain?

Go ahead and guess, because I'm not going to talk about it.

My Talent makes clinging to a cold, gritty wall with one tenuous handhold and on tiptoe not exactly easy, but possible. I brace myself, then hop from my one foot to swing my other hand up to the edge. From there, it's a simple pull up, so long as the edge of the tower holds.

It does. I flop onto the rooftop and roll away from the edge, safe at last. Then I finally roll onto my side and curl into a fetal position like a grown man ought to.

~What good luck!~

"Good?" I croak out.

~The eye you tore off the gargoyle fell into the bushes, and the guard happened to be far enough away not to hear it.~

I can only groan. *Lucky me.*

I've barely stood up and dusted my hands and tunic clean when I hear a voice below, shouting, "Stern! Kylar Stern, I know you're here!"

Aware that a crossbow bolt or a blast of magic may be waiting for me to pop my head out into view, I approach the edge carefully, but the speaker isn't lying in ambush. He's standing under a covered patio almost directly below me. It can only be Lord Repha'im himself. He must be packed between bodyguards who can't be happy he came outside—not to mention mages, too, because I can see little balls of variously colored light spinning out from the patio, dipping into shadows, hunting me.

Next he's going to tell me to come out and fight him like a man.

"Stern!" he shouts again. Then his voice goes quieter, though I can still hear it without straining. He's got one of those voices that carry. "You think you know how this ends. You're wrong."

The glowing balls zoom around one last time and then disappear. I hear the door bang shut and the loud scrapings of bars magical and mundane being thrown home.

I'm wrong, huh? I think, pooling the black ka'kari into my hand. *Guess we'll find out about that.*

I stand, and with the whole of the tower itself safely blocking the ka'kari's magic from the view of those below, I simply cut through the lock on the door.

I take a moment to gather my will for the ugliness that's to come.

The responsibility is mine alone. My guilt is immeasurable, inescapable, unspeakable—but it's not mine alone. You and your family welcomed me into your home as a son, Count Drake. It's my fault my sister is dead. But *I* didn't throw her from that balcony. *I* didn't deface her body. I can't make myself pay for what happened, but tonight someone will.

I wrap dampening weaves of air around the hinges to cover their squeaking and slip inside to do some killing.

Chapter Four

A Convenient Monster

*S*eems a waste to climb all the way to the top of the highest tower in a place only to descend all the way to the heavily guarded cellar, doesn't it? Especially when that tower has numerous choke points that can easily be held by any disciplined guards, much less mages.

In this tower, Lord Repha'im has teams of guards every few floors. He has such teams guarding *every* approach to his inner sanctum. At least five of the teams consist of a guard partnered with a mage.

That's a lot of mages for some new lord from nowhere. And all of them, guards and mages alike, are now on high alert. It's almost as if, in addition to being wealthy, the man is smart and careful and doesn't want to die.

That's fine, though. Lord Repha'im's defenses aren't going to be any problem. I trained as a wetboy. So that means I'm a super assassin who can walk through walls, kill whoever I want, and disappear before the body hits the ground, right?

Oh, that's right. You used to hire wetboys, back before you took me in, didn't you, Count Drake? Back before you changed.

There are two doors off the narrow central stair serving the apartments at the highest level of the tower: a servants' entrance, and a fancier door for the lord or his guests. I hesitate here in the darkness, considering how sound will carry down the spiraling stone staircase.

I don't know much about Lord Repha'im, but I know a lot about Cenaria. I grew up in the slums, and its courts are as vicious and not much cleaner. No one comes to Cenaria unless they're willing to get dirty. Certainly no one comes here and gets suddenly wealthy unless they're very good at being very bad.

So call me a cynic, but I'm betting Lord Repha'im has a guilty conscience.

Not that he *has* a conscience, but you know what I mean.

The level below me is some kind of parlor, divided into two sides by tall bookshelves, with large windows on every side to take advantage of the views of the city. On my climb, I already saw that there's a guard and a mage inside, but what I hadn't seen was that rather than the spiral stair continuing through this level, the stair enters at one side, and then a new stairway begins on the opposite side of the room.

It's an annoying level of paranoia. If your enemies have taken your castle except for the highest room of your tower, you've already lost. But, inconveniences aside, it means I'm probably right.

The reason I didn't kill the kid as soon as he showed me the way in isn't because I'm nice. It's because I'm a cynic. I didn't have time to scout this job properly, so I made some guesses: dirty noble, guilty conscience, fearful, careful, egotist?

Add them up and I figure this noble's got some nigh-impregnable safe room for himself.

But you see, that's not a problem. It's a solution.

Assassin breaks into a heavily fortified estate? Everyone rallies to the boss, because everyone assumes the assassin has come to kill the boss.

In this case, everyone's wrong.

The alarm has called almost all the guards to positions where they can defend a man who doesn't concern me.

Lord Repha'im probably deserves killing. I don't know. I'm not here for him. I'm here to kill one of his guests. One who I believe is in this room.

If Repha'im is a good man, he'll have brought his guests with him into his safe room. If he's a bad man, he'll have left them to fend for themselves. Maybe with a single guard or two—like the two men in the parlor.

This is the real gamble, because I don't know Repha'im. My master would never have gambled in such a way. But me? Now? I have to.

That there are still guards here tells me I'm probably right. That they haven't been called away suggests there's something valuable in the apartments at the top of the stairs. Or, I hope, someone.

Breaking into the apartment may be noisy. What I'll do inside definitely will be, so I have to take care of these men first.

And not kill them. No massacres, for Logan's sake. My arm trembles, and I blink against the sudden reminder of my exhaustion.

I can hear the men talking, though I can't make out any of the words. It means they're about to switch stations, though I've lost track of how long it's been since I climbed past the window. My master Durzo would know exactly which one he'd see next. He also would have known exactly what kind of trigger they had to set off their own alarms—which could be as simple as mundane whistles, or as difficult as magical beacons triggered any of a dozen ways, some of them very difficult to stop.

This job is looking more and more like a tremendous mistake.

Even now I can call it off.

But Trudana Jadwin is right here. Her treason doesn't concern me as much as the fact that she assisted those who murdered my foster sister Magdalyn and used her body for what she calls *art*: turning her body into a perfectly lifelike statue made of undecaying flesh and put on display for the vulturous titillation of others.

If I leave, the duchess gets away with all of it. Her crimes will be pardoned under High King Logan's postwar amnesty. She's been in hiding since the last battle, but after today, she'll walk out of this tower and rejoin society. Not at the bottom, either; she'll jump back in near the top.

I won't allow it. You understand, don't you, Count Drake? The thought of you going to court and seeing her laugh and drink wine with her friends? She's the kind who would seek you out, too, who would gloat, knowing you've sworn yourself to a life of nonviolence.

I understand why you got out, but the world needs men who will walk the werewolf night, who will wade through blood to stop what's wrong. Men like me.

I remove my weapons belt and pack and stash them out of sight up the stairs. I open two tins; first I wipe an insulating layer of grease on my fingers, then scoop up two daubs of my knockout poison. I will the ka'kari to sink back into my skin, leaving me naked.

Then I hesitate in the shadows of the staircase. This seemed like a much better idea last night.

I see that the man on my side of the parlor is the mage, and I call on the ka'kari to hide my Talent from his sight, just in case.

"Psst," I say.

He's standing against the windows, looking out at the rising dawn coming up over the city. He is much bigger than I'd realized. I'm going to have to give him both doses.

How'd I miss *that*?

"Psst," I say again, louder. My shoulders are hunched, and I have my hands crossed to cover my nudity, everything about me speaking vulnerability.

He turns. "What the—?"

I wave him over with one hand, embarrassed.

"Dannil?" he says, but not loud. Must be the other guard's name.

I shake my head, as if mortified at being seen naked, pleading.

He walks toward me. "What are you doing here?" he asks, not quietly.

"Shh, please," I say. "I'll lose my job if my master finds me out. I've been trying to get out of here since the alarm went off."

"What are you doing here?" he says again, eyes narrowing. He's got a delicate glass bauble in his right hand, with his big thumb poised on it.

"I was…with…you know, last night." I jerk my head toward the stairs. Trudana Jadwin is famous for her prodigious sexual appetite and her preference for men about half her age—which is to say *my age*. I say, "When the alarm hit, she kicked me out of her chambers! And she won't let me back in. My *clothes* are in there!"

He snorts. I see the tension go out of him. He's barely holding back a laugh.

"Please!" I whisper. He's wearing gloves. There's very little skin exposed for me to use the contact poison. "You've gotta help me. Do you have any idea the degrading things she made me do last night—and did *to* me? I'll be spending the rest of the week in a bathtub trying to scrub away the…ugh. If I lose my job on top of that? Please, sirrah." I fall on my knees in front of him and reach up to take his hand in both of my own. I smear the contact poison around the front and back of his wrist, then hold his hand in supplication with both of mine to confuse the touch.

It's an old pickpocket's trick. A lone touch is easily felt, but a brief light touch can be overwhelmed in the senses by a firmer, broader touch right before or after it.

"Dannil!" he says louder, amused. "Come see this!"

"Oh, come on!" I whine, still on my knees. "Really?"

He pulls his hand away from me with distaste and tucks away the glass alarm trigger. "You should know not to consort with your betters, boy."

Then he blinks.

"What is it?" I hear the guard on the other side of the wall ask.

The big mage blinks again, then totters.

I'm behind him before he notices, striking the back of both of his knees with my fists.

He folds into my waiting arms, and I wrap him in a sleeper hold to ensure his silence. He goes limp, and I release him immediately. Can't cut off the blood flow to the head for long; that risks death, and besides, I want the knock-out poison in his brain.

I vault over a low bookcase as the guard is coming around the corner.

I imagine the last thing he was expecting was a naked man leaping into the air, knocking his hands wide, my right leg going over his shoulder, left leg stabbing below his right armpit, missing my target. But I pull his head down and with my full weight bearing him down, we fall together. I slap the floor to break my fall, and he drops on all fours on top of me. He manages to stand as my legs snake around him, hoping to lift me and then slam me to the ground. But I block his heel from stepping back as he tries to balance our combined weight.

Tripping, he falls onto his butt even as my legs complete the triangle around his head. And that's that.

From him spotting me, to fighting me, to lying unconscious took less than a ten count. It never even occurred to him to use his most dangerous weapon: his voice.

I release him quickly. Again, it's too easy to kill a man without intending to. I grab his weapons and find his alarm trigger tucked in a pocket. Then I bring the ka'kari to my skin to sheathe me as the Night Angel once more. There's no telling how long a man who's been choked out will stay unconscious.

In this case, it's not nearly long enough. Instead of the flutter of eyelids signaling him drifting back into consciousness, his eyes open fully and suddenly.

I don't intend it. Don't want it, but perhaps the proximity of our faces, perhaps the fear in his eyes, something triggers my powers: The Night Angel—whatever the hell *it* is, whatever the hell *I* am now—can sometimes see a person's crimes in their eyes, like an indelible stain writ directly on their soul, impossible for anyone else to see, impossible for me to miss.

As fast as I can, I break eye contact. Without intending to, I've crossed the space between us, pinned him with a knee, wrenched his head back with one hand and drawn a blade with the other—poised for a killing blow; jaw clenched, teeth bared, the Night Angel mask sheathing my face, smoke leaking from eyes of blue flame, burning condemnation.

My averted eyes take in his livery. Somehow, I'd missed it before now.

These men aren't wearing the Repha'im coat of arms; they wear *Jadwin* livery. This man was involved in kidnapping Mags and... and I don't know what else. I'd looked away as soon as I saw the beating he gave her.

I can't kill this man.

I can't *not.*

"Magdalyn Drake," I growl at the man beneath me. My Night Angel mask is made of the same black ka'kari-skin as the rest of my outfit, but instead of hewing closely to my own features as the rest does, the face is a sinister blank of judgment. Mouth minimized to a hint of a scowl, eyes hooded, sometimes dancing with an illusory blue glow for curious eyes—but now, by reflex, flaring to red fires, illusory smoke curling up as from the hellfire within waiting for the condemned.

"I never laid a hand on her!" he says.

It's a lie, though I can tell even as he says it that *he* doesn't realize that. Has he forgotten beating her?

My powers do this to me sometimes, presenting me with seemingly contradictory information. I guess by 'never laid a hand on her' he means that he never raped her. But at the same time, in his eyes I saw a flash of him grabbing her breast, twisting it, and laughing at her pain and terror as she cried out, terrified what he'd do next. But he'd never raped her. He didn't have that kind of hunger—

I can't do this. I can't judge him. Not here. Not now. I can't risk digging too deeply. I know that if I see certain kinds of guilt, I'm going to kill him regardless, consequences be damned.

"Hell's wrong with your eyes?" he asks, squirming beneath me.

I look up, meeting his.

He loves intimidating, loves hurting. The only music that moves him is the percussion of blows on flesh, the sounds of pain pitching higher; the averted eyes of the humiliated stirs him like coy teasing, and tears are better than—

I force myself to stare at his throat instead of his eyes. I shudder, my limbs tensing as my desire to end this *thing* crescendos.

He's not afraid of me in the least, but it would be wrong to think him courageous. I see fear in my work, know it well. As everything else can break or go wrong in this world, so can that. Some people don't understand fear, don't feel it. You'd think that's a gift. It's not. In its proper place, fear is a gift. Fear is evidence of a soul, evidence that a person values something. A man like this'll lie to your face—not because he's cunning, but because he's unafraid of you catching the lie. He either doesn't understand consequences or is unable to care about them.

Now that I know what I'm dealing with, I go cold. "Can you write?" I ask, cutting his sleeve open from wrist to shoulder with my thin, sharp blade.

"Can I what?" he asks, looking bewildered as I cut the sleeve free.

"Write. Your letters, man. Do you have your letters?"

"Naw, I don't write. I look like some smooth-nut book sniffer a' you?"

"Good," I say. "Then you get to live." I wad up the sleeve.

"I get a' what?"

"You won't be able to tell them any more about me than they already know."

"What?"

I sheathe my delicate knife and draw his. It's got a wide, heavy blade.

"You ain't got the belly to kill me," he says. "Or you already woulda. You think you're gonna scare me silent?"

I shake my head and avert my gaze yet again. Perhaps he takes it as a loss of nerve.

"What's going to stop me from telling them everything, huh?" he demands.

"Not this," I say.

With a rapidity he isn't expecting, I seize one of his hands, pull on it to extend the sinews, and slash the hand free of his wrist with the heavy blade.

By the time he gasps, I'm ready with his own wadded-up sleeve to gag him and muffle his cry—and then the scream that follows it as the ka'kari burns red with power and cauterizes his stump to keep him from bleeding out. It smells like—well, you don't need that detail rattling around in your head.

"You've been a man who preys on the weak," I say, "so I sentence you to weakness. You will survive only by the compassion of others, or not at all. But compassionate people are vulnerable people, and I'll not loose you as a wolf among sheep, so I'm going to take away your ability to hurt anyone."

All right, I've come back later. I realized that before I go on, we should probably talk about our deal.

Yes, yours and mine, listener or reader or whatever you are. Turns out this isn't going to be the private tale for Count Drake's ears only as I'd planned, so I need you to understand a couple things.

On the few occasions I've offered to tell any part of my story, people always tell me they want to hear it all.

They never do. Not really. You *don't, either.*

Hey, I get it: You listen to a hired killer tell stories, you expect to hear hired-killer stories, right? Maybe you start by asking the question that anyone who's ever killed just adores: 'How does it feel to kill a man?'

As if killing a man always feels the same. As if killing a man always evokes any feeling at all.

But I understand, maybe you honestly believe you're different, you can handle it, you do *want to hear everything.*

Well, I don't trust you. You'll want extra gore when my deaders are particularly bad. But when I've got to kill some wretch just doing his job, trying to put meat in his kids' bellies once a week by serving a good man who serves a good man who serves a bad man that I need to kill, you'll want a bloodless, easy death for him. Won't you?

As if the world works that way.

If you want to feel comfortable with what I do, get the hell out. If you came here to enjoy murder vicariously, get out now and go take a good hard look in the mirror, friend.

If you're curious about what I do, though? That I understand. I had that curiosity myself once upon a time. But I was a kid. I didn't know better.

All that said . . . if you've got a reasonably strong stomach, you can trust me about this. I'll tell you all you need to know to understand how I got here on this precipice, about to . . . do what I'm about to do.

But beyond what details are necessary for clarity? I'll be the one deciding how much you need to hear about the awful stuff. If you don't like that, my lord—or my lady—or whoever the hell you are, you can stop listening at any point. Or put down the codex and stop reading, if my words someday reach the page. Believe me, I'll tell you plenty to sate your curiosity and a bit more besides, and if the violence gets to be too much—and it will—I'll tell you when to look away.

Enough interruption. Back to Dannil and the necessary carnage.

None of the rest of my not-killing him is all that noteworthy. It's enough to say that he quickly passes out.

Now I stare for a moment at the appendages I've flung about the hall like an adolescent scatters clothing around his bedchamber.

It doesn't seem right to leave what looks like a butcher's shop here, so I gather his eyes, hands, and the front half of each foot. (I decided he'll need to be able to stand but never run or kick anyone.) For the life of me, though, I can't find his *tongue*.

Where in the world is his bloody tongue?

I give it up—his friend the mage won't stay unconscious forever, and if he wakes while I'm here, he'll be much harder for me to deal with. I decide to go on to my main objective.

My gaze falls on the man's pile o' parts. I'd intended putting them all together to be a conscientious act: like a carpenter sweeping up the sawdust or a chef cleaning the kitchen after his work.

Unfortunately, the neat stack gives a rather different impression. I'd cauterized his wounds, but not the wounds on the detached parts. So it's a pile of little bloody parts. And, really, I'm trying to make this not sound sick, but what *does* one do with loose eyeballs?

Point them out from each other, so they look wonky? That's hardly appropriate. Point them in, so they look cross-eyed? Even worse. Both pointing left, toward his own unconscious body, as if he's staring at himself? Away from him, so he seems ashamed? *Oops, misplaced my eyeballs! How embarrassing!*

I do the best I can and then cover the whole thing with his handkerchief.

Smearing the last of my knockout poison on Dannil, I leave.

Ah...blast it. Never should've said his name. You don't need to remember it. He doesn't show up again—at least, he hasn't until now, and I could hardly imagine a cripple hopping his way up this mountain—but me telling you his name personalized the bastard, didn't it?

But if you feel sorry for him, don't. I didn't tell you half of the sick stuff I saw in his eyes.

Anyway, I'll leave out the irrelevant details next time. Cut me some slack, I'm new to this telling-it-as-I-go business. I'll get better with practice.

Probably.

I go to the fancy door and rap on it. "Lady Jadwin?" I say, sounding for all the world like a gentleman caller.

"Who's there?" a woman calls out. Despite the thick wood muffling the sound, in her nasal voice I hear a quaver.

"It's Kylar Stern. I'm here to kill you. Won't take but a minute."

Chapter Five

Death and the Artist

If you pay attention, people will surprise you with how dumb they are every day. But sadly, Trudana Jadwin doesn't open the door for me.

I sigh as I unlock the door with the guard's key. Often nobles like her are so far out of touch that they think having people to do things for them is a sign of their own importance, and Trudana Jadwin has shown herself in many instances to be the worst sort of noble—but I still have to assume she has one of those glass-bauble alarm triggers.

As the lock clicks, I hear her scream. She must now have realized there are only a few ways I could've gotten that key, and for her, none of those is good news.

In case she has a crossbow or a silent, armed companion in the room with her, I stand out of the direct line of fire as I turn the latch at shoulder height and push on the door.

It's barred from inside.

I hear her laugh scornfully. "Stern?" she asks, directly on the other side of the door now. "Logan Gyre's poor relation from the countryside? The one with the hideous clothes?"

Ah. The scream was a tease. A setup so she could mock me.

"Not a relation," I say. "Merely a friend. A friend with a minimal sense of fashion and a maximal..."

The ka'kari puddles like iridescent black oil in my palm and slips through the crack in the door, becoming like a thin crowbar. I lever it up and down a few times and am rewarded as the wood plank that was barring the door on the other side goes crashing to the ground. "...grudge," I finish, irritated. I thought that was going to sound a lot more menacing.

Eh, maybe I'll fix it later.

I push the door open with a foot.

The twang of a crossbow sounds almost atop the thump of bolt into wood—not the sharper sound of iron hitting the stone of the stairwell behind me, as I'd expected.

Trudana couldn't even shoot a target the size of an open doorway from—I poke my head around the doorframe, incredulous—seven paces?

Lady Jadwin's backing away, the crossbow now held limply in her hands. Her eyes are wide, aghast. She isn't trying to reload. Probably she doesn't know how. She trips over a stool and goes crashing into one of the many easels set up around the periphery of the room. Her art clutters even this large space: Folios thick with drawings obscure every desk and stool, canvases lean four deep against every wall, and one corner is coated with marble dust and stone-carving tools.

No one else is in sight.

That could be a trap, though. I spend precious seconds making sure it's not.

"Look what you made me do," she says. There's fresh fire in her voice. In falling, she's destroyed one of her paintings. I glance around the room and guess that all of the paintings here are her creations. "How dare you!" she says, standing.

She has the hawkish beak—it's really so much larger than a nose that Logan would call it a... *what's the word?*

~Snout?~

Proboscis... I think. Anyway, she has the huge nose and the long horsey face and watery eyes that you only get with a certain deeply inbred subspecies of nobility, but sadly none of their better features.

She does, however, have excellent aesthetic sensibilities. Even the dressing gown she's wearing at this early hour, with lavender and a seafoam green of perfectly complementary shades and with textures in a perfect counterpoint to the layers of her underclothes beneath, reeks of a rare confluence of money and good taste.

Her art is beautiful, too. I hate her for that.

I'll admit, in my darker hours I had fantasies about how I might punish her appropriately for what she's done. I was going to kidnap her, hide her away somewhere, and give her food only when she gave me paintings, or sculptures, or whatever moved my fancy. I'd force her to make whatever it was she hated, over and over again. Or maybe what she loved. I dreamed of spurring her to the greatest heights of Art she might climb, and then destroying what she'd made in front of her, so that she might know no one would ever see what she had done.

I was planning to experiment: Destroy her art in front of her every day? Or perhaps one day a year I would destroy all she'd made in the previous year? Which would be more soul-crushing?

Such fantasies are unworthy of a professional, I know.

"I'm here for Mags Drake," I say.

Her piggy eyes squint. "Who?"

"Magdalyn Drake. You turned her into one of your corpse statues."

"The broken girl? You can't be angry about *that*! I did astonishing work with what I was given. She'd jumped to her death! I put her back together. I gave her beauty back to the world."

I blink. I shouldn't be surprised. It must be all the sleepless nights catching up with me. Denial of wrongdoing? What's next? Finger pointing?

Finally noticing the look on my face, she howls, "It wasn't my idea! I had to do it. He made me! Said it was research. He said..."

I rub my temples. What did I think I was going to find here? Sorrow for her crimes? A bit of self-reflection? Penitence?

~Peace?~

Shut up, I tell the ka'kari.

This woman murdered a prince. In cold blood. After having been his lover for a while. She helped eliminate the royal line in Cenaria, helping guarantee that the Godking's brutal invasion into Cenaria would find only fractured opposition. The threads of a million evils in this land pass through this woman's murderous hands; a bit of guilt for every one of them surely stains them.

I could look at her soul and find out. My rage would blind me, perhaps. It would help me do what I came here to do. What I worked so hard to be able to do in time.

Yet suddenly I have no heart for it.

"After I kill you," I say very quietly, "I'm going to set fire to this room. And for the rest of my life, whenever I come across your work, I'll destroy it, regardless of the cost, regardless of the consequences. It would be better for the world had you never been born. You should've been strangled in the crib. But as it is? Nothing of beauty should ever be known to have come from you. And I will make it so. Your work will outlive you, but not by much. Instead you will only be remembered for your crimes."

It's a cruel thing for me to tell her, but she's a cruel woman, and she deserves it. This is retribution.

It takes some time for something like what I've told her to sink in, though, and even longer for her to believe it.

I walk to the corner with her carvings. I can't tell what it is yet, but something is taking rough shape from the black marble, like a child forming in the womb. I'm hoping she sees the open path to the door and runs. There's something about seeing prey in flight that triggers the primal predatory instinct. I want her to help me do what I must.

But she doesn't run.

"I have powerful friends," she says. "You aren't going to hurt me."

See? I was right after all: If you pay attention, people will surprise you with how dumb they are every day.

Soon she'll be telling me how I won't get away with this.

I blow off marble dust from her stone-cutting tools.

I pick up a chisel and a hammer.

Chapter Six

The Basics of the Job

It's getting dicey because somehow I seem to have forgotten the fundamentals.

I should've killed the kid. I told him I would if he alerted them. I should've put that arrow through his neck. They still would've sounded the alarms. They still would've been diverted as I planned, and I still could've done my job. Difference being that right now I wouldn't be facing the rectal rearrangement that's looking increasingly likely.

How many missions have I run? How good am I, really? I got in, killed my deader, and...this guy? The Night Angel himself? Yep, him. *He* left himself with no escape plan.

It's like an experienced pearl diver forgetting to take a deep breath before diving.

I don't dare try the tunnel I used to get in—I didn't kill the kid, and I heard them asking him how he got in, so I have to assume they'll have mages' traps set in that tunnel now. So here I am, checking every room, every outbuilding, trying to find some weak point. Yeah, that's right. I'm not finding my exit *before* the job. I'm doing it *after* the job, when the grounds are locked down tight, crawling with mercenaries and magi looking for me. Like an amateur.

I mean, you want to know what my job consists of?

Get in. Kill. Get out.

That's it. That's all my job is.

If you're a professional, you can fail repeatedly at your infiltrations and still have a career. You can almost always finish the job some other time, some other place.

You can also get access to your deader and fail at the kill itself now and again and still find work.

But the one thing that's non-negotiable is that you can never *not* get out after a kill. Those who trade their lives for their target's aren't professionals; they're madmen, zealots, fools, *assassins*.

Of everyone I know in wet work, with my experience, with my magic, with my tutelage under the greatest of us to ever live, how could *I* fail at this?

~On purpose?~

Ha. Not funny. That's not who I am, and you know it. You know what it'd cost if I got killed.

~Yes, I do. Have *you* forgotten?~

That's not even an option for me. Failure never has been, and since I learned my immortality's cost, it's a thousand times worse. If I die, I come back—but someone I love dies in my place. Someone like my foster sisters.

Their deaths are on me, though I didn't know it at the time. I didn't imprison them. I didn't make Mags jump, but I might as well have. One of my deaths triggered hers. I don't pretend to understand it, but it's a deep magic, a balancing of the scales: For me to live again, someone has to die.

It's why I had to avenge them, why I had to kill Trudana Jadwin. No matter what I do, one person responsible for my sisters' deaths—me—will walk free. I won't let it be two. That's my problem. This wasn't a job. This was personal, and when you let things get personal, you press on where a professional would know to ease off. You make mistakes.

I'll be lucky if it doesn't get me killed.

The guards are agitated, all of them working in pairs or larger groups, keeping their backs to the walls as much as possible. The sun is rising now, and they've had no sign of me. Lord Repha'im is clearly wealthy and paranoid, but even he can't afford to have dozens of magi, so eventually I make my way into the kitchens despite the guards outside it.

Though subterranean, the kitchens share a wall with the compound, and as I hoped—but, stupidly, didn't *know* beforehand—there are a couple chutes here, one for wood and one for coal. The chutes angle from the kitchens up to the street outside to make fuel deliveries easier and cleaner. Lords don't like coal haulers traipsing through their great halls. Both chutes are locked, which won't be a problem, but the wood chute is filled with a few cords of wood, maybe more.

The guards check the kitchens every minute or two. There's no way I can clear out that chute without making a terrible racket, the guards raising the alarm, and then me having to kill some of them.

But with every passing minute, the odds of Trudana Jadwin's murder being discovered ratchets higher. When they find her dead, they may well realize Lord Repha'im wasn't my target at all, and many of those guarding him are going to come flooding through the rest of the mansion to hunt me.

The coal chute is about the same width as from my elbow to my fingertips, and it's a coal chute: pitch black even to my sight and full of black dust to make breathing an agony. But it's not full of coal, yet. An estate this size must take deliveries daily, though, so I can't count on it being empty for long.

I examine the lock but have to stop as the guards' footsteps come closer. The good thing about my tripping the alarm is that there's no kitchen staff about. Doubtless they're all either huddled fearfully in their rooms or locked outside the front gate. What I'm doing now wouldn't be possible if the kitchens were as busy as they normally would be in the early morning.

The guards check the kitchen, grumbling about jumpy mages and making jokes about the kid getting a whipping for the false alarm.

Amateurs. They should be *more* afraid because they haven't seen anything, not less.

With the ka'kari, I quickly open the lock to the coal chute, hide what coal is still piled inside in one of the great black kettles nearby, and take my unstrung bow from my pack. I'm flexible enough to fit into such a small space, but I won't be taking anything extra with me. I stow the bow behind one of the neat piles of wood along one wall, tie one end of my bowstring around the latch of the coal chute door, and tie the other end to my foot so I can pull the door closed behind me.

I hear the guards coming to the kitchen again. Early.

Somehow, I wedge myself into the coal chute and begin to wiggle my way up into it. But I haven't pulled my feet all the way into the dark tunnel, much less closed the chute door behind me, when I hear one of them say, "What's that?"

In my exhaustion, I actually freeze instead of acting immediately. Do I throw myself back into the room and start killing, or flee?

"Alarm!" another voice says. "Murder! Upstairs somewhere! C'mon!"

I wait until I hear them running, then wiggle forward and pull the chute's door shut behind me with the bowstring tied to my foot, closing myself into the darkness.

The chute is as unpleasant as you'd imagine, thick with dust, smelling slightly of rotten eggs, and not cut smooth. It takes me a few minutes to make it to the grate at the top. It's locked. Seriously, why couldn't the full-time staff here be as incompetent as the mercenaries?

I would've been in real trouble if I didn't have the ka'kari to cut through the hinges for me.

~Is that *appreciation*? Finally.~

I ignore it as I so often do and flop into the street, coughing, spitting grit, thankful for the sweetness of the relatively clean air.

But I don't allow myself to lie there in the alley. The rest of the city knows nothing of what just happened, and morning bustle is in full force, the only change being the large knot of tradespeople stuck outside the mansion's locked front gate, demanding to know why they can't come in.

I climb to a vantage point down the block as shrill whistles cut the morning air. I've gotten away clean.

Well, not *clean*. I need to find someplace safe to bathe—and sleep. Using the ka'kari and my Talent so much takes it out of me, and I haven't slept in... I'm not sure how long it's been.

But maybe now that Trudana's dead I'll be able to sleep again.

I turn the thought over as I see men saddling horses inside the mansion's walls, rushing about. I see the red magical shielding come down.

No. Probably not. Good sleep isn't in the cards for someone like me. But I can flop unconscious into a bed for a few hours before the nightmares visit again. That's probably the best I can hope for, after all I've been through. After all I've done.

Daytime is no time for a living piece of the night, so I'm about to melt away safely from the morning light when something down a side street below me catches my eye. It's a raggedy street kid young enough that at first I can't tell if it's a boy or girl, hair cropped short against the lice and fleas. Intentionally going around a corner from the bigger kids who might take his prize, the kid pulls out a ball.

Not a ball. *The* ball. I can tell from the kid's delight at his new treasure. He must have found it wherever it landed after the mage tossed it out of the estate an hour ago.

The crowds at the front gate are parting, tradesmen and horsemen yelling at each other, and suddenly I know exactly what's going to happen.

I don't know where the horsemen think they're going. Surely they can't think they're going to find me, but I see them splitting up, maybe thirty of them, going different ways in groups. Maybe taking messages to friends or superiors, maybe hoping to head me off somehow.

They're getting jammed up by the morning crowds.

The kid's down an empty side street, but that's precisely what's going to put him in danger. I just know it. One of those knots of horsemen is going to come charging down that empty street five abreast with no room to maneuver. They're gonna come around that blind corner, and...

And it's not my problem.

I've gotten away clean; I left no compelling evidence that I was Trudana Jadwin's killer. If I go down there now, I could ruin everything.

Besides, the kid could move at any time. It's his own fault.

~Who are you trying to convince?~

I'm already moving. Not to save the kid. Just to get closer.

I see the horses break free of the crowd, and everything happens exactly the way I knew it would. The horses run over the stupid kid, sending him flying, with one of them stomping on the stupid kid's head and smashing it open.

~That's what you want me to record? You want to skip the part where you fell to the earth like a meteorite burning with sapphire flames, made two of the horses throw their riders, scooped up the kid, deposited him safely a few blocks away, and then disappeared?~

I was planning to skip that, yes.

~So then... should I cut out the earlier bit about you being honest?~

Would you obey me if I told you to leave it my way?

The ka'kari doesn't answer, and now isn't the time to find out what would happen if push comes to shove.

Fine. Leave it however the hell you want. But saving that kid was a mistake. It gave me away, confirmed Repha'im's suspicions, and put Momma K's head on the block. I should never have done it. The rest of this wouldn't have happened if I'd let the stupid kid die.

Chapter Seven

No Contract, No Pay

The rooftop of my building in Elenea is high enough to be removed from the bustling city below and windy enough to be perilous. The night air is cold enough to be bracing and clean enough to be refreshing, and yet it does nothing to clear my head.

I didn't tell you how it went when I talked with Count Drake. I hadn't thought it through beforehand. Story of my life, huh? I'd meant to offer the account to him. Scribble it all down in my little black codex and drop it off with his porter, maybe. But I didn't do that. I just showed up.

He was overjoyed to see me until I told him why I was there. Said he didn't want anyone killing anyone for him, said he got out of that line of work a long time ago—that there was nothing that could more imperil his soul.

Yeah, he still loves to talk about his soul. And mine too, if I'm not quick to head off the conversation.

I thought that meant he was sort of glad I'd done it without him asking me to. Foolishly, I said so. Shouldn't have. I wasn't in a good frame of mind, but then I haven't been for a long time.

He said some things that were all fair and true and hurt like hell.

I said things I regret.

Honestly, I don't know why I thought he'd want to hear about me killing Trudana Jadwin in the first place. Me, regaling him like a drunk veteran trying to impress some new recruit? Given Drake's history, it was more like a kid hot off his first battle bragging to an old master sergeant about all his fighting experience. The hell was I thinking?

That he'd break down in tears because I'd given him closure, that I'd given his daughters justice? That he'd tearfully admit I've redeemed all I've become because I used my skills for him?

That he'd be impressed?

Gods, I wanted him to tell me I did good, didn't I? I thought I'd stride back into the Drakes' lives and things would somehow be good again, normal. That we could just talk.

I've got no one to talk to.

How did Durzo do it, being alone all those years?

Hell, I even managed to louse things up with *him*, quarreling with and driving away the one person in all Midcyru who really could understand, and maybe even help me.

Maybe I just need to talk. I mean, I'm not *weak*. It's good enough to put it all into words, like this, to the ka'kari. It's good to hear yourself, and good to see what you've said later, so you don't keep going in the same circles, stuck in your own head. I don't have the patience to journal and the ka'kari can record things in real time, so I've decided to keep this up for a bit. There's something soothing about a flow of words, even if they're your own.

There are people down there in that moonlit city, people who'd be happy to fawn over the war hero Kylar Stern. People who want things from me. Funny how all the ones who really know me are angry at me, have left to go do better things, or are dead.

I mean, don't get me wrong. I don't need any more than this. This life is good enough. Good even! I've got all I need. I'm not starving. Have a warm place to sleep. Things to call my own. Everything I wanted as a kid on the streets? I've got it all.

Maybe the night air has cleared my head. There's something rattling around in my chest, a hollow discontent, but maybe no one ever gets rid of that; maybe that's just the pain that lets you know you're alive. How could I want any more than this? I'm fine.

Chapter Eight

A Visit from Mom

*T*he tulip is dead. Has been for a while now.

I think it died while I was in Cenaria killing Lady Jadwin. Nothing I've done has revived it. It'd probably be dead by now regardless. I should throw it out. Every day, when I can't bear them anymore, I crawl out of my twisted blankets on the floor, and there it is, cheerily desiccated, the only adornment in my aggressively bare apartments.

Logan wanted to give me a mansion in his new capital city, wanted to honor me in a hundred ways after the Battle of Black Barrow. He's a good man. I think he's even a good king, despite his taste in friends. I didn't want honors. Didn't want a huge house because I don't want staff. I don't want to be tied to anything. Any people I had would be a hindrance. I would put them in danger. I would *be* a danger.

After I refused, he gave me this building instead, seven stories tall, filled with luxurious apartments for visiting diplomats and wealthy traders and lords who are all scrambling to set up business in the high king's new capital. Logan took care of the building's staffing and security, appointing a trustworthy chatelaine—this place is too fancy for a mere landlady—who collects the rents and does... whatever it is such people do. Apparently, my profits are deposited into accounts with numerous banking families around the city. I don't know. I've never checked.

I occupy the cavernous top floor myself. Have my own entrance. Have secure exits from the roof if I need them. No one bothers me anymore.

There were some attempts on my life in the first couple months. Nothing serious.

But something feels wrong this morning. Some intuition of danger stirs me.

As if unaware, I ease the tension in my muscles and scrub the sleep out of my eyes, checking the empty room in quick glances.

Nothing.

I check the sight lines in through the windows before I move, in case a marksman is out somewhere, lining up the shot. Then I do my usual: checking my traps and mechanically putting hardtack and jerked meat in my belly. Maybe it's a false alarm. It happens. I had a pigeon trigger one of my trip wires once and spent half the night lying in wait, ready to ambush attackers who never came.

I leave my blankets in a pile and don't change or wash my clothes. What's the point? I'll be training in them later. I don't shave my scraggly dark stubble. My fingers catch as I try to brush my unruly hair out of my eyes. It's not only sticking every which way, it's starting to mat. If I don't wash it soon, I'm going to have to cut it off. Funny how I'm rich now, and I probably looked better when I lived on the streets.

In my left hand, I pick up my dead tulip in its white pot and take it out to my balcony to give it some sun. The flower is withered and ugly, the leaves yellow and brown. I should give up on it. I know. I know how to care for and harvest dozens of the most common poison-yielding plants, but nothing I've tried has brought my tulip back.

If it were a regular plant, I'd give up. But it's not. And the only thing I can think of that might bring it back is magic.

Unfortunately, finding someone who might do that kind of magic means leaving my apartments. It means talking to someone. It means trusting someone not to destroy my last reminder of her.

I've barely started on the rope work portion of my morning training when there's rapping on my door. My heart stops and I flip silently to the floor, landing on my toes.

People aren't supposed to be able to get access to my private stairway.

"Kylar?" a woman's voice says.

I walk to the door. It has a spy hole, but I don't use it.

"You," I say, as I pull the door open. It comes out ruder than I meant, so I try to make amends with "How is it you look younger every time I see you?"

"Shut up and get out of my way," Momma K says, pushing past me as if I'm a recalcitrant child. She waves at her bodyguards to stay outside. They obey without question.

With her perfume filling my nostrils—head notes of neroli, maté, and ambrette seed, heart notes of jasmine and orange blossom and maybe tiare flower, and a base of cedar, black ootai, and chestnut?—I close the door behind her like a doorman. It's a new perfume for her, just as expensive as her old scent, but more regal.

"Please do come in, Your Grace," I say to her back, sarcastic.

She's staring around my place with obvious displeasure, then at me, disgust yielding to disappointment.

The woman known as Gwinvere Kirena Thorne, or Duchess Thorne—or merely Momma K to us old guild rats and gutter kids—is never less than well put together, but she's the soul of cold style today, in loose casual dress of cerulean silk that probably cost more than all my tenants together pay in rent. Lean and graceful, with eyes as sharp as the knives she so long directed, she looks perhaps forty, though she's at least a decade older.

"They told me," she says, sniffing at my mess. "But I didn't think you'd let yourself sink so far."

"May it please Your Grace," I say, sweeping into an elaborate court bow, "I have not yet begun to sink." Momma K taught me whatever courtly manners I still have, and this goes over as well as expected.

She gives me a flat stare, but I'm not a street kid shivering in her parlor anymore. She says, "I brought you a present. But that's not why I'm here. I've been trying to avoid it for both our sakes, but the real reason I've come is to hire you."

"Good! I was hoping this would be a short conversation."

"You owe me, Kylar."

I purse my lips. "Get someone else."

"I've tried. It's an impossible job."

"There are no impossible jobs, only impossible prices," I say automatically.

"Exactly what Durzo used to say, right before he'd gouge me." She smiles, amused, and the room's chill goes balmy, but my numbness insulates me even from her.

"Then why don't you make him do it?" I ask.

She looks away, and I see her spinning a ring on one finger with her thumb. It has only a small white opal on it. The rubies she wears today make it look almost comically small and modest. A wedding ring perhaps?

"He's...unavailable," she says, forcing a smile.

Starting life on the streets gave me a keen sense of when someone might get violent, at the cost of being worse at differentiating other emotional states, and

Momma K is such a skilled liar I shouldn't be able to tell that she's forcing that smile, so either she wants me to see the pretense for what it is, or her pain is so sharp she can't hide it.

I'm guessing it's manipulation. She wants me to ask about Durzo. Or if her pain is real, she's probably planning to use it to get me to do this job for her, whatever it is.

"That's too bad," I say. "Thanks for coming by."

I walk toward the door to usher her out.

Instead, she heads out onto my balcony.

I feel like a petulant child, but I don't follow her. I walk back to my ropes and am about to resume my exercises when I see that she's busy with something out on the balcony.

I'm there in an instant.

"Put that down!" I say.

Her back is to me. A knife flashes in her hands, and a brown leaf drops to the ground. Then another. Another.

My tulip. But I can't even move to stop her.

"It's not a kill," she says.

"What? The flower? Stop!"

She sighs, as if she expects better from me. "The job. Anyone else doing the job would have to kill people to get it done. Innocent people. And if we hesitate, innocents will die regardless. You're the only one who can do it cleanly. One little heist, Kylar. It might save Logan's life. Maybe more. Maybe much more."

"A heist? Heists never work. And why me? I'm a wetboy, not a thief." She knows how I feel about Logan. I don't want her to press me on that. "Hell, I'm not even that anymore."

"A heist's not so dissimilar from an assassination, is it? And they can work if you keep them simple. Just do what you did at Lord Repha'im's estate—minus the torture and murder and being spotted like an amateur."

I don't bother denying it. I'm not going to discuss that job. "For the last time—"

She gestures out at the city. "Have you thought through the implications of building this city on top of a magically preserved ancient battlefield?"

The shift in topic baffles me. "Haven't been worrying about it, no," I say.

"I have. The dome and the magic that kept people out of this area for centuries also protected some things inside it. Most of what people brought to that last battle long ago has decayed, of course, especially the magical items. But some survived. Of those, some were stolen immediately, before I realized no one else was placing guards out there and decided to do it myself. You see, I consider everything recovered from Black Barrow to belong to our new high king. I want those things back. All of them."

"That's nice," I say. She hates it when I give her that tone.

"Trouble is, the people I'd send to find powerful or intriguing magical items are all . . ."

She lets the sentence hang, quizzing me. "Mages themselves," I say, begrudgingly playing her game. I know where this goes next, so I say, "And mages are precisely the people who have the most to gain by keeping whatever they find."

"See? There's that mind I love, Kylar. Sharp as a splitting maul."

"Aren't splitting mauls—?"

"Exactly. Follow along now. In the midst of doing everything necessary to guide the setup of not one kingdom, but four, I've had to trust people, and then I've had to trust the people I set to watch over those people. Problem: Not all of them are worthy of trust."

"That must've been a shocking revelation for an old crime boss," I say. "But I don't like where this is going. It sounds like this job comes with a side of assassination after all."

Momma K has never taken betrayal lightly. Before she switched which side of the law she worked on, Durzo had worked for her, and he'd done a *lot* of work for her.

"*No one* likes where this is going," she says pleasantly. "We should all just get along. We should agree Logan is the best king any of us is likely to see for a hundred years. We should serve him without reservation. Isn't it nice that when people see what they should do, they do it with no further prompting?" Her tone is sweet, but impatient.

"No need for that," I say. I feel sullen. Worse, I sound it.

"We want the same thing, Kylar," she says.

"I want you to leave me alone."

"Happily. But we both want Logan safe."

"I want that because I believe in him," I say. "You want it not only because he's the only noble who would've ever taken a risk on you, but because he still is. You keep Logan safe because it keeps you safe and in power. Logan goes, and so do you."

She sighs. "Still have that stubborn streak of righteous idealism, huh? Even after everything. The question is: So what, Kylar? So what if I'm being purely selfish in this?"

It takes me off guard, because, in truth, I know I'm being an ass. On most days, I'd tell you Momma K is as hard as her circumstances have always required. Momma K pretends that everything she does is in naked self-interest. The truth is that she turns her better nature into also serving her self-interest: feeding and sheltering and saving the lives of street kids? She could never admit she hates seeing starving, abused children. No, she declared that was simply an investment, because the street kids of today would be the criminals of the future. Earn their loyalty now, she'd say, and the best of them will stay loyal forever.

She fishes in one of her pockets and tosses me a silvery band. I catch it. By the weight, I guess it's white gold, not silver, a bracelet with a deeply cut endless knot in some ancient style I can't place. "This is my gift?" I ask. "Jewelry? You shouldn't have. And I mean that."

"That's not my gift. It's a trinket. At least that's what Durzo said when he asked me to pass it along. Holds the ka'kari for you when you want it close but not touching your skin. Said you might figure out when that would be wise in a decade or two."

Ouch. That does sound like Durzo. "Magical?" I ask.

She snorts. "That's what I asked, too. He said no, but platinum resists devouring. Subsequent tests verified it's not magical."

"Ah." Platinum. Not white gold. And of course she tested it.

"Speaking of ka'kari," she says.

"Were we speaking of the ka'kari?" I ask. "I thought we were on to talking about the gift you have for me?"

"No. Ka'kari. Kylar, you have the greatest of the ka'kari. We know that a few of the others are safely guarded in Ezra's Wood, but—oh, I have your attention now."

I hadn't even noticed, but I took a breath and braced myself as soon as she said *others*. "You have word of another ka'kari? Hidden here?" I ask.

"I have rumors. Cold trails. Tales of magic gone awry. Mount Tenji spewing fire and ash for a hundred days after the battle. The Tlaxini Maelstrom collapsing. Sea serpents in the Black Waters off Friaku. Tidal waves on Gandu and the Silk Coast. Magic gone awry. Omens. Terrified priests. All the usual noise.

But the greatest danger I can imagine to Logan—and to the rest of us—comes from the ka'kari. The mages are hinting at bad days coming. This is a long-term play I have for you, Kylar, but it's a big one. One skirmish in a long war with a hundred fronts. It's my job to foresee threats to the man you say you love so much."

The man *I say* I love so much? That nettles me, but I see it's a hook, a trap, a manipulation. She gets me to talk about Logan, and then what I owe him, and then how I can serve him—by serving Momma K. So I swallow my anger, ignore her bait. "You want me to hunt rumors? That's not a heist, that's spy work."

"What's been stolen is an artifact. Translated it's called the Crepuscular Compass."

"The come again?"

Momma K sighs. "The Twilight Compass, then, either the time between times at either morning or night. Maybe it only works at those times. Maybe something about it is particularly shadowy. I don't know. What matters is we need it. It will help us find who holds the ka'kari...or at least who last held them."

"How's it do that?"

"It's got another name. One you should find most intriguing. Its only power is that it helps find people. Supposedly, you do whatever's required to activate it; then you speak the name given at birth to a person and it points toward them. It doesn't tell you how far away they are, or even if they're living or dead. It merely points toward them. A very limited artifact, as such things go, but..."

I frown. "Limited? I can think of a thousand uses for such a thing. *Especially* for wet work."

She smiles with genuine affection for me, and if I don't miss my guess, with a certain joy at being understood. "Me too," she says. "Which I'd guess is how it picked up its other name. A demigoddess, a daughter of Mother Night herself, she was an early avatar of retributive justice. The one who follows: implacable, merciless, ruthless, relentless in her pursuit of the guilty. Remind you of anything?"

She isn't asking if I know the goddess's name. She means that the goddess sounds a lot like a Night Angel. In some tellings, the first of us. I ignore the chill down my back. "It reminds me of a superstition Durzo once laughed about."

"Durzo can afford to laugh about a lot of things the rest of us should fear. But that's beside the point. Even if Nemesis never existed, even if this artifact has no connection to her whatsoever, I believe this Nemesis Compass is real. We can't afford *not* to act as if it is. The mere possibility that it exists tells me that it's worth a lot of effort to make sure no one else gets it. You understand?"

I do. More than she'd like. I see now how carefully she crafted her pitch. The connection to the Night Angel, the magic, the fear of losing something powerful to some enemy. "Sounds like a real important job," I say. "But I've got an important job already. I'm a landlord now."

She scoffs, amused. "Kylar, if you were going to retire, you'd've done it. You wouldn't have done that job at the Repha'im estate. Some of my best agents have been doing 'one last job' for me for twenty years, Kylar. Truth is, people like us don't get new jobs. We're lucky if we get new masters—a thousand times luckier than most if our new master is a man like Logan. No matter how you lie to yourself, you'll get pulled back into the life, and the longer you wait to do what you must, the more heartache and grief you'll cause everyone around you."

I cut her off. "I'm glad you've found work that'll let you sleep at night. Good for you." I pause. "But then, you never did have a troubled conscience, did you? No matter what. Guess that's just me and my weakness."

For a moment, I see a flash of real anger in her eyes, but then she glances at the sun and sheathes her little belt knife. "Please do excuse me. I've been commanded to appear before the high king today. I knew the nobles would move against me—an old whore, in charge over them? I knew they'd find it unbearable—but I didn't expect it so soon. I'm being put on trial for gross misuse of power and murder. So either Lord Repha'im is a fool, or...well, we'll see, won't we?"

"Murder?" I ask. "You? What murder?"

"Yes, Kylar. You didn't think you were *solving* problems with that little stunt of yours, did you?" She finally turns to face me. "Lord Repha'im is alleging that Trudana Jadwin was assassinated on my orders. Cenaria is my city. My turf, my responsibility."

She hands me the flowerpot, which I take dumbly. A bare brown stem jutting from bare brown earth is all that's left. "I may have saved the bulb from the rot setting in, though you won't know until next year," she says, as if she hadn't just announced she was heading to trial for a murder I committed. "In gardening, death requires management, Kylar. One must neither rush it nor delay it too long. You've done both, but perhaps this may still bloom again."

"Answer's still no," I say.

She produces a handkerchief and wipes her hands. She's never minded getting them dirty, but one can't appear in court with visibly soiled hands.

"Kylar, you have no idea how much it's costing Logan to protect you while you've been here pouting like a child, and he can't afford it. Cut the stem off in a couple weeks," she says, patting my cheek. The maternal kindness of the gesture is belied by the stone in her gaze. "One way or the other, I won't be here to do it for you."

"Hey," I say. "I thought you said you brought me a present. Where is it?"

"Not it. He. He's in the hall. Actually, he's a good example of the last thing I wanted to tell you." She squints in distaste as she looks at my face. "Do something well or don't do it at all. That includes growing a beard."

"Why don't you just say it?" I demand.

"What is it you want me to say?" she asks, as if she doesn't know. Being treated as if I'm stupid has always been an easy way to get me furious.

"Say it! 'She's dead, Kylar.' 'Get over it, Kylar. Move on.' 'You've had your time to grieve, Kylar.'"

She looks at me as if I'm a puzzle to solve. "I won't say any of those things because I don't say idiotic things, Kylar. You'll never get over Elene. Either your character or your circumstances will force you to start moving forward again. That's all. And she won't move with you, because she's gone. And that will hurt. And then someday you'll start to forget her from time to time. And that will hurt too. And then you'll forget her for longer and longer, and that will hurt more. You won't be able to recall her face exactly, and that will feel like betrayal. And on, and on. No one's saying there's no pain, Kylar. Pain is part of the deal. Maybe it's the whole deal."

"It's a bad deal," I say, though this conversation echoes one we had long ago too closely for comfort.

"There is no other deal," she says softly. "So grow the hell up."

She goes—and it irks me that she doesn't even have the common decency to slam the door.

Chapter Nine

The Weight of Shadows

The Chantry's scholars posit three types of immortality. Only the One God himself—if such a fiend exists—might have the highest type: total invulnerability to time and to the sword. Below that, the elshaddim never age, but when embodied they are partly vulnerable to the sword: Though their essences are undying, their bodies may be killed, and such a death banishes them from taking on flesh again. The highest kind of immortality a human might hope for, even with the most powerful magic, is the lowest type. "Don't call it eternal life," the scholars say in their measured speech. "Call it life indefinitely extended, where aging is slowed perhaps to a stop, but otherwise, all else is as before."

They say all this with the great confidence of women who are entirely wrong.

I know, for I am what they say cannot be. Not only am I invulnerable to time's patient knives, but given enough time, my body will Heal me of anything, even death.

Of course there's a catch. Several. No one explained to me how it works, and it took me several lives to figure out the worst part: Every time I die, no matter what, someone I love dies in my place.

I have a thirst for justice I can't suppress. All my talents are for violence. I grew up on the streets, where I was trained by a legend. Everything I am has been shaped for fast, lethal action.

Everywhere I go, I see suffering calling out for my skills—but is there anything I can change that's worth it slowly causing the deaths of everyone I care about? If I slip, the innocent die for me. My failures have already cost me the one light in my world of darkness.

This is why I must be perfect. This is why I have to find out what's caused this curse I bear, and end it.

My name is Kylar Stern. I am the Night Angel, and this is the weight of shadows.

The preceding page had originally been written in a slow, meticulous hand—but over the entire page, Kylar had slashed an angry X. Below, in a fast, loose hand, he'd written more.

I don't know how to tell this damned story. Everything I try is a lie. A story's a promise, isn't it? This isn't the story of how I tried to end my curse. Maybe it should be. Remind me to come back and try something else. This is all wrong.

Viridiana exhaled slowly. And again, blinking against a tide of emotions she could never name.

Kylar hadn't come back to fix it. Hadn't tried something else later.

She knew why.

Chapter Ten

A Godking in Ruins

You're too late," the man says, coming inside, the words rattling rough from a rusty throat. Softening his hard-angled face, he has a magnificent, neatly trimmed black beard. At the moment, he doesn't look like a madman.

But he doesn't look like a former king, either. Momma K's 'present' is none other than Dorian Ursuul, formerly a renowned Healer and mage, and later formerly Godking Wanhope, king of Khalidor and Lodricar. He is a man who's disrupted my life more than once.

His clothes are fine, but disheveled, as if he sleeps in them. Rather than a deposed king or a madman, however, he looks like a kid who's getting away with something and is pleased with himself about it. His black hair is awry, but not dirty, and he doesn't have the pinched look of starvation, which tells me he's only recently escaped his handlers.

As I understand it, Dorian spends the majority of his time catatonic, sitting in one corner of the castle or another, unresponsive. He'll chew and swallow food given to him and give signs when he needs to use a latrine, and follow where he's led, but that's it.

Logan had him examined by every sort of magical and medical authority he could find, and they were unanimous in concluding he's not faking his condition, whatever it is. Nor does he try to evade responsibility for his misrule when he does come to his senses for brief interludes.

A harder king, or perhaps a wiser one, would have executed him.

Dorian is a prophet, though no one agrees exactly what that means.

He has a long beard now, and his icy blue eyes are going glassy, slowly losing their focus on mine.

"Nice to see you looking well, Dorian," I say.

He snaps back to the present. "Sane, you mean?"

"Yes," I admit. "Too late for what?"

He interlaces his fingers and twists them sharply. "You're looking quite fit," he says. "Everything about you looks even better than before—"

"Occupational hazard. I train all the—"

"—except your eyes."

I clench my jaw.

"You're one of the slow casualties of war, aren't you?" he says, unfazed. "And you can't afford to be. How are we ever going to get you moving?"

"You're the prophet; I'm sure you've got just the trick."

A flash of irritation crosses his face. "You know, I can't get used to that. Being treated like I have nothing to offer except my one thing. As if I, Dorian, am nothing more than the most inconvenient talent I possess. I who have been a Healer, a king, a student and a master of many of the world's most difficult magics, reduced in everyone's eyes to the mad prophet." '

"Too late for what, Dorian?" I ask again.

"Tell me about the boy."

"What boy?" I ask.

"The one you didn't kill."

"You think I kill children so often that that narrows things down?"

He stares flatly at me. "I don't have all day, Kylar."

"If you know enough to ask about it, you know everything about it."

"No," he says. "The black ka'kari interferes with my vision. I lose things about you. Miss things."

"Oh. Good news at last. You're telling me I can use one irritant to block another? Though I have to confess, it does seem like donning a cloak of mosquitoes to fend off a swarm of bees."

"Why didn't you kill the boy?"

"Lost my nerve," I say.

He squints at me, as if he's wondering if I'm lying.

"I know I messed up. How much is that gonna cost me?" I ask.

He looks off into the distance. I can't tell if he's gone again, and I'm about to ask when he says, "Maybe it's better to save one child than to save the whole world."

"The whole world? Is that all?" I ask. "Wow. Just some kid off the street, too! That's some power!"

"As I recall, you were just some kid off the street."

"You know the trouble with prophecy, Dorian?" I say, my heat rising.

"A bit," he says, his affect flat. "But please, do lecture me."

"The problem with prophecy is prophets."

"Oh, let's not make this abstract. You mean the problem with *my* prophecies is *me*. And, yes, I fall short, no doubt," Dorian says. There is nothing weak or apologetic in him now, though.

"No, no, no," I say. "I mean people assume that the prophet's merely a vessel for a message, that he doesn't change the message to steer things how he wants. But I've seen what you do when you have knowledge others don't, Dorian. You knew Logan was alive when you seduced Jenine. You let a grieving bride think her husband was dead so you could marry her yourself. I don't deny that you try to do good too, but you're the last person I'd trust with 'secret knowledge.' "

Dorian levels a hooded gaze at me. "My failings obscure my message. Yes. As I said. You're accusing me of what I admitted."

Oh. "Then why are you here? Are you helping Momma K? You clearly have some plan to manipulate me into doing something I don't want to do."

A melancholy too deep for words settles around the man who once was regarded as a god. He says, "No, Kylar. All my power is for nothing. My son needs me."

Something about how he says that is odd. "Son? Only one of them needs you?"

"There only is the one. Ask Vi if you still don't understand. I don't have the time to explain. Jenine and I are united in this much at least. Our son needs us, and we can't save him. I know all our efforts will be in vain, yet we can't help but try."

"So you're going to trick me into doing it," I say.

His eyes flash, and he talks slowly, as if speaking to an imbecile. "No, because that would be my power changing things. Which I already said won't work. You don't even want to hear me, do you?"

I move to speak, but he cuts me off, saying, "Let me try it like this: You ever play pockets?"

"I *have*." Smooth table, ivory balls, a stick, and unsurprisingly, pockets as goals. I say, "So far as I can tell, it's another excuse for noblemen to gamble."

"Imagine that instead of everything being known and uniform as it is in that game, instead the balls were each different sizes, that you don't know the number of players, or even the location of all the pockets. Imagine the table is always changing, that sometimes there are grooves and lumps hidden under the felt, and that all the players strike simultaneously and repeatedly. Oh, and the balls have some power to change their own courses. Some even change size in midroll. That's the game I'm condemned to playing, Kylar, as are we all. In a universe that is free and vast, prophecy is merely being able to see a bit more of the table than most others do."

"Uh-huh. Right. I still wouldn't wager against you."

"All my powers are a breath in a gale, Kylar."

"Pretend whatever you like." I raise my hands, palms up. "You're still *here*. Swinging your stick at my balls."

"Kylar, do you know what happens to a man too long isolated?"

"What—?"

"I do."

I squint. "You do...know?"

Dorian's lips thin in frustration. Then he expels a great breath. Then he stops. He cocks his head suddenly, as if at a sound only he can hear. "No time for follow-ups, I'm afraid. It appears I have only about a ten count of sanity left."

I don't want to interrupt, even to urge him on. I don't want to look eager. This is all a manipulation. It's all about power. It always is, with these people.

But even though I'm not going to believe a word out of his mouth, I can't help but be curious what it's going to be.

Even as the moments slip by, he stares at me hard, as if daring me to yell at him and waste his remaining time.

He finally says, "The Night Angel judges, but who judges him? The truth is, I'm not here to change your path, Kylar. I'm here so that when you don't, you remember that you *chose* not to. My revenge is that you judge yourself."

His eyes go glassy. The mad prophet is mad once more, locked in the solitary confinement of his own skull, and what stares at me now through the bars of all his past decisions has nothing of the divine spark in it. He is an empty vessel in an empty cell.

Chapter Eleven

The Wrong Man to Ambush

After Momma K's people take away the now-vacant-eyed Dorian, it takes me only a few minutes to sponge bathe, pull my hair into some order, dress, and—sliding back lock after lock—finally confront my weapons closet.

"Different battles require different arms, eh, Master?" I say.

I talk to myself these days. Not because I'm lonely; it moves the tumblers around the locks of my mind differently. In the echoing canyons of your own brain, you can repeat a thought a thousand times and never realize it, never escape it. If you start doing that out loud, you pretty quickly realize you sound like a lunatic.

I hope relating things to the ka'kari like this will help me stop the habit.

I grab a single belt knife and a gladius whose chief virtue is that its jeweled scabbard matches the nobleman's foppery I have to wear. When you go somewhere you'll need to let yourself be disarmed, don't bring a weapon you'll mind losing.

Two minutes later, at the street, I ask the building's porter, "Carriage?"

"None available in the last hour, milord, what with the goings-on at the castle. Could get you my brother's horse. Ten minutes?"

I start running.

You'd think I'd own a horse. But again, that's something else to take care of, or a contract to keep paying for. Either way it's a tie for someone to use to find me. A danger. It takes a certain amount of sophistication and constant care to secretly keep up safe houses and transportation and even weapons.

I have the sophistication.

My old master would point out that I'm living in one place, openly, under my own idiot name. What additional danger does owning a horse add?

None. So I'm inconsistent even at breaking my own rules. Fine.

I run past a mugging right away.

That's not usual this close to the castle, not in this city. Not that I've been out and about so much, but the scum doing the mugging seems weird somehow.

Poor people can't afford to migrate to a new city in the first wave. They'll come in time. What would a city be without the poor? But for now, we have a better class of scum. So maybe that's all it is. Three men hassling a shopkeeper. Extortion? But their cloaks match, and so do their boots. Seems like a mercenary company rather than the normal thugs.

But then, I guess even mercenary companies need to eat. Maybe they came to the city looking for work and haven't found it.

A couple blocks later, in a high-walled alley between two estates that I take for the shortcut, three women are beating a man.

I grew up in Cenaria. I've seen violent women; these women are eerily quiet. Only one speaking, all of them noticing me instantly. It's strange. Men will sometimes sink into a primitive silence when they turn to violence, but women rarely so. And regardless of gender, communal violence is never quiet.

Everything about this begs me to take a closer look.

"Please, help!" the man cries, his hands up over his bloodied face.

But I'm not looking at his face. His boots match the earlier mercenaries', and the women's.

The one at the back raises fingers to her lips to whistle.

Ambush.

The answer to any ambush is No.

There is a tenuous moment before a trap springs where the ambushers wait, frozen, focused for the instant their quarry steps too far. There's a story the hunters tell themselves about what their quarry will do, believing that fear and surprise will overtake its rational mind, and then it will fly into the greater danger they've prepared.

No.

I dash forward, reaching full speed in a few Talent-aided steps, dipping my hand into the second purse I carry, a purse full of steel shot.

Their eyes widen at my attack. They step back, clawing at the weapons they'd kept ready but concealed.

I fling a handful of the shot before me.

Caught in the act of drawing their weapons, with something—they know not what—flying through the air toward them, they can't help but flinch.

I'm upon them a moment later, the gladius only coming to my hand at the last moment. I sweep out and down, slashing deep through the first woman's thigh. I dive through the opening window of their blades rising, roll up beyond the second woman and barely sweep the short gladius through the meat of both of her buttocks.

Parry the spear of the last woman with my left arm and pin her to the building behind her through the guts, blade barely missing her spine.

She stares at me, wide-eyed, as I pull the gladius away and as the other women clatter to the alley amid their weapons.

But she doesn't fall, or try to wrench the spear from my grip. Instead, bravely, she brings her fingers to her lips to whistle.

Or would have, but the gladius relieves her of her fingers, and then stoppers any shout from emerging from her throat, a bloody metal cork to her windpipe.

The others are moaning on the ground, the first likely dying. The second may die. Neither has the presence of mind to shout.

The other ambushers must be out of the line of sight, thus necessitating the whistle.

Only now does the man they were pretending to beat up straighten. Fear and anger duel in his eyes.

I can feel the power gathering in him. A magus.

No. I lunge left-handed with the stolen spear.

The spearpoint dips into his torso and emerges from his side. He twists, and his body tears the spear from my one-handed grip.

I dash around the corner. No time to ensure the kill. The rest of the ambushers may appear at any moment.

Then I hop from a door handle to a rain spout to the top of an estate's wall.

At the main road, ten horses wait saddled under the guard of two men. It dashes my hopes of stealing a horse to be my getaway and get me to the castle. I can't kill two more men.

Well, I *could*.

But I shouldn't. Not on the main road, where it'll be seen and look unprovoked.

I hop across an alley, landing atop another estate's wall, drop into the estate, cross a lovely garden, wash my blade clean of blood in a burbling fountain, wake a rather large dog, and leap out into the next street before it can snap at my heels.

By the time I arrive breathless at the main gates of Castle Gyre, my mind is only beginning to grapple with all the obvious questions.

Was that a trap for any nobleman heading to the castle or for me in particu-lar? Most mercenary bands can't afford the services of a magus. Magi aren't supposed to do anything that could bring their respective schools into disre-pute, and mugging the new high king's nobles has to count as A Thing We Really Do Not Want to Be Associated With.

But again, people gotta eat. Even mercenaries. And just because I'm oh so spe-cial, that doesn't mean every strange thing that happens in the city is all about me.

Surely, if this had been another attempted hit—number six, I think?—they would've been more careful.

It all seems like one more reason to get the hell out of this city permanently. What am I gaining by staying in Elenea?

This isn't what Night Angels do. Sitting around with a target painted on my back? Who does that help?

I've been passive for months—far too long. I can't keep it up.

Soon, I step into the huge castle courtyard.

Places like this unnerve me a bit. Durzo taught me to avoid this kind of place. Hundreds of people, dozens upon dozens of angles of attack, no way to watch them all—and here I am, walking in as myself. The feelings of exposure and vulnerability are so sharp my stomach turns.

I know there are lords who want me dead. Some of them even have good reason for it. More are simply jealous but hide their hatred under false faces. To them, anyone closer to the high king than they are is someone pushing them further away. They're playing games I don't care about, that I don't have any intention of affecting—but that could get me killed.

What am I doing here?

What does it mean about me that I've come? What kind of fool am I?

I can't answer that. But if there's a price to be paid for my killing Lady Tru-dana Jadwin, I'm not going to leave someone else to pick up my tab.

For all her honeyed word-knives and deep plots, Momma K didn't really get me here by her arts, even though she'll think she did. She could've simply said, *They're blaming your kill on me. If you don't tell them the truth, I'll hang.*

I don't mind killing those who deserve it. To tell you the truth, with a certain class of the bad men, yeah, sometimes I even enjoy it.

But innocents dying so I can live?

Hell no. I've had enough of that for many lifetimes. No more. Never again. No matter what it costs me.

Chapter Twelve

A Villain at Court, or Two

*I*f you're listening to this, I suspect you're familiar with Castle Gyre, so I won't describe every glittering dome and flying buttress. For one thing, when the guides of the two-copper tour start talking about balconets and clerestories and entablatures, I honestly have no idea what they're talking about. I mean, I have eyes. I can see when a fancy thing is on top of another thing at a corner, and I can tell when it's done artistically, but mostly that stuff doesn't matter to me unless I need to climb it.

~I could help you with the vocabulary, if you like.~

I'm not gonna ask the left nut of darkness to define words for me.

~No need to get testy.~

That said, those who call Castle Gyre one of the wonders of the world aren't lying. Even aware as I am that I might be going to my death—exile seems more likely, though, knowing Logan—I feel a grudging awe.

It's all white marble with red veins and huge windows and stained glass and bright mosaics and immense tapestries. The entry hall alone comfortably holds perhaps a thousand people right now, half of them hurrying here and there, already inured to their surroundings after a few short months. The other half glance about from time to time, as if still disbelieving they're here, or that this castle is here.

I was part of this coming to be. A small part, truth be told. My Talent and the Talents of about a dozen of the most powerful mages in the world were harnessed together and amplified by Curoch and Iures—the Sword of Power and the Staff of Law—to make all this. And by all this, I mean not merely the castle, but the entire city. Dorian directed all that magic. Mostly, he says. Doing so broke his mind.

I'm not sure if all the rest of us are much better off. When I last saw him, Durzo seemed unaffected. Vi seems fine too. But some of the other mages were shattered, magically or mentally or both. My own mind seems—well, let's not talk about that right now.

Dorian claimed that this castle and much of the city newly created atop the ruins of Black Barrow didn't spring from his imagination alone. He said he simply restored what he felt was already here, as if there were an echo in the air from ancient times. Added to what was unimaginably old, the magic also wove in bits and pieces from each of us, knowing and unknowing, things from our imaginations or hopes or latent within our psyches.

I hope nothing of me got added. I certainly didn't try to add anything but my power, letting those stronger and wiser direct it. I can't imagine what horrors this city could hold if the magic had taken any cues from the dark, dead-end alleys of my brain.

Regardless, this new castle and new city has given our new high king a new start, a place removed from the corruption and failures of Cenaria and the murderous intrigues of Khalidor and Lodricar and the incessant clan wars of Ceura.

The great doors of the audience chamber are closed today, and the fussy polearm-wielding guards don't know me by sight. I really have been out of circulation too long.

"I need to get inside. Right now," I say. "Has Momma K gone in yet? Where's her case on the docket?"

They look singularly unimpressed.

"Who'd you say you were again?" one asks.

"Look..." the other tells me, "watch your tongue. You'll be in twice as much trouble as the duchess is right now if you don't refer to her properly. She's got a lot of scary friends who won't take kindly to anyone referring to her by that old name."

"Oh! Right. Duchess Thorne, I meant. I'm—uh, how to say this?—one of those scary friends. I'm Kylar Stern. You mind?"

One of them snorts.

"No you're not," the other says. "I've seen Lord Stern with my own eyes, near enough to touch. He's taller than the high king himself and exudes such power you're lucky if you can catch half a breath if you're in the same room. Power like he's got? You feel it in your chest fifty paces away."

These men are reminding me why I don't like people. "Really? He makes it hard to *breathe*?" I ask. "Just by being in the room? Doesn't sound terribly subtle. Isn't he supposed to be sneaky?"

I throw my hands up, a big motion to misdirect the eyes so I can *subtly* reach hands of magic unseen to rest against each man's diaphragm. I start pushing, gently at first.

"Well, I suppose, he can"—the guard who claimed to have seen me before takes a shallow breath—"turn it off when he wants to. You know, being the Night Angel and all. That's...mmm." He grimaces.

The other man rubs his belly.

Then, after the next time each exhales, he finds he can't take a new breath.

As confusion turns to fear, I say, "Just get the admissionarius or the cubicularius or whatever Logan's decided to call them out here, would you?"

One opens his mouth, eyes widening as he still doesn't breathe.

I release them before panic sets in. Perhaps before understanding has set in, too, because the men both gasp a few times, then look at each other.

I'm standing with my hands crossed, shoulders stooped, feet close together, trying not to look threatening.

"You're...you're..."

"Yes. We covered that," I say. "Now will you please go get someone who can order you to open this door?"

They look at each other, one turning white, the other rather green.

In two minutes, a round woman with iron-gray hair in a bun and an enormous key dangling from a chain of office around her neck is showing me not through that main door but instead to a side waiting room.

"Apologies again, Lord Stern," she says. "We do have so many new faces on staff. Half of them think you're a ghost. The other half a giant. Won't happen again."

"No, I don't think it will," I say flatly. Not for the reason she thinks, though, but because in about ten minutes, I'm going to be exiled or worse. "Has Duchess Thorne's case been called yet?"

"Where have you been?" she asks, puzzled. "That started yesterday. They're doing final recapitulations and apologias right now."

"Apologias?" I ask. One of Logan's many tasks has been trying to decide which legal traditions his new country is going to adopt. It's all borrowed traditions and borrowed titles and borrowed roots. No matter how strong, no matter how carefully chosen, is there any way a new empire conjured from thin air can work, or is this all doomed from the start?

She says, "After the complainant gives their version, the defense gets one last chance to rebut the case or, if their position looks dire, to beg for clemency."

I try to imagine Momma K begging. I injected her with a lethal poison once, and she didn't so much as ask for the antidote. She won't beg. Ever. She hadn't even told me that the trial had already started. And she might be speaking even now?

"Can you let her know I'm here?" I ask.

"No. The high king has ordered no surprises. He wishes the first royal trial of this magnitude to be orderly and just. No posturing or mummery, he said."

"Can you tell the king I'm here?"

"Of course. After the trial convenes. Else I wouldn't have brought you here."

"I mean now."

She stops dead in the hallway and turns to examine me. Her eyes are as sharp as her figure is round.

"I'm here on his orders," I say.

Her eyebrows come down and together, lips tight. "If that's true, he'll send for you."

"He'll send for me if you tell him I'm here."

There's sadness in her, but it yields to stone. "You were friends, weren't you?"

"We *are* friends. Best friends."

She shakes her head slowly. "A friend would have been here for him in these past terrible months."

The hell's that mean?

She leads me to a guarded door. Royal guards open it for her without question.

There are a few lords and ladies in the room, most of them consulting in low tones with counselors or each other, or looking over papers to memorize last-minute details regarding their cases, or trying to listen covertly to the trial in the next room. I don't recognize anyone.

Not good.

The admissionarius hustles through the doorway that leads to the royal courtroom to check up on whatever she'd missed by getting me.

"Oh, you made it. How unfortunate," a large, handsome nobleman with an elegant black beard and pale blue eyes says to me. I don't recognize him. He's seated, legs propped on a table, ankles crossed, a small codex open in one hand, the very picture of youthful lordly indolence, but his eyes are quick. He looks Khalidoran, but who can say, these days? I've got dark hair and light blue eyes myself.

"Do I know you?" I ask. There's something familiar about him.

"Bright side: You are too late, and I'm guessing you saved me some coin."

His words catch me, and I reappraise him. He's a big man, not young as I first supposed, but with the ageless look some bards and athletes have that seems to put them endlessly in their prime. I don't know him, and I can already tell I don't like him. "Excuse me?" I say.

"The mercenaries I hired to delay you. The job was technically to stop you altogether. And as they've obviously failed, I do hope they all had the courtesy to die trying? Saves me the second half of their fee."

The door to the royal court opens. A rotund herald with a booming voice calls out, "In the matter of the allegations that Duchess Thorne commissioned murder, His Royal Majesty will examine the plainants personally before rendering judgment. Lord Repha'im, come forth!"

"Your pardon," the nobleman says, standing, and he's much taller than I'd realized when he was lounging in the chair, "that's me." And now, too late, I recognize his voice from the estate. He tosses his book aside. "But let's do continue this soon."

Chapter Thirteen

On the Lethal Art of Diplomacy

The trial had to be the first time that I've had my life in imminent danger and felt bored.

Later, I realized I was bored because of my ignorance.

I'd like to give you the full account of how Logan saved my life and Momma K's and his entire kingdom within the course of about five minutes, but I can't. I was paying attention to all the wrong things, and not paying attention at all to the right ones.

When I watch martial artists fight, even those trained in arts I don't know, I can roughly judge the level of their training within moments. The untrained eye, however, needs scale, needs to see a master demolishing other fighters in order to know him a master. Even this is flawed, though: A trained fighter demolishing untrained ones can look the same as a master demolishing merely trained fighters. A lucky blow can look the same as skill.

To the untrained eye, the initial maneuvering of three masters, the feeling out of weaknesses, the preliminary attacks abandoned instantly when an inauspicious counter is offered—all of it looks like a lot of standing around, shuffling feet, moving forward, stopping, circling, stopping: a dance with none of the beauty of a dance. Boring.

When watching masters, if you blink at the wrong moment, a fight may end, and you won't even know what happened, or why others are applauding.

I honestly don't even have much of an excuse. At Momma K's feet, I was trained a little in the courtly arts of dialectical positioning and knife-edged words, even legal wrangling. So maybe, to find myself so bored that I was lost, I may have been more sunk in myself than I realized.

~May?~

Shut up, you.

Momma K—ugh, *Duchess Thorne*, it's hard to call someone by a new name after a lifetime—is a master of these arts, but her position was the worst of the three. Lord Repha'im seemed to have only aggression, and played as if his position was stronger than I thought it was. Wrongly, as it turned out.

He was playing up the offense he'd taken at my attack on his estate, demanding justice for the failed attempt on his life. Logan played as if weaker than I would've expected—him being the high king. He seemed either distracted, or exhausted, or was balancing far too many clashing demands to bring his whole attention to this matter. (All of these were true. Apparently I do still know my friend.)

I tried to make myself visible through the guards' halberds, which barred me from the Hall of Winds, but I was far off to the side, and Logan never glanced that I could see.

That is, until the end, when the admissionarius approached me from behind and said quietly, "His Highness asks that you do something subtly but unmistakably magical when he calls you forth."

I look at her. "Like what? You talked to him?"

"He sent me a message."

"In the middle of all this?" I hadn't seen Logan so much as whisper to an aide during the whole time I'd been watching. "Did he say anything more?"

Vi rubbed her eyes. This was turning out to be more complicated than she'd first expected. This was the second or third time Kylar had clearly gone back and added to or amended what he'd narrated before, but there were no markings to show edits in the text, no extra pages tucked in to allow for the extra words. Clearly, at some point, Kylar had gone from narrating for Count Drake's benefit alone to changing his mind and narrating his story for himself (or so he said), but also obviously for someone else—who? Several times he had made reference to expecting listeners, not readers. How much of what she was reading was the original? Had anything important been lost?

"Lord Kylar Stern," Logan announces. He's got a magnificent voice, strong and clear. It carries effortlessly. It's a more valuable talent than you'd guess in a commander or a king. But then, Logan has always had the whole package: tall, handsome, brilliant, brave, strong in every way. If anyone can make this new kingdom work, it'll be Logan. "Come forth."

The guards pull back their halberds.

The hell am I supposed to do now? My master trained me in subtlety—lots of training in that. He even trained me a little in magic, despite my previous handicap. But the magical stuff was always supposed to complement the subtlety, not undermine it.

Flashy little delinquent that I once was, though, I couldn't help but practice a bit on the side.

I stride forward.

You want to help me with this or am I on my own? I ask the ka'kari.

~Happy to help.~

The edges of my figure blur intermittently as I walk, tiny whips of darkness extending from me, snapping in minute tongues of blue flame as my arms swing and at each step. It's subtle enough to look like the blue iridescence of sequins flashing in the light, except there's no light, no sequins, no blue.

A hush goes over the large crowd in the audience hall. People are wondering if they just saw what they think they saw, but I have eyes only for the king.

He nods, as if to say *Yes. More.*

So between one step and the next, I disappear into a smudge of darkness—

And then reappear before the next footfall.

His smile flashes for a moment as whispers break through the crowd like water gushing in all directions from crashing surf, then he schools his face to stillness.

When I come to a stop before him, Logan doesn't address me. Instead, he says, "Lady Trudana Jadwin was a traitor and a murderer. As we all learned too late, she assassinated Prince Gunder by her own hand, aiding Khalidor's invasion and causing our beloved home kingdom to fall. Then she served our enemies, and was directly and indirectly involved with the murder of at least twenty of our subjects, including children of noble station, such as Lord Drake's daughters Serah and Magdalyn, Lady Eveline's son Draccos, Coreen Bellmont, and the Vashiel twins Korran and Karrin. In her depravity, she desecrated the bodies of the dead and set them up for display. Upon our victory, she fled our royal justice and went into hiding."

Logan levels his gaze at Lord Repha'im. "In your house. Where you sheltered her."

I see only now what Logan is doing. Rather than defending one of his advisors, Logan is going on the attack.

"I only hope, Lord Repha'im," Logan says, before the man can say a word, "that new and naïve as you were, that you were somehow unaware of Lady Jadwin's many crimes, and of our warrants for her arrest. For the time being, we will choose to believe that you were, and we will look forward to seeing you demonstrate your loyalty in fulsome degree in the future to make up for your errors in judgment.

"Now as to the case at hand. In the matter of Lady Jadwin's killing, Duchess Gwinvere Thorne protests her innocence. This I know to be true—"

"Your Majesty, I have witnesses who—" Repha'im tries to interject.

"I know her innocence personally," Logan says more loudly, and with him drawing attention to it, I realize that he hadn't slipped up in using 'I' rather than the royal 'we,' "because I sent Kylar to execute Trudana Jadwin myself."

The Hall of Winds must be holding two thousand people right now, and for a moment, I don't think even one of them breathes. Execute, he says, not assassinate. He's playing a tricky balancing act between his public persona and his private knowledge here that I can barely follow.

"It's not how I wished to handle the matter," Logan says. "But I only found out where you were hiding her—I mean, that she was staying, perhaps under a false name? at your home—after I'd already dispatched the general amnesty to all the corners of our realm. I ask all of you good people assembled here for your forbearance, for that provided me with an intolerable dilemma: first, that we might allow our royal amnesty to apply to a vile traitor whom it was never intended to cover in the first place, or second, that we might appear to suborn our own amnesty by bringing her to trial after the amnesty took effect, making everyone wonder if we intended to hold true to our own royal word in future cases. So I ordered Kylar to dispense the high king's justice on the traitor *before* the amnesty took effect in Cenaria.

"And so he did. Her abhorrent presence was removed from our sight, the stain on our kingdoms expunged; she was brought to justice, and it was all accomplished before our amnesty took effect. Though I admit, very near it. Uncomfortably so. Which is why, my good people, we have believed you all deserve this full and public accounting of our reasoning, that you may not fear our justice, but that malefactors will."

I don't know how many of the people listening realize how finely Logan is parsing this. He's claiming that rather than intending his amnesty to apply as soon as he signed it, he only intended it to go into effect as soon as it was announced in the various parts of his realm.

When the man who wrote the law tells you what his intent for it was, it's hard for you to argue with him that his intent was something else entirely.

But Logan isn't giving anyone time to catch up or contradict him. I'm only following it this well because I had to think about the very same problem for the entire time I hunted Lady Jadwin. I had decided to parse it in exactly the same way—how he figured that out without me telling him, I don't know. I guess he's just that good at this sort of thing. Or Momma K is.

He goes on, "I'll have you know, Lord Repha'im, I asked Kylar to kill only Lady Jadwin if possible, but his writ was broad enough that had he deemed anyone a material obstruction to bringing the full weight of justice to that traitor, he was empowered to deal with them as necessary. So you may begin your own new, post-amnesty life by thanking him for his mercy."

The chamber goes very, very quiet.

"Y-yes, Your Majesty," Repha'im says after a long moment. His jaw is forward, eyes tensed, visibly trembling. Not with fear. Rage.

"We mean *now*," Logan snaps.

"Yes, Your Majesty," he says. His tongue, a little pink snake, darts out to wet his lips. "Thank you for your mercy, Lord Stern," he says, loudly, clearly, and abruptly without rancor, as if thanking me for passing him a pitcher of wine.

He doesn't even look at me, though, only Logan.

"And you may thank us for ours," Logan says. "For had we known you were harboring a traitor, you might have found yourself quite unable to bring *this* frivolous case before us. As it is, count yourself fortunate that your scandalous deeds are covered by the broad tent of our amnesty, and that we shall not withdraw its protections and mercies from you."

A brief twist to the corner of his lip reveals Lord Repha'im's contempt for Logan. "Thank you, Your Majesty," he says. "You are truly a man of your word."

There is nothing of defeat or humiliation in Repha'im's posture or his tone. He doesn't seem to even understand how much this hurts him.

He sees me staring at him, and he smiles. Another puffed-up noble born on a mountaintop, crediting the view to his own climbing skills. He doesn't seem to realize that he hasn't only offended Logan, a man known to be merciful when he can be; Repha'im's gone after Momma K, a woman who's climbed out of slipperier places than he could possibly imagine. She's been underestimated all her life, by smarter, more vicious men. All of whom now feed the worms. I only hope I get to see it when he gets a properly rude awakening.

I smile back at him.

Chapter Fourteen

A Friend in Need

I've a modicum of trouble," Logan says. His valet is brushing his dinner jacket and laying out his formal evening attire, but otherwise, we're alone in one of Logan's tidy dressing rooms.

"A moiety?" I ask, though I'm not sure I'm using the word correctly.

"More."

"Are we talking disquietude or distress?" I ask.

"Perturbation, not imperilment," he says. He flashes a brief grin. It's a game we used to play: me catching Logan and teasing him for his habit of using words rarer and longer than a razorbeak glaive, and Logan doing his best to double down on them.

"A tribulation?" I ask.

"More a travail."

"Zounds, you win. Don't know that one."

"*Zounds?*" he says. But his grin fades immediately. "You've heard the rumors, I'm sure. They're...not inaccurate."

"I haven't heard any rumors." My stomach tightens.

He pauses halfway through stripping his tunic off his chiseled body, then completes the action and throws it over a chair. "About Jenine?" he asks, a hint of incredulity in his voice.

Then he sees my face and clearly believes me. "That you *don't* know the intimate details of my life should be refreshing given the panopticon I've been living in, but..."

Before he was a king, he didn't speak with long pauses. Now it seems that weighing his words has become second nature. Even with me.

A friend would have been here, the admissionarius told me.

What's been happening that's so bad?

"What's going on with Jenine?" I ask.

Logan rubs his still-unlined forehead with one big hand. He changes into a fresh pair of dark trousers and a white linen tunic. Most tailors must dress their clients to diminish negatives or to emphasize positives. Logan's tailors are spoiled with choice, choosing how many of his positives the occasion calls for his attire to reveal. Lean, muscular, tall, long-legged and broad-shouldered, I think Logan looked better when starved, grubby, and wearing his prison rags than I could look dressed in all the silks of Ladesh.

As his valet finishes with some buttons, Logan makes a sign that the man understands as a dismissal. "I'll send in your hairdresser in five minutes, Majesty?"

"Ten."

The man pauses by the large door with gleaming brass fittings and made of some exotic striped wood, maybe bocote or tigerwood. The luxury here is stunning, and the white-gloved valet and Logan fit right in. I do not. "Your Majesty asked me to remind him that he didn't wish to be late tonight and give Chef Vayden offense for a third time this week."

Logan grumbles, defeated.

The valet says, "Ten minutes, but I'll send all the ladies in at once?"

Logan grunts his assent. "Thank you, Arixus."

"And Mistress Brises reminds you of the fragility of the mother-of-pearl, and asks you not to attempt the Allorean boot lacing yourself."

"Yes, yes! Go!" Logan says.

The valet leaves promptly but without fear. The heavy door swings shut on silent hinges.

As he exits, Logan says, "I tell them to tell me things, then I yell at them when they do. I've begun to think the only thing worse than being a king is serving one."

I smile. "Is this where I assure you that serving you isn't so bad, and that somehow segues into you asking me to serve you in some new and onerous way?" I ask. "Then I feel duty-bound to accept because I just said serving you wasn't so bad?"

"And you claim you're no good at these games." Logan sits heavily. "That's about the size of it, yes. These days I manipulate even my friends without intending to, Kylar."

"I expected you to exile me today, if not have me executed," I say. "You can just ask."

He studies me, not only taking in the state of my clothing but staring into my eyes. "You did make me work pretty hard there to save you." His handsome face lightens, and I can tell he's proud of how he managed the situation, thinking on his feet.

But our time's almost up. I say, "It's not like you to have to warm up to a conversation."

His smile fades. He rubs his forehead again. "You ever have that fear that once you put a thing into words, you're going to be committed to a course of action? As if it isn't real until you say it out loud, but once you say it, there'll be no going back?"

"What's wrong with Jenine?"

He avoids my eyes and doesn't answer for a full minute. I say nothing.

"Her pregnancy with the twins was hard on her. Not, uh, not just on her body. When we won the battle, there was so much magic and she was so close to everything the twelve of you did...she's convinced it did something to the boys."

"Something to the boys?" I repeat.

He scrubs his face with his hands. "Crazy talk, Kylar." He flinches, maybe at his use of the word *crazy*.

To prompt him, I say, "We used enough magic to kill an army and build this city. Somehow. Wouldn't surprise me if all that magic did other things. Strange things even."

"She says everything changed about her pregnancy then. That the boys quickened during the deluge of magic. She...she fears Dorian did something to them."

"As I recall, Dorian was kind of busy," I say. Dorian was sane until after that battle. He sacrificed his sanity to help us win, to help undo all the evils he'd been part of, wittingly and not. "Sane or insane, Dorian isn't the kind of monster who would hurt a child."

"I'm not saying I believe her!" Logan snaps. His face falls. "I mean, I tried to believe her. I consulted midwives and wise women and chirurgeons and barbers and half a dozen charlatans. All the ones who weren't trying to sell me something said sometimes the strain of childbirth can wound a mother's mind for a time, but that she'd likely heal soon. I had the Chantry's best Healers examine her, too. They agreed too. But instead, she...I love her, Kylar, you know that, but I think she's getting worse. She tells me about these dreams she has, and I know dreams are often—very often—outlandish. Right? But these? They're not normal. I don't even know how she can dream at all, she sleeps so little."

"How long's it been since the boys were born? Two months? Isn't this still pretty early according to how such things go? Maybe time will—"

"She's getting worse, not better. I'm afraid she'll—no, she, she wouldn't..."

The agony on his face pierces me. He doesn't want to say it, or can't, so I do. Sometimes a friend can't be brave for themselves, so you stand in the gap for them. "You're afraid she might hurt the boys?"

"No! Yes. Or herself. It's only a fear. There's no chance—not a big chance, you understand. But enough that I think I should preclude the possibility." He can't meet my eyes. Logan is very big, as physically powerful as he is politically, but now he stands small, shrunken in on himself.

"I'm so sorry, Logan."

It seems like he doesn't hear me. "Some of her dreams, Kylar. They're apocalyptic. Paranoid. When the Chantry Healers examined her, they sent for backups immediately. That can't be a good sign, can it? When they finally spoke to me, they were the opposite of encouraging. Magic can often cure the body, they said, but the soul almost never."

Here I thought I was the only one carrying soul wounds after our great triumph. Amid all the celebrations, I believed I was alone in my mourning.

"How can I help?"

I say it without thinking, but as soon as I do, I think maybe this is my way out. Maybe my despair can be eased by helping someone else out of theirs.

He grabs on to it. I can tell he's got a plan. "My new empire has raised fears everywhere in the world. Everyone thinks that to have seized three kingdoms so quickly I must be aggressive, that I must want more territory. Whatever they claim, half the diplomats visiting us have only a single item on their agendas, and that's to figure out where I'm marching next. Not if. Where. For the moment, the Alitaerans are the only ones who have the means to do much about it."

"That's good news, isn't it? Alitaera is so far away."

"Yes, but with all their might, if they *do* decide to do something about us, no one's going to be able to stop them, certainly not us. I've decided I have to make a trip south to forge a treaty with them."

"A trip? Surely you don't need to go personally?"

"Need to? No. I can do what all my advisors are telling me to do, and send some skilled diplomat to handle things."

"Then why don't you?"

"Because I don't want war."

"I know you don't," I say, "but—"

"Every ruler would expect my diplomat to come and say all the right things. That's what diplomats do. A diplomat would say the same things regardless of whether I'm planning never to attack or I'm planning to attack tomorrow. Everyone knows that. But if I show up myself..."

"If you show up yourself, they'll take you captive! It's idiotic."

He flashes a quick smile. "That's a little blunter than how my advisors put it, and you're not wrong. But I do have some cards up my sleeves."

"Such as?"

"If I told you, they wouldn't be up my sleeves, would they?"

I don't know if he's trying to tease me, or if he's worried about listening ears even here. Either way, the case is closed. He's the king. "You're putting your life on the line for your subjects," I say after a moment. "As I always have, I respect your courage and your motivations."

"And you think I'm a fool," Logan says.

"Not a fool, but being foolish, yes."

He smiles sadly. "See, you could be a diplomat yet!"

"Yeah, me, meeting kings and empresses. I'm sure that'd go great."

He gets a funny look on his face, as if I've just given him an idea. "Openly sending the world's best assassin as my emissary—"

"Wetboy," I say. "And I'm not the best—"

He waves it off like I'm being humble. "Most famous. Close enough. Sending you openly *would* cause quite the reaction. It would have to be the right posting..."

"You're teasing me," I say. I lower my voice. "You are teasing me, right?"

He flashes a sudden grin, and for a moment, I see the old, boyishly handsome, irrepressibly confident Logan again. "I'm stalling to avoid telling you the next part."

His youth turns geriatric before my eyes.

"That bad?"

"I need Jenine to come with me. Her strengths complement mine. She sees things I don't, and people say things to her they'd never say to me."

"I thought she was too fragile to travel."

"No, the twins are. At least at the speeds I intend to go. I've got horses set up at stations ahead of me, so I can switch off teams and go and return as quickly as possible."

"Wait. You mean to take her but leave them? They're two months old. How does Jenine feel about this plan?"

"She . . . she doesn't know yet."

"You're going to separate a distraught new mother from her babies?" Does no one tell our new high king when he has colossally dumb ideas?

His voice goes quiet. "I can't leave her behind, Kylar. If she stays, even if I were willing to insult her forever by appointing a regent to rule over her, she'd still be the queen. Who can get between the queen and her children? If she comes with me, she might save tens of thousands of lives. If she stays"—his voice goes lower still—"she endangers three."

The door opens and Logan's valet, Arixus, pokes his head in. He holds out two fingers, then disappears, closing the door once more. Two minutes.

Logan sighs.

"Is it like this all the time?" I ask.

"Always. And will be until I get the right ministers in all the right positions. Then instead of getting all the decisions passed to me, I'll only get the most difficult ones. Joy."

Time to cut through the fluff. "So what do you want from me? To go with you, keep you safe? You know I'm not a bodyguard, but . . . your wish is my command."

"No. I mean, usually, I'd take you up on that in a heartbeat. It'd be wonderful to have you with me for your company, even if I weren't heading into danger. No. Jenine's paranoia . . . she thinks the boys are in danger. She thinks she's had a vision that someone's going to steal them or kill them or something."

"So . . . what? You want me to take care of your kids?"

"You, take care of babies? Ha! Don't take this wrong, Kylar, but you're the least paternal man I know!"

I chuckle as if it's just a good-natured ball-busting, which is all he means it to be. He doesn't know.

He doesn't know Elene was pregnant when she died, that my whole world was changing before my eyes. I could no longer be a kid myself; I was a husband; I was going to be a father—even a *dad*.

He knows I lost her. He's careful about everything around that. This? I can't hold him accountable for jabbing a wound he doesn't know is there. I'm the one who never told him about it, after all.

Best friend? A good friend would have been here for Logan. A good friend would have let Logan be here for him, too. Would've shared my own wound.

I'm a failure in every way.

Except for killing. I'm good at that. I thought once that I was escaping the shadows' embrace, but the shadows cling to me wherever I go.

"I want you to watch over them," Logan is saying. "I know you're not a bodyguard or a nurse. They'll have those. I want you to skulk around, check the routes that you'd take if you were going to try to hurt or kidnap some kids. Nothing's going to happen, but it gives me something to tell Jenine to reassure her, to let her know I'm doing everything to make sure they'll be safe."

"Logan, she's gonna lose her mind over this." He flinches and I realize it's a poor choice of words, so I hurry on. "*Any* mother would. You can't take a mother away from her babies. Give it a few months. Send your diplomats on ahead for now, and go when things have settled down a bit. A couple months will make all the difference."

"By then it'll be too late. In a couple weeks, Empress Caelestia and her court leave Alitaera's eastern capital. After partying in the Summer Isles, they end up at Castle Stormfast and then sail west at incredible speed, driven by the Great Storm. Once in Borami, she'll oversee her new under-king's rule for six months before she heads back east overland and repeats the process. Point is, once they leave Skone, she's out of reach. Borami's too far away, with too many enemies along the routes there. Even if it were safe, if I went I'd be gone for far too long. But there's more.

"Kylar, I've read my histories. Gwinvere's spies have had the other rulers' speeches reported to me. I see the signs. Suddenly, rulers throughout Midcyru are levying new taxes to fund lavish projects—monuments, palace expansions, and the like."

"That seems like what royals do during times of peace and prosperity. Isn't it?"

"It is, but not like this. Few rulers are patient enough to raise all the money for a new palace first and then pay for it all at once. They raise a small amount to begin the foundation work, paying for the excavation and the stone. The next year, they levy a new tax to pay for the masons and carpenters. It irritates the nobles less and it gets a project started immediately. This isn't that. This is countries raising a lot of coin and not spending it. Why? Because money is fungible. A wily ruler can raise money without it looking like they're preparing for war, then at the last moment take that money and fund an army's weapons and food and everything else they need to march. So I've *got* to go; it's got to be now. Jenine coming with me could be the difference between success and failure. Otherwise, when the empress marches from the western capital Borami next year, it could be at the head of an army."

"I hoped we were done with war," I say. It's one thing to kill a murderous traitor. It's something else to kill some teenager whose only sin is marching under the wrong banner, convinced that you're a threat to his family.

"That's my job," Logan says grimly. "To help my people thrive. To protect them. To make sure we are done with war, if not forever, then for as long as possible. My work's too important for me to be the kind of father I ought to be, Kylar. Or husband. I'm a king. My people's lives are more important than my happiness."

"And your wife's?" I didn't mean to say it out loud, but Logan forgives me.

"She was born a princess, raised every day with the knowledge she would someday be queen. She's known the likely costs of her position longer than I knew mine."

I'm sure that's true, but I'll be happy not to be present when they have *that* conversation.

"I'll do whatever you need, Your Majesty," I say, heading to the door. "And... thanks for not exiling me. Or worse. I was asking for it, but... I couldn't let it go, you know?"

"I miss Mags too," he says. He averts his eyes. "And Serah. And Prince Aleine, for all his foibles. And everyone else. Trudana needed killing. If you'd asked, I would've sent you myself."

There's a bit of an accusation there, and hurt. Why *didn't* I ask his permission? "I only found out where she was the same day I heard of your amnesty. I thought I had to get there first." I almost let it sit there, partly honest, but only partly. "And... I'd been gone from your court so long. I didn't know what you'd say. I didn't think I could obey you if you said no."

He smiles sadly. "That's kind of who we both are, isn't it, Kylar? Men who'll always do what we think is right, no matter what anyone else says. I only wish we always saw eye to eye on what that is."

"You're a better friend than I deserve."

"Nothing to do with being your friend. I'd be a fool of a king to exile my secret weapon." He quirks a smile, and we both know he's lying, but only partially. Logan's power is an integral part of what he is now. Even though he's most often motivated by higher ideals, in order to survive, he has to think always about the taking and maintaining of power. "Will you join us for dinner?" he asks.

I cough. "I think I'll keep my, uh, mystique instead, thanks."

"You're still going to say no, even if I tell you that there's a guest you'll be particularly interested in?" Logan asked.

"I'm a better secret weapon for you if you only pull me out when you need me." I open the door, and a line of servants bustles in. "If it's really that important, after the dinner you can send him to me."

"Him?" Logan says.

"This guest?" I say.

"Oh, it's not him. *Her*," Logan says. "And if you don't come, I'm pretty sure she'll find you."

My stomach sinks.

Chapter Fifteen

Love Is Not Enough

I'm not sure why everyone lies about it: Newborns aren't cute.

I mean, newborn *animals*, sure. I'll ooh and ahh with the best of them over a puppy or a baby alligator or whatever. Newborn humans? With their squished features and total lack of awareness?

Maybe one in a hundred is actually cute. If that many.

These two? No. Sorry. Not remotely.

"They're adorable!" I say with as much enthusiasm as I can manage.

"They really are, aren't they?!" Logan says, lofting one of his sons high in the air, making the nurse nervous. "And me? I'm a man who doesn't think every baby is cute. You want to hold him?"

"No, no, I'm fine." I just know I'll do it wrong somehow.

Logan throws me a cloth. "Drape that over your shoulder. You never know when something's going to go squirting out of one end or the other." He laughs as if this is adorable too.

He was hard to resist *before* he was a king, but now Logan's warhorse personality has been given full barding and a slap on the butt.

I force a smile, not really putting my heart into it. "I'm really quite fine without—"

He hands me a small, slack, somnolent sausage. The one with the wispy dark fuzz on its oversized pate.

Logan's head cocks disapprovingly at how I hold it, but he says nothing, as if he's trying to give me the benefit of the doubt. Then, as it suddenly wiggles, and its giant cranium threatens to topple off its muscle-less neck, Logan says, "The head. Kylar! Support Kiern's head, man!"

I spread my hands out as if balancing a precious artifact. No, it's worse than that. This little lardball is a prince.

"Against your chest, man. Try not to kill him, huh? It's like you've never held a baby before."

"I, uh, I haven't," I say.

"Ever?" He looks stunned. "Oh. Right. I'm sorry. I just didn't realize how blithely I put the future of my kingdom in your hands."

"Nah, you're good. If I break this one, he's got a brother, right?"

Logan laughs and helps me hold his child correctly. It's still awkward. The thing is a floppy, eminently vulnerable noodle.

There's a tingle where the child's head touches the skin of my chest and neck. I don't know if it's my dormant paternal instinct, or just the fact that I'm holding a future high king.

Regardless, I don't like it.

"So...they look different," I say. Not that I can usually tell one human prune from another, but the one I'm holding has dark hair. "I thought, Kiern and, uh, what's-his-name were twins?"

Logan palms his face, and I'm not sure which dumb thing I said caused it. But before he can speak, an advisor comes up and whispers in his ear.

It leaves me alone with His Royal Pudgeness. I look down to see it yawn.

Okay, the yawn? That's cute. A little.

Oh gods. It's waking up. I start bouncing it like I've seen people do. *Please stay asleep. Please stay asleep.*

Did someone ever hold me like this? Did someone see me as a little terror, and hope she could ditch me at the earliest opportunity?

I mean, I am an orphan. At least, I was abandoned early enough I have no memories of any parent. It couldn't have been too early, though. I wouldn't have survived on the streets if I'd been too young. The gangs don't take in anyone who's so young they're too much trouble.

Would I have tossed me out like so much trash?

Kiern opens his eyes. I stare into those baby blues and a lump forms so fast and hard in my throat, it's as if the little brat has put his tiny little fist down my gullet.

"What? You didn't say—" Logan says to the advisor. He curses under his breath, and I'm relieved for the excuse to look away from the kid. Logan stares at me, then at the door, as if making some terrible choice, though it only looks as if he's deciding whether to reach to take back his son.

Then his jaw sets, and he forces his hands down to his sides.

"What's wrong?" I ask.

Too late, I guess.

Then I realize what must be coming, but the door opens before I can hand the kid back.

High Queen Jenine Gyre has seen a lot of life: Born Princess Gunder of Cenaria, she married Logan, thought he was murdered at the same time her entire family was assassinated, was then abducted, then "saved" by Dorian, who married her, making her Queen Ursuul of Khalidor, Lodricar, and Cenaria, and then (pregnant with Dorian's children), she learned Logan was still alive after all—and that her husband Dorian had known all along. She left Dorian, annulled their marriage, and got back together with Logan, who agreed to adopt Dorian and Jenine's yet-unborn children as his own.

Despite all that, Jenine isn't yet twenty years old. When I last saw her, she looked even younger.

Not now.

Dark circles rim her eyes. Her face is puffy.

She freezes when she sees me.

But only for a moment.

"Not *him*!" she shouts, pointing. In a whirlwind of fury, she snatches the child from my stunned arms. "How could you, Logan?"

"Honey, it's fi—"

"No! How could you let that *thing* touch our child?!" she shrieks. "You told me—*you* admitted!—that he's the most dangerous man in the realm. What are you thinking of, bringing him—?"

"He's my best friend, Jenine! He—"

"His kind doesn't have friends. They only have targets."

"Jenine, my love—" Logan says.

"Don't you 'Jenine my love' me!" she spits, body shaking.

"Not true," I say.

She stops.

"*My kind* doesn't have targets. Assassins have targets, because it's possible to miss a target. Wetboys have deaders. Because when a wetboy takes a contract, the condemned person's death is merely a matter of time. But do go on." Jenine's acting like a scared child, and it's starting to piss me off.

"Deaders? *Deaders!*" she says.

"*Kylar*," Logan says, pleading.

"I should go," I say, flipping my hood back on. "I'll abide Your Majesty's will. I can see you two have—"

But at the moment my hood falls into place, Jenine's eyes grow wide as if seeing me for the first time.

She starts keening.

My heart lurches with pity, not only for her, but also for my friend who loves a woman who's lost all moorings to sanity.

I see an attendant rush into the doorway, waiting for permission to come in. She's holding a goblet, and I see the brown grit of poppy floating in the wine.

They had it prepared already. This is not the first time Jenine has done this sort of thing.

I catch one last sight of Logan's face before I leave to try to spare him further embarrassment, and it's all cracking stoic resolve, a man confronting the kind of battle where he cannot fight, only stand; a man lifting again a burden so heavy he knows not how to carry it, and yet carry it he must.

We lock eyes, and part of me thinks I should stay. Do I stay, for the friend I love, or go, for the sake of the woman he loves? My presence seems to be making Jenine worse.

I turn to go.

"Stay, Nameless One!" Jenine shouts.

I freeze. Not because I'm obeying my queen, but because the last person to call me that was the White Seraph herself, and before that, the Wolf. And I wouldn't call either of them a *person*.

"You think I'm crazy," she's saying to Logan in a tone that makes everyone in the room certain that she is. "Want me to prove I'm not?"

"I never said that," Logan says gently.

"Never *said* it," she snarls.

"I don't believe you're crazy," Logan says, and I believe him.

He's wrong, but I believe him.

Jenine hisses, "A man's going to come in here with a message for you, and you're going to have to leave."

Logan shoots a look at me, awkward to be fighting in front of me. "Honey... that happens a hundred times a day. That's not exactly a—"

A courtier steps into the room, and Logan stops abruptly. He waves the man over. The man makes quiet apologies and hands Logan a note.

"Not this man," Jenine mutters, and her face looks troubled. But I think I'm the only one who hears her.

Logan reads the note, then shakes his head and sends the courtier away. "See? I'm staying—"

"Not *that* man," Jenine says.

Logan throws his hands up.

"I've told you a hundred times. Tried, anyway," Jenine says. "Dorian *did* something that day. Not just to the boys. To me." Her voice cracks as she says the last; her face contorts suddenly, but she stops herself from breaking down.

"I don't want to hear about Dorian!" Logan snaps.

"I didn't have stretch scars on my stomach until that day, Logan! I felt the boys twist in my womb. It was as if they suddenly doubled in size and strength. Perhaps they were too small, too weak to live, and he Healed them. He was one of the Hoth'salar's greatest Healers of all time, you know that. There are legends about him there—but I'm telling you, I think he also accidentally passed on his—"

"Stop this! Stop it!" Logan says. "The boys are fine!"

"I know him. I know he wouldn't have hurt them on purpose. But there was so much magic—"

"You *know* him? Dorian told you I was dead! *Everything* he told you was a lie!"

"No! No, Logan, it wasn't."

Logan's face falls as he studies her, disbelieving. "By the gods..." he breathes. "You still love him." I don't know how he made that leap, but I see a flash of guilt on Jenine's face.

Then Logan glances over at me, and it's a look that holds a thousand thoughts and a mud stew of feelings.

I can't escape. I'm intruding on an unbearable moment, observing a fault line in a marriage at the very moment it slips and threatens a full earthquake, rending all their life asunder, heaving the very foundations of Logan's reign into the air.

I see his embarrassment at being seen in such a moment, helplessness at the scope of his problems, but there's some gladness too, that of all people to see this, it's me.

He is slow to anger, Logan is, with those he loves. And he loves Jenine more than anything. But...

What if love is not enough? Can love save a mind in reckless retreat from reality, heedless of harms, flinching fearfully from even the most sensitive, strongest, steadiest hand?

In his helplessness, I can see Logan's anger awakening. His fair skin is reddening. The pain, the betrayal, is twisting within him. Logan has given her so much, and she repays him by still loving the man who took Logan's place? The man who deceived her into bigamy, seduced her, and impregnated her. The man who knew all along that Logan was alive, starving in a dungeon. How dare she love him?

Jenine must have stepped gingerly on this ground in the past, but now, with me here, she's being reckless.

Before Logan can speak, Jenine says, "I know you're planning to force me to go with you to Skone."

It takes all the wind out of Logan's building rage.

I look to the door, wondering how I can make a graceful exit. Or even an ungraceful one.

"You what? How do you know about that?" he asks.

But she's gone quiet.

"Who told you?" he demands.

"The dreams—"

"Always the dreams!" Logan roars, as if happy to have found something he can safely be angry about.

"It doesn't matter how I know then, look! Taking me away from the boys is the stupidest thing you can do right now. I'm sorry, not stupid. The worst-advised. They need me. I need *them*, Logan. They're all that's keeping me afloat."

"They're *drowning* you."

"I'm begging, Logan. Don't take my babies away from me. Please."

Jenine looks suddenly haggard, as if a hundred sleepless nights are catching up to her at once. In her pregnancy and before it, she was young, vibrant, and full of life, and in this moment, she looks none of those things. Hollow-cheeked, bloodshot eyes, shoulders sagging.

"Milady, how long has it been since you've slept?" I ask, trying to smooth the waters.

She stares pure poison at me. "Silence, *snake*."

"Jenine . . ." Logan says, softly.

"I'll go," she says. "I'll go with you. But please . . . bring your wolfhound with us."

"I've already got a better idea," Logan says.

"If this murderer is in the castle, something bad is going to happen while we're gone," Jenine says. "You have to believe me."

Logan says, "If something bad happens, he's the best person to *stop it*."

The door opens, and a courtier with downcast eyes comes in silently. He whispers in Logan's ear.

"That's the man," Jenine says with a sigh. "That's the one."

But I don't think Logan hears her.

In a moment, Logan says, "I have to deal with this. We'll...we'll talk more." He looks at Jenine, then at me. "Kylar, you're, uh, you're dismissed."

He leaves quickly then, and before I can get to the door behind him, Jenine says, "No, you're not. Stay."

I have faced literal monsters in my life, and I don't think I had as much dread then as I do now as I stop and turn to face this small, aggrieved mother.

"I'd seen you around before. You know, before all of this, back when you were masquerading as a relation of the Sterns. But now I know you," Jenine says, that mad gleam in her eye. "I *know* you."

There's nothing for me to say. She's either crazy or she's not. Regardless, there's no winning an argument with a queen.

"You're a worse man than Logan thinks you are. He sees the best in people, and though he's not as naïve as he used to be, you're still a blind spot for him. He'll believe in you no matter what. Because he needs that. I can't be everything to him; I know it. He is hanging on by his fingernails in this court. He needs someone *good* in his life to be his friend—and instead, he gets *you*." She's practically spitting with disgust. "I hate you," she says. "I'd try to kill you right now if I thought I had any hope of success."

I take a step back. The last thing I need is to defend myself against the queen. What happens if a dozen royal guards come swarming the room to find me fending off the woman in actual combat?

That might go much more poorly for me than she thinks.

She says, "So understand how much this pains me: I..." Her mouth twists.

But then she kneels on the floor.

"I'm begging you, Kylar. Please. Don't do it. Don't you do it. You have a choice. I don't care what you think. You do have a choice." She lies fully prostrate on the floor and starts weeping. "Please...*please*..."

All thoughts of beating a dignified retreat forgotten, I flee.

A brusque servant bearing poppy wine shoves past me to tend to the mad queen.

Chapter Sixteen

The Sulky Silence of Teenage Boys

I had the most disturbing dream last night," I tell the ka'kari.

It says nothing in reply. I sigh, realizing I'm not touching it. I put one fingertip on it and repeat myself.

~I heard you. Good for you.~

"So you can hear me if you're within vocal distance, but you can't speak in my head unless I'm holding you."

I take my finger away, pause for a few moments, then touch it again. "Ah, and you can't hear my thoughts unless we're touching either."

~Let me guess: You just loudly thought something you hoped would be offensive to me to get a response. I'm so curious what I missed.~

"No need to take that tone," I say. "Let's talk."

~This always goes well.~

"Who made you? What can you do? Why do you help me sometimes and not others? How do I get you to help me more? Why'd you choose me?"

I ask all those questions and others over the next hours, in every way I can think to ask them. It doesn't help.

The answer is mostly silence, and finally, the ka'kari says, ~I've had enough.~

The ka'kari is like a huffy teenage boy sometimes, prone to sulky, impenetrable silences.

Did you get that part? I ask.

~'Sulky, impenetrable silences.' Once again, your wit skewers with all the subtlety of a claymore, milord. I am cajoled into revealing more than intended by your sly manipulations.~

I sigh. But then, I pretty much knew this wouldn't work.

Sorry.

~Now you're trying *kindness*?~

Whatever my purpose is, the ka'kari isn't going to help me find it. I wonder if that was intended by whoever created it, or if that's a residue of Durzo's effect on the thing, it having been carried by him for so long. Then again, foolishly or not, I rejected Durzo's way. Would I even accept whatever guidance the ka'kari might provide me?

Maybe I wouldn't help me either. Maybe I'm unteachable, only able to accept what I learn the hard way. Maybe the ka'kari knows it. Or maybe that's too much agency to believe of an artifact that is, after all, ancient and impressive magic, but merely magic. Its creator clearly made it with certain instructions embedded in it. It seems that I have to do certain things—hidden, untold things—before the ka'kari will respond. After I first bonded it, it was months before it finally spoke to me at all, and that was only a single word to try to save my life.

There are echoes or intimations of a personality in the ka'kari, but not, so far as I can tell, actually a personality itself. The Maker of such a thing might, I guess, design it so it wouldn't speak to any new holder for a certain number of months. A Maker might worry about someone unworthy taking the ka'kari and immediately having access to all of its powers, all of its knowledge.

That's easier for me to imagine, and more in line with what I've experienced than the ka'kari having a real personality. Even Durzo wouldn't have been able to sit silently watching, all day long, day after day, while I made mistakes and fumbled around for month after month and not say a single word. Especially not after the years (a decade?) that it spent in isolation after Durzo lost his bond with it.

A *personality* would be starved to speak after so long. This can't be that. It's a magical construct with rules I have to figure out.

What do you want? What are your rules?

~I want you to become the Night Angel in truth.~

All right! Now we're getting somewhere! What does that mean*?*

Silence.

We've done this enough that I know it's not going to broach anything first. Its silence might as well be a parent screaming, *This conversation is finished!*

"So this dream I had," I say. "Kinda throwin' me. Like I put on a too-small jacket and now I can't get my arms out of the sleeves. One of those dreams that feels really real? Dreamed this image of me pounding a spike into a rock wall, and the spike was connected to a chain and the chain was connected to a manacle covering my whole forearm. Guess you probably don't give dream interpretations, though, huh?"

I sigh. Because it doesn't answer. As I knew it wouldn't.

"I can't tell if you're the best person to talk to or the worst. Seeing how you're not a person. But then again, you're the only company I have."

Well, hell. *That's* depressing.

I don't want to think about that.

I don't know. There's no point to me narrating anymore. I don't have anyone to share it with anyway. I'm done.

Chapter Seventeen

A Drink with an Old Friend

I missed something important that night, and trying to remember it now isn't as good as if I could go back and examine every moment as I experienced it.

The poisoned wine didn't kill me, obviously. If it had, you wouldn't be hearing this. Hearing? Reading? Will a minstrel set this chronicle to music someday? Will copyists pore over every line and doodle in the margins?

I'm probably flattering myself to even consider it. Tale's not heroic enough— not heroic at all. Not on my part.

After Logan and Jenine left for Skone, I was on the roof of the palace. I'd begun making this record to let Count Drake know how I avenged his daughters. But he didn't want it, and with the world leached gray by Elene's absence, I couldn't see the point in keeping up the effort, so I stopped committing my observations to the ka'kari. But stopping was a mistake. If I'd been narrating everything I saw that night, I might've captured something that could help me now. So this isn't for Drake or anyone else now. It's for me.

But fine, I loused up. Best I can do is tell what I remember now of what happened.

~And constantly narrating to me going forward is your solution? What have I done to deserve such a gift?~

None of that.

It looks like the only thing worse than writing such a chronicle may be doing it with 'help.'

~Would you like to try doing it *without* my help?~

Would you like to go back in your box?

The ka'kari is silent for a long time.

I'm basically immortal and it's basically indestructible, so a war of wills between us could last a really, really long time.

Anyway, it was one of those new-moon nights where the lustrous cloak of heaven swirled wide and the divines above us danced and twinkled, messengers cutting fast or slow from horizon to horizon, the great planetary powers shining in their glory. It was a night to make a man of action philosophize, but I'll spare you my further cerebral susurrations.

~'Cerebral susurrations,'~ the ka'kari repeats, deadpan.

A little too much Logan there?

~No, no, it's fine, fine. But, uh, you're right. From here on out, you should just narrate as we go. You maybe overthink your phrasing when you do it later. Just a smidge.~

I can't tell if it's mocking me.

~I am mocking you.~

I'd been up on the various roofs (palace, keep, chapel dome, Hall of Winds) for three or four nights before I realized how strange it was that I could see the stars at all. The government buildings are all on the highest hills of the city, but they are still within a city.

In other cities there's a constant riot of lights after darkness that dim the stars. Even poor cities like Cenaria where few people can afford to burn lamps all night, there are businesses and guardsmen and various tradesfolk who have to be out and carrying lights, pouring their buckets of muddy light into the crystal waters of the sky.

The keep has a defensive view of the whole city, but large parts of the other buildings were shielded from the cities' lights below by trees and high hedges. Plants and hedges, full grown, in a city that isn't even a year old. The next day I checked and saw that throughout the city, all the mounted lights and lanterns were hooded, so as not to cast light toward the castle or the sky.

When we created this city with magic, the bulk of the work was done by Dorian, but each of us had time to add little flourishes. Who would have done this? Only someone with a deep concern about beauty.

Elene, my love, had used her time to plant early-blooming tulips in every yard and sill. Elene must've grown these trees and hedges as well. Her touch lingered yet in this city, though the tulips had now died. The beauty of this starlight was her gift to all of us. To me.

It pierced me. Just when I thought I could forget her for one day . . .

"I knew it wouldn't be easy for us to see each other," a voice said, shocking me from my reverie. "But I didn't think you'd avoid me for my whole stay."

"Vi," I said. I felt like a jackass, just as I knew I would.

"The Sisters say I'm supposed to correct anyone who calls me that. It's Viridiana now."

"Right," I said.

I was supposed to make some comment. Something about how healthy or happy she looked, or how great it was to see her.

Instead, I stared at her stupidly. The changes would've been merely interesting on another woman: Vi is wearing a dress, but more shocking to anyone who knows her is that her long, flame-red hair is unbound. Oddly, the white magic-streak I remember growing in after the battle is gone, either dyed or carefully tucked out of sight. But... the dress.

It's *dowdy*. It is the only attire I'd ever seen her wear that makes her look less than gorgeous. High-necked, ill-cut, lumpy in spots where I know she's not lumpy underneath, all in a terrible pastiche of oranges and yellows that clash with her hair color and skin. Despite all this, she still didn't look bad—but she did look the worst I'd ever seen her look. I was probably too slow to hide the what-the-hell in my eyes.

"You were able to climb out here in all that?" I said.

"*That's* the first thing you have to say to me?"

I think I stuttered then. "It's the twelfth thing, but all the others were gonna sound even worse. How's the Chantry treating you?" There, that was safe, right?

She waved a hand at her outfit and gave a pained smile. "They say they're teaching me life lessons, but I won't bore you."

"Your hair's unbound," I said suddenly, then cringed. I knew better. Vi has a strange, intense relationship with her hair. I've seen her with her hair down, but only in private moments. This was like me pointing out she's naked. If a woman's talking to you while she's naked, she's probably aware of the fact.

She was holding her hands folded in front of her, and I noticed the knuckles go white as she stopped herself from lifting them to her hair. "Another of those lessons," she said, then she turned away. "Nice night."

Why did it sound like there's an ocean of pain just beyond the shores of her voice?

"I've been enjoying the stars," I said.

"Yeah?" She shot me a quick look, gave me a sudden smile. "I always hated how cities make it so hard to see the stars. I guess I—I mean, I barely thought about it. It just happened."

"You?" I asked. "You did this? *You* blocked the lights when we built the city?"

"Uh-huh. What? You don't think me capable of it?"

"No," I said. "Yes? I mean, I know you're capable. Very much so."

That it wasn't Elene's doing, that I'd been crediting her for something she hadn't done, seemed to take it away—and take her away from me. Grief shot down my tight throat.

But Viridiana was already talking. "I was standing right next to you when we used Curoch and Iures. You must've added some of your own touches to the city too, right? What did you do?"

That made me feel again like I was worse at magic than everyone else. How had they had time to add grace notes to the city? But my mouth was already going. "I was a little more worried about stopping the gigantic army of monsters trying to kill us all. Didn't really occur to me to—" I stopped. This was not how I wanted to do this. Quieter, I said, "I thought it was Elene's doing. Like the tulips."

I didn't mean to say it aloud.

It was as if I'd punched Vi in the gut. Her hands came up to cover her mouth, and then she smoothed her hair.

"This is not how I wanted to do this," she said, voice tight.

How did you want to do it? I wanted to ask her. I didn't.

Why did she seek me out? Our lives had overlapped for a time, and it had been pretty intense, but there was no way it could go on. She was training at the Chantry now, and would be for years—decades for all I knew. The Sisters weren't going to let their hooks out of her; she was too Talented, and to them, that meant too important.

The Chantry is the one place I *can't* be within leagues of. Not with who I am. Not after what I did last time I was there. For all that I can be pretty stealthy, there have been times in my past when I . . . was not.

"We're just too much alike, aren't we?" she said. She drew a wineskin from her little pack. "One of the servants gave me this. Said it was the good stuff. I thought we might need it." She mumbled, "Though not so soon."

"Too alike for what?" I said without thinking. I should've let it go.

As she quickly drank to give herself a moment to answer, I realized again how dumb I was. 'Too alike for what?' Gods!

"No bad guys out tonight," I said. "Not that I think there's anyone looking to hurt the twins or anything. But I should get moving over to my next station. You want to come with?" I pointed out my circuit. "How is Jenine doing, anyway? I assume you're part of the health delegation?"

I was blathering, putting as much distance between us and my stupid 'Too alike for what?'

I'm cringing even dictating it now. Maybe I should skip the worst of it.

~Later. Get it down correctly first. Worry about fixing it after we finish.~

Yeah, you're right.

Viridiana walked with me to my next station, striding along a steeply pitched rooftop at midnight in her frumpy housedress as if walking down a city street. Even her shoes are wrong. I almost suggested an easier route for her, but even I'm not dumb enough to insult her that way.

"We couldn't find anything wrong with the queen," Viridiana said. "And the Sisters have finished up the business they had in the city—the king donated a building for the Chantry to keep a permanent embassy here, and there's a lot of setup to be done. But the group I'm assigned to has finished their part and... we're heading out first thing tomorrow."

"Oh," I said, manfully doing my part to keep the conversation flowing.

"They're staying at an inn on the outskirts of the city so we can get an early start home in the morning. *We* are, I guess I should say."

"You rode back just to see me?" I said, surprised but with some pleasure at the thought.

Did I really have to say it out loud? Sometimes I want to hit Past Kylar.

"Uh... Actually, I wanted to see the babies."

"Oh. Right. Right." Gods, I could just die recounting all this. He's a smooth operator, that Kylar Stern. Hells.

"I like babies," she said. "I never want to have any, but I do like 'em. Especially when there's a team of nursemaids to handle all the, you know, and you just get to cuddle them." She flashed a private smile at the thought. Vi's always had a killer smile, but that moment of unself-conscious joy skewered me for some reason.

To see her happy, even in a small way, even at a memory, warmed me like frozen hands warmed by a fire. It's good, but mostly it aches.

My breath frozen with my thoughts, I managed only, "Yeah. Sure." Or something like that. I can't even remember. In that instant, I couldn't even decode what she'd said.

I think I understand for the first time why some weak men hate a beautiful woman. At any moment, she might reveal a kind of power to which he has no answer. This is the reason beauty is the handmaiden of truth, for beauty glides past the mind's tight-shut barbican and into the citadel of the heart. And at the sight of her, we wither, or cheer, or long to seize, and in our response, who *we* are is shown truly, if only to ourselves. Beauty unveils us, and some hate what we see.

I felt a surge of longing so sudden and so strong it left me shaken. I haven't felt like that since—

No. It's mere lust. Must be. I have nothing purer in me than that. Not anymore.

"That's what I told the Sisters, anyway," Viridiana said, with a sudden devious smile that sent another bolt through the bars of the cage wherein I draw breath.

Gods, I was stupid-horny. That's all it was. I haven't slept with a woman since Elene died. That's all.

And now I'm cringing again. It's only occurring to me right now what she was implying with that latter part. She told the Sisters she merely wanted to hold the twins one last time, but it wasn't true. Which meant . . . she *did* want to visit me.

Ugh, my stupidity is too painful to tell. But okay, fine, I'll get it down now and edit it out later.

Regardless, I was so caught up in my own responses that I didn't actually see *her*. Didn't hear what she was saying at all.

It's awful, how blind I am in certain situations. I mean, I know *why* I'm clueless, not that it helps. I'm maybe twenty years old, and for something like fourteen years I've spent sixteen hours a day learning disguise-crafting, poison-making, armed and unarmed martial arts, climbing, how to lie convincingly, and making many attempts at magic; and then learning all the skills necessary to the baronet I was pretending to be as my cover: studying politics, histories, the personalities and rivalries of all the major players in Cenaria, then back to evenings working on human anatomy, tending plants, doing menial chores for my master, and all the time training training training at all the arts a professional killer needs to master—to the exacting standards of the most legendary killer of all time.

It shouldn't surprise me that the price of becoming very good at a host of obscure skills is that I'm completely useless at normal ones. I haven't had any practice being normal.

I missed her hint. And then again, as she scooted closer to me on the railing I was leaning against and touched my hand. "Have you had any aftershocks? Wounds?" she asked.

"From the magic?"

"I'm not supposed to talk about it, but two of the Sisters who helped us, at Black Barrow? Burned out their Talents. Couple more have memory loss in odd ways; like, they've forgotten people they've known for years, or simple spells—but nothing else. We think four of the Brothers have serious injuries, but of course they won't let us examine them. Want their own Healers."

"Didn't it change you?" I ask, brushing a bit of her bright red hair back to look for the streak of white I thought I remembered her having.

She shivered and closed her eyes, melting toward me, turning her head so my hand cupped her cheek, and only then did I remember about the hair.

"Oh—uh, sorry!" I blurted out. I jerked my hand away.

Her eyes flickered open and she shrank away from me too. "No, no, it's nothing," she said with a forced smile, not meeting my eyes. I felt somehow like she was ashamed, even though I was the jackass.

I'm a hard friend to have.

"Yeah," she said. "So far as the Healers can tell, the hair's the only thing wrong with me. If you even call it that. Makes for a fun party trick. Can't complain, when others got real wounds. They still aren't sure why. Maybe the difference between how much each of us tried to do versus how much Talent we have. Dunno." I didn't know what she was talking about. Fun party trick? But before I could ask, she said, "You haven't had any problems?"

"All sorts," I said, trying to smile. "But, you know, not the magical kind."

She accepted the lie.

My body Heals itself. I have no reason to think that my mind won't do the same, in time. I'm sure I haven't forgotten anything important.

Finally, she withdrew her hand from where it was touching mine on the rail. I wasn't sure why she seemed disappointed—at my stupidity, I see now, or my apparent rejection of her.

Vi seemed tipsy from the wine. She sat down on a precipice, idly kicking her feet. "Logan convinced Jenine to go with him. We don't know how. The Sisters are divided on whether it was the right thing for him to do. There's some soul wound in her that our magic can't cure. I suppose we all have some of those." She offered me the wineskin. "Sit with me?"

"Did the Sisters examine the twins?" I asked. I knew I should head on to the next stop of my rotation, but even with as awkward as it was, I wanted to stay with her. The warmth of her company was starting to feel more good than achy.

"Oh, they examined them extensively. That was Jenine's whole concern. Didn't you hear? She's worried the magic hurt them somehow. I mean, the king asked us to come so we would examine *her*, but with the state she was in? We tried to save her feelings and covered it up by examining everyone. And...I shouldn't have told you that."

I chuckled at that, finally starting to feel at ease. I took a quick drink. Yeah, I think that was my first drink. No smell that I recall. Maybe there was a hint of something that I dismissed as Vi's perfume, though?

"That's ridiculous, though, isn't it?" I said. "I mean, Jenine didn't even take part in the magic at Black Barrow, and no one there wanted to hurt her unborn babies."

"It's not that simple," Vi said.

"Why isn't it? Dorian was controlling all the magic. It's one thing for someone to make flowers for the city or make sure the lights are pleasant, but Dorian wasn't insane yet—and there's no way he would let anyone hurt the woman he loved. Or his children."

"Even still, Kylar. I guess there's no reason you'd understand magic on such a scale, but..."

"What's that supposed to mean?"

She sighed. "I'm not belittling you, Kylar...I mean that the Sisters are scared. They say that what Neph Dada and the Khalidorans did here? That alone might have been enough to upset some old, precarious magical balances around the world. There are things—old things, barriers, gates—held together with the magical equivalent of spit and string. Neph may have wrecked some things in raising all those monsters. *We* may have wrecked more with what we did to kill them all and build this city. Magic of that magnitude is going to have aftershocks and unintended consequences. We didn't mean to, but the Sisters think we woke up some things that go *bump* in the night."

"We woke up things? What we did is *killed* the things someone else woke up. Thousands and thousands of them! The Sisterhood is going to turn that into something bad? They're going to blame us—"

"No one's saying we didn't have to do it. The Sisters wish we'd been a little more subtle, that's all."

"And they put it that politely, huh?" I sneered.

"Well, no," she admitted.

Typical of the Chantry, I thought, but I managed to keep my mouth shut for once and not say it aloud. "You should've had Dorian help you," I said, mostly joking.

"What?"

"Feir told me that back in the day Dorian was an incredible Healer. When Dorian first foresaw that he was going to lose his mind, he hoped maybe the Healers' school could teach him how to cure his own madness. Obviously, that didn't work, but maybe he learned something that could help Jenine now. You know he'd help in a heartbeat."

"Yeah, I suppose," Vi said, seeming troubled. "But with their history? Anyway, he's catatonic now. Has been the whole time we've been here..."

There was a question in her voice, but I didn't want to go into what Dorian said to me, so I said, "You know, I held Kiern the other day, and it was probably just in my head but..." I took a quick drink, marshaling the words to describe what I'd felt.

Suddenly, a look of horror shot across Vi's face. She sniffed sharply, then— with blinding speed—slapped me. Wineskin and wine went flying and blood started filling my mouth.

I jumped backward to defend myself, but Vi instantly wobbled and collapsed onto the edge of the battlement.

I barely grabbed her before she fell off the height, and as I hauled her away from the edge, she said, "The wine. Kylar, the wine's poisoned!"

Vi stuck her fingers down her throat, retched, vomited. She fell to her knees, too weak to stand, and then did it again.

I had no medicines. I couldn't help her. I could carry her to get her help—

The twins! If someone was trying to poison me—

I ran. Maybe it was the wrong thing to do. Maybe I should've identified the poison first, asked Vi what it was, smelled it myself, or made myself throw up like she had, but all I could think of was getting to the twins.

I reached the edge of the keep's roof, but as I was leaping, a black pulse rolled through me. I couldn't tell if it came from within me or from outside, but suddenly, my Talent went blank.

My muscles weakened to merely human strength, and instead of landing five or six paces onto the roof, I didn't even reach it. I slammed with my full body into the side of the keep, face ricocheting off my reaching arms and into the wall, my fingers tearing at stonework even as my breath whooshed out of my lungs, ribs cracking. My legs swung under the roof edge, prising my grip from unyielding stone. I fell—

—and landed flat on my back on a balcony that I hadn't even known was there.

I staggered to my feet, feeling not only the pain of broken ribs and a face pounded to putty, but also drunk with the poison. Poppy with something sweeter and more deadly beneath? Have to hide the bitterness, though a new wineskin would help conceal odors. Feverwort? No, I could still feel my fingertips. Aedensbane? Well, if my back started sweating soon, I'd know. Maybe quorkswallow? Probably too expensive, and I was still alive.

I reached the balcony door. It was locked.

It took me a befuddled moment—*What do I do now?* Oh, I'd drunk poison, so maybe…following Vi's lead, I made myself puke. Sometimes that makes poisonings worse, but I had no charcoal to swallow, nor any hope of reaching my antidote kit at the rate this was hitting me.

I spat to clear bile, dragging a sleeve across my teary, grimy face. Then I threw my strength into the door, enough to tear it off its hinges.

Except it didn't budge. My Talent was gone, and thus, so too was all my magical strength.

I clambered back up to the roof with difficulty. Woozy, and with all the world swimming, I made it to the skylight above the nursery. I staggered and fell across the reinforced glass. I caught a glimpse of a nursemaid sprawled in the room below, unconscious or dead.

I pulled out a dagger and smashed the pommel against the glass.

Once, and it cracked, and with the second blow it shattered.

The fall went better than I had any right to expect. I didn't lacerate anything on the jagged glass or stab myself with the dagger. I rolled as I hit the ground, apparently uninjured. Or at least not injured further.

I ignored the nurse; she wasn't my problem now. As soon as I could stand, I made my way to the cribs, checking for danger as I went. A door was open, but I couldn't hear anyone else. Not that I would, necessarily. I was in a bad way. My head was swimming, blood running freely from my broken nose into my gasping mouth, down my chin. A lot of blood.

The first crib was empty. There was a silent child in the other. What did that mean?

Please be sleeping, I thought. *Please don't be dead.*

The infant was swaddled, rolled on his side. I leaned over his crib, dripping blood everywhere. I couldn't tell if he was breathing.

I picked up the bundle. Baby Caedan's eyes fluttered open.

I expelled a great breath in relief. It blasted blood from my broken nose out in a cloud, but luckily not onto the kid. I brushed his fuzzy hair back with a thumb. His eyes focused on mine.

Something there hit me with the same force I felt the day I'd bonded the black ka'kari.

Jenine wasn't crazy. There was something intensely magical going on with this kid.

"What's going on here?" a woman's voice said behind me. "Please don't— Lord Stern?"

As I turned, I saw one of the nursemaids. She looked terrified of me, or of the blood, her eyes darting repeatedly to the unconscious woman on the floor, but she steeled herself and stepped forward, taking the baby from my arms, shushing either the child or perhaps me. She checked him for injuries.

"It's all my blood," I said, barely holding myself up as I gripped the railing of the child's crib. "Pull the alarm rope..." But she was already striding over to the rope. "Someone's..."

I couldn't figure it out. Why was the one child here while the other was gone? Luck? A midnight feeding? But the nurse on the floor seemed to suggest it was neither of those.

The nurse didn't make it to the ropes in the corner to pull the alarm bell. At the last moment, a big man in dark clothes streaked into the room and slapped her hand away. He snagged her in a headlock so hard she almost dropped the baby.

There was nothing she could do to resist. Even if she hadn't been holding a child, the man was huge. He threw a look toward me, and then, apparently satisfied I was no threat, dragged her across the room to the other child's bed, looked in, and cursed.

I willed my body to Heal itself—but instead I was feeling worse with every passing moment.

Pushing away from the railing, I stood. Wobbled.

"Repha'im! That's far enough," I said.

He stopped, and slowly smiled. "Far enough? Oh, Kylar. I'm doing far more than saving this child. You think I've gone far enough? I'm willing to go much farther than this. The real question is, what about you?"

"What about me what?"

"How good are you with that knife? I heard amazing things about you, but so far I'm not impressed."

"What knife?" I actually didn't have a knife. I'd lost my dagger when I fell, though I saw it then, too far away. But I did have the ka'kari gathered in my hand.

"The knife you're planning to throw at me," he said. "Tougher to throw a knife accurately than people think, isn't it? It'd be easy to accidentally kill this girl instead of me."

He'd already twisted her around so she was in front of him. Armed as he was, a knife held to her throat, the only target I could hit that would do what I needed would be a low throw, angled high through his throat and into the stem of his brain. Pierce that golden triangle, and a human goes limp instantly. Hit elsewhere and they can thrash and fight long enough to hurt others on their way to the black gates.

Dizzy and nearly seeing double, I wasn't sure if I could hit him at all, much less strike such a small target. Nor was accuracy the only problem. Throwing a knife isn't as instantaneous as loosing the bolt of a crossbow. The throwing motion takes time, not much, but time in which he could react, duck, move the woman.

The nurse was tall. Her neck was in the way of his. I needed her to dive at the exact right moment—but she met my eyes, then looked away, looked at the baby, her eyes dripping tears, paralyzed with fear. There was no way she would see a signal and drop for the floor without him seeing it first—and now she wasn't even looking for my signal.

My chances—and hers—went from slim to practically nothing.

"Count her as lost," Repha'im said. "You have to guess I'll kill her on my way out anyway, right?" He reached a hand up and pulled her neckline down. She whimpered. "Right here? Through the soft tissues of her neck, and into mine? That's your only chance, isn't it? What does she matter, anyway? Her life, for the prince's? She probably took an oath to put the twins' lives first! You'd not even be taking something she hasn't freely offered."

"Please," she choked out, and then started crying.

"See?" Lord Repha'im asked. "This is you, Kylar. One moment you commit atrocities, and the next, you're not even willing to put a dying woman out of her misery, not even when the stakes are everything—because you're too *good* for that. You're a farce. Your moral contradictions make you weak."

He's right. The baby's only hope was for me to kill her and hope I took Repha'im out too, or at least slowed him enough to give me a chance, or maybe someone else a chance—but regardless, if I wanted to stop him, I had to kill the woman.

But Repha'im didn't wait any longer for me to decide. He bulled forward, pressing the woman toward me, and at the last moment, his long arm snaked up. His right hand nearly took off my jaw with an open-handed slap that clipped jaw and neck and ear.

It dropped me to the floor, nerveless.

I might have gone unconscious, if only for a moment, because the next thing I saw was Lord Repha'im handing the swaddle streaked red with my blood off to another cloaked figure. "Go," he said, "I'll catch up."

On the ground in front of me, the nursemaid was dying, blood spreading in a pool around her. He'd cut her throat while I was down.

Her eyes were open and she was breathing rapidly, but even as I watched, locking gazes with her, her breathing slowed, and her eyes dimmed. She lost consciousness as the blood still pumped, the body stubborn for life, pumping, pumping the blood pool broader, trying to feed a brain that will never know enough again.

"Two minutes. No more," the other cloaked figure whispered. They were lean, but I couldn't tell if it was a woman or a man.

I knew I had to move. The nursery was large, with numerous comfortable chairs for nursing the infants, bright patterns on the walls, a large shuttered window, and several doors, all of them closed except the one the kidnapper was leaving through.

Most importantly, there were summons-bell ropes in the one corner. One of those was an alarm. Any of them could be an alarm if I pulled the right signal.

I lifted myself up on an elbow, judging my strength.

I almost passed out. Was that the blood loss, or the poison?

With effort, I kept myself from vomiting again.

Maybe not vomiting was the wrong move long term, but I couldn't take the moments of incapacity to worry about the long term.

But by the time I looked up, the big man had taken one step closer, narrowing the angles between him and me and the alarm rope, as if taunting me, not closing off the possibility but making it very improbable I could get there first.

Impossible, in the state I was in.

Lord Repha'im threw back his hood. "You know, Kylar, Night Angel," he said, "you baffle me. Really you do."

"Oh? We have something in common, then," I said. Would my Talent answer me now? My body tends to process poisons faster than most bodies do, and I hadn't had that much poisoned wine before Viridiana knocked it from my hands. Maybe she'd saved me. Maybe she'd given me a chance here.

Repha'im said, "You murder people for a living, and you don't realize you're the monster here, do you?"

"That's a fair point. Very convincing with you standing over an innocent you just murdered," I said.

"You think I'm the bad guy," he said, incredulous. "What would you do to save thousands of lives, Kylar? How about the world? Worse than this, I think."

"Saving the world? So you're the good guy," I said, rising to all fours, glancing over at the alarm rope again. "Does that mean—?" I grimaced with feigned pain.

Not completely feigned. I huffed a few breaths as I glanced down to figure out what had gone wrong with the ka'kari. Could it hear me? Would it do what I needed it to do?

I heard the sound of a sword clearing a scabbard.

"Does this mean we get to have a fair fight?" I looked at his stance. He'd taken a Long Tail Guard to conceal the length of his blade and tempt me to try my luck, but I always note weapons first. I'd already seen that his sword was forged to fit his expansive frame and limbs: His Long Tail Guard is long indeed.

He smiled and lifted his chin toward the alarm rope. He knew exactly what I was doing.

So he thought.

"A fair fight?" he said. "Against the Night Angel?" He switched guards, the motion at first seeming like he was mocking me: The Crown does look like a salute. The switch is the kind of thing a skilled swordsman will do; let you plan your attack against a particular guard and then switch, then switch again, sowing confusion, looking for weaknesses, stealing initiative. Unarmed or with a dagger at best, I didn't have good options against a competent swordsman. If I could close the distance without getting skewered, I might use surprise to disarm—

"Well...you *do* have a few things in your favor," I said, weaving drunkenly as he changed his stance again, now to the Leopard, a half-swording stance that sacrifices reach for leverage. As I had no sword, his reach was still much greater than mine; with one hand on his grip and one on his naked blade, any attempt at disarming him had morphed from *unlikely* to *suicidal*.

But I thought my Talent would respond. Maybe.

I'd have one chance. One.

"Oh, Kylar, you should know better. I said I'm not the bad guy. I didn't say I'm good."

We moved at the same instant. He lunged to intercept me, cutting off my approach toward the alarm rope. But I leapt toward the window.

The window shattered as my Talent surged, though not with all the strength I'd hoped. I slammed into the locked shutters, and my weight pressed them outward, but they didn't break open.

He recovered and lunged back toward me.

I slithered through the gap at the bottom of the shutters a moment before his swordpoint skewered them.

His thrust broke the shutters open. Instead of dropping straight down, I was sent spinning.

My feet hit a balcony railing on the floor below, but I was off-balance and tumbled out into space.

Twisting, I caught a bit of the railing in my fingers—and lost it—but it was enough that I swung in and hit the next railing a floor below and fell inside it with a crunch of grinding bones and blood.

Next thing I knew, I'd rolled onto my back and was staring into the night sky, thinking I should probably try to figure out how bad my injuries were, just as soon as I could get a full breath. Then I caught a movement.

Two floors above me, I saw Lord Repha'im leaning out of the broken window as far as he could. His hand began to fill with red-black fire, but it sputtered, popped. He looked at his hand angrily, tried again. Again his magic failed. He tried something else, and managed only a shower of sparks that made him flinch away.

He disappeared, then he reappeared a moment later, holding something, leaning out again. His hand moved whip-fast, and I couldn't process what he was doing before I heard the *thunk* of something hitting the balcony railing near me.

The dagger ricocheted off the railing and went spinning glittering into the night.

I've practiced throwing daggers—and that was an incredible throw.

I watched him lean out again, measuring the distance to try again.

I tried to roll out of the way—and couldn't.

This blade hit next to my shoulder and ricocheted into me, but didn't cut, at least as far as I could tell.

His hand went to his belt again but came up empty. He was out of daggers.

I blinked against the encroaching blackness and saw him with his sword in hand, clearly weighing whether it was worth trying to throw a sword from that far.

Throwing a dagger's hard, but throwing a sword accurately from that distance is well-nigh impossible. If I were him, I'd count it a wasted effort not worth the loss of a sword.

On the target side of things, I didn't feel so confident about my chances.

But I never saw the throw. I lost consciousness.

In hushed tones, later, they said that when they found me there was a sword stuck into the marble—yes, stuck into *marble*—right next to my throat.

Chapter Eighteen

Unraveling Bonds

If only I hadn't given Kylar that wine, Vi thought. *It's my fault. All of this.*

She sat, staring into space and thinking how it was going to feel when she had to read about Kylar realizing what she'd done. But mostly staring into space. Shaking herself, she stood and walked over to where the sun was shining bravely through the little library's small window.

The Chantry was many stories tall and housed within a floating island-statue called the White Seraph. This library was high up, but its window didn't give her any view over the lake or to the beautiful surrounding mountains; the window was placed high for reading light, not a view.

Viridiana had skipped breakfast and now had spent so long she might have missed lunch too, so she decided to jog downstairs to try to grab something to eat before the kitchens closed. Before she left the first stairs, she got the old itch that she was being followed. The Sisters following her weren't bad—or weren't following her at all. Despite that it might cost her lunch, Vi took a circuitous path to the dining hall. One of her possible tails followed, but then walked on past the dining hall as if it were coincidence she was passing this way. Given the number of Sisters tightly packed in the White Seraph, that was entirely possible. It was also exactly what a good team tailing a target would do. The other woman Vi had thought she'd spotted was already eating, didn't so much as glance at Vi when she arrived, though the woman was seated where she could see every entrance and exit.

Troubled, Vi grabbed food and headed for the nearest friendly faces. Some of her training partners hailed her with obvious joy. Their ranks had been thinned, not by war but by success. Three of her closest friends and lieutenants had accepted plum postings far away. Two of them had even asked her permission—her *permission*! as if she were their commander—before accepting. She'd had no reason to say no. There was no war, now. War mages were forbidden by the old Alitaeran Accords, so even though the Chantry had been glad to have Vi and her compatriots and their war magics at the Battle of Black Barrow, now that the imminent threats had been vanquished, the war magae were an embarrassment.

"You going to be in the big meeting?" Gwaen asked. She was tiny, muscular, and relentlessly optimistic, even in the face of a deep shoulder wound she'd taken from one of the red insectoid monsters at Black Barrow which had rendered her left arm almost useless. She'd killed a *buulgar* with its praying-mantis-like blade arms by herself, over the bodies of numerous of her Sisters and half a dozen soldiers. Others had broken and run. Gwaen hadn't. Nor had she left Viridiana's shrinking platoon in the time since.

"At the end, I think. They gave me a big project to work on," Viridiana said. "How's the therapy?" The Healing required Gwaen to strengthen her atrophying shoulder muscles, tearing them away from the significant scar tissue and reattaching them magically until each layer of muscle was flawless. To Heal Gwaen's wound fully was requiring skilled Healers to work one layer at a time, cutting the muscles away from the scar, excising the scar tissue itself, stretching the muscle fibers to reconnect them over a magical lattice, and then leaving it to heal naturally. In between every session, Gwaen had to do painful exercises daily to keep the muscle from atrophying from disuse. Despite that, Gwaen never complained.

"Sister Assaen says maybe forty more sessions over twenty weeks if I keep up my exercises. Says I scar 'funny,' because of my 'foreign blood.'"

Vi winced. Gwaen had dark skin from her Ladeshian ancestry, but her family had lived in Waeddryn for four generations. Apparently, though, pucker scarring was rare even among the Ladeshians. Healers on the continent didn't have much experience with it. "She's just taking out her incompetence on you. Think one of the Sisters coming to the big meeting might be any better?"

"I've already started asking around. Whether Sister Assaen will take advice is a different matter. As long as it's not one of the Chattel, maybe. But it's not so bad. It's working. Not fast, but if I weren't at the Chantry, I'd have lost the arm. I'll get there."

"We'll help," one of the others said, and everyone at the table agreed to quietly make inquiries for Healers. It warmed Vi to see them having each other's backs.

"What about you?" Gwaen asked. "You need anything?"

"A handkerchief, a poppet, a blankie, and if those don't stop the tears, a lot of poppy wine," Vi said, flashing a grin at the end to try to turn it into a joke.

No one laughed. The table fell silent. Every eye turned to her.

"You don't cry," the pallid, black-haired Sarren said.

"It's this project," Vi said. "It'll bore me to tears." A few of them looked back and forth at each other, those who knew her less well looking to those who knew her better. Before they could ask more, she said, "Any of you see Uly?"

Sarren said, "She poked her head in earlier. Said she had the notes for you from your Developments of Current Governments lectures. Think they just started Modai."

The others groaned. Willowy Aeryx said, "That was the worst. I swear there were like fourteen men from those two dynasties who had about three names between them, so everything was like 'Zilpaz the Greater, but the one during the Second Interregnum, not his great-grandfather of the same name, during the first one.'"

The other women laughed.

Everyone else at the table had finished their lower schooling years ago. Viridiana, on the other hand, would sometimes go from a morning of drilling women decades older than herself to attending afternoon lectures with twelve-year-olds who knew far more than she did. The older women—even her friends—often forgot she hadn't had the same experiences they had.

Still, she was here with friends, even if she had lost the closest of them to the Chantry's machinations—but she couldn't tell even these women about the book. She finished eating and made her excuses, saying goodbye with a real smile, but one that failed to connect her lips to her heart.

Sister Ayayah Meganah had threatened Vi's continued membership in the Chantry if she didn't find Kylar's body, but Vi felt like the bonds of Sisterhood were already unraveling in her hands. There were good women here, women Vi loved and trusted with her life.

A pang that she refused to call a premonition hit her. She'd already lost Kylar. Was she going to lose them, too?

Chapter Nineteen

Harder than Impossible

I had the weirdest dream.

~Was that the one where you get tenderized like cheap steak?~

That was real, huh?

Could have used some more help there.

I'm in an unfamiliar bed, and I think for a moment how this happens to me way too often. And it's never because I drank too much and ended my evening with a beautiful woman.

Although...

That reminds me of the other dreams I had, actual dreams. There was the one with Vi. For a moment I luxuriate in the memory of it, but then I feel an old familiar pang of guilt. You're not supposed to have those kind of dreams about your wife's friend. I wouldn't have those kind of dreams if I really loved Elene. She's not even been dead six months yet.

~Eight.~

Huh? Oh. I guess it has been that long.

It's supposed to get easier with time, isn't it? Why isn't it?

I sit up and try to banish the thoughts as I look around the room. Not a dungeon, so that's good. From the marble and the hardwoods, it looks like I'm in the palace somewhere.

There's clean clothing laid out for me, and a note folded on the bedside table, with my name written on it in Momma K's hand.

I dress.

There are more than a few strange things about me, but one of the weirdest is how my Healing functions. When I get gravely wounded and wake up, I'm not only healed—I feel great. I mean, I feel better than after a normal night's sleep. It's all backward. I *know* that my body has just expended vast amounts of power. I should feel terrible, totally drained.

But nope. My broken nose is set perfectly; I have no bruises, and even though I was poisoned, I feel wonderful. Better yet, there was no visit with the Wolf in the Antechamber of the Mystery while I was unconscious, so that means I didn't die and come back. That means no worries about the cost of my immortality this time, either.

Finally, I pick up the note:

Twins kidnapped. No good leads. Viridiana alive last I heard. Healers have taken her back to Chantry. Please come to me immediately to debrief. —D.G.T., Regent

The D.G.T. throws me. I fixate on it, can't think about the other news yet. Duchess Gwinvere Thorne, instead of M.K. for Momma K like I'd expect.

Again. People changing on me. Why sign it at all rather than assume I'd recognize her handwriting? To remind me of where things stand, I suppose. But why Regent?

Oh, to remind me that Logan left her in charge while he's gone.

Logan. Logan's kids. Oh hells. A wave of nausea hits me so hard, I have to sit back down on the bed. I was supposed to protect them. Logan trusted me.

It's night out. I don't know what day. It's the flip side of my waking up feeling great—when I'm gravely injured, I do tend to sleep a long time.

I hope not *too* long. My guts twist again.

Gods, no. My mind flashes to the fight, the falls, to Logan, to Jenine who was so certain I'd mess things up, to Logan again, and to that whoreson Lord Repha'im. He's surely fled, and if I want to catch him, every moment counts, and I've been unconscious for some unknown time. I feel sick with helplessness.

But there's no faster way to get on the right trail than to talk to Momma K. I put my hand on the latch but then hear a voice in the hall. I pause until I hear the steps recede as they continue past.

I don't want to talk to anyone. Don't want to be questioned or held up by well-intentioned guards who have no clue what they're doing. I pull the ka'kari over my skin and go invisible.

When I get to her rooms, I peer through a crack in her door. I see that though she wears a dressing gown as if for bed, she's seated at a desk, as she so often is, going over correspondence and reports. I don't know that I've ever seen this woman relax. I suppose that's how one climbs from gutter to glamour: unceasing effort in private to make everything in public seem effortless.

I knock on the door, drop my invisibility, and step inside.

As soon as the door is shut behind me, leaving us alone, she sets her quill in its rest and says, "We have our suspicions, but you were there. What can you tell me?"

"Thank you, I'm doing well, surprisingly enough. But fine, let's get to it. Is Vi alive? Are the kids all right? How long have I been out?" I ask.

She stares at me with hard eyes.

"Lord Repha'im," I say. "With at least one subordinate."

She blinks, and I'm shocked to realize she didn't know who was behind all this, or at least she wasn't sure. I can almost see the tapestry weaving together anew instantaneously in her mind's eye, but she's already speaking. "How'd he come so close to killing you?"

"Vi and I were poisoned. Something that blocked my Talent." I frown. Is that right? It has to be. I suddenly wish I'd been narrating everything to the ka'kari so I could go back and dissect what happened. I'll have to go back and fill in the blanks as soon as possible. "Did she . . . did she make it?" I try to keep the question casual but stumble a little.

Momma K notices, naturally. She notices everything. But instead of asking about it, she says, "She was alive last I heard. I don't know how bad her injuries are. The Sisters took her back to the Chantry with them. So either she was well enough to risk the trip, or so gravely ill they needed to risk the trip regardless. They wanted their best Healers to work on her."

"I thought the ones who came here to see Jenine *were* their best."

"I raised that point myself. They said they are *some* of the Chantry's best, but for a case like Viridiana's, they wanted the help of some of their oldest Healers who are too frail to leave the Chantry."

"You think that's true?" I ask.

"I think they sent High King Gyre good Healers, maybe very good ones, but they keep their best safe at home for themselves. For reasons of diplomacy, they can't say that aloud."

"So she's in a bad way," I say.

Momma K gives the smallest shrug, and I know her well enough to read it as *How many people have we seen die, Kylar? This is our world.*

"She said a servant gave her the wine. The poisoned wine," I say.

"Did she say when?" Momma K asked. "Any other identifying details?"

I think back but can't remember for sure. "Don't think so. Was she conscious?"

"No. And she looked poorly, so I let them take her away. With the number of servants who died or disappeared, I'd not give us good odds with that lead. Nonetheless, I'll do what I can to re-create your friend's path."

A dead end, then. "Don't suppose they asked Dorian to help Heal her," I say, but it's just a complaint. The Chantry would never go to Dorian for help—even if he weren't who he is, he's a man. Any individual Sister might seek a male mage's help, but the Chantry as a whole doing so? No way.

"There was an attempt on his life as well. At least, we assume he was the target," Momma K says. "His friend, the mountainous one?"

"Feir Cousat?" I say.

"Yes." She flips through some parchment and writes down the name. She keeps files on everyone and everything. "Feir killed six armed men who tried to break into Dorian's little hut. A seventh intruder got away but was wounded."

"Feir's a second-echelon Blade Master. He can fight." Still, taking on seven men?

"Indeed?" She makes a note of that as well. "We tracked the wounded one to a warehouse. Someone got there first. They'd slit his throat."

"To keep him from talking, or maybe from slowing them down as they escaped. I assume there were no identifying items on any of the attackers?"

"None," she says. "Even the weapons they carried were of various national origins. Dorian apparently never came out of his trance through the whole thing, or afterward. I've given Feir permission to take him into hiding."

That seems uncharacteristic, given that he might be useful, but then her play dawns on me. "And you had them followed."

Momma K shrugs. Of course she did. If she knows where Dorian is, but no one else does, she gains something of value.

I'm not sure she's going to be successful in tracking a man who can see the future, but that's none of my business.

She takes a deep breath. "You're *sure*."

She means about Repha'im, not Dorian. "Certain," I say. "How'd this happen? Where were the bodyguards, the royal guards, the nursemaids—I mean, I saw two of those, but Logan wasn't taking chances! My presence was supposed to be a ridiculously overcautious last line of defense, not the only one."

"One wet nurse and some other staff are still alive. Four bodyguards and four royal guards are all dead. Skillfully murdered, bodies tucked away. Professional wet work. Some guards in a nearby outpost were drugged. A few guards are still unaccounted for, bribed or panicked and fled, I assume. We're searching for those now."

"All this, right under our noses?"

"The Commander of the Royal Guard has submitted his resignation—not that I can accept it without Logan here. And I wouldn't anyway, barring evidence of complicity. It's a new kingdom, Kylar. *Everyone's* new. People show up to take a vacant job and say they have experience in the work? It's not like we can check with their former employers. The people who come here have come to start a new life. I've walked past women in the palace halls who worked for me for a decade yet pretend not to recognize me and now go by other names." She crosses her legs and takes a slow sip of ootai, which must surely be cold. She seems not to notice. "But you're certain, Kylar? You *were* drugged. No masks, no illusions, no misdirection?"

"You know how you hate it when you have to repeat yourself?" I say.

Her demeanor goes frosty. "The stakes are high, Kylar. For all of us."

"It was him. But why keep asking? You think I'm lying?"

"You wouldn't lie, not about this. I know that. But you are my sole source vouching it's him. That's puzzling. He covered his tracks so well everywhere else. Until this moment, I didn't know who took the boys. I didn't know why. So many of the staff are new that few even noticed any strangers coming through. Reports of possible strangers' hair color, height, build, even gender are inconsistent. Maybe three people? Maybe eight! Maybe two different teams? Three? Maybe a team for each child in case the other got caught? Kiern and Caedan both had several magical beacons placed in their clothing and on their persons. Those were all removed and destroyed before they even left the nursery. We brought in hounds to track them, but they quickly lost the trail, which may have been magically scattered—if such a thing is possible. It's a professional job through and through. So how did Repha'im do everything else right, and then let you see his face and live?"

"He underestimated me. I messed up his plan," I say.

"Did you? Or is this another part of his plan?"

"How good am I at fighting, Momma K?"

" 'Your Grace,' " she says, with a note of irritation.

"How good?" I insist.

"Possibly the best in the empire at the moment…other than Lantano Garuwashi. Maybe Feir Cousat. Come to think of it, I'm sure there are others I don't know about. War and opportunity does tend to draw such men, and create more of them. Clearly your master. But yes, to your point, very well, you're *one* of the best."

It's a fair assessment, but I can't tell if she added all the qualifiers merely as she thought of them, or as a way to take me down a peg.

"You do have a point, I imagine?" she says, still cool.

She didn't say Durzo's name. What's that about?

I don't jab back at her. We're both frustrated, but not at each other. I say, "Lord Repha'im's a sound fighter. Good posture, grip, and speed, and he can throw knives—an uncommon skill. But he's not remotely great. I can usually tell when someone's pretending to be worse than they are. Masters do it with their pupils all the time as they teach. I know when someone's actually trying to kill me. And he tried magic, too, but couldn't pull it off. So he's not well trained with it. This wasn't part of some master plan to let me live so I'd go do something else he's already foreseen."

"No?" she asks.

"No. I lived because I'm just that special." Which is also true, but I'm also saying it to take her down a peg.

She scoffs instantly, though, which stings.

"To give him his due," I say, trying for some rapprochement, "he did do a pretty good job of killing me to keep me quiet. How long have I been out?"

"Three days."

It's a gut punch. If I'm actively using my Talent, I can Heal myself faster, but it's not like I usually get a choice in the matter. When I'm out, I'm out until my body heals itself.

I shouldn't complain. In a fair world, I'd be laid up for another six months with the injuries I took—if I weren't dead already. But it's all so terrifically *inconvenient.*

"So where do we start?" I ask. "Does Repha'im have a place in the city?"

She looks troubled. "No, he's gone. I've tracked everyone's comings and goings, but I couldn't imprison the entire city; by the time my orders arrived, I knew anyone with good reason to flee would already be gone. If I start sending soldiers to detain nobles, half the nobles in the city might run. If they run, they'll be slow to come back. If they're slow to come back, Logan's legitimacy will suffer. If Logan's legitimacy suffers..."

"Fine," I say. I don't care about all the political stuff. "So he'll be back in Cenaria in his mansion. Great. Can't wait to visit again."

"No," she says. "He sold that property immediately after you killed Jadwin. He hasn't bought any comparable manor to replace it yet. Not in Cenaria or Elenea anyway. Not that I'm aware of." The old lines between her eyebrows are reappearing.

She's having the same worries I am: Rich properties and the many servants they require usually make nobles easy to find. He got rid of his, right *before* doing all this? That means he's got a lot of money on hand and few ways to track him.

I say, "This seems all far too involved for him to have cooked it up just since Logan humiliated him in court the other day."

"I was thinking the same," Momma K says. "But if he was planning to run away already, why go after me and, by extension, the high king himself so publicly in the first place? Regardless of how his confrontation with me went, why make himself the face of Logan's opposition right before planning this kind of treason? He has to know it makes him the first person we'd suspect—and it has. I already have people checking into everything about him."

"Why invite that, then?" I ask. Then I answer my own question. "Assuming he didn't mean for me to live…then the truth is, he doesn't merely look like Logan's enemy; he looks like *yours*. You going after him now could be made to look like you were using a crisis as cover to weed out your political rivals and enemies. That could make everyone who's been against you—"

"Thus pretty much everyone," Momma K interjects.

"Right. It could make pretty much everyone nervous that they're next in your sights, especially if you do anything they think is unfair."

"And how am I supposed to be *fair* when we've lost the future of the empire?" she snaps. "Logan will be furious if I *don't* turn every suspect's house upside down, nobleman or not. It's what *he* would do. The difference is, he could get away with it."

"And the nobles will be outraged that they're even suspected if you do it. Well, you're in a pocket nob with a woo basher, a'ncha?"

Her brows tighten at the old Cenarian street jargon for a tight spot: A pocket nob's a dead-end alley with high walls and a basher's a muscular thug, often a mugger. Never really understood what *woo* means, it was just part of the phrase, but she ignores it anyway.

"Kylar," she says with sudden intensity. "*How* ambitious is he?"

"He told me he's saving the world."

"A zealot?" Momma K closes her eyes and rubs the bridge of her nose.

"What?" I ask. "You figure something out?"

"I hope not. But there are only so many reasons to kidnap heirs to a throne, especially when they're mere infants. Murdering them is much easier. I own… hundreds of properties in Cenaria, and many beyond. If Lord Repha'im wishes to destroy *me*, when Logan comes back, Repha'im can simply let it leak that the boys are being held in one of those properties; they break into an empty house a few hours before Logan can raid it, murder a few of Repha'im's own lackeys who don't know anything anyway. The more obscure the place, the better. Within days, Logan tracks down who owns that place, and..."

"And it's you. And you look like a traitor. And you do own a *lot* of obscure properties," I say. "Too many to watch them all, all the time. And it probably takes a few days to get reports sometimes, huh? Small problem of coming in from the underworld."

"But I'm not worried about that," she says.

"Why wouldn't you be?"

"Because the real reason Repha'im risks publicly making himself the face of the opposition is to differentiate himself from all the other nobles in the event of a general rebellion. He's not from an old family; he bought his title. He's one of the crop of new nobles Logan's been raising to rule these lands, balancing giving existing nobles of the four kingdoms plum lands in other kingdoms to knit the new land together and also bringing in needed revenue, and hopefully settling the wide swaths of empty land in the east and north. Point is, there are many nobles old and new, all jockeying for position, and Repha'im doesn't have a solid base of loyalty to count on, so he needs to be seen as important, even if in a negative way.

"So his reason to do that, and then kidnap infants, is not because he wants the babies found in an inconvenient place; it's so they're never found at all. Logan and Jenine are both currently the last of their family bloodlines. If he's as ambitious as you say, Lord Repha'im wants the throne. If he murders babies to get it, though, that would mark him as so bloody-minded that even possible allies will avoid or abandon him. Even if he won, having murdered children to get the throne would delegitimate his rule. He'd be forever tainted, inviting rebellions against him. But if the princes simply disappear...or their deaths can be pinned on someone else, he gets the best of both worlds. Rivals gone and a clean throne."

I feel sick. "But surely...after all these kingdoms have been through...I mean, would any nobles follow him?"

"It doesn't matter," Momma K says. "I mean, in the short term, it doesn't matter to us if his plan would work. What matters for now is if he thinks it will. And obviously he does. Kylar, there's only one way for a man to emerge from total obscurity into prominence in so short a time—by being willing to gamble everything and winning, several times in a row. He's done that to get where he is now. What's to say he wouldn't gamble everything again, one last time, for the ultimate prize?"

"Do you think Caedan and Kiern are already dead?" I ask, my throat tight.

She thinks about it, and almost instantly, I see a change in her face from the worried but warm Duchess Gwinvere Thorne to the old cold Momma K, who had to deal every day with criminals who ran the gamut from con men to killers of every persuasion, from those who killed for power to those who killed for fun. "He left the first wet nurse alive, and she would've been a big risk. That gives me hope that he can see a difference between degrees of threat and isn't purely bloody-minded. But he killed the second because she could identify him, which tells me he's willing to do anything it takes to win." She sips her ootai again, measuring her words. "That kind of man? He won't kill the children until he's sure that there's more to gain than to lose by it. Which means..."

She goes quiet, and I try to think about it too, but I have no idea what it means, or what she thinks it means.

After a while, I break the silence. "I have no idea what it means," I say. "I'm just sitting here pretending to think hard."

She doesn't so much as crack a smile.

"I'm trying to think how we use you, Kylar."

"What do you mean? I'm going after them."

She levels a flat gaze at me. "Of course you are. And *where* are you going?"

"I...I don't know. But I can go chase down leads as well as anyone."

"As well as anyone. But not better than anyone. I have a thousand people working on this, Kylar. Literally. And now I have a strong focus for all that work."

The thought strikes me suddenly. "Logan is going to go out of his mind. Jenine—"

"Let's not even talk about her just now," Momma K says.

She's right again. "Logan needs to know I'm doing everything I can about this."

But she jumps in before I can go on. "Kylar, don't take this the wrong way. You are very, very adept at a very, very limited number of skills. Do you think that with your abilities, contacts, and wealth, you can do a better job of finding Lord Repha'im than I can with all the resources at my disposal?"

I grit my teeth.

"It's not like back in Cenaria, Kylar. We're the law here. We can do things openly. There may be a few jobs you can do more efficiently than anyone. Papers you can procure quietly—"

"You're gonna turn me into a cat burglar? What's that, just something to keep me out of your way? You have people for that, too, don't you?"

"This is not a task for which you have any skill, Kylar!" she snaps.

I recoil as if she struck me.

"I didn't mean that," she says, averting her gaze. "It's not been an easy few days."

I pick up her pot and pour her some fresh ootai. "You're not wrong," I say quietly.

Then I sit, heavily.

"What about that job?" I ask.

"The papers?" she asks, puzzled. "Many of the nobles aren't eager for us to see their ledger books, and following the money may—"

"No, not that job. The one from before. The compass."

Her cup of ootai freezes at her lips. I can see her mind working at its dazzling speed.

Then she sighs. "No. Sounds like just the thing now, doesn't it? A compass, to show us directly to the children!"

"And afterwards to Repha'im, to kill him," I say.

She shakes her head. "I'm happy to send you, if you wish. But it's a waste of time. It won't work."

"What do you mean it won't work?" I demand.

"Kylar, finding the Twilight Compass was a one-in-a-hundred chance, albeit with a thousand-to-one payoff—a week ago, when I tried to hire you. To tell you the truth, I don't even know if it's real. If it is real, I don't know if it still works. If it still works, I don't know if *we* can get it to work. You want me to go on?"

"Yes, actually," I say, "yes I do! Because it's exactly what we need."

"Oh, a magical artifact to solve all our problems is exactly what we need," Momma K says scornfully. "No it's not, Kylar. What we need is to do the boring work of chasing down a thousand leads. Carefully. Methodically. This is my kind of job, not yours. You can't rush in and save the day here."

"A lot of people in my life have told me what I can't possibly do. I think you've had people do the same in yours."

She sits back in her chair. Sets down her delicate cup. "It was practically impossible before, Kylar. At this point, given the time frame? No."

My chin rises defiantly.

"No, no, I know what you're going to say," she says. " 'I'm Kylar Stern! I have a knack. I always find a third way!' And you have. You've done stunning things, things that no one thought you could do. I'm telling you, this time, even you can't do this. And frankly, I'm worried what it will do to you when you try and fail."

That strikes me. It's oddly personal, and I realize how abstractly I've always thought of this woman. She's always been this towering figure—in the slums, but somehow above them, always masterful, at ease, in charge. I hadn't really thought of her as a mere person, hadn't thought of why she did the things she did. "Are we friends, Momma K?" I blurt out. It sounds stupid as soon as the words are out of my mouth. "I mean, Your Grace."

Somehow, that sounds even worse.

I've caught her off guard. "Kylar," she says carefully, "I saved your life early on, but since then I've lied to you, manipulated you, almost cost you the most important relationship in your life, and nearly gotten you killed. You've deceived me, defied me, and jabbed me with a lethal poison. Even in the Warrens, that's not what friends do. So, no, I don't think that makes us friends." She raises her cup to me. "I think that makes us family."

I laugh. "We've had a *few* good interactions!"

"A few," she admits with a mischievous smile.

"Mostly when I was doing what you wanted me to," I say. "Huh."

"Huh," she echoes back at me. As if I'm on the brink of a terribly obvious epiphany.

It brings to mind something Durzo said, and that makes me think of him. I say, "Given the stakes, if the job's that hard, maybe I can team up with Durzo."

The air seems to go cold. I see her knuckles go white for a moment on her ootai cup.

It won't be a pleasant meeting, given how the last one went, but I'm willing to do whatever it takes. Even apologize. And Durzo likes Logan.

Her face doesn't move from its carefully neutral expression. She says smoothly, "Durzo isn't available."

"Where is he? When will he be back?"

"I don't know."

"You don't *know*?" I say. "Your husband."

For a long moment she says nothing. But neither do I. She's the one who taught me the power of silence.

Finally, she seems to remember that fact. "We had words," she admits.

Her too? "About what?"

"Adult stuff," she says sharply. "You wouldn't understand. Get out, Kylar. I'll send you word when we find a lead."

I clench my jaw and take it. I don't have any right to know about their marital problems, but I have every right to be furious that she's driven away my master. It's not worth fighting about it now, though. Or at all. I can see she's not going to answer anything about him.

"You know I can't do that," I say.

She recrosses her leg and rubs an immaculately lacquered fingernail against her thumb, thinking. "Do you know what I like about you, Kylar?"

"Many things."

"Many things," she concurs, with a fleeting but genuine smile. "But the relevant one at the moment is that you have a ferocious tenacity that reminds me of myself in my best moments. Do you want to know the problem with that?"

"No. I'm well aware of my flaws, thanks."

"Hmm, maybe you are. Now. Maybe you're no longer the filthy scared kid who stood in my parlor years ago, making demands." She raises her eyebrows at me, and I don't like to remember the parallels between now and then. "Kylar, no matter what happens here, you're going to get out of this room, and you're going to decide I manipulated you into doing what I wanted. So before you go, I want you to decide if this is what you really, really want to do. If so, I'll give you all the help I can."

"You still haven't told me anything about the job," I say.

"Does it matter? Is there anything I can say that would dissuade you from taking it?"

"No," I grumble.

"Then let's put that aside for the time being."

She smiles beatifically, and much as I hate to admit it, some part of me still— still!—feels warmed inside by her approval. Maybe it's that she was a mother figure to me when I was that orphan on the streets. Maybe it's her surreal confidence that she knows what's best, or that she almost always does. Maybe it's that everyone wants to please people who are charismatic and seem to care about you. Maybe I'm simply weak. Regardless, she's always had that power: Whenever she gives me a scrap of approval, I want to do whatever I must to get more.

"It's not all bad," she says.

I can tell it's a lie the moment she says it.

If she makes a joke of it and finishes . . . *it's worse*, I'll let it slide.

"I'm sending help," she says.

That is worse.

"By 'help' you mean a fine horse and a full purse, right? You know I don't work with partners."

"Of course," she says.

I can tell she means *Of course I know that*, not *Of course I'm not going to send you with a partner.*

"As it happens, you *are* the help. I already have someone attempting the job."

"I'm not gonna be the help."

"Of course not. The plan will have to change."

That seems too easy.

"What's the catch?"

"Kylar, you're the Night Angel now. I respect that."

I search her face for any hint of sarcasm but see none. A moment later, it bothers me how important it was to me that I not.

She says, "Let's cut to the chase: You tell me all your non-negotiables, and I tell you what the job requires. Then you decide if we can put those together. I already told you what I think of the idea, but it'll be your choice."

Finally, progress. It is actually nice to be playing on the same side as this woman. I wouldn't stand a chance if we were truly working at cross-purposes. "You have to pay me. Durzo rates. Not 'cause I need the money, but because I need to know we both have skin in—"

"Not happening. My money's already committed elsewhere, for Logan and the children. Tell me the real ones."

I think about it. There's a lot of things I'd like to demand, but time is of the essence, so I try to think only of the real non-negotiables. "Three rules," I say. "First, no travel—I have to be the one to go after Lord Repha'im as soon as we get a good lead, and I have to be here when Logan gets back. Second, nothing that pits me against the Chantry. I've already got history with them, and they have good reasons *and* the ability to put me on a table and dissect me. I need to steer clear of them for about the next hundred years. And three—"

"Third," she corrects.

"Right. Thank you. Now, I know you've known me since I was a child, and sometimes I think you can't help but still see me as that clueless kid. I'm not that anymore—"

"Clueless, or a kid?" she asks, deadpan.

"I'm all grown up. I've been trained by the best. I know how you work, and I know how you want to be in charge every step of the way. I don't need some nursemaid to tag along because you don't trust me. So, *third:* no partners."

Chapter Twenty

A Rich Prize

Look, I don't want to hear it. You've never been in a room with the woman. I mean, yes, I described part of that meeting to you, but words don't adequately express...

~Are you stalling? In a monologue?~

It's embarrassing, all right?

~This is far from the most embarrassing thing I've seen you do.~

It is?

~Remember that time you humped a bridge?~

I did not—*you are totally mischaracterizing—you're not recording this, are you?*

~Recording?~

I hate you.

Yeah, so, I guess I'll cut that stuff out later. Where was I?

Yes, I'm on a horse, outside the city, and heading even farther away.

Yes, I'm on my way to meet a partner.

And, yes—you saw this coming, didn't you?—my mission is to steal something... from the Chantry.

The good news? I don't even know how!

Wait. That's bad news too, isn't it?

It's cold and raining now in this mountain pass, and all I can think about is the warm glow I felt inside at Momma K's approval of me when I agreed to do everything she wanted, minutes after I'd sworn I wouldn't. It felt so good to betray my principles.

~With all that work Durzo made you do to increase your flexibility, he'll be so proud to learn that you folded like wet paper.~

As I've been riding south, it's taken me a week and a dozen attempts to narrate even this much, and it still isn't satisfactory, but for now I abandon my attempts to clean it up because I see something.

Up ahead there's a glow in the woods.

The borderlands I'm riding through are in the midst of the paroxysms of vast social change. One of the first things Logan did when he established Elenea as his new capital was secure the major mountain passes into the country. A major new city means merchants from all over Midcyru hastening to be the first to arrive to set up shop—which means bandits trying to get a piece while the getting is good.

Logan immediately secured his side of every border and sent messengers to the neighboring kingdoms of Waeddryn and Ossein imploring them to do the same.

Now those kingdoms are scrambling to push in soldiers and roads and edicts and dictates and lords and ladies, so that they can take away wagonloads of silver in tolls and taxes. The people who live here like the new possibilities for trade, but they don't like the sudden influx of bandits or the soldiers who sometimes don't seem much different than bandits. They don't like at all that their entire way of life is going to change forever because of decisions made by people far, far away.

It all means that little remains of the homespun hospitality I encountered the first times I traveled this way. A young man riding alone, leading two horses? To the locals, I look like a bandit. To bandits, I look like a rich prize: Rob one man, get three horses? Who could resist—?

Chapter Twenty-One

The Capacity of a Grub

The words suddenly disappeared from the page. Vi snapped her eyes fully open, thinking she'd fallen asleep. She looked around the little library, but it was deserted. There were only three tables in the place. Then she heard humming, coming from the bookshelf in front of her. No, not from it, from behind it. As the humming got farther away, the words slowly reappeared on the page, as if it were sensitive to human presence—even through a wall.

The squeak of a chair being pushed across a wood floor was next. Whoever was on the other side of the wall wasn't attempting stealth. Slapping the book under its dome and flicking the lever to activate the protective magics, Vi found herself standing, feet wide, hands up, ready. She scanned the room, looking behind her in case this was a feint, but there was no incoming attack.

There was a telltale scuff on the floor by the bookshelf that she hadn't noticed before. A scuff in an arc. Not what a chair would leave. More like... where a secret door swings open.

Instinctively, Vi's hand shot to her belt to draw her blade, but there was no blade there.

"Aha!" she heard the muffled voice say from behind the wall.

Click.

Only as the bookshelf popped open and swung in on hidden hinges, scraping across the wood floor in its arc and revealing Sister Ariel, did Viridiana realize she hadn't even thought of using magic. Here, in a school full of mages, she'd fallen back to her martial training and completely forgotten her newer and far more formidable tools.

"What are you doing here?" Sister Ariel said. "Oh, oh, this is where they hid you away? Huh! No wonder there's a guard on the front door. Mystery solved."

"Mystery solved? Guard?" Vi said, dropping her hands from her defensive position. She felt foolish.

"Oh dear," Sister Ariel said, looking down at three volumes she held in her arms. "I got quite sidetracked, didn't I?"

"What are you—? There's a guard on my door?"

Sister Ariel waved it away. Pointed over to Kylar's book. "Are you finished reading it yet?"

"Finished? I've barely even started!"

"Really? How long can it be? I'd not have figured prolixity one of our mutual friend's vices. If it is indeed his. His book, not vice, that is. Which it must be, if you're still working on it. Yes?"

Vi stared at her, lost.

Sister Ariel stared back at her, equally puzzled.

"By 'our mutual friend,' you mean Kylar?" Vi asked.

Sister Ariel shouted, "No!"

Vi flinched.

"There may be—oh, very well."

Sister Ariel drew out reading glasses and tapped them a few times in a specific rhythm, chanting under her breath. Then she perched them on her nose and walked around the room, nose close to the bookshelves, her glasses giving a tiny blue shimmer now and again. "Nope, none!" she announced. "Can't believe they haven't done that yet. Sometimes it's a mistake to overestimate one's enemies, I guess."

"Enemies?"

"I suspect she'll remedy it soon, however. So. Best not to say anything in here that you don't want overheard. Or if you find something you must speak about, give me some warning. If it's important enough, mind you. In the meantime, help me bring in my books, would you?"

Vi was still too scattered to protest. She went into the narrow hidden room where Sister Ariel had erected a veritable tower of codices, scrolls, and tomes on a study table. Along the opposite wall was a pallet with a few blankets folded at its foot. The room had a similar tiny window to the outside world for light, and another, currently closed and opaque. Vi slid it open; it overlooked the Grand Council Chamber.

It took numerous trips to move Sister Ariel's things from the hidden room to one of the other desks in the little library.

After Vi set down the last of the books, Sister Ariel said, "To answer your question, yes."

"Question?" Vi had forgotten which question out of all the questions she had that she'd actually put into words.

"I did mean Kylar."

That didn't help. Oh, the mutual friend was Kylar, and Sister Ariel had been asking...

Reading the look on her face, Sister Ariel said, "The codex they recovered? It really is his diary?"

"I'm not sure if I'd call it a diary," Viridiana said. "But it's his voice. Can I ask you why you have access to a room that spies on the Grand Council Chamber?"

"Are you looking for the pertinent or the proximal answer?"

At Vi's blank look, Sister Ariel went on, "Do you mean, 'Why do you have a spy hole on a room that's always open to the public?' Or do you mean why do *I* in particular have access to this room?"

"I guess the second question, but now that you say it, also the first one," Vi said.

Sister Ariel shrugged. "The hidden chamber used to spy on a far more interesting room, but it was renovated. The Grand Council Chamber was expanded a long time ago now and made it obsolete. Can't recall the year offhand. But why I, in particular, have access to this room? I have rooms next to most of the libraries. It's the main thing I use the ever-dwindling remainders of my relationship with my sister for."

She meant her literal sister, who happened to be the Exalted Istariel Wyant, the Speaker of the Chantry. If Istariel Wyant were an entirely political creature (and very good at it), Ariel was entirely scholarly (and great at it). If there were one person in the world who could call Viridiana stupid without offending her, Sister Ariel was the one.

Under her uncombed hair and behind her baggy, mismatched clothes, the older woman had the kind of mind that could remember pages of text she'd read decades before. On the other hand, she might not remember a Sister she'd met a dozen times. One of these simply didn't matter to her.

"But...I feel so lost," Vi said. "What are you doing here?"

Sister Ariel pursed her lips. "Looking for some books. But also you. Well, I was. I knew Sister Ayayah must've prevailed upon her superiors to keep you isolated until you can report to the full Council. Afraid you might infect others, I suppose. You don't mind if I use that chair? Best one for my lumbago. Thank you. So I figured, with a magic-imbued book, you'd be in one of the libraries equipped to deal with such things. Which left me with only six options.

"I'm afraid in the second I noticed a pamphlet written by Grekian Lazar that I could swear doesn't appear in the master registry at all. Got me sidetracked completely. Total dead end for the purposes of my own treatise, unfortunately. Not one of Lazar's travelogues as I was hoping, but one of his other kind of stories, if you know what I mean." She gave a significant look to Vi, who didn't know at all what that meant.

After a long, awkward moment, Sister Ariel went on, "Anyway, I figured while I was searching the libraries, I might as well grab some books in case I needed to wait for you to finish reading yours." She winced. "I haven't arrived too terribly late, have I? You haven't—no, no, that's right, you said you haven't finished. Well, then, carry on! Don't worry about me. I've got plenty to keep me busy. My *mustelidae* await."

"Uh…" Vi said. "Can we go back to the part where I have a guard on my door?"

"Yes."

But then she said nothing further. They looked at each other.

"Why is there a guard on the door?" It was taking Vi everything not to go open the door to check—though if there *were* a guard there, confronting her could force an issue Vi might not want to force. She didn't even know what the issue was.

"Lest you corrupt others, I suppose. I thought you'd understand that when I said 'infect' I meant metaphorically. Or maybe to stop you from coordinating testimony with other members of the team. Everyone on your Special Problems and Tactics Team has been explicitly forbidden to speak about what happened at the end on the storm ship when you exited in such spectacular fashion, so naturally, several of them appear to have started gossiping about it immediately. Or at least I'd guess Sister Ayayah has, if I were a cynic. Which I am. Regardless, many of the Sisters do not appreciate the rumors they've heard about your actions on the storm ship. So you're being isolated. In case you're disloyal."

"They're questioning my *loyalty*?" Vi asked, aghast.

"Kylar makes a lot of people here nervous. Me included. Worse than that, he's embarrassed a lot of people, Viridiana. Including the Speaker herself. I don't know if she's party to this, but she never forgives a slight, and Kylar did more than slight her. He made her feel weak. Worse, he made her look weak, publicly."

That wasn't really fair. Kylar had embarrassed people? Well, maybe he had.

But he'd saved far more, *including* Sisters. Vi said, "I knew I'd be punished for my mistakes on the ship, but how does this connect? Sister Ayayah said Kylar carried an artifact. She ordered me to find it. But that's hopeless, isn't it? First, for the obvious reasons, there's no way we're going to even find Kylar's body. Second, even if we did, someone would've taken the artifact off it already. And this story? Like, what does Sister Ayayah think Kylar's going to do, spell out where it is? No kid from the slums is going to tell anyone where he keeps his treasure. And no professional would, either. Kylar's both."

"Oh, I don't think she expects you to find anything. I'd bet she's content to have set you on an unreasonable task that will waste your time and take attention away from her. Sister Ayayah was one of the leaders of an expedition that turned into a disaster. Blame will need to be placed. Someone will need to pay for that failure. She won't let that someone be her."

Vi's breath caught. "So what do I do?"

Sister Ariel paused halfway through a page flip. "Do you know that reminds me of a story? Remind me to tell you later. But to abstract the moral from it: When someone boxes you in with an unreasonable task with shame and failure on every side, there really is only one option, which is quite a delight as it reverts all the failure and shame they'd prepared for you back on their own head. So do that."

"Do what?" The trouble with Sister Ariel was that she was constantly speaking over Viridiana's head. She never meant to, and for all that Viridiana hated being treated as if she were stupid, she wasn't sure if it was actually worse to be treated as if you're smarter than you are. When someone treats you as smarter than you are, you have to either constantly nod your head and pretend you understand things you don't and pray you never get found out, or you have to constantly correct them: *No, sorry, I'm dumber than that.*

Nope, still dumber!

Yep, please, speak as if I've the mental capacity of a grub.

Sister Ariel seemed to be reading even as she said, "When set an unreasonable task where the price of failure is shame or destruction, the only acceptable option is to succeed."

Destruction? Vi thought, pulled right back to her situation. How serious was this?

Maybe Sister Ariel was exaggerating, or maybe she was talking generally about other cases, but Vi didn't ask to find out.

Woodenly, she went back to her desk, put her hand on the ward to unlock the glowing magic around the book, pulled the lever to open it, and leafed through it to the place she'd marked. She stared at the page but couldn't bring herself to read.

Then, at a thought, she flipped to the very end of the book. The last page was blank. She sighed, disappointed. But then, Kylar wouldn't have known exactly how many pages his diary would require while writing it. It would end whenever it ended, not necessarily on the last page. She flipped a blank page, and then another, another, working from the back of the book toward the front.

"What are you doing?" Sister Ariel asked suddenly.

Vi looked up at the scholar. The woman looked scandalized. "I'm, uh, flipping to the end. If I need to find out where the..." She remembered then that Sister Ariel likely had a very good idea that the artifact in question was the black ka'kari, but she couldn't say that out loud. Not here. "If I only need its location, there's not really any need for me to read the whole book, is there?"

"Kylar's telling you his story and you're skipping to the end?" Sister Ariel's eyebrows seemed to have merged with her hairline.

Now Vi felt like the one who'd been asked a very obvious question that couldn't possibly need an explanation.

"I'd thought you respected him more than that, that's all," Sister Ariel said, still obviously aghast but trying to work through it.

"You never flip to the end of a book?"

"Sure. Reference books. History books. Books with chapters delineated by subject. Books made for flipping. But you tell me, when you meet with a friend, and she's telling you the story of some recent heartbreak, do you hold up your hand and say, 'Can you skip to the end and tell me if this means your old flame is available now? Because I really like him. Would you mind terribly if I meet with him for dinner tonight?'" Her voice had risen to unusual volume and passion by the end, but she seemed not to have noticed.

Vi pulled her head back as if someone had swatted her nose. "I...I don't think I've ever had a friend tell me about her heartbreak."

"Well, me neither. But that doesn't mean I don't know how to behave if one were to do so!"

Vi had the feeling that either one or the other of them was being very stupid. Usually, between the two of them, she would be the stupid one. But this time? "Okay, but...this isn't a friend. It's a book," Vi said. "It can't get its feelings hurt if I skip ahead."

"Do you think Kylar put together his tale with less care than your hypothetical friend would tell hers while four ale flagons deep into her tale of connubial woe? Huh!" Sister Ariel tutted, then seemed struck by a thought. Her head bobbed back and forth as if she were having a quick internal dialogue. She came to a conclusion in a heartbeat. "Maybe it's a generational thing. You go ahead, then. Maybe I'm too quick to condemn. Maybe I fail to understand." She turned back to her own work, but her lips pursed as if it took every bit of her self-control for her to ignore Viridiana's continuing sin against the vengeful reading gods.

Scowling under the weight of the Sister's judgment, Vi turned back to the end of the book. She flipped another page. Another. Blank. She pinched a stack of pages and bent them so they fluttered back toward the front of the book, rapidly approaching the place she'd stopped reading. She was intensely aware of Sister Ariel watching her out of the corner of her eye. With one more page turn it became obvious.

All the pages were blank—until the page Vi had been reading. She finished reading the last two sentences where she'd left off, and then flipped to the next page. Writing had appeared on the page that had been blank a moment before, as if it had been there all along.

"Ha!" Sister Ariel said. "Not a generational thing after all. It seems our young diarist agrees with me. I like him more and more. You'll have to read the whole thing in order if you want to get his story. Clever bit of magic, too. Must've hired someone who knew what he was doing."

Thanks, Kylar, Vi thought.

She sank back to the task. Sister Ariel was right. Not about the reading-in-order part—but about her options. If Sister Ayayah Meganah wanted her to fail so badly, her only option was to succeed. She didn't know why reading this book mattered, but she knew she was powerless unless she did.

The panicky feeling didn't leave her throat all through the rest of a weirdly brief chapter about his travels. Kylar's tone changed from how he'd been telling about things as they went to suddenly being very clipped, very brief.

In the course of a few paragraphs, he told about getting jumped by bandits (that went exactly how Vi expected), a little about a picturesque valley and finding a moose and a wolverine, and escaping what he called razorbeaks (immense, intelligent condors?).

She had the sense that he must have come back and edited this part, probably because he decided it didn't have anything to do with the rest of the story and it didn't matter.

Unless that was precisely the opposite of the truth, and somehow this section was the key to everything.

Stop it, Vi! Breathe. Breathe.

Vi couldn't second-guess herself, not with so many pages to go. She had to press on and trust her judgment.

'Cause that worked out for us so well on the storm ship?

She tried to shake off the thought.

She turned the page.

Chapter Twenty-Two

A Warm, Welcoming Fire

After weeks of punishing riding, first on the easy highways that head toward Alitaera's eastern capital, Skone, then veering onto the well-maintained byways that have led me south through several days of rain forest, I should feel relief as I come over a ridge and see at last the coastal city of Tover in the distance. That's where I'll be able to finally stop riding tomorrow. It's where all my questions will find answers.

The city is a chromatic carnival. The wide gold beaches ring a sapphire bay. Lush emerald green trees line the steep streets of the outlying favelas as if to point to the gardens and palaces of the city center, where orchids and other flowers bloom in a bounty of color matched only by the flamboyance of the architecture. The magical, scintillating spire of Sho'fasti seems to proclaim that here the bounty of nature is matched by the brilliance of mankind. Those who told me of this view and this city uniformly used words like *wonder* and *delight*.

But I feel only dread.

All of Alitaera is a world apart from the hardscrabble squalor of Cenaria, where I grew up. It's also old, where Elenea is new; rich where Logan's empire is poor. Everything here feels established and well-maintained. At one point, I was more than a hundred leagues from any sizable city, and ten leagues from any town at all, and the highway passed between beautiful rows of purple glories planted carefully before rows of immensely tall jequitibá-rosa trees, which the local who told me their names said would be even more beautiful when they flowered pink. The trees had been spaced widely enough that their roots, even centuries later, didn't disrupt the cobbles passing below and between them, and their branches intertwined overhead, giving homes to the golden monkeys with heads reminiscent of lions and toucans and parrots of nearly iridescent green. Even that far from major cities, new trees were cleared and the branches of the old trees were kept trimmed back to keep from impeding wagons or riders that passed beneath them.

That kind of forethought? That kind of money? That kind of stubborn belief that the labor you do now will ultimately benefit your kin and country centuries hence?

I know I may be overthinking this, but Alitaerans have a reputation for incredible arrogance. When you run into someone with incredible arrogance, the first thing you should do is look for signs it's deserved.

My master has such a reputation, and his arrogance was earned, not overweening. Worse luck for me, as I'm looking at the city of Tover below me, I think these people's arrogance might be earned too.

What's that make it, if there's a lot of it, but it's not overweening? *Just* weening *arrogance?*

~Are you seriously asking me this?~

Uh. Yes?

The ka'kari doesn't deign to answer.

Just making conversation.

Sometimes I get the impression it thinks I'm too stupid to talk to.

Tover's on the northern end of the Gray Sea (and, given the bay's color here, clearly wasn't consulted by those farther south who named it) and is the only bay for many leagues deep enough for large boats. Deep, eternal springs burst from this hill I've just crested, and most of the buildings are made with the rust-red rock common here, and all the homes have flat roofs that serve as additional rooms where people dry their clothes or hang cloth shades so they can escape the heat and catch the cooling winds of the afternoon.

There is one building that is conspicuously not red, nor the white of the preceptor's palace.

I don't know how it is in your time, listener, but despite some recent overtures Vi's told me about, the Chantry and the various men's schools of magic are still split in my time. It's a hell of a thing, probably driven as much by certain coincidences and big personalities as by the centuries-old massacres usually cited to keep them apart, but in this era, Tover is proudly the home of Sho'fasti. Magic plus politics always gets needlessly complicated, so I'm not going to go into all that. What matters is that, beneath their jargon and schisms and even the lesser splits—like between Sho'fasti's kineticians and the kinematicians, and no, I'm not making that up—the blue mages are known as the

Lords of Motion. Two of their specialties are likely to become highly relevant to me soon, because Sho'fasti produces two main kinds of war mages. The first use magic to move other things (projectiles, their opponents, and in stories that I hope are wild exaggerations even *mountains*). More rarely, some of the schools teach their pupils how to use magic to move *themselves*.

I can't remember the Old Jaeran terms for those two, so for the time being, I'm going to hope that I don't need to explain anything more about them. If I get in a tangle with one or the other in the next couple days, I'll tell you more then. If I live through the encounter.

The most prominent building is a sapphire blue tower. From where I am, it could be a trick of the light, but the stories say it's not: The tower seems to literally float twenty or thirty paces in the air, held to the earth by huge chains, each link taller than a man.

It's evening, so supposedly, the tower will soon come down to rest, as it does every night, but I'm too far away to see that in any detail. Besides, I have other worries.

I'm supposed to meet my *partner* tonight. Momma K said, 'partner,' but I heard her loud and clear. This woman will be the partner who has all the information, who points me in whatever direction she wants and tells me what to do once I get there. She's in Tover already, not because she's from there, but because Momma K sent her on ahead of me when I first refused the job to find the Nemesis Compass. Her orders included a contingency to look for me in Tover, in case I changed my mind and took Momma K up on her job.

Momma K's that confident. And as usual . . .

But she hadn't known the princes would be kidnapped and I'd be nearly dead for days, so I'm days and days behind where I would've been if I'd done what she asked in the first place. I'm doing exactly that same thing. It's just harder now.

To put it lightly, this is one of the things about Momma K that never ceases to vex me.

But that's not my big problem.

Two days back, I met a merchant laboring to fix a broken wheel on his wagon. For an hour of my help, he was happy to tell me news from Tover: upcoming festivals, important local people and factions, areas of higher crime, that sort of thing. He recommended some inns and taverns and told me to mention his name.

I probably don't need to tell you I didn't have the slightest intention of taking his advice. You never know when someone's setting you up.

But then I asked about the meeting places on my list. Depending when I caught up with her, Momma K's agent Phaena was scheduled to stay at different places on her journey to Tover. She'd obviously made good time, because I hadn't caught up to her, though I had heard word that she'd passed through all the places she was supposed to.

I'd ridden like hell to catch up with her for the last two days since I talked to that merchant I helped, because as soon as I'd mentioned the next inn on my list, he'd shaken his head sharply.

"Not there. Don't stay there. Was never a proper inn, only a large home that let out a couple rooms. I don't know if it's still there at all. But the new lord of that prefecture's no good, y'understand? Leaves the woods nearby lawless. There's pressers in there, and when Lord Bunton comes to hunt 'em, his men come banging pots and ringing bells, if you get me."

I did. Lord Bunton's on the take, turning a blind eye to the slavers, if not behind the business himself. Slavery is illegal in Alitaera. Any Alitaeran would assure you they're far too morally upright to tolerate such a barbaric practice. No, no, *they* only allow indentured servitude for debtors who don't pay their debts in time and for those convicted of serious crimes.

In practice, indenture can be pretty close to slavery, but the bureaucratic Alitaerans will have careful records of everything to assure themselves it isn't. They'll have records of the crime, where it occurred, the witnesses, the judge who passed the sentence, and the date at which an indenture expires.

I said, "Pressers need forgers to get papers. They get those in Tover or somewhere inland? Probably Tover, huh, some bad neighborhood close to the water? In case their forger doesn't come through they can always load them onto a ship? Local Sa'kagé must have someone at the harbormaster's office they can count on to turn a blind eye."

"Galleyside, aye," the merchant affirmed, but he looked at me suspiciously. "How you know about that kind of thing?"

"I'm from Cenaria," I said. He recoiled at the mention of the city. Everyone knows the pit of corruption that is Cenaria. "Even the honest men there need to know how the dishonest ones work."

"And are you one of those?" he asked.

"Yes," I said.

"I mean—"

"I know what you meant. Friend of mine is supposed to meet me at that inn."

"Then you'd better hope he's tough."

The merchant grimaced as I simply stared at him, questioning.

He spat to the side. "I don't truck with all that, y'understand? Rumors is the pressers break 'em first. Beatings and...other things, ya know. Repeatedly. Man or woman. Them who's to be sold for farmin' or the mines or as domestics, they ship far away from here to make it harder for 'em to run away. The unluckier women and boys get sent to other coastal cities, after they been broke. If you're one a' them what uses the pillow workers in town, like I used to—" He spat again, mouth twisting at some memory. "Just know that no matter what they say, they ain't likely free to leave, or free at all, and they don't get to keep but a pittance of any coin you give 'em."

I swore under my breath, and the man straightened.

"You really gotta friend goin' there?" he asked.

My expression told him all.

"Then get outta here. I can finish up alone. A few minutes' difference might make *all* the difference. Go on. You ever come across Marius Naggle again, you owe him a favor. That is, if you save yer friend. If ya don't, let's pretend we never met."

Marius gave me directions to the old inn and advice on where I might leave the road to avoid the pressers' lookouts.

That was two days ago.

Where I grew up, a stranger helping you and giving you advice on why you have to hurry in order to avert some disaster was usually sending you straight into an ambush. I'd been that treacherous little cocklebur myself. 'Oh, mister,' I'd say, looking as unthreatening as an emaciated, grubby child of seven can, 'don't use that road! There's a gang down there setting an ambush. They're mean. I don't like them. You can get around if you go this way—' And I'd point to the narrower alley where my gang actually was setting an ambush.

And yet, you can't distrust everything. I paid close attention as I came to the place where he'd recommended I leave the road. It didn't look like a good site for an ambush, so I took Naggle's advice.

And it wasn't an ambush. Turns out there are good people in the world. A few. We've all got a shadow, every last one of us, but some folks—some few—turn their backs on the shadows.

I used to think I was one of those. Used to count myself morally superior to the worst that humanity had to offer. Maybe I was just better at lying to myself.

By the time I catch sight of the old inn, it starts raining this odd warm rain, warmer than the cool night. It turns to fog immediately.

The glow ahead is too bright for the farmhouse I'm expecting.

The odds I've taken a wrong turn are high; I'm not that great in the woods, but I keep going. It's full dark now, and I don't dare spur the horses forward to a canter. Sometimes I'm reckless with their lives, but I'm not insane.

Though the undergrowth and foliage is thick, I catch glimpses of the fire. Too big to be the light of windows to a farmhouse. It's either a bonfire outside against the mounting cold, or...

Despite the sound-dampening rain and fog, I hear yelling from up ahead, and I know this music. Angry voices, demands, the kind of cruel laughter that always sets my teeth on edge.

I slide from the saddle, trying to think as I tether the horses, taking agonizing extra moments to make sure I secure them correctly. This is exactly the kind of situation where a man who thinks he's a hero gets himself killed. Time is of the essence, so it's easy to rush into the middle of things without knowing what you're rushing into the middle of.

I shuck off my cloak. The ka'kari rushes black over my skin and clothing, and I jog through the woods with the toe-striking stride of barefoot distance runners and sneak thieves. Wind and rain will cover any sound my feet make, but I still dodge tree to tree. I never know when a mage will show up and be able to see through my invisibility, and when that happens, it's always at the least convenient time possible.

Fifty paces out, through the heavily shambling silhouettes of the trees and mist lit orange, I see that the fire is... a burning outhouse? A tool shed, maybe?

That doesn't bode well.

There are four people outside, figures illuminated by the firelight. Two victims on their knees and two bandits, if I don't miss my guess. Undisciplined, both of them, standing too close to the kneelers and to each other, stances too narrow, neither taking care not to stare at the fire and ruin his night vision. One has a crossbow pointed at the man and woman kneeling before him, but he moves with jerky, nervous motions, not keeping his aim steady, his fingers resting on the trigger plate. He's got a long knife in his belt. The other bandit is loose and easy, maybe drunk given his big, sloppy motions, holding a short sword in one hand and a butcher knife in the other. He's got a staff laid aside, too far away to do him any good.

He's also laughing that idiotic taunting laughter that transcends creed and culture. It's the same in every language. It says *I'm destroying your stuff and you can't stop me.* It says *I'm a piece of human garbage.*

Today, it also says *I'm gonna die.*

But wary of a trap, I don't charge right in.

Besides, before I start killing people, I prefer to find evidence they deserve it.

If I come across a man sinking to hell, I don't mind climbing up his muddy back and stepping on his head to postpone my own arrival, but heaving a heaven-bound soul up to his reward only pushes you deeper into the muck.

Not that I believe in heaven, but I know how it feels to kill good people who'd fit in there. Not great.

Even as I pad toward the bandits on silent feet, I look toward the house. I have no idea how many other bandits may be in there. I look to either side, scanning the woods. I look behind me.

"...deal," the bandit holding the crossbow is saying to the kneeling man.

"No I didn't! She's gonna be here for days! I was gonna flag you in the morning! Please, I'm sorry. I'll give you anything," the old man says. "Just don't hurt..."

I can't hear who he doesn't want to get hurt, but it doesn't take a lot of imagination: He's trying to put himself between the kneeling woman and the crossbowman.

No, not a crossbowman, I realize as the bandit starts yelling.

He's a kid. Maybe thirteen, fourteen years old. "Get away from her!" the bandit-kid yells, gesturing with the crossbow. He's got that excited-panicky edge in his voice you never want to hear from anyone who's armed, friend or foe. "You stay still like I—"

The old man's head explodes, a meaty, melon-splattering sound layering over the twang of the crossbow. The kid flinches so hard that he drops the crossbow.

The old man's kneeling body topples over.

The laugher stops laughing.

The kid curses over and over, panicky.

The kneeling woman is frozen.

"You farker!" the man says to the kid.

"I didn't mean to! It just went off!" the kid says. He can't seem to take his eyes off the dead man.

"Now we gotta kill her, too, you farkin' piss-chewer. It woulda been a can-ing or losing a thumb at the worst before, but if they catch us now we'll *hang*."

"What? What?"

"We can't leave a witness," the laugher says. He's not laughing now. He's older, yet still not out of his teens. With awful teeth and bad skin, they share the pinched look that proclaims these are not highly successful bandits. "They broke the deal, anyway. We told them to tell us when they had lodgers or they'd be sorry. It's on them. Take care of it!"

Now, finally, the woman moves. But not to attack, nor to flee. She throws herself over the body of the dead man and starts shrieking. I think she's saying his name, but her cries are so tortured, I can't make out her words.

The kid had pulled out a belt knife at her sudden move, but now he looks at it as if it's a serpent in his hand. He looks from it to the man he accidentally murdered, and to the woman red with her loved one's gore. "I—I can't," the kid says.

"Fine," the laugher says, snarling. "I'll do it."

He takes a step toward the woman, then stops, grunting, as my knife punches into his abdomen.

"Sower of the wind thou wert," I whisper low in his ear. "Now reap thou the storm."

I open him up from groin to breastbone, then slash either side of his neck before letting him drop.

"Chelton?" the kid says, only looking over as the laugher hits the ground. "Chelton! What're you doing?"

I shimmer into visibility, with the ka'kari making its mask over my face—glowing blue slits for eyes, then flashing to red as I look at him with the inhuman, disapproving face of Judgment—my stance a Four Keys appropriate to a knife-on-knife fight: disarm, break, block, and throw, each more difficult than the last. He's only a kid, but if you abandon the fundamentals, you'll pay the price.

The kid sees the ka'kari-blade in my hand, dripping blood, which shimmers a lambent deep red on black in the flickering firelight. He bolts.

I'm faster.

I snag him before he takes three steps.

All the fight goes out of him at once when he feels my forearm around his throat, my leg tripping him and holding him off-balance. "Please," he says, both hands grabbing on to my forearm to keep himself from strangling. He'd dropped his knife without a thought. "I didn't mean to hurt anyone!"

"I do," I say.

He grunts a complaint as I strike him in the chest. He says, "I didn't mean to! It went off all by itself. I swear it on my soul. I didn't even touch it! I swear by all the gods!"

"I don't believe you," I say sadly. "But maybe the gods will."

It doesn't change anything. It's too late for him anyway.

I pull the blade out of his heart.

It's a funny thing—a lot of funny things happen when you're in the business of killing, if you look at 'em right. If you work with death all the time, dark humor's the only thing that keeps you half sane. Funny thing is, you can kill a man without him even realizing it. Or you might see a body that you're certain is dead, and then it tries to stand and have one last go. Or a guy gives a teary dying speech and collapses, but wakes up later and lives another fifty years. Or a guy pitches over two hours after the battle's finished, and no one realized he was even hurt—not even himself.

~You're right. That's downright hilarious.~

I hold the kid upright until I'm certain he's dead. As I do, I study the woman, still weeping over her husband—her dad?—maybe it's her dad. She's a good twenty years younger than he is, anyway.

Was. Than he *was*. Now he's nothing but meat and broken expectations.

She doesn't look up. I don't know if she even realizes the bandits are dead. I don't know if she'll care.

I double-check to make sure the kid is dead. I check to make sure the laugher will laugh no more. Given my own powers, I'm a big believer in making sure the people I kill are truly dead.

Moving into the deeper shadows of a larger tree, I finally break in on her grief. "Miss," I say, masking my voice, lowering it. "Are there others?"

She looks up then, lips pressed in a white line. "The boss. And our guest. They went inside together."

Something about the phrasing and the flash of anger in her eyes catches me, but I can't afford to be too late again. I sheathe myself in the ka'kari once more, and let it devour whatever light hits us. It's not full invisibility, not in a hard rain like this, where I deform the drops, and rivulets run visible down my form. But I don't know what I'm going to find inside, and I'll take every advantage I can.

I move to go, then stop. It feels inadequate to speak, but cruel not to.

"I'm sorry I was too late," I say.

But her head is bowed over the man she loved, and I can't tell if she hears me.

Chapter Twenty-Three

The Squeamish Bandit

𝘋urzo was paranoid, but he wasn't often wrong. He taught me to assume all helpful witnesses are cowardly stupid senile liars with cataracts. (Conversely, one must assume witnesses to your own crimes will always be brave honest eagle-eyed geniuses with eyedactic memories.)

That can't be right. Eyedactic *isn't a word, is it?*

~No. I would've asked you about that, but I didn't want to distract you as you were heading into danger. Did you mean *didactic, eye-dactylic,* or *eidetic*?~

Uh, eidetic. *I must've heard Logan say it and not read it myself.*

~Ah, that's too bad. *Eye-dactylic* could be an eye that fingers people, which by happy accident would've worked surprisingly well: a hostile witness with an eye-dactylic memory. If it were a real word, that is. You want to go with it? I know it's a bit poetic for you, but writers *are* allowed to take certain lib——~

No! No.

So as I head toward the house—it isn't quite an inn; I'd guess they merely have an extra room or two they rent out—I don't assume I'm heading toward one bandit and one hostage.

It might be two bandits and a hostage. Or three. It might be a trap.

I don't know what waits for me inside. This doesn't look like a trap, but then, traps aren't supposed to.

One more thing slows my steps: The grieving woman hadn't said *the bandit forced her to go inside with him* but instead *they went inside together*—as if maybe they were partners. Perhaps the apparent hostage had scouted out the home for the bandits?

I'm sounding paranoid myself, I know. This seems to be the right house for my planned meeting with Momma K's agent, but I'm not even certain of that much in this weather and the dark.

So I hope you'll excuse me for not going and busting down the front door to save the damsel in distress.

Durzo used to say, 'When time's tight, take your time.'

And if you can figure out what he meant by that, you're smarter than twelve-year-old me, or fourteen-year-old me, or sixteen, and…Yeah. I always just hoped it was his version of the old standby 'Haste makes waste.'

Durzo is almost always right, but a part of me is screaming that a bandit—a slaver—took a woman inside and made his buddies stay outside in the rain. Why? So he could have privacy? Why else?

You wouldn't think that the words *squeamish* and *rapist* could apply to the same person. If you think that's too messed up to be a real thing, I applaud your faith in humanity.

I don't share it.

Instead of going through the front door, though, I force myself to slow down—even though I know what my delay might mean for the woman inside. I find a side window. It's not glass, worse luck. Glass is a luxury out here. The ka'kari bores a pinhole in the flattened, shaved-animal-horn window.

I can't see anyone inside, but then I do hear a murmur right under the window. Maybe a moan of pain?

I might be too late.

I move carefully to the back of the house, and even peek around the last corner. No horses anywhere.

Find another window where I'll have a better view. Bore another hole.

And…that's awkward.

A man and a woman are embracing against the wall under the window I first looked through. Lips locked.

Not a rape, thankfully. They both seem quite enthusiastic.

So this woman's a spy for the bandits after all. Not my new 'partner.' Something about that seems even worse than regular banditry. A bandit threatens your life, then takes your money; it's all very straightforward. This woman? She came in, accepted hospitality, and all the while was planning to betray and rob these people. It got one of them killed.

Well, she's about to get what's coming to her.

I plan my route past the furniture so I can be upon them before they can react, then give one last glance. And stop.

He's holding a bared knife.

But it's forgotten in his hand. *His* back is against the wall, not hers.

Now, I'm not an idiot. If a man with a knife says *Kiss me*, many perfectly intelligent people are gonna kiss him. And if he says *Make it convincing*, they're gonna try to be convincing.

But in the middle of the most traumatic experience of their lives, most people are not actually going to be convincing.

Then I think of a thing I've heard about: that sometimes in the middle of the most awful moments of their lives, counterintuitively, some people will fall for the very person who's putting them through that hell.

It never made sense to me. Watching it happen—maybe?—it still doesn't. But it's the only thing I can put together. Why else would he have a knife out?

With the ka'kari, or maybe simply as part of my own powers apart from it, I can do that Night Angel thing where I sort of...delve into a person's soul. It's often not very pleasant; what I See sticks to me, and I sure as hell don't want to delve into some madwoman. But with this situation, to figure out how much this lady is and was working with the bandits? I might—

Okay, now she's kissing down his stomach and kneeling in front of him, undressing him. He still holds on to his hunting knife as she removes his belt. He knots his fingers through her deep black hair, dominating her.

Whatever the hell I end up having to do with *her*, I decide this world isn't going to have to endure *him* for much longer.

Momma K said her agent had midnight hair, didn't she?

Oh please don't let this be my new partner.

I open the back door a crack, my Talent gathered, preparing to leap. The woman is shaking her hair out from its coils as she pushes the bandit's trousers down around his ankles.

"Lean back," she purrs. "Enjoy this."

Then I freeze as my assumptions are shattered once more. Her left hand is on his thigh, and she's studying it—and not in a way that suggests she's considering its erotic potential. Her right hand is curled in a fist around something she'd pulled out of her hair—

I only see a brief metallic glitter.

Then her right fist slams into his thigh, and as he gasps, I see her grinding the hair pick back and forth, deep in his muscle. Then she rips it out of his leg.

Blood shoots forth with all the surprising force that only comes from a cut artery.

She throws herself backward, but the bandit's grip convulsed around her hair as soon as her fist hit his thigh.

She's snared.

Some men are stunned by any attack. Some want to understand what happened before they do anything. But many criminals are more like animals; they strike back instantly at whatever surprised them.

This one's like that. He can't have even realized the seriousness of his injury and already his big hunting knife is on a wide looping swing toward the woman's neck.

I barrel in, launching off the doorframe, the force of my Talent lifting me nearly horizontal, vaulting over a table and above and past the woman. My left hand blocks the wrist of his knife hand, stopping his fatal attack. My right forearm—not quite elbow—catches him across the chin an instant before the rest of my weight crushes him into the wall at an angle.

The woman goes flying. The man and I bounce off the wall. I yank on him, imparting my momentum into his body to make us both spin, keeping my grip on his wrist and ducking under the blade as it cuts the air over my head, and then I spin with him and in behind him.

His arm comes up behind his back; I break the wrist, smack his head into the wall to stun him, and then settle into a choke hold, behind him, one of my legs wrapped around his to keep him off-balance.

As a lightning strike shocks and then is gone, stunning as much by the abruptness of its departure as its coming, suddenly, the violence is finished.

Instantaneous, overwhelming, incapacitating violence. It's everything Durzo taught me.

There's a weird silence as the two of them try to come to grips with my unexpected appearance. The only sound is a patter of arterial blood landing as it spurts rhythmically onto the polished wood floor.

The woman didn't merely nick the artery; she cut it entirely.

Then there's only that sound and the harsh huffing of the bandit's breath.

"You've got about a sixty count before you lose consciousness," I tell the bandit. "In twice that you'll be dead. If you've got any gods you want to talk to, now's the time."

Telling him that? That's the Night Angel's mercy.

He lurches against me, fights, then screams when I grab his broken wrist to keep him in my grip.

In the time he has, he does not, as far as I can tell, pray.

His breathing goes from the defiant, raspy heaves of one gathering his strength to fight to a calmer sound, to fighting for consciousness, to calmer once more, quieter, quieter.

I hold him until he goes limp, hold him as the fountain of blood from his thigh goes from a pulsing jet to a stream down his leg, to a rivulet barely discernible as it joins the sopping-wet fabric of his trouser leg.

The woman is frozen for the whole time, sitting on the floor, watching him bleed out, her eyes darting from his face to mine. I've gone visible and removed the mask of Judgment. I think I did that when I crashed into the two of them. Forgot to mention it.

Even after he goes unconscious, still she waits, as if I'm a wild animal that might attack at any careless motion she might make. Aside from the chair I knocked over when I leapt in, there are only a few signs of a struggle in the house: A stool knocked over. A vase on its side, water spilled. The house's lone book, splayed open on the floor. A lyre smashed into a mess of wood splinters and strings. But nothing important: no dangers, no hidden others lying in ambush.

Finally, I release his broken wrist. It flops down limp. Despite the excruciating pain a living man would certainly feel from that, no muscles tense. He's dead.

Definitely dead.

So you can go ahead and plug your ears for the next little bit. It's gonna sound unnecessary and gross ... but in an occupation like mine? In a world like mine with magic, illusions, and crazy Healing? A professional always makes sure. So still holding the limp bandit up, braced against the wall, I set my hand against his upper back, a bit left of the spine. The ka'kari knows what to do.

With a softer sound than you'd imagine—take two fingers and tap them against your ribs through cloth—the ka'kari flicks out of my open palm like a stiletto, punching easily through cloth and flesh with that little sound like *tun*, and as it pierces his heart, the points of the blade split and blossom like a black lotus. I twist.

He doesn't flinch. Truly, safely dead.

I pull the blade out, clean it on his tunic, and finally let the body drop.

Although the woman has been staring at me while I held the bandit, I haven't really thought about her at all. Part of me disappears in those moments or minutes of action, reducing humans to Threat or Not-Threat, looking at exits, examining attack angles, escapes, possibilities.

She stands and scrubs a sleeve across her lips. She takes her hair pick off the floor, stares for a moment at the blood on the narrow shaft, then looks quickly away. Her hand suddenly begins shaking.

Coming down from the blood surge can do that to people, even to veterans. It's purely a bodily reaction. It's wrong to ascribe cowardice or even fear to it.

But she seems embarrassed, putting her hand down at her side quickly as if it's betrayed her. She looks at me sharply, her chin rising in challenge.

"Kylar Stern, I presume?"

I purse my lips.

"Of course you are," she says. "There were two more, outside . . . ?"

I cock my head, lift my eyebrows briefly, to say *Yeah, there* were. I say, "They killed the old man before I could stop them."

"Ah." Sorrow flashes over her face. But after a moment, when she says, "I see," her voice is level. She takes a deep breath, then meets my gaze. Her eyes are so dark they're almost black.

"Thank you for saving my life, Lord Stern."

"Kylar."

She doesn't follow it with her own name, seems scattered. I don't blame her. Momma K told me she wasn't a trained fighter. Given that, she did incredibly well.

"And you?" I finally ask.

"Huh?" She's looking around the cabin, at the broken stuff, anywhere but at the body.

"Name?" I say, though at this point there's not much question who she is. She matches the description, she's at the right place, and she knows who I am.

"Oh. My name is Phaenarete Alcina Emiliana Speranza, but please, you can call me Phaenarete Alcina Emiliana."

"Thanks?"

"Joking. I was joking. Call me Phaena. I'm—I'm trying to pretend this, this sort of thing happens to me, I guess . . . I guess maybe it does, now. You, uh, you were supposed to have something for me?"

"What were you told?" I ask. I'm almost completely certain she is who she says, but in my work, you make sure.

God, I'm becoming as paranoid as Durzo.

"Duchess Thorne said you'd be joining me. She told me about you, at least as much as she thought I needed to know. And, you know, what I hadn't heard in the stories. But then she said you weren't coming after all. I guess you changed your mind?"

"I . . . yeah, that's about the size of it."

"She gave you new orders for me?"

I nod. In a sealed bag, no less. Which I could've opened, but not without revealing I did.

They're sure to be in code anyway. And I'm trying to trust Momma K on this.

After all, we're 'family.'

If Phaena has any more questions about that right now, though, she seems to have forgotten them. She's pallid, with a light sheen of cold sweat on her face. She can't stop stealing glances at the body. She swallows. "I know it's night and it's raining and this is not exactly convenient, but, Kylar? Can we get as far away from here as possible?"

Leaving now means sleeping cold and sleeping wet and not sleeping very much at all. There are no threats left here. Plenty of reasons to stay. No good reasons to leave.

"Not a problem," I say.

"Thank you," Phaena says. "Now if you'll excuse me, I think I need to vomit."

Chapter Twenty-Four

The Perfect Reader

Υou're wasting time," Sister Ariel said. "Go to bed. You'll end up reading all these pages four times and have to read them again tomorrow. Worse, you'll not be sure if you missed something even earlier. Trust me. I have some experience with reading too long."

As Sister Ariel walked away, having given her advice and now unconcerned if Vi followed it, words reappeared on the page.

It was hard to argue with Sister Ariel about study, so Vi marked her place, closed the little book, covered it, and pulled the lever that reset the protective magic over it. At Sister Ariel's suggestion, she'd decided to sleep in the hidden cell behind the secret door so as to lose as little time as possible.

Early in the morning, when Vi stumbled out to her table once more, Sister Ariel was still at the same table she'd been at yesterday, albeit with several new books open, and an ink smudge on her forehead. A platter of food, cold and half-eaten, sat on a table nearby, as if pushed out of the way. Vi approached it more than the bookish old woman.

"What are you working on? May I?" Vi asked.

"You're making conversation, aren't you?" Sister Ariel said. "Take the food. My newest treatise is about ritual interactions with *mustelidae* in the early Cabisinnian empire, specifically the gulo gulo—though I'd settle for middle or even late Sepharatic era at this point. So far I've translated the relevant sections of twenty-four compendia on ritual sacrifice—filled with all sorts of things I'm not happy to have committed to memory, thank you very much. I've reread seventeen bestiaries, and just now finished my...forty-seventh travelogue, and still the most intriguing bits I've found have come from the confirmed liar and fabulist Grekian Lazar, whose account got me started on the whole sorry endeavor in the first place. So, most likely I've wasted at least several weeks, meaning my own treatise will only itself be valuable to later scholars wishing to examine how accurate Lazar is or is not. Intellectual rogue, really. Adventurer, wit, sophist, scoundrel, gambler, soul of poetry, but it appears, oddly enough, that the only things out of the forty books he wrote—to be fair, only twenty-two are extant, so perhaps he was less mendacious in the rest of his work, but—what was I saying? Oh, the only things that are probably true are the tales of his many and lushly described romantic conquests. Page upon page of descriptions of seductions and bedplay. Those volumes are constantly being borrowed from the libraries, though I'm not sure why. I don't see scholarly value myself. What? What is it?" Sister Ariel asked. "You look constipated."

But Viridiana wasn't about to get into explaining to the older woman why those books were popular. If she did, one or both of them might learn a whole lot more about each other than was comfortable for either. "How do you figure it out?"

"Constipation?" Sister Ariel asked, taken aback. "Do you know, you may have stumbled upon something I'm not overly cerebral about. I'd like to say I consider my recent diet's impact on the likely variance from my average bowel movement frequency, but—"

"No! I mean, I mean—do we have any listeners?"

"Very subtle, Viridiana," Sister Ariel said. She stood, irritated, and did her sweep of the room. "Still no. A good sign, though far from dispositive. You were saying?"

"You say that guy, Lazar or whatever, that he lied about all sorts of stuff, but not the things you'd expect. How can you tell when someone's lying in a book?"

"Well, first, you never forget they might be. In Lazar's case, we know he had a lot of instability in his life. He claimed expertise in a highly unlikely number of subjects, so when you read that he's a master of botany in a letter to a minor king who is known to have an interest in botany, you pay attention. Skeptical attention. On the other hand, we've found several secret diaries of some of his paramours speaking in highly complimentary ways of him. We know that women he claimed to have taken to his bed were later divorced by jealous husbands, sometimes with no mention of any scandal, but other times with dates known that align awfully well. When you read closely, you get a sense of the man after a time, but you still always check. But you've got no interest in Grekian Lazar, do you?"

"I feel like...um, *our friend* is trying to be honest, but—"

"He can't. No autobiography can be fully honest."

"Not even if he's totally unsparing of himself?" Vi asked.

"Does that volume make sense?"

"Huh?" Vi asked, confused.

"Does it have a flow? Can you follow it, or are there constant references to things only he would know?"

"I can follow it," Vi said. "Mostly. I think."

"Then he's selecting details for readers, and omitting others."

"But he wrote it for himself. He said so."

"He said so?" Sister Ariel said. "Maybe he was even being honest when he said it. But maybe he changed his mind as he wrote, or after it was done. Trickiest of all, maybe he deceived himself about who he was writing it for. But never forget one fact as you read."

Sister Ariel waited until Vi said, "What fact is th—?"

"The magic only allows *you* to read it. Kylar could've burned that book. It's highly unlikely that Kylar had the skills to craft this enchantment himself, so that means he had to hire a specialist to make sure that you and only you could read it. If he was writing for himself initially, at some point he decided he wanted you—out of everyone, *you*—to read it. He wanted to tell this story to you. Why?"

"Maybe he thought I was the only one who could understand," Vi said, her chest feeling hollow.

"Be a little more sophisticated than that, child. That may be true. On the other hand, you're *here*, and—as far as he's concerned—you're loyal to the Sisterhood. He surely knew that you'd be pressured to share everything you read with women he has good reason to see as his enemies. He might've selected you because you understand him. Or maybe he had some completely different reason in mind."

That rattled Vi. But...what other reason could there be? Viridiana thought about it for a while, got nowhere, and with the thought hanging over her like a dark cloud, got back to work.

DAY TWO

Chapter Twenty-Five

At First Blush

*I*t's all fairly awful, but only in the normal and predictable ways. I get my horses, rub them down in the stable and feed them, then deal with the bandits' bodies. My Talent makes the digging go faster than it otherwise would in the root-choked clay soil, but burying a body's still a miserable job that the dark and the rain make even less pleasant.

When I finish up, I'm surprised to find that Phaena has cleaned up the lake of blood inside. Her own pallor tells me it's the second-to-last thing she wanted to do, but that she believes inaction is even worse. She wasn't going to leave that bereaved woman to deal with the mess. That tells me a lot about her. It helps me understand why Momma K trusts her: She'll pull her own weight.

The innkeeper eventually lets me bring her father's body inside. Father, not husband. I don't want to learn anything more about her, or him. Don't want any more details for my guilt to latch on to like burrs in the heavy woolen tunic of my failures. Her name is Letizia—I couldn't avoid learning that much, even as she cursed me and blamed me for her father's death.

Why couldn't I have come earlier? It must have been my fault that boy pressed the trigger plate. I startled him, didn't I?

It's not fair, and I try not to take it to heart. Sometimes people need someone present to yell at. People say horrible things on the worst day of their lives. I've seen a lot of people on that day, and often enough I've been the reason for it, and many times they weren't brave enough to hurl the insults at me that I did deserve, so on this day when I don't deserve it, I take it quietly. She takes my refusal to defend myself for an admission of guilt and screams more.

I hope it helps her.

I dig a better grave for Letizia's father, but she's not ready to see him in the ground yet, so I do no more than that. Like so many of their problems in life, some people need a corpse to start putrefying before they'll bury it, even if they'd have had help if they'd done it right away.

By the time we've finished and I've resaddled the horses, there isn't much night left. Nonetheless, I see a desperation to get away from here in Phaena's eyes.

I head out as if it's my idea. We lead the horses until it's light out. By itself, the danger of them breaking a leg in the dark negates any value in an early departure, but right now, the act of traveling is what's important, so that's what we do.

On my recent days on the trail, I had a lot of time to think. I've thought about why I failed Logan and lost the twins, and I think the answer is entwined with what it means to be the Night Angel.

Though, you know, someone could just tell me *all about that.*

The ka'kari says nothing. Not that I expect it to. I'm sure it'd say it isn't allowed to tell me about that, or that it'll mean more to me if I figure it out on my own. Or something.

I wait, but the ka'kari still isn't baited into answering.

Anyway, here's what I got: The Night Angel is the Avatar of Retribution. It has three faces: justice, mercy, and vengeance. So far as I can figure, a Night Angel protects the innocent at all costs—especially to himself.

From Durzo, I learned a thing or two about excellence. I learned about the prices you have to pay if you want to be the best. Those go beyond the obvious. People say words like *time* and *dedication* and *sacrifice* as if those concepts are simple but hard.

They are hard, but they're not simple.

Take training to be an athlete. You don't train until your body hurts and then simply keep going longer than anyone else will. That would be simple but hard. Truth is, if you train too far into the realm of pain, you'll injure yourself and slow down your training. It isn't simple to learn the difference between intense discomfort and mild injury. It takes experience to know when your body is lying to you or when your slippery, devious, lazy mind is actually telling you the truth. It can be either.

I failed to save Logan's children—I failed as Night Angel—because I found it preferable to sit and shoot the breeze with an attractive woman rather than do my rounds.

No one screamed at me for being two minutes late like Letizia screamed at me this morning for being two minutes late. But they should've.

I told myself it wasn't important, that nothing would happen, that a few minutes wouldn't make any difference.

It made all the difference.

That's what sacrifice means. A Night Angel protects the innocent at all costs—especially to himself. All costs. And sometimes that's simple but hard, like staying on task when it doesn't seem to matter.

I don't ask Phaena any questions, though I have more than a few. She's innocent in what happened, and she deserves the Night Angel's mercy and Kylar's compassion. I don't even give her any compliments, though I have some of those, too. It's not time for that yet.

The rain stops by dawn, which means the only thing our unnecessary extra hours on the road gained us is wet clothes. But I don't complain about it.

Nor do I open my mouth as we take numerous extra bathroom stops. What did the Sage say? 'If you want to go fast, go alone. If you want to go far, go with another'?

Even sages can be wrong.

It turns into a beautiful day as we get nearer to Tover. Farms and outlying villages with water-wheel mills and furnaces for the nearby pot-throwers yield to a city of iron-red bricks, whitewashed walls, and blue accents. Unsurprisingly, the river, which in the early morning farther upriver had been blue despite last night's rain, turns to the usual trash- and sewage-choked urban gray.

Humans. All in all, we're kind of terrible.

We stop at several inns on the way but never go inside. Phaena goes to the front door each time, inspects the doorframe, and then we leave.

I don't ask her about it. I'm feeling off. Morose, I guess?

I've been feeling it all day. I'm kind of dumb about that, putting labels to my emotions, I mean. Like, sometimes I'll go days and days and only when I'm feeling better will I realize that during all that time, I was depressed. I dunno, this thing of dictating everything as I go is awkward. It forces me to examine things that usually float along, chained behind me in an amorphous cloud.

It makes those things more real.

I don't know if I like it.

Maybe it's that old man. I know his death wasn't really my fault. But I don't know why it happened at all. The younger bandit said something about a deal? I think?

~Yes. He did.~

Oh, hey, there you are. I wasn't really talking to you, but thanks. Now go away.

~I live to serve.~

By this point, you can probably guess the ka'kari's tone of voice as it said that, huh?

The bandit mentioning a deal would've made me think that the innkeeper was working with them. But maybe the old man had second thoughts about handing over Phaena?

Or maybe he actually meant what he said about planning to send a message to the bandits today and handing her over into slavery. Maybe he deserved to die, after all.

I'll never know. Durzo taught me long ago that was one of the prices of wet work: We don't get the whole story. We swoop in and end the story. That doesn't entitle us to knowledge of the whole thing.

Except those times when it does. Sometimes, I think Durzo vacillated between training me to be just another famed wetboy like he had become, and training me to be a Night Angel. So sometimes he lied.

Or maybe he didn't mean to lie. Maybe he was teaching me the rules before he taught me the exceptions to the rules—and we never had the chance for me to get far enough to learn those. I wish we'd parted on better terms, but it's too late now.

We pass a fenced-off field where a dozen teenaged boys in faded blue tunics are horsing around while twice that number of locals watch them for entertainment. As we get closer, I hear the boys jeering at each other. Immediately, I angle my horse around Phaena's so that she's on the outside. I recognize the tones in those voices: teenaged boys, jockeying for status against a rival gang. The bandying of insults is the first couplet of a sonnet that ends in bloodshed. I start to look for alternate routes.

Phaena is riding on at the same speed as before, distracted by what I'm doing but still focusing on the boys, her speed forcing me to maintain mine. Two camps, I see now, not evenly split six and six, but instead with seven boys in blue and five boys in lighter blue with a yellow stripe on the left shoulder. Lopsided odds, that's worse. The outnumbered boys might skip the preliminary posturing and jump right to violence, hoping surprise will even the odds. Only one of the boys has a weapon—a training bow with such a low draw weight it looks completely ineffectual—but that doesn't matter. With whatever training they've gotten, even at their young ages, these boys themselves are weapons.

"Want to watch?" Phaena asks, smiling.

She's not the only one. The locals are eager, too, with more drifting over. But there's a discordant note: It's not the eagerness of the audience at the Death Games. It's not bloodlust. And no one's taking cover. Don't they know the danger here?

The boys are as puffed up as any guild rats would be on the streets of Cenaria, but none of them betrays stark fear underneath his bravado. None looks ill at the prospect of killing or petrified of dying. These boys aren't taking the confrontation to the next level. They've simply . . . stopped escalating. Some even turn away from each other, showing their backs.

That never happened in Cenaria. Confrontation always meant humiliation, loss of territory. That meant starvation, desperation, blood. I've read this all wrong. This isn't the preamble to bloodshed. It's play. A friendly competition.

"Ready!" the boy with the training bow shouts. He's got a quiver on his right leg, and he's standing all wrong. A blue glow surrounds his right hand. "Throw!"

Three of his fellows throw balls into the air, far downfield. The archer draws, fast. The glow transfers from his hand to the arrow. His draw is awful: The bow is extended straight before him rather than to the side, his elbow's down, the bow's too weak to shoot that fa—

A blast of red powder in the air marks the first target exploding, then the second. There's no perceptible flight time, though the path of the arrow burns a blue afterimage on my eyes. As soon as he releases the arrow, it's at its target. He misses the third with his first shot. Draws again, aims carefully as the target plummets to the ground some forty paces away, and releases.

He misses, and groans along with the crowd as the final target hits the ground and breaks.

But I'm gobsmacked.

There was no leading the target. The arc of the shot—well, there was no arc. It was a straight line. From how careless the boys seem to be with their gear, I doubt the arrows were perfectly fletched. Nor were they long enough for such accuracy.

Another boy steps forward from the yellow-striped group. He holds out his hand with what might be stones or round lead shot such as you'd use for a sling. They're surrounded by a similar blue glow, and they start orbiting him, crackling with little yellow lightning bolts. "Ready!" he says. I can hear a hum of energies building up around him and the air itself within the shots' orbit turns into a crackling blue shell. "Throw!"

His compatriots throw, and four missiles shoot out in quick succession nearly as if he were a sling himself. Again, two targets hit out of three.

"Yeah, that's great if you show up to the battlefield lugging half a king's treasury," says one of the boys on the solid blue team. With a little crackle of magic around his fingers, he splits open one of the boy's round shot to expose a core of gold. "You 'motes. I always heard you pretty boys threw gold away. Just didn't think you did it literally. How many of those arrows do you actually recover when you miss?"

There's a whoop from the neighboring field downrange of where the archer was shooting. A neighborhood kid among a group of at least twenty others has raised his fist in the air, holding one of the arrows as if it's a great prize. As everyone here looks at him, he turns and runs away with it, followed by all his friends.

"All *we* need is our bodies," the boy insulting the first ones says to finish, patting his chest with the supreme self-satisfaction of cocky adolescence. "And our far superior skills."

Gold. There's literally gold in every arrow and shot? I've always known gold had properties that make it useful to mages, but this is something else.

The kids jeer at each other back and forth. Clearly, there's a class distinction between the two disciplines. One is poor, or takes a vow of poverty maybe— though it's clear that not one of these kids comes from real, abject poverty. They see themselves as harder working, more manly, more like soldiers than court mages. The first group sees them as fools, poor because they're stupid.

And yet, Sho'cendi has channeled these rivalries into bloodless competitions. And maybe—from their talk—the occasional fistfight they keep hidden from their instructors. But not murder.

The bragging kid has moved down the field. I think he's planning to have the others throw the targets—which I see are fist-sized clay balls—*at* him. But one of the older boys from his group is eyeing me, and I want to get moving. Seers aren't common among male mages, but I don't need to take chances.

"Ready!" the teen says, taking a solid defensive fighting stance, blue light blossoming around his fists and maybe his feet, though I can't see those through the crowd. "Throw!"

I'm too far away to see exactly how he does it, but the targets all explode in the air near him—even one that was thrown several feet off target. He must've extended his reach magically for that one.

"Let's go," I tell Phaena quietly.

She doesn't ask any more. We go immediately. I see the one teen—an older one of the body mages in the solid blue—still eyeing me. It makes me uncomfortable. These kids are on their way to becoming blue mages, and most mages only ever master one discipline. The Solons of the world are rarer, and the Dorians are once-in-a-century lightning strikes, but some mages have additional Talents that don't neatly fit into their primary discipline. Rarely is it enough for them to go someplace else for more specialized training, but I have no idea what this baby mage might see when he looks at me. My Talent, or even more than that? Best not to tempt my luck.

We head deeper into Tover and its eerie, floating blue spire chained to earth. The streets yield from dirt to cobblestone, the fields shrink and disappear altogether, the brown river widens and slows, and the crowds swell. Tover is a port city on the Gray Sea and it's as cosmopolitan as Cenaria. Though pink and tan and olive skin tones dominate, I never see one Lae'knaught black tunic, despite seeing every other mode of dress. I have to imagine they have plenty of spies here, but the anti-magic sect probably doesn't go over well in a town that depends so much on the blue mages.

Finally, Phaena finds an inn with something carved into the doorframe that satisfies her.

I stable the horses, throw my saddlebags over my shoulder, and take a look at the symbol as I go inside. It's not exactly hidden, but you wouldn't see it unless you were looking: a stylized sun over a line, as of the ocean horizon, with another sun beneath the line, as if a reflection. I get a chill.

The top sun symbolizes life, the line death, and the reflected second sun life after death. It's a symbol for the Society of the Second Dawn, a secret organization that would love to learn everything I know about immortality, supposedly as a purely scholarly endeavor, but Durzo always believed that it was ultimately so they can acquire immortality themselves. Momma K is part of the Society, or uses them, anyway.

As I come in, Phaena finishes speaking with a woman at the bar and heads to meet me in front of the stairs, now carrying a leather folio.

A barkeep with his eyes closed grabs a thin stick and comes over. He guides the stick as lightly as any swordsman, taps my shin, and moves past. He moves with such certainty up the stairs and to the guest room that it takes me a few moments to realize he's blind. The stick only quests into places where he suspects some possible danger, but he has no problem showing us the room.

As in many inns, this room has only a single bed, though it's large enough for numerous sleepers.

"This room yours, mine, or ours?" I ask.

"Ours," Phaena says, as the barkeep pulls a folding privacy screen from a closet.

Without saying a word, the barkeep clears his throat to get our attention. He shows us a few of the normal things about the room, tells us where to get water for bathing, and promises to bring us the necessaries for washing our clothing. Then he bars the door, and as he settles the bar home firmly, I hear a click from the window. He pushes some curtains out of the way from around the tiny window and pulls down hard on one of the hooks. A latch releases, and he shows how an entire panel opens to the roof.

"Should you require an alibi," he says. "There will be others downstairs at all hours who will swear there's no way you could have left your room without being seen."

"Others?"

He opens his cloudy eyes and turns toward me, nonplussed. "My own testimony as an eyewitness isn't much respected, I'm afraid." He smiles joylessly. "Let me stop you before you add a punch line."

"I wasn't—"

"As you will," he says curtly. "Rules: We're not criminals. We'll do this one thing for you, and that's it. You hurt anyone on this side of the bridge, deal's off. No matter how high and mighty they are, or who they know, we don't let visiting dogs crap in our yard. Got it? Good."

He leaves before either of us can answer.

"Visiting dogs?" I say.

"Have I just been called a bitch?" Phaena asks me, but she smiles.

We settle ourselves in. I lay out my kit, examine the weapons and tools for those that need maintenance first, then look at my clothes. They badly need laundering. Phaena busies herself with her own things on the other side of the privacy screen.

I begin washing my spare clothes. I have to plunge them by hand, because some other guest was using the only agitator. I say, "So. About the job. If I need to go out tonight, will it be worse for me to be slightly damp or very dirty?"

I hear a muffled grunt. Pain?

"You all right?" I ask.

"What? Oh, the job. Right," she says. She tosses her dress up over the privacy screen. "My instructions say you need to steal a bracelet. There are three possibilities. Or were, as of two days ago when we were supposed to arrive here. You can—or could—get one from any of three magi here. Each of the men is fearfully powerful in his own way, and you have to do it before they leave the city. If they haven't left already."

"That's the heist, a bracelet?" And one of three? There can't be three compasses.

"Of course not. The bracelet is your pass into a certain...meeting that you'll infiltrate later. Without a bracelet, the job doesn't happen. Originally, you were going to steal one from a courier before he arrived in Tover. Easy job. But it's too late for that now. So you'll have to decide on your target, then kill or delay or otherwise disappear him without the others finding out, because if anyone tells the...hosts of the meeting that your target isn't coming, that bracelet will either be deactivated or *armed*, with apparently lethal consequences for whoever is wearing it."

"Ah. So I'll be going out dirty rather than damp, then. You want me to wash your dress?"

A pause. Then she says, "Sure?"

I grab her dress off the privacy screen and get to work. I don't mind confessing that I use my Talent. Durzo tried to indoctrinate me to only ever use magic in emergencies or for work. But have you ever washed trail-filthy clothes entirely by hand? At least there's a wringer for getting things mostly dry before I hang them up by the fire.

"Anything else?" I ask.

She pokes her head around the privacy screen and looks at my extended hand oddly. "You don't mean about the job, do you? You mean my clothes?"

Exasperated, I say, "I'm not stupid or a child. I know why you've been back there so long. You're on your blood. I'm not asking to handle your menstrual rags. But surely you have stockings, shifts, another dress? I'm washing the clothes. You want help or not?"

She looks chagrined. "Oh, right, right. I just…" She disappears, and moments later, she tosses more clothes over the screen. "It's not that. I mean, it's not just that. Before you got there last night, that…man…threw me against a wall and bruised the hell out of my chest. Scratched me up good, too."

That did explain a time or two earlier when I'd seen her wincing with her hand at her chest and looking embarrassed about it.

"Why aren't you already planning what you're going to do next?" she asks.

"Any of these need to be washed cold?"

"Huh?" she says.

"Cold water. And I *am* planning what to do next. This is how I plan. I think while my hands are busy. Now tell me about these mages," I say.

She tells me about all three of them, then directs me to the files that were in the package she picked up from the woman downstairs. The files are loaded with details: names, places, prominent servants, favorite social spots, favorite foods, bedroom predilections, lovers. It's all up to date, including where each ate dinner last night.

Though I haven't read half of it, I can see it's good intel, and all the right intel for the work. Momma K doesn't do things by half measures.

But it's also *a lot* of intel, and most of it doesn't turn out to matter, so I've come back later and erased all that stuff so I wouldn't bore you with it.

In fact, let's quick establish a rule of thumb. If I ever do something that looks rash or even dumb, you should go ahead and assume that there were very good reasons for me to act the way I did—the way *I do*? The way *I'm about to*? Tenses are hard.

Anyway, if I do something that looks dumb, assume that there were some details that I forgot to include that gave excellent reasons for why I should do that thing.

~You meant 'the way I did,' because the time at which your listeners will be hearing what you do now will be after you did it, regardless of—~

Right. Much appreciated. Go ahead and fix that part for me, then.

Somehow, and this is how I know the ka'kari is powerfully magical, lungless as it is, silent as it is, I can distinctly hear its sigh.

"Can I ask you something?" Phaena asks, as I hang up the last of our laundry.

I stare at her.

"You never asked me for proofs that I work for . . . who I work for," she says.

"Nope," I say. I feel like I'm coming across as terse as Durzo, but really, I just don't know what to say.

"Were you going to?" she asks.

"Now you've ruined it. I was planning to wait till you were asleep, then I was going to leap on the bed, point a bodkin arrow at your eye, and start screaming questions. You know, to make sure this trip started on the right foot for you."

For an instant, I see the blank flash of fear.

The woman has just been traumatized, idiot. She was certain she was going to die not even a full day ago. She doesn't know I'm being wildly, over-the-top ridiculous. She doesn't yet know what I would never do.

~Do *you* know what you would never do?~

She recovers quickly, though, and chuckles.

It's a social chuckle, like what I said wasn't at all funny, but she's trying to give me the benefit of the doubt.

I'm a jackass.

"Duch—" Phaena looks around, as if remembering there might be eavesdroppers. "Our mutual friend said that you might be . . . that you might require a lot more convincing than you seem to be requiring."

"Did she say I'd be difficult?" I ask.

"That word may have come up," Phaena says carefully.

"Did she also call me surprising?"

"Uh-huh."

"So which of those two would you like me to be?"

Phaena looks at me like I'm a puzzle cube. "Surprising?"

"Then I'm going to surprise you by not being difficult."

"You are?"

"Are you surprised?"

"Yes."

"Then she was right about me."

"Half right," Phaena says.

"And that worries you. It needn't. The difficult Kylar will come out, I promise."

"But now that you've warned me, I won't be surprised," Phaena says, with a little smile.

"Oh, I think I—" I catch myself.

I'm about to start *flirting*. It's like I never learn anything.

Maybe I should describe Phaena. I hardly ever notice clothing unless I'm at a fancy party. But I know other people do, so, uh, the clothes she's wearing since we got to our room has three places she might conceal a knife or other weapon, but from her motions thus far and with her lean body type, only one remains a possibility.

That's what I look for, when I look at clothes.

Not very helpful for most purposes, huh? If you're the kind of person who uses words like *chartreuse* and *puce*, I'm probably not giving you any of the details you care about. When I intervened with the bandits, I examined Phaena for certain telltales: looking whether she had dirt packed under her fingernails and on the back of her neck, greasy hair to tell if she'd been living in the woods as long as they had. I looked at the musculature of her shoulders and for any veins standing out on her forearms which, given her leanness, would tell me if she trained extensively with spear or sword. But here, knowing she's not a foe, and myself exhausted from the days of long riding and little sleep, the shield of my professionalism was too heavy, and it slipped down.

If I tried to describe her how I was seeing her moments ago when I was about to start flirting, I'm afraid my description would've sounded more like a very, erm, *lonely* young man who hasn't been intimate with a woman in nearly a year describing body parts, not a woman. You can guess which parts.

I'll try not to embarrass both of us by going on. But in my defense, I would like to note that she does work for Momma K, and Momma K is a firm believer in hiring attractive people. And sometimes she is very successful.

And that's why I almost started flirting with her. Despite that being the whole reason I'm here. I got sidetracked chatting with Vi rather than doing my job. Forgot what it means to be the Night Angel, the sacrifices required. I'm not the only one paying the price for that. The whole kingdom is. Logan and Jenine. Vi might be dead, or crippled permanently. And here I am getting sucked into that same human weakness of mine again.

I won't do that with Phaena. Besides, she's older than me, with the first hints of smile lines and the air of someone with a lot more life experience than I have—normal life experience, the healthy kind, not my kind. She's pretty, yeah, but not an option.

But I guess I just went through all that and still didn't describe her, did I? Let's try average height, slim, dark eyes, wavy long dark hair, currently in a ponytail, warm tan to almost olive skin? Not quite Sethi tones but—

Why do they call it olive skin? A person could have green skin and it would be olive skin. I wonder how many times in tales someone had green skin and I thought the bard meant they were really tan.

Anyway, she's got light olive skin. Not the green kind. And a chartreuse skirt.

~That's not chartreuse. And, Kylar. She's waiting.~

"Huh?" I say. I think she asked something about me not being difficult while I was in my head here, doing my best not to describe her chest. "Momma K wants to keep me in the dark on this job. That irks me. I told her so. But she's still persisted, right?"

"Yes," Phaena says, and I appreciate the blunt response.

"I've had time to think about it on the trail. And she picks her battles. She knew I hated it, and she decided it was important enough to do anyway. I can't come up with any reason she would do that to hurt me right now. Even if she and I aren't exactly friends..." We're family, she'd joked. Right. "She wants the same thing I do."

No she doesn't.

And at that moment, it strikes me why she wanted the Nemesis Compass even before we lost the twins. It's a person-finder. Why would she want a person-finder enough to ask *me* to look for it, knowing I'd likely say no and I'd give her a hard time?

Because she doesn't know where Durzo is.

And of course she couldn't admit that's why she wanted the compass. Certainly not to me. Certainly not after I started being an ass about the whole thing. Huh.

"Getting the...twins back, yes," Phaena says.

"Right," I say. "So I'll play along. She thinks it's important I not know things for a while? Fine. It still gets under my skin, but I'll do my best not to take it out on you. She had good things to say about you."

"She did? Like what?"

"Like I'm not supposed to tell you," I say. Then I grin.

"That's revenge, isn't it?" Phaena says. "For all I'm not telling you."

"Uh-huh." I smile more broadly.

For someone who doesn't really know how to flirt, I feel like I'm edging dangerously close back toward it again, so I try to back down. "She said your skills and abilities were basically the opposite of mine, and that she trusts you.

I think she hopes you have a future in her organization. Wasn't really clear if she meant in its newer parts or the older ones." I assume when I say this that Phaena will understand I'm talking about whether she's on the legal or the illegal side of things.

Phaena beams. "That's nice to hear. Though I'm not sure I have the ambition to take over the . . . things she wants me to do."

"Oh?" I can see she doesn't want to divulge specifics, so I go with a pleasantly interested tone.

She shifts. "I, uh, work for her kind of irregularly? In sort of a specialized capacity?"

Momma K has everyone from stable boys to maids to enforcers to sneak thieves and counts working for her. Phaena isn't narrowing things down for me. Given her discomfort about her work, I'm guessing Phaena isn't a courtesan. Courtesans don't embarrass easily. "Oh, like a spy?"

"No, more like . . . in one of her pleasure houses."

"Sure," I say. Phaena surely knows where I grew up and some of what I've done, so I'm not sure why she seems to think I'd judge a courtesan. Maybe she's got her own reservations about her work. I certainly have reservations about mine.

She says, "With what I do, I'm able to work a few days a month and still make enough for my family to get by, without me being away much. It requires absolute discretion, though, so the duchess has learned that she can trust me. And since I haven't been regularly or openly at any of her establishments, she thinks no one will recognize me here or at our next stop, or connect me to her even if they do."

"I see," I say. But I don't. Momma K is sending us somewhere where she fears we might run into some familiar faces—but in Tover? How many Cenarians could be here? "You a hedge mage?" I ask suddenly, though I shouldn't have. I know Momma K has prostitutes who use magic either directly in their work or for self-defense and the like, and though she's never said anything about it, I'm sure she tries to get training for those as much as she can without sending them to the Chantry—where she would lose them altogether.

Phaena shakes her head and doesn't seem offended. "Only insofar as music is magical," she says.

"You're good?"

"Pretty good," she admits.

Aha!

So . . . a musician/courtesan who makes a month's wages in a couple nights. That, with her looks, means she entertains the kind of lords or ladies who like to sleep with the talent. I could see how that would fetch a premium. But not that much of a premium. At a few nights a month, supporting a whole family? That has to mean they're living pretty lean.

With a woman as pretty as Phaena, I can't believe there's only that much demand, so I guess that she doesn't work more because she doesn't want to. She wouldn't be the first woman I've met who hates the work but has no better options.

I feel suddenly awkward. Knowing that she's a musician should open up all sorts of topics for conversation. But I don't know very much about music. I haven't seen an instrument among her things, either.

"The job gives you time to be with your family, huh?" I say, mostly to fill the silence. "Tell me about them."

I think I've put it together now. We're going to a secret fancy party with lords and ladies in attendance. Momma K wanted Phaena rather than someone the lords and ladies might recognize as one of her rent girls, so the party will be nothing so vulgar as an orgy, but rather the kind of event where a beautiful woman might seduce or at least distract a target while I steal the Twilight Compass.

Phaena gets a wistful smile on her face as she thinks about her family. "A brother and two sisters, we live with my dad. Renzo's fifteen and angry a lot, but seems to have settled some since he made journeyman. Boatwright, loves finish work. Ticia and Treya are eleven and incredibly sweet—half the time. Er, more than half. Much more than half. Okay, maybe only half. Twins, obviously. Mother died some, eight years back now? Muggers. They knocked her down and she hit her head and . . . never woke up. Father's great when he's himself, but he's going senile before his time. Can't hold a job. The duchess, she sent a mage to look at him—no charge to us, you know, we couldn't afford that, but . . . it's not the kind of thing magic can fix."

"I didn't mean to . . ." I trail off. I'm suddenly stuck, trying to figure what exactly I did wrong.

"Express interest in me as a human being?" she asks with a muted smile. "It's fine. People do, once in a while."

I can't tell if she's teasing or if she's referring to how people don't generally treat rent girls like human beings. "Uh, no. I meant—I meant I'm sorry if I dredged up muck."

She shrugs it off.

"So you're supporting your whole family? Alone?"

I stop.

And now I've brought up her work.

Great job, Kylar.

Phaena smiles ruefully. "I couldn't make this kind of money working for anyone else. But it does make it pretty hard to tell Her Grace no when she asks for something. Even if she asks for something like this."

I immediately think of teasing her, saying *Something as awful as working with me?* and pretending to take offense.

Flirting, in other words.

"Ha," I say instead. "She doesn't pay me at all, and I *still* can't tell her no." It's the right move. Suddenly, we're just two normal people complaining about the boss. "Speaking of the boss," I say, "gimme that file on the second guy. I've got an idea."

Chapter Twenty-Six

The Trouble with Dogs, of Both Varieties

*H*anging here by my fingertips, I think I've finally figured out why dogs hate me. Imagine waking up in your bedroom to find a dog. Your house is closed, door locked. Your bedroom door is closed. It's locked. No windows. How'd the dog get in? It's awfully large. Now it comes close and, trembling, you reach out to pat its head. Your hand passes right through it.

What would you be feeling?

Is it a dream, a hallucination? No—now the dog nips you, playfully, and you feel *teeth*.

Freak you out a bit?

To dogs, that's how I am. When I'm wearing the ka'kari and maybe for a while afterward, I give off no scent. None. Even my breath doesn't smell. For dogs, to whom every crap on the street is a scent rainbow of fathomless variety, history, and depth, it must be like stumbling upon a creature that lacks a basic dimension of being.

All that to say, while I like dogs and can evade them more easily than the average cat burglar can, when they *do* see me, they react like I'm the average cat.

Add me showing up armed and in places I don't belong? Well, imagine the dog you wake to find in your bedroom is a war mastiff, taller at the shoulder than you are, wearing spiked barding, growling.

The image of a war mastiff is particularly vivid just now, as there is one on the wall above me with jaws that could fit my entire head between them, and it's sniffing very near my fingertips.

Gently, gently, I shift my weight to my left hand and carefully release the edge of the building from my right.

My body swings left, my rubber-tree-sap-soled shoes stopping my motion with hardly a sound.

The monster's ears prick up.

"Petti?" a voice calls. "What you got there, girl?" A moment later, a man with a draft horse's shoulders pokes his head over the edge, where he doesn't see me. He's got a face only a dog could love.

But I dunno. Maybe he smells really nice.

Satisfied there's nothing below him, the man says, "Cats again? Love to torture you, don't they, girl?"

He starts baby-talking the war mastiff, and Petti—Petticoat's her name, yes, really—calms and licks his face. He doesn't mind, not even when the dog's giant tongue crosses his open mouth. He laughs.

I've seen a lot of nasty stuff in my work, but I am not immune to the peculiar pleasures of disgust. I saw where that dog had her tongue two minutes ago.

People are gross.

I keep swinging hand over hand along the edge of the wall until I get above the balcony I want.

I've been following Philanthes Magnarius for most of the night. Scouting trip, unless I find and get the perfect opportunity to lift the bracelet. So far, I haven't even established he has the bracelet, much less with him.

I did View him, walking past him on a crowded street, meeting his eyes momentarily.

He stopped afterward and looked around. These mages, some of them, sense it.

As if I didn't have enough to worry about with them.

But he went on, apparently not too troubled.

Between his profile and Viewing him, I've learned he's a vain and venial man, a flatterer, a liar, and a backstabber—but only in the metaphorical sense. Not a good man, but he's got no guilt in him that demands death.

Philanthes Magnarius is a Tover native who's risen high within the labyrinthine halls of power in the blue tower. Fifty years old, with chestnut brown hair and an oiled mustache, he has a mage's youth about him to where he could seem thirty if you don't look at his eyes. He's married to a sickly woman who has not been equally spared the ravages of time. He has three children who all hate him, and considerably more lovers, who are partly why. He's been very busy tonight, visiting various women, trying to get any one of them to travel with him. I've heard him repeat the same lines—

"...just think," I hear Philanthes say through the open window, "we won't have to sneak around!"

The same words. Three times now.

"Sweetheart, please," this woman says tiredly. "If I go with you secretly, that *is* sneaking around."

"Ah, you wound me!" he says. "Come now..." And then his voice lowers and I can't hear the words, only the rising and falling cadences of seduction.

It's odd. This man has convinced at least these four very attractive women to cheat with him.

~Mysterious, isn't it? How in some quarters, rich, powerful, handsome magi are found attractive? So strange!~

Shush. I understand that *part!*

What I mean is that none of them has turned him away, so he's either keeping four affairs going at once, or he's been able to break them off without hurt feelings. That's impressive enough, and yet, these also aren't young girls who've been swept up in the whirlwind of a romance with a rich older man. Tonight, the two of us have visited his tailor, a married noblewoman, a bored rich widow of some sort, and now, a successful brewer. Not one simpering simpleton in the lot—and yet not one of them has taken him up on his offer of a free trip that he promises is going to be all parties and fun.

How does a man find such women?

~I think you think you mean that as a rhetorical question, but I don't think you do.~

Huh? What are you trying to imply—?

Wait, what's that?

There's a strangled noise.

I drop catlike onto the balcony. I peek in.

Oh.

~I think your answer's coming any moment.~

Right, okay.

Look. I'm not gonna describe what's going on inside with Philanthes and the brewer. Not because I'm embarrassed, but because the ka'kari has no body, and it gets jealous.

~Mmm-hmm.~

But seriously, I don't really watch. I commit enough necessary violations in my work, and watching them now? That's an unnecessary one. And I mean, honestly? Usually when you intrude on such a moment, you don't want to see what you're seeing. Most people look a lot better with their clothes on. And if you *do* want to watch, that's even worse.

> *Men controlled by the sign of the horn*
> *will do anything to get theirs wet and warm.*
> *And just so do they*
> *Turn from hunter to prey,*
> *And thus become food for worms.*

I wrote that myself, years ago, thinking my master would be impressed. He wasn't. He said, 'A horny man makes mistakes. Don't be that man.'

I sit down on the balcony, back to the wall, just under the window.

Violation or not, sometimes you stay in such situations in my line of work, and often you really should, because pillow talk is a real thing.

However, and I really shouldn't say this—I'm not lingering on this, I swear—but I've figured out the reason Philanthes is able to maintain these lovers all over the city despite everything: sex magic.

That's not really something I thought I was going to talk about, so let's not.

~All that buildup, so close to a resolution, and you're just going to leave your listeners hanging there unsatisfied?~

Yes.

After a few not-very-quiet minutes, and one very-not-quiet minute, Philanthes says breathlessly, "I'll introduce you as my very dear friend. Believe me, I've been to a hundred of these parties. No one makes any assumptions, and no one comments afterward on each other's companions."

"You'll tire of me by the time we get to..."

Of course her voice is muffled just at the moment she says the name of the place where the party is going to be as she pulls her clothes back over her head.

"Tire?" he says. "Of you? Never!"

She laughs, clearly disbelieving him, but not angry.

"Yulina, you know my word is good. I will take you there, and I will bring you back here with me, none the worse for wear, I swear it. And yes, if either of us finds more amenable companionship the night of... well, such things happen. If it does, we each aver now to tell the other before the night is half-gone, and regardless, next day at noon, we come back to Tover together. No questions asked."

"You're lying," she says playfully, ". . . about returning me none the worse for wear."

He laughs. "Perfect. I'll pick you up tomorrow night at our old favorite place outside of town. I promise a night of delights untold, and we'll depart at dawn, *together*, not sneaking around at all."

She groans. "That's not picking me up, Philanthes. That's meeting me at the last ratty inn before Roshlington. In other words, sneaking around," she says. She sighs.

"Just until we're out of town," he says.

And that gives me my deadline, and if she wasn't speaking metaphorically, it may even give me where they're meeting. It also tells me this party I'm trying to infiltrate is not in the city—and is at least far enough past Roshlington that it's worth it for these two to travel together rather than simply meet at the destination.

I hear the sound of an interior door opening to take them farther inside her brewery. Her departing voice says, "Please tell me you're not bringing that god-awful hound. What's . . . ?"

But of course I can't hear his response. That'd be too helpful.

Sun's almost up. I'd hoped to scout out at least two of my possible targets before dawn. It's already past time I get back to check if Phaena's got any more guidance or news for me. I've got to investigate the other two magi, figure out which of the three to rob—and how! All before Philanthes is out of my reach.

I've got less than twelve hours before Philanthes departs for his inn on the outskirts of the city and maybe twenty-four before he leaves the city altogether. Scouting three jobs, deciding which has the best odds, planning the job, and pulling it off?

It's far too much to do in one day, but that's what I've got.

Chapter Twenty-Seven

Dead Weight

I loused up," I tell Phaena, throwing my cloak over the back of a chair. "I took too long. I'm not gonna have time to scout both of the others."

"Do you have time for one?" she asks. She looks flawless this morning. While I was hanging off a roof by my fingertips, apparently Phaena was getting her beauty sleep and doing her makeup.

Seems fair.

"Which one do you think I should check out?" I ask. "You've had more time to look at those papers than I have. Not to mention a full night's sleep. After a couple nights without any at all, I'm gonna start making bad decisions."

Her chin rises sharply and lightning flashes in her eyes like a summer storm on the far horizon. Perhaps I only imagine it, though, because she says, "I saved you some biscuits and sausage. Bit of fruit?"

I take it with a thanks, and realize I'm an ass for the five hundredth time in my life. The bad decisions that start to pile up after two full nights without sleep? Sometimes they begin showing up with you treating those close to you badly.

"Sorry," I mumble around a mouthful.

My master couldn't bear to say sorry. It's the only thing I'm better at than he was. Is, maybe.

She doesn't appear to hear me. She sits on the bed. "Did you read the file on Grandmaster Glaucon Vitruvius?"

"Yes," I say, knuckling my forehead. "The . . . what is he? An old mystic, monk of some sort? I read the file. But some of it was over my head, as if I know how everything works here with the . . . collegial brothers? Like, they each have their own sects with their own little fiefdoms and terminology, but they're mostly but not totally under the central authority? My eyes kind of glazed over and I couldn't figure how much of it was important for us."

"Don't worry," Phaena says. "That's why I'm here. I had to learn all that so you don't have to. Not much of it matters right now. You know those young men in blue outside the city?"

"You mean the ones with and without the yellow stripe measuring the length of their Talents against each other?"

"Both groups are kineturges, which is why they're rivals. The group with the yellow stripe uses missiles. They hurl other things—the yellow stripe symbolizes lightning. The ones without the stripe impart speed to their own bodies. That's Grandmaster Glaucon Vitruvius's sect, usually called the Hands of the Storm, though they call themselves the Cogitants of the Storm. There's lots of nicknames. You want me to tell you more?"

I'm lost, and I'm so tired I really don't want her to tell me anything else, but I hear Durzo in the back of my mind, nagging me, saying you never know when some detail might make all the difference, so I say, "Please do."

"You look so pained."

"How rude. I was born looking like this."

She smiles. "It's simpler than it seems at first. But you're right, at first it doesn't seem simple at all. Each of Tover's collegial brotherhoods—colleges to outsiders—investigate movement in their own ways, some purely through academic study, some through worship and dance and music, and some through the martial arts, like those boys showing off outside the city. The blue mages describe all of it as investigating the Prime Mover, which is kind of another name for the One God, though I think they imagine It as more of a force than a person or even a deity. At least for some of them. Doesn't matter.

"Each of the Blue colleges or sects or stoas or academies or studios—they think of themselves in all those ways, and the differences matter to them, but not to us. Anyway, each of them investigates one or more of the Three Great Mysteries of Motion. Those mysteries are the things that move other people or things, often in unseen ways, or are themselves the ether through which other things are moved." She pauses. "I'm losing you, aren't I? Anyway, the Great Mysteries are Wind, Music, and Light. Sometimes Breath and Water are included under Wind. And Magic is always included under Light. There are, apparently, long-running debates about how all these things fit together."

"All right, that's... weirder than I was going to guess. How does Music fit with—?"

"I was going to skip that part, because I don't think it's relevant. But I have studied it all, so I can give you the one-minute or the ten-minute version. Which would you like?"

"Neither," I say quickly. "You're right. Maybe some other time."

She sits on the bed and seems to have lost her place. "If you see any man here wearing blue anywhere above the chest—collars or shoulders or shoulder tabs or even hat or hood—he's a mage. Tover enforces sumptuary laws that bar anyone else from wearing blue, though naturally some daring dandies will wear faded purples that are very close. Each college has its own sigil, but most full brothers only wear theirs on formal occasions. You want to know them?"

"How about just the ones we saw on the field?"

"The Storm Keepers—the boys with the yellow, who use projectiles—have a yellow lightning bolt on blue. Sometimes with storm clouds. Those are the ones you're not investigating. Grandmaster Glaucon Vitruvius's school's sigil is a figure seated in meditation, sometimes radiating power."

"Cogitating?" I guess.

"Huh?"

"Cogitants. Thinkers. Because they meditate on the storm. Right?"

She frowns. "I actually don't know. That wasn't in the file. But maybe so? Anyway, Vitruvius lives with two to three hundred of his fellow warrior-magi-mystic-monks—for some reason it's hard to get a solid number—along with twice as many outsiders who come to pay them for martial or magical training but either don't commit to becoming Storm Fists themselves or aren't able to finish because they don't have the Talent or the discipline to do so. They become Storm Fists if they complete the martial training, but all the acolytes are known as Hands of the Storm as soon as they begin. It's complicated and I don't think it matters to us."

She goes on, "Their compound has a number of intriguing features—"

"Stop, stop. That's enough. Hundreds of highly disciplined warrior-mage-monks sleeping in a barracks together and I'm supposed to steal from *him* in the middle of all of them? Sounds like my nightmares."

"Mine too," Phaena says.

"Scratch him off the list. We'll have to steal from one of the others. Tell me about Vonn Atreus," I say.

"No need," she says. "I already went after Vonn Atreus myself."

"You what?"

"I eliminated him, unfortunately."

"You *what*?!"

"No, not *eliminated* eliminated. Not your kind of eliminated. Eliminated as a possibility," Phaena says, smoothing her skirts over her knees. "Lord Atreus Sa'fasti is not going to—um, attend the gathering we wish to attend. He had a recent death in the family. He sent his bracelet back a week ago—too long for us to catch up with the messenger."

"How'd you find that out?" I ask. I thought she'd been sleeping in while I was out.

"I asked him." She gestures to herself, indicating the makeup and the tailored dress as if I'm being dense. "Did you think I dressed like this for you?"

"Wait, you what?"

"You don't always need to stab your problems in the back of the neck, you know. A little subtlety goes a long way. I forged a letter of introduction, bought some samples of cloth, and pretended to be a merchant selling draperies in the newest style. We had a lovely chat. My greatest difficulty was extricating myself from his very sweet reminiscences about his dearly departed cousin. He even tried to give me a large down payment on an order for new draperies."

"You..."

"I declined," she says quickly. "I'm not in the business of scamming grieving old men."

"But...you?" I'm not doing a very good job of reversing out of my assumptions.

She frowns. "If you keep this up, Kylar, I might start to feel insulted. Has it not occurred to you that *you* might learn a few things from *me*?"

It actually...hadn't. Not that I mean to say it.

But I'm tired enough that I must have let my surprise at her competence show on my face. I see that summer storm brewing in her eyes again, and I say quickly, "So usually, I'd take a full day to scout this Grandmaster Vitruvius's place, make a plan, poke holes in it, throw it away, make a new plan, repeat that process a few times until I found a least bad one. Then I'd sleep and regroup, realize I'd missed some things in my best plan and amend it, and then I'd scout the next target the same way. Then after I had all my best plans side by side, I'd make a decision which target to go after. Give or take, that'd take about a week. You eliminated Lord Atreus. That saves me maybe two days. I still need four. We have less than one. Any ideas how I can sneak in to spy on these monks?"

With a certain glee, Phaena's rouged lips curve into a smile. She says, "Why yes, I think I do."

Chapter Twenty-Eight

Into a Coil of Blue Vipers

$\mathcal{M}$y job is terrible, no way around it. But sometimes I do love it.

The sun is as high and bright as a lofted executioner's axe. It is the threat of justice and the promise of expiring time.

This is only scouting, I tell myself, pulse quickening as I approach the monks' compound. The streets here are wide, so despite the nice tall buildings lining it, many of them reaching three and four stories high, the floating blue spike of Sho'fasti half a league away looms over all. Spindly staircases and thin, impossibly undersupported bridges are the only entries and exits from that gleaming sapphire dagger over the heart of Tover.

If I weren't so pressed for time—and if I didn't have a small fear of one of its mages seeing through me with some kind of Talent I don't know about—I'd go to the spire to see it up close. It's a wonder of the world.

I wonder, is it all still there, as you read this, whoever you are? Or has the world gone to hell? They say magic is changing. How much *can* it change? How much can we lose, really? If you're listening to this fifty years from now, do you think I'm exaggerating to impress, that such a building can't exist?

~Hold a moment. I thought this record was for you alone. To help you remember details.~

I shrug. *It's a lot of trouble to do this all just for myself, isn't it? You know. Like how making a fancy meal for one seems like a waste, but if you're setting a table for the whole family it's worth it.*

But then, maybe you don't know that. Being a metal ball and all. Anyway, I thought I might get some more use out of all this, maybe. You know, if I look heroic enough at the end of it, maybe I'll let a bard see it.

~Didn't someone once say, 'When you tell a story, if you tell it *to* someone, you've lost all hope of telling it honestly?'~

What is it with you and my honesty? You my conscience now?

~Your character over time determines which of my powers you might be granted access to in the future. And that's all I can say about that, so don't ask more.~

Why does that sound like a threat?

No answer.

Tell you what, I'm telling you everything because the most important thing for this record to do is to keep an accurate account for myself. We'll go over it later together. You're right, though, I'm probably fooling myself. I'm not gonna share this with anyone.

~I'll remember you said that.~

You know, for a moment there, I'd felt that telling my tale as if someone might benefit from it in some nebulous future was helping blunt the loneliness, the utter isolation of my livelihood. The ka'kari's taken that away from me now.

Thanks, friend.

It doesn't answer.

Where was I? Something about the spire? Well, luckily I'm not going there. Instead of visiting the spire, which is full of mages who are politicians, bureaucrats, and scholars, I'm going to visit the Hands of the Storm.

I didn't say it was good luck.

The Storm Hands' base is in a district called the Waters. The compound has only one wall (an ancient remnant from whoever held this territory before they took it over, Phaena says). There are no overt guards. All blues are magi of motion, thus the water thing—I don't know that they have any particular affinity for water, except as a metaphor for complicated motions. The Storm Keepers don't believe in stopping attacks or even intrusions but instead seek to bend them and redirect forces. This applies even to approaching their stoa: Those who are unwanted end up choosing not to come this way, often apparently of their own will.

The monks accomplish this in a dozen ways, most of which people don't even notice—I wouldn't have, if Phaena hadn't briefed me on them. I do see the ruts for wagon wheels in the flagstones. First, they're filled with terrible, bone-rattling bumps, whereas side routes are clearly smoother. Then by shifting the distance between the bumps, the roads might hang up or slow carts.

Sections of the road show routine flooding, with flagstones raised for comfort-able walking—for adults, but uncomfortably far apart for children's shorter legs. When children play on them, as children do, they generally go no farther into the monks' compound, and adults who need to travel past banish children from loitering too much.

Changes to the cobbles winnow those visitors who ride horses to a single lane and suggest an easier route down broad avenues off to either side. Those avenues lead to attractive markets, easy travel, and good entertainment. The buildings here, though tall, are widely spaced: There is no rooftop highway for law-averse people like me.

I don't understand all the tricks in play, but I do admire them. In my plain messenger's clothes, no one stops me. No one even looks at me twice, but even I almost turn off the road several times, for reasons I can't explain.

But soon, a dull roar I've barely been aware of sharpens. And here, right in the middle of a flat city on a floodplain, I turn a corner to see the Gate of Waters.

The Sisters of the Chantry often create gathering places and monuments of astonishing beauty, but it seems to me that everything male mages make, they make to instill awe.

This? It's nearly half the height of the blue tower itself, half a league east of here, and it has no readily apparent source, magically pumping up all the vast volume of water it then drops as if from some secret spring. Nor does the waterfall crash into the ground and throw mist over the next three city blocks. Instead, the water pours through the level of the street, plunging into the cis-terns or the river that recycles the falls.

Near the gate, the cobbles of the street yield to quartz, or glass, or maybe some magical equivalent. With the wash of waters on them, they remain eerily clear. One approaching the waterfall feels as if he's walking from safely solid street into unsupported air, flying rather than walking toward the pounding falls, looking down through a watery window to where the waters crash and roil on the rocks in subterranean caverns far below. It is highly unnerving.

Yet even as I watch, numerous people approach the gate, unperturbed. The monks are all male, every ethnicity I know, all with close-cropped hair or shaven heads, all in voluminous trousers of various colors, and all in sleeveless shirts, again in various colors (though blue predominates) and with various sigils announcing, I presume, their rank or accomplishments or college.

I hear a voice behind me. "First time?"

I nod to a young monk. Well, he's only a few years younger than I am, but he's got a young look about him. You know what I mean? I've seen twenty-year-old soldiers who have an old look about them, and I've seen boyish men of fifty. This kid is a kid.

"It's not as scary as it seems," he says. "Walk straight at it with a firm purpose in mind, and it'll open right up. Your shoes'll get a bit damp is all."

"Firm purpose?" I ask.

"Like me wanting not to be later to my training than I already am," he says with a grin. He jogs on ahead of me, and the waters part from above like a curtain being drawn back. He strides right out onto the glass of the chasm without hesitation, and it holds him.

"Does it matter what purpose?" I shout after him.

"If it's delivering a letter, keep left. See the sign of the scroll? If you want to roam and see what we do, that's good enough!"

"How does the gate know? Does it read your mind?" I ask.

"It's just a gate!" he says, and then he's gone.

Just a gate, my left gonad. *Just a gate*, indeed. When magic is involved, sometimes a gate is just a gate, and sometimes it's a gate that flays your mind, sounds alarms, and drops you into an abyss if it finds something in your mind it doesn't like. Sometimes I really hate magic.

I forgot to describe Phaena's plan. It's got a lot of moving parts, but I'll see if I can artfully condense those and translate all the specialized professional jargon into terminology that a mere civilian can understand. They do say that a sign of real mastery of a subject is when you can explain it to a layperson. So here it is.

One, dress as a messenger. Two, walk in through the front gate. Three, look around.

Startling, isn't it? It's one of those plans that's so beautiful, so audacious, that in hindsight, it seems obvious. You think, *Why didn't I think of that?*

Looking at the big, obviously magical gate with unknown magical properties in front of me, I have my answer. Still, there's nothing for it. There's no time to interview locals and winnow out the knowledgeable ones from the merely superstitious in order to ask them questions about it, no time to find a library where I might read up on the gate's abilities. Here we go.

I approach, stepping out into the abyss, and feel the glass underfoot, right where it's supposed to be.

The waters part, and I walk through.

Easy. Just a gate.

Phaena's plan looks brilliant once more.

I see my young monk ahead, hurrying to join a class training in a wide, open square. There are about a hundred monks there, but surrounding them are other people. Most of these are spectators, but there are also people who are joining the exercises: men and women, dressed for exercise, each in the fashion of their own people. Tover is a port city, and as cosmopolitan as any other, if smaller than the great cities of the world.

Watching the monks move, snapping from form to form, I remember that Feir Cousat trained here ten or twenty years ago.

Despite being the size of a small continent, under this training, Feir learned to move with such speed and precision that he became a second-echelon Blade Master.

These exercises, however, are fairly basic.

"Alphas!" the slender, bare-chested monk leading the class announces. "With me!"

The monks at the head of each of the rows step forward, salute, and move with alacrity to follow him.

I shouldn't follow, but I'm curious to see if there's anything I can learn from the most advanced fighters among the Storm Fists. And who's to say that maybe Grandmaster Glaucon Vitruvius won't be wherever we're going? Maybe he likes to train the best pupils personally.

In minutes, I'm standing behind a pillar in another large area of engraved stone and beautiful wood pillars, splashes of greenery, spartan statues, and even a few growing flowers, surreptitiously watching the alphas sparring at half speed. They're good; there's a crisp snap to their movements, the speed of flexible limbs, the ease of bodies honed hard by long training.

My cover, if you want to call it that, is that I'm a lost courier. A nosy lost courier is, I hope, something they see frequently enough that I won't be in much trouble if I'm found out.

It wouldn't actually be a disaster for me to get caught, I hope. At least it would show me how tight their security is. For later. This is just scouting, after all.

The alphas' trainer, a bald dark-skinned middle-aged monk with a hitch to his step, barks out, "We'll start with a postception. We'll make it visible for those of you still struggling with the dual sight while in motion. Tawniel, rise. Rain on Palm Leaves at four, eight, breathe, then positions two and six into The Lions at Sunset with an extra spearman at two and with number seven mounted. No force pads."

The young warrior he addressed has shucked off most of his clothing by the time the trainer finishes speaking to stand in no more than a loincloth. He conjures a glittering blue cloud in front of himself and walks through it on his way to the room's open training space. The magical cloud twines around his body, sticking to his skin, flaring bright, then dulling.

What's this?

Bowing, the young monk says, "Unless you prefer otherwise, I'll do the morning variant of Rain on Palm Leaves, Master Trainer?"

The trainer can't help but smile. "Showing off, Tawniel?"

"Pushing myself, Master."

"Then please do."

The kid blitzes through the forms. He wobbles only momentarily on one tricky leap that requires him to land on one foot and pause with his other leg extended in a kick.

His hands flare with magic at several places, but it dissipates instantly. I assume that these are to give him the proper recoil and thus balance for what the form imitates: here, the throwing of magic at one's opponents.

The last flying side kick is the kind meant to unseat a horseman, but here the jump is magically aided so that one could clear a fourteen-foot lance and strike the head of a horseman on a big destrier. In other words, it's a jump that is both inhumanly long and high.

It puts my heart in my throat. And this kid is still in training? These are not people I want to fight.

"Thank you. Be seated," the old monk says. "Critiques? Merkaelus, comment?"

Another of the young monks points out some minor errors of foot position and balance, and then others chime in. All standard stuff for training.

But then the old monk says, "And now we see how well you all saw."

The blue cloud that had clung to Tawniel glimmers and spins away from his skin, and comes to rest without him in the space where he'd done the form.

Now, his glittering cloud-doppelganger moves exactly how Tawniel had, blooming with various colors as it moves. From my own training, I can guess that pressure is red, muscle tension a gathering green.

No one else in the room seems particularly dazzled. I am.

They advance Tawniel's glittering doppelganger, pause it, bring it back, slow it down, examining in minute detail not only where he went but how his body managed even the trickiest transitions from one motion to the next. Then everyone gets up and tries to emulate the tougher motions. I would've had to watch my master perform these moves repeatedly over a course of days if not weeks to figure out things that here must be obvious in an afternoon.

"Now with force pads," the old monk says.

Tawniel repeats the form, but this time, at every strike, his fists and kicks are met by moving ghostly forms of men that offer resistance. He's much sloppier this time: When you kick empty air, you know exactly what to expect. Kicking a head might mean hitting a tensed neck; you might catch hard skull or softer nose.

The class dissects that next, and then copies it.

All this within a quarter of an hour, as if this is warm-up.

"Enough," the trainer says, and the class lights up with anticipation. "Today, we start preception. Merkaelus, up. Free form. Improvise."

He throws another cloud at Merkaelus and then simply watches for half a minute.

"Now see it how I saw it," the trainer says.

He makes Merkaelus's doppelganger replay the forms once more, but this time the ghostly figure is surrounded by a cloud of ghosts that jump out from it in every direction at each moment.

You don't have time for this, I keep telling myself, but there's no way I can leave now.

At first, it's baffling, but the trainer slows the motion to a fraction of what Merkaelus's speed was, and then I understand: Each ghost is a potentiality, dozens popping and disappearing with every heartbeat as he moves. As Merkaelus shifts his weight to this foot, suddenly all the possible moves requiring his weight to be elsewhere vanish, to be replaced by new potential moves. Some of those ghosts are brighter, more vivid. As Merkaelus gives the first two strikes of the form Floodwaters Rising, the ghost showing him completing the third strike of the form goes bright.

Preception is a visible shortcut to the kind of teaching all masters of the martial arts do constantly. If I see that your hips are in this position, I know you can't move in these ways. If you stand like so, I know that you might do this or that.

But here the feedback is immediate, visible. Errors can be identified and fixed so quickly that it's no wonder the blues shave years off the usual time it takes to train to mastery. And if used in a fight—invisibly, as it sounds like they learn to do—preception might give only a tiny advantage at the highest levels, but at the highest levels, the smallest advantages matter the most. For everyone else, it must surely help the merely competent perform as well as the highly trained.

I wonder, if you could filter the visions (either magically or simply by experience) with what you know of your opponent—say that you know he always likes to uppercut with the left, or that he's trained in the martial art val torpa so he loves kicking—perhaps the advantages of preception might not be so small after all.

Perhaps a blacksmith wider than he is tall could become a second-echelon Blade Master.

Thinking of Feir Cousat learning preception, I can't help but think of Dorian. He came here too, didn't he? Did he come to learn to fight...or was he more interested in learning how to forecast the future?

How far *can* preception push into the future? Is it connected to, or analogous at all to what Dorian does? Is *this* how he sees the future?

"You watch as if you understand what they're doing," a voice says behind me.

Cringing that I got so involved that I let myself get caught, I say smoothly, "I trained a bit when I was younger. Got pretty adept at the old fisticuffs." I turn with a smile and take up a fighting stance that's slightly wrong, so I look like a clueless braggart.

It's Grandmaster Vitruvius himself.

My heart drops and my smile falters. Without meaning to, as I lock gazes with him, my gift comes over me and I look *into* him.

"Goodness. What was *that*?" he says.

"What was what?" I ask, cursing myself.

"In your eyes," the grandmaster says, his expression going from amiable to troubled. He glances at my clothing. "You're not a messenger at all, are you?"

"I, uh..." I've loused up, badly.

"You're coming with me. Now."

Chapter Twenty-Nine

Serpent and Charmer

*I*t was the gate," the grandmaster says. "If you're wondering."

"The gate?"

Grandmaster Glaucon Vitruvius looks old at first glance, but he's not. He's got prematurely gray hair, but with white at his temples that to my eye isn't natural. It's not the white of age, it's the noon-sun white that speaks of some extremity that led him to using so much magic that it nearly killed him. The fingers stroking his oiled black beard are manicured, the nails longer on the right hand. A lutist, then, not a harp player, if I correctly spy fretting calluses on his left hand. Tall and lean as bamboo, he wears no insignia of rank. He inhabits that odd intersection of fame where hubris and humility are indistinguishable: He wears no mark of rank but needs none because everyone here knows who he is. He wears a plain black cotton tunic and matching trousers, no finer than the lowest student's, and with no adornment, so perhaps he is humble after all.

Everyone we pass recognizes him, many nodding, some even bowing—though this doesn't seem to be required. Anyone blocking our way scurries aside to give us plenty of room. Without fail, everyone we pass goes silent. We travel in a bubble of serenity, interrupted only by little escaping gasps, at his presence, not mine, I think.

We climb several stories into the polished stone heart of the monastery. Every passing step makes my escape less likely, the knot in my stomach tighter. But we are attended by no guards, and when we reach the grandmaster's modest chambers, he sends the young assistant waiting by the door out for 'refreshments.'

Perhaps that's a code. Perhaps a hundred murderous monks will descend at any moment.

Whatever his level of suspicion, though, he clearly has no fear of me whatso-ever. He believes he can handle me alone.

Having seen his underlings train, I'm not certain he's wrong. I might've bragged about my skills to Momma K, but I'd want to know far more about this man before I put them to the test.

He offers me a seat.

I politely decline and choose a narrow stance, composed, alert, but not hostile.

He sits and crosses his legs, ankle over knee—not a posture from which he could quickly start fighting.

It occurs to me that he's doing *his* best not to make *me* feel threatened. That makes him even scarier.

The grandmaster interlaces his fingers on the desktop and gently, to some unheard rhythm, rubs his thumbs together. My entrance must have drawn him from this very spot, for his desk is littered with parchments and open books, here a ledger, here a journal, here an unstopped inkwell with quill standing in it, with drying sand and a tiny quill-sharpening knife nearby. Bronze book-ends loosely hold together a half-dozen volumes on the table, with gaps like a broken-toothed smile where he's pulled out the books he's working on.

Then my heart leaps. Holding down some parchments as an ad hoc paper-weight is an ornate bejeweled bracelet. *My* bracelet. Or it will be soon.

I try not to react.

He says, "It requires a tremendous and a focused will to pass the Gate of Waters. Many consider it the first trial of joining our order."

I take a breath but can't decide what lie best fits before he goes on. I had no idea it was supposed to be hard to walk through. That stupid monk out there had given me no sign.

"*You* seem not to have even noticed it," he says.

"Perhaps it was broken?" I say. I have a terrible thought.

Did you *break it?* I ask the ka'kari.

"Oh, it is broken. Now," the grandmaster says. "There's a hole in it."

You did*!*

~I was hungry! And you were lousing things up, so I made a way we both got what we wanted.~

This is not what I wanted!

"Lucky for me, I guess," I say. "Guess that explains how I made it through without even noticing it."

"You misunderstand. Before something devoured its magic, the gate did manage to perform its secondary function. See, it measures magical potential, your glore vyrden. Ah, I see you're familiar with the term."

I swallow.

~Couldn't just walk through the messenger's gate, could you?~ the ka'kari asks.

You're trying to blame this on me*?*

"You're saying it detected magical potential...from *me*?" I scoff. "It really is broken!"

"Not mere potential—potential such as hasn't been seen here since before my time." He leans forward, resting his elbows on his desk, and gently taps his forehead against his still-interlaced fingers, peering at me through the O of fingers and thumb, exasperated.

"I'm not a mage," I say, as if this is all too stupid to be believed. "I've been tested. Check me again. You'll see. Surely you've got another...whatever to test me again with. Or I can walk through the gate where it's not broken, if you really want to waste your time and mine going all the way back out there..." Where I will definitely run away.

"The gate is not a finely tuned instrument. It's merely one sieve among the many we use. It signals only a few degrees of difference: black for no Talent, blue to signify enough Talent that a person may be trained. To identify possible initiates arriving, you understand? Yellow reflects a developed Talent as most of us here possess, or tells us when a mage from one of the other schools arrives."

"Security," I say. "Handy." He's given me no clue how many people see those test results. If other monks have been notified I'm here too, there may be a noose settling on my neck even as we have this very civil discourse.

"Indeed, very," he says. "We only see red when someone terribly dangerous enters."

We. And there's my confirmation that he isn't the only person who sees the warning beacon. Others know that I'm here. Hell save me.

But I compose my face, as if this is merely of academic interest.

"Only a few times in the last hundred years has anyone pushed through the Gate who burned our warnings white hot. The most recent was before my time as grandmaster, but—if I'm right about where you've come from, maybe you can guess who it was."

"Where I've come from?" I ask, raising my eyebrows.

"Cenaria originally, though likely Elenea most recently. If you're going to play stupid, make more of an effort. You're not terribly convincing so far."

I sink even further into myself. "Dorian Ursuul?" I hazard. "I heard he trained here. At one of the colleges, anyway. Was it yours? But how do you know where I'm from?"

Maybe he's merely guessed from my clothing or my patterns of speech that I'm Cenarian. It's possible. Right?

He snorts. "No. And Dorian was too canny to ever walk through the gate. No, I meant his friend, Solonariwan Tofusin. How are those two?"

I don't bother with denials. I still hope to avoid open conflict. But I feel that noose tightening. I can't help but glance out his window, overlooking the court-yard where classes train. It's empty now. Perhaps that's a coincidence. "Well, Dorian's mad, and King or Emperor Tofusin or whatever he is now is co-ruling the Sethi empire, facts you must surely know as well as I do. The whole world does by now, right?"

"Mad how?"

"Crazy mad, not angry mad."

"Got that. I meant how is his illness manifesting?" He's impatient, as if I'm being intentionally thick.

"I hear he's catatonic, mostly. Delirious when he's not that. I hear he wanders the palace grounds, and they suffer his outbursts because of the high queen's old love for him, and try to keep him out of the way because of her equally abiding fury."

"I still marvel that the high king suffers his old rival to live. In his own pal-ace, no less."

I want to say that Logan's a good man, but that might suggest how well I know him, so instead I shrug as if I know no more. Not defending my best friend feels like a betrayal.

"Grandmaster," I say, trying a new tack, "it is a pleasure indeed to speak with you, but I'm afraid your gate is a faulty scale indeed, and I fear that when you realize that your broken scale has told you an ant is an iron bull, you'll take out your displeasure on the ant. Please, I don't want to waste your time. Test me again."

"I already have," he says. He pulls his interlaced fingers and circle-forming thumbs apart, and something crackles in the O and dissipates. He'd been staring at me through that space. I'd thought it was strange that he was doing that, but I'd dismissed it as a quirk. "And from my examination, you appear to have as much Talent as one dead."

"So that's that," I say. "I'm sorry for taking up your precious time, my lord. I'll just be go—"

"Stop." His voice is quiet, but there's the snap of authority in it.

I stop.

"Sit."

I sit, feeling my hopes for a peaceful escape slipping through my fingers.

He looks at me for a long time, and I realize how poorly I've planned all this. I don't even have an in-depth cover: Am I miming the sort of man who would look away from a challenge, or one who would stare back defiantly?

So I take a stupid middle ground, and look back pleasantly, which as soon as I do it, I realize is far too self-assured for a person in my tenuous position.

~Kylar, I don't feel good about this. He is not nearly worried enough. Which means *you* aren't nearly worried enough.~

Finally, he says, "Have you ever lost a faith?"

"A faith?" I ask, doe-like.

He stares at me intently, weighing.

If this man can fight as well as I guess, I've stepped thigh deep in the sewers, and I need to walk away clean. Because when I Viewed him, I saw something much worse than I expected: He's innocent.

I don't mean he's some kind of a naïf or a saint. I try to avoid it like chugging iced water in a mouth full of cold-sensitive teeth, but whether it's my inborn Talent or the ka'kari's work or a gift of Night Angels past, I see sometimes, somehow see the scum that accumulates on a soul. I don't know how it works or even whether it sees guilt or crime or sin.

But I know this: Though not a saint, Glaucon Vitruvius is not only not a bad man deserving death; as far as I can tell, he's a good man.

I can't kill him. I can't kill an innocent without betraying everything I am.

"Ah," he says finally. "I think you have lost one. Tell me, what was it you had faith in? A god? A lover? Your family? Your place in the world?"

The peaceful look on Elene's face as my blade slid home rushes to mind before I can banish it.

My voice level, I say, "Happy endings. I used to believe in happy endings. You?"

"Myself," he says. He smiles wryly, but there's sorrow to it. "I was born to a title, more wealth than most of my peers, intellect, relatively good looks made all the more comely by the best tailors, and vast self-assurance, and when the time came, I evinced the Talent, strongly. Honestly, young me would've been baffled if I'd *not* been Talented, and greatly so. Everyone believed I was special, none more so than I."

"Then something happened," I say. Why is the grandmaster telling me this? Is he stalling me? Is this his mystic monk act? My eyes flick to the door. The novice still hasn't come with the 'refreshments.'

I don't think he'll be returning alone.

"Something, yes. Or perhaps I should say some*one*." As a seasoned gambler might shrug after a single bad night at the tables, he shrugs it off. Gives a lop-sided smile.

That's how I know that whatever happened, it utterly broke him.

The old bitter Lodricari epics mock men for this. There's a line that goes something like, 'O'er a sliver in his hand, a man will rage the rivers red, but a mortal wound he endures in stolid silence.'

"That where you earned the white hair?" I ask. Too late, I realize I shouldn't have said it. That connection isn't something everyone knows.

His eyebrows lift, surprised I know, perhaps, but not denying a connection. "That's a story for another time. Suffice it to say, I emerged from my crisis of faith smaller but somewhat better. And I learned something paradoxical and troublesome. By giving up my belief that I was so special, I can do more now than I could do previously. I can do things thought to be totally unbefitting an exalted figure such as I used to be."

"And doing those things, in the eyes of many, makes you even more special and exalted," I say.

"Indeed!" He claps his hands with real delight. "You understand! The big problems—the besetting problems—those don't get easier with long experience, do they? They get deeper, worse. They strip us to the core and demand to know what we really believe, and how much we believe it."

"They break us," I whisper.

He sits back in his chair. "Indeed." His face becomes somber. "And what's your problem, friend?"

"Different than yours," I say brusquely. Opposite his, really.

My problem isn't that I think I'm special even though I'm not; my problem is that I know I'm special and I hate it.

"I don't know why you're here," he says, "but it doesn't seem that you've come to kill me, so I'm guessing that you're here to steal, either some magical bauble you believe I have or some intelligence you think I hold. You won't tell me which, will you?"

I think on it. "No. It was a scouting trip, and one I obviously botched early on."

I don't know why I tell him the truth, but it's clear he doesn't believe me.

He falls silent, pensive, gathering himself, then seems to make a decision. "Let me cut to the chase: You mayn't steal from me unless you're willing to kill me to do so."

"You paused," I say.

"I paused?" His eyebrows tent.

"Before you said I'd have to kill you to get what I want, you paused. You were making sure you meant it, weren't you?"

He nods, warily.

I say, "Funny thing. As a man who carries an integrity-shaped hole in my heart, I recognize real integrity when I see it. I can't kill you, Grandmaster. Won't. I would sooner get a splinter than take a true man out of this wretched world."

"A splinter? You'd go so far?" he asks dryly.

"You are an extraordinary man," I say. "I hope we never meet again." I stand and step toward the open door.

"Kylar Stern," he says. "Stop."

I feel as if I've been hit with lightning. I stop without meaning to. He knows my name.

Do I try denial? I ask the ka'kari.

~Did it sound like he was making a wild guess?~

I turn back toward him. My heart thuds so loudly in my ears I doubt I could hear the telltale sounds of footsteps running up the stairs even if they were there. "I didn't think my fame had spread so far," I say with a grin I don't feel in the slightest.

"Much farther even than Sho'fasti, in certain circles," he says. "Young man, early twenties, ice blue eyes, dark hair, slight build, supremely gifted in the martial arts, but alternately appearing highly trained with his Talent or ignorant of even the basics. He was one of the Twelve Magi at Black Barrow, and possibly one of the more gifted ones, given that he appeared to escape that magical cataclysm without injury.

"Blue mages were there at Black Barrow, Kylar. And red. And green. What you Twelve did there is of the greatest interest to every magical brotherhood and sisterhood in the world. Do you even know what you've done?"

"Not really."

"Ah, yes, 'nonchalant' is key among your descriptors. Even when allegedly facing the White Seraph of the Chantry herself and humiliating several hundred Sisters. Did that really happen?"

"I...I don't know how you heard the story, so I can't say."

"I'll take that as a yes," he says. "It makes me want to like you, imagining the look on Istariel Wyant's face, the haughty old cow."

"You have my permission to like me," I say.

"Ah yes, 'inconsistently charming' they said, too."

"Inconsistently?" I say. It's ridiculous to be offended, given that I may soon be fighting this man to the death, but I am.

"I'd love to hear any insights you have about what happened at Black Barrow," he says. "I'd expect the rumors of monsters in isolated villages and forests that we've heard. That's the sort of thing one always hears about when there's great social upheaval and wars. Given that there were literal monsters at Black Barrow, I imagine some of those rumors might even be true this time. But do you know the Tlaxini Maelstrom collapsed some months back? The straits there are a shipping lane again. Something is different with magic itself. Ripples are being felt all over the continent, maybe the world. The scholars among my brotherhood are hollow-cheeked and dark-eyed, buried in the texts looking for clues. Frightened."

Something in his words tugs at a memory. Something I'm supposed to remember. A warning, but I can't quite grasp it. "I don't know anything helpful," I say. "We were all dumb muscle. I was, at least. Dorian directed everything."

"So it comes back to Dorian, the most dangerous man in the world."

"The most—what? That seems a little harsh. Did you know him?"

"Know him?" Grandmaster Vitruvius says, eyes flicking up and to the side as if gathering his memories. "I met him briefly. Didn't like him. But I daresay that was due to my own youthful insecurities. When he was here, he gave every indication of not being terribly interested in what we had to teach, so I thought him arrogant. Apparently, he alternately baffled and infuriated all the masters on the theoretical side, but he was never interested in fighting, so we moved in different circles. And by all accounts his main gifting was in Healing! The stories beggar belief, but those few our agents were able to check turned out to be true. By the time he left Hoth'salar, they brought him all the most desperate cases. A hunter accidentally gutshot with an arrow lived. Elderly people with clouded eyes came to see again, allegedly even better than they had when they were young. A newly pregnant woman with terminal lungworm came in begging not for her own life but for her child's. They say he moved the fetus to her sister's womb, and then after three days of constant magic, he moved the wriggling mass of lungworms out of the woman too. Our people found her, still alive, years later, with more children. She swore it was true.

"Even his failures were successes. A merchant with tumors riddling his liver came in—and Dorian removed them *without breaking the skin*. The man was joyous, but Dorian told him he'd bought him only six months of life, for the cancers had already spread and taken hold everywhere else in his body. Any lesser man would've let the merchant leave amid the applause—for he looked a hundred times healthier than he had before Dorian touched him, and none would have guessed he wasn't fully healed."

As much as I want to hear everything the grandmaster has to say about Dorian, I feel like an arrow drawn back on a bow, trembling with the effort of holding still.

He goes on, though, "It was said, half-jokingly, that if you'd been dead less than a day, Dorian could bring you back. An agent of ours asked him about it once, and Dorian irritably said it wasn't true: It completely depended on how you'd died, and even then, he could only help within six minutes at the best of times. The full-day revival was an exceptional case because the man had been ice-fishing and had fallen into the hole.

"He was like that. Even in minimizing his own accomplishments, he revealed the breadth and depth of them. But as you might know, there's a trap excellent people fall into. It's all too easy, when you're really, really good at one thing—or at four or five things, in Dorian's case—to think—"

But I hear a footstep on the stairs, and the grandmaster is distracted. As much as I'd like to hear everything this spider has to say, I'd rather not have the conversation in his web.

I dart out the open door, expecting magic to smash into my back despite my speed.

But it's only a few steps, and I make it. Then I dodge aside, out of any line of fire. Then, with my Talent, *up*. I leap to the ceiling, sinking claws of ka'kari-black into a beam and swinging my feet up to hang inverted.

As I expect, a moment later he rushes through the open door of his study below me, hands filling with blue fire, body radiating power.

"Brothers!" he cries. "To me!"

He checks the empty hall, sprints to the corner.

As I drop from the ceiling and slink back into his study, I hear the pounding feet of several monks. I hear their alarmed voices.

I go to his desk. No time.

~Maybe don't be too hasty with——~

I snatch the bracelet off the table.

Or try to.

My fingers pass through the illusion with only a slight catch of resistance.

Resistance?

A trigger.

I leap instantly for the exit, but my fingers just miss grabbing the door slamming in my face. Shutting me in.

The clang of oak and iron resounds heavy through my chest. The clang of locks engaging is a slap.

Trapped.

I fly to the window in a blur, my foot drawing back to blast it from its frame with all the force of my Talent.

Then I stop. I bring the ka'kari to my eyes. A snare sits there, sinister.

Something magical glitters there that will grab my leg harder the harder I kick it.

You said you were hungry, right?

~I already ate. I'm stuffed.~

Eat the magic, you worthless trash!

~It's a trap! He knows we devoured the magic out at the gate. He set you up, and now you want to spring another trap on purpose?~

I curse.

I hear the sound of feet pounding up the stairs, running down the hall, yells getting closer. I throw the interior bar across the door.

"Give up! Anything you do now will only make things worse!" the grandmaster shouts.

Almost certainly true.

"We don't want to hurt you!" he shouts.

Almost certainly not true. Regardless, we do things we don't want to do all the time.

I'm a rat in a snare, but the difference between me and any regular rat is that I've been considering escapes since before I set foot in this office.

Like I said, I'm special.

"This is gonna hurt," I say.

~It always does,~ the ka'kari says, rushing to cover my skin.

Chapter Thirty

The Arrow and the Ring

*G*athering my Talent-strength, I grab Grandmaster Vitruvius's table by one leg, spilling its contents everywhere as I spin with it like a discus hurler. I heave it through the magic-trapped window.

The ever-satisfying music of shattering glass is followed by the timpani-drum boom of magic breaking and a festival's worth of fireworkers' searing lights bursting in every color. Acrid yellow smoke blasts out of the walls even as the entire window and its wall explode, the magic shearing in unexpected directions.

But I only register all that moments later. As soon as I hurled the table, I leapt up with all the force of my Talent—yes, *up*. Right into the ceiling.

And *through* it, gods of mischief be thanked. Apparently they have some use for me yet before they cast me aside.

From the attic I find myself in, I don't pause to see if my ruse in the room below works. If it doesn't, I'm about to have a hundred warrior-mages attached to my backside more firmly than a tail.

I hear some shouted warnings between the mages about the yellow smoke being poison, and my heart leaps with hope it will delay them a long time. But I'm not about to slow down. I'm hurdling old furniture in the attic, sliding under the scythe-arms of training trees, flipping to roll over training pads.

I'll never not marvel at the oddities you notice in the middle of life-threatening situations. Here, it's that the attic isn't dusty. No dust whatsoever.

Magic, part of me thinks. In most places, magic is a finite commodity, and mages are Important People, so magic is only used for Important Stuff. Here, they have access to so many mages, they use magic to keep things tidy.

Best not to get on the wrong side of people who can afford to use magic for trivialities.

Why do I always realize the things not to do after I've already done them?

I reach the window, and stop, rather than jumping through or kicking it apart.

I bring the ka'kari to my eyes. No traps. At least none I can see.

Trying my luck, I test the latch. It opens nicely, letting in the smell of smoke from the burning floor below. Regular smoke, though, not poisonous, so far as I can tell.

After I poke my head out, I see the trickle of black smoke from the burning frames of the windows below. Below that, I can see the shattered glass and window frames and masonry littered in the training yard, with a few faces upturned, staring, and more sure to join them soon. The fire isn't spreading fast. I'm sure the monks will contain it soon.

Not that they're going to forgive me simply because I didn't *quite* burn down their home.

Even as I look for handholds to climb to the roof, I hear a shouted "Go!" from the burning room. I think it was the grandmaster's voice.

Yellow smoke poofs out from every empty window frame at once, like wet dog crap squishing out from under a bootheel. Side by side, at every window simultaneously, I see monks appear, each with a tower-shield-sized wall of force in front of him pushing the smoke out.

Their speed and coordination baffles me. They clear the room of smoke entirely in moments. The shields disappear, and I hear the tones of men reporting—reporting my absence, surely.

The most obvious option for me to climb to the roof is using one of the stoa's signature rain chains. They're musical or something, swirling the rain down in famous ways. Obviously magical too, to gather extra rain to them and do... whatever they do. Can't risk touching those. Their magic might have security embedded in it, like spikes to impale cat burglars and friendly Night Angels.

Mercifully the ornate style of the building gives me plenty of handholds. With the visual distraction of yellow smoke, I decide to go with magical invisibility rather than mundane invisibility, and start climbing. Even though it costs me time I probably can't spare, I carefully shut the attic window behind me until I hear the latch click.

I always hate that first step, when you leave firm footing and swing out into the unknown, but the carven stone knotwork of the building's wall holds my weight, and I scramble to the high, lightly angled roof.

Did I say I hate the first step? What I really hate are the *last* steps when climbing. You know, the ones where you leave firm jagged stone holds to grab on to a dirty, steeply sloped, smooth, slippery, slick surface.

What's the difference between slick and slippery, anyway? I think at the ka'kari as I inch on my belly up to a place where my body's friction will, hopefully, keep me from plunging off the roof to an ugly, broken death.

~You're asking for definitions *now*?~

You're right. Let's come back to that later.

I stand, heaving breaths. I peer off the edge to see how things are going.

Man, do I hate heights.

They don't paralyze me immediately, but I feel like if I think about heights too much, I'm gonna get vertigo. I have to stop myself thinking when I look over a precip—

The window I'd so carefully latched behind me shatters as a blue-wreathed form blurs through it. He snags the rain chain, setting the whole thing swaying with his momentum. It rings musically as the magic up and down the chain shatters in waves in response to the swinging.

Grandmaster Vitruvius gathers himself for a single heartbeat.

Then I see why people call the blue mages the lords of movement, *sa'celeri*. With glowing blue gauntlets at his hands and feet and a glowing blue prehensile tail anchoring him to the chain, he begins *sprinting* upward—as if climbing a vertical chain is as easy as dashing up a few stairs.

I run, sprinting away along the spine of the roof, my Talent lending me speed but also making my feet tear away the concave rain-music roof tiles until I reach full speed. Making a guess, I now make myself invisible to mundane light and throw a glance over my shoulder as Grandmaster Vitruvius lands lightly on the roof.

His eyes dart to where one of the roof tiles I tore free is clattering rhythmically down one side of the steep roof.

Then his eyes come back, lock on a tile sliding down the opposite side, and I can see he knows—the only way for tiles to be going down both sides is if I was recently on the roof's spine.

The far edge of the palace roof looms ahead of me. I can't see the next building over yet, but on the way in, I noted that all the buildings were widely spaced, didn't I? What if it's fifteen paces? Twenty?

What if it's thirty?

The grandmaster's hands slap together, some kind of magical field knitting together between them. Viewing magic?

I have to either jump—and stay in sight but put more distance between us—or dive for the edge of the building to hide, switching invisibilities.

I dive, trying to minimize my silhouette and switching to magical invisibility.

I catch one glimpse of him, shoulders knotted with effort, hands stretching open a glassine portal that glows yellow. His eyes, magnified through it, loom large. I can't tell if he sees me.

Then, still skidding, I reach the edge of the roof and flip over.

I dangle off the other side, see another rain chain. But here there are no spectators in the garden below. My momentum swings my feet back to hit the building, and I immediately use the brief instant of leverage to push off and leap away from the building.

One of my feet slips off some decorative nub or another as I leap, and I fly crooked, snag the rain chain in only one outstretched hand, and spin in spirals down the chain, shattering magic in a way that is not at all musical.

I pull my other hand to the chain only at the last instant and manage to slow my descent enough that when I hit the ground amid the rock garden, I almost manage to keep my feet. Until I don't. I stagger, nearly do the splits as I slip on lovely green decorative moss, and finally go down in a near faceplant in a spray of gravel, wrenching my neck to keep from braining myself on a small boulder.

On the plus side, my fall was barely twice as loud as an iron bull stampeding through a bell bazaar.

As concerned bystanders and monks begin appearing, I dodge under the canopy of a spreading red maple, switch to mundane invisibility, and then roll out of the far side. No one here is thinking of using magic to look for me, so no eyes follow me—at least as far as I can tell.

Glancing up to the peak of the roof, I see Vitruvius appear, scanning the crowd, looking down the open street between two buildings for me. He shouts a question I don't hear to the monks and twists open that portal again, looking for me.

One more building over, there's a wall that surrounds this inner part of the stoa. Much as the monks make of not needing a wall, and as ostentatiously humble as they are about simply redirecting unwanted traffic away from their home—nothing really serves as a wall quite so well as, well, a wall.

~Gonna want to revisit that phrasing later too, are we?~

No, no, I'm actually kind of pleased with that one, I think, sliding into shadows and dodging past places where the grandmaster is likely to spy me from his vantage.

Then half a block away, I drop both kinds of invisibility and run for the face of the wall. It's rough stone on this side; all the perfectly smooth edges face outward. With its open design, the monks' compound was never intended to keep people *in*. So it's an easy climb, made trivial by my Talent.

I go slower than I could—if I'm being watched, there's no need to show the true measure of my skills—but I don't want to tempt fate or the Hands of the Storm by going too slowly, either. They've already shown that they're even better than I guessed an hour ago.

Reaching the top of the wall, I stand for a moment, skylining myself like an amateur and glancing back, hoping to present a figure he can't miss—

And hoping like hell that if they have any archers, they do miss.

But the grandmaster isn't on the rooftop anymore.

I don't know if he sees me at all.

I want to hide the hook, but maybe I've hidden the bait.

But I can't afford to gamble too much. Not with these people.

I leap off the far side of the wall. Slide to the ground, climb the next building, which is stuffed with wealthy apartments, and rest on a balcony, fully visible in both senses, but also utterly camouflaged amid chairs and tables and flowering plants in a dozen colors and climbing vines.

The long, wrapped package is still where I left it. I count that as good luck. I've had such things disappear, even when left for less time and hidden better than this one.

This isn't the only bundle I hid, and I'd hoped not to use any of them, but here we are.

I unwrap the bow, carefully warm the wood between my hands with my Talent to make it more pliable, and string it.

~A bell *bazaar*? I don't think I've ever seen one store devoted solely to—~

Shut up.

I part a curtain of vines to see the top of the wall where I disappeared, conveniently right where some steps reach the top walkway. Any moment now, if I'm right.

Maybe I should have clung to the wall instead, sprung my trap up close and personal.

He doesn't appear.

Maybe I did bury the bait. Maybe he didn't see me at the end there.

I'd decided to give it five minutes before I'd leave, lest some countertrap envelop my trap.

Having met the grandmaster, I decide to give it two minutes instead.

One minute passes, and I start to think about my escape routes from here. I didn't scout them as fully as I'd like.

That's the trouble with rushing into a job. If things go wrong, you can be left with nothing.

And things always go wrong.

The second minute is moments from expiring when I see a movement—not in the place I expected. Twenty paces off to one side, I see a head pop into view.

He dives for the edge of the wall and slides forward, a crossbow in his hands. His body stops sliding, giving him a perfect shot at the spot where I had almost decided to hang.

Then he flips over, aiming down the wall in the other direction.

I breathe.

That close. I was *that* close to getting my dumb ass shot.

Then he stands with an air of resignation. With the crossbow to his shoulder, he sweeps it over the roof of the building I'm in, searching, his fingers carefully away from the trigger plate, clearly cognizant that he's pointing a loaded weapon at a building full of civilians. He scans the balconies, squinting, the setting sun in his eyes.

I see his shoulders sag as he sighs. He lowers his bow, and as his eyes turn from me, I raise mine.

The grandmaster digs in a pocket and pulls out a gleaming circle. The bracelet. He holds it up in the air, outraged, waving it toward the building where he somehow knows I am.

"This? This is all about *this* stupid trinket?! I wasn't even going to go to her stupid party! I despise the empress! But now? I'll be going now, I promise you that—and I'll stop you, Dark One! Whatever you're planning, *I will stop you.*"

I'll only get one chance at this. If I had one of those boys' enchanted bows, I could make this shot for sure. But I don't have one of those. This is a long shot for me, and I'm not as good of a shot as I wish.

The bowstring kisses my lips with the dry unsoft farewell of an angry lover.

But Grandmaster Vitruvius twitches at some sound or sight or holy intuition, and he snatches the bracelet—my target—aside. My arrow streaks through empty air to thud into a building far behind him.

Blue light blossoms everywhere around him, but he doesn't dart away.

What's wrong with him? What is he doing?

And now the blue light dissipates from around him, and his tensed muscles relax. He shifts out of his instinctive fighting stance.

Slowly, he turns to face me fully. He moves the bracelet so that its empty circle rests over his heart. Daring me to shoot, to claim the bracelet I desire at the cost of his life.

I've already nocked the second arrow, already drawn it back.

The grandmaster stares at where he knows I must be, though I feel sure he can't see me. The last rays of the setting sun climb the wall and abandon him to the shadows.

Even with Talent, with this bow's draw weight, I can't hold it fully drawn forever.

I Viewed him. I know he has none of the darkness that demands death. He's an innocent. I'm the Night Angel. I can't kill him for the bracelet, no matter what the stakes.

I've got that much right, don't I?

~The Night Angel doesn't willfully kill innocents. There's a lot of gray area, but that doesn't mean there's no black and white.~

Disgusted at myself—though whether at my failure to kill an innocent or how near I came to trying, I don't know—I relax my draw.

In the center of the city behind him, I see the great floating plinth that is Sho'fasti lower slowly back down to its foundations. With a grating rumble like a brief, distant earthquake, it settles into its base. The whole blue spire flares once with royal blue fire and then goes dark.

I stand up, the blue light briefly licking my skin.

I don't know why I do this, why I let him see me.

"So you do have a code," Vitruvius shouts across to me. "And you're living by it, though it vexes you. Tell me, Kylar, isn't making sacrifices to live by one's code a sure sign of integrity? Yet you claim to have none. You are more than your greatest strength, young man, though you've refused to see it. Let me tell you this, if I have any claim to wisdom: You think you're already broken. I think you're not yet hanging from the precipice from which you will fall. But I think that you have a long way to fall indeed, and you're on the path to it. Your code creates an inescapable tension with your work. So what will it be? What will finally destroy you, Dark One? Breaking your code? Or keeping it?"

In the shadowy tower behind him, mundane yellow lights perforate the night chink by chink as windows illuminate, curiosity pickaxes piercing the darkness one strike at a time, as the sages and scholars within settle down to work deep into the night.

Chapter Thirty-One
An Imperfect Heist

How many more things could I possibly be doing wrong right now?

~One? Two? No more than three, surely. Are we trying for a new record?~

Do you know, I'm lucky to have you, ka'kari. You're a loyal, dear, and true friend. I can't imagine how lost I would be without your assistance.

Hey! That isn't remotely what I just said! Are you changing *things I say?*

~Oops! Changing things? No, no. I must've misheard you.~

I haven't scouted the inn or even the neighborhood. I don't know if Lord Philanthes is here, how many guards and servants he has attending him, or if his lover Yulina has arrived yet. I don't know what room they'll be in, or if they're planning to stay overnight, or if they'll simply meet outside, pack up, and go.

What I don't know dwarfs what I do. It's daytime. There are people everywhere. I have no safe houses nearby. Only a floppy hat and a battered cloak as a disguise. If things go poorly, my option for escape is to...ride until I lose my pursuers, I guess. I'm not being impulsive; I'm merely making all the mistakes an impulsive idiot would make.

~Could be worse. You could be marching into the Chantry and making demands of the most powerful women alive!~

I know it was stupid, all right? You don't have to rub it in. Vi told me once that she would protect me from her new sisters, but I know that's a hopeless task. I didn't only frighten the magae; I didn't merely offend them; I didn't solely humiliate them; I did something worse.

I *intrigued* them.

And now I have a thought that feels like a lead ball dropping into the pit of my stomach. Momma K told me I would be in a race against the Chantry to acquire the Nemesis Compass. That was bad. I have no desire to cross the Sisters again. But I hadn't deeply considered the consequences of failure. I need that compass to find Logan's kids. If I don't get it, I won't be able to find them.

But what if the Chantry gets the compass instead? How will they use it? To find the twins? Maybe. But that's not the only thing they'd use it for, is it?

At some point, sooner or later, the Chantry will use it to find *me*. Not merely to find me. To hunt me.

No matter my disguise, I will never be able to hide from them, not anywhere in the world. And they will come after me. How could they not? If they even have a suspicion that I hold the black ka'kari, then they'll believe that what I hold is so powerful, it's their moral duty to take it away from me.

Running away from a group of thousands or tens of thousands of magic-using women spread all over the world is not something I'd relish. But my master taught me a few tricks that should make me pretty good at hiding.

Against the Nemesis Compass, those tricks will be useless.

And the Chantry never forgets. It's got institutional memory, and institutional grudges.

The Society of the Second Dawn is a group of hobbyists pursuing immortality, which means pursuing becoming like *me*—sometimes by helping me and hoping to learn by observing me, and other times by challenging me and daring more aggressive responses. But the Chantry? They're professionals. Long-lived personally and immortal institutionally, if they decide to pursue a person, it's only a matter of time until they catch them—and together, they have all the time in the world. With the compass...

At best, Vi might fend them off from coming after me for a decade, but not a century. Not forever. That is, if she's still alive. *Dammit, are you all right, Vi?* My throat tightens.

So there's nothing for it. Phaena told me that I absolutely must get the bracelet before Lord Philanthes leaves town.

Why not steal it on the trail?

I asked that.

The answer is because Lord Philanthes will be leaving on one of the new, experimental flying carriages.

That was the first time I'd heard the term, too. Don't get excited. They don't truly fly. They don't even float. The Sa'fasti are experimenting with magics to make loads lighter, and they've attached those magics to a carriage and to harnesses to lighten the carriage horses' very bodies.

According to Phaena, the roads they use have to be specially maintained; the magics have to be refreshed by magi twice a day at purpose-built stations on the way; and the horses have to be extensively trained for their unnatural task—all of which makes such travel very limited and very expensive, but also very, very fast.

In short, there's no way we'd be able to keep up with such a carriage, much less overtake it.

I walk to the stable of the inn on the edge of Roshlington, glancing at roofs, at passing traffic. No bodyguards. I pause by the open door, next to an unhitched wagon.

There's a kid inside brushing a beautiful stallion. He's enrapt by the animal. It's surely the nicest horse he's ever stabled.

I think that means my man is here.

There are no saddlebags on the horse. Too bad. I couldn't be lucky enough that Philanthes would simply leave the bracelet where I could snatch it, could I?

~Like off a mage's desk?~

While you're at it, kick me in the other nut, why don't you?

I lean my head against the wall of the stable. Plan: Go inside, sneak past the mage, rifle through his belongings, avoid any traps, steal the bracelet. It might even be easy.

It's now or never. Ready or not.

I'm not. But here I go.

I take a deep breath and start gathering the ka'kari.

Something light slams into my back.

I leap to the side by pure instinct, roll under the wagon, and embrace the shadows. I search the street but see nothing, no one moving in suspicious ways, no one looking my way. I touch my back, draw out my hand.

No blood.

Only then do my eyes fall on the arrow lying nearby. Practice arrow, blunt tip. It has a bit of parchment bound tight around its shaft.

I hesitate momentarily. Grabbing the arrow means going back out into the line of fire.

But whoever shot me decided to hit me with a blunt practice arrow, rather than a bodkin arrow or a broadhead. They're not looking to kill me.

I snatch the arrow and sit back in the lee of the wagon to read the note in safety.

In block letters, either like someone concealing their handwriting or an ignoramus who barely knows their letters, it reads:

Bracelet gone. Repha'im's men on way to kill Phaena.

It sends a chill through me.

Sure, it's *garbage*. A friend doesn't give you this kind of information by shooting you in the back with it. Besides, I don't have any friends here.

But whoever did this knows Lord Repha'im.

And they know I'm seeking the bracelet.

And they know Phaena.

What friend would know all that? Durzo? My heart leaps. But no. Durzo would do something more painful, and he'd tell me how shoddily I had done something or other. And at this point, why wouldn't he just show himself?

Who else would help me? I don't have any friends left.

So what friend of Logan's would do this? Someone keeping themselves secret, obviously.

Maybe I've stepped into something the Society of the Second Dawn is doing? Who else knows I'm here? Maybe they're trying to steal the bracelet at this very moment, too, and this is their attempt at delaying me so they can get to the bracelet first. I could be screwing up their operation here.

Who else would want to stop me, but not hurt me?

Nothing is as important as getting the bracelet.

But what if the part about Phaena is true?

So what if it is? What's Phaena to me? Not a friend. Not really. A person I'm friendly with, maybe. But friendship? In this business? Friendship in the shadows always means turning your back toward a backstabber and hoping for the best. We're not friends.

~You sound like a real hardass, Kylar.~

Go on, say the rest. I know there's more. There's no way you're going to end any statement to me with a compliment.

~That you think being called a real hardass is a compliment shows how young and callow you are.~

See? Knew it.

~So if you're such a hardass, Kylar...why are you already running to save her?~

Well, since it's obviously not plain human decency, there's only one pos-sible reason left.

~Pray tell.~

Seeing how I'm so young and callow? Breasts. The answer is breasts. Phaena has them.

Oh, and she also has our orders. She alone knows where we're supposed to head to next; she knows who's there to help us and how to contact them.

In fact, I'm kind of completely lost without her. That'd be a good reason to save her—but I'm sticking with breasts.

"What is it with men and breasts?" Vi said aloud.

Across the room, Sister Ariel looked up curiously. "Actually—"

"I don't—I don't think you're the right person to answer that," Vi said. "No offense."

Sister Ariel didn't seem offended at all. "Do you know that when I was about your age, a young visiting scholar once wrote an encomial sonnet to my left breast?"

"To your—What?"

"It struck me the same way. I had no response at all. The next week, he wrote another to my right." Her eyes flicked up toward the ceiling, and then Vi's worst fears were realized as Sister Ariel began reciting it from memory: "The rose-bud hue of thy tender nipple / Doth call me to come forth and nibble—"

Vi made a strangled sound, and Sister Ariel stopped.

"I know. It's offensive, isn't it? The scansion is so wrong! He asked me if I would meet him to give him my thoughts on it, so, naturally, I corrected the metrical errors and slant rhymes, clarified the progression of his imag-ery around the eight/six turn, and made a note that my nipples are more of a dusky than a rosebud hue and returned the poem to him. Oddly, he was quite offended! 'If you're going to be like that, why would you come meet me here anyway?' he demanded. And I said, 'Well, I don't know why we're meeting in a hayloft in the first place. If this is where you come to write poetry, it's no wonder you're such a poetaster.' But I was young and awkward then."

"Then?" Vi said. She hadn't meant it to say it aloud.

"I've matured and learned a lot in my years. So there's hope for you yet!" Sister Ariel said with a kindly smile. "Oh, did you want the results of the research I tracked down on why males fixate on mammaries? I discovered three competing theories."

"You know," Vi said, "I'm...really behind on this reading. Maybe later."

Sister Ariel was looking into the air. She said wistfully, " 'Only you can slake my thirst, / My innards swell, I'm fit to burst.' I mean, come now. How can one be thirsty—a condition of emptiness—and simultaneously full to bursting? That boy...clueless. Kinda cute, though."

Chapter Thirty-Two

First Job, Last Job

ᴲour horses. There are four horses I don't recognize outside the inn Phaena and I are staying at, saddled and warm, with the stable boy holding their reins. He says he's been paid to hold the horses. They don't expect to be long. This late in the day? Then again, maybe that's not suspicious. When the heat of the day gets oppressive here, many people nap at midday and extend their usual business into the night, so maybe I'm overreacting, reading things wrong like I did with the teens outside town. Maybe it's some friends meeting for a quick drink.

The kid passes all their traces to one hand and reaches out to take mine, but I don't dismount.

"Four riders or three?" I ask, pointing at the horses. I toss a coin to him.

He juggles the coin in his free hand until he catches it. "Four," he says. "Why?"

Then if I'm not overreacting, they're here to murder Phaena, not kidnap her. I pull my horse around into the alley and pull it roughly to a stop under our window. I stand up on the saddle, then leap lightly onto the roof outside our secret-exit window.

From inside, I hear a doorframe splinter. Through the window, I see a couple of armed men rush in.

"They're gone!" one announces.

"Search everything!" an older man in the hallway orders. "Remember what he said about the secrets here. We got outside. And, kid!"

Secrets? What secrets do they know? Most of the four-paned window is smoked, but there's a clear section at the bottom of one pane to let returning guests like me check that the room is clear. I can see the kid in his mid-teens and the older man in the hall—but not the man deeper in the room.

"What...sir?" the kid is saying, frustrated.

"You don't let 'em talk. 'Specially not her. Pretty girl, all soft and helpless lookin'. You cut her down the moment you get the chance, you understand? Him too. They got magic. They'll burn us all from the inside out without a second thought, you got it?"

"*Dad...*" the kid says, as if his father's embarrassing him. "I got it."

"First job's never easy, and this is a hell of one. But I know you can do it."

"Dad. I got it!"

The men at the door disappear. A moment later, I hear a click. These guys know at least the first part of how to open the secret exit. Whether sold or stolen or broken, the Society's secrets have been compromised.

I glance around, judging. The lamplighters are at their work in the busier intersections and markets staving off the oncoming night, but it's not yet dark even where their lights don't reach. I'm only about ten steps into the alleyway, and it's a busy street. Lots of eyes, though few glance this way.

Things are about to get noisy. And bloody, I'd guess. Consider yourself warned.

Farther into the room, I see that the other man has switched his short sword to his left hand and is running his fingers along mantels, searching.

I wrap only a single arm in the black skin of the ka'kari.

The kid's face looms in the window, scowling. He leans close.

I punch my fist through the bottom windowpane, snag his lapel, and yank him forward, using his face to break the rest of the upper windowpanes. One pull, two, three. Smash, smash, smash. Top, left side, right side. I smash out almost the whole window in less time than it takes him to blow blood out his demolished nose in surprise. The whole window—except for the saw-toothed shards stuck in the bottom frame.

Then I release his lapel, grab his hair, and pound his neck down on those jagged shards.

Heaving myself up, I roll up and over his back to land in the room as I draw a long dagger—ducking low barely in time to avoid an awkward left-handed slash from the other man.

He pauses to shift his short sword to his right hand and jumps back as I slash at him.

"Ha!" he says, as we both take fighting stances despite the confines of the room. "You're not so fast!" His position is something like a Full Iron Gate that seems ill-adapted to a short sword. I take a perilously low Boar's Tusk, trying to invite an overhead slash.

But he doesn't switch to a High Guard, seems stuck in his favorite.

I scoot back, and though it takes my guard off its line, I wave my blade toward his belly.

He didn't raise his voice much, but I listen for the others.

I gesture again. *Go on, look.*

Tell you what, not one person in fifty will try to talk while in a fight to the death. But there's always that one guy.

At first he refuses to look down. Then he blinks. Maybe he feels the wetness, the something-is-wrong-ness you get when you realize you're wounded. When he looks and sees the red line from kidney to kidney, he gasps. The motion tightens his stomach muscles.

I'm not going to describe how his guts squirted out, because even though it was cut and sticky with blood, his tunic somehow contained all his intestines as they spilled out of his body. Still, it was like watching a homeless man drop his trousers and defecate into a sack while still covered by his tunic—even if his body is covered, you know what's happening: You can see the bag bulge and squirm, and you can certainly *smell* it. I don't recommend it.

From the look on his suddenly pasty face, I'd guess the sellsword wouldn't recommend it either. He drops his blade.

"Who are you and who are you serving?" I ask him.

He's a talker. It's worth a try.

But I see sudden defiance in his eyes. He's about to spit on me, not answer.

I ram my blade up under his chin, twist, and rip it out.

His body falls with a wet burble, air escaping from—well, never mind, you don't need to hear all that. I've done this enough that I've already stepped far enough away not to get splattered, but before I tuck my weapon away, I see that my twisting it inside the man's braincase has snapped the blade.

I toss it aside. This is why I carry too many knives: There's no such thing as too many knives.

Pulling the shadows about me, I hop back out the window, stepping on the kid's back—not trying to be disrespectful: It's the only safe place to step. He doesn't move.

I see the kid's father mounting up, with the other man from inside on his heels. But then I hear the pounding of hooves as another four men join them.

Great. Two men? Generally not a huge problem for me. Six men? All mounted?

"Someone inside thought she was going to a nearby market," the man from inside says. "Yonder, at the waterfront."

As I ghost closer, the commander says, "Tob, you wait for Tacks and Jaemun. Then you all follow quick as you can without raisin' a ruckus."

Then the five mounted men pound away, sending pedestrians scurrying.

My blade penetrates Tob's chest and he gives a little yelp. The stable boy looks over at him, but seeing nothing amiss, he quickly looks away. I brace Tob against the wall and leave him standing there to die.

The five men aren't able to ride fast with how crowded the streets are, but I still have to run at a full sprint to even start to close the gap. Probably should have ridden as well. Too late for that now.

A block ahead of me, one of the riders lags behind the others. They turn down a street. I turn a block before they did, racing parallel to catch up, then dodging through an open bazaar, this one flowing fabrics—doubtless where Phaena picked up her samples yesterday.

There's an art to moving quickly through crowded streets, and it's one I've practiced a lot. It must be a market day—or market night, given the hour—because the streets are packed. That's good and bad. On the one hand, there are a lot of eyes to see any disturbance or anything out of the ordinary. On the other, the light is bad: Deep shadows alternate with dim flickering torchlight and fulsome lantern light around the shops, throwing dancing shadows every which way. There are plenty of ways your eyes can play tricks on you in such a setting, so plenty of ways people can dismiss any oddities. Plus, with the crowd, anyone on foot can only see so far ahead, especially with wagons in the mix and if everyone is being noisy—as they are tonight—people can miss what's happening a mere dozen paces away. Angry rebuffs and sharp words are the expected music of the streets, and anything below someone screaming bloody murder fades into the background.

Generally, chasing someone who's rudely pushing through a crowd is far less conspicuous than pushing through it yourself. But there's no way to be subtle with how much ground I need to make up.

Dodging and turning, alternately sprinting a few steps and then jostling my way through tiny gaps in the crowd, soon I have to leap over tables, slide under mules, and bowl over a smith three times my size carrying bars of pig iron across his shoulders that go ringing across the cobblestones and into the legs of other pedestrians, who shout with pain and alarm, but I disappear into the crowd before he can even start cursing me. As I pass under the eaves of a shop, I leap into the air and grab the sign, pulling myself up to be able to see over the crowd.

They're not too far ahead. I should be able to intercept the riders right where a butcher's fully loaded open wagon is blocking half the traffic, slowing everyone as the driver and another man shout at each other.

I reach the wagon as the last rider finally clears the bottleneck and goes around it. A father picks up his daughter and puts her on his shoulders to keep her from getting crushed in the press of the crowd. That gives me all the room I need.

As the ka'kari whooshes over my skin and I go invisible, I leap, one foot pushing off the wagon wheel, barely touching the stacked sides of beef and then the rail of the wagon bed. Then I cartwheel to fly just behind the last rider. In the air, I grab for my dagger—

Empty sheath.

I grab the next, pull it out—too slow!—slash!

It's late. The blade's ripped out of my bad grip. Wrist twisted, body thrown off-balance. I hit the ground with my feet sideways, barely missing a woman carrying a basket on her head. I don't fight the fall but roll instead.

A passing wagon wheel almost rolls over my head. I start to stand, bang my head on the underside of the wagon, then duck and let it pass, rolling to dodge the low metal hitch at the back of the undercarriage.

When I stand, I see my deader still riding, but limply now. My blade is stuck in his neck, halfway through, caught in his spine. I can't tell if he's only stunned or paralyzed, but he's definitely on the one-way trip.

Strangely, in a crowd of so many, no one's noticed yet. But it's only a matter of time.

The other riders, still slowed by the press of the crowds here, die quickly. One a stab to the kidney, then a slash to the artery on the inner thigh, sending a quiet river of blood into his pants and the saddle, unseen.

I grab the spear from his saddle. Dip it through the back of the next rider, slash across the neck, then poke through the back of the neck and up into the skull of the rider in front of him—and finally the first cries ring out, for only now has anyone seen the men going down in sprays of blood to an invisible opponent.

The commander wheels around, alarmed. His stopping allows me to catch up. Invisible still, I dodge under his horse's belly even as he's bellowing questions to his dying men. As the cinch strap parts for my blade, I slap the horse's flank and grab on to the commander's tunic.

In an instant, the horse jumps forward in surprise—but without saddle or rider—and heaving on his tunic, I slam the commander onto the cobblestones, head first. His skull cracks with a crunch.

His body starts twitching in little seizures, fingers dancing, but his eyes stay wide, scared, searching but maybe blind.

"My boy! My boy!" he wheezes.

"At the inn," I tell him. I don't know why. I didn't mean to break his skull, but now that I have, the only thing for a professional to do is to dispatch him cleanly. I'm not going to interrogate him in the street.

"So my boy, he's—he's alive?" the dying commander asks, desperate.

"No," I say. "You got him killed."

"His mother. She'll never forgive me. Ines, Jaemun, I'm so sorry!"

"You were right about one thing," I say.

"Huh?"

A hammerblow stab through the cup of the collarbone, into his heart. A hard twist, and pull out. "When you gotta kill someone, gains you nothin' to let 'em talk first."

I slip through the crowd that comes collapsing down on the suddenly, mysteriously dead man in the street. The air fills with wild tales, and someone starts shouting for the bazaar guards.

I find Phaena several blocks away, oblivious to the near-riot that I've kicked off by killing so many people invisibly. She holds bags full of fresh bread and produce and a smile on her face.

The smile proves fragile.

She's shaken but recovers quickly when I tell her I still have work to do. We think there's no more imminent threat to her, but that she shouldn't go back to the inn. She knows of another one that should be safe, and though she's briefly fearful about me leaving her, she rallies. "Go," she says. "I'll be fine."

Funny thought occurs to me as I travel once more to the inn in Roshlington where Philanthes Magnarius was meeting his lover. The Night Angel protects the innocent, right? How about that young man, Jaemun? He was attempting to murder Phaena and me. I didn't View him to know, but for the sake of argument, what if he'd never killed anyone yet? His father did say it was his first job. What if he'd never even hurt anyone? Was Jaemun an innocent too?

Maybe I protected his innocence. It merely happened to cost him his life.

I don't feel bad about it. Maybe that says something about the state of my conscience. Or maybe this one was a shade of gray—but it wasn't *that* gray.

Despite the late hour, when I reach Philanthes's inn, I find a scene as chaotic as the one I left. A woman I identify as the owner of the inn is arguing with Philanthes's head valet or some kind of important servant.

A noblewoman is screaming in the main room. It's Lord Philanthes's wife, Lady Magnarius. She's demanding to be allowed upstairs. A defeated-looking innkeeper is holding her back. Philanthes's wife loudly communicates her displeasure at being touched. Phaena's intel said the woman was sickly. She doesn't seem sickly to me. But then, intel's like that, isn't it? I could imagine someone describing Jenine Gyre as sickly, and they wouldn't be wrong exactly, but you'd take it to mean all the wrong things.

Invisible, I ghost past them. The door of the largest room upstairs is open, with the innkeeper's key still in the lock. Inside the room, Philanthes and his lover are entwined in bed together, awkwardly naked and more awkwardly dead. They're pinned to each other and to the bed with Philanthes's own ornate longsword. One thrust, two hearts.

~On the contrary, I'd say there were at least two thrusts.~

Huh? I check Philanthes's back to see what I've missed, but I don't see any other wounds.

~Never mind.~

Whoever did this acted with the brutal efficiency of a professional. Either the killer stole the key and opened the lock with it himself, entering unheard while Philanthes and Yulina were distracted, or they got in and out some other way, and left the door locked when they left.

It's too much to hope that whoever killed Philanthes left the bracelet, but first things first. You never know. I go through Philanthes's and Yulina's things quickly and carefully. No luck. Then I turn back to the bodies to see what they can tell me about who got here first and stole the bracelet I need.

I hop up on the bed, planting one foot on either side of the pinned lovers, and try to judge the angle of the murderer's stab. But I can't tell what I'd hoped. I'd thought I might be able to guess if the killer was taller or shorter than I am, but the strike wasn't meant to be the most convenient for the killer; it was meant to get both victims through the heart. Maybe even...

I check their faces. Philanthes has no blood flecking his lips; Yulina does. The killer not only got them both through the heart, he or she seems to have done it in between breaths.

It's too early for postmortem bruising to be easily visible, so now I'm only guessing, but it makes sense to me that the murderer stabbed them and then crushed them. Caught breathless, Philanthes couldn't scream. Yulina was crushed by her lover on top of her and by the murderer too, so whatever breath she got out was muffled—and could easily be mistaken for other sounds.

It's one of the more difficult ways to kill both of them at once, but it is *clean.*

Withdrawing the blade would've had them bleed out more quickly but also would've meant a lot more blood. In a second story in this not-well-maintained inn, that risked blood dripping into the tavern hall directly below this room. But to hold them pinned, breathless, impaled until they lost consciousness—which can be a five or even fifteen count—meant that the killer either was supremely confident of holding them still and unable to draw even a single breath, or maybe had some way to silence them magically.

For that matter, Philanthes himself might have magically silenced the room for his lovemaking.

Regardless, drawing Philanthes's own sword from its scabbard, hopping on the bed, and landing the death stroke at the precise moment, at the perfect angle? It's impressive wet work. I can't help but admire it.

And then, Yulina's wide, staring eyes and blood-rimmed mouth shift before my eyes from a puzzle to be solved to the tragedy, the crime, that any normal man would see first. This woman was murdered for nothing more than that she fell for the charms of the wrong man. It needn't have even been her. Philanthes had asked three other women first. And, whatever his faults, Philanthes was murdered for nothing more than a magical bauble.

For it's too much of a coincidence to think this has nothing to do with the bracelet, isn't it?

Could the wetboy—for it must have been a wetboy to be this good—not have simply stolen the bracelet instead? It's what I was trying to do.

Durzo could've done this, of course. But I think he would've done something subtler. Poisoned the man to make him sick for long enough that he stayed home, and swapped a counterfeit bracelet. This is as effective, but more brutal than his usual mode. And the woman? He never liked killing anyone unnecessarily.

He did it if he had to, it's true.

So who warned me off with that blunt arrow? Was that the killer? Or some other party, as they claimed?

I'll find no more answers here, though. As I'm figuring out my own exit, Philanthes's wife—I never did catch her name—breaks through the innkeeper.

Lady Magnarius storms into the room, giving me space to slip out behind her. She must've been told who was there and that they were dead, for she shows no surprise.

Which is not to say she takes any of it calmly.

Shrieking obscenities, she tears the sword out of the dead lovers' flesh and heaves her husband off the woman he'd mounted. It's even more graphic than you'd guess. Blood settles to the lowest points in dead bodies and with how these two were entwined—well, I won't describe any more.

Ah, two thrusts. *I get it,* I think at the ka'kari.

The black humor would've struck me as funnier if I weren't watching Lady Magnarius doing this now.

In a rage, Lady Magnarius pulls the naked, bloodied, limp woman out of the bed and begins kicking and stomping on her dead body, cursing her, blaming her for Lord Philanthes's infidelity and his death.

I think I've said before that in the bitter business, I see people on the worst day of their lives, and that means I often see them at their worst.

Exciting, huh? Enjoying yourself? Is this the kind of thing you were hoping to hear?

Violence. It's fun, huh? Add some sex and it's all so marvelously titillating, isn't it?

I find Phaena where she told me to meet. The hopeful expression on her face dies as she sees the haggard look on my face. I give her the update and as I close, I say, "So, now that we've failed to do the only thing we came to this city to do, what now? Any other leads?"

I think about going back to Grandmaster Vitruvius and trying again. With him knowing I want what he has, it'd be a suicide mission.

"No," she says, her face a stricken mirror of my own. "If there were other Sa'fasti invited, they've already left. Or at least, I haven't heard about them. I guess...I guess we improvise."

"Improvise?" I say. I feel so, so exhausted.

"We go where we were always planning to go. Stormfast."

"Stormfast?" I say. Tover is at the northernmost part of the Gray Sea. Stormfast is so far south, it's beyond the Gray Sea entirely, east of the Dragon's Teeth on Alitaera's southern coast, opposite the Summer Isles. "That's a long ride. And...Tover is not exactly on the way there from Elenea. I'm so glad we took this little detour."

"Oddly enough," she says. "Coming here *is* the fastest way there."

"Huh?"

"We'll be attending the Alitaeran Summer Court's departure party at Castle Stormfast." She clears her throat and smiles gamely. "That is, if we can figure out how to get in. That's what the bracelets are for."

"The—the imperial departure? As in, when they leave for Borami? Isn't that soon? I mean like, isn't that really, really soon?"

"The parties are actually a week-long series of parties. And those are... going on already. But the only one that matters is the final night."

"And that's when?"

"It's past midnight now, so I guess...four days?"

I rub my brow. "Never mind that we don't have the bracelet that is apparently our key to get into the most exclusive party in the entire Alitaeran empire, attended by the empress herself and protected by some of the most competent fighters and mages in the world. Never mind that we don't even have a plan to get one. Let's put all that aside. If we walked outside and found the two fastest horses in Tover and rode day and night, there's still no way we could even make it to Stormfast in four days. It's impossible."

"Not impossible. Just very, very expensive." She gives a joyless smile as she pulls something out from the neckline of her dress. "Or it would be, if I hadn't managed to come into possession of these." She holds up two gold-embossed vouchers.

"And what the hell are those?"

Chapter Thirty-Three

The Flying Carriage

The ground is rolling past the flying carriage at such speed it's nauseating. The horses have been pulling us for hours at the kind of rate that before today I've only seen horses gallop for short distances. I've never liked riding, and I like carriages even less, but this is something else entirely.

We stop every two hours to change horses, for the magi to refresh the magic, and to check that the ultralight carriage isn't falling apart. I'm not exaggerating that last part. They tell us explicitly that this is what they're doing, which doesn't make me feel better. After eight hours, our exhausted magi swap out with others. We pass numerous crews working to smooth the road as we go. Despite their work, every time we hit any little bump, it feels as if we go airborne, and when we do, I'm never sure that when we land it will be on the road.

Whatever else this is, it's got to be a massively expensive experiment for the blue mages. Despite how expensive our tickets would normally be—Phaena told me the sum—they can't begin to cover the costs of what I see.

Making the whole thing worse, Phaena seems to be having the time of her life.

The cabin of the wagon must have been made by some nebbishy first-year blue mage, because in addition to being so cramped that I'm thankful for the first time in years for my slight build, the seats have been designed with little reference to the geometry of the human body, all sharp angles and clean lines that look nice and feel terrible. Worse, it's airtight. This makes things quieter, which initially seems great, but eventually the cabin becomes as swelteringly hot and damp as a swamp. The windows are tiny and don't open, and the doors won't open a mere crack: They're either fully open and we freeze, or they're fully closed and we're sweating puddles.

Whatever the blues hope, I do not see this as the transportation of the future.

Phaena, on the other hand, cheerfully bundles up or strips down, as required. The latter is awkward, for one of us at least. With one cramped seat on each side, we sit facing each other, so close our knees touch. She's wearing practical woolen traveling clothes: a maroon rain cloak, light blue tunic, fawnskin breeches. Or she was wearing those, until the heat got utterly stifling. Now, her rain cloak and tunic are wadded up for a makeshift pillow, her undershift is turning translucent from sweat, and without layers over it, her tight breeches reveal a figure that's hard not to appreciate.

I've made my decision about her. The Night Angel doesn't get certain things in life. I try not to even look at her. Mostly, I'm successful, I think. I'm probably imagining it, but part of me thinks she almost sees this as a challenge. She closes her eyes and yawns and stretches, putting her arms back and her chest forward.

I'm probably wrong. We're cramped in here. She's stretching. Simple as that. Not everything a woman does is about me.

Anyway, if Phaena is flirting with me, even just to pass the time, it means she feels safe. She feels safe with me, despite knowing some of what I am.

Then again, extreme situations can make for poor decision making.

And really, she's probably not flirting. I'm flattering myself. And even if she is, it doesn't matter.

But as much as I'm trying not to think about any of it, some part of me that I'd thought dead is stirring. Like fingers frostbitten brought near a fire, I suddenly ache. I'm not fit company for anyone. I've got nothing to offer a woman.

The golden hazy-warm fantasy of sitting together over a meal with a beautiful woman, her head thrown back in laughter, her hand on my leg, her hair cascading past her shoulders in glorious red waves, a smile on full lips, eyes bright, leaning in close—

That's not for me. I take a shuddering breath. Stare at my hands.

Vi stopped reading, confused. Elene's hair had been blonde. Phaena had very dark hair. Which meant that the redhead Kylar was fantasizing about—even as this older, more experienced beauty was throwing herself at him—was . . . *her*?

It shouldn't have made her feel better. She had no reason to be jealous of Phaena. And no right to it, either! She had no claim on Kylar, certainly not to how he felt back then.

He hadn't even noticed it himself. It seemed to pass right by him. From another man, it might have been a put-on, but this was Kylar. He could be clever, but not with women.

It was as if even here, before everything else that had happened later, she'd somehow slipped through his defenses. The thought settled in her stomach like a stone.

That's not for me. I take a shuddering breath. Stare at my hands.

I get the joys of magic. Of mastery of physical arts. Of mastery over others, of violence. I don't get the simple domestic joys. That's not the path I chose. It's too late for that, too late for me. I had that life, once upon a time, for all too brief a time. I had a season of undeserved grace, of happiness.

I lost her.

Phaena wakes from dozing, or trying to, or pretending to, but at the look on my face, her sunny smile fades.

When I say nothing, after a time she says, "Can you explain this to me?"

"This?"

"Like, all this. The flying carriage. How does it work?"

"No idea. It's magic."

"I know, but you know all about magic, don't you? I thought..."

"It's kind of a big topic," I say. She leans forward, intrigued, and I become aware of her cleavage. Manfully, I don't glance. "What do you want to know?"

She purses her lips. "I guess...What can these mages do? Are they more like technicians making a fancy machine work, or are they archmagi who can do everything? Because I swear one of them looked at our tickets funny, and I'm wondering how vulnerable we are."

"Ah," I say. "Good questions. See, the trouble with magic—I mean, there are lots of troubles with magic, but...you'd think magic comes with a handbook. 'You're a blue mage. That means you can do this, and this thing over here, but not this and that, only red mages do that.' That'd be nice, right? In truth it's like...say, take a Death Games champion. Is a champion tall? Lots of times yes, because a long reach is helpful. Is he a fast runner? In a range, yes—usually between somewhat faster than average and ludicrously fast. Is he strong for his size? Always. Is he skilled with a spear? Almost always. How about a sword? Depends if that's his sidearm. Is he a good long-distance runner? Only sometimes.

"A mage is like that champion. Knowing he's a blue is like knowing which gladiatorial school a particular champion trained at. Certain schools always train certain skills, but once a gladiator is finished with one art, they might go train in a completely different art next. A blue mage may innately be better with fire; he simply didn't realize where his talents lay when he was young and went to attend the only place available to him.

"The trouble doesn't stop there. You have to consider that mages lie; and all the places that teach men magic have to compete with each other for students and for preeminence, and thus *they* lie, too. Mages who make advances in the arts of war or magic? That's right; they might exaggerate for prestige. You're sensing a pattern here?

"On the other hand, mages may make breakthroughs and keep them secret instead to protect them. They may pass them on to no one, not even their students and confidants, so as to maintain their own advantages and reputations.

"Then cultures and even followers of certain gods have their own restrictions, whether due to sacred texts or bad experiences. Like, how much is it acceptable to experiment on dead people? That's a cultural or religious question, not a magical one. So, there might be a mediocre blue mage out there with the potential to be the world's best Healer, but he'll never find that out because he or his culture isn't willing to 'desecrate the dead' to learn about living bodies. Or whatever.

"It's a mess. That doesn't mean there aren't things that are always true about magic. There are underlying verities; you just can't trust that the person in front of you knows what those are. Even if they do, you can't trust that anyone who says they're telling them to you really is."

"Except you?" she says with a little smile, teasing.

"Come on. Don't be like that. Yeah. *I'm* being honest."

~Do you think 'I'm being honest' has been said more times by people who are telling the truth or people who are lying?~

"I'm trying to, anyway," I mumble. In the confines of the closed cabin, I can smell her fresh sweat and a simple perfume of tangy bergamot, the softness of iris, and the warmth of vanilla, lightly applied. I resolutely don't think about any other situation in which I might be speaking in soft confidential tones while pressed close to a sweating woman, smelling her body and her perfume.

"I believe you," she says. "But . . . was all that to say you don't know how this carriage works?"

"I hadn't thought of it that way, but yes. You got me."

"Huh. Maybe mages aren't the only ones with egos," she says, her eyes dancing.

"Ego as inflated as an aneroid," I admit.

"An aneroid? What's that?" she asks. It was some kind of weather box Logan showed me once with a bladder. Or the bladder part. Or something.

"See? All this and smart too." I realize what I'm doing, though, and hurry on. "Thing that matters more than how the magic works is your other question. How much are they suspicious about us? I'll spend time with them tonight and see if I can detect any hostility."

"And what are you going to do about it if they do?"

"There are things I can do, if I have to." I purse my lips.

"None of them good?" she says.

"None of them good, not for them, and not for us."

Then Phaena looks down and flinches.

"What's wrong?" I ask as she crosses her arms despite the heat.

"Could you...?" She motions for me to look away, so I do. She unwads some of her shed clothing and puts it back on, despite the heat. "I'm just—" she says.

"I'm not asking," I say, still looking out the window.

Which doesn't mean I'm not guessing. I can't help myself. I'm guessing she noticed that she had sweated through her undershift and was maybe suddenly realizing how translucent it was. But I wouldn't know that, because I wasn't looking.

I'm an oak.

She acts oddly later, not piling out of the carriage the moment it stops at our next station, but staying behind in the sweltering box for a while by herself. She emerges in fresh, dry clothes, with her dark wavy hair limp with sweat. As we've gotten away from the coast and slowly ascended, the land has shifted by degrees from jungle to high desert, and though it's not nearly so humid here, with the sun high in the sky, it's painfully hot. Phaena remaining in the carriage means that she cuts short one of her few chances to stretch her legs, and all too soon we have to fold ourselves back into the carriage.

We leave the doors open for this leg, and it's much more pleasant, though noisy. We dry off in the wind, and soon, despite the heat of the day, the speed of the wind actually makes us both unpleasantly cold.

As we rattle over another bump, I notice her wincing, putting a hand to her chest. "Doesn't help the bruises, huh?" I say, with an attempt at a smile.

"Huh?" she asks, over the wind.

"That guy. You said he bruised you? Are they feeling better?" I studiously don't glance at her chest and cringe. " '*They*' the bruises, not 'they' your—I mean, are *you* feeling better?"

Idiot! Why'd I bring that up?

"Ah, right. Yeah. Yes, they are. The bruises, that is. Not as fast as I'd like, but I'm getting better."

She gets quiet, pensive.

My further attempts at conversation fall graceless to the floor. Her answers are polite, but brief. I can't tell if her huddled body language is all because of the wind.

Just had to bring up one of the worst nights of her life, didn't I? *Good, light topic, Kylar. Well done!*

Our way station for the night is a little three-room house next to a large stable. Phaena begs some privacy and hurries to the room we'll share. I stack up our few bags outside the door, while the men who maintain the way station mock me good-naturedly for being barred from our room. They think we're a couple, and as our tickets indicated we needed only the one room, they think me being locked out must show I've made Phaena angry in some lovers' spat.

As I don't want to invite further scrutiny, I take their gibes ruefully.

I don't notice any of the veiled hostility or forced amiability among the men that I would expect if they were preparing to attack us. So I ask if I can help prepare dinner, and they soon let the teasing drop. They're nice enough, but I take care not to leave much of an impression on them.

Once dinner is ready, I take Phaena's and my portion back to the room and report my feeling that we're reasonably safe.

We chat about inconsequential things for a time—like, literally the weather and what good time we're making, but I can tell something's bothering her.

Finally, as I'm about to turn in for the night, she says, "Hey."

I look over.

She smiles wanly but then looks away, staring unseeing into the darkness outside our window. "I just wanted to say thank you. For...saving my life. I know I hurt that man bad, but I...He would've killed me before he...before he died, huh?"

Yes.

But I don't say it aloud. Does she want to hear that she wasn't as close to dying as she really was? Some people are really shaken up by their first kill. What's Phaena looking for? Does she want to hear that she didn't kill him, so it's not on her conscience? Or does she want to hear that she definitely did, so she can believe she's strong enough that she doesn't have to be afraid?

"You did great," I say. "You kept your head, and that kept you alive long enough for help to arrive. Not that I'm going to thank you for that, you know. I mean, with a little more training, Momma K could've sent you without me. So it's kind of your fault I have to come do this thing at all."

I give her a lopsided grin, but she doesn't even look at me.

"I feel gross," she says quietly.

I don't know if she means the violation or her seduction of the man or her killing him, but she's already going on.

"I just kept thinking about this thing my father told me once," she says. "He said that if a man threatens to hurt you unless you go somewhere with him, no matter what you do, don't go with him."

"*Don't* go with him?" I ask, not sure if I misheard.

"Because he's taking you from a place that's not safe for him to one that is. He wants to get you where no one can hear your screams, where no one can help. A man trying to put you entirely at his mercy is a man who has none."

Having seen what I've seen of the world, I can't help but agree. At the same time, it takes more insight and more guts than most people have to force a crisis right away rather than wait and hope for the best. It also takes a certain dim view of human nature: the realization that, say, the smiling, handsome man who seems merely pushy could actually be setting you up for torture, rape, murder.

People who grow up in nice neighborhoods don't want to believe they live in a world where that sort of thing's possible. People who grow up in slums know we do.

"If he trusted you with that sort of advice, it sounds like your father thought you were pretty tough."

"Or maybe I wasn't tough enough, and that's why he needed to tell me."

I goggle at her. I literally saw this woman stab her would-be rapist in a major artery. She must have known that even trying it meant she'd get beaten badly afterward, with only a slim chance of escaping death—yet she'd gone for it.

If I tell her she's not giving herself enough credit, I'm going to come across like I'm trying to flatter her, but it's true; the woman isn't giving herself enough credit.

So I say nothing. Phaena was nearly raped. Now she's isolated, sharing a room involuntarily with a man she knows is more dangerous than any bandit. Last thing she needs to worry about is my flattering her.

I give a disaffected grunt, and hope it voices some degree of disagreement.

She doesn't seem to even notice. She says, "You ever think that there are currents within you that even you yourself don't understand? Like, that night? I was thinking about what my father said, and what did I do anyway? I went inside with that bandit. I was scared, but, but I wasn't panicked. I felt like I was thinking clearly, but...but I went inside with him. I mean, I *suggested* it. Why would I do that? So other people wouldn't watch while he...while he did what I thought he was going to do...? Is that it? I wanted to be *comfortable* while he—" Her emotion is rising.

"Stop," I say sharply. "I figured it out."

"Huh?"

"That deep current in you. I can tell you why you were remembering your father's words. You'd think of it yourself if you took a minute. Swap the good guy for the bad guy in what your father said and you'll have it."

I remove my shoes, then sit down on top of the blanket on the bed we'll be sharing, and spread my cloak to serve as my own blanket.

"What?" she asks.

"There were three bandits outside," I say. "You couldn't fight three."

"So?" she says.

I lie down and turn my face away. "That bandit didn't take you to an isolated place where he could have his way with you, Phaena. *You* took *him*."

Chapter Thirty-Four

Nothing Easy

I wake to the best and the worst feelings in the world. A sleeping woman snuggled into me, my face in her hair, her breast in my hand, and the pleasant, eager warmth blossoming inside me at the realization that—given that we're under my cloak and hers, but on top of the blankets—*I* didn't move in the night to join her; she moved to join me. Which means the way her hips shift against me now may not be accidental.

The second feeling is the one that flashes through me as I hear a whisper again outside our door, a whisper with a hard edge. It's a sound I know well: the sound of men planning something more sinister than breakfast.

I roll over atop Phaena, and her eyes snap open, surprised at my boldness, but also receptive, hungry. She shifts her hips further open as I lean close to whisper in her ear.

"Up!" I whisper. "Get dressed. Fast. Quiet. Pack what you can. Stay out of view of the keyhole."

I can tell she doesn't understand yet, but I slip off the bed.

The ka'kari rushes over my skin, and as if on cue, at that familiar old sensation, my mind banishes every human concern, every embarrassment. A couple fingers of my left hand feel wet. Doesn't matter, I'm moving toward the room's one, high window.

It's small, not quite as wide across as my shoulders, and narrower. With one foot on a post of the bed, I cut the glass soundlessly with the ka'kari, pull it in through the empty frame, and toss it on the bed.

Phaena is gaping at me—or should I say at the Night Angel? I gesture sharply for her to get moving. To her credit, she does.

Then I go invisible and slip out the narrow hole.

I drop lightly to the ground outside the little house and peek around the corner. It's barely dawn, and two of the four mages at the outpost are standing in the road, soaking up sunlight for power.

"I'm almost ready," one of them whispers. "Maybe one more minute."

The other nods and mutters agreement. I know that mages can also soak up power from fire, but many prefer sunlight for reasons I don't fully understand. Different mages are also more or less efficient with converting sunlight to fill their glore vyrdens.

Suddenly, I don't know if I'm panicking over nothing. These men need to get magic ready to do their normal work on the carriage and the roads. There's nothing incriminating about this. Maybe they're whispering so they won't wake us. But I thought the whispering came from outside my door.

None of these are bad men. I know. I looked into their eyes last night.

If the blues had some way to tell that our tickets were stolen, I would've expected trouble when we embarked, not after they've taken us halfway to Stormfast.

Another mage, a young Modaini with an aquiline nose, emerges from the stable and says, loudly, "Hey, I got the first harness done. You all going to come help me charge the—?"

"Shh!" a lanky blond says. "I was just outside their door. They're still asleep. You mind not giving our advantage away?"

The young Modaini drops his hands to his sides in frustration. "Are we really doing this?"

"I concur with Hrothlan. I do not feel good about this course," the tallest man mutters. He's as dark-skinned as a Ladeshian, and though he has no accent at all, his speech flags him as a foreigner of some sort. "Though there is something strange about them, I do not believe this man to be a malefactor, nor the woman he accompanies."

The lanky blond looks at them all, furious, as if this was an argument they'd already settled. "I worked for Lord Philanthes for a year. This is *his* ticket. No marks of transfer on it. It's *stolen.*"

"They might've loused up the markers when they reassigned it," the Modaini says.

"And we'll ask them about that—after we've subdued them," the lanky blond says. "Did none of you notice how he looked at us last night? Have you ever seen anyone less impressed by four magi? That's not normal. I'm telling you that in addition to being either a thief or a murderer, this man is something else. Something dangerous. We take him down first, then we ask questions. If he's got good answers, great. We go on our way, no harm done. If not? Then I'll have kept us all alive. Again."

"You think he might have something to say about that?" the chubby one says, emerging from the house. Oddly, last night he struck me as the most dangerous of the group, though he seems to have the lowest status. "My mother had a saying: 'When the steel sings, no sword gets to choose the other's song. And no singer seeks the same finale to the duet.'"

"I am not familiar with this. What does it mean?" the dark-skinned mage asks.

"It means I'm done convincing you all," the lanky blond interrupts. "Hrothlan, you got what you need?"

"Enough for this, I guess," the young Modaini mutters.

"Good! We do this my way. Now!"

They head inside, and I follow them into the common room. Here's a truth you won't like any more than I do: Men reluctant to kill you but still willing to do so are still men who will kill you.

In these men's eyes, I saw outlines, intimations, shapes of deeds that I couldn't tease any meaning out of. Perhaps those were things these men have done that are wrong, but nothing as dark as murder, nothing obviously crying out for their blood.

The lanky blond who's trying to get them all killed? He's actually a pretty good person, though you couldn't tell it from how he's acting right now; he simply likes to be in control—he's only situationally a bastard.

This isn't a war, where sometimes you have to kill a good man because he's fighting under the wrong banner. These men are trying to apprehend us for something we're actually guilty of. We *did* steal Philanthes's tickets; we *are* dangerous; they *should* capture us first lest we do something about it.

I know how to kill these men. I've already got a plan and a backup and an escape plan. Granted, the odds of me being wounded? Against four mages? Pretty high. But they're heading into an enclosed area—the little hallway outside Phaena's and my room, lit by only a single lantern, and pretty tight for so many bodies. They don't know I'm behind them, and they have no idea what I can do, who I am.

But I don't want to kill them. I don't know if I *can* and still be the Night Angel. I haven't murdered an innocent since before I bonded the black ka'kari.

I'm beginning to formulate a new plan, but it requires me to go outside first, before they get to the—

Time's up. Can't do it. They're already stacked at the door. The lanky man produces the key and checks one last time that all the others are ready.

You ever train in the martial arts, or for a sport? Maybe your master or coach told you what Durzo once told me: 'Never try something on the field that you haven't done a dozen times in practice.'

It's good advice.

I'm gonna have to ignore it.

The common room has a fire burning low in the fireplace. A full pot of gruel is warming off to one side. There's a small kettle that ... maybe, if I have to, I can ... and there are also assorted cups and bowls—wood, nope, too light.

The lanky mage holds up his hand, fingers up. Waves a tempo, then starts counting down: five, four ...

I snatch the kettle, transfer it to my left hand. The hallway's lantern is burning—mages, needing light, tend to hate the dark. The storm lantern, with its glass chimney, is the only source of light in the hallway.

Three ...

This is not going to work.

Two ...

I pluck a knife from my harness. Not the one I snapped the other day, unfortunately. Hate throwing away expensive knives. I hurl it at the lantern, straight spike style. Even as the glass of the lantern shatters, I throw the entire kettle at the lantern.

The satisfying smash of crockery and the merciful lack of flame tells me I extinguished it. I knocked out the lantern. But I'm already grabbing the nearby chair.

There are cries from the mages. The lantern is beside them, so they don't immediately turn my way.

I throw the hallway door shut and jam the chair under the knob.

Now the thing I've never practiced. I dump the pot of gruel directly into the fireplace. It sizzles and bubbles. Most importantly, it *smokes*.

Here goes nothing: I try to tap my Talent to spread it out in a bubble or a bag to capture the thick smoke.

The hallway's door rattles as a body slams into it—already?

I snatch my magic bag o' smoke and shuffle toward the door, not even daring to blink. My Talent is fundamentally body magic, and something about holding the hot smoke feels like I'm shredding skin off my forearms.

I drop to my knees, tuck the neck of the bag under the door, and squeeze—venting all the dark, hot smoke under the door and into the pitch-black hallway with the mages.

Plunging a mage into darkness isn't at all the same as throwing someone else into the dark—any kind of mage can make a light. These men have filled their glore vyrdens.

But the thing is, what men *can* do and what they *remember* to do instantly when under duress are very, very different. Mages are men first. And mages and men both are terrified of the dark. Adding the smoke, they can't see or breathe.

I hear screaming. The door bulges again. Some are shouting. Coughing.

I'm out the front door already. I round the house at a sprint in time to see the second of our bags sail out the window of Phaena's and my room.

Going visible, I run at the house and jump, diving through our bedroom's narrow window. I roll as I hit the floor inside our room and slam up against the wall.

Phaena is staring, wide-eyed. I'd nearly collided with her as she was halfway into trying to climb up and out the window herself.

There's cacophony from the hall, and I hear rattling in the lock. I lunge, extending my Talent just a bit beyond my reach—this, this I *have* practiced. My little finger of magic pokes the mage's key right out of the lock.

I hear a curse and maybe the rattle of the key on the floor on the other side. Maybe.

Without needing to say a word, I boost Phaena up and she slithers out the window.

"No! Don't use fire!" I hear the lanky man scream from the hall. "The lamp—"

Then there's a whoosh and a strobe of orange light under the bedroom door. Someone's fire magic just ignited all the lamp oil on the floor from that lantern I shattered.

I dive out the window, misjudging a bit and scraping the hell out of my stomach. Slowed and thrown off angle, I fall on my head on the other side.

The sound of the door exploding open behind me tells me that the mages have finally remembered they're mages.

Phaena is already halfway to the stable, running awkwardly, carrying her bag. I snatch up mine and follow. Smoke is billowing from every crack in the house behind us.

The horses' glowing blue harnesses are all laid out neatly in a line for the magi to charge them with magic this morning. There's even one of the distinctive saddles, more akin to barding than an ordinary saddle, all with magical panels to reduce the horse's weight.

I heft it and shove it toward Phaena. "Saddle the biggest one!"

"It'll take too long," she says.

"You have a better idea?" I snap.

"Yes! I'll be right back." And she disappears into the barn.

Is this going to work? I ask, drawing the ka'kari into the form of a blade in my hand.

~It'll work.~

I slam the ka'kari-dagger into the first of the glowing harnesses. The ka'kari shifts and squirms in my hand, attuning to what it's about to devour.

Then the harness goes dark and something in it shatters.

I slam the ka'kari into the next. It goes dark, its power devoured almost instantly.

As fast as I can, I go from harness to harness, and then to the wagon, jabbing every magical blue thing I can, draining and destroying them. I hesitate before I punch the ka'kari into the glowing saddle. But then I decide to trust Phaena, and I destroy its magic too.

I only save some glowing blue tracers and wrap them around Phaena's and my bags.

The wall of the house behind us shudders once, and then explodes.

"Find them!" a man shouts, then descends into a coughing fit.

Phaena emerges from the barn riding a big stallion saddled in glowing blue barding and extends a hand down to me, leaning hard the opposite way. Snatching her forearm, I leap up and land behind her.

As soon as we cross the boundary from dirt onto the blue road, I feel our tracer-entangled bags and the very horse itself beneath us shift as its weight is halved by the magic of road and saddle interacting.

Phaena digs in her heels and then we both hold on for dear life as the horse leaps forward down the road. Lightened by the blue magic and trained to this work, the stallion almost immediately reaches full, incredible speed.

Missiles of blue force go flying by us, but none are even close. Within a few breathless moments, we're a hundred paces away.

"How'd you know this one was ready?" I ask Phaena.

She laughs from the exhilaration at the ride and our escape. Over her shoulder, she says, "All the stations keep one horse saddled and ready at all times so messengers can switch horses and ride on without delay. You didn't notice at the earlier stations?"

I shake my head, though she's in front of me and can't see it. If we'd tried it my way, she'd still be wrestling a saddle onto a horse that didn't know her, and I'd be fighting a bunch of mages.

"Stop the horse," I tell Phaena.

After some distance, she does so, with difficulty. This big bay loves to run.

I turn and then stand on the horse's rump so I can see the men behind us, and they can get a good look at me—still in my underclothes, as it turns out. I pull my coin purse out of my bags and say, "For the horse! We're not thieves! Sorry for the inconvenience, gentlemen, but we have things to do that are too important for us to allow you to tie us up and question us. Which is very rude behavior, by the by. Good day!"

I hurl the coin purse back toward them, happy to see that they're all still alive, though several are bent over or on hands and knees, hacking and coughing.

They answer my good manners by trying to murder us, but the distance is too great for any of their sizzling bolts or blue missiles to have any hope of connecting.

"Get the horses!" the lanky mage yells.

"If he's this mad now," Phaena says, "he's not going to take it well when he finds I chased all the other horses away."

"Oh, now that's just mean," I say. "They already had no hope of catching us."

"*I'm* mean?" Phaena asks. "And everything you did to them was what? Sweetness and light?"

We hear a petulant howl of rage from the barn.

"Fair point," I say. Mindful of how fast this horse gets started, I hold on to Phaena's hips. "Shall we?"

My hands on her hips is awkward. I hug her midsection, accidentally brush her breasts, clear my throat, and try to hold my hands in an iron loop that only touches her lightly.

"You weren't so shy this morning," Phaena says, turning in the saddle and arching an eyebrow at me.

"I wasn't *conscious* this morning!"

She laughs as she kicks the horse into the gallop. I squeak and scramble to hold on, all decorum forgotten.

"Can we stop so I can put some clothes on?" I say.

Phaena just keeps laughing.

Chapter Thirty-Five

The Quiet Before Stormfast

*A*re we ready yet?" I ask irritably as Phaena returns from another of her latrine breaks. Fifth one today. It's getting to where these breaks are putting us in danger. Depending on the other mage traffic on this road, and how much spare magical equipment they have, we may be only hours ahead of pursuit.

Even if I destroyed the harnesses the mages would've used to chase us, there may be other horsemen or carriages coming today—each with their own harnesses. Those may need powering, but any advantage we have over those carriages is destroyed by the fact that we can't recharge our own horse's harnesses at all.

We've already dodged three horses and one carriage heading the opposite way. I'm not sure if any of them saw us before we were able to hide in the scrub.

"Uh-huh!" she says. She flashes a cheerful smile, but do I see the hint of tightness at the corners of her eyes? Is she merely mad at me for being mad at her, or is there some guilt there?

She tucks away her little laundry bag and then swings up in the saddle behind me. She groans as she settles back in, hugging me hard to shift her own weight around. "Ooh, next time, can we steal the whole carriage, please? Does your butt hurt as much as mine does?"

"Nope."

"Right. Have I told you how much I hate you yet?"

"Once or twice," I say. I can't help but smile as I nudge the big bay forward. He's a helluva horse—I see now that I underpaid for him—and at least the frequent breaks have given me chances to treat him right.

I'm not a smart man. I stew all afternoon while we ride. I stew until evening when we've finished setting up camp.

See, I hate being *handled*, and in my work, I get handled all the time. Whether it's getting orders without the rationale behind them, outright manipulation—

~I think that's an oxymoron.~

Oh, you're still there, are you?

~You tend to keep me close when you feel scared. Did you not notice?~

I'm not scared!

~Uncertain I meant, not scared. I misspoke. Please don't tuck me away now. I'm curious to see what you do here.~

Phaena isn't merely holding out on me. She's lying, and I don't know exactly how or why.

I could've started a fight about that this morning, and maybe by now we'd be ready to make up. And if early this morning was any indication, that making up might've taken a deliciously physical form.

But no. Me? I've gotta go and do this. Now.

"Are we ready yet?" I ask. Again.

"Ready?" Phaena asks. "For bed, you mean?"

"Um…" No.

"I couldn't help but notice you only put out one bedroll, and, Kylar, I have to tell you—"

"It's for me. You can roll out your own."

"Oh! I thought you were—I'm sorry."

"Teasing," I say. "I was teasing. There only is the one bedroll."

She laughs and puts a hand on her forehead.

"You…" She pulls her dark hair out of its ponytail and rubs her scalp with both hands. "You confuse me, Kylar Stern. Do you know that?"

"Can't see why. I'm a simple man." This is not the direction I was intending to take this conversation.

"No. Simple men don't say they're simple. They just are. You're a puzzle box. One minute you're that icy killer taking out mercenaries and bandits as if you could do it in your sleep. You're utterly indifferent. You don't even look at me as if I'm a woman. You answer in monosyllables. Then…" She takes a deep breath and looks down, blinking tears away. "Then last night, you see right to the heart of my fear and call me brave? Put me back together when I've shattered. You crack a joke? Tease me?" She looks at me, eyebrows knitted together. "What came along and made you suddenly so human?"

Jiggles, I want to say. I want to joke about our ride in the carriage, the enforced closeness, the sweat, our sharing a bed without sharing a bed. I want to tease and laugh and find comfort in her presence tonight, and maybe in her bed.

Maybe if I bed her, I can defuse her mystery. Maybe I can be like Durzo and use sex to numb my longing.

I used to look down on Durzo—though I would've denied doing that, because I didn't realize that's what I was doing. I used to think it was so easy: You get up every day and fight today's battle. Simple. I didn't realize that each time you fight, you add a little burden, a moment of fear or a regret, exhaustion or disgust or surprise or elation. Thus, in every battle, you carry every battle you've ever fought. That weight of experience can ground you, can save you. But the burden builds and builds until your back aches and your shoulders burn and God forbid you ever have to swim, lest you drown.

"Kylar?" Phaena says. "Wow, did you go far away. I didn't mean to hurt you."

I snap back to the present. "What, by treating me like a human being?" I ask. "People sometimes do." But my smile is false, and I think she can tell.

"Kylar," she says, glancing over at the bedroll. "I'd love to make love with you tonight."

I open my mouth, stunned.

I know what I should say. I know what it means to be the Night Angel, how I have to treat distractions. I should deflect. I should come up with some graceful way to extricate—

"But I am exhausted," she continues, "and after a whole day in the saddle— even with the stirrups!—my body is shaken misery. Especially the lower half. Which is in agony. And I can only imagine tomorrow I'll feel worse. If you're still interested, can you give me a few days? Because I am. Interested, I mean. If you are."

In an instant, without warning, twin hydras wake within me. The dormant sempiternal longing for a woman, selflessly for a woman in all her glory, and for all the ways a man can participate in that, and also selfishly for all a woman can mean to a man: the cool hand on an evening walk; the devious private smile across a table; the moment embracing bodies settle together, eye to eye, breath mingling, the strain and the release, pupils flaring; the long talks, the old wounds revealed and washed in new tears and somehow eased.

But that hydra named Longing is matched, head for head, by its twin, Grief. It says, *No, that's not for me. I'm the Night Angel. That's not the deal I made in this life. That's not the deal I get.* I can only see Elene, her body laid out on a cold bier. My wife. My love. No. Never again. To hold only means to lose.

Phaena has been watching me for any response. She has, I slowly realize, just propositioned me. But my face is as still as my heart.

"Phaena," I say finally, and it feels as if I'm lifting an immense weight.

"And in a few days," she goes on in a rush, "I'll also be out of the red tent, and you know, I don't know if that bothers you, but I always feel freer to be intimate when—"

"I think it's time for the truth." I sigh.

Her brow furrows. "The truth?"

"Those aren't menstrual rags," I say, gesturing vaguely to her laundry bag.

"What?"

I stare at her flatly.

After a moment, her shoulders sag. "It was just easier not to talk about it."

"I'm listening."

"I am a musician, but the music, the shows...They're not enough. Haven't been, for several years. I was part of an ensemble, but just as we started doing really well, my husband left me. He thought he was the talented one, that we were all holding him back. But mostly, he just didn't want to be a father. It wasn't fun anymore, he said. So I became a wet nurse and tried to still sing here and there. But then my father got worse. He forgot things at work, or even where his workplace was, so he lost his job. You know what being a wet nurse pays?"

"Not much."

"Not much," she says bitterly. "The only halfway decent jobs are for rich people who want you to live at their home, to be at their beck and call at all hours. I couldn't do that and take care of my siblings, my father, and my daughter. I tried everything. I filled in as a wet nurse at a few brothels, for mothers who needed a break or were having problems feeding or those who needed to go on work trips with clients. From there I came to Momma K's notice, and it turns out there are a few lords who will pay well for..."

"Things other than music," I say. So she lied to me. I knew she couldn't be making a month's wages off one or two performances a month if music was all she was providing.

She looks down at her hands. "I need to be lactating for that work, and it solves all my money problems in only a few days each month, so if I hate it, so what? Everyone hates their job, right? If I do well on this mission, though, Momma K said I can stop doing all that and move up in her organization. She thinks I have potential. Maybe I can move up again higher when my daughter's old enough that I can be away from home more."

She looks at me as if daring me to judge her for what she does.

"So that's it?" I say. So I was right, that was why my fingers were damp this morning, after I'd been holding her. Breast milk. "You've been holding us up, and sneaking off in private so you can...what do you call it, hand...milk yourself?"

"Hand express. Yes."

"Well, knock it off. Do it while we ride."

"While we ride?"

"We can't afford to stop so much."

"But, but—all right, mechanics of doing that aside..." Phaena says, as if she got all wound up and now has nothing to do with all her energy. "That's it? That's all you've got to say?"

"No, it's not. What's your daughter's name?"

She looks surprised I would ask. "It's, it's Istarah."

"Pretty. How old is she?"

Her mouth presses to a line and her eyes fill with tears. "Four. She's... everything. I miss her so much."

"I'm sure you do. Phaena?"

"Yes?" she asks, very quietly.

"Don't ever lie to me again. It might matter next time."

We say nothing more as we go to bed together, each wrapped in our own cloaks, though we share a thin blanket. I pretend to sleep, and she pretends to believe I'm asleep as she cries with her back to me.

Elene used to cry like this, sometimes. Once, when I thought she was crying about me after I'd done some stupid selfish thing, Elene had to tell me, 'I'm not crying about you, you big dumb oaf. I'm crying about the whole world.'

It didn't make any sense to me then, but right now, on a cold night not quite warmed despite the body next to me, with the beauty of stars reaching down toward me but not quite able to touch my unseeing eyes, it makes sense.

I think of Logan and Jenine, surely on their way home by now. Maybe today they got the news that I failed them, that their children have been stolen, the future they imagined for themselves and their family shattered. I think of

Momma K trying to hold this new infant kingdom together while forces on all sides want to smother it. I think of her retiring to her chambers after another long day and having Durzo not be waiting for her. I think of Count Drake and his wife and his daughters who will never come home. I'd say I think of Elene, but I'm never not thinking of Elene. But now for a moment I think of the child we were going to have. I think of Phaena's husband, running off and leaving his wife and child destitute, because taking care of an infant isn't *fun*.

Phaena weeps, and I feel every echo in the hollows of my chest. In this world, there is everything to mourn.

I wish I could cry about it, too. I wish I could feel that human again.

Chapter Thirty-Six

Into the Eye of Stormfast

This is foolish on many, many levels," Phaena says, not pausing in brushing down our big stallion at the rail outside the inn.

"I'm aware of that."

"Actually, every level I can think of, Kylar."

"Uh-huh," I say, handing her a carrot. The big stallion likes her more than me anyway.

"We shouldn't do it. It's painting a big sign for the blues that we're here."

"You're absolutely right."

"Don't you care about our success?" she demands. "Because I do!"

"Go do what I told you, or I'll do it myself." We both know if I go, it will make things a lot worse.

Phaena throws the brush to me with more force than necessary. "Fine!"

"Don't forget to tell them about the trap!" I call after her in my friendliest voice as she approaches the front door of the first inn one encounters when entering the villages around the city of Stormfast.

She gives me the monodigital salute that I deserve. Stabling the horse here virtually guarantees that the blues chasing us will find it. But that's the point. It served us well, and it deserves to be back with them.

I'm no thief.

Not when I can help it.

I stuffed the saddlebags with the blues' magical harness and all, and put a trap on them. Hopefully the innkeeper will believe Phaena about the trap to dissuade any thieves. And hopefully the innkeeper will pass on the existence of the trap to the mages, who will undoubtedly be eager to reclaim their highly trained horse and its magical accoutrements.

In reality, the trap is merely a stink bomb to panic anyone who gets too curious before the mages reclaim their property.

Phaena's absence gives me a few moments to examine the city. From the high desert interspersed with dry forests we've been traveling through since Tover, here the land turns strange. Stormfast is the gateway to the Summer Isles, the pleasure islands where all the Alitaeran nobles vacation for a month or two before Empress Caelestia moves her court from Skone to Borami. On the Rims, north of and above the city, where we are now, there are a scattering of normal enough desert towns, albeit with many inns to serve the yearly crush of visitors for the Festival of the Wind that's going on right now, or at least those visitors who can't afford to go closer to the coast. Low and round buildings dominate up here.

The land then ramps down toward the great rock into which Castle Stormfast is built at the edge of the ocean; on its far side—invisible from here, but I've heard of it—the immense imperial storm ship is docked.

The Alitaeran empire's armies are sometimes likened to a great storm, but it's only now that I understand why a mere storm would leave such a deep imprint on this people's psyche. The yearly Great Storm has reshaped the land itself from the Rims where I stand down to the sea. Instead of soil, the ground is scoured granite in speckled reds and blues and shimmering quartz whites, the rock sandblasted into smooth grooves and eddies and whorls by the force of the storm. Fine red dirt or sand currently fills in some of those grooves and forms drifts around anything that sticks up too far out of the rock, but it doesn't seem permanent enough to rightly be called soil.

Tents and pavilions stud the sloping rock down to the sea, but it looks as though many of those are in the process of being dismantled even now for the Great Storm's coming in three days. The storm's first harbinger, an eerily regular breeze directly from the east, is already blowing, but it's currently light enough that it doesn't kick up any dirt.

Two great lines like parallel claw gouges cut the stone down near the castle, but I can't tell what they are from here. The nearer one seems to be *smoking*, but that could be the dust in the air.

More attention-grabbing are the palaces blooming like flowers clinging to rock everywhere on the far side of those two gouges. They're lavish with white and red stone and decorative brick and hammered gold and polished copper roofs, but most of all in greenery. On the bare rock of this wind-scourged desert storm-plain, gardens are the ultimate sign of wealth, and here as everywhere, neighbor seeks to rival neighbor, vines and flowers of every color spilling everywhere over the walls.

Oddly, given the number of palaces, there's no correspondingly large city. No city at all, really. There are wandering roads every which way between the various suqs, and one golden road straight as an arrow to the castle, currently packed with festival-goers, but no homes. Does every local worker walk half a league or more down into that rock bowl and back out every day?

How does that work? For that matter, how does any of this work?

It seems to me that Alitaera is like one of those precarious boulders in the wilderness that a traveler goggles at, sure it will tumble any day, never knowing that their great-great-grandfather passed the same way a century before and thought the same thing. It is, by rights, too large a country to hold together, but with two capitals and peerless roads and its rotating court and lots of magic, money, and might, it's managed it somehow for centuries now.

I look at the castle in the distance, but I don't really see it. How are we gonna get in there?

This is the kind of job that might not have been too hard if I'd arrived a week ago.

Which, yes, was when Momma K tried to get me to be here.

I grimace. There must be bracelets in at least half of those palaces down there. Security is sure to be lax at one of them. But I don't have the intel to know which one to try. If I hit the wrong palace, I'll alert the best of the Alitae-ran empire to the presence of a pro—and with their history, they know how to defend against wetboys, stalkers, drop thieves, cons, and aggrieved would-be assassins from every sort of breakaway tribe and ethnic group.

Hell, after I get in, what if the compass is broken? What if I can't figure it out? Do I dare consult a mage and try to use its powers to find the twins imme-diately myself, or do we make the trek all the way back to Elenea first?

I need to find some magical gewgaw just so I can steal some other magical gewgaw. Have I told you how much I hate magical gewgaws?

~Pardon me?~

Gewgaw. Has that word suddenly lost all meaning to you like it has to me? Gewgaw. Gewgaw.

An impossible job, Momma K said. Good thing I charged her so much for it. So far I've made permanent enemies out of one entire school of mages, which includes the most elite warriors in the world, but on the bright side, at least I...Nope, actually, I don't think I gained anything positive at all from Tover. Just pursuit.

I hear the sound of familiar footsteps. Phaena joins me.

She makes an appreciative moue. "First time here?"

I grunt an affirmation.

"Me too," she says. "But the duchess hired a local to tell me everything she could remember or I could think to ask. I got us a tilbury and a ticket. Shall we talk as we go? What do you need to know?"

"A tilbury? A ticket?"

"A ticket for the Via Aurius. Cost a fortune. We could walk, but I thought you were worried about our friends in blue catching us up. Tilburies have curtains."

As I follow her gaze, I say, "Don't they also usually have a horse?"

"There are rules here about who and what can go where. This is the fastest way to get where we want without attracting attention."

The tilbury is simple and very small. With two wheels and drawn by a single man, its main amenity is that the broad roof and gauzy curtains give shade for its crammed occupants. Or, ordinarily, from the sour look on the man's face, its occupant, singular. But he sizes us up, decides we're small enough, and soon we're off.

"Our first stop will be to get you some acceptable clothing," Phaena says.

"I find my clothes perfectly acceptable."

"That's nice." Phaena finds a fan and begins wafting us as we rattle along, and she does cool both of us, because we're packed tightly enough against each other that we're sharing body heat.

If the sun weren't beating down so relentlessly, being pressed tight against this woman would be distractingly wonderful, despite the decisions I've made. As is, it's mostly hot and sticky. Plus there's something very awkward about talking to someone so close your breath mingles. Eye contact from a handbreadth away is far too intense for a normal conversation.

"To answer your question," I say, looking away, "I've heard about the Great Storm. Storms? Whatever. Other than that, I know only what I can see. I'd rather talk about how we plan to chase down—" I glance at the tilbury puller, and though he seems far enough away not to hear us, I say, "our entrance fee." I tap my wrist.

"I know," she says. "I'll be meeting with some brokers here."

"Sa'kagé?" I ask quietly.

"Same thing I asked," she says. "Apparently that's a complicated question. I'm to collect another package, but if everything goes to hell, the boss has given me permission to deal with a lovely local they call the Clipper. And I think we can fairly say things have gone to hell."

"This gets better all the time," I say.

"I know, I'm not exactly looking forward—" Phaena freezes, looking past me. "Kylar, don't turn your head." She squints against the distance. When she speaks again, she barely moves her lips, whispering. "Blue mage. On horseback. We're going to go right past him."

She grabs at the ties holding the curtain tight to the frame of the tilbury. Getting the breeze was nice, but it'll be nicer to stay alive. I grab the curtain on my side and untie it, too.

They both roll down at the same time—and reveal themselves to be the widest weaves of bad lace I've ever seen. Totally useless for concealing us.

Our eyes meet. Phaena looks scared. I say, "I can—"

"No. They know what you look like," she says, pulling out her ponytail and shaking out her hair into big black curls. "But they won't recognize me."

Then her lips are on mine, and she rolls half on top of me, putting her hand up on my face to obscure as much of me as possible.

For a moment, I don't respond. Can't.

Then for a moment, I kiss back impartially to keep up the pretense, thinking about the mage, and making my plan for what I'll do at his first yell: roll Phaena over, launch over the side with my Talent, pull the ka'kari to...

Then time drifts away from me. The softness of Phaena's lips, the invitation of her tongue brushing my lips, gentle, playful. The insistence of her hand on my face, pulling me in. Everything pliant and welcoming in her makes all my iron battlements feel rusted out and brittle, and without meaning to, I trust her. Something in me cracks.

Part of me yells, *This is not the time for this! We are in danger, Kylar!*

I feel as if I'm tottering on a precipice, simultaneously sizzling with awareness of my surroundings, alive to the faintest shift in the air that will warn of danger—but also losing awareness of what's outside for what's within. The hydra has wakened, and it's roaring to the surface. I am suddenly, terribly, all need. All hunger. All longing, insatiable and wounded—

Phaena moans as I squeeze her tight to me, but it doesn't sound like the right kind of moan.

It's pain. My eyes snap open, and I freeze, not sure how long we've been kissing. I search Phaena's face.

"Well, that confirms two things," she says breathlessly. Then she gives a suppressed whimper of pain as she pulls back from me. But there's no fear in her now. The danger has clearly passed.

"Wha—? What two things?" I say, struggling to make my voice level, to reclaim my lost dignity.

"Everything still hurts from riding, and my eyesight at a distance is still terrible."

"Your eyesight?"

"That, uh, that wasn't a blue mage," she says, chagrined. "Just a large woman in a blue cloak. Sorry."

She doesn't sound very sorry.

"What? You know I might've—"

"I know. I like that about you." Her eyes twinkle.

I expel a great breath in frustration.

"You can, um, take your hand off my butt now," she says.

"I can? That's nice," I say. I squeeze it instead. Firmly.

She yelps in pain and mock outrage, and then lowers her voice and bats my hand away as our driver turns his head to see if everything's fine. "All right, all right, I deserved that! But how are you not sore?"

"Oh, I am," I say. "Very sore. I can barely move."

"Liar," she says. At first, I thought we would trade off who got to use the stirrups to lessen the jostling from the stallion's incredible galloping. But it was immediately clear that Phaena was getting the worst of things, so we'd wrapped the extra blue weight-lightening straps around her waist as a belt. The magic wore off those thin straps after the first day, with the horse's gear lasting somewhat longer. I'd realized my fast Healing while I sleep is a huge advantage, so I'd let her use the stirrups the rest of the time, but neither of us is a skilled rider, and being on a galloping horse for days would beat up anyone.

Unfortunately, something's gone wrong and I can't do ridiculous-fast Healing on the fly like I did at Black Barrow. I asked Durzo to teach me more about it after the battle. He'd often told me he'd have to teach me many things once my Talent finally awakened—but he got a funny look on his face and put me off, and hardly taught me anything before the quarrel. Then he disappeared. Thanks, Master!

We make stops at two of the shops among the many in tents and pavilions that line the golden road. The larger shops are permanent, either cut into the rock itself or housed in low-domed stone buildings behind their storefront. Like the colorful head of a turtle, each shop bursts out into the open with long vibrant banners and flags, and bright cloths drape overhead to give shade all along the golden road.

The golden road, as it turns out, is not gold but merely rock painted yellow, which is simultaneously disappointing and a relief. Even the Alitaerans aren't that rich.

At the first, Phaena buys me 'acceptable' clothes as quickly as possible. The pedestrians and the shops along the road would be at home in the richer districts of any cosmopolitan city. I see people wearing—and shops selling—everything from Modaini half togas and breeks to Ladeshian silk dresses to Friakian leathers, but most of the locals wear brilliantly colored sleeveless cotton tunics over billowing slitted pantaloons, the women adding lace or silk wraps over their shoulders bound by large brooches. Hats are rare and small or tied beneath the chin to combat the persistent wind, though some sport dangling veils of gauze or tinkling gold chains. Religious jewelry and charms abound.

By law, the Alitaeran empire follows some sect of Count Drake's One God, but in practice, I see shops devoted to many of the hundred gods, with men and women who are obviously priests and priestesses selling bowls and shrines and incense burners. One has a sign that these items are offered strictly as art pieces.

"Did you pick up the boss's orders from that shop?" I ask Phaena.

She shakes her head. "At the next one. Maybe." She seems nervous.

"Need me to—?"

"No. Please don't."

The tilbury's wheels clatter onto a new surface. Suddenly, there are no flags draped overhead to give us shade, nor any shops to either side. I sit up and see that we're crossing a low bridge over one of the great gouges I'd seen from the Rims.

"That would be the Below," Phaena says. "Or I think they just say Below?"

I'd wondered where all the locals live. This is my answer. Carved into the walls of the deep canyon below us is an entire city. Or perhaps I should say a vast slum. There are remnants of nice buildings, especially close to the surface; wood and rope walkways stretch from wall to wall everywhere, many in poor repair, some drooping off one side or the other, and masses of people are jammed together in the few open places. The stench, reminiscent of the Warrens I grew up in, but with the spoiled-eggs odor of sulphur added, reaches us high above, along with a fair amount of smoke, some of it steam and some of it woodsmoke. From my angle, I can't see how deep it is.

Phaena says, "When the Great Storm started centuries ago, it scoured away all the topsoil down to the rock, but here the people found these two big seams of sandstone. The masons and mages who built Castle Stormfast dug into it to make themselves safe homes, but soon the wind began scouring it away, deeper every year."

"How deep is it?" I ask. "It looks like it...Does it go below sea level?" I'm horrified by the thought. The sea isn't that far away.

"Far below it. Those in the Below have cut their own tunnels into the sandstone in every direction, usually with no thought to sewage or ventilation or roof supports for the caves. Cave-ins are common. My local said that down there everyone knows that someday, someone will weaken the wrong wall and let in the ocean and drown half of them."

I don't call them insane. I don't ask why people keep living down there when they could move to the Rims half a league away. When you're poor enough, you don't plan for the maybe-someday catastrophes; today has so many catastrophes you don't dare think about tomorrow's. If you do, you'll despair and die.

"I'm really hoping this one's Hell's Gorge," Phaena says. "Because if the other one's worse..."

Then with one last rattle, the tilbury is back on smooth road, and the bridge is behind us. We say nothing for a full minute between the two canyons. I close my eyes.

"What are you thinking about?" Phaena asks.

"The job," I lie.

Another rattle announces that we're crossing the second canyon. There's no stench, only gleaming homes, beautiful edifices carved into the walls, wind scoops spinning magically for ventilation, scaffolding for new construction, soaring bridges, clean streets, many lamps. People in the bright colors of clean, new clothing.

Something about it all sits on me, heavy as the memories of my childhood. Everything about this city is different from Cenaria, but it's got exactly the same human awfulness.

"So," I say thickly, "gleaming palaces on one hand and a putrid warren filled with all manner of misery on the other. Great. Why is it I know nothing about this job and yet I'm willing to bet where I'm going to be spending most of my time?"

In a few minutes, we stop outside another store; before we go inside, I say, "Hey, Phaena, I wanted to say sorry about the . . . back there."

"The kiss?" she asks, her eyebrows pushing together.

"The . . . enthusiasm. There's, uh, there's not going to be anything between us. I can't be distracted. I'll make mistakes. I can't do that."

She looks stung. "Does this have to do with—?"

"Just has to do with me." Anything more I can say will only make it worse, won't it?

"All right," she says. "Thanks for being clear." She gives a quick smile, but her heart doesn't seem to be in it, and then she goes inside.

This shop seems to be a tailor and a haberdashery. The two women usher us into their domed shop, which is magically cool—probably literally magically cool, come to think of it. They start stripping Phaena down immediately, making much of their joy to be working their arts on such a canvas.

I watch her try to fend them off. "Surely you don't need to take off—?" she says, as they unlace her underthings, but I look away. Enjoying her awkwardness, much less spying on her getting naked, seems to directly betray what I just said.

Why can't I keep my dumb mouth shut?

But I was right. A lovely distraction is the worst distraction, for me.

The two shop owners have that irresistible bossiness certain professionals get. Phaena surrenders to them hopelessly, laughing, while I study my hands.

They soon bully her into a back room, where servants bathe her while they argue with each other happily about how best to dress her, half of it in terminology I can't even begin to follow.

"Now you," the tailor says eventually, with considerably less eagerness. "Strip."

"I already got clothes. I'm good."

She crosses her arms. "Strip."

They make no move to help me undress. And when I'm naked, they make no move to take my measurements. The tailor wrinkles her nose. "Bath first."

They provide me neither with a robe nor any dignity. I have to walk nude back to the bath room, where Phaena's head alone is visible above the rim of her tub. She's grinning devilishly at my discomfort, and not turning away at all.

She is pretty great, but it's only weakness that makes me want her attention. I can't even tell in my heart of hearts if I'm interested in her or merely lonely. Can a lonely man be friends with an attractive woman? Can he be friends with her if she's clearly open to more?

I'll probably just hurt her, and hurt her more the closer I let her get.

In the next few minutes, I'm soaped and scrubbed. Then they take my measurements brusquely. Then they banish me. They tell me I'm in the way, somehow, though I'm not. I'm forced to sit outside the shop in the heat, in only a robe.

Sure, *now* they have one available.

"Can I have my old clothes back?" I ask.

The tailor sniffs and doesn't deign to answer me.

A servant tells me that all my clothes have already been taken to a laundry.

"I only wore some of those for like an hour!" I protest.

"The mistresses are very particular," the young woman tells me.

"Hadn't noticed."

"Oh, they are."

I look at her flatly.

For the next two hours, the partners lavish attention on Phaena, trying out different fabrics and styles. It's wasting time we don't have, but I don't have any better options. I'm half-naked, clad only in a robe—and while the ka'kari could remedy that for me, I don't have anywhere to go.

I mean, I could pick one of these estates at random and attempt an impromptu infiltration and see if I can find a bracelet—but if I choose the wrong noble, the bracelet's absence or the noble's own absence from the party because I have their bracelet will be obvious. Beyond that, either absence will be reported immediately, and I've got to guess that the detail-loving Alitaerans are tracking each bracelet separately and will know who has a stolen bracelet before I even get to the party.

My only other option is to wait for Phaena and trust her and Momma K. If I'd trusted Momma K from the beginning . . . this would be substantially easier. Exactly like she said.

Another merchant with several armed guards shows up to show Phaena jewelry that, according to all the oohing and ahhing I hear, plainly complements this or that of Phaena's features in superlative ways.

None of this has much to do with my tale, so I could skip all this or edit it out later, but I have to endure it, so you have to, too.

You, uh, already erased my rather enthusiastic *descriptions of Phaena when she, uh, was in a state of deshabille, right?*

~Oh, must I? I thought you were at your most poetic there. A true loss.~

You really think so? I thought I might've been a bit over—

~No, not really.~

You know, I was just going to say thank you.

~Really?~

I'm tempted to say *No, not really,* just to needle the ka'kari back. *Yes, really,* I think at it instead, not least because I like to throw it off-balance by surprising it once in a while. *When I just admitted Momma K was right all along, I was sure you were going to take the opportunity to stab some little gibe into me. You didn't. I appreciated that.*

~You're welcome. In future, if you need to be particularly eloquent, I could help you with that, if you'd like.~

You?

~There are linguistic and conventional expectations one learns over time that you seem not quite to have learned, despite Momma K's attempts to teach you. But I'm sure you'll get there——~

Don't say it.

~——in six or seven centuries.~

You said it. Tell me one thing: Did you bust Durzo's stones like you do mine?

~Oh yes.~

I grin to think of Durzo being truly exasperated by someone—well, some*thing*—that he couldn't intimidate or simply kill. No wonder Durzo stopped wearing the ka'kari.

In two days, the yearly magical storm that gives this city its character, its danger, its fascination, and all its importance will arrive.

Two days before the storm ship leaves. Two days for me to steal a bracelet, then use it to sneak into the fancy party, find and steal the compass. Two jobs in two days.

No. That's not right. The Great Storm arrives in two days...at dawn. Which means the last night of the departure party spans the night before that. Which means I've only got a day and a half. Two nights, one day.

I sag back in my seat.

Time passes.

Ten years later, Phaena emerges looking radiant. She smiles at me and hands me a folded bundle wrapped in a ribbon, which turns out to be my own laundered clothing. "You are going to be very, very expensive to clothe appropriately, Kylar Stern."

"*I* am?"

"At least that's what I'm gonna tell the duchess. To be fair, she did say the words 'Spare no expense' to me. Not that she'll ever say them to me again."

On another day, I would admire her audacity.

"Then again," Phaena says, "it was Momma K who taught me to take whatever joys thankless work might send my way. Perhaps she'll understand."

"Thankless work?"

"What have you been doing out here while I've been working inside?" Phaena asks.

"Working?" I feel like all my words have been stolen, leaving me only able to repeat those she drops for me.

Phaena produces a folio. "Momma K's agent dropped off reports for me. I've been reading while Dido and Demetra were picking out things and arguing. What do you think this is, Kylar, a pleasure cruise?"

"A pleasure—?" Now my temper is rising.

"I also spoke with the Clipper." She holds out her fingernails, which are freshly trimmed and lacquered. "Not at all what I expected from a crime lord. Seemed like such a kind and sweet old man. Until he gave me your job. I think I should feel scared, but for some reason I don't."

"Job? You were—"

"Ah! Here's our ride." A big, ornate wagon is pulling up, emblazoned with a coat of arms I don't know: some kind of raptor and a serpent. "Let me do the talking. You're my bodyguard and, by open secret, my consort, so we can share a room. Now get inside and get dressed—quickly, or I'll give you the dumbest pseudonym I can think up."

"Yes...milady," I say, nonplussed.

"Quickly, *Braxby*. The countess doesn't like to be kept waiting."

I make a face as I head inside. "Braxby?"

"Blodgert if you prefer."

"You wouldn't dare," I say.

She raises her eyebrows. "Of all days, are you sure today is the day to test my daring?"

Chapter Thirty-Seven

Prelude to a Prize

I don't know how much time we'll have after you finish tonight, so I need to fill you in about tomorrow," Phaena says, coming out onto the palace balcony in a layered flowing blue muslin dress that dances behind her in the persistent evening wind. She comes to stand beside me and moves as if to place her hand on mine on the railing, then changes direction and puts it beside mine instead, not touching.

When I say nothing, she cocks her head at my silence, then shrugs her shoulders and begins. "The empress uses the Festival of the Wind to keep her nobles off-balance. I'm sure she's meeting with them even now. Each day, a new tier of the ziggurat is opened, and fewer nobles ascend. On the seventh day, after everyone is locked in, at midnight she gives everyone their assignments and positions for the coming year. No one who goes into the party knows if they will be heading with the empress to Borami or if they'll be staying behind, nor what their position will be until she returns. Lords and ladies don't know if they'll be promoted or demoted. Lovers don't know if they'll go together to the west or be separated. After the decisions are handed down, there's nothing anyone can do about them—the more powerful half of the court is simply gone, along with the empress herself. There are no appeals for the decisions she makes. Not to mention how many people are deathly terrified of the passage itself."

"Longing, uncertainty, social climbing, and desperation? Sounds like a great party."

"It's worst at the highest levels. Do you know about the empress and her consorts?"

"That she has them?"

Phaena gives me a look.

"And she tends to go through a lot of them...?"

Another look.

"I've kind of had my hands full with Sa'kagé and Cenarian and Khalidoran politics up until now."

"Caelestia became empress young, at sixteen, I think. It took her six years to rid herself of the advisors her father had left to help her rule but who tried to rule over her instead. In the twenty-four years since, she's been playing the lords off each other in all sorts of ways, but not least with the hope of marriage.

"Because Alitaera has two capitals, she can obviously only rule from one of them at a time. That's caused everyone else before her problems, but she's turned it into an opportunity. Yearly, as she departs from the western or eastern capital, she appoints either a new king or a regent to rule in her stead while she's away. A regent has fewer powers, but if he proves himself, he may move up to being King in the East or King in the West the following year. If a man is appointed king, he's also the royal consort. They rule together for four months if in the west or five months in the east, and if he gets the empress pregnant in that time, they'll marry and he'll become emperor to rule with her. This year is extra exciting because she's already announced that the east is going to be ruled by a regent—Lord Tezzani Serapis, who's been regent of the east twice before. He's old and sharp and well trusted, obviously."

"That sounds...the opposite of exciting?"

"It's exciting because a mere regent of the east means she's far more likely to be choosing a new King in the West tomorrow night, rather than having a regent. It means the big prize is open."

"What happens to the old kings when she's done with them?" I ask.

"Nothing. Unless they cause problems. Early on, a couple of them did, consolidating power while she was gone and then announcing a rebellion once he felt ready. Each was assassinated within an hour of his announcement. The empress didn't even come back; she knew it was coming and already had plans in place for who was to take charge if they went through with it. Since then, the kings have obediently rotated out when their reign is up, somewhat richer, more experienced, and outspoken about their loyalty. Sometimes the good ones do get a second term a few years later, but never back to back. She doesn't want anyone to accumulate power against her."

"So all these nobles vie to become king—and maybe emperor if the empress likes them enough? And no one knows until tomorrow who wins the prize?"

"It's the crowning moment of the party."

"I bet," I say. This country is mad. Hundreds of nobles, all competing for one woman and the throne and beginning a new dynasty?

"What about all the nobles who are married already?"

"Oh, any of the men can become a king. She doesn't mind. If the man she chooses is already married, his wife is stationed in the opposite capital."

"A hostage for the king's good behavior?"

"Or a way to split his house's power. And the king can't become emperor unless..."

"Unless they give the empress a kid. And if they do, what? A quick divorce? The wives can't be thrilled about that."

"At that level of power, everyone understands exactly what they're getting into, Kylar. None of these lords are plucked from obscurity to suddenly become king. They've all been vying against each other for years. It's just that in most kingdoms where it's the same five or ten families, here it's thirty or forty. Which sounds like a lot, but when you ignore everyone too young or too old, too obviously crazy or incompetent or too stupid to learn the job or too corrupt, and then—for the empress—everyone too poor or too likely to infuriate certain of the others, the real pool isn't that large at all. Maybe twenty men? Probably more like ten, with twenty others possible depending on what you're willing to compromise."

"And she's been married to or slept with, what, all of them by this point? How does that go over?"

Phaena shrugs. "She's not just any woman. She's the empress, and though it's said she is a woman who quite loves men, the truth is the normal rules don't apply to her."

"No, but they do to the men she sleeps with. If she's juggling them against each other, that means some of them probably feel led on, lied to. She makes them feel special and they get their hopes up, and then they feel scorned, discarded, and jealous of the next man. She's playing a dangerous game."

"Maybe she knows exactly what she's doing," Phaena says sharply.

"Maybe she does. Or maybe she only thinks she does. When you start sleeping with people, or with people's husbands, eventually you're going to find someone who doesn't take it well."

"She seems to have done pretty well for herself."

I raise my hands, confused. I'm not arguing that, and I don't understand Phaena's obvious offense about the point.

"I don't think she promises these lords anything she doesn't give. She's a woman who loves men. There's no crime in that, is there? By all accounts, she's faithful during her marriages and for a time before, so if she falls pregnant, no lord will have need to wonder if he is indeed the father."

So she's a woman with self-control. It makes sense, though. No noble who was jockeying for the position of king hoping to impregnate the empress would want the possibility that the child who becomes his heir is the seed of his predecessor.

Of such suspicions and jealousies do empires fall.

Which makes me think of Logan adopting Dorian's sons, covering by his magnanimity stresses that could break a lesser king and kingdom. He's a good man, my friend is. He deserves more than the pain he's going to get as soon as he finds out I failed him. But that's a worry for another day.

"So it's a charged atmosphere," I say. "And I'm sure I'll have more questions tomorrow, but it seems like maybe we're talking about the wrong job first?"

"This one seems straightforward, doesn't it? Grab the guy, get the information and the bracelet, and leave, right? Is there anything else you need to know?"

I look at her. "You skipped the part where I murder him."

"I thought it went without saying."

I study the woman but can't see through the new veil of sophistication and beauty, distracted by my own weaknesses from what I really hope to see.

She's embraced her role as a countess from near the Waeddryn border but far from the main arterials, and gladly employed our hostess's resident aesthetician's magical arts. Did you know that when you get to a certain level of wealth, you can employ magic-users to make sure that your artfully tousled hair retains exactly the artful tousle you desire all night long? I didn't either, until now.

Hate what humidity does to your curls by the end of a long night of feasting and dancing? We can fix that! Maybe you have one perfect ringlet that just begs for a twin on the other side that nature cruelly denied you? It can be yours! Love that adorable dress, but hate continually hauling up those little straps to keep it in place? Easy!

All you have to do is exploit a few thousand peasants, and you too can afford to employ magae even for this. And let's be honest, you were gonna exploit them anyway. Your life is hard! You deserve it!

Cenaria doesn't have that kind of wealth and frivolity, not even at the top.

"I'm ready," I say. "You think the Clipper was telling us the truth?"

"I told him you would know if he weren't. He said he had no intention of playing any games, and that Cenaria's wetboys have enough of a reputation to deter anyone who did. I believed him. And he wants to 'explore certain mutually beneficial business opportunities' with my employer. He said that he hoped your professionalism lives up to its billing. Some of his people are going to be quite irritated that he brought in outside talent. I told him they won't have any occasion to be irritated, because they won't find out about it at—" She stops, looking in the air toward the castle. "Huh, would you look at that."

I turn. Our balcony overlooks the cramped gardens of one of the tiny oases on the plain, but Castle Stormfast, though its base is set lower down the slope toward the sea, looms immense over the southern horizon. The castle is a ziggurat spiraling around and built into a small mountain in six many-arched circles to the heavens, with immense gardens and squares at each level, flowing with greenery and waterfalls and flowers of every color. Tonight, as it has for the first five nights of the festival, it roars with life, the castle top dark, but now the first six levels of the ziggurat alight with party-goers, light, and magic.

But Phaena wasn't enrapt by the castle or apparently thinking of the armies of carpenters and masons and magi it must take to maintain it. She's looking at tiny pink flares of light in the sky. Borne on the burgeoning winds, at first the lights seem like fringes of sunset peach cloud in the east. But now they advance and appear like fireflies, not dense in the air, but simply so many, over such a broad swath of sky that they are hard to differentiate.

And now as the lights are blown closer, I see one blow past us on the wind, elongated and delicate, more like a sky-bound jellyfish than an insect.

"What the hell is that?" I ask.

"It's your cue," she says.

"But . . . what are they?" I ask.

"Did I leave that out of the briefing? It doesn't matter. They call them fairy lanterns. It's the sign that the storm's coming. Magical. Harmless. They're supposed to be lucky. But our hostess said we might see a few dozen if we watched all night . . ."

I look and see people everywhere coming outside from their own houses, crowding the bridges, give gasps of wonder and delight.

A few dozen? There must be a hundred thousand of those things.

I feel suddenly queasy as I think of what the grandmaster and Vi said about what we did at the Battle of Black Barrow changing things, that our magic messed up ancient balances. "Good luck, huh?" I say. "Phaena, what causes the Great Storm?"

"You're asking this now?" she asks, tearing her eyes away from the fairy lanterns. "The gods are fighting. Or the god of wind had a vendetta against the old rulers of the city that used to be here. Or a star fell in the east and still attempts to escape its captivity every year. They have a bunch of explanations, but the truth is that nobody knows. Do you really want to spend an hour talking religion and ancient history?"

"No," I say. "You're right. Focus on the job at hand."

"Kylar," she says hesitantly. "I know that you don't kill innocents, and I believe the Clipper that Aemil Wesseros deserves to die, but even if he doesn't...if we can't get into the party, we'll never find Logan's children. Do what you have to, all right?"

"And that means killing Wesseros, regardless?" I say. Not because I don't know, but because I want to make sure she knows what she's asking.

She swallows. Then something fierce enters her eyes. She nods sharply.

I look at her for a long moment. "You know, Momma K took a gamble when she sent you."

"She told me the same thing."

"You're doing a hell of a job representing her."

"Thank you."

"It wasn't all compliment. Momma K was broken early, like me. I don't think you ever recover from the kind of things that happened to us on the streets. I'll never not be the kid who was willing to do whatever I had to do to stop being afraid, and abandoned his friends to prove it. Momma K will never not... well, her story isn't mine to tell. Suffice it to say we both seem to be broken in ways that make us useful, but there's no telling what we would've been if we hadn't been forced to become what we are. Better, I think. Maybe a lot better. Be careful, Phaena. When you start giving orders to have people killed, the biggest danger isn't that someone comes after you for revenge. The real danger is that you start to like it. Have a good night."

She looks pensive, compassionate. She reaches out as I turn to go, but stops short of touching me.

"Kylar, wait. You said something to me earlier. About you and me. I've been thinking about it. Momma K foresaw this, you know."

"This?"

"Said she suspected I was lonely, given everything, and she knew that you were too. Young. Lonely. In danger. Together on the road for a long time. She didn't forbid me to sleep with you. She only asked me to take a few days before I did so, to decide if it would be a good idea for either of us."

I shake my head. Momma K, keeping me from getting laid, from hundreds of leagues away. Some family.

But even that thought sends a pang through me. I never had a mother, and though she taught me for years, Momma K never tried to be that to me. I think she tried quite the opposite, in fact.

"I don't have to guess what you've decided, do I?" I say. "I'll admit, you gave me a little less reaction than I expected, back when I told you. Are you going to tell me it's not me, it's you?"

"Oh no, it's totally you," she says. And then she laughs at my surprise.

But then she sighs, as if worried she hurt me.

"Kylar...I'm a mother. I've got a little girl. That changes everything for me." She shrugs as if that explains it all, as if the conversation is over.

It should be. I'd told her I'm not ready for any relationship. She's now told me she's not either. That should be the end of it. No need for anyone to be embarrassed. No need for anyone to feel rejected. *Let it lie, Kylar.*

"And I'm not fit to be a father?" I ask. My mind flashes to Elene, pregnant with our child. I was going to be a father. For a little while.

"I didn't say that," she says quickly.

"You're not wrong," I say, throwing in a little wry smile, as if the acknowledgment doesn't rip me open.

She looks pained, apologetic. "I...I think you'll be a great father someday. And I don't think you're ready for that yet. Probably not for a while. Right? I mean, why would you be? You're so young. Kylar, if we started sleeping together, I'm afraid I would fall for you. And I can't do that. Momma K said..." She heaves a sigh, knowing she's stopped too late.

"You can just say it," I say.

"She said that you're more fragile now than you realize, that you'd fall for me if I wasn't careful." The hint of a smile touches her lips. "And at first, that didn't sound so bad. But..."

"But you realized how immature I am? Is this the part where you ask if we can just be friends?" The bitterness that steals into my tone isn't fair.

This is not her fault.

Her eyebrows draw in at the shot. But she doesn't strike back. That proves her maturity, as I just proved my lack, I think. She says, "I think both of us need a friend. A friend can save you from taking a bad situation and turning it into absolute hell. I know I make mistakes when I get isolated. The voices in your own head can lead you astray. You know what I mean?"

Heh. The voices in my head. Did you like that part, voice in my head? I liked that part.

But she's being somber, and I've been enough of an ass. "Yes about the making mistakes. But no about the part where friends save you from them. Suppose you've gotta have friends for that."

"Maybe you'd find a friend closer than you think, if you'd look," she says sadly. "But maybe you're right. Maybe we can't be that for each other."

Longing wakes in her nest in my belly, rakes her icy fingers up my chest, and grabs my throat, constricting my breath. "Well, this has been fun," I say. "I gotta run now, but I'm really glad we had this talk."

"Kylar..."

"I'll be back by dawn." I draw the shadows about me, and their weight is welcome. The darkness hides me. It's my home. There's no shame in the darkness. No exposure. And lest I hear Phaena's curses or her pleas or her tears— each worse than the last—I flee into the night.

It's what I do.

Chapter Thirty-Eight

Over a Barrel

*I*n the dank cellar, the nobleman coughs on the niter in the air. His face drips sweat. His arms spread like a child begging for a hug, he's lashed to a tun barrel taller than he is. Imagination is the best torturer.

The tun lies on its side. Half full of vinegared wine, it's as heavy as ten or twelve men put together. The way Count Aemil Wesseros is tied, facing the barrel, he could push off from his toes and make it roll—if he wanted to crush his own head when it continued rolling him down on the other side. With his hands and feet lashed close against the barrel, though, he can't get the leverage to do anything else.

"I admire your courage," I tell him quietly from the shadows, and I'm not lying. "I was once tied up like you are now. I didn't much care for it even before the torture started. But a virtue like courage is meaningless unless it's used in the service of some good, don't you think?"

He grunts. "Oh, so you're the good guy now?" They're the first words he's spoken since I broke his nose and gave him that blood mustache.

It annoys me. It's uncomfortably close to what I said to Lord Repha'im.

"Good guy?" I say aloud. "Huh." I start unfolding a package on top of the smaller hogshead barrel I set on its end to make a table. We're in a cellar in an old abandoned house now being renovated for new owners in Hell's Gorge. Up near the top, though, where oddly enough the homes aren't that bad.

This is not the house that the Clipper told Phaena I could use. I don't trust him enough for that. I've got a pretty good nose for truly abandoned buildings, a skill I developed as a kid when looking for safety in the slums. Sleep is always a vulnerable time for people on the streets. But if the Clipper had people following the count to see if or how I did the job, and if they're sufficiently good that I've missed them, they may know I'm here anyway.

I checked my perimeters and have seen no one.

It's dark in here.

Actually, it's too dark. I forget sometimes that not everyone can see perfectly in darkness.

I light a single candle so my noble friend can see a little. What fear he was going to feel from hearing from a creature like me in the perfect darkness has already been juiced from his flesh. The sweat on his body attests to it.

Now to give his imagination new fruit to pulp for nightmares.

I set the candle where he can see the implements laid out on the hogshead barrel table, barely, if he cranes his jowly head back as far as he can.

I peel off my tunic. Carefully turn it right side out. Carefully fold it. That I'm of medium height and slender is generally an asset in my work, aiding in stealth and frustrating descriptions of me, but it does mean big, fat men who were athletes in their youth don't find me threatening.

As if something small can't kill.

People are irrational. Can't change that, so I work with it. I've been training for hours every day for more than half my life. It's not pride to note that I've an impressively muscled physique.

But I don't act as if he's supposed to be impressed. He'll pretend not to be. Machismo is irrational, too. Instead, I move the hogshead forward a bit so he can see it better.

I unfold the cloths on the table to reveal a graduated hollow metal cylinder, some olive oil, a live mole trapped in an open glass bottle, and a length of rope.

I bow over the table, reverent. I light another candle, this one red.

"*Ch'torathi sigwye h'e banath so sikamon to vathari. Vennadosh chi tomethigara. Horgathal mu tolethara. Veni, soli, fali, deachi. Vol lessara dei.*" I do my best to make the words sound like a prayer to some dark god. In truth, it's the blessing Durzo spoke over me a long time ago. I'd never heard the language before, and haven't since, and though my memory is very good, it needs refreshing now and again lest I forget the words before I find the translation.

I sigh. I really don't want to do this.

I bow my head again as in prayer, tenting my hands in front of my chest. Aemil's head is cranked as far toward me as possible. He's gonna have a crick in his neck tomorrow if he keeps that up.

On second thought; no, he won't. The dossier the Clipper gave Phaena told me enough to know that Aemil Wesseros won't weigh heavy on my conscience: A scion of an important noble family that rivaled the Gunders, he fled Cenaria when Aleine Gunder came to power. He used his wealth (some of it stolen) to buy himself a title in Alitaera. He's been angling for years to climb the greased pole of power higher, and believes that when he saunters into the empress's presence tomorrow, she'll swoon at the sight of him and immediately name him King in the West over all other suitors.

Self-deception isn't a country that belongs solely to the wealthy, but they are overrepresented in those lands.

Since arriving in Alitaera, Count Wesseros has cheated business partners and lovers; married two women at the same time; forged the wills of both after their deaths, which both happened in suspicious circumstances; embezzled imperial funds; and, when he almost got caught for that last transgression, framed yet another business partner for it. That man 'hanged himself' in his prison cell, cementing his guilt for the embezzlement in the eyes of the crown and ending the investigation before the man could testify against Wesseros.

According to the Clipper, Wesseros paid a prison guard for the deed.

The prison guard faithfully carried out the murder he'd been paid for. What he didn't do was seek the warden's approval for the murder first, which meant the warden didn't seek the Clipper's approval for the murder first.

It turned out the Clipper had had a plan for that noble, so he was irked when the man committed suicide, and when he found out it wasn't suicide, the Clipper was far more than irked. Ordinarily an unsanctioned hit commissioned by a lower noble would earn that noble a visit and an extraction of promises to cut in the Clipper on some future work. If he were particularly disrespectful, the noble might receive a careful beating, too.

But the Clipper had been dealing with some breakdowns of discipline in his organization. He needed to make an example. Wesseros, as a count, but a friendless and corrupt one, was the perfect candidate. It was why the Clipper wanted to use an outsider for the job, too. When someone a crime boss wants gone simply disappears and no one in their organization knows how he did it, it makes all of them wonder what other scary people he has on the payroll. It announces to would-be rivals that the boss has weapons the rival doesn't know about, and thus can't neutralize.

That buys a lot of respect and more fear. Fear restores discipline.

I take a dab of the olive oil on my fingertips and take a deep breath, as if bracing myself.

~I love this part.~

I draw the oil in a strip down my chest.

Steam escapes. I grunt, pursing my lips. The skin bubbles, and jet-black metal is revealed beneath torn skin.

I take a few deep breaths and extend the line down my belly. Again, hissing and bubbling. I moan to cover the lack of a sizzling sound. It takes me hours of practice to prepare a simple illusion, and so far I can only do visual ones. Aural illusions would be awfully handy. What's more, I know they can be done. Scarred Wrable is known for being able to throw his voice and even other sounds.

I can't do that. Not yet.

Durzo's left me, and the only other people who might teach me anything would rather kill me or capture and study me instead.

"To answer your question, no. Not a good guy," I say. "A good man wouldn't do what I'm going to do next."

I smile at him, and as I smile, my teeth go ka'kari-black.

You give them little glimpses.

Because fear is irrational, too.

I look away. "I want you to know something, Aemil. I'm not here for you, but when the Night Angel is upon me, don't meet my eyes. If I look into your eyes then, I will judge you. I will see your every sin, and I will *punish*."

A lot of the rest of this is mummery. The gibberish, the illusions... but this last is all true. Durzo once said that for a time, after holding the ka'kari for long enough, he became so sensitive he could see a lie as a man spoke it. I'm not that sensitive. Maybe I never will be. But when I see awful, awful things in a person, I move to end them, because some monsters I will not suffer to live.

"Has the poison started working yet?" I ask.

"Poison?" His voice is suddenly tight.

"Didn't notice, huh?"

"You didn't... You never..."

"Should be some discomfort in your belly by now."

He goes silent.

I grin, flashing black metal teeth again. "Don't fret. It's only a laxative."

"A, a what?"

I imagine he's heard of laxatives, so he's not wondering what I said; he's wondering why.

"I need room to work," I say.

After a befuddled moment, he demands, "The hell does that mean?!"

"Any time now. You want your trousers off, or on?"

He curses me repeatedly.

"Expensive ones, too. Pity."

He groans at a stomach cramp. "Off, dammit. Off. Please!"

The ka'kari makes one hell of a knife. It snaps out of my hand like a stiletto, but then I morph it into a little hook from my finger. I slide that finger down each outseam, and his trousers and underclothes fall off.

He's livid that I cut them, swearing more at me in words damp with fear. As if I were going to untie him so he could take off his trousers. I scoot a chamber pot between his legs with my foot, and step back, lean against a wall, and wait, casual, patient.

Time hunts us both, but it will devour Wesseros first.

It doesn't take long. Cramps rack him, and he tries to hold back, but he makes the inevitable splattering mess.

Odd thing, even though the ka'kari isn't covering my face, I can't smell anything.

~I was assuming you'd prefer not to.~

You assumed right.

The ka'kari's never been in a hurry to tell me its secrets, and I usually stumble across them like this. I had no idea it could do that. Wiping out my sense of smell? That is an odd kindness, though, isn't it?

When Aemil is done, I slosh water generously over his butt and legs until he's clean.

"I'll kill you," he says. He's so flushed he's gone almost purple. Sometimes I forget how easily people get embarrassed. "I swear to all the hundred gods I'll kill you."

Anger covering humiliation, fear.

Maybe I won't have to do it after all.

I slap a foot on the tun, a thumb's width below his manhood. He starts in fear. More afraid of getting kicked in the stones than of demons in the dark.

Aemil's an odd one.

I push hard, and the barrel rolls.

His bonds lift him off his feet, and when he's lying mostly atop the tun, I kick blocks beneath it to keep it from rolling farther. Then I adjust his bonds to draw his knees out. He fights against it, but he's got no leverage. Soon he's sprawled froglike, ass in the air.

I slosh water again on his further exposed nether regions. Then, with the dispassion of a mortician, I rub him clean and dry with a cloth.

Oh, I'm sorry, does this offend your delicate sensibilities? You know what kind of man I am. You know the work I do. You know what's at stake for me: a friend, a kingdom, innocent lives.

Why are *you* here, reading this or listening to it, judging me? You don't have to be here. I do.

But don't worry, I haven't forgotten our deal.

"What are you doing?" he asks, and this time his mask of anger is thin as rice paper.

"In Cenaria, the Sa'kagé was constrained from the top. Our Shinga had a code. She weeded out our monsters. Thought they were bad for all of us, that they invited investigations, interference, repercussions, vengeance." Numerous as my problems with her are, Momma K is a singular character, and I respect her more than anyone. If anyone can successfully make the transition from crime lord to duchess, it will be her. "But other cities aren't so lucky with their scum. One time, I was visiting the Sa'kagé in—well, never mind where—and they were torturing this woman. They didn't care whether or not she died— which, as a professional, I can tell you is something that not enough people decide before they start torturing. They had this method that turned out to be one of the most disturbing things I've ever seen. I'd tell you all about it, but I'm not much for words. Always get halfway through a story and then realize there was a thing I needed to tell at the beginning. So rather than tell you, I'm going to show you. Not really sure if it'll work on a man. Guess we'll find out."

Piquing the imagination.

More inchoate cursing follows.

I dribble olive oil down his butt crack.

Oh, right, we were talking about your delicate sensibilities. You're curious about the work of a killer—and now a torturer, sad to say—but you don't want to hear anything *too* disgusting. You're an odd bundle of contradictions, aren't you?

But I can hardly condemn you for that, can I? I've got a few contradictions myself.

Anyway, I haven't forgotten. I'll warn you when it's time to turn away. You can trust me. I won't describe his hairy hole or his shriveled scrotum or the humble manhood he had so proudly hoped to introduce to the empress.

Who knows, if we're both lucky—I mean, you and me, not Wesseros—turning away won't be necessary at all, at least not today.

More cursing. He flails against his bonds so hard that if I hadn't used silk rope, he'd have bloodied his ankles and wrists and knees by now.

"I've got friends," he yells. "I'm not here alone! They'll be here any moment."

"Friends, huh? Well, I envy you that. Were there only the six, or was that seventh one of them too? I couldn't tell. He moved like a civilian, but I took him out as well. To be safe."

Silence.

Then he says, "Dear gods."

I didn't kill them. Not that he needs to know that. A knockout poison and a lot of rope. I mentioned you have to be careful with knockout poisons: can't really use them on kids. But there are problems even with adults. What's a lethal dose for one person, another person shakes off in an hour. Durzo figured out some of the factors that affected that: Good physical condition, habitual drunkenness, and oddly, vegetarianism can all push sensitivity up. But when you don't have time to ascertain a deader's full chirurgical history, you make do with rope and gags.

Like so much else in wet work, you need to have solid fundamentals to back up the magic and the toys.

Good thing, I suppose. Killing a man is too easy. Getting away with it oughtn't be.

I move to the table again to draw his attention to the items there. He looks at them blankly.

Not the blank of terror. Just . . . blank.

This one's imagination appears to be a blunt instrument.

Fine, then.

I pick up the hollow graduated cylinder and smear oil generously on it.

Then I put it down, disgusted.

That much isn't an act. "I don't think I can do this," I say, wiping my oily hands on a rag. A lie. I'm capable of a great deal worse. I wait to give Aemil time to get hopeful, then I finish, ". . . but *he* can."

I'd thought *he* would be an obvious enough reference to the Night Angel, but Aemil merely looks confused.

Very well. Hints and intimations have done nothing. Time to drop the subtlety.

I grab at my bare chest and groan. Then I start digging at the skin, as if cracking open the heavy covers of a book. As the skin peels back over my sternum, a single iridescent blue line is revealed along the black skin. I'm still experimenting with my Night Angel persona, but I like this deep burning cool blue as an accent. Don't know why. I might be immortal; I might yet live seven hundred years and get jaded like my master, but right now I'm still twenty years old, and I think it's scary. And kind of awesome.

Count Wesseros's eyes bug out.

I brace myself, and with a yell, I tear my skin off like I'm shucking off a coat. It is pretty horrific-looking, if I do say so myself. Skin clings to my hands, and at my neck and above, it's bleeding from being torn. My chest beneath is all gleaming obsidian muscle and blue accent lines burning in the darkness.

I walk out of the line of his sight. He turns, looking for me, but he can't turn far enough. Sweat drips down his cheeks, dampens his hair, trails down his naked back. His breathing is quick, labored. Finally.

I grunt and groan, as if in more pain, but really to make noise to cover the sound of me taking off my trousers and underclothes. The ka'kari could simply devour them—but then, when this mess is done, I'll be without trousers and underclothes.

~You're bringing that up *again*?~

I let the ka'kari come to my skin. It covers me perfectly and silently in black metal curves and—begrudgingly—burning blue accents. I keep it free of my head, though—best to do this in stages if I don't want to have to go through with torturing Wesseros.

As I step back into view, he gasps, then says, "Gods, what are you?"

"Not a good guy. Not that." I'm still working on the voice. I haven't had to speak much as the Night Angel. It should sound different than my regular speaking voice, though, shouldn't it? I want to be intimidating, like the Night Angel is possessing me or something—as if I'm not fully in control of my actions—but I don't want to be goofy raspy.

Also, should I only do the voice when I'm wearing the entire outfit? What about now, when it's not covering my face? Decisions, decisions.

I say, "I am the imperfect avatar of an immutable ideal. I am the hungry maw of Justice. I am the reaching hand of the curse. I am the sharp teeth of Vengeance. I am the open throat to hell."

I can't tell if his silence now means I have a great future as a torturer, or none.

~I thought it was perfect. This level of eloquence suits you. This is you, Kylar.~

The praise strikes me as if I'm a baritone being lauded for not trying to sing soprano, with all the implicit barbs about how well I wasn't performing before when I tried it.

But now isn't the time to get into it with the ka'kari. I go on. "I'm going to tell you exactly what's coming, and if you're completely honest with me, I'm going to leave you a dull knife you can use to cut your ropes and escape."

"You idiot, you fool! Release me this instant! My men are on their way even now. Don't you know who I am?"

Ah, progress.

"You were the brother of a duke. Now you're merely the count of some Alitaeran backwater. A man who plans to try his luck with the empress, and then if that fails, will try it again in attempting to reclaim his dead brother's titles back in Cenaria. Aemil, even if your men somehow guessed where you are, they don't like you much. Not enough. Truth is, no one knows we're here. No one's coming to save you. I'm not the best at what I do, but I am very, very good. Quite good enough for tonight."

"What do you want?" he asks, his eyes bulging.

Finally. "You got a bracelet to get into the empress's party. You're going to tell me how you got it, and you're going to give it to me."

"Go to hell."

"Undoubtedly. In time."

Strangely enough, though, that's the one problem immortality solves entirely for me.

~No it doesn't. You merely displace your hell from eternity into the present.~

I have no reply to that, so I head back to the table and pick up the bottle to check on the mole.

The ka'kari is at its worst when it's right. I can hear a hydra roaring, and it's no mystery which one as it gnaws at the edges of every bit of life that makes life worth living.

"What—what are you going to do to me? You just got this look on your face."

Imagination is the best torturer, but some men have no imagination. "This funnel goes in your rectum. I force the mole down it and inside you. Then I tie your legs together so it can't get out the way it went in. The mole panics. Tries to dig out some other way. Good diggers, moles, and don't need much air. They'll carve through muscle or bowels with ease. Apparently, sometimes they burrow all the way out of your body before you die."

"Oh gods have mercy."

"Tell me everything and you live. Last chance, Aemil. Don't make me do it. I don't like killing the innocent."

His face goes slack with fear. "I'm not...I'm not entirely innocent."

"I was talking about the mole."

And without my quite meaning to call it forth, the black ka'kari comes up over my face in hues of cold fiery blue judgment, and I stare into his eyes and *See*. He's a tick bloated fat with the blood of evil.

Remember that thing I promised? About telling you when you should turn away?

Now would be a good time.

As it turns out, imagination is only the second-best torturer.

Chapter Thirty-Nine

A Slavering Beast

As the sun's first rays set fire to the highest spire of the ziggurat behind me, I hop onto Phaena's balcony. I pick the lock to her door. I slip into the dark warmth of her room.

Disturbed by the gust of wind that followed me in, Phaena rolls over in her sleep. I pause inside as she kicks the covers off and settles back to sleep. I suddenly remember her momentary blank terror at the idea of waking to me looming over her, and I freeze, unsure what to do.

As I stand still, I'm assaulted by unwelcome memories. Elene, rolling over in bed to find me awake, again compulsively checking our old room for danger, my lifetime with Durzo slow to lose its grip on me. A soft, hazy smile on her face—I remember it so keenly!—and a beckoning finger, 'C'mere, you,' she said, and I went. To her arms and her comfort, I went and all was well, all the storms within me soothed. And I remember Vi, hair tumbling in waves of liquid sunrise, her face startlingly soft in sleep, unguarded.

But Phaena is neither of those women, and vulnerable as she is, I'll terrify her if I wake her like this.

I unlock her door and slip out to the hall. Once outside, I knock.

She calls out something and a minute later opens the door. She's put on a thick robe but looks concerned.

"How'd it go?" she asks, ushering me in. She goes and pulls open one curtain, letting in the swelling morning light. Then she stops. "You look awful. Exhausted. Are you hurt?"

"Me? I'm fine," I say.

"Sit," she says. And in moments, she's seated next to me on her bed.

I hand her the bracelet with its single, faintly luminous blue gem and two clear crystals.

"You did it!" she says.

I sink into a sulk, though I'm not sure why. "This can't really be our only option."

"What are you talking about?" She searches my face.

"I don't like it," I say. "Wesseros wasn't exactly the epitome of competence."

"Wasn't?" Phaena asks.

I have no energy to answer.

"Was that a problem?" she asks.

It takes me a while to summon the words. "Not after I learned some things about him. He won't keep me up late." But even as I say it, I wonder if that's true. That someone deserves killing doesn't mean that the killing doesn't leave a mark on the killer.

"So do you not want to use this?" she asks, waving the bracelet. "After everything we did to get it?" Her voice is level, but I hear anger underneath it.

I don't answer. I don't know what's wrong with me.

"What do you want to do instead?" she asks. "Try a frontal assault? On the most feared imperial guards in Midcyru—including their battle mages, hunters, seekers, illusion-throwers, maybe a few praetorians, and gods know what else?"

"It's a heist, right?" I say. "I could sneak in. I'm pretty good at that sort of thing, you know."

"If it were that easy, the duchess wouldn't have bothered working so hard to get us a bracelet. Castle Stormfast has hundreds of mages—more than anywhere else in the world outside the Chantry itself. And the gods only know what kind of magical defenses. Assassinations have been attempted there, Kylar, by serious people. How long would it take us to concoct a plan and put together a team to sneak you in, much less get you out? Tonight's the last night of the party." But then she takes a breath, and softens. "I get it, Kylar. Everything about this job is desperate, and improvisational, and maybe literally impossible. But you're the one who still wanted to try it."

She lets that sit—on me, not on her, which tells me once again that she has been taking lessons from Momma K and her lethal silences.

"It's fine. If we don't, we'll never get Logan's kids back," I say. "There's nothing for it. It's worth the stretch. I guess I'm just tired."

Phaena relaxes. "Okay, then. Okay . . . Two things, though."

"Go ahead."

"Someone broke into this room last night."

"Huh?"

"The door wasn't barred when I came to let you in."

"Oh. That was me," I say. "I didn't want to wake our hostess or her servants and have witnesses that I was out all night. Figured it would be faster to climb in."

"So you walked past me and went outside to knock? Why didn't you just wake me?" she asks.

"I . . . I didn't want to scare you, and . . . You'd thrown off most of the covers."

She looks down at her now-robed figure. "Oh." She clears her throat. "I, uh, always sleep nude at home. Finally felt safe enough to go back to normal, I guess. Sorry."

"Sorry? I'm the one who broke into your room. I didn't mean to—I hope I didn't take away that feeling of safety from you. I didn't . . . you know, ogle you. Once I saw."

She blushes and seems on the verge of saying something, then changes her mind. Gets more serious. "You seem tired," she says.

"Exhausted. And I need to get a few hours' sleep before tonight or I'll make mistakes. But I don't know if I can. Lack of discipline, you know. I start thinking about things I should leave well enough alone." I don't know why I tell her that.

"Strip off your gear. I'll sing you a lullaby."

"A lullaby? Am I acting like a spoiled child again?" I ask wryly.

She suppresses a smile. "Come on now. My voice isn't the best, but the luthier isn't going to be able to deliver my new lyre until later."

"Lyre?" I ask, coming to her and, at her insistence, laying my head in her lap.

"You know, to replace the one the bandits smashed?" She says this as if I should know what she's talking about.

"Oh, right," I agree, because her voice sounds strained to be recalling the bandits, but I'm pretty sure I never saw a lyre.

~You did.~

I did?

~When she killed that bandit, you noted 'A lyre smashed into a mess of wood splinters and strings.'~

Oh. I guess I did. Hey look at you, being useful! Volunteering, even!

The ka'kari doesn't quite huff into silence, but it doesn't answer me.

Phaena starts humming, stroking her fingers through my hair, and then she sings. Her voice is rich and capable of swooping lows, and between her fingers on my scalp—why does that feel so good?—and the soothing balm of that voice, I don't even try to pick out the words of the song, which is somehow familiar. Maybe I heard other children sing it, though I don't think anyone ever sang it to me. My childhood didn't feature many lullabies.

"What is that?" I ask. "Something I'd know?"

"No. It's new. You might've heard me humming parts of it on the road," she says. "I'm still trying things out. It's a motif for you. It'll sound better with accompaniment. And maybe even *good* once I figure you out a bit more. I'm still trying to figure out how the Night Angel part fits with the Kylar parts."

"Ha. You and me both," I say. I settle in to her smile, and there in the softness of her lap, I surprise myself by not making something sexual out of something simply soothing. I've become awfully mature recently.

Or maybe I'm just that tired. Regardless, there's something refreshing and comforting about her. To a man with limbs heavy from hunger, she's a touch of honey on the tongue.

It is breathtaking, as if, freed of apprehending a woman solely through the tiny aperture of my libido, I stand suddenly at a hilltop, seeing the rising sun of her in her full glory, as she takes on depth and color I'd never noticed before, whole horizons unfolding: not woman merely as potential lover, but as friend, as confidante, as potential soul mate, as someone's daughter, a sister, a mother. A woman whole, enmeshed in the rich weave of her relationships, of which the least is some few flirtations with me.

To see her this way is alluring, enchanting, and not as intimidating as it ought to be. Maybe because her fingers in my hair feel so relaxing.

"I can tell you a little Night Angel story, I guess, if you think it'd help your song," I say.

She makes some noise of encouragement.

"It was something my master told me before he—well, not too long ago. He said, um, well, enough with the excuses: Five thousand eleven years before the coronation of Jorsin Alkestes to the Siege Perilous, Ashur Ram Mandaru, last of the Ramranah-tarib, plotted his great abomination to culminate at midnight on the longest night of the year, a night his astrolographers had told him would be, from a unique conjunction of the planets and the new moon, the darkest night in a thousand years. He believed that if he reached a certain pinnacle of depravity at that moment, he would ascend and become one of the gods beyond the veil.

"Instead, after all the preparations were done, after the slaves had spread the caltrops and the fathers had their bodies shaved and their heels bolted bloody to the ritual stones, and the mothers had bathed their children in the oil and shushed them from their cries, as Ashur took to the dais with his blade of hammered bronze, and the ten thousand lanterns were extinguished as one, and the whimpers of the condemned rose with the priestesses' clouds of incense, before the great king could speak into that unholy darkness, a new star was born suddenly, brighter than a full moon. A star that burned with such intensity that it cast shadows even during the day for two years before it disappeared as mysteriously as it had arrived. But that night, that temporary star appeared from the darkest corner of the darkest sky in a thousand years. In so doing, it ruined Ashur Ram Mandaru's ritual and perhaps his ascendance to godhood.

"It is said that from that light, that fragment of a dying star—or, some say, from the doubly dark shadows it cast—stepped the first Night Angel, and she slew the mad emperor in front of his whole court and those held in his thrall."

I look to see how she's taking this, but from her lap it's hard to read Phaena's expression.

I say, "I've never heard of those places or titles or people. I don't know if any of it's true. But supposedly, that is why the darkness welcomes my eyes, for some part of me was born of darkness. I am supposed to be a light in the darkest night, hope for the despairing, and despair to those who crush hope. Light to those who stumble in the darkness, and an abyss in the night to those who deserve to fall." I shrug, feeling suddenly far too serious. "Or, you know, maybe it's a silly story." I smile up at her, tiredly.

"Yeah. Silly," she says. She swallows.

I hadn't noted it in the story before, except as a curiosity, that Durzo referred to that first Night Angel as 'she.' When I'd asked, Durzo had said in some versions of the tale, the first Night Angel was male, but he preferred this way. He hadn't elaborated why, and I could tell what was a closed door with Durzo.

Was that Nemesis? Was she real? "That was a terrible story. Sorry," I say, closing my eyes.

"No, no, it's fine," Phaena says. I can't read the emotion in her voice. I'm too tired.

"Kylar," she says, an instant later, oddly far away.

Jarringly, her voice comes not from above me but from across the room. My eyes flick open, hurling my consciousness toward unwelcome alertness. She's standing facing me, walking back from the door, a folio in her hands. A pillow is now propped beneath my head.

"How long?" I ask, sitting up.

"You slept most of the day. It's time to get ready now. You drooled a little," she says, smiling as if it's cute.

"I droo—I did not!" I wipe my chin—ugh, it's wet! "I did! You know, I'm gonna blame you for this. When you said you didn't have the best voice, I thought you meant it wasn't very good, not like literally, *Hey, my voice isn't the very best voice in the whole world but maybe only the second or third.*"

She gives an embarrassed smile. "You're too kind."

"No, not at all. I'm just the right amount so you never tell Momma K I was drooling all over you. Literally."

"Kylar. Please. I would never tell her about that. Unless..."

"Unless what?" I ask.

"Unless it gave us a good laugh at you."

"I'll never forgive you!"

She laughs and glances quickly at my lips. She's standing close, holding something in her hand, but she seems to have forgotten it.

I remember myself and step back. Because I'm a damn oak.

She seems to come to herself. Hands me the parchment. "You'll have no choice but to forgive me when you see what you get to wear. That or you'll hate me twice as much."

I look at the parchment. It's got a highly detailed description of an ornate blue chest and how to open its false bottom and a good drawing of the lock mechanism.

"Is this...? Is our thing inside this?" I'm not going to say anything about the Nemesis Compass out loud.

"I sure hope so. Because that's as much as we've got. When you're finished, burn it."

I toss the parchment in the fire, having memorized what I need. "Wait, did you say something about what I *get to* wear? Does that mean I have a choi—?"

"Get to wear as in, have to wear. But trust me, you'll look smashing."

Chapter Forty

An Admirable Ambush

The sweat trickling down my spine has nothing to do with the heat in our fancy carriage. Phaena and I have spent several hours waiting in queues at the various gates ascending Castle Stormfast, and now we're before the seventh and final gate's security. She is a vision in midnight blue silk skirts and white brocade and delicate gold chains and dazzling jewels; I am her more demure complement in a lean-cut black jacket with inset red panels and gold brocade. She wears Lord Wesseros's ill-gotten bracelet, I my anxiety.

There is no talk. There is no backup plan. We're nearing the front of the queue.

I hear a scream outside, ahead of us.

Our carriage driver curses quietly. "Poor bastard," he says.

I poke my head out of our open window into the evening air. Up and down the line of carriages, circling the seventh spiraling level of Castle Stormfast, others are doing the same. "What was that?" I ask.

The carriage driver says, "'Nother un tryner sneak inna the party. He fourt 'em, and they just trew him off the side." The driver looks at me, eyebrows raised. "Their captain don't seem too nithered. They're 'lowed to do thet." He curses again and shakes his head. "Some whut think they're so special, oi?"

I pull my head back in and sit.

"That was the third one, huh?" Phaena asks. Her skin is ashen.

"The others got away with a beating," I say. "So if they get us, don't fight back. Momma K will get you out. Eventually." I adjust my own bracelet. Mine isn't magical, but decorative: the platinum bracelet Durzo gave me, currently without the ka'kari, which I hold inside my body.

"Are you going to follow your own advice?" Phaena asks.

If I fight, what does winning mean? More soldiers, a general alarm, the elites coming down on our heads like the wrath of gods. It'll get Phaena killed, that's for sure. "This is a terrible idea," I say.

Phaena fidgets with the bejeweled bracelet on her wrist. Wesseros told me that the single large sapphire on it, next to two pieces of clear crystal, denotes that he's a noble, albeit at the lowest of three levels attending tonight's party. I know there's magic in the bracelet, but I haven't examined it too closely, afraid the ka'kari will devour something important in it and get us killed.

Minutes pass. The carriage continues its halting progress toward our doom.

"Kylar," Phaena says, "if this goes badly..."

"It will."

"Could you be the strong silent type for me, just for a few minutes?" she says.

I grunt.

She sighs, looks away, then takes a breath as if summoning her courage. "It's about my work."

"You don't have to justify it," I say. "I'm the last person who'll judge you for that." I realize as I say it that this is not exactly true. Judging people is kind of what I do. But, you know, there's judging and there's judging. "You know what *I* do. You lie on your back to keep your family together and safe? So what? I'm not gonna condemn you for that."

"See, that's the thing," she says, shifting uncomfortably in her seat, and inside my head the alarm bells start going off. "That's not...exactly my job? That's what Momma K told me to tell you—ordered me to tell you, really—that if, um..."

I get a sick feeling in my stomach. "If *what*?"

She says nothing. She stares out the window at the desert and the sea spread below the castle, as if too ashamed to meet my eyes.

I say, "Why do I get the feeling that it's either far, far too early for you to tell me what you're about to tell me or far, far too late?"

"I've been trying to tell you ever since you took my cover story so well, Kylar..."

Whatever it is, part of me thinks, *this is not the time for you to tell me this. I need to be coming up with a plan for what to do if that idiotic bracelet fails us.*

But another part of me is thinking this is exactly the time for this, and I'd better pay attention and make her spit it out quickly, or something's going to interrupt her and she'll never tell me. Because my life is like that.

"I'm not a—" she begins.

There's a knock at our carriage door.

I curse. "You have got to be kidding!" I hiss. "No. Ignore it," I tell Phaena. "Go on."

The handle rattles.

I grab the handle and hold it in place.

"Go...on..." I command Phaena, my voice a deep growl.

"I'm not a prostitute. That was the embarrassing cover story to keep you from asking more—"

"Kylar?" a woman's voice calls out quietly from the other side of the door. "Please let me in. It's important."

I freeze. I know that voice. What is she doing *here*? I stare unseeing at the door, then at Phaena.

She returns my look blankly. She doesn't recognize the voice.

"Kylar," the voice says. "If you don't want to die...Let. Me. In."

Dazed, I open the carriage door, and Viridiana Sovari hikes red skirts up her long, svelte legs, and gets in the carriage. Sitting across from me, she looks me up and down. "See? I knew it wouldn't kill you to try to look fashionable." She tosses a bundle of neatly folded clothing into Phaena's lap.

With her hair teased up into intricate plaits, artfully applied cosmetics, and a gown perfectly tailored to her perfect physique, Vi is as far from looking as dowdy as she did on the rooftop of Castle Gyre as can be. I can't find my breath, and I'm not sure if it's because she's alive, because she's here, because she's here like this, or if it's simply that she's like *this*.

"Put those on," she tells Phaena, all business. "We're almost to the front of the queue."

Phaena holds up the clothing Vi tossed her. They're servants' woolens. "Excuse me?" she says.

"That's trash," Vi says, pointing at her.

"Excuse me?" Phaena repeats, looking at her own expensive clothing, affronted.

"Not your clothes. Wesseros's bracelet. It's no good."

How does Vi know about the bracelet? "Do you have any idea what I did to get that?" I say, finding my voice.

"Does it matter?" she demands. "Each bracelet has a unique identifier, and that one's been reported stolen."

"That's not possi—"

"Not your theft from Wesseros. Wesseros's theft of it from its rightful owner. If they find you wearing it, it's gonna get you both killed."

Phaena curses before I can. "How do you—? Who *are* you?"

"Clothes, woman!" Vi snaps. She snaps her arm up and Phaena shrinks back, thinking she's going to be hit, but Vi is only brandishing her wrist—which has one of the bracelets on it, though hers is adorned with a faintly glowing stone in ruby red rather than blue, followed by two clear crystals. "Mine is real. I can bring one guest and one servant. Kylar's my guest. So do you want to get into the party or get tossed? And by tossed, I mean tossed *off the mountain*."

Vi has never been one for subtlety.

Anguished, Phaena looks at me.

"Do it," I say.

Phaena pauses for one more moment, then starts stripping down. Vi and I help her, and Vi plucks pins out of Phaena's hair, making her beautiful coif droop artlessly.

"Not the hair..." Phaena says plaintively. But hurriedly, she pulls the woolens over her head and, half-standing in the cramped confines, shimmies the hem down past her hips.

There's a knock at the door.

"One moment!" Vi says.

The door is wrenched open just as Phaena settles down onto her seat, her finely tailored clothing hidden away at the last moment.

Vi thrusts her braceleted wrist toward a sour-faced guard. He stares at the three of us, then waves a magus over. The magus bends so close to Vi's bracelet that his impressive mustache nearly brushes the ruby.

Then he stands and goes back to a lectern to confer with a guard there, perhaps consulting a list.

The three of us look at each other, and I see the tension in Vi's face. She flicks her eyes down to herself, then to the far door of the carriage, then at me and to the nearer door, signaling that if this all goes wrong, which way she's going and which way I should go.

I raise my eyebrows. She wants *me* take the more dangerous route?

"My dress," she says under her breath. "It's supposed to tear easily for certain eventualities, but I wasn't allowed to test it."

I look at her formfitting dress. It is not attire in which one could easily run.

"Certain eventualities?" Phaena says, clearly thinking this is a sex thing.

"Running or fighting," I say.

"The other eventualities too, if necessary," Vi says to Phaena without elaborating.

She never was averse to using all the tools at her disposal. It was required by her apprenticeship to the sick twist Hu Gibbet, who'd hurt her terribly.

"I thought you'd changed," I say. "More than your clothes, I mean. I thought you'd left all that behind."

Vi looks at me like I slapped her. "I'm *trying*, Kylar. It's not been as easy as I'd like. How's *changing* been going for you? You want to tell me what you did to get your bracelet?"

She doesn't mean the platinum one on my wrist. I think about what I did last night, and I shut my mouth. It's surreal to be sitting here, in a distant country, with Vi. I can't wrap my mind around it. I didn't even know if she'd lived through the poisoning. I certainly didn't expect her *here*.

Why wasn't the first thing out of my mouth how glad I was to see her okay? The first thing I say is 'I thought you'd changed'?

Why am I such an ass?

The guard's return keeps me from apologizing. He looks bored, which is a good sign. He hands a plain bracelet with one clear stone to Phaena and a slightly more ornate one with three clear stones to me.

In a voice that makes it clear the rest is rote, in a monotone he says, "You'll be searched at the gate. Any contraband, including alcohols and other intoxicants, inhalants, and narcotics, will be seized and not returned to you. If you wish to leave your carriage here, you may continue on foot. If you have anything to declare, you may do so there with small civil penalties assessed according to the violation. Those undeclared and later found will be assessed a treble penalty. Criminal violations will be dealt with severely, including loss of titles and lands in perpetuity. Sign here to show you understand." He sticks forward a quill and a parchment pinned to a board.

Vi hesitates, her face going blank. I can tell she's trying to remember her assumed name.

"Sign here to show you understand," the guard repeats, annoyed.

Evidently, though, the name comes to Vi's mind and she signs.

The guard leaves but doesn't close the carriage door.

Vi twitches as if to close it herself. Then stops, she looks over at Phaena. "Phaenarete? Phaena? Or is it just Fay?" she says.

Viridiana knows her name? How does she know her name?

Phaena reaches across Vi and closes the door. "Phaena, if it please milady," she says demurely.

The smile disappears as soon as the door is closed, and there's cold fury in Phaena's eyes.

We sag into our seats.

With the immediate danger past, I finally think of Lord Wesseros's bracelet. His useless bracelet, and what I did to get it.

What I did, for nothing.

"The Clipper double-crossed us," I say. "That bastard. After all that talk—"

"Did he?" Phaena asks quickly. She juts her chin at Vi, disgusted. "Who is she? How do you know *she's* not lying about it?"

"She wouldn't," I say. "I know her. She's the kind of woman you want on your side in a fight. This is Vi, Phaena."

"Viridiana," Vi says brusquely.

"Viridiana, right," I say, placating.

"Mage?" Phaena asks, flicking her eyes to the red jewel in Viridiana's bracelet.

"Yes," Viridiana says.

"And you think you can trust her," Phaena says, looking at me. She rubs an eyebrow.

"She's always come through for me," I say. "And I think she just saved our lives."

"We don't know that. But I can bet it's going to cost us as though she did," Phaena says. "That was...the boss's take on the Chantry, anyway."

Viridiana pulls out the count's bracelet and extends it to Phaena defiantly. "Take it then. Put it on and tell the guard you'd like to enter under your own name. See what happens. Leave Kylar here, though. At least until we see how that bracelet works out for you. You can do what you want, but I don't want him to have to try to learn how to fly."

Phaena eyes the stolen bracelet but doesn't take it. "What are you doing here?"

"I want to hear you say it," Viridiana says, her eyes flashing. "I hear you've got all sorts of hidden talents. They teaching nursemaids to fly these days?" She shakes the bracelet. "Take it. Take it or shut up. Or do me one better: Take it and then shut up."

"Vi..." I say.

"Viridiana," she says sharply, still holding Phaena's gaze.

"Viridiana...it's so good to see you," I say.

"You can say it, Kylar," she says, her chin drifting up, but she barely glances at me.

"I was really worried about you back in Elenea. I thought you might be dead."

"Not that," Vi says, but half of an apologetic tone creeps into her voice. " 'What the hell are you doing here, Viridiana?' That."

"I was warming up to that." I wasn't actually. Or hadn't thought of it, yet. There *is* something soothing about seeing her. Even like this.

Phaena snatches the bracelet. "You win. But I'm going to get this checked out later. And if I find out you lied to me..."

"You'll do what?" Viridiana asks.

Phaena purses her lips. "I guess you'll find out if it comes to that."

"Vi—" I start.

"Viridiana," she says.

"Right, 'cause you're *so* different now." It slips out.

Her eyes flash. Her lips go tight.

Whoops.

Then she says, "There you are, Kylar. Always could find my sore spots."

I'm doing it again. Messing up everything. "Thank you for saving us," I say. "I—"

"There are conditions," she says quickly.

"Huh?"

Phaena settles back in her chair, as if it all makes sense now. "This is a Chantry operation, isn't it?"

Now I'm doubly baffled.

"What do you want?" Phaena asks Viridiana. She doesn't defer to me to handle this. I'm merely the hired muscle here.

"Same thing Kylar does," Vi says. "We're on the same side."

Phaena snorts.

Vi stares daggers at her. "You're to go with the servants. An older woman wearing three coins on a necklace will take you by the arm and give you your instructions."

"You *are* here with the Chantry," I say.

"Maybe a little quieter with that? Hmm? Of course I am," Vi snaps, gesturing to her ruby bracelet, as if that explains everything. "And they're competent and have a plan, unlike you two, bumbling around and alerting everyone you come across. I mean, really, Kylar, not only do you come in here with a stolen bracelet, but you also had to drag the blues into this? Like...all of them?"

"I didn't drag all of them into it!"

"No. You're right. You only brought in the most dangerous one. Grandmaster Vitruvius, a man the Sisters painstakingly nudged in a dozen ways to make sure he'd be too busy to attend. Successfully, I may add. Until you came along."

They had? I scowl. "Why don't you want him here? For that matter, how do you even know about him?"

"Kylar, you don't understand the Chantry at all, do you?" Viridiana scoffs. "I mean, I probably should've realized that from when you attacked the Speaker herself and humiliated her inside her own offices, but—"

"I did not *attack* her! I...only scared her a bit."

Granted, it was not my wisest hour. It did feel good for a few moments, though.

"You did what?" Phaena asks me.

Viridiana rolls her eyes. "Point is, the Chantry knows everything. It's how they survive. Women from all over the world receive an education at the Chantry. Even those without enough Talent to complete training are allowed to stay until they can read and learn some skills. They learn history, learn their countries' laws and their own rights, and form deep ties with other women. They go home changed. Noblewomen doubly so, because even if they can't learn magic themselves, they learn how it's used and its limitations. Men believe everything is about power. Women know that everything is relational, even power."

"Oh, all men believe one thing. And all women know better, huh? They teach nuanced thinking at the Chantry, too, don't they?" I sneer.

I sound like a snotty child, I realize. But the whiplash of emotions is too quick for me to think clearly.

"I saved your life. A little gratitude?" Vi says.

"What are you *doing* here?" I ask, slightly more contritely.

"Same thing you are," she says, as if it's obvious. "Making sure Logan doesn't end up dead or on that storm ship, which is pretty much the same thing."

I'm dumbstruck.

Vi frowns at my reaction.

"Logan's *here*?" I finally manage.

"You *don't* know Logan's here?" Viridiana asks. "Why are *you* here, then?"

I look at Phaena, who looks as shocked as I feel. She didn't know about Logan either.

I think. Unless she's that good a liar.

"Why the *hell* is Logan here?" I demand. "Of all the idiotic...He can't be *here*! He's got a kingdom that's threatening to fly to pieces."

"You agree with the Chantry on one thing, then," Vi says.

"What *happened*?"

She looks around, to see if she's got time for this, then says, "You know he and Jenine went with only a token honor guard to meet the empress."

"Yeah, so he could move as quickly as possible, and not be gone for too long. But he told me he was only going as far as Skone. That's like, hundreds of leagues north of here."

"The empress wouldn't meet him. And then she *insisted* on him accompanying her here. With only a dozen soldiers, he didn't have much choice. Any choice, really."

It's exactly what I warned him about. I rub my forehead.

"But why's the Chantry got its nose in this?" I ask. "What's it want?"

Viridiana says, "It wants friends near the levers of power, always. Peace, whenever possible, and stability so they can continue their work. The Speaker's convinced Logan is trustworthy and, more importantly, a whole lot better than any of the other alternatives. They—we—want to make sure Logan gets his treaty and gets back home alive in time for him to still have a kingdom when he gets there."

"And that's all?" Phaena asks.

"The Chantry is never fully on anyone's side except their own," I say.

"I'm sure it's not all," Vi says, "but it's all they told me. I'm the new girl on the team, remember? And I wouldn't even be here except that they found out you were coming. They say you, uh...always have the capacity to change situations completely."

I sag further into my seat. "I'm sure that's *exactly* how they said it."

She flashes a sudden grin and puts on a crone's voice as she says, " 'That man-child always louses things up if he's allowed to run loose, so we'll make him help us instead.' "

I snort but can't help a little smile, too, at least at the first part. Then the second part hits me. Help them? Help them how?

Viridiana's grin fades too. "But...Kylar, if you didn't come to save Logan, why are you here?"

I look over at Phaena. She's stony-faced, but I can tell what she *doesn't* want me to say: *I'm here to find a small royal-blue chest with a peculiar gold scrollwork border, steal the Nemesis Compass that's inside it, make it out alive, figure out if the compass still works, figure out how to use it, use it to find Logan's kids, and bring them home. Preferably before Logan realizes they're gone. The plan's a bit fuzzy at the moment, but I have the utmost confidence it'll all work out.*

I mean, I've had bad plans in my day, even bad plans that worked, but revealing a plan this ruinously bad, to someone who just saved me from another terrible plan to get inside?

Nah.

I say, "I heard this was a killer party. People dying to get in."

Vi deflates. "So that's how it's gonna be? Or are you just showing off for the girl?"

"Girl?" Phaena asks. She's eight or ten years older than Vi.

I look away. I came here to get an item to help me save Logan's kids, but now Logan himself is here and in danger. All the most powerful nobles of the most powerful empire in the world are here. And so is the Chantry. And so are some unknown number of the most dangerous of the blue mages, who know my face and are hunting me. And so is the most elite, magically adept imperial guard in the entire world.

I came here with little hope and less preparation to attempt to do one job. Now, in one night, I have to do two?

'There are no impossible jobs,' Durzo once said.

Why is it only *now* I remember that Durzo's been wrong before?

The carriage rattles to a stop. A commanding voice outside says, "Everyone out for searching, please."

Phaena moves to go first, as a servant ought to. She looks back sorrowfully at the clothes left behind on her seat. "I really loved that dress."

Then she opens the door. The night is a beautiful monster festooned with lights and color, music and laughter. She leads us into its maw.

Stormfast

Chapter Forty-One
Among the Eagles

This is like no party I've ever seen. Even as we join yet another security queue before the last fancy wrought-iron gate that will let us into the palace atop the ziggurat, there are musicians and dancers and sleight-of-hand acts and acrobats to entertain the nobles as we wait. Male servers, bare-chested and wearing little wings and diadems like eagles' beaks, carry trays of appetizers and drinks of every color and provenance, offering them up and down the line. More than a few of the nobles before us greedily gulp theirs down.

"You can get through this, right?" Vi asks, taking my arm.

"You mean security?" I ask. "I'm not armed. Why would it be a problem?"

"They test everyone for Talent. If you've got any, they give you a choker. It reacts to any use of magic. Apparently, the stronger the magic you attempt, the tighter it gets," she says.

"Oh. Lovely," I say. *You've got this, right?* I ask the ka'kari.

"Yeah, it's terrifying," Vi says. "The Sisters said if I slip up and use my full strength it might *accidentally* kill me. The chokers aren't at all calibrated for people like you and me."

"No, I meant you," I say, because it's the first thing that pops into my head. Because I just noticed her as a woman dressed up for a party, somehow for the first time. Even noticing that at this late moment isn't because I'm marginally observant. Instead, I've noticed a bunch of other men—and women—in the line looking her over. Some of them not at all subtly. Momentarily, I was worried something was wrong with her.

Yes. I am that dense sometimes.

"Me?" Vi says.

"You look lovely."

"Oh," Vi says, a cascade of emotions passing over her face as if it's the last thing she expected me to say. "Um...thank you?"

A woman in front of us smacks the staring man beside her with a fan when he doesn't notice that she's advanced ahead of him with the queue, and drags him away from his ogling Vi.

I have a hard time imagining what life's like for Vi. In normal clothing, she gets as much attention consistently as I probably get when I'm fully in my Night Angel skin. Today, she is not dressed in normal clothing.

"You're not using a glamour, are you?" I ask. She did, the very first time I met her. She was trying to kill me.

"*No*," she says, abruptly angry again.

Smooth as a metal rasp, that's me. "I meant..." I trail off. What did I mean? "I meant, uh, I thought your hair was growing in white—or some of it was?— after, you know, after Black Barrow. So I thought maybe now you're using magic to hide that. I mean your hair is naturally such a beautiful red, and with it styled like this, it's, um—not that it looked bad with the white! I mean, I'm glad they let you dress up." She'd said something about the Chantry forcing her to wear those frumpy clothes before, hadn't she? "You look stunning," I finish lamely.

I didn't mean to say the last. It's true, but I don't know if the truth has done me any favors, ever.

Viridiana meets my eyes, surprised once more, then looks away quickly, reaching a hand up to touch her hair, then stopping herself. "Yeah, the hair's strange," she says, as if that's a safer topic. "It's a rare side effect, I guess. I asked them to Heal it, but the Chantry doesn't classify it as an injury. They have this thing. They say when magic leaves its mark on you, you shouldn't take it away. That everything's for a reason."

"I don't understand," I say. Back in Elenea, she'd said something about a fun party trick, but her hair looks normal to me.

"Oh, right, right," she says, flustered. "It's magically reactive. The team had to show me the exact right blend of magics to make the color to match my natural red." She looks away, almost shyly. Maybe apologetically?

Hell, I don't know. I don't know how to read Vi. It's why I like how blunt she usually is. And what's magically reactive hair even mean?

"Team?" I blurt out. We're almost to the front now. She's said *team* twice now, I think.

Hey, you never did answer me. You are *going to cover my Talent, right?*

The ka'kari doesn't answer.

Vi sighs. "The Sisters, I mean. We're, uh, we're going to go meet with them, first thing."

"A team, though."

She scowls. "Hadn't meant to let that slip," she says.

"I love that you're terrible at keeping secrets," I say. I smile my biggest, goofiest grin.

"Jackass," she says, resigned.

~Yeah, don't ask me to change that later. I'm leaving that one in. You deserved it.~

That one? Out of all the things I've done, you choose that one as deserved? Wait, now that you're awake again, you want to tell me you've got the check-point handled?

But the ka'kari goes silent again.

I'm starting to think it enjoys torturing me.

We finally reach the checkpoint at the fancy wrought-iron gate before the palace steps. I'm sweating but trying to keep the tension off my face. What would it mean if I couldn't use my Talent tonight? I'm nothing without it.

The ka'kari wouldn't screw me completely, though. It'll come through. I'm sure of it.

Pretty sure.

A woman in an eagle cloak and a lot of weapons searches Vi while a beefy man head and shoulders taller than me manhandles me. He too is wearing eagle-themed attire, but in his case, it seems perfunctory, his eagle-hood thrown back from his bald head. "You seem awful nervous," he grunts, patting down my legs.

"Oh, it's capable of speech," I say. "Everyone's nervous."

He raps my stones with his knuckles. "Whoops," he says, no trace of apology in his tone. "Hey, Daefia, double-check this one. I've got a bad feeling about him."

"Are you serious, Kylar?" Vi says. She's through her check already, now with a silver anti-magic choker with a large ruby on it in addition to her matching bracelet. It's actually very pretty.

I never did describe that dress, did I? I don't want to look panicky as the mage searches me, so maybe now's a good time. Uh...it's a shiny red that matches the red stones of her bracelet and her new magic choker perfectly, as if she planned for it. Which I guess she probably did—or her Sisters did.

The mage reaches me and stares intently into my eyes, obviously scanning me somehow. I force a smile, then look away, like a normal guest nervous about being stared down by a mage would.

The dress has got those what-do-you-call-them? the things that pull fabric in? pleats? darting? pulling the fabric to a fancy brooch thing at the side of Vi's waist to emphasize her slender athleticism. The fabric is pulled again to the small of her back in those little soft folds that probably have some other name. It's ankle-length, tight from top to hips, but more flowy below that, slitted up one leg, and with a strap only over one shoulder, with a cloth...um, thing hanging down the back. Not quite a sleeve, not quite a cloak?

The mage pulls my chin toward her with a finger, stares hard into my eyes again. I can feel the magic delving hard into me this time, brushing something hidden deep.

Maybe that dress sleeve thing'd be good for strangling someone? Not a garrote, unless it's got a pocket for a stone—very important to crush the trachea. Much faster than simple strangling.

But no. It's probably just a half-sleeve, half-cloak thingy. Probably has a name.

Remind me never to attempt describing women's clothes again, would you?

The mage turns away, finished with her examination. "No Talent whatsoever," she sniffs to the guard. "But please, do rough up our guests some more, moron. The commander always appreciates the complaints, especially when they're relayed to him by the empress herself."

The man grunts. Maybe it's an apology. To her, not to me.

I'm sensing a theme in my life.

Vi takes my arm as I rejoin her. Then immediately drops it. She swears quietly. "Forgot."

"Forgot?"

"I've got things to do here, Kylar. Things best accomplished if I appear to be very much unattached."

We walk up the twisting stairs together. I can hear the roar of the party through the many open doors. Light growls into the night from hundreds of broad windows.

Inside, we're devoured by noise and spectacle, lights and glitter and the crush of thousands of the empire's elite and all those necessary to entertain and serve them.

In a former life, I learned that to be invisible, I have to look ordinary. Here, that doesn't mean stooping, eyes at the floor, hurrying to my destination. Instead, I straighten my back, paint on a wide fake smile, and cast my eyes about as eagerly as any empty-headed young lord.

I hate parties. Bad things always seem to happen at them for me. There's always too many things to keep an eye on, too many dangers. Is Grandmaster Vitruvius here already? Does he have men keeping an eye on every door for me? Maybe not. Maybe he too was only able to bring in one guest and one servant.

"This way," Vi says.

"I'll be a few steps behind you," I mutter, openly staring at some beautiful woman other than Vi that a number of other men are staring at, too. Vi herself is too conspicuous for me to stay too close.

Suspended either from wires or by magic, eagle-costumed dancers fill the air above the raucous party, dazzling with acrobatics and flashes of magic both. But many of the nobles ignore these sights, jaded even to this.

They aren't jaded to the virtues of alcohol, though. Enormous trays of empty glasses are being replaced at every moment by new trays of full ones, and from the noise and flushed faces, those present are partaking liberally. From the pupils of many of the party-goers—some with pinprick pupils, others with unnaturally dilated ones—alcohol isn't the only drug being enjoyed.

Vi glides through the crowds ahead of me, and while appearing interested in everything else, I follow her. At one point, I see a man grope her as she goes past.

She stops immediately and turns. There's a smile on her face. She bites her lip but then ducks her head shyly. I can't hear what she says first, but the middle-aged man who did it steps forward with a swagger.

She takes his hand in both of hers and appears to be about to kiss it, but she looks around, as if demure.

Vi, demure.

Oh hell.

"My lord," I hear her say as I finally get close enough. "If I did something outrageous right here, would you make a scene?"

"On my honor, no."

"Mmm," she coos. "On your honor."

Don't do it, Vi.

She draws his hand down and leans in close toward him to whisper in his ear. I'm watching the hand. I see the quick twist as she dislocates his thumb and breaks at least one finger.

His eyes bulge and he yelps. His companions laugh, thinking it's because of something Vi has said.

She slips away. "I'll see you then," she says, winking. "Don't disappoint me!"

I've accidentally caught up with her. Maybe not completely accidentally.

"Don't you dare chastise me," she says. "I already know what my Sisters will say."

"They won't hear about it from me."

"Really?" she says, meeting my eyes.

"That man was, um, about to spot me, so you had to act quickly to keep me safe. You did."

"I did?" she says. "He was?"

"No. But that's what I'll tell them if they give you trouble."

A look of gratitude and something near happiness washes over her. "You know, Kylar…" Then something melancholy enters her eyes and she concludes, "Upstairs, second room on the right. Bring me a glass of something bubbly."

Then she drifts away, as if I were merely another suitor unsuccessfully trying his luck. I shrug as if to signify *oh well, I tried*, and mingle another direction.

A bit later, I follow her.

Huge hall opens to huge hall, each in their own style of decor and music, each a feast for the senses. Here a young musician's lute throws sparks every time his finger plucks a string, different colors for every note as he dazzles his way through arpeggios with the easy facility of a prodigy. Over there, a tower of four acrobats balances upon one hugely muscled man who is himself balanced on a single hand. Impressively, they're doing it without magic, but with all the magic going on here, they're ignored, as everyone assumes what they're doing is aided by magic, too. In another corner, high above the floor, two feather-clad servants suspended on wires take drinks from a tray, put them on tiny magical disks, and drop them from above to float coruscating down from the sky to the waiting hands of lords and ladies below.

As I pass from room to room, I see that the chambers are representative of different regions of the empire: golden grasslands to verdant forests to rusty deserts, with the various cultures' artistic versions of the imperial eagle soaring over all of them in some way, emblem of the empress's power and sharp-eyed beneficence—not to mention her ability to drop out of the clear blue and wreak bloody havoc, as one mock battle between costumed dancers illustrates graphically, complete with exaggerated spraying blood, to the cheers and fake shrieks of horror but really the delight of those who gather round. The music and foods change with the rooms, but the waiting-for-lightning feeling among the party-goers only intensifies. The stairs are guarded by yet more mages and imperial guards in resplendent armor.

Maybe they're only allowing certain nobles—higher nobility?—upstairs.

Might have mentioned this, Vi. Did your team figure me in to their plans? Or did they forget me?

I've noticed bracelets adorned with many colors. I'm guessing they're meant to simplify things. The various regions of the empire have differing styles of dress and different markers of status that I'm sure not everyone in the other regions knows, so the room for slights and therefore fights abounds. So far, I've guessed that those with yellow gems are imperial servants. Nobles get blue gems, and mages red? Obviously, in each case more jewels means more important or greater access. Clear stones for guests?

How far do mine get me, though?

Above my head, wire-borne performers all in heroic golds and gleaming whites begin a reenactment of some battle of gods from ancient Alitaeran lore. Illusion-throwers cast explosions and the various musicians in this vast hall suddenly join in one swelling chorus. Heads turn everywhere.

Except the guards' heads and the mages'. They barely even glance up, carefully eyeing the crowd from their post at the bottom of the stairs.

Total professionals.

Hoping that I know what I'm doing, I approach them.

Chapter Forty-Two

Special Problems and Tactics

I'm not ten steps from the checkpoint at the base of the stairs when I see him. Grandmaster Glaucon Vitruvius is approaching the checkpoint himself at an angle ahead of me. I only now see him as he turns his head to watch the spectacle above us. A hat is hiding most of his face, which explains how I missed him before now.

He's too close.

I look left and right for any escape, but the guards at the checkpoint have seen me coming. The senior officer's eyes narrow. He's noted the hitch in my step, the furtive glances. If I do anything else that's remotely suspicious, he may come after me. I'm committed now.

As if enjoying the reenactment, I cast my gaze up as I approach the checkpoint. I pass within arm's reach of Glaucon Vitruvius, my skin tingling, heart racing.

The guards at the checkpoint give my bracelet a bored once-over and let me through without a word. The senior officer lets his eyes flick over to the next possible threat, dismissing me.

I head up a long, broad, spiraling ebony-wood staircase as quickly as I can walk without drawing attention. This is where it'd be nice to be tall so I could nonchalantly take two steps at a time. Near the top, I risk a glance over my shoulder and see that Grandmaster Vitruvius has turned from the spectacle and is now in friendly conversation with one of the guards.

He hasn't seen me.

The second level is more intimate. The ceilings aren't so massively tall here, and there are hallways and numerous rooms. From the jewels on men and

women both—mostly two blues with some three blues scattered about—and
from the fineness of the fabrics of their clothing, this is clearly where the richer
and more important people enjoy the evening.

And they do seem intent on enjoying it. The halls are crowded, the talk loud,
boisterous. Laughter punctuates the chatter, some of it nervous, but some free
and jubilant. For some, it is the triumph of their lives merely to be here. The
party has reached a pitch already that most parties only reach after midnight.
Imperial guards in light laminar armor stand at every intersection, eyes roving, reeking of professionalism. They're armed to stop fistfights, not to wage
war: Most have cudgels padded with leather or narrow staves or brass knuckles
nearest at hand, with a gladius at their hips for emergencies, but the only polearms I see are the pole-and-lasso man-catchers they keep propped against the
walls behind every third station.

Every last one of the imperial guards is Talented, and the women among
them doubly so.

At some sixth sense, I throw a quick look back down the stairs. The officer is
pointing up toward me. Grandmaster Vitruvius's eyes lock with mine. Alight.

Disaster.

I don't bolt. Don't dart away. That's not how you melt into a crowd. Even as
he runs up the stairs after me, I merely step into the streams of people coming
and going.

Now? Now I'm fine with being short.

I slip past four imperial guards standing outside the first room to the right
and look for refreshments in a room ringing with the noise of a chamber
concert—odd instruments and weird sounds with a woman singing to an enrapt
crowd, somehow splitting her own voice to harmonize with herself. Soon, I
snag something. There aren't many plausible reasons for covering your face in
public for long, but holding food and drink is one of them.

I slip out the side door, into the next room.

It occurs to me only now that many of the imperial guards must have trained
in Tover—they're not just mage-trained, most of them are *blue*-mage-trained.
And that means a significant number of them must have trained under Grandmaster Vitruvius as Storm Fists.

If their old grandmaster asked them to keep an eye out for me, how many of
them would say no?

I thought I'd only had to look out for Grandmaster Vitruvius, his one guest, and one servant. But now I see the truth. I have to avoid every male imperial guard, which is most of them—and they're everywhere.

Eating the cracker I'd picked up for this, I use my hand to obscure my face as I pass four more imperial guards. I step through heavy doors into the room where I'm supposed to meet Viridiana.

It's a book-lined parlor, all done in acacia wood with elegantly curving armchairs and a roaring hearth. The moment I cross the threshold, a pretty woman with auburn hair and a smattering of freckles takes my arm and pulls me in. She wears a bracelet and choker with three rubies on them—a Chantry mage with lots of access—so I let her lead me back to a smaller room behind the hearth, a little reading nook, apparently.

There's barely room for the five women and one man who share the space with me. All of them adorned with glowing red jewels.

The woman releases me as everyone's heads swivel toward us. The group is perhaps the most ethnically diverse possible, their clothing and skin tones spanning the sprawling Alitaeran empire and beyond—but there's an essential sameness about them. Wherever they were born, these women all were selected by the Chantry and raised to be proud, commanding, fearless, smart, and powerful.

"Kylar," Vi says, "I'd like you to meet the Special Problems and Tactics Team."

"Perfect. I have a special problem," I say, as if I haven't just fled one dangerous mage to find six more subtle and equally dangerous ones. "Grandmaster Glaucon Vitruvius is after me—"

"We know," a woman even shorter than I am says. With cool light skin and ash blonde hair that appears to be literally tipped with gold spikes, she's got one of those faces where you can't tell if she's in her teens or twice that. Pretty, but her expression regards me as if I'm something she stepped in.

"You'd know more if you didn't interrupt," I say. "One of the guards at the stairs pointed me out to him. I may have lost him. But it occurs to me he must know many of the imperial guards. Some will've trained with him, and many may be willing to help him look out for me."

"I got it," the wholesome, softly feminine woman who'd grabbed my arm says, volunteering. She has a voice I could listen to all day. Beneath her finery, she looks like the pretty farmwife next door who would bring sweet baked goods by your homestead to welcome you to the community when you move in. She breezes past me out into the hall.

The rest of them seem unperturbed, as if utterly certain the woman can handle whatever comes her way.

"Who was that?" I ask. "And is she as good as she thinks?"

"That's Melena," Vi says. "She's the best. All of them are."

I notice two things: Vi says, 'Them,' not 'us.' And all of them accept her compliment as if it's a matter of fact.

Now, these Chantry types *believing* they're the best and them *being* the best might be two very different things.

I'm afraid I'm about to find out.

"Well, then. It's a unique opportunity to meet you all," I say, inclining my head.

"I hate him already," the short, haughty blonde says.

"Well, aren't you the cutest little thing? It's an equal pleasure to meet you, little missy," I say. Short people just love it when you patronize them. I'm pretty short myself, so it's not often I get to play the height card. "Maybe when you grow up, you might learn some manners. What's your name, sweetie?"

"Petaria Feu," she sneers. "Not Pet. Not Aria. But save your breath and don't talk to me at all."

"Petaria's our pickpocket," Vi says. "None better. Not even in Cenaria."

"She also has some issues with self-control. Petaria, give it back," a dour older dark-skinned woman says. She's tall, and lean, with short-cropped hair, a gold diadem, and large earrings. She has such presence she draws the eye more than anyone. There's no doubt she's in charge.

Petaria grumbles and holds up my gemstone bracelet. I hadn't noticed her take it. I hadn't even thought she'd come close enough to me to snatch it.

"I didn't think those things could even be opened," I say.

Petaria snaps it shut but doesn't hand it back to me. "They can't."

"Wow, you're a real bitch," I say.

I'd seen the one man in the team but don't notice his approach until it's too late. He's merely my own height but three times my weight. His punch is at my stomach before I can stop it.

I've been hit a lot. I know how to take a hit. I know the differences between people who know how to punch and don't, and the differences between a punishment punch and a punch intending to inflict injury, but I can't tell if this bastard means to hurt me or not. He hits me *hard*.

I stagger back a few steps, groaning.

"*Kylar*," Vi says, as if I'm embarrassing her.

I look around. Apparently, they're all prepared to ignore the fact that the man with veins on his forearms thicker than my neck just assaulted me.

"Petaria," the cold woman in charge says quietly.

"I need it. For the *thing*," she says. "It's a swap, not a snatch."

"Ah, very well."

Petaria slouches away from me, sneering, still holding my gemstone bracelet.

"Oh, she's *that* kind of thief," I say. This time I noticed. She's good, and to be honest, I wouldn't have noticed her snatch my other bracelet—the platinum one Durzo gave to me—if I hadn't been warned about her. "Can't stop herself, huh? That's dangerous, Sisters. Person like that's a danger to the whole team. Give it back, won'tcha, Pet?"

The others look at me, confused, thinking I'm demanding back the gemstone bracelet that she needs to swap for the job. But I can tell Muscles is considering hitting me again—not for that, but for calling her 'Pet.'

"*Kylar*," Vi says. "You're making this harder than it has to be."

"You know, it occurred to me, I never washed my hands after I tried to help that steer give birth yesterday. Had my fist in there way up to the elbow. Never was able to help it, poor thing. Kept trying, too. Wore that platinum bracelet the whole time."

As Petaria looks down at her fingers, disgusted, Muscles snorts. His suppressed grin disappears before Petaria's hot gaze hits him.

Before their leader can speak her reproof, Petaria produces my platinum bracelet from a pocket and shoves it toward me, eyes full of hatred that I caught her. I smile at her as if she's adorable, holding her gaze.

It's a mistake. Not because it elicits her fury—I meant to do that—but because without intending to, I look deeper into her eyes than I'd intended. I feel something triggered deep inside me, and suddenly, in my mind, it's as if I'm thrown bodily against a wall, my face slammed repeatedly against a peephole into Petaria's past.

I see hands, flashing in a blur of flying blood, stabbing a man repeatedly as he tries and fails to block, his forearms and hands dripping, slashed open, ineffectual before the speed of the onslaught. A woman jumps up to run away, half-naked, but I'm faster. I snag her long hair before she can take two steps, and even as her body snaps back from the whiplash, my blade slashes up through hair and throat.

This wasn't the plan.

I kneel over her where she's gasping on the floor, her hands at the wound on her throat, trying to stop the blood spreading in a pool, soaking her chemise, her plaited blonde hair. There's no saving her from this. She's dying. Probably won't be conscious in even a minute.

But at least I can make it a painful minute. I reverse the dagger in my hand, and attack her teeth.

Her teeth!

I tear my eyes away from Petaria's, falter.

Petaria smiles triumphantly, as if it's a victory that I couldn't hold her gaze.

I'm shaken, revulsion arcing through me, but try to hide it.

What am I gonna do? Tell them what I saw?

Hell, maybe they already know what she did to that couple. Maybe it was long ago. Regardless, the only thing worse than them not believing me would be if they did—they'd want to know how I saw it.

"You've met our muscle," Vi says quickly, a flicker of concern in her eyes. She noticed that something happened, and she seems to be covering for me.

"His fist anyway," I say, forcing a smile.

"Jasmine Jakweth," Vi says. "Jasmine's a former blue mage—"

"No, I'm not. Expelled before I finished," he interrupts. Jasmine—is that a nickname?—is either from some ethnic group I don't know or mixed race. He's got skin the color of warm sand, but it's paired with a huge head of long brown hair in corkscrew coils, dark eyes, and a prominent nose.

"From the top of your cohort!" Vi says in a way that makes it clear they're friends. "Anyway, Jas is one of the best. Jasmine, Kylar."

"I like this one," Jasmine says when I don't inquire about his name. "Knows how to take a punch."

"I like you, too," I say. "You seem like a good kid who's fallen in with a bad crowd."

His smile fades. So does Vi's.

"Forget what I said," he says, "I'm with Melena on this one, now."

"Meant it as a compliment," I say.

"I'm so glad to have the chance to meet you in person, Kylar," the farmwife says, heading off any more barbs, coming back into the room as if she'd merely ducked out to grab a drink. She looks quickly at the dark-skinned older woman in charge. "I set a Vilian Sparrow at naught six."

"Six?" the boss says, her eyebrows climbing.

"There was an RG clogging the lane, so I thought it best."

"I suppose we'll know in exactly two minutes."

Melena turns back to me. There is no trace of anxiety in her. Suddenly, I appear to be the center of her world and all her attention, and she appears to like what she sees. Her eyes twinkle, a genuine smile spreading across her face.

"If he's the muscle, and she's the thief, and she's the boss, does that make you the brains?" I ask Melena.

She smiles further. She's one of those people who go from pretty to beatific when she smiles. "I'm the team's lodestone. No good in a fight, sadly, but for whatever reason, it seems people like me. Oh—you should probably hear this from me..." She's suddenly apologetic, her eyebrows gathering in. "I voted with Reyhan. In my defense, that was before I met you."

"I hope to give you the chance to make many more poor choices," I say.

She laughs and puts a hand gently on my forearm. The laugh, like her whole demeanor, is open, responsive, encouraging, but brief enough not to be sycophantic. She looks away quickly, as if she likes me but is shy.

I don't think this woman is shy. I like her, though, even though I know I probably should be scared as hell. She may well be the most dangerous of the bunch.

"And what was that regrettable proposition you—erm, proposed?" I ask the woman who hasn't spoken yet.

Proposition she proposed? I was doing so well there for a moment, then my gold tongue had to turn to lead halfway into a sentence, didn't it?

Under a loose beaded headdress, the last woman of the group has wavy dark hair and warm golden skin, but she shrinks back at my attention, mousy, blinking, and bewildered as if under siege.

"That's not Reyhan," Vi says quickly. "This is Sister Aashvi. Aashvi can speak, but she mostly doesn't. Safe cracker, lock picker, code breaker. The only puzzles she can't crack are the human ones." She gives me a look that says *Kylar, could you not be an ass for a minute?*

"Right. You've got Melena for the human puzzles," I say.

Aashvi shoots a glance at me, confused, and when she meets my gaze she seems to panic, flushing and looking quickly away, twisting her beringed fingers against each other. She's older and weirder than the rest—but then, I suppose they're all weird in their own ways.

I can't exactly judge on that count, can I?

"So where's Reyhan?" I ask. "And what's her job?" I've got an idea *what* she is, and why I can't see her: She's their killer. None of these others fit the type.

It's been at least a full minute now, and still there's no tension on any of the team members' faces. What happens at minute two when Melena's Vilian Sparrow at naught six—whatever that is—runs out?

The dour old woman says, "Sister Reyhan Alaq was killed whilst honorably serving the Chantry in ... in very difficult circumstances. She is sorely missed, and she will be avenged. One day." I can tell that this team is close, and that they're veterans from the way emotion shows briefly on their faces around the circle followed by stony determination. Reyhan's death hit them as the death of a comrade-in-arms.

"So. Does the boss have a name, or do I not rate that?" I ask.

"I am Ayayah Meganah, Sister Ayayah will suffice."

"Sister," I say, inclining my head. "So what is it Reyhan wanted to do with me?"

"She thought that you were a greater threat than anything else," Sister Ayayah says sourly. "She thought that we should abandon our current quest to kidnap you for the Chantry."

"And if kidnapping didn't work, I suppose she advocated the obvious ... ?" I ask.

Sister Ayayah gives me a look as if she hadn't expected me to be so shrewd. "Yes."

"Killing me. Figured. So did the proposal lose or merely get put off until later?"

Flat glances all around, except for the con Melena, who has the grace or the miming skills to appear embarrassed.

"And you?" I ask Vi.

"I'm not given a vote," she says coolly. Apparently she's still mad I'm not playing nice with her new friends.

"And that's two minutes," Sister Ayayah says. "You were right again, Melena. Well done."

"Why not?" I ask Vi.

"I'm the trainee."

"The trainee? Not the new killer? Sounds like there's an opening."

That gets flashes of anger, as I expected, and also tells me that there probably has been discussion of the possibility. A good team never likes it when a rookie joins up; rookies make mistakes and endanger everyone, and replacing a dead veteran the team loved or at least respected is the worst situation a rookie can step into.

"Viridiana's best Talents lie elsewhere, though she needs another decade or two to develop them," Sister Ayayah says. "But we've taken enough time."

"So what's the plan?" I ask.

"You don't need to know most of it. As far as we can tell, the empress has no plan of letting Logan within a hundred paces of her tonight. She has no space on her schedule to meet him, and she has rooms reserved for him and Jenine on the *Storm Racer.*"

"She's planning to bring Logan to Borami?" That would add months to Logan and Jenine's absence. There's no way his new kingdom will survive that long without them.

I'm still reeling from hearing he's here. I came here to save Logan from unbearable heartache, but now his rule and even his life are on the line. What am I supposed to do?

Sister Ayayah says, "Our mission is to make sure he doesn't get on that ship—without precipitating war and without the Chantry being seen to interfere. We're going to give Logan a chance to plead his case in . . . an hour and six minutes?" she asks Aashvi, who nods.

"Or an hour thirty-one minutes, depending how Viridiana's part goes," Melena says.

"The empress is a woman who lives by her schedule, and she uses this night of nights to her advantage," Sister Ayayah says. "If things go according to plan, Kylar, you won't have to do anything but eavesdrop from a spy hole on a meeting we've orchestrated. But if the meeting goes poorly and it looks as if the empress is going to force Logan onto her ship despite whatever he says, you'll barge into the meeting with terrible news. Coming from you, Logan will believe it."

"What do you want me to tell him?" I demand. I've got a wild guess that it's *not* the truth.

"The truth. Tell him his children have been kidnapped, and that he's needed at home immediately. That the plans for recovering them are in disarray. The empress is a hard woman, but she has a soft spot for families. In private discussions, she's already alluded to having reservations about keeping Logan away from his children."

"Private discussions you're privy to, somehow."

Sister Ayayah ignores this. "If any of us comes and tells you to do something, you do it, immediately and without question. We saved your life so that you can help your friend. I assume we can count on your help?"

What am I going to do? Tell them to go to hell? As far as paying the Chantry back for saving my life, this seems like I'm getting off easy. Besides, this party is huge. Without them, I don't know if I can even find Logan, much less help him. I can't get him a meeting with the empress myself, and I certainly can't smuggle him and Jenine out of here. This party's locked down. No one in or out.

"Of course you can count on me. I'm sure it will be as much of a delight as ever to serve the Chantry," I say.

Vi sighs and rubs the bridge of her nose.

"Everyone else," Sister Ayayah says, "you know your assignments. Questions?"

In the stories, someone would say, 'Let's go over the plan one last time,' and I'd get to hear it all. In the stories, none of it would be in jargon or even shorthand.

But I'm not that lucky. Irritatingly, these are professionals. No one has any questions. I get no hints, nothing.

And with that, they all begin leaving.

I look around. "I thought this was the briefing," I tell Vi. I don't know what anyone's doing, not even me.

"It was."

"Did you get to hear the rest?" I ask.

"Like I said, not a full member of the team. They tolerate me. They told me my part. That's it."

"Oh, hey, Petaria," I say before the woman can leave.

"What?" she snaps.

"When this is all over, we should get drinks or something."

She sneers and leaves.

"Ya little thief!" I call after her. "You've already stolen my heart!"

I grin at Vi as she and I are left alone.

"You're kind of an ass," Vi says.

"You have no idea how satisfying that was," I say. I look at her choker. "Seems like those are no fun."

Vi dismisses it. "Sister Aashvi says they're easy enough to disable, but they're checked constantly for the duration of the party, and putting them back on and covering the tampering is the tricky part. So we leave them alone."

"Any lock can be disabled with enough time and knowledge and the right tools?" I suggest. It's something Sa'kagé sneak thieves used to say.

But if I'd hoped that hearkening back to our mutual past might bring her a smile, I'm disappointed. She murmurs an assent, but she's clearly distracted.

"What do we do now?" I ask her.

Before she can answer, Jasmine Jakweth pokes his head back into the room. "Kylar, you wait here. Someone will come get you. Should be Petaria with your new bracelet. Should be about forty-five minutes. Viridiana...he's in the zone. You're up."

Viridiana pales and takes a deep breath. Checks her hair.

"He?" I ask.

But no one answers me. Viridiana pats my shoulder with a worried smile, already mentally off on her assignment, and leaves.

It occurs to me for one insane moment to grab a book off the shelf, enjoy myself, sit around, do nothing. But no. I'm not staying in the room. I didn't come here to be the Chantry puppet.

~No, you came here to be Momma K's puppet. That'll show them.~

Shut up. I came here to pull a heist. I can do both.

I look down at my bare wrist. Forty-five minutes, with no gemstone bracelet at all, with Grandmaster Vitruvius and two unknown magi looking for me—plus hundreds of other magic-using imperial guards, the best in the world, who might be on the lookout for me.

Things can never be easy, can they?

~Some might even say this job is *impossible*. But not you, huh?~

Then a horrible thought occurs to me. If I'm here for two jobs, who's to say that the special team isn't, too? In fact, what if they're here for the *same* two jobs? If they have eyes and ears everywhere, then they too might have learned about the existence of the Nemesis Compass.

If they know about such an artifact, helping Logan is surely a distant second in importance to them; nabbing it would certainly be first.

I have to get the compass, and I absolutely must make sure the Chantry doesn't.

A sick dread floods my guts with ice. But a small chance is better than none, and I've got no chance at all if I stay here like they want me to.

When you gotta eat feces, you get one choice: Savor the flavor, or swallow it quick.

I don't want to savor the flavor.

I'm good. I'm great. I can do this.

I poke my head out the door quickly, drink in hand near my face, shooting a glance one way. I chuckle as if at something someone says back in the room, pull back inside, push open the other door, and glance the other way as I say, "—I never say *that*," as if concluding a conversation.

Then I slip out, head down, shaking my head to myself, simply another party-goer, having the time of his life.

I just hope it's not the *last* time of my life.

Chapter Forty-Three
Old Friends, Old Raisins

I have to get to Phaena, and she should be making her way to the baggage, though she can't have any idea that my time constraints are so tight. One mistake here, and I'll lose everything. I'm not even talking failing Momma K and destroying Logan's stupid empire, or losing Logan and destroying his stupid empire if I let the empress take him to Borami. It's worse than that.

I'm surrounded here by people who can dissect me—not merely kill me, but take me apart, magically. That process could be quick, or it could be slow, but if I'm discovered, the Alitaerans won't let me go until they've broken the ka'kari's bond with me—someone told me once magic can do that, though it takes time. And once the secrets of the black ka'kari come out, what might someone else do with it?

Truth is, Sister Reyhan was right, if probably for all the wrong reasons. I'm a bigger threat to the Chantry than anything, because I'm a bigger threat to the entire world. The safest thing would be for the Chantry to lock me in a room and never let me out. No, not even a room.

Given the stakes, someone would come to that room, eventually. Immortality is the ultimate prize, the only prize that matters, really.

Who can be trusted with true immortality? With my powers, who wouldn't become a monster, a tyrant?

I've barely made it ten paces out of the parlor, and my stomach's clenching. I've been trained not to show my tension, but training can slip at any moment when you let yourself think too much. My body's rigid; sweat's cold on my forehead. An imperial guard gives me a long look.

These people are trained to notice when something is off about someone. The good news is that lots of people are tense at this party.

Still, the guard nudges the man beside her.

Durzo used to tell me, 'The nerves go away if you focus on what you're doing.'

"I adooore your cape!" I say to a woman nearby walking the same way I am. She's wearing a ludicrous feather cape and two sapphires at her wrist. "That is *not* phoenix feather from House Wai'Len, is it?"

There are no phoenix feathers, only peacock feathers laboriously dyed and edged with gold and sold to gullible foreigners.

"And those silks!" I say, as we step past the guards. "Those are *not* true mulberry, are they?!"

I pretend to notice the imperial guard looking at me for the first moment, then nod absent-mindedly at her, then turn back to the noblewoman.

The noblewoman glows at my flattery. "It's from House Vaygar."

"Noo! I couldn't even get *in there* when I last visited—and you wear it so well! Oh, oh, pardon me—must catch this friend. Have a wonderful night!"

We're past the guards, who haven't stopped me.

I turn down the next hallway. And then the next, holding the crystal goblet up to cover my face—

—and I see, not thirty paces away, Grandmaster Vitruvius. Heading my way.

I turn on my heel, right in front of the squad of imperial guards. Two of them eye me immediately. The other two, with considerable discipline, keep their gazes down their own halls, but I know they're all paying attention to me.

"Something wrong, milord?" one of them asks.

"Old ex," I say apologetically, voice pitched up. I flash a quick grimace of disgust to suggest a bad breakup or a man who couldn't take a hint. "If he asks...you haven't seen me? Oh no, he's coming this way."

"Think I saw you down the next hall," the woman says encouragingly, like someone who's been there. She's got a deeper voice than the men.

"Thank you!" I whisper, beating my retreat.

I throw a look back when I reach the next intersection, and see that the guard is as good as her word. She points down the opposite hall.

Yes!

But then as Grandmaster Vitruvius steps into my view, she glances toward me, and Grandmaster Vitruvius stops, noticing her look.

No! I do my best to disappear.

I don't know if he sees me. Want to be noticed in a huge crowd? Make eye contact with the person looking for you. I looked away, this time.

But I have to assume he's seen me. I have to assume I'm that unlucky.

Which means I might have to pull out the next, double-edged weapon in my small arsenal: No one here knows I'm a magic-user. I can use my Talent to create an illusory face to disguise myself.

Sounds like an obvious thing, huh? Something I should have done long ago? It's not.

As soon as I use magic, to every mage looking for mages, I will feel and look like a magic-user. It's one of the reasons every squad of imperial guards has at least one woman in it. Women are usually much better at seeing others who have the Talent. They still have to be looking for magic or magic-users, and it's easier to forget to look for it than you'd imagine.

But the women in the Alitaeran imperial guard are among the best guards in the world.

And I don't have a mage collar on. If they see a magical aura and no collar, nothing Grandmaster Vitruvius is doing matters—whether they know him or not, whether they're willing to do him a favor or not—here a magical aura plus no collar surely means *lethal threat*. That meant instant death outside; it'll mean it twice as much in here.

Twice as much instant death as instant death?

No, that doesn't make sense to me either.

I'll have to come back and fix this part later. If there is a later.

"Excuse me," I say, bumping my way through the crowd.

It takes me an embarrassing four attempts—on four different targets—to snag a bracelet using the technique Petaria used on me.

This one has three blue gems on it. Higher rank than what I started with. Not bad. But as I put it on my wrist, I notice that the blue gems don't glow. I did something wrong. Or maybe the bracelets with more gemstones have more security built in.

It takes me trial and error to figure out that I can loosen the bracelet without the gems going dark, but if the two sides lose contact completely, the stones go dark. That makes lifting them much harder—I have to pull the open loop down past the mark's entire hand.

Once I've secured a bracelet with two functional blue stones, I make my way to a desk where dozens of ledgers are being presided over by a pudgy little servant with ink-stained fingers wearing a bracelet with three yellow gems. He's also wearing a ridiculous little hat with the imperial eagles on it. "It's the third room there on the left," he tells a woman in the queue in front of me, aggressively polite. "Under the *enormous* sign?"

"Excuse me?" the woman asks, affronted.

"The sign that also has the picture? For those who are illiterate?" he asks, as if being helpful.

The woman huffs her way off to the latrines.

I put my hand to my mouth as if sharing amusement with him. It doesn't matter how little it is, some people love to use whatever power they hold to belittle others.

"Your pardon," I say with a smile. "First time here. Can you tell me where our servants were directed? I seem to have missed that."

He glances at my bracelet but seems unimpressed. "Your servant is unavailable until dawn. Her Imperial Majesty's staff will gladly assist you with whatever legitimate needs you have. Next?"

He looks past me, as if that's gonna fly.

There are times in life when violence or threats of violence won't get you your way. They're rarer than you'd think.

I glance down toward one intersection, then the other, putting my hands on the high desk.

"Milord?" Master Pudge says impatiently.

The imperial guard responsible for keeping an eye on this part of the hall looks the other way to share a comment with his squad, and I vault lightly over the table, landing right next to the fussy little bureaucrat.

He's so taken aback that his chin turtles so deep into his neck I wonder how he can breathe.

Which is just as well, because his next sound is something like "Heh gick."

The lady in line behind me also seems astonished, her bone fan stopping midflutter. That was for my leap. Then her gaze trails down to where my left hand disappears below the bureaucrat's high table. I hold up a finger on my right hand toward her, as if to say *One moment.* And then tap it to my lips with a wink. *Quiet.*

The pudgy servant hasn't said a word.

"It was a simple question," I say. "Why don't we try again, though? Can you tell me where my servant might be?"

He looks at me, wide-eyed, but no words come out of his mouth.

I give him a little squeeze of encouragement with my left hand.

He squeaks. "They're all expected to help load the *Storm Racer* and make the last-minute preparations."

"So the servants are told who's embarking?" I ask, surprised.

I'd thought no one at all knew who was leaving until dawn. But maybe that's not possible. How could they leave at dawn with all the baggage aboard if no one knew which luggage needed to be loaded by dawn? And nobles never travel light.

"Only the chatelaine has the master list, and she updates it as necessary through the night as the empress tells her. No servants load their own employers' things. Everything's compartmentalized," he says. "How could you not know this? How provincial can you possibly be?"

He swallows another yelp as I squeeze him gently.

Yes, my hand is fully down his trousers. Skin on skin. Sack in fist. Grapes shriveling to raisins.

No, I don't like doing this. Inspiring terror in murderers and thugs? I'll admit I do enjoy that sometimes. It's an ugly pleasure, but an abiding one. But terrifying some idiot who's merely rude? I don't enjoy this.

~Not at all?~

Maybe a little. But I recognize what I'm doing is revolting and wrong.

It's far from the most revolting thing I've ever done.

"I'm going to let you go now," I say. "And the first thing you're going to think of doing is a mistake. So…*before* you call the guards, give yourself a few moments to consider your options. Here's the question I want you to consider: Is this really the story you want everyone to be snickering about whenever your name comes up? Because it will, Raisins…for the rest of your life." I smile at him.

He blanches and folds even further in upon himself. "Raisins?"

Naturally, with all this happening, he's not been paying the least attention to what my right hand was doing.

"One last thing," I say. "Could you please be as polite as possible to my friend here?" I nod toward the noblewoman next in line. I smile and wink at her. She's been watching the whole thing, enrapt.

Her fan flutters at double speed.

"Raisins?!" the man says.

"Well, they're not stones, are they? I'd say not even grapes." I withdraw my hand and wipe it daintily with a handkerchief.

"I'd advise you to do as my new friend here suggests, *Raisins*," the woman says, with a broad smile at me. "And you...if you're not busy later..."

I smile and wink at her and go.

~That was somewhat reckless.~

A calculated risk.

Fine, more of an uncalculated risk.

I heave a sigh. I shouldn't be burning through my luck like this, spending it on things that barely matter.

But I got it. Took me way too long, but I stole Raisins's yellow-jeweled bracelet from his wrist. The yellow denotes a member of the imperial household. Three jewels, too, so it'll give lots of access. And I managed to lift it without breaking them, too.

I don't know if it'll be enough, but it's something.

Without wasting any more time, I head for a servants' door, snatch a parchment from a drinks table as I pass, and lift my wrist to show the bracelet and obscure my face, which I turn down, as if reading.

I make it through into a sub-kitchen. The room is a mess of bodies working in harried concert, sous chefs delivering platters of canapés, others quickly arranging appropriate assortments upon the serving platters, beautiful male and female servers standing in lines, fixing each other's costumes or hair, patting off sweat, applying body powders, spritzing each other with perfume, gossiping and giving warnings about problematic guests. A few report the worst offenders to a guardsman, who's conferring with a protocol official to write down names.

There's a stack of spare men's wings and loincloths near the stairs down. Aware that I can't stand still long without someone wondering what I'm doing and who I am, I push through toward them. I grab wings and a loincloth as I head down stairs.

"Hey," a woman says to me, "what are you grabbing those for?"

"Orders," I say with a shrug. "Hell if I know why she wants 'em."

I don't wait, and apparently it's good enough. She doesn't pursue or call after me.

I make my way down to the next level, past the prep kitchens, past the burly servants rolling kegs of wine and carrying foodstuffs and bottles of liquor to them, past scullery boys, through hallways full of servants passing this way and that.

I keep going down into the guts of the palace until I see an older man's eyes alight on me. He's got three yellow gems on his own bracelet. That's the worst.

Servants high in the hierarchy and at the same level are going to know each other or of each other. At the least, it will be clear to him that I don't know things I should know.

With a clear air of authority, he moves to stop me, and I approach him directly, shifting my burdens from hand to hand and taking the moment to slip the two-gem blue bracelet onto my wrist instead. "Hey, do you have a good spot I can change clothes?" I ask.

"Change? Down here? The changing rooms are—but why are you—?"

"Look," I say, exasperated. "Let's just say, be smarter than me, and never, but *never*, irritate someone far enough above you that she can order you to get half-naked and dressed ridiculously for her amusement."

"Her amusement?" the man says, suspicious. "Whose amusement are we talking?"

I show him my blue-gemmed bracelet, with an air that suggests that I'm no mere peon. "I'm not at liberty to discuss *her* amusement," I say, as if I mean the empress—but giving me enough wiggle room to pretend I didn't if that lie collapses. I purse my lips.

He curses, commiserating. "Good news is that you must not have irritated her very much, and she doesn't usually kill her playthings. But...if you take the advice of an old coal hauler, my lord?"

"Be glad to!" I say, letting some desperation into my tone. He clearly hasn't been just a coal hauler in many years.

"Don't give her any attitude. Obey instantly, no matter how foolish her commands make you look, and you might walk away from tonight still holding all your lands. My office is over here."

He takes me to his office, and I wonder how many minutes have passed. I think it's been about twenty.

Not yet halfway to when I have to be back to the library.

Also not yet nearly halfway to my objective.

I strip down while he waits for me, and when I come out, he looks at my muscles. "Huh. You might have a chance to come out ahead in this after all. She do like 'em pretty."

"Uh...thanks?"

"And none too bright. So you might be perfect," he says. But he says it with a smile.

I purse my lips again. "You have something I can keep my clothes in?"

He gives me a little bag. "Where are you supposed to meet her?"

"I don't know if it was going to be her... herself, you know? But they said down in the staging area where the servants are loading stuff?"

He gives me a side-eye. "You sure someone's not pulling your leg?"

"I don't think so, no. But thank you for giving me something else to be terrified about." I knuckle my forehead. "Only thing worse than showing up like this if she *hasn't* called for me would be... not showing up like this if she *has*."

"I could make inquiries..." the man offers.

"No, no. I'm running late as is. If it's a prank, I'll take my lumps now and get my revenge later. It's good to know who wants to make a fool of you, anyway."

"A brave stand, milord," he says, in that way veteran servants have when they want to tell you you're being a moron.

"Thanks for your input," I say, in the way veteran noblemen have of reminding servants that they're servants.

He smiles and demurs, his face saying *Enjoy the self-immolation, friend.*

It takes me another ten minutes and a few more bluffs to make it all the way downstairs and out onto the huge wharf where the *Storm Racer* lies. I also get my butt grabbed twice, a nipple tweaked, and a full-on groin grab once. The last is a man with only one blue jewel alight on his bracelet—a low noble. When I flash my own two-gemmed bracelet and glower at him, he stutters an apology and practically flees.

I don't feel too put out, though. I feel like I deserve it after what I did to get my bracelet. I oddly kind of like it when it feels the universe balances the scales with me quickly. When you go through life doing stuff you know is wrong all the time, it's like scuffing around a carpet in your stocking feet. The longer you wait to touch something, the bigger the shock you're gonna get.

By the time I get to the wharf, though, I've gotta be past thirty of my forty-five minutes. If I had a lick of sense, I'd admit failure and head back right now.

The *Storm Racer* is an immense presence tied at many places to the wharf and even the castle itself. It's almost too large to comprehend, but I barely pay it any heed for the moment. I'm scanning the literal thousands of people streaming toward it: all the laborers, overseers, and nobles' representatives tasked with the last-minute loading of the great ship. The castle is embedded in the cliff above and beside us, with ramps like spiderwebs connecting to the vast open trimaran pontoons of the storm ship and to the hull of the ship itself. I'm merely in the largest loading area, but others go east and west from here, not to mention up and down.

Looking on the throng, all guarded by hundreds of soldiers keeping the loading areas secure, I despair.

Even if I'm in the right zone out of maybe nine possibilities, how am I going to find one woman of average height dressed as a servant amid all this? If the crowd were merely idly milling about, I might hope to see a knot of attention, men's glances drawn like iron filings by her beauty. But now? In the hustle and crush of the impending deadline? Everyone has so much to do they can barely waste a glance at anyone else.

So I scan, relaxing my gaze to find the patterns, not seeing the men and women as individuals. Though the laborers are loading everything they can, much of the activity seems to be simply sorting things. Huge tents block our sight of the end of the docks nearest the ships, where nobles' things are put in waiting. Those aren't being loaded onto the storm ship. They must be waiting for the reading of the lists, like everything else—the people here held in suspense as is everyone else.

The knots of inactivity tend to be around overseers as longshoremen wait for their turn to get orders. A fight has broken out to one side, where laborers collided, smashing something. My eyes rove onward.

A tall man snags my eye—very tall, in a forest green cloak that flutters like silk in the wind. Too rich for here.

A servant in white and red appears from behind his form, walking away, and he snatches her arm, speaks angrily. She lets him, doesn't pull away.

I know that man, and it hits me like a kick in the stones, snatching my breath away. Lord Repha'im, the man who stole Logan's kids, the man who almost killed me.

Of all the places he could be, what in the world is he doing *here*?

More shocking, I know the woman, too. That's *Phaena*. I'm not surprised she's here, but what is she doing talking to Logan's mortal enemy as if she works for him?

And then, despite the crush of thousands, despite that I'm surely eighty paces away, and not tall, and not conspicuous in this crowd, Lord Repha'im lifts himself suddenly to his full height, attuned like a spider whose signal line has been struck. Like the predator he is, he turns with a snap, exactly the right way.

Before I can shrink and hide, he sees me. Locks his gaze to mine.

And smiles.

Chapter Forty-Four

Flight and Fire

I flee.

I don't think about what I'm doing or why. I get caught up in the doing itself—breaking line of sight while I dig into the bag of my clothes. You might not think Dressing Quickly would be one of the career skills necessary for a killer for hire, but if you think it's not, you'll have to take up your complaint with Durzo Blint, who did.

Stuffing the wings into the bag requires bending the stupid things in half and ruining them, but I do it. If you drop bits of your outfit as you change during an escape, you leave a trail of where you've been and a clear sign that you're changing disguises. In less time than you'd expect, I'm in my old nobleman's clothes, augmented with a new hat I steal as I walk back upstairs.

Only when I'm far away does it occur to me to be ashamed at running away. I should've gone and killed the guy. Demanded some answers.

But that shame lasts only a moment. Durzo had no use for the words *bravery* or *cowardice*. To him there was only doing the job, or not. Utility, not praise or censure. Bravery, he said, can make you ineffectual as surely as cowardice can, so bravery is irrelevant.

Bravery goes into the same category as 'a fair fight' in war. It's not imaginary—there are plenty of times and places where it matters, but it's a notion that can make you predictable and get you killed if you let it rule you.

There's something about Lord Repha'im that makes my skin crawl, something that tells me that he's supernally dangerous. I can't attack him at the time and place of his choosing. It has to be at mine.

I'm running behind time now. I need to be upstairs back in the parlor in something like five minutes.

I come upon another of the many checkpoints—this one at a landing in a great spiral stairway—and it suddenly looks like there's no way I'm going to make it. The queue here alone will hold me up for ten minutes. I throw a glance over my shoulder, looking for Lord Repha'im. Nothing.

But when I look back up, there's a man I don't know off to one side of the queue, scanning it. He looks at me with a strange intensity.

He's wearing the ruby collar of a mage. A blue mage. He's one of Grandmaster Vitruvius's people.

The man darts off into a side hallway.

And then, hot on his heels, out of the crowd behind me, I see Lord Repha'im suddenly emerge and go running after the blue mage.

Maybe he thinks it's me.

I hunker down, taking deep breaths and trying to remain inconspicuous. I've got to get out of here before one or both of them come back.

"Come with me," a voice says at my elbow.

It's Melena, the farmwife lodestone of the Chantry's team. She's in far richer clothes than she was before, a black dress with many laces, different makeup, no mage collar, and a bracelet with four blue jewels and an imperious air. She pulls me from the line. "Like so," she says. She pulls me past the queue, leading me like a woman leading a new lover to an assignation.

Vi said that it was easy to remove the magical choker collars but very difficult to put one back on without it being obvious it had been tampered with. But then I suppose solving difficult problems is kind of what the Special Problems Team does.

There are currents and undercurrents here that I don't get to know. It's not comforting.

It's only then that I notice the entire party has taken on a new air. Where things were tense before, everything's doubled now as the party has progressed. People are raucous, laughing too loud, drinking way too much, kissing in the queue, pulling each other off to nooks to do more. At the back of the queue, a fight breaks out, and the guards move unhurriedly toward it—on this night of nights, this is expected behavior.

Melena pulls me through the checkpoint, then pulls me forward so we walk hand clasped in hand, with her a little in the lead as my social superior.

"Those clothes won't do," she says. "I've got a change for you. You've made our lives difficult. In here."

She pulls me into an oak-paneled room with a lyre player, a harpist, and a singer telling a mournful story to twenty or thirty nobles who are avidly ignoring them, sitting on each other's laps, giggling and snorting or even licking various substances from hands or even cleavages. Melena pulls me behind a screen, where a couple is, ahem, rhythmically encumbered with each other. They notice us but don't seem to mind our presence enough to leave off what they're doing. She leans past them and lifts a bag from the ground as if this is all normal.

"Clothes," she says, as if I'm a slow child. "Off."

Then she helps me strip down and dress again, in white silk trousers of all things, fitted down the leg and calves—not to mention the butt—with flamboyantly laced high red shoes. No one should wear white silk trousers, especially not ones as tight as these. A frilly white shirt—which is not even butt-covering tunic length, merely a shirt!—and a red leather weapons harness (sans weapons, or even sheaths) completes my attire. It doesn't complete my look, however. She slathers some goop into my hair, styles it quickly into spikes and curls, then applies kohl to my eyebrows, blackening them to a single heavy brow in the Modaini style, and then blackening my lips as well. Then she powders my face with a pink-tone talcum.

She leans back, scowling at me like an artist. "Too fresh." She looks around. "Water . . . water . . ." But none of the goblets here hold water, only wine, and she mumbles about not risking red stains.

"Sorry," she says. Then she spits in her hands, rubs them together, and smudges the talc and a bit of my unibrow at one side. She squishes me in a sudden hug, startling me. Steps back quickly and pinches those rumples into creases on my shirt. "Hold still," she commands.

She puts fresh rouge on her lips and kisses my neck right at the collar line. It sends a shock right through me.

Then she wipes the excess rouge off my neck—but not off my shirt.

"There. Congratulations, you're now a lightly used dandy. Now let's go let Petaria have her way with you."

"Excuse me? I feel like I've already been—been—been hadded your way withed," I stammer, but Melena is already pulling me out from behind the screen, leaving behind the couple who never stopped what they were doing and barely even spared us a glance.

Melena steps out into the hallway, holding me in place while she looks both ways. Then we head to another room, this one magically empty—which I imagine might have been the hardest feat of all for the team to pull off.

Before Melena closes the door behind me, Petaria is there, cursing at me in half a dozen languages, standing way too close to me as she does so, making me wish I could back away, but there's nowhere to go. Petaria snatches the imperial bracelet off my wrist so quickly, you'd not even think it was locked on. "What am I supposed to do with *this*?!" she demands.

"Uh…"

"Where's the bracelet with two red gems Jasmine gave you?"

"I never—"

"He stepped out," Melena says.

"The plan called for me to swap—How am I supposed to …? Damn you, Kylar Stern. Do you have to make everything difficult?"

Without waiting for an answer, Petaria slaps a different bracelet on me, and takes mine. She stretches her own neck, where her choker with purple stones is now tight enough to bite into skin. Then she disappears.

"What's with the purple choker?" I ask Melena.

"Red plus blue?" she says.

It takes me a moment. "Nobles who are also mages? But—"

"Did no one tell you? With any magic we use, the choker gets tighter. Easy to make yourself pass out, and Pet's had to use a fair bit tonight—not least for you. Gotta go."

The door opens, and Melena goes but holds the door open. Vi pokes her head in. "Kylar! Come on! Now!"

Vi snatches my hand and hustles me down the hall. I only now note the bracelet on my own wrist. Four blue stones. *Four.*

The locks on these bracelets get more complicated with their scarcity. Even a thief with Petaria's skills needs to use particular magic to steal the four-gem bracelets.

"Hidden room," Vi says. "Once we're in, no talking. We wait for the signal from Sister Ayayah. You don't interrupt Logan and the empress unless she signals, got it? Because if I don't see her signal, I won't give the coded knock. If I don't give the knock and you go in without it, the imperial guards and the magi will attack instantly. May even be praetorians in there, if Jasmine failed his second task.

"As it is, if you have to go in at all, the agent who's getting you and me into the eavesdropping room will probably pay with his life for allowing the intrusion. The Alitaerans are *not* keen on surprises. Don't put that blood on our hands unnecessarily."

"So Sister Ayayah said you've got other, better talents. Or Talents. Are you using those? What are they?"

"No, I'm not, and no time to explain."

"You're theirs completely, aren't you?" I ask Vi. "The Chantry's, I mean."

"No, Kylar," she says, her eyes hard. "I don't belong to them. I *am* them." She takes me into a narrow, winding service corridor, then stops at a corner. "Now," she says, "for one miserable time in your life, will you please do what you're told?"

I raise my hands in surrender.

"You will get us all killed if you don't." She twitches as if receiving a message I can't hear. "He's already in there. No Talent! Follow me."

She checks the hallway again. A hand darts around the corner with three fingers extended. Melena's hand, maybe? Then two fingers.

Ah, a count. Why do I have the familiar, sudden, sharp, sick feeling that I'm caught up in events vast beyond my comprehension?

One. Vi puts her fingers against a stone above her head, her other hand poised. And—

Vi pushes hard against the stone, and a door pops out, the edge glimmering with the unmistakable shimmer of magic. She ducks inside.

The hard sick knot in my stomach spasming, I follow on her heels.

Chapter Forty-Five

An Empress and Her Equal

*O*n the opposite side of the spy screen, Empress Caelestia stands with hands spread helplessly, twitching between expressions. Her irritation is like a bird fluttering about the room crowded with functionaries and guards, looking for a perch. With every beat of its wings, the bird seems to be morphing. First swift as a hummingbird, then quick as a sparrow, but rapidly shifting into the mighty imperial eagle. No one wants those claws to rest on them.

"This meeting," the empress says, speaking slowly, eyes casting about for someone to blame, "is *not* what I had scheduled."

"I echo your disappointment, Your Imperial Majesty," Logan says. I can't see his face from Vi's and my position hidden within the wall, pressed tight together. "Your ministers promised me that we should have this meeting long before tonight."

"Did they?" she asks, unconcerned. "Caradzi? Did we not have an appointment with . . . Overlord Rotans of the Lae'knaught scheduled for now?"

A stump of a deeply tanned man with no neck squints through a monocle at a tiny codex in his hands. He and the others of the empress's inner circle all wear bracelets with lightly coruscating gems. "I had thought so as well, Your Imperial Majesty, but . . . uh . . . When did I put this in?"

From the expression on his face, the notation must appear to be in his own hand. Brilliant. The Chantry had forged it well enough to fool the imperial secretary himself?

"I don't recall adding this . . ." he says, apparently genuinely puzzled.

The empress levels her unblinking eagle's eyes on him. "Caradzi . . . I don't mind most of the bribes you take, but I think it's about time we see how zealous you have been in our service, against how zealous you have been in using me to serve *you*."

The man looks as if he wishes to drop through the floor. "I'll get my books immediately."

"Not your books. Your bookkeeper. Commander Atu, there's a woman named Elsapeth Romari in Lord Caradzi's entourage who will have his real sets of books either on her person or nearby. Go get her. She may be interested in a new line of work. Indeed, I hear she's so talented that she may be a candidate for Lord Caradzi's own position within the Exchequer. Let her know she is being considered for this. I will have ten minutes for her later downstairs, thirty minutes before dawn. She will have until then to supply me with ironclad evidence either for Lord Caradzi's innocence of excessive embezzlement or for his guilt. There is no third option." She looks over at a secretary, who nods.

"Majesty," Caradzi says, "that woman is a climber. She may say any—"

"I know this," she interrupts, and he shuts up immediately. "Dismissed."

He bows low, a sudden sweat pouring from his forehead.

Empress Caelestia gives no sign she's even aware of his continued presence. "Now, where were we, Logan? Ah yes, I see you're not a man without resources. Very well, but you must have suspected I'd know you made this happen."

Vi glances my way within the confines of our tiny cell, which was not made for two. She grimaces, and not, I think, from having to snuggle up with me.

"I welcome my chance to finally speak with you, Your Imperial Majesty. But I had nothing to do with this," Logan says evenly.

"You must know I could simply have you bundled onto the *Storm Racer*."

"You *could*, but you'd be breaking your word," Logan says. "Doesn't seem your style."

"Intriguing." She turns her back on him, leaving me guessing what her face must say now. Then she says, "You make others want to be better, don't you?"

"I consider that part of my portfolio of responsibilities as a leader. Don't you concur?"

She expels a breath, shakes her head, and finally turns back to him. "You're audacious. I'll give you that. Maybe idealistic—"

"But not naïve. I left that behind me some time ago."

"Oh? Did you really? When?" she asks, turning back to him, curious.

"The day I practiced cannibalism," he says without hesitation. By the gods, he hadn't even told me about that. His time in the Hole was a wound, and when I saved him, I knew better than to stick my fingers in it by asking questions.

"I heard rumors about that," the empress says. "I'd have expected you to deny it. They say it was some common criminal?" She means who Logan *ate*. Dear gods. It's got to be some way of testing him, rubbing his face in what he did at his lowest moment. Or perhaps she is without any empathy at all.

"Not common at all," Logan says. "In fact, I found him very rare."

She's turned toward me, and I see half a dozen expressions pass over her face so fast I couldn't name them—confusion? astonishment?—and then she laughs involuntarily.

But I'm already looking at Logan, who's now turned a bit. He's trying to conceal it, but he looks a bit sickened by his own joke. "Your pardon," he says. "That was uncouth. It was the worst of times for me. I survive the memories by making light of them."

"Sounds like my first marriage," she says. "Pardon granted."

"Then I hope you will forgive a further importunity. I came to you seeking an alliance. Your letters encouraged me to believe that this should be a prompt, simple matter. Which I believed. I was given guarantees. Unfortunately, Your Imperial Majesty's ministers have held me hostage in a gilded cage. My rule will not survive my further absence. If I leave for home later than today, I have every reason to believe I will be a king in name only—at best."

The empress studies Logan, and I study her. She's slender, ensconced in a cream dress of deceptive simplicity, the threads seeming at first randomly pearlescent, but as I watch, they subtly shimmer more to draw the eye in flattering directions. Cinched around her narrow waist, she wears a black fur of obvious softness. Around her head, floating rather than touching her head, nine spinning opals winking with interior fire give the impression of a crown. Her eyes also glitter like opals and then shift even as I watch to emerald—which the points of her floating crown now appear to be, too. Her face is severe in some way that puts it beyond classical definitions of beauty, and either cosmetics or magic makes it difficult to tell her age.

"Why have you put yourself into my power?" Empress Caelestia asks, stroking her black furry stole almost as if it's alive.

~Oh, it *is*. That's a black farix! I haven't seen one of those for centuries! Slippery, faster than your life flashing before your eyes, and with venom that reacts spectacularly with magic, though it's lethal regardless. Durzo tried three times to capture one alive for its venom. You know, if you wanted to apologize to him, that'd be just the gift.~

As if—and I'm not the one who owes anyone an apology!

"To stop us from having a war," Logan says.

She glances around, and I get the feeling she misses her throne. She is not a tall woman, and Logan is nearly seven feet and proportioned like the muscular gods of Ilyrian art. Nor is he one of those tall men who stoops so as to make others feel less threatened; at least he hasn't since the diadem first graced his brow.

He goes on, "To show that I am willing to risk trusting you, hoping that it will inspire you to trust me in return. The emergence of a large new kingdom such as mine is bound to make other powers leery."

"I should hate to come across as leery," she says, eyeing Logan up and down with evident pleasure.

"Your caution is entirely understandable. That's why I made the trip," Logan says. Ah, sweet Logan. Once upon a time, he would have missed her insinuation. Now I'm pretty sure he's ignoring it.

"You're very brave," she says. "They told me that. They told me you are imposing, too. But I think they sold you short."

"*Short* is one thing I've not been called," Logan says. I wish I could see his face. There's only so much I can guess from his tone.

She laughs, touches her hair, but then stares at him boldly. "They didn't tell me you were gorgeous."

"I...can imagine several reasons for that," Logan says.

"Is she *flirting* with him?" I ask Vi, very quietly.

Vi gives me a look of disgust. "Are you joking? *Look* at him."

I've looked at Logan many times, and right now all I can see is his broad back. But I take her point. Logan is one of very few men I know whom I'd feel comfortable describing the same way the empress did. He *is* gorgeous. He's also commanding, kind, brilliant, strong, rich, and powerful. And he has great hair. So yeah, sure, I guess maybe he's the most attractive man I've ever seen.

If you care about that sort of thing.

Clearly, Empress Caelestia does. In my asides with Vi, I've missed one interchange between the empress and Logan, and now she asks Logan abruptly, "What do you know about my kings?"

"Little enough, but still too much to waste your time with idle guesses. Can you be more specific?" Logan says.

"I choose a new King in the West tonight. We journey together to Borami, where I'll spend the next four months seeing if my new consort is competent enough to rule the west for me until I return. Then I begin my imperial procession back to Skone. He'll rule the west until I return next year."

"By all accounts, a system you've used ingeniously," Logan says, nodding.

"Are you offended by my promiscuity? I've heard you yourself are quite abstemious."

"I don't think it's promiscuity at all, so I respectfully challenge the assumptions of the former as well as to the latter: for I'm not abstemious, simply married."

"Happily?" she asks.

He hesitates. The only weapon Logan lacks in his large armory of giftings is a forked tongue. But his pause is momentary. He says, "I have been afforded greater joy in my marriage than I ever believed my life would hold. I regained what I lost once, and intend to treasure it forever."

I don't know if the empress notes the past tense, but I can't not hear it. *Oh, Logan, my dear friend, it hurts to see you hurting so badly.*

"In fact, I wish she could be here now," he says, and I know he's feeling disloyal for not having been more effusive in his praise of her.

"I'm so glad she's not."

Deciding to ignore the implications of that, Logan says, "She's good at this sort of thing—"

"And you're not?" the empress interrupts.

I realize then that Jenine's exclusion was entirely intentional. The Sisters got Logan here. They could as easily have gotten both Logan and Jenine here. Why exclude her?

"I bumble a bit, I'm afraid," Logan says. "Speak when I should be silent. Hold my tongue when I should speak."

"A bumbler? You? Apologizing for one's lack of rhetorical gifts is the oldest rhetorical trick, isn't it?" She doesn't wait for Logan to answer. "So if you don't judge me harshly, how do you judge me?" the empress asks, shifting the conversation as quickly as a martial artist who sees her opponent off-balance and presses the advantage.

"I'm not sure how that's relevant to—"

"Indulge me," she says, and her voice cuts cold. She is an empress indeed.

He cocks his head, perhaps taken aback. I really wish I could see his face. I know Logan the man very well, but Logan the high king has been taking shape out of my sight.

"We pay with what coin we have, don't we?" he says, sounding more human and less formal. "It seems to me that maneuvering your nobles the way you have has probably defused a half-dozen rebellions, any of which might've cost your empire many lives. You have taken it upon yourself to save those not only on your own side but also those opposed to you. I find that laudable in ways most people never see and certainly can't understand. I imagine that doing so is and has been sometimes a distasteful duty. That sounds like sacrifice to me. I could guess it might even be a terrible one, if your heart has ever had some great favorite whom you could not choose because of politics."

I see her chest rise with a sharp intake of breath, a brief pause, as if she were stricken. This is not a woman accustomed to being understood.

But she smooths it away quickly, absently petting again the creature wrapped around her waist. "Not always distasteful," she says with a smile. "Today I approach my choice with great anticipation. My system has served me well. I could maintain it for decades yet, if I had no interest in producing an heir of my own blood. But I do. The One God makes things harder for queens than kings in this, as in so many things. I'm thirty-eight years old, Logan. If I wish to produce more than a single child—which seems prudent, given the dangers inherent to our stations—I haven't much time left. A fact not lost on my nobles."

"Thus the heightened tensions here, I suppose," Logan says. He seems to be trying to pull the conversation in another direction. "Everyone wants something of you—even me! Which—"

"There's a reason I stalled you," Caelestia says. "Beyond mere caprice, I mean."

"Many reasons, I'm sure."

"One, really," she says. "I needed time to investigate you, your character, your associations. Every person you've talked with since you arrived in Skone was sent by me, all part of a singular effort. I planned to meet with you tomorrow morning just before I embark and after . . . some other things were decided. But you are here, and he is not, and I am busy, so let me be blunt."

"Please do," Logan says, mystified.

He? Who's the absent man she's talking about?

"We could marry," the empress says, studying Logan's face.

"Excuse me?" Logan says.

Everyone else in the room seems equally stunned, but the empress ignores them. "There would be difficulties, naturally. These are surmountable. Indeed, trivial, compared to the likely benefits of uniting our two empires."

"You . . . you know I'm already married," Logan says, confused.

"Surmountable difficulties, as I said."

"Not for me," Logan says, quickly, loyally.

And now I wonder at the Chantry keeping Jenine out of the room. Did they know this was coming?

"Take a moment, Highness, and remember yourself," the empress says carefully. "I can make you lose your kingdom with a word. A year from now, imprisoned in my court, powerless, friendless, and only trotted out from time to time at our royal banquets as the once high king of the north to be ridiculed or, worse, pitied; in hindsight what you say right now may appear very foolish to you."

I see the sinews in Logan's neck go tight.

The empress says, "Your wife bore another man's sons."

"They're my sons now."

"For now. Will you feel the same when Jenine Gunder bears you sons of your own blood? Will you be happy to see another man's seed take your throne after you're gone, ahead of your own sons? What if Dorian Ursuul's madness lies latent in them? But with a marriage to me, you'd be secure enough politically to put your wife aside. Not to mention many other benefits. I know you've had troubles."

Logan is silent for a long moment. "Your Imperial Highness, you're right. Such a proposal requires all due consideration—which, given the constraints on our time, I have now given it. Tempting as the proposal is, no."

"Excuse me? You're telling me no." A noble shifts nervously into my way, and I can't see the empress at all as she says this.

"Yes. I am."

"Just like that?" she says, her fire rising. "You think I throw myself at every man who crosses my threshold?"

Vi nudges me, and I look toward one of the empress's ladies-in-waiting. It's Sister Ayayah, the Chantry's Mastermind. Her hands are clasped together, but she's twitching them forward, giving me the signal to break into the room to tell Logan about his lost children and hopefully tug on the empress's heart-strings enough to make her let him go.

Vi moves to her hand to knock her signal to whatever agent is standing out-side our hidden room, but I grab her wrist. Not hard. I hold it, hoping she trusts me, not willing to tear my eyes away from the empress and Logan to see if she does.

I trust Logan. He's got this.

Logan says nothing, but he takes a deep breath, stands taller.

Suddenly, without any sign I see, he is surrounded by imperial guards. My confidence evaporates. There are dozens of them. Weapons ready. They obscure my view of Sister Ayayah. But I'm not waiting on her judgment.

Vi pushes against my grip, but doesn't tear her hand free, which she could.

If Logan tries to fight, how many of those men can I kill before they get him?

"You won't reconsider?" the empress asks quietly.

My hand weakens on Vi's wrist, muscles coiling.

"I will not," Logan says, with the tone of a man who knows he's signing his own death warrant.

I know my plan, who I take out first, whose weapons I'll grab—but it's too far, too far!

"Then please forgive me," the empress says. "I've much to accomplish this night, and no time to waste. You're a man who remains loyal in difficult cir-cumstances. You'll be a worthy ally. I'll sign the agreement you came seeking."

She waves a hand, and the imperial guards melt back away from Logan.

My heart starts beating again. I breathe. I release Vi's wrist, and we share a look.

"That was *a test*?" Logan says quietly. "You test my honor for your amuse-ment?" He is clearly struggling to control his temper.

No, no, no, Logan. We're coming out of the danger. Don't bring it back!

"Not purely a test. It was an honest proposition. I should quite like to take you to my bed. Consider it still. If things worked out, our children might rule a continent united. It would mean an end to war in all Midcyru—not in our time, but in theirs, perhaps. As it is, we shall be allies—not as strong a bond for our countries as a marriage would provide, but perhaps less fraught." She drops off. Her hands flutter but I've no idea how to interpret that from her. "What's this? I've finally affronted your delicate northern sensibilities?"

Logan's mouth moves for a moment. "As we enter into an alliance, I should quite like to believe that oath keeping is not solely a northern virtue."

"I *have* offended you." She taps her folded fan to her chin. "However can I make it up to you?"

I know Logan, and though I can barely see a quarter of his face, I can see he's still furious. His marriage has been such a misery for the last months that someone daring to question his commitment to it isn't merely someone else questioning his honor, it's making *him* question it. So I'm impressed that he answers her immediately. "No duties on goods your traders export to my kingdom, nor tariffs on ours. Trade will bind our lands together better than even a necessarily distant marriage could."

"For what term?" she asks, her chin rising, immediately all business.

"Twenty years."

Her eyebrows climb at his audacity. "And your trade with us will also be free of duties and tariffs and excise fees?"

"*You* insulted me, not I *you*. Your Imperial Majesty."

A thin smile plays on her lips. "Cap your own fees at two percent. The term will be ten years, and you pay for maintaining both sides of all border crossings."

"Three percent gross, and we will remit fees equaling our own border maintenance expenses to you, twice yearly—we are simple people in the north, and our betters of the mighty Alitaeran empire might beggar us should we attempt to keep up with the luxury of your border crossings. Naturally, your chosen representative will be given full access to our ledgers to confirm that our numbers are true—not a small concession, I think you'll agree."

"Hmm." She seems amused. "I haven't made my finance ministers apoplectic for months. Done. Now if you'll pardon me, I have other men to infuriate tonight. But, Logan?"

"Yes, Your Imperial Majesty?"

"In private, call me Caeli, please. And do consider what I said. Marriage is too precious for a person to only ever have one."

I see Logan twitch to hold back the first reply that comes to his mind. He says, "You are very kind. Caeli, it has been an...alloyed pleasure. I look forward to failing to match wits with you for many years to come."

She laughs with real joy.

I see ministers shoot first her and then each other surprised looks.

On her way out the door, even as all the men bow and the women curtsy low, she pauses. "I remember my own first years on the throne, Logan. This alliance

is a great victory for you and your people, but a quiet one. Too quiet. Too boring. At this point in your rule, you need not only calm, long-term victories that
enrich your people for years to come but also the appearance of victories and
confirmations of legitimacy. Good trade terms aren't shouted from the roof-
tops. Speak with my steward. He'll make sure we announce the treaty and our
eternal friendship in appropriately lavish fashion. X!zorriss, see to the gifts.
Level five."

The Friakian steward blinks rapidly. His pause is all the protest he offers.
Then he says, "That will take some time, Your Imperial Majesty, but I will
expedite it as much as possible."

She stops at the door. Her jaw sets. She doesn't turn around.

"Even if I have to exhaust my own accounts to do so," X!zorriss adds quickly.

She doesn't move, merely exhales frustration.

"The treasure train will depart within two weeks," the man says quickly, his
throat bobbing as if he were attempting to swallow an orange whole.

Without so much as a thank-you, the empress floats out of the room, leaving
a dozen powerful men shaking in her wake.

Including Logan.

And me.

There's something profoundly discomfiting about interacting with someone
who not only routinely changes the lives and fortunes of everyone around her
but is entirely comfortable doing so.

No one should have so much power.

~Hey. Kylar.~

What?

~A moment ago, you were prepared to kill the empress of Alitaera, her highest officials, and everyone else in the room who posed a threat to your friend.~

Yeah. So?

~Nothing. Never mind.~

Chapter Forty-Six

Lies and Loyalties

Come with me," Vi says, taking my hand.

We've barely stepped into the hall and closed the door to the spy room. I glance down at the hand she's holding, and she drops it awkwardly.

But I snatch her hand out of the air, already sorry. With Logan and his rule now safe—something I'd be celebrating if I weren't so wound up—the Special Problems and Tactics Team should be done with me. Certainly, I'm done with them. Maybe I'd feel better if I'd been part of Logan's victory in that room. How much time and effort and treasure did the Chantry expend to get me there? And in the end, the most important thing I did—even when it seemed like I had better act or there would be devastating consequences—was nothing. I did nothing.

~You had faith in your friend. That's not nothing.~

My master would kill me if he knew I'd sat there doing nothing while letting others decide the fate of the world.

~Durzo put his whole faith in a friend once.~

Yeah, back when he was Acaelus Thorne—and he lived to regret it, didn't he?

The ka'kari has gone silent, though.

"Where are you going?" I ask Vi. I'm not sure if I should go with her. One of my two jobs tonight has miraculously sorted itself out. Unfortunately, I don't think I can expect the Nemesis Compass to find itself for me.

"Fourth-floor auditorium, the Privy Hall, they call it," she says. "For the reading of the lists. The highest nobles get the news first. They also have the best treats. Legendary honey cakes." She smiles at this; she adores honey cakes. I'd forgotten that about her.

Her innocently conspiratorial smile does something funny to me. I start to smile back, squeezing her hand, then something freezes up inside me.

"No, no, I gotta go," I say. I drop her hand. I can hardly breathe.

"Go do what?" she asks.

"Just—I just—" and I flee.

Time passes. I find myself hiding in a side room, trying to control the hammering of my heart, gasping deep breaths, sweating profusely. Elene, gods have mercy.

Then, I don't know how long later, I hear a voice I know.

"There's nothing here," Logan says. "Jenine said if I still didn't believe her to enter the second room on the left after the fire-eater. That's this room, isn't it?"

"You're very forbearing, milord," a woman says. It's Melena. Melena?

My heart drops. I'm hiding in the room, nonmagically, merely ducking behind a bookcase. As Logan goes to check behind it, I step around the side—right in front of Melena's flashing eyes. When Logan comes back around, I dodge back into the shadows.

What's happening?

"Well, then, I guess that's that," Logan says, his voice that of a man retreating far into himself. "I guess she really is...lost to me." His voice is devastation. I swear that my liege, my friend, is on the verge of tears. I've given him proof that the wife he fought for is insane.

He puts a hand on the doorframe to steady himself.

It shakes me out of whatever pit I'd fallen into.

I don't know what to say to Logan. I don't know how I can talk with him without lying or compromising my mission. But he's my friend.

I step out from behind the bookshelf. Logan's back is turned. Melena's eyes lock on mine. She shakes her head, eyes fierce, mouths, *Go! Now!*

"Your Majesty," she says smoothly, taking his arm, turning him away from me, "perhaps we can—"

All I have to do is do nothing, for a few more moments. But my problems are alone in this room with me, and I don't know what I can do about them. Maybe nothing. Logan's look so much easier. Maybe I can help with his.

"You're right," he says. "Keep moving. That's best. Keep moving. So much to do—"

"Logan," I say.

He turns slowly.

Melena gasps, as if shocked to see me. "How did you get here?"

Logan's face breaks into that broad smile that melts hearts in seven kingdoms. "Ky—!" He stops himself, seeing my disguise, and perhaps my sweat, and he instantly realizes I must be here on business. "My friend!" he says quietly, fiercely, eyes alight. "Yes, Orlana, he...does this sort of thing." He smiles again, like he can't help it, like he can't stop smiling.

Orlana. That's Melena's cover, huh?

But then I see the look I was afraid of enter Logan's eyes. *What are you doing here?*

"My liege," I say, bowing appropriately. "I see you trust this fine lady. You can use my name."

"Lady Orlana Betissian, this is my dear friend Kylar. Baronet Kylar Stern... that is, unless you decided to take me up on that duchy?" He's still playing the part of the well-mannered nobleman, making introductions, but that flicker is still in his eyes. He's troubled, but covering it.

"Too much responsibility for me, I'm afraid," I say. "I'm quite enjoying quietly getting rich while doing nothing."

"Kylar's been my friend since we were boys, and he has a nose for getting in trouble, not always his own. In fact, he's saved my life an embarrassing number of times and once even sprang me from prison."

"As I recall, you'd already escaped. I merely found you wandering about and brought you home."

"Carried me, as I recall," Logan says. "Out of an inescapable hell."

"You were a touch delirious at the time, Your Majesty. You may have made it more dramatic in your mind than it was in real life."

"Oh, really?" he says, amused. He rubs his left arm, where the moon dragon's blood left him with a mark he always keeps covered.

"Kylar Stern?" 'Lady Orlana' says, pretending to connect things. "You're *that* Kylar Stern? The one who...oh. Oh my. My lord, it is a great privilege indeed to meet you."

"Kylar..." He shakes himself from what he was going to ask, and gets back on the polite track. "Lady Betissian is my deputy head of mission at my embassy in Skone. She has accompanied me to help smooth things out as much as possible during my...extended stay with the empress. And she's done so brilliantly. If she's not careful, Lady Orlana will find herself full ambassador soon!" Logan says.

There's an art to introductions, giving each side a quick sketch of who the other person is, with enough conversational hooks sprinkled in so that if you're paying attention, you'll have something that you find interesting to ask questions about. Though I'm sure Logan has less than zero interest in me and 'Lady Orlana' having a conversation, he's been so thoroughly inculcated with the courtly arts that this is second nature to him.

"A post I should be deeply flattered to accept, Your Highness," Melena is saying, "as soon as my three young children are older and my aging father's health has recovered, or...well. Family is of paramount import to me, as I know it is to you."

"You shan't put me off forever!" Logan says with a smile. "I know talent when I see it. But, you know, speaking of family...Lady Orlana, would you excuse us for a moment?"

"Of course, Your Majesty," she says.

"But don't go far!" Logan says. "I do want to finish that conversation."

She smiles pleasantly at him. To me, her smile is more strained. And I realize that she gave Logan that segue to 'family' on purpose. I'm messing with her work? She'll mess with mine. She heads a discreet distance away, admiring some art displayed around the room.

On a professional level, I'm once again impressed with the Chantry's work. Melena inserted as *deputy* head of mission in Skone? That puts her two steps below the ambassador, making a full vetting of her by Logan's people unlikely. But the ambassador can't leave to go with Logan, so usually the head of mission would go. Get that person out of the way and put in Melena, and then you have a new problem. If Logan trusts her—which you want—the new king is likely to promote her. But Melena has a full-time job for the Chantry; she's too important to them to be saddled with a real full-time job working for someone else.

Her job and her excuses for not wanting a promotion put her in a place where she can re-insert herself into Logan's life and court at any point in the future—if Logan has a future. Or, she can quietly disappear and few will notice she's gone.

Logan waits until she's far enough away not to overhear. His pleasant expression melts to concern. "Kylar, what's happening? Why are you here? Has something happened? Is everything all right with the boys?"

How do I tell him I failed? I got distracted, and everything's falling apart.

"I'm, I'm here to help you. Or I was. The Chantry brought me to this party to make sure you didn't get trapped by the empress."

"What? The Chantry?"

"I was watching your meeting with the empress. They arranged it. You were brilliant. I was supposed to go in with terrible news if it looked like she wasn't going to let you leave."

He closes his eyes, shaking his head, trying to absorb all this. "The Chantry arranged that? And you were *there*? Why are you working for the Chantry, Kylar? And..."

His eyes snap open. "Kylar, what terrible news were you supposed to bring—"

Oh no. Through the fog of irrelevant but interesting questions he could ask me, Logan's somehow seized on exactly the right one. "Not working *for* them," I say quickly. "Helping them help you. I didn't even know you were here until an hour ago. I'm here working for Momma K. For you."

"Kylar. What terrible news? What terrible news were you going to bring in?"

I glance over at Melena, who happens to be taking that moment to hook a fingertip into the side of her strapless dress by her armpit and adjust it on her chest. I don't know if it's because she's done as many costume changes as I have today, or if it's merely one of those strapless dresses that slips down no matter what—but she manages to adjust it with far more elegance than I've ever managed when adjusting my trousers. I flick my eyes away, worried she'll think I'm staring at her breasts.

It's always the wrong details with me.

Why is it so hard to say, *The boys have been kidnapped. We have no leads. I'm here trying to find something that will help us find them*?

Logan's been through so much. Lost his whole family. Lost his wife, got her back, now is losing her again. I remember the joy in his eyes as he held one of his sons, called him adorable, blind exactly the way a father should be. As soon as I tell him, he'll have lost his sons, too. And find out his old best friend has failed him.

But all that's at least half a lie, isn't it? I'm worried about Logan, but I'm more worried about how he'll look at me, aren't I? If I can return with his sons, it'll be like I never failed him, like Jenine's damning words about me were wrong.

"Kylar!" Logan says.

And what am I preoccupied with? Worrying about whether Melena will think I'm staring at her chest.

Suddenly, I feel like I've been punched in the throat. What had I thought sardonically back on the trail? 'Breasts. The answer is breasts. Phaena has them.'

Lord Repha'im is here. In the carriage, Phaena was trying to confess something to me about her work.

Phaena was talking with Lord Repha'im.

Oh *no*.

I can barely breathe. Melena sees the look on my face and comes over toward us, fast. I can tell she's afraid I'm going to louse something up.

"I have to go," I choke out, taking a step back.

"Kylar," Logan snaps. "We're not done."

"My liege," Melena says smoothly.

"Not now!" Logan barks. "Kylar, where are you going? I have questions!"

It'd only take me a few moments to tell him the boys have been kidnapped—but what will Logan do if I tell him that?

"I know you do," I say. "And I'm getting answers for them—but if I don't get them now, I won't be able to get them at all!"

But before I can slip away, he lashes out with one of those damnably long arms of his and snags my sleeve. With all the times I sparred with Logan, how could I forget how quick and long he is?

"Kylar, I'm not letting you go until I hear this terrible news."

"Then ask the person who can give you all the answers you want," I say, looking over.

Melena's eyes flare with shock and outrage, and Logan catches the expression before she can recover.

"Why don't you fill him in, Lady Orlana? Or should I say, Sister Melena of the Chantry?"

"Sister—*what*?!" Logan demands. His grip on my sleeve loosens and I twist the cloth out of his grip and bolt for the door. "Kylar! You can't go!" he shouts.

But he's wrong. I'm already gone.

Chapter Forty-Seven

No Longer Impossible

I can't believe how blind I've been.

I shoot a look over my shoulder down the hallway, but Logan doesn't come after me. He knows how fast I can disappear.

When I'd first seen Phaena talking with Lord Repha'im, I'd been too stunned to think straight. And then he'd seen me. Before all my attention turned to flight, I'd only felt the jolt of fear that she was betraying me, that she was working with him.

A bell rings, and everyone in this hallway stops. There's a collective intake of breath.

But there's no reason to believe Phaena is Lord Repha'im's.

Other, similar bells resound in faraway halls and atriums. The nobles all begin heading the same direction.

Far more likely is that she's doing exactly what Momma K ordered her to do.

My thoughts are interrupted by the imperial guards being reinforced and starting to form up.

What is this?

Oh, right. It's nearly midnight. At midnight the lists are read: who's going to Borami, who's staying, and dozens upon dozens of appointments to various positions.

A herald with a high voice that cuts through the din declares, "Anyone visiting, please return to your own level immediately. Everyone with three gems or more on your bracelet, advance to the Privy Hall, please. Have your bracelet ready for inspection."

I shrink toward a wall. I need to think. That we're almost to the reading of the lists might change what I need to do first.

Where was I? Oh, far more likely is that Phaena was doing her job as ordered. Phaena and Momma K lied to me to obscure what they wanted me to do, and Phaena concealed her lactating, then told me the embarrassing 'real' story, and then felt guilty about telling me that? Why? It's obvious now. Because that story was a lie, too.

I should've put it together long ago. But the timeline distracted me, because it seems out of order.

Lord Repha'im is here. Lord Repha'im, who kidnapped the princes.

Phaena was speaking with *him*, out of all the people at this party. So they're connected. Phaena, who tried to confess that she isn't a prostitute who serves particular appetites. Minus all the misdirections and feigned shame and lies, I'm left with three facts.

One, Phaena knows Lord Repha'im.

Two, Repha'im—the man who kidnapped the princes—is here.

Three, out of all her possible agents, Momma K sent Phaena.

Four, Phaena is lactating.

Five, Momma K always picks the perfect tools for the job, which means—

~Ahem. Didn't you say *three* facts?~

What are you, the Abacus of Shadows now? The Digits of Darkness?

~More like the Scribe of Screw-Ups lately. I wanted to know if I misheard you is all. Go on.~

Shaking my head, annoyed, I return to my thoughts. I may not be able to count to three without reaching five, but if you give me a few tries, even I can add two and two. I haven't been sent to steal the Nemesis Compass; I'm not here for a heist, I'm here for a rescue.

But why wouldn't Momma K tell me that? I want to save them. That's all I wanted all along!

No...not *all* along.

What doesn't make sense is the timeline. Momma K wanted me to start this job before Logan even left Elenea. That was *before* the kidnapping.

That's too lucky, even for her. Out of all the cities on the continent, she sends me to exactly the right one, with exactly the right help for me to be able to bring the children back alive?

How could she send me to rescue children who hadn't even been kidnapped yet?

Had she changed her mind and sent me on a different job than she'd first intended, and used the Nemesis Compass heist as cover? No. She'd already sent Phaena on ahead of me for *this* job, and she'd sent her *before* the kidnapping.

Does that mean she's in on it? Is Momma K working with Lord Repha'im? Is she pretending to do so, to double-cross *him*? Momma K once told me she'd vowed never again to be at the mercy of any man. Does that include Logan Gyre? How ambitious is she, really?

She and Durzo had fought about something recently—something serious enough that Durzo left. Was it *this*? Durzo had limits. There were always jobs he wouldn't do. She'd said once that when she'd led the Sa'kagé and she'd had those kinds of jobs, she'd had to hire others to do them.

Momma K was always willing to do the things even Durzo wouldn't.

But this? This doesn't seem like her. Kids were always her soft spot.

It's a problem, and a big one, but not one I can solve with what I know right now.

What matters now is that if I'm right, the princes are here; I'm supposed to rescue them, and Phaena is supposed to serve as their wet nurse, caring for and feeding them until we get home. Gods know it would've been an enormous stretch for me to steal infants and *then* hire a wet nurse on the spot who would've been willing to travel halfway across the continent—likely while pursued by traitors willing to murder anyone to catch and kill us. Without a wet nurse, rescuing the boys would likely mean condemning them to starve to death. A wet nurse is a key to the whole job.

Seems like there must be magic out there to feed babies, right? That's the kind of thing practical people unlike me would've figured out. But again, finding a person who knows that magic and who would be willing to travel with me doing it—and who wouldn't immediately report to the Chantry—is a different matter.

So Momma K lied to me, but she also gave me all the tools I need to succeed.

If she has her own plans for what happens when I get back to Cenaria with the boys, I can deal with those then.

I don't like even entertaining the idea that she might double-cross *me*, but that too is a problem for later.

Mostly, I feel a rising joy. Having put all my worries off for another day, I feel—dare I say it?—optimistic. A few minutes ago, this job was (1) track down ancient artifact, (2) steal artifact, (3) hope artifact still works, (4) learn how to activate artifact, (5) activate artifact, (6) hope artifact can be activated repeatedly, (7) travel to wherever the twins are held, (8) gather allies and supplies, (9) rescue twins, (10) return twins home. Any of those steps could've turned out to be impossible. Most of them would've likely taken months. Now the job is (1) rescue twins, and (2) return twins to Logan and Jenine, who are already here and about to head home themselves, safely, with their own guards and an imperial escort.

I thought everything was doomed, including my friendship with Logan. Now? Now it all seems achievable.

Not easy. But no longer impossible. Not for Kylar Stern.

A surge of hope floods my body with light. I can't help but smile. Maybe I can even rescue the boys before Logan and Jenine ever find out they were gone.

The imperial guards are fanning out, checking all the side rooms, flushing out guests. To my left, a coughing man reeking of derivan leaf with his tunic loose, hopping on one foot trying to put on his second boot, is followed by an older noblewoman who looks perfectly put together except for the rouge smeared from her lips to one cheek and, improbably, a perfect rouge lip print in her cleavage.

Nonplussed, an imperial guard attempts to hand her some large yellow undergarments.

"Those aren't mine," she says, feigning offense. They match her dress perfectly, and appear to have a word embroidered on them in the same red of her dress's trim.

"I was posted in the smoking room for the last half hour," the guard says, bored. "You can take these now, or I can have a servant bring them around to your estate. I can't guarantee that will be at an hour when your husband isn't home."

Outraged, the woman snatches the undergarment and huffily walks away.

The imperial guard sees me watching. I smirk quickly and she smiles back. "And to think," she says. "It only gets wilder after the lists are read. Good luck, milord."

The reading of the lists! It'll be pandemonium. No one knows which way they'll have to jump until the lists are read. No one, not even Lord Repha'im, which might have been what he was hoping to figure out down at the docks. But if that's right, it means the princes won't be loaded yet or stay until Lord Repha'im's name is read—or isn't. The nobles' stuff was being held on the docks, but people will have to walk or be carried across last.

Which means I'm going to need help. I'm going to need someone I can trust, and I'm not totally sure Phaena is that, anymore. And though she's smart and resourceful, she has no powers, no fighting skills. There are two sets of ways onto the *Storm Racer*: a bunch of ramps down below at the waterline for the servants, and then a set of causeways up top, for the nobles and their most trusted advisors. I need to watch both for someone carrying babies.

I can maybe handle watching all the ramps down below. If I see the princes, I can do something to save them before they board. But Phaena doesn't have clearance to be up here. And even if she sees them, she won't be able to do anything to stop them from getting on the storm ship.

Which leaves me with only one person I can trust to drop everything and help me. And she's up here somewhere, probably already in the Privy Hall.

The imperial guard I'd spoken to has been relaying orders to her squad when I see her head cock, not twenty paces from me, as if her memory's been jogged by something. What if it's a description she heard of me?

I duck into the crowd as her head snaps in my direction, searching for me.

She starts pushing through the nobles, scanning.

This just keeps getting better, doesn't it?

By the time she reaches where she spoke with me, though, I've disappeared.

I hope.

Chapter Forty-Eight

The King in the West

I might need you any moment, I tell the ka'kari.

It gives me no response.

Hey, you awake?

This time I swear I can feel it twitch, as if it's smiling while feigning sleep. Gods, I'm getting to know this thing.

And now it seems to sigh.

Ahead there is yet another bank of queues. These all pass through large empty frames, giant doorways with great crystals overhanging each. For magic, I guess. Those guests wearing red-gemmed chokers are being funneled through one off to one side. I see Petaria Feu blinking as she approaches the frame but otherwise giving no hint she's nervous. She steps through and the crystal above her blooms a very pale blue.

A royal mage speaks sharply to her, a warning of some kind? But she lets her through without any more trouble.

Need you to cover my Talent.

Of course the ka'kari doesn't answer me, but I'm not too nervous as I choose a different, quicker line. This is the reason I haven't touched my Talent yet tonight, trying to avoid leaving any magical residue on myself that I can. I'm not sure how these detectors work, though.

I walk through, staring skyward, not at all nervous. The crystal does nothing at all, but on looking up, I notice that a line of gold wire along one side of the frame has been snipped. No wonder.

I take a breath. Hadn't realized I was holding it.

"Keep walking," a man grunts behind me. It's Jasmine Jakweth, the special team's muscle.

I scan the queue behind me and see Sister Ayayah Meganah is in it as well.

"Oh, has someone been naughty?" I ask.

He merely glowers. I get the impression he spends a lot of time doing that. But I'm not here for him. They don't say anything else to me, so maybe they haven't heard about me blowing Melena's cover to Logan yet. As I make it through with him hard on my heels, I'm already looking for Viridiana. She's not in the queues, nor in the areas outside the immense ebony-wood doors inlaid with silver that open into the Privy Hall.

So inside, probably.

Jasmine Jakweth shows no interest in speaking further with me, which is fine; I'm not fluent in Grunt.

I push through thick velvet curtains hanging beyond the great doors to dampen sound and separate those inside from the mob outside. I hate curtains. I can see through darkness, but curtains? Not at all. I think, briefly, of going invisible as I step through them—but as soon as I touch my Talent, I'll have ruined my disguise, right in the middle of hundreds of royal guards who are on the lookout for people exactly like me.

It's quieter in the Privy Hall; voices still buzz, but here in whispers. I step into the room, getting my first glimpse of the opulent heart of the palace when I notice that the curtains to my left seem not to have parted totally freely, as if there was a wall there—or a person.

Not every surprise is a lethal one. Bumping into a person unexpectedly at a party? How many times have you done that? How many times out of those was it someone trying to kill you?

I hesitate, balancing the dangers of making a spectacle of myself against the dangers of not.

A big hand closes around the back of my neck.

Made the wrong call.

"Kylar Stern! The Night Angel himself!" a jovial, familiar voice says.

A charge passes down my trapped neck. Please don't be—

"Lord Repha'im. Just the man I'd been hoping to see," I say, staring up at the big man. My heart is in my left pinky toe. I'm sure my grin is entirely unconvincing.

"I didn't know you were here! It's sooo good to see you again," he says. "Come! Come with me!"

He folds my right arm in his left, as if we're dear friends in the Modaini style, or possibly lovers in the Alitaeran, and holds his right hand over my hand, pinning me, while making me seem either a close friend he's protective of or the junior partner in a relationship.

If I'm willing to make a scene, I can get away.

Well, maybe. He's outwitted me so far. Why do I think pulling away would be a move he wouldn't expect?

I tense up, only thinking a stream of curses as he walks me deeper into the room, stepping onto a carpet so thick my feet sink in every step like snow. The Privy Hall audience chamber is so lushly opulent I wish I could describe the scenes etched into the walls shimmering magically, illustrating moments from ancient battles, famous loves, and noble sacrifices. Religious iconography dominates elsewhere with gold and rubies and pearls and mother-of-pearl, and recessed in subtly lit nooks so as not to dominate the room are the heads and stuffed figures of monsters, some of which I've fought.

I'd like you to think I'm this cool, collected person who always knows what to do. But I freeze up. Brain locks. I walk with him at least halfway across the room like a witless cow wondering why my human is wearing a butcher's apron and carrying a big knife and a bleeding pan.

It's the sight of Vi that snaps me out of it. She walks in front of us with a plate full of honey cakes, taking a deep, chesty breath to inhale the smell that has got to be on purpose, though she doesn't even glance our way. Lord Repha'im definitely notices her.

Which, I guess, proves he has a pulse. Most of the people nearby do.

Notice her, that is. Not have a pulse. I mean, that too, but—never mind.

He makes a little growl of approval low in his throat. "Mmm. I've always had a weakness for human women."

"Excuse me?" I say.

~Oh no.~

"Good thing is, it's reciprocated."

I notice then that he's attracted as many eyes as Viridiana. He releases my arm as if unconcerned now that I'll run away.

It's bold, but also accurate. I can't exactly run away. I'm in the middle of the room. I don't have anywhere to go.

"Food, too, sometimes. Though these I don't understand," he says, pointing to something on the table. "Chili-stuffed dormouse? If I wanted to eat rodents again, I'd return to—but never mind. This blood sausage, on the other hand? A delight, don't you think?"

"I prefer blood on my hands, not in my mouth," I say. It doesn't sound quite as tough as I'd hoped, but I'm still off-balance.

He barks a laugh and hands me a plate. He grabs slices of the sausage by hand and plops them down on my plate. "Do you know the great thing about power?" he asks.

"You're going to tell me, aren't you?"

"Yes." He sucks his fingertips clean, one by one. "The answer is everything. But one of the best is watching people's eyes as they see you doing something that they couldn't get away with. You tell a joke that isn't funny, and everyone laughs, and the one wit in the crowd gets this look in his eyes of pure hatred. I like to catch his eye at that instant. The two of you share a holy moment there, both of you seeing the truth, both of you knowing in that instant the truth doesn't matter, because you're special and he's not. Watching a man—what's the phrase?—eat his own heart. That's one of the things I love. There's more. I'll tell you about them some other time. If we get the chance."

"Where are the boys?"

"Kylar, do you know how to turn a mere warrior into a perfect weapon?"

I do have an idea or two about that, but I'm not interested in being side-tracked right now.

He says, "You break off all the inefficient human bits. You leave only enough humanity to keep him loyal. That's your grip. The rest is extraneous. Some-one's already broken you that way. Which might be very convenient, but with you I'm not sure the loyalty piece is salvageable. Better to discard a sharp blade than to cut oneself, don't you agree?"

"Where are the boys, Repha'im?"

He heaves a sigh. "And they said you would be the greatest threat to my plans. I only see a broken old dog. Is there more inside you that I haven't yet seen? Do you have hidden depths, Kylar Stern? Some secret well of resolve you haven't yet tapped...but surely will, at the last moment?" He smiles cold contempt. "Kylar, you're not my goal. I'm not aiming to take away everything you've ever loved or hoped for. Which is not to say I won't. I likely will. But it'll be incidental, a by-product of greater plans. You're simply not that important. If you left now, if you walked out those doors without a word, I wouldn't pursue you. You're not worth that much effort to me."

He sets down his plate. "My question is, did the Chantry bring you here, or someone else? Pardon the bluntness, but you don't seem capable of a whole lot on your own. Mostly hired muscle, aren't you? My money's on the Chantry. It's remarkable, really. Even though they suspect what I am, they still think they can pull one over on me. On me! And you people have such respect for the Chantry's long memory.

"But then, every so often they do need to be taught a lesson. Like a dog that nips your heels, a good quick cudgel across the eyes teaches more than a thousand sharp words. I'll be teaching them soon and bluntly. And maybe you, too, if you belong to them. But you don't quite, do you?"

"Who are you, then, that I should be so scared?" I ask.

"Was it luck, then, what you did before? Or was that all Durzo Blint's doing? Durzo the charging destrier, and you the drifting leaf in his wake? Maybe I should've had Ishael knife you in the curtains as he wanted. Or before that. You've *got* to have guessed by now." He examines me closely. Wrinkles his nose. Finally, he says, "No? Really? Huh. Well, enjoy the party. Or don't. What a disappointment you are, Kylar Stern. Just another man, not willing to do what he must to be of consequence. How old are you, Kylar? Late twenties or so? Not yet thirty, surely . . . and already a has-been."

I don't know why it stings, but it does. Not yet thirty? I'm not yet in my midtwenties. Lord Repha'im despises me—and I'm even more pathetic than he realizes.

"Tragic," he says. He picks up his plate and walks away, dismissing me.

Immediately, he's enveloped in a conversation with half a dozen high officials, seamlessly taking the center of their attention.

He doesn't look back.

What's going on? What just happened?

I haven't been treated as if I were irrelevant for a long time. Why now?

Because it's already too late for me to stop him.

Or at least he believes it is.

But he can't know that. He can't yet even know if he's getting on the *Storm Racer* or being left behind. Can he?

Something about being dismissed makes me feel . . . relieved. Feeling relieved makes me feel embarrassed. Embarrassment boils.

I want to pick a fight with him.

I want to tell him how he's going to wake some morning choking on his own blood, and how my smiling face will be the last thing he sees.

Taunts? Threats? It's as if I've forgotten everything Durzo taught me. How...unprofessional.

Threats are the refuge of the impotent, shouting at an indifferent world how he's gonna sodomize it good, while the world regards his sad, limp phallus and mocks.

A threat gives away your intent, binds you to it, and makes it less likely to come to fruition. You only make a threat if you can't be stopped and if you accomplish more by making the threat than by simply taking vengeance.

"Hi," an unarmed woman, no hidden weapons, unlikely to have martial training, says to me, "could I..."

We have a pleasant conversation. I eventually realize she's flirting with me, or perhaps with my four-blue-gemmed bracelet—she's a three and I realize fours are quite uncommon, and the woman keeps angling to get my name out of me. I break off our conversation and do what I can to keep my bracelet out of sight. Then I circulate carefully, talking with as many people for a few minutes at a time as I can. Because I've finally seen Vi.

She's circulating, too. Laughing in conversations, throwing her head back, throat exposed. She's magnetic, and were she not moving on constantly, a group of men would form around her. Indeed, it does somewhat anyway, slowly drifting after her quick, artful steps away.

As the minutes pass, she throws me quick hand signs: 'No.'

A minute later. 'Go away.'

Five minutes later. 'Stop.'

She tries a few longer messages, delivered in quick, staccato flashes when no one else will observe them, but truth is, I can't decipher those. My own grasp of the Sa'kagé's hand signs is rudimentary. Durzo taught me only things that would be immediately useful to him if we worked together: 'I take the one on the left.' 'Gap, armor, at neck.' 'Go on my count.' He never imagined me working as part of a larger team, and always said there were too many useful skills for him to teach me already in the time we had, and he'd get back to the lesser skills if I lived long enough.

Finally, she gives up and angles herself toward an alcove, where she pretends to chat with Sister Melena. I approach behind her and bend to fix the fussy laces of my high red shoes.

Turned toward Melena, Vi says quietly and angrily, "Did you not see what I said?" She smiles at Melena.

"Oh, that's lovely!" Melena says. Then, under her breath, "You ruined a cover I spent six months building, you son of a whore. And now you're endangering us all."

Vi pulls out a tiny mirror from a clutch and pretends to touch up her cosmetics. But her eyes are locked on me in the mirror. I know I have only a few moments.

The most helpful thing for the Chantry to learn is that Lord Repha'im believes the Chantry is plotting against him, whether or not he knows specifics, and that he plans to teach them a lesson, soon. Or maybe I could tell them he has delusions of being superhuman.

But I'm not here to help them. I'm here to get Vi's help.

"Repha'im's got Logan's kids."

I take a chance and look at her face as I say it. She freezes as if I've knocked the wind out of her. She goes green.

Then she smiles it away, dabs one corner of her mouth as if fixing the rouge, and tucks away the little mirror.

When did Momma K think I would figure all this out? Was the description of the blue chest purely to throw me off the real job? That doesn't make sense. No, she'd have given me the right description or one that was close enough. That way, if I didn't figure out the heist was a rescue until I found the chest—which might not be a chest at all, but would have to match the description closely enough that she'd be sure I'd check it—I'd still find the babies. In reality, the chest is probably a bassinet, and Phaena was supposed to tell me the truth at some point tonight, once I was already in the party and committed to the job.

And now that I think of it, Phaena *was* trying to tell me, maybe even a little early, when Vi came to our carriage and hijacked everything.

Moving my lips as little as possible, I say, "The children are being transported inside a blue chest or bassinet, maybe two. Golden stripes, ermine trimmings, adorned with birds of prey, maybe accompanied by a brunette woman in red and white. I'll be watching the loading areas downstairs. I need you to watch up here."

"I'm a little busy," Vi hisses, smiling at Melena and patting her arm, clearly preparing to leave.

"If I ever meant anything to you, Viridiana...please."

I don't know how she takes it. I don't have any other options, any other hope.

I set my laces and head in the opposite direction.

Melena says something sharp, but I don't know if it's to me or Vi. I don't turn back.

I don't know if I'm being watched, but I circulate through the party more, chatting with random people, standing near others and seeming to talk to myself, even feigning bigger emotions as if I'm secretly speaking to them—all the things you need to do to increase the noise of false signals and increase the clutter of leads spies will have to chase down if you're being watched.

The air is changing here as midnight approaches, and then, according to the most elaborate water clock I've ever seen, passes. I notice that there's no alcohol being served now. No doubt there've been problems before. Seems like a good idea to give people a bit of time to dry out when they're waiting for the most stressful announcement of their year, or their lives.

I stare at the water clock; it's a brass and silver monstrosity, with its whirling gears, gold-dust-infused drips, and spinning statuettes of characters from Alitaeran history and mythology—every five seconds, two spearmen in different desert robes come spinning together and clang tiny spears against each other before retreating.

"Are you going to talk to the entire team and mark them all for death, or do you think you've done enough already?" I hear a woman say to me.

I don't turn to her, though her demeanor tempts me to.

Sister Ayayah Meganah is standing beside me as I fill a cup with some pink juice. I turn slightly farther away from her and pick my nose to let her know what I think. "I was hoping to talk to you," I say. "I don't know what your plans are, but Lord Repha'im knows you're all here. He's toying with you."

"Why would you think our plans have anything to do with him? What reason do you have to believe he knows anything about us?"

"Because he told me."

The tall woman actually relaxes. She doesn't believe me. "Our business with you is finished, Kylar Stern. Go now, lest we decide collecting you is the best use of our time after all. It was a near thing on our last vote."

"And what won the vote? Not keeping Logan here—that business is finished, yet you're still tense, which tells me it wasn't your only goal."

She grinds her teeth. "Every moment you speak to me endangers me. Don't make me your enemy. Don't."

"Is it the children?" I ask, risking a glance at the moment to see her reaction. She blinks, then instantly seems to realize her reaction's given it away.

"Child," she murmurs, and it's an admission and a decision. "They split them up. We lost one's trail immediately. That's who you should go after, Kylar, considering—"

She cuts off.

"Considering?" I prompt.

"Considering we're already recovering this one."

"*Recovering*, not *rescuing*. Because you think of him as property. Valuable property." My face feels hot, gut tight.

"Rescuing," she says smoothly as if she'd misspoken, but her smile is tight.

I take a sharp breath at a thought. "You don't mean to return him."

"Of course we'll return him," she says. But there's something off in how she says it. She's lying. The Chantry never gives something for nothing. They plan to couch it soft and sneaky, but they plan to *negotiate* the child's return.

"What are you planning to demand? Some kind of concessions? This is their child!" I'm struggling to keep my voice down. "Do you have any idea what he'll do if you demand a ransom—?"

She flushes. "I have nothing more to say to you."

Her eyes burn with the sudden hatred of a person perfectly willing to take out her frustration at her own errors on someone else.

I turn and start walking, my mind reeling from what I've just learned: one child, not two...not considering...not returning...It's all going in circles. Any of it could be a lie, or wrong, but I don't think it is.

I'm still thinking, wondering if it's all too late, when a curtain is pulled back and a herald comes out to speak, before footlights that illuminate him. The other lights in the room come way down. A hush descends.

My gorge churns.

Someone taps my shoulder, and I turn my head to look up. "You're going to love this," Lord Repha'im says.

I hadn't even noticed his approach.

There's only one time to enjoy your enemy smiling at you. That's when you know something he doesn't.

This is not that time.

Somehow, Lord Repha'im knows what's going to happen here. That means he knows if he's getting on the boat—or not. Or thinks he does. But I have no idea which of those would be better for him.

"Have you ever been to one of these?" Lord Repha'im asks me in a whisper.

"No." I consider knifing him right now. We've been searched and searched again for weapons, but nothing can stop the ka'kari.

There are a lot of imperial guards around. A *lot*. Even I wouldn't get away alive. If I kill him, I'll die for it. If I die, that means I'll trade the life of someone innocent who loves me to stop him.

Maybe it's worth it, but I'm not willing to let anyone else pay the price for my rage, my failures, my insufficiency.

The herald finishes whatever he was saying—I didn't hear a word of it—and the Privy Hall goes dark. Not a little bit dark, but dramatically dark, cloudy moonless midnight-in-a-tunnel dark.

With my powers, it doesn't bother my eyes, but after a few long moments, a sense of uneasiness ripples through the crowd: These nobles are here with their friends, but also with their enemies. They're protected by imperial guards, but if those guards can't see anything either, how protected are they?

In the end, darkness is not an argument. Darkness's power is preternatural. Darkness strides past the mind and speaks a language the mind knows not; it speaks directly to the heart.

I realize it's too late already even as it occurs to me that if I'd been paying attention, if I'd been planning ahead, out of everyone here, I could use the darkness like no one else. I steal a glance at Lord Repha'im.

He's staring straight at me, eyes no longer pale blue but luminous with an inhuman poison-oak green, his pupils horizontal slits. Then the slits rotate from the horizontal to the vertical: caprine to feline, and he smiles. I take an involuntary step back, and he shakes his head at me indulgently, as if he'd expected an attack in the darkness, and is disappointed to see me afraid.

Rebounding from my fear, ashamed, angry, I reach out to View him—

~Don't!~ the ka'kari snaps—quietly, though, even inside my own head, as if afraid to be overheard.

So I don't View him.

My fists curl, jaw goes taut, rage rising. My vision narrows to his mocking face, his alien eyes. 'Tight is slow, taut is stupid,' Durzo says in the back of my mind.

But Durzo's far, far away. And I'm about to make a mistake. I know it.

~You can't make mistakes with this one, Kylar. Not this one.~

Light flashes from the stage, startling me.

Without conscious thought, I lash out—

And find my wrist trapped by Lord Repha'im's huge hand.

"Let's not spoil the moment," he whispers.

And he lets me go.

He's so certain of what I will and won't do, I feel like a child whose very tantrums are predictable.

And he's not wrong.

Onstage a feathery cocoon descends from the ceiling with no visible supports. Lightning flashes, strobing light across a rapt audience, and timpanis roll thunder. Lines of blue light up, sketching feathers to a heartbeat pulse, the lines of wings. The cocoon rotates, revealing the tucked head of the eagle, and the crowd murmurs as if surprised.

Everything's eagles here. What's the surprise?

Then the wings unfurl with a snap and a great flash. To the gasps and applause of the nobles, the empress descends from the eagle, her own arms spread, hands making some religious sign of blessing or another. With each gesture, she flings gold dust infused with magic that makes coruscating shows of color all the way to the floor, or onto her fortunate subjects themselves.

The empress is resplendent in a white and silver gown. She literally glows.

But I lose all sense of enchantment as soon as she begins, for she's not foremost an entertainer but a head of state, and the novelty of useless, colorful magic dies by asphyxia as she starts her speech by thanking those who've put together the festivities and the lords who served their term so faithfully last year—the usual boring stuff that greases the skids in a bureaucracy.

I can see it on the faces, again with each spotlighted by magic as the empress speaks. Their thoughts are obvious: *Everyone else's name is a boring item on a list, but* my *name is sweet music and all my neighbors and rivals heard the empress herself recognize me.*

Repha'im whispers to me, "I do believe that the empress would love to make everyone wait all the way until the end for the main announcement, but as soon as you start naming the lordlings downstream it's obvious what's going to happen upstream to the lords they serve, so unlike most of these dull affairs, we won't have to wait long for the real fun."

I look up at him, still wondering what he's doing.

"Oh! Here comes my little moment," he says with a dashing smile. "Don't blink. You might miss me!"

He makes his way along a wall in the semidarkness, oddly unobtrusive for a man so big.

Man?

Maybe not a man.

Those eyes could have been illusions. The magic isn't that hard.

But my gut turned at the sight of those eyes. They didn't feel like illusions. He said he wasn't human. What if he's not?

I should run away. The rest of this is probably a trap. If he's happy, something bad is about to happen, and whatever it is, I'm not ready for it.

But after I make my way to the rear of the Privy Hall and check to see that no one is going to stop me from leaving, I can't go. I should. But I have to know.

He hasn't been onstage yet. There have been a few and surprisingly brief speeches from high nobles, but not once has Lord Repha'im been onstage. Not that I've seen anyway, not in my quick glances as I surreptitiously made my way through the crowd.

Did I miss him as I made my way back here? Was his moment as brief as he warned?

The empress is speaking again. "As you know," she says, "it is one of my great pleasures from time to time to name and ordain the King in the West, whom we entrust with half of our empire, along with other things . . . equally dear to us."

The audience laughs. I don't get it.

~Sex joke.~

Ah.

Why is sex weird in its own way in every culture? Here, nobles were having sex in half the side rooms. The empress often *officially* takes two new lovers every year . . . but even a vague reference aloud to that fact is scandalous enough to be funny?

I don't get it.

"Without our new king serving me from afar, I know I'd be pulling my hair out. But with him near, I shall be glad to have someone else pulling my hair." She gives a conspiratorial wink to the crowd as they go wild.

She looks down, puts a hand to her forehead to cover her face briefly as if embarrassed—though careful not to smudge her cosmetics—then waves them down. "I should *not* have said that. My friends, you have to *promise* not to tell anyone."

~Oh, she's good.~

I can see what the ka'kari means. The nobles are eating this up. This is what their power is for. This exclusivity. Being part of the innermost circle is why they do all the scheming and backstabbing. The empress herself, sharing her secrets with them, telling ribald jokes?

The woman even abandoned the royal pronoun as she did it, going for the personal instead. I don't know if she does it by pure instinct or intentional genius, but she knows how to bind a room to her more closely. Even after all her years on the throne she doesn't take her people for granted. She makes them pay dearly to be invited into this room, but she knows how to make it worthwhile.

This is a woman who knows how to ride the tiger named Power.

"We..." She clears her throat, fanning herself as if she's hot from blushing. I'm too far back to tell if she really is. She straightens up, taking on her formality again. "We, therefore, with no further ado, are immensely pleased to name the new King in the West..."

The lights drop down again, dramatically.

Through the shadows, I look to the sides of the stage. Is Repha'im a member of the new king's entourage? The rest of this political stuff doesn't matter to me. If I cared more, I'd already know who Repha'im's lord is. Because, given Repha'im's hints, I now realize that *this* is how he knew what was about to happen here: His lord is going to be the King in the West.

That isn't good. I'm not sure how bad it is, but it's bad—for me, for Logan, for the Chantry.

And then I see a noble in the darkness of the stage, approaching the empress. A single noble, no entourage accompanying him.

No. No no no! My throat clamps tight. That's not how this works! It can't be—

The lights come up.

The sound of gasps fills the Privy Hall.

"Lord Rabisu Repha'im," the empress announces, taking his hand. "Your new King in the West."

I can't hear whether there are gasps, can't hear the applause that follows, though I see the blurry crowd between Repha'im and me moving, making the motions that should be accompanied by that sound. I hear nothing but the roar of my pulse, see nothing but him, as if at the end of a long tunnel.

There are at least seven hundred people in this room. Maybe a thousand. I'm standing near the back, not where I was when Repha'im left me. There's no way he should be able to find me in this crowd, but I swear, without having to scan the crowd, he locks his eyes on me, as if he notices no one else.

"My consort, O loyal one, your people," the empress announces. "My people, your king."

Everyone in the room drops to one knee. Every head bows.

I hesitate. Not long, but long enough that eyes start flicking toward me, questioning, scandalized. The royal guards stiffen, their entire bodies speaking their questions about why I'm standing: Rival? Troublemaker? Traitor?

I too lower myself to one knee, and bitterly, bitterly, bow my head. At the first possible instant I can do so without it looking like treason, I glance up.

Lord Repha'im—now King Repha'im—is basking in the attention and doing the royal thing, returning little nods out into the audience to particular favorites, acknowledging the lords' and ladies' obeisance graciously, reflecting the attention back to the empress and leading the applause for her.

With most eyes diverted from him momentarily, he glances back in my direction and grins. I can't be sure he's even staring at me, he seems to have so many friends here, but I feel it nonetheless, that he wants me to know he's seen me take the knee. His victory over me is complete, and with barely a flicker of that triumphant grin, his gaze moves on. I'm nothing to him now; he continues basking in his victory.

My guts go crashing through the floor. I don't know what it means yet, but I know, without a shadow of a doubt, this is not a setback; this is disaster. This means catastrophe and death and probably war.

I'm in the middle of it. I'm in way over my head.

And I can't see any way out.

Chapter Forty-Nine

Walls That Magic Can't Break

$\mathcal{M}$y emotions in riot, I stand dumbly with the rest, though a hush of delighted expectation ripples through the hall. Some servant hands King Repha'im a sword. No, not a sword, a metal rod? People start looking from the king to the back of the hall.

To me? For a moment, my heart seizes. Then I see that people aren't looking toward me, but above me.

King Repha'im has set the rod into the floor. Not a rod, a lever. He gestures as if asking the crowd if he should pull it.

They roar approval.

It's his big moment. He soaks it up, and then heaves on the lever.

The wall behind him opens on an unseen seam and splits open to the night, wide enough for three oxcarts to pass abreast.

I follow everyone else's gaze, as from some hidden gallery above all of us in the Privy Hall a giant form sweeps into view—and swoops past, over me and then over the crowd in a rush of blue and yellow feathers.

Flinching along with half the rest of the people around me, I nearly embrace my Talent to attack, but it's not an eagle; it's a man strapped to a frame below two wide, stiff wings. Right behind him come two more, smaller.

A young woman in front of me grabs the woman beside her, squealing with delight, "Pilot wings!"

The great eagle glides the length of the hall, and out into the night, passing within feet of King Repha'im. As it sails into the darkness, two flares on the pilot's legs ignite, blue and yellow: Repha'im's colors.

A few moments later, I hear distant cheers from below, even over the sound of the burgeoning wind. Then the other pilot wings launch into the night, turning left and right, and light up blue and yellow as well.

Belatedly, I realize this is how they announce who the new king is to everyone on the lower levels and at the docks and the city.

Suddenly, the doorways at my back become a rush of movement: servants filing in with drinks and platters and tables for the party that will last through the rest of the night until it's time for the nobles to cross the upper loading bridge onto the storm ship just before dawn.

The servants at the wider docks below will have to work through the remainder of the night to load the correct nobles' items—doubtless right now overseers are flipping through their contingency plans to find the unlikely one labeled with Lord Repha'im's name.

As imperial servants stream into the Privy Hall, dozens of messengers are already crowding the exits to go take word of the development.

The faces around me are a stormy sea of emotion, from the haunted faces of those contemplating disaster to mild disappointment to hunger to elation.

I start fading back, toward the line of the messengers getting out, but I can't take my eyes off the man dominating the stage as if he's grown in size. He radiates presence. I see him flick his fingers in toward his leg, subtly summoning someone.

The empress heads back to the center dais to walk down the stairs into the crowd. She pauses, waiting for King Repha'im.

He's whispering to a man like a whip, dressed in black slashed with Repha'im's blue and yellow, and a feathered cap. The man searches the crowd with hawklike eyes as Repha'im speaks to him.

I know instantly who he is, and what he's looking for.

This must be Ishael, the one who wanted to knife me in the curtains—and he's looking for me.

Me. I want to snap my back to him so he doesn't see my face, but I hunch and turn, slowly, slowly. Quick movement draws the eye.

When I dare a glance back, Ishael is gone and Repha'im has joined hands with the empress. They proceed down the stairs into a congratulatory sea of nobles.

He's accepted, supreme in his confidence, admired, an outsider who's successfully become the ultimate insider.

The stab of hatred that twists in my guts is so sharp that I actually miss a step and bump into a young messenger. She pushes me away angrily, ignoring my mumbled apology.

Logan's kid is going to be loaded onto the storm ship in minutes, if not at this very moment. Repha'im's people had to wait for the flares with everyone else. There's still time, but I need to get down to the lower docks.

I'll have to hope that Vi is going to watch up here.

Sometimes the best way is the least expected. So I glance back, beyond King Repha'im to the nobles' bridge, reaching across space to the upper decks of the storm ship. Pyrotechnics are bursting in the night air outside, blue and yellow mixed with the empress's purple and red. I count no more than ten imperial guards and maybe five huge men each in unique armor who must be some of her famed praetorian guards.

I'd guess there's maybe another half-dozen imperials out of sight on the dais. If I can get past all of them, I could cross to the storm ship itself—or perhaps there's a ladder I didn't see on my first trip.

But the night wind is blowing in, ruffling dresses and hair, and even as I look, someone pushes the lever and the great doors to the bridge begin grinding shut. I suppose they won't open again until just before dawn, when it's time for about half of these nobles to board.

It's too far away. If I run, I'll blow my cover. If I blow my cover charging toward the empress, I'll be attacked by the imperial guards and her hulking praetorians and maybe even a bunch of nobles in this hall. It's suicide.

I hesitated too long. My options, like a noose, are tightening, tightening, cutting off my breath.

In the crowd, I catch a glimpse of the whippish, feather-capped Ishael. He sees me, too, a hawk catching sight of his prey.

I turn, threading my way through the crowd, dodging quickly into every gap I see, then stepping slowly in the way Durzo taught me to move through a large crowd while remaining inconspicuous. Here being slight is my greatest advantage.

Out of the hall, I join the messengers streaming toward every stair and exit. The oak-paneled music room where Melena gave me these clothes isn't far, so I jog toward it. Even hiding my four-gemmed bracelet as well as I can, I may be the best-dressed of the messengers hurrying to give their lords the news, but all of them have more pressing things to do than gawk at the strangeness of others.

I find Melena's bag behind the screen where she'd grabbed it to help me change, and hastily strip and then pull on the less-conspicuous nobleman's clothes that I arrived in, happily saying farewell to the tight white trousers. Mercifully, the woman has a whole cosmetics kit in the bag, so I'm able to scrub off the heavy kohl she adorned my brows with, too. I sop up as much as I can of the oily goop in my hair with my white silk shirt, breaking my hair out of its stiff points and curls and back into a more anonymous style. Then I tuck everything away and hurry on.

By the time I emerge, the air is raucous, festive, loud. Musicians play in every corner and in galleries overhead. People laugh too loud, men roaring, women shrieking. A young man is weeping inconsolably. Knots of wild, intense emotion clog the stream, whole groups looking crestfallen, angry snarls hidden under the gaiety and forced gaiety and noise.

I flash my bracelet at the overwhelmed-looking imperial guards at a servants' entrance, and they say nothing as I pass. I think I hear a shout as I disappear around a corner, but neither comes running after me.

I've barely stepped into an art gallery reeking of vomit, with servants already on their knees with rags, when a fistfight breaks out between a young nobleman and an old one. The men are spitting images of each other: father and son? A whistle shrieks and I see imperials coming running with man-catchers. They almost shouldn't bother. Father and son both appear to have trained most in the martial art known as shout-and-shove, with only a rudimentary knowledge of grab-and-flail. Their purple-faced enthusiasm sends them careening off-balance right toward a masterful still life of a codpiece.

An imperial mage with a long-suffering expression on his face slaps a hand on a golden button on one wall, and steel plates snap up in front of every painting in the room. The men bounce off one of the plates but I'm gone before I can see what happens to them next.

In the servants' areas, everyone is moving at a solid clip. Not running, but moving fast with the air of people who know they'll need to be moving fast for the next five hours and they can't exhaust themselves.

No one pays any attention to a man like a flitting shadow, never getting in the way, flashing his bracelet at every doorway. When questions arise, the four blue gems on my bracelet silence them quickly.

I make it to the lower docks in minutes, pushing out in the warm night air from a side exit, slightly elevated over the streams of wagons organized tightly into entry lanes and exit lanes. A wagon suddenly sags to one side, perhaps with a broken wheel. But instantly, longshoremen with levers and jacks and spares of everything swarm in like bees.

But I dismiss their emergency. It means nothing to me. My eyes rove, seeking the blue and yellow wagons I hope not to find—

Right at the front.

~That is ... not good.~

From here, I can't see how close they are to loading. I can't quite tell how much imperial presence there is before those wagons get on the ship, either. I feel an ache in the back of my throat. Though a part of me knows what I'm going to find, I plunge into the crowd.

It takes me too much precious time to push my way to the front.

As I go, I'm looking for exits, other ways, new opportunities or new threats.

The things that didn't matter before could be vital now, so I examine the storm ship.

Despite everything, my neck tips back as I take it in. I forget to blink. There's no way to regard this monster without being aware that one is beholding one of the wonders of the world. Its size alone—hundreds of paces long and high enough I feel like I'm walking through a great canyon—speaks of the labor of many thousands, the resources of an entire now-lost world, and unimaginable magics, and yet this leviathan has a unity to it that speaks of one megalomaniacal or genius vision.

I don't remember the name of the emperor who commissioned it, but he'd been some idiot who believed courage was the highest good. So he dared only the bravest of his nobles to join him as he relocated his court from one capital to the next in ten days of insane travel rather than the months-long procession always taken by his predecessors.

Somehow, he survived and became famous for his bravery, rather than derided for his stupidity.

Thus was born an idiotic tradition. His successor couldn't hope to hold power if he wasn't brave enough to do the same, and then *his* successor couldn't hope to hold power if she wasn't brave enough to do what they'd done, and so on to the present day.

Depending who you believe, after all these years, the voyage to Borami is now either safer than ever or far more dangerous. The magi and navigators now have generations of experience, but the storm ship was constructed using techniques no one now living can even comprehend, much less duplicate, and there are evidently magics in key areas with the same problem, so a catastrophic failure is either very unlikely or long overdue. Apparently, the imperial mages say it's harder every year to hold the ship together, but the nobles say that the mages have been saying that for generations and are merely looking for more funding.

Regardless, there's no mess of ideas or decoration: All the ship's beauty is in serving its one function efficiently.

The *Storm Racer* is so specialized that she has a brutal beauty reminiscent of the great white sharks that process through the nearby waters like cumbrous kings. The ship's body is unnaturally smooth to the wind, with no open decks at all. Its only nod to its occupants' desires is the glassed-in observation deck at the front capped by a tiny observation globe, surely all magically hardened. The ship is silver-skinned to a straight-on glance, but refracting the distorted moon an ominous blood red from this angle. Round above the waterline, the hull cuts sharp and deep in the water for stability, and, like a shark's dorsal fin, a central tower rises into the air to flex against the coming gales.

To either side of the smooth selachian body rise gull-like wings, not far above the water. The wingtips terminate in sleek trimaran pontoons, like dolphins swimming escort to the great white shark of the central hull, each with their own deep keels below and round wind-cutting dorsal fins above.

The spiderweb of a bridge from the Privy Hall spans across to the great central dorsal fin, high above me. Everyone else will enter across the docks I'm crossing now.

Beneath that bridge, Castle Stormfast and the mountain into which it's built are sheer. Whatever windows grace this southern side have now been shuttered and surely sealed with magic against the coming storm—and against men like me.

Even if I could get one open, the gap between castle and ship is much too far for a grapnel throw, and what would a grapnel catch on?

The crowd jostles me back as I push through it, throat tightening, tightening.

Could I break through a window and climb across on the underside of the nobles' bridge?

But then I see the knots of spikes protruding under the nobles' bridge every ten paces. The Alitaerans, paranoid about assassinations, consulted with wetboys, Ymurri stalkers, and every other kind of sellsword and burglar they could possibly hire. Those spikes won't be mundane only. There will be magical traps in each one, and in between them.

With the ka'kari, maybe I could make it, given enough time.

But I have to get on the ship, find the kid, and take him back—all before dawn.

Oh, not to mention getting away. I keep forgetting that part recently. I have to escape. With an infant in tow.

I snort aloud. This is ridiculous. It's death to even try it.

I don't have to stop to ask myself what Durzo would do. It's reflexive, constant. Though in my private life I reject his intuitions, his approaches, and his conclusions, in professional matters he is my high priest and high king; he is the law and all the prophets and every commentary; he is a sardonic dragon in a world of swaggering geckos.

Durzo's tenacity was patient. He would back off, ride a horse to Borami, contact some trusted local intelligence network, and do the job from—No, actually, he wouldn't. Durzo didn't do rescues. An important person of the kind he was hired to assassinate always had to emerge eventually. Power can't be maintained forever from a distance. An infant? Anyone can hide a kid.

If I take a horse, I'll get to Borami more than a month later than King Repha'im. Borami will surely offer him an entire network of agents who can take the child any direction he wants. He'll have all the power and connections of the Alitaeran empire at his command. I would arrive late, in a foreign country, in a city I've never visited, where I have no friends or even associates, attempting to find a child hidden by a man with all the connections and money in the world, a child who may no longer even be in the country by the time I arrive.

Momma K told me I was the wrong person to be looking for a kid in the city of Elenea, where we had all the advantages. How much worse would I be at scouring Borami for him?

I could look for years and never even hear a whisper of what I'm hoping for. I would barely know where to start. No wonder Durzo never took this kind of job.

I'd like to tell you I immediately come up with a new plan.

I don't. Despair chokes me. I let the crowd pull me forward, no longer pushing my way through. Up ahead, I see the last of Lord Repha'im's baggage train being waved through onto the great sloping loading dock.

I'm too late. There are dozens upon dozens of soldiers and imperial guards and mages here. For pity's sake, at the edges of the docks there are divers shivering in the cold of the night's wind, holding their long cloaks closed around their near-nakedness with one hand while the other hand holds a long dagger, their eyes searching the waters. The security here is ready even for someone who might dive off the edge and swim toward the storm ship.

I cast my eyes about, chest tight, swallowing, trying to find some third way. But minutes pass, and all that becomes clearer is just how much worse everything is than I'd thought. The soldiers, guards, and mages form a literal wall of humanity. With that mass of bodies, going invisible won't help me—some of the mages are scanning for magic at all times, and I'm hemmed in by the crowds anyway.

They are too, part of me thinks. Maybe I can take advantage of that?

But it's not enough. Some mages are positioned in low towers, scanning the crowd from above. Others are on the ground. All of them are trained in combat magics. Without any room to maneuver, if I try to push my way onto the ship, I'll be going against at least a hundred of Alitaera's best fighters. With plenty of backups. That's not *I'd only have a slim chance.* That's suicide.

On the ramp, disappearing into the great ship, I see a woman in red and white turn and look behind her: Phaena!

She's made it aboard! But she turns before I can think to wave. Doesn't see me.

Not that she could do anything to help me. It's astonishing she got herself in. My throat clamps down.

I'm almost to the front of the line. What am I going to do? Hope that the guards flub checking their lists and miraculously wave me aboard?

Even when my luck's good, it's not that good.

I'm about to turn back when I see a streak of light, as of something aglow on a string sliding down from the top of the castle toward one of the elevated guard towers. A parchment? An officer there snatches it out of the air—a message, clearly.

He shouts an order to the guards below him, but I can only catch snippets of it, and it's in some kind of jargon.

But the effect is immediate, the change in intensity instant. Every guard and mage is suddenly on high alert. "...about this tall," the officer says, gesturing. And then what must be a description. "Last seen with a four-sapphire bracelet!"

I look at the bracelet with four sapphires on my wrist.

I curse under my breath. I came to test Death's defenses. Now Death is looking for me. Checking my pocket first to make sure I still have the yellow

gemstone bracelet I took from Raisins, I start fiddling with the sapphire bracelet. It won't open at first, so I yank on it, hard. Something snaps loudly enough
that a few people in the crowd look around to see what the sound was. I hide
my wrist and don't look down.

When I can safely spare a look, I see that the bracelet's clasp is open, and the
four blue gems are cracked and no longer glow. Well, that's that, I guess. It's far
from the worst thing that could've happened when breaking a magical security
device.

Reckless, Kylar. I slip on my three-yellow-gemmed bracelet.

With all my years of practice, I melt back into the surging crowd. It's no easy
feat. Any block in the flow of a packed mass of humanity causes eddies, ripples. I begin dodging, slipping from side to side, making anyone's missed step
as they go forward last only a fraction of a second, staying low. Finding gaps.

A family party advancing together, eight people across, stops my progress:
parents holding convulsively to their children's hands, fearful of being separated, and themselves hemmed in by carts. I can't smooth away the blockage,
so I stare up, as if enraptured by pilot wings wheeling overhead.

Not every eddy in a packed crowd is a fugitive, after all. There are plenty
of gawkers, and the last thing an assassin would do is stop to stare at the show.

The wind is now a firm breeze, and the half-dozen pilot wings swoop and
swirl at different heights, tethered to the castle against the wind like kites.

Tethered from a central balcony.

With a grumble, the father releases his daughter's hand and takes it again
immediately after they pass me.

Durzo once said, 'Don't improvise. Don't ever improvise. Unless you have
to. Then improvise like Pytharius when he was caught in bed with his lord's
wife. If you move fast enough, even something stupid can work if it dazzles
your opponents into inaction.'

I am one of the most dexterous and coordinated people I know. Durzo
wouldn't have taken me in if I weren't. I have outstanding gross and fine motor
control. But I'm not an idiot.

~Ahem.~

Well, *usually* I'm not an idiot. I know I can't grab one of those gliders and fly
it safely on my first try. That's like saying *Hey, I've spent my whole life using
my voice. I shout a lot. Ergo, I could be a soloist for the Waeddryn Royal Rep-
ertory Choir.*

But maybe I can—

~Ahem, Kylar. Kylar! Wasn't talking about that. You need to move. Now.~

I start to move. What's the—?

A whistle blasts nearby.

Every eye goes to an imperial guard fifteen paces away as she blasts two more alarm notes, and then all those curious eyes shoot to where she's pointing—at me.

The Alitaeran security apparatus is a wall of human intention, overlapping responsibilities, and focus, made seamless with constant practice and thick with discipline.

And now that entire wall falls on me all at once.

Chapter Fifty

Man in Flight

*C*an I tell you something insane?

I love this.

As the first hand reaches out to grab, to stop me, to arrest me in my flight, my world contracts, becomes a heartbeat: Expands—observation. Contracts—action.

Movements practiced and chained together a thousand times become single volitional chunks, faster than a gasp. A civilian's hand snags my tunic, and my only thought is *Off!* but my body translates: My right hand comes up, traps his against my chest as I step in, flexing past him, pulling him forward off-balance, twisting his wrist, extending his arm, my left palm coming in sharply, popping his elbow out of joint.

I'm beyond him before he gasps, three paces away before he yelps in startled pain—but his yell is muted to my ears; it's not the yell of an incoming attack, so it's inconsequential, even as my senses expand once more.

A blur of civilians' faces, undifferentiated, unimportant. Whether those faces speak fear or confusion or anger, their bodies show no readiness to attack, their centers of weight recoiling.

I duck, lunge sideways, blurring my trail. A tall imperial with a man-catcher is rushing to head me off behind a heavily laden cart. Seems to have lost me for a moment.

Durzo used to give me this drill I hated where he'd have me steal badly from merchants in crowded marketplaces. Most thieves try to steal as well as they can. Durzo explained that he wanted me to learn the exact line where failure lay. How *bad* can you be at lifting items and still get away with it?

It was a lie. That was hardly even a secondary point of the drill, though he didn't tell me that for years. He was training me how to flee through crowds where space is tight, where civilians might intervene, might be unaware, might move unexpectedly or not at all. One thing I learned: Keep your tricks to yourself.

If I give away that I'm Talented, the whole situation changes immediately. Forget worrying about man-catchers. If I look Talented, no one's going to try to catch me alive. A magic-user *is* a weapon. To stop him safely, he must be killed.

But that doesn't mean not using my Talent.

I duck in front of the heavy cart, finding a bit of exposed axle, and drop, swinging underneath it and launching myself with my Talent the entire length of the cart.

My legs sweep the imperial's out from under him. He drops flat on his face. I'm up and even as he grunts out his air, I slam both hands hard into his armored back, driving the rest of his wind from his lungs.

But I've exposed my back to his shorter partner, whom I hadn't seen. Startled into action, she lunges at me with a short spear.

Dodging, rising, I trap it under an armpit, cloth parting, maybe my flesh parting too. But I'm already spinning in, relentlessly in, always in, there's no time in this kind of situation for anything other than total aggression. The spear snaps and my left hand whips in, unblockable, changing only at the last moment from a killing fist to an open hand across her entire jaw.

She flies, boneless, into the crowd.

Their gasps and shrinking back might as well point a giant finger at my location. She fell back the way I want to go, so I press in toward the gap her inert body has made. Noticing I still have the broken haft of her spear in my hand, I lean over her and grab the helmet that's rolled off her head.

Dodge, push, dodge. Duck and shove the helmet onto my head. It about rips my ears off, it's so small. Now finally with a hand free, I touch my armpit even as I start echoing the imperials barking, "Make way, make way! Imperial business. Where'd he go?" I stand tall and hold up the unbroken side of the spear.

For those who can only see my head over the heads and shoulders of those in front of them, the illusion is good enough. They shrink back, creating a path.

I push through as rapidly as those pursuing me. Most of the civilians who see me come into view wearing an imperial helmet but none of the rest of the uniform assume I'm some sort of un-uniformed officer, or perhaps they think nothing at all, standing blinking like cows chewing cud. It's enough to make them freeze momentarily as they try to figure it out.

As long as I keep moving, it buys me time, so I push on.

I glimpse another soldier through the crowd, brows furrowed. I shout at him, pointing off to my left, as if demanding he seek over there, intentionally ducking a bit so my signals are garbled. I don't know what hand signals the imperials use—should've paid better attention, I think, cursing myself.

A moment later, I see him again, having taken a few steps the way I pointed, but now reconsidering, and pushing back through disgruntled people tired of being pushed around for a second time.

I stoop as if to tie my laces and remove the helmet, nearly tearing off my ears again.

Then I weave through the crowd like a rat zigging through grass while hawks circle overhead.

Four sharp blasts of a whistle sound. I leap to lie flat, nearly get stepped on by a huge peasant, then roll.

There was no incoming attack, but when you hear a signal you don't understand, you don't turn to look, you don't wait to see what's going to happen, you guess and you *go*. I roll under a cart, let it drag me the wrong way for a time. I can see nothing, though, but legs. In moments, we roll past a soldier. Maybe the same one, and I roll to my feet again behind him.

He's standing tall, waving a hand with three fingers outstretched. He lowers his hand. "Coming," he grumbles. Then starts complaining about his superior officer.

He doesn't notice me, so I trail in his wake, walking smartly as he hollers and clears a path.

When facing overwhelming force, it's all too easy to get warblind. When taking your attention off your immediate surroundings for even an instant may mean death, it's easy to forget everything else. But you can't. Not taking moments to get a longer view, to look behind you, to look far ahead, may lead you straight into a blind alley.

I've made it farther than I'd thought. I'm almost off the great bridge now—but ahead of me and my point-of-the-spear soldier clearing the way for me, the imperials are trying a new tactic. They've shut down the entire bridge. They've formed up and made a wall of their very bodies.

Behind them are hundreds upon hundreds more people waiting to load, and now, as the wall of imperials solidifies, a gap is opening before them. The people loading onto the storm ship proceed forward and the wall of soldiers stays still, facing me with an ever-widening open area to cross into the teeth of a trap, a trap yawning wider by the moment.

The wall of imperials and mages is the width of the bridge and three soldiers deep. The first line is packed shoulder to shoulder, with spears lowered—though the spears lift here and there as soldiers like the one I'm following hurriedly join the ranks. The back rows where the mages and archers stand aren't so tight. Off to the sides and a bit behind their line are the low lookout towers that flank the bridge at intervals, now bristling with archers and mages.

Behind all of that are tight-packed crowds of civilians, stretching almost fifty paces back to the great doors that lead into the palace, which are also choked with soldiers and shut down.

As we approach the gap ourselves, I think, *What odds do you give me?*

~Three to one.~

Really? Didn't expect you to believe in me so much. Sort of warms my heart.

~Not *for.* I meant *against.*~

The ka'kari rushes over my skin moments before we break free of the crowd, setting me invisible to normal sight. This is why you hold off showing your Talent.

This is the one thing that gives me a chance.

I keep myself to the low jog that my soldier is maintaining, wishing he were bigger. I know I'll be visible to the mages looking for magic, but with his body in the way, they might still miss me. If my aura seems to be glowing around him, they might simply think *he's* Talented.

We're halfway across the gap.

Farther.

Someone in the line shouts out a challenge.

My soldier answers.

Spears lift helpfully to let him take his place in the line, and I see a gap opening.

If I dodge into that one instant before he does, wending my body in that narrowest of spaces, any bumping I may do through the second and third lines might be excused as the unseen jostling of any crowd of restive soldiers.

The gap opens and I shoot forward—but a yell rings out from one side.

I throw up a magical shield just in time to catch a blast of force that flips me off my feet.

Skidding, I tuck, roll, and pop back up, but my invisibility has been blasted away.

I'm crouched in front of a line of hundreds of highly trained imperial guards, all looking for me—and now that I'm visible, they've all found me.

The attacks are instantaneous.

I throw forward an illusion of myself running forward, sprinting straight ahead at frightening speed, and drop to the planks of the bridge and go invisible at the same time to present the smallest possible target to anyone not fooled. With the illusion of me, I throw a blunt block of force, so that even as the illusion shreds apart as their attacks pierce it, the force crashes into the wall of imperials.

They immediately collapse in around what they think is me, surrounding it, trying to rescue their comrades who've been blasted off their feet.

I'm already running, invisible, sweeping parallel to the line.

Several mages look right through me, inadvertently having reverted to normal sight. But one, suddenly exposed into the front line as the line before her dissolves, doesn't. She yells—

But *everyone* is yelling, screaming at each other, confused.

The mage already has a fireball between her hands, is already lunging forward for the momentum to throw it hard—but then she stops herself, noting what's behind me like a good archer would. If she misses me, she'll demolish an entire section of panicky crowd, so she holds.

Only after I make it past her, going sideways now at incredible speed, do I finally leap over the line. My move pinches her line of fire, but she throws the fire into the night sky anyway.

She can't throw a second fireball because I'm passing between her and the guard tower, where so many of her associates stand.

One of them I hadn't seen, less disciplined, shoots a missile of blue force at me.

I twist catlike in the air, and it grazes my foot—enough while I'm airborne for it to blast me into a spin.

The rocks flanking the head of the bridge rush up to meet me, and though I've practiced falling a thousand thousand times, there's no way to adequately compensate for a five-pace fall if you land on your side.

At the impact, I lose a moment—

But it must be only a moment, because I'm still alive. More yelling everywhere.

I stagger to my feet, stumble, but don't fall. Pull the invisibility back over me.

Gasping with pain, I try to get moving, try to will myself back into the tempo of battle. Body hurts, but it moves. That's all that matters right now. Weak right ankle, can't try too much with it.

The lines of the human wall have been shattered by the young mage's errant attack. Everyone's shouting, furious, disoriented; an officer in the guard tower has the offending blue mage by the tunic and is spit-screaming into his face, even as the young mage tries to gesture toward me.

I look up, certain the imperial guards at the doorway back inside will have broken ranks and come rushing to help their friends and colleagues in this disaster.

They haven't.

I have to look again. They *haven't*?

Their discipline is that ferocious. While their colleagues have been decimated, it seems all the soldiers here have done is make all the civilians trapped between them and the soldier-wall get down on their bellies.

"All mages, front! Now now now!" one of the back-rank officers bellows. "Archers ready!"

There's no way I'm getting through that. I twist the ka'kari to make it absorb magic rather than light. Here in the dim darkness, I'd rather be a slight man moving alone against a bright, flaring, chaotic background than be invisible to some while being a burning beacon to all the mages.

The door is to the left of the corner before me, but to the right I stare at the looming, unnaturally smooth stone wall of the palace, and by smooth, I don't mean smooth considering that it's stone, I mean the stone of this wall is as slick as glass.

It could only have been polished to this by magic. Which is not comforting.

If magic did that to the wall, what other magic is at work here?

Someone shouts and points at me and suddenly all that doesn't matter.

I could run away. I could leap for the water, give up, admit this was impossible even for me.

But the Night Angel doesn't give up. The Night Angel doesn't lose.

I draw the ka'kari to my fingers to make little claws. Ten more steps and I can reach the wall.

Odds now?

~Worse than before.~

"Archers!" the officer bellows. "Loose!"

Chapter Fifty-One

The Climb

*W*hen eight or ten trained archers loose arrows at you from twenty to thirty paces, how many arrows hit you is all down to misdirection and luck. There are moments that descend upon me, unbidden, and usually not when I'd most wish, when I might track the intentions of ten opponents, and the trajectories of ten lethal weapons—when the magic that seems to live in my skin partners with me to make the most beautiful of the ugliest art.

This is not one of those times. I get lucky. I snap to a sudden stop on the guess that most of them will be leading me, and then I duck and dive and roll and somehow make it around the corner and to the wall, uninjured.

I did all the right things, but I'm not going to lie, it was luck.

Wait, did I say uninjured?

Scratch that. I feel something stinging hot across my shoulder blades. But I don't feel the weight of an arrow jutting out, impeding my movement, so it's not serious enough to kill me immediately.

I flicker out of visibility as I hit the wall. If I can confuse half of my attackers half the time, I'll double my chances. Right?

I leap and stab ka'kari-sharp fingers into the stone of the wall to begin my climb.

But my fingers bounce off, find no purchase.

I drop to the ground and, surprised, fall on my butt.

I pop back to my feet, shooting a look at the line of archers running forward toward the corner of the wall now, to get a line of sight on me.

I slap my hand onto the wall, arch my fingers to claws again.

Nothing. It's not simple stone. It's fortified with some sort of magic.

But the ka'kari shimmers through half a dozen colors in a heartbeat, as if picking a lock.

~Won't be perfect—but *go*!~

I trust it and leap once again, as high as my Talent allows. My fingers stab into the stone now, but it flares and spits sparks as the ka'kari punctures magic and stone both.

It's like climbing a wall of ice, kicking feet in to get each grip, slamming hands home hard. And each time, little gouts of molten rock and snapping magic spit out into the night.

I'm not going to be invisible to anyone.

That's bad. Also bad? The force necessary for each kick and each slapped hand against the rock naturally pushes me away from the wall. To keep from launching myself out into the air, I have to pull on all three limbs *hard* at the same time that I slap or kick for each new hold.

An arrow ricochets off the wall directly in front of my belly, missing by just that much. Others fill the air, but I can't pay attention to them. I don't.

In a few more moments, I've got the hang of the necessary chain of motions, and I clamber at high speed up and sideways and up.

Projectiles of magic burn the night behind me.

Something flares nearby as it hits the wall and sticks, and then a magical *something*—like a creature made of tar, given legs and tiny wings and set afire—begins scuttling across the wall toward me.

I stab out a foot and kick it off the wall.

It twists like a living thing as it falls, and a moment later it explodes, buffeting me against the wall. I lose a handhold and my other foothold, dangle for a moment by one hand.

Then I regain my grips one at a time. Burning tar from the thing clings to my ka'kari-encased leg, but the ka'kari sloughs it off with a pulse of magic even as I climb. I make it to a heavily shuttered window. The ka'kari lifts the latch and I haul the shutters open.

But before I can open the window, I catch sight of another fireball curving through the air behind me, beating tiny wings and swooping toward me. I throw myself through the glass, the ka'kari encasing me in liquid metal as the explosion blasts me through and inside.

Woozy, I stand and pull the shutters tight. I think I'm deaf.

~You should be. Would be, if not for me,~ the ka'kari says as it recedes from covering my ears.

I untie the fancy cord holding the curtains open and pull them shut, too. Shuttered and blocked now, from below it may be hard to identify which window I entered.

It's only when I turn back that I notice I'm in a fancy bedchamber and that there's a couple busy on the bed, staring at me, aghast at my intrusion.

No, not that kind of busy.

The man and woman, plainly servants, are round-eyeing me over open luggage on the bed. A pile of bags and chests with all sorts of different nobles' colors and insignia have been lined up to their left. Another mixed pile waits by the door as if they've already finished with those. The man had just heaved a new bag onto the bed. The woman is rifling an open bag.

A small pile of jewelry is on the bed.

Thieves.

I scan the luggage. Have an idea. I can't be this lucky, can I?

I look around quickly for blue-striped luggage with ermine trim. If I can find the Nemesis Compass, then all isn't lost! I could still—

Then it hits me again. There is no compass. That was a lie to get me here. I'm looking for a child in a bassinet, attended by wet nurses. Not even an idiot is going to stuff an infant into a chest.

"This isn't what it looks like," the man blurts out.

None of the luggage matches the colors or insignia of the nobles getting on the storm ship. This is the luggage of all the losers, those *not* going on the storm ship.

So, no, I'm not that lucky.

"Please," the woman says, tucking a necklace heavy with garnets slowly into a bag, as if I won't notice.

I stride over to them, looking first in her bag, then his. I snatch out a cloak, tunic, and trousers.

"You're...you're not going to report us?" she says, as if she can't believe her luck.

"I'm not your problem. You're not my problem," I say, pulling the tunic over my head. I grab a hat that's lying out.

Wrong size. I toss it aside. See a woman's wig collection. Grab one with short blonde hair. Not a perfect fit, but I'm not in any place to be picky.

I throw the cloak around my shoulders and walk out the door.

Then I stop in the hall. Sigh.

"Quick question," I say as I come back into the room.

They freeze in the midst of piling the jewels into their little bag.

"How's it look?" I ask, pointing to my wig.

The woman, struck dumb, slowly, tentatively gestures to her temple.

The man is standing next to her, wringing his hands as if he doesn't know what else to do.

I step close so she can adjust the wig. She pulls it around and tucks in my hair at several places. I smile sheepishly. "Better?"

She nods, slowly, brow furrowed, as if this is too surreal.

I snatch their heads and smack them together. While they're stunned, I tie them up with the fancy rope from the curtains, then spill the bag of jewels all over them. I snatch the man's servant's bracelet, which has two yellow gems. Not terribly helpful, as the one I'm wearing right now has three yellow gems, but more options is better than fewer. I tuck it away as I examine them, irritated.

"You are not my problem, but I'm always putting my nose into things that aren't my problem," I tell them as they groan from the floor. "I know, I know. It's a flaw."

I tuck a nifty jeweled eyepatch into one pocket, then leave. I close the door behind me and walk down the hallway. I walk straight up to the first imperial guard I see.

"Sirrah? Excuse me," I say, making sure my own staff bracelet is out of sight. "I think I just saw some servants pilfering jewels from the luggage in that room down there?" I turn as I point to give him as little time to look at my face as possible.

"Which room?" he demands. "Second, or third?"

"Second, definitely the second," I say, as he goes. "Uh, maybe the third?"

I get all the way to a corner beyond him. Just around the corner where I need to go, I see half a dozen imperials in conversation around some written orders. "Nah, nah, that's this tall," one says, holding his hand up at exactly my height. "Lean build, early twenties, tight white trousers and shirt with a red weapons harness and red boots, dark hair, light eyes, and black brows, but he's a pro, so expect him to be using a disguise..."

I shrink back from the corner.

A looking glass mounted on the wall near me reveals a man exactly that tall, lean built, in his early twenties, albeit with black trousers and blond hair.

Bollocks. There are six of them, and if I've got one hair out of place from under this ill-fitting blond wig—

And my hair is out of place, my own black hair peeking out several places. It practically shouts 'disguise.' I step close to the looking glass to try to quickly tuck the hair away.

Then the imperial I'd sent toward the thieves shouts an alarm from the third room down. "Huh?" I hear from around the corner. I don't dare peek. They'll all be looking this way, now.

I pull my hand away from the wig; imperfect as it is, messing with it any more now will only announce I'm wearing a wig. I can't face them, not looking like this.

As I hear footsteps, I step closer to the looking glass, open my mouth, and start picking at my teeth as if I have something trapped between them.

All six of them rush right past me without a second look.

I slip around the corner out of their line of sight and take a deep breath, then keep walking. Go figure. Saved because I put my nose where it didn't belong. Sometimes doing the wrong right thing turns out to be the right right thing after all.

Maybe my luck has turned. Maybe it'll be smooth sailing from here on out.

After a few perilous minutes searching for some service door out to the pilot wings' balcony, with my heart thudding louder and louder in my ears, I accost a servant. "Sorry, new here," I say, frowning and flashing my bracelet (carefully so she can't see how many jewels are on it). "Can you tell me where the pilot wings' balcony is? Can't seem to find the door. Message. Not my job, but it's my job tonight, you know?"

"Don't I know't, love. Worst night the year," she says. "Gorta go out the Griffin Hall. Big doors are locked; our door's right side, black."

I smile my thanks and go.

A friendly, helpful servant who doesn't examine my credentials. That's two pieces of luck.

Luck always comes in threes, right?

My idea—I won't call it a plan—is almost too stupid to tell you. I know there's no way I can fly one of those big pilot wings. I'd crash immediately. Stealing one of those wings would be too stupid for words, right? Right. We agree on that. So I won't steal one. I'll hijack it. I bet one of the large ones can hold the pilot's weight and mine—at least long enough to glide me over to the storm ship. It'll still most likely mean a crash, but potentially a nonlethal one.

Logan's kid is on that ship. He's this close. I can't give up now.

I make my way to the lower nobles' wide hall, which I hadn't noticed earlier is bedecked with griffins. Griffins everywhere. Griffins big and griffins small. Hundreds of griffins. Can't miss 'em—though somehow I did earlier.

The sound that hits me as I walk into the hall is a sloppy sledgehammer. Servants who had been nowhere to be seen earlier are now attending their lords and ladies from discreet distances. I see one swoop in to catch his lord as the old man passes out midsentence. The other nobles simply laugh.

I realize this has descended into—mostly—the losers' party. Everyone here is staying behind this year. For most of them, that is not a good thing, and they're taking it about as well as expected.

But I can't spare them any more than a glance.

Weaving my way past a few nobles and servants, I see my doorway, a sally port beside the enormous double doors of the Griffin Hall that reach three times the height of a man. A few nobles stand near it in hushed conversation, but...this can't be true. My luck can't be this good.

But it is. There's no one guarding the servants' door.

All right, all right. Let's not get ahead of ourselves. I may have to pick the lock.

I glance at the nobles. They're huddled together soberly, not two paces from the door. My jubilant heart freezes.

One of them is Queen Jenine Gyre. No. That can't be. Why is she even here? Why isn't she upstairs with the upper nobility?

She's turned half toward me. Her eyes flick across my face—

—and away. My disguise has held.

Nonchalantly, I test the door, my back carefully toward Jenine, my muscles tensing.

Locked.

I pretend to knock a quick rhythm as I feed the ka'kari into the lock.

Four seconds. Five at most. Unless I want to completely melt the lock, but that'd cause its own problems.

The pins click, click...click. One more...

A finger taps my shoulder. "Excuse me?"

Click. And that's all of them.

"Sorry, milady," I mumble, head down, trying to disguise my voice. "Got orders. Big rush."

But the woman grabs my arm, steps close, and hauls me around. Her noble friends are staring at her, alarmed.

Jenine's eyes flare wide. Then they narrow sharply, as her face twists with rage and grief. "You! You murderer!" She's got my arm in a death grip.

My blood congeals in my veins, dread slowing my reactions. I've never done anything against this woman. I've only ever helped her and her husband. I've given everything for them. She wouldn't have a kingdom if not for me. And she's attacking *me*?

For the moment, everyone within fifty paces is only looking at us, curious, wondering if this is some kind of joke.

"Jenine, I swear to you, I'm only—"

But revulsion rushes over her face. "I've seen this," she mumbles. "I'm not crazy. This is exactly—" Then she screams, pointing at me, "Assassin! Stop him! Help! Help!"

From every side, guards come running.

Chapter Fifty-Two

Born to Fall

I dodge out the door onto the balcony and collide with an imperial guard coming rushing toward the yelling. He's big. He looks down at me. "What's going on there?" he demands.

"There's a woman losing her—"

I club the side of his neck with the blade of my hand and shove him hard.

He practically flies backward, skidding on the ground, not unconscious, but stunned.

I've got mere heartbeats to make my choice.

The balcony jutting out from the castle and the cliff face over the sea and toward the *Storm Racer* is enormous, and mostly empty. The wind has picked up enough to be unpleasant. Any nobles who may have come out earlier have now gone back inside, leaving only the pilots and their teams working at the edges of the balcony beside enormous winches, which spool out the great lengths of ropelike kite strings to the pilot wings flying far above us.

From here, if I climb the wall to the roof of Castle Stormfast, I might reach safety—but I'll surely fail.

Climbing the wall means giving up on Logan's kid. It means admitting my humanity, my limitations. It means admitting defeat.

I'm off and running before I realize I've made my choice.

Even as I run, a pair of men are winching one of the pilots and his wing back to the balcony. He touches down, and with a speed that shows their long partnership, his team secures him with a safety chain and then instantly starts disassembling the framed wings that held him aloft.

The other teams and their winged contraptions are all either taking apart their own gliders or are sitting in the lee of small structures built to shield them from the wind.

I knew that stealing one of the gliders was even stupider than hijacking one of the pilots—there's no way I can safely manage one of the things—but as I run forward, it looks like I won't have either option. Every glider that's been pulled in is already at least partially disassembled, and there's no way I can put one back together by myself, not in moments, certainly not in this wind. And how can I force a team of five men to do it for me?

Looking back, I see how much I've loused up. Imperials are pouring out behind me—too many, too many.

I hit the railing at the end of the balcony, look down. If there's an overhang, I'll be shielded from attack. I'll have a chance.

There's no overhang.

I shoot looks left and right, not looking back where death is coming like the morning's storm.

There's a single pilot wing still aloft, tethered to the balcony by his long cable like a human kite. He's the captain of the group from his insignia, with the largest of the crafts, performing last-minute tricks to delight the crowds in the castle and on the docks below. He completes a barrel roll that brings him to a point in the air between the castle balcony and the storm ship.

The idea that springs into my head is idiotic.

I look back at the charging imperials. An archer looses an arrow, but it's snatched off-course by the wind.

The other flight teams have noticed me now. They look bewildered.

The archer's already got another drawn to his lips, adjusting his aim.

No new ideas have rallied to my mind.

This is never gonna work! I think as I spring toward the last pilot's team. I catch them blind, totally focused on their job, eyes skyward. In a blink, I launch them toward the other teams. Men go flying, sprawling out of the horizon of my thoughts.

They're unimportant now as I look at the winch, judge the length of the rope, the distance to the storm ship. With double the weight on the glider, it'll lose height—but then, he won't want to crash, so he'll pull up, right? So if I'm going to swing across the chasm, I need to make sure I have enough rope to reach the storm ship. If I reach it, but I'm a hundred paces in the air when I do, that's not gonna help me.

The solution is obvious. I need slack. Slack gives me options.

I slap the brake off the winch and throw a ton of slack toward the pilot.

Then, as he struggles to cope with the sudden change in the forces on him, I step around the winch and grab the rope—*this is stupid, this is stupid!*—and I yank on the rope behind me, pulling coil after coil off the winch.

Now I just need to cut it so it's no longer anchored to—

Suddenly, my left arm is nearly yanked out of the socket as the rope I'm holding goes taut with incredible force. I wasn't ready. I'm flung into the sky, spinning, flipping, the ground and sea and lightening sky a sickening blur.

I slap my other hand on the rope and swing my legs to grab the rope too, but miss. The pilot, somehow having already recovered, throws a rapid spin down the rope at me. I'm thrown in a tight circle, burning my hands, but I don't lose the rope.

Again, I swing, and this time, I catch the rope between my legs, and twist it around one leg and lock my feet together.

For long moments, I have no way of telling what's happening. I see the pilot staring down at me, his teeth bared, eyes flicking up toward the palace.

It's clear that the one thing I was sure was true is not true: I was certain our combined weight would force the pilot to descend.

Then I see a new problem looming. By not severing the rope, I've put us in a place where we're going to run out of slack very, very suddenly.

The pilot is fighting to fly higher, higher. The droop in the rope caused by my weight is like a bowstring being drawn back—and I'm about to be the arrow.

Already I feel myself being lifted, lifted.

If I let go with one hand to cut the rope, where can I cut? What if the slack runs out before I make the cut?

I shoot the ka'kari down to my foot, stab it through my shoe, and slash.

It works and I slash the rope just as it jerks taut—but all the pent-up forces are released through my body, as if the bowstring snapped.

Flung skyward, above even the pilot, clinging to the rope with all my might, all I know is that nauseating forces roll through me. I look up and find I'm looking *down*. Rope tight between us, I'm staring at the pilot as he fights to control his craft, and beyond him isn't the sky, but ground. Twisting, spinning, I lose all sense of what's up or down and merely cling to the rope with all my might.

Then he pulls out of the spin.

I bounce, hover suddenly slack in the air, my rope loose, and when I crash back to the full length of the rope, the pilot is thrown off-course again.

This time, he recovers quickly.

And the danger is past.

I try to get my bearings.

Fine. Fine, I don't have as much rope as I was hoping, but . . .

I look down. We're not over the storm ship.

In fact, we're not over the palace or the docks, either. We've been blown hundreds and hundreds of paces downwind, and we're over land. The rocks below do not look particularly soft.

But the pilot seems to have a plan. Though my weight drags at the pilot wing and I see him glancing at one wing where it seems something has torn away because it doesn't match the other, he remains absolutely in control, his motions smooth, even as his craft shudders and bucks against the forces arrayed against it, the wings flexing, straining, little bits tearing from the broken surface. Then he dives into the wind, picking up speed, heading back toward the palace balcony.

All right. That's vaguely the right direction. At least it could be worse—

It is worse.

He's heading straight back to the balcony, glancing down at me, up, down at me again, bleeding off speed, gaining more.

I'm dragging below and behind the craft like a pendulum swinging on the rope behind the pilot as he accelerates. Despite his apparent aim, I know he's not planning to ram himself into the balcony.

He's planning to ram me into it. He's going to flare right before he gets to the balcony. He'll land gently on the balcony, and I'll be flung into the side of it at incredible speed.

I start climbing, hand over hand over hand, Talent lending me speed and strength—but I've got a long way to go and I'm no Grandmaster Vitruvius, virtually sprinting up a rope.

He looks down, blanches. Then adjusts his speed and his aim to cut it even closer.

The guy is unflappable.

Now it's a race.

The balcony looms like a giant hammer and the pilot flares.

I leap and snag his legs as he shoots up, maybe too late.

Imperials scatter, at the last instant pulling back the polearms they'd intended for me so they don't impale the pilot instead.

The wing shakes as a wingtip clips the railing. We shoot skyward but are thrown into a roll, still soaring upward and in toward the castle, losing speed—

And then we crash.

We skid up and across something hard and smooth, and I'm thrown away from the pilot, rolling and tumbling.

I don't think I lose consciousness, but I think I cushioned the pilot's fall, because when I get to my knees, he's already cursing and messing with his glider.

He's ten paces away, holding his body low to the ground, his eyes frantic for some reason I can't tell.

Then as he lifts his head to look at me with alarm, he accidentally also lifts the front edge of the wing's frame. The wind pulls the craft and the pilot tethered to it skidding across the roof. We must've hit the side of the castle and then settled atop its wind-rounded roof.

If the wind pushes him much farther, he's going to fall off the edge of the roof, probably to his death.

He's dropped down flat, trapped. He's holding the wing's frame down to the lowest profile possible. "Leave me alone!" he shouts. "The wing's broken. It can't hold both of us!"

My gift doesn't activate every time I look into someone's eyes, but unhelpfully, it chooses this moment to do so. I see into this soul in an instant and know this is a decent man.

I run toward him, looking at the wing. It doesn't look like it's broken that badly. Maybe he's lying.

"Get me to the storm ship and I'll let you go," I tell him.

His eyes widen like I'm mad, but he's my last chance.

"I couldn't make it there even alone like this! Look—" He points to the crumpled wingtip, and him releasing his grip on the glider with even one hand for one moment lets the nose rise and he's pushed farther toward the edge.

I snag him and pull him down. As soon as the glider tips over the edge, it'll be shielded from the wind entirely.

With no speed, and no wind to pull against, if I let go, the wing is going to drop straight to the ground. The wing not only can't support two of us—without a running start into the wind, it won't support one.

Lying on my back as I am, kicking my heels into the stone with the ka'kari's devouring sharpness, I gather my Talent and roar—flinging the pilot up and into the wind as hard as I can.

He shoots up into the air with astonishing speed.

For the barest instant, the rope flashes in front of me, and I snatch after it. My last chance—

I miss.

In the air above me, the pilot wrestles for control of his craft, and finds it. He turns wide, shaky circles above the palace, staring at me in wonder.

Then he goes in for a landing on the balcony.

I sit up on the cold stone of the windswept rock dome and look out to the *Storm Racer*. It is impossibly far away.

I've failed. Dawn is only minutes away. The nobles are filing onto the ship even now, surely all a-titter with rumor of this year's excitement on the loading docks mere minutes before.

I've tried everything in my powers, everything I can think of, and I've failed.

It was a stupid plan from the beginning, a job I should have turned down, and I knew it. Barely any plan, barely any advance preparation or intel, and I thought I'd march in here in one night and do the impossible?

Durzo would say I did everything in my power *to* fail.

What was I thinking? That I'd just be so special I'd improvise my way in where dozens of others who were better prepared and better informed have failed?

I shouldn't be devastated. It all makes too much sense. Maybe I'm not so special after all.

"Kylar Stern!" shouts a voice over the wind behind me.

I know that voice. Grandmaster Vitruvius.

"So we finally meet again!" he says cheerily.

He stands between me and what had been a hidden door in the lee of the wind. That door behind him is the only way off this roof, and the wind is picking up by the minute.

"You owe me a fight, young man," he says happily. "And there's no getting out of it this time."

Chapter Fifty-Three

Biggest Fish, Biggest Pond

*G*randmaster Vitruvius advances toward me with the feral economy of a jungle cat. He's traded his party finery for the simple, loose clothes he wore back in Tover. He's also wearing some kind of pack, strapped tight to his back—full of weapons, I assume. You always have to guess the worst-case scenario. But he hasn't drawn any weapon, not yet.

Why?

He raises his voice over the insistent susurrus of the incipient storm winds. "How do you want to do this?"

"I'd rather not do this at all," I say, still looking at the chasm between me and salvation. I can see the nobles in a great line far below, crossing their high bridge, passing single file between hundreds of imperials. That way onto the storm ship is impossible. Even for me. Even for Durzo it would be.

"Even I couldn't make that jump," says Grandmaster Vitruvius, coming up almost even with me but giving me a good ten paces to the side. "But then, I'm too smart to try. You might not be. Not that I plan to give you the chance."

"Are you precepting me?" He does seem to be hanging just far enough back that he could cut me off before I could reach the door he used to come out onto the roof.

He smiles ruefully. "We don't make it a verb, but no, I'm not using preception on you. I don't know the extent of your gifts, so preception might hurt more than help. It could wrongly rule out as impossible things that *are* possible for the gifted apprentice of the legendary Durzo Blint."

"Nice to hear you have some limitations."

"Many. And you?" the grandmaster asks.

"I just ran forcefully into one." The admission plucks a chord of self-loathing that runs from the center of my gut to the base of my spine. Failure. "How'd you know I was up here?"

"It's where I would've come. I would've come here first, so it's been a long and boring night for me. It appears it's been more lively for you."

First. Son of a...I shake my head.

"But..." he continues, reaching into his pack slowly with a single hand as if not to alarm me. "It doesn't look like you have one of these. Which makes me happier than I can tell you."

He pulls out what looks like a costume.

I cock my head.

"No?" he says. "You didn't see...?" The grandmaster is downwind of me, and as he holds the one-piece garment by the collar, I see it's got some kind of webbing between the legs and also from the arms to the hips. Rather than a fully externally framed wing, this suit has boning integrated like a bat's wings. "Wingsuit," he says. "It's what the sky dancers use for the second half of their performances, as the wind picks up speed. Do you have flying squirrels in Cenaria? No? You'll see, soon enough."

I still don't get it, but suddenly I remember how the teams on the balcony stayed outside, hidden in their little shelters after they'd disassembled the framed pilot wings—rather than going inside as they would've if they were finished for the night. A second act. I hadn't even thought of that.

But if they can use wingsuits, then maybe I can, too! Maybe I can steal that one from—

The grandmaster tosses his wingsuit off the edge.

The wind snatches the fluttering garment away instantly.

My gut lurches as if a last lifeline was just jerked away.

"They can't soar for hours with these like they can with the external-frame wings, but with rising winds off the hill, they can glide for a time. Worse luck for you, some of the imperial guards are trained with them. So, even though I blocked the way up the stairs there, come dawn, between me and them, I expect you're going to find yourself in a tight spot."

"Unless I do exactly what you want?" I guess.

He shakes his head. "I'm not here to make a deal with you, Kylar. I'm here to stop you. I didn't block the stairs to help you. I blocked them to trap you. Same reason I just threw away my wingsuit. If you were able to kill me, you might've taken it. If you of all people seize whatever magic the Chantry's going after here tonight, the entire world will pay. I'm not going to let that happen."

"Magic? What magic is the Chantry going after?" I glance at the crowds entering the storm ship below.

"Don't play dumb, Kylar. Why do you think my men and I didn't intercept you earlier? You were seen speaking with several members of the Chantry's best Special Problems Team. We know they smuggled you in here. I also know now that they worked to keep me away."

I've been on the lookout for any members of the team since all hell broke loose, wondering if they'd try to help or—now that they don't need me to help with Logan—if they might try to capture me, either to take back to the Chantry or to ingratiate themselves with the empress.

I don't know if they'd do that to me, but I know enough to be wary of the powerful, and every one of them is that. So as part of my situational awareness, I've been searching the crowds below whenever I dare take my eyes off the grandmaster. And now I see them: a knot of women passing across the upper bridge; it's the team. But they're not looking for me. Indeed, they seem to be chatting as happily as any of the nobles around them. They're getting on the ship. All of them.

I say, "They said they needed my help making sure Logan wasn't forced to get on the ship. If he had been, he'd be finished as king and his realm would fall with him. The Chantry thinks it'll help them to have a stable, reasonable, friendly power in the north. That means Logan. But honestly, I don't care what they want. I was glad to help my friend. But why didn't they want *you* here? What do you have against Logan? Why would you have stopped us?"

"I wouldn't have!" he says, baffled. "I have nothing against the high king. All the men's schools have found him quite well disposed toward us. Far more so than the previous rulers. None of us have any reason to act against him that I know. I certainly wouldn't pit myself against him and the Chantry unless I had an existentially compelling reason to do so. I can't afford such enemies.

"As far as the Chantry, they may be happy to have High King Gyre in place, especially if they think he'll owe them. But they did work to keep me away. So was that merely to limit the number of players at the table, or were they worried about something else? And—" He cuts off, shocked, staring toward the storm ship. "And *why* are they getting on the storm ship?"

"Hitching a ride to their next assignment?" I say, though I know better. "It is the fastest way west."

But the grandmaster seems troubled. "You think it was easy for them to arrange their passage on that ship? You think they simply asked? Do you think the empress is in any mood to do the Chantry favors right now, mere months after she found out they've been making war mages?"

I open my mouth but find nothing to say that won't make me sound stupider.

He goes on, "I've been tapping every source I can reach, and I've learned that there's some item, some artifact, something of incredible power here, and it has a strong connection to Logan Gyre. The Chantry wants it. That's why they'd want to keep me away. They want it badly enough to risk infuriating the empress of the most powerful nation in the world when she's *already* incensed they broke the Alitaeran Accords. Picking a fight with Alitaera is not the kind of thing the Chantry does lightly. Saving High King Gyre's reign may help them someday down the line, yes, but the fact that they're putting two Special Problems and Tactics Teams on the *Storm Racer* tells me they've got other plans."

The Chantry's after an *artifact*? No, that's not right. Maybe Vitruvius's people conflated some of the same rumors I did. Were they led astray by hearing rumors about the Nemesis Compass being here, like I was? And then they put that together with the Chantry coming to town hunting something important?

But that doesn't mean I have to blurt out everything to Grandmaster Vitruvius. "Two teams?" I say. The Sisters have now disappeared into the metal monstrosity.

But I wonder, how sure am I that the Nemesis Compass isn't real? I'm so confused. I thought I'd figured out that Momma K had made that up to get me moving here. Then, if she did make it up, she could've had her people here plant rumors about it for me to find—rumors that made their way to Vitruvius.

All right. That's plausible. Maybe wrong, but it's the best I've got to go on right now.

Vitruvius says, "Maybe keeping High King Gyre off the ship is merely the Chantry clearing players off the board. Looks like they took you off, too, huh? Gave you something supposedly vital to do at the party? Something that froze you in place and kept you from interfering with their plans. You walk away with a smile on your face, knowing you've helped save your friend, happily thinking everyone wins, when really, the Chantry played you for the fool. Oh, don't feel bad. They're the best in the world at this sort of thing."

He's right. They played me. And now I'm stuck.

"You talk a lot," I say. I don't know why I say it. I should keep him talking. But I'm too angry, too stupid.

Anger flashes over his face but is gone as fast as it came. "Maybe I'm freezing you in place, too," he says.

"It's wasted effort. I'm already beaten."

"You're far too dangerous for me to imagine a setback like this will stop you for long."

"Guess my imagination is better than yours, then," I say. "If I were any more stopped up, I'd be looking for laxatives."

He attacks, crossing the space between us in a blur so fast I can barely bring up a guard.

I go sprawling from his kick, rolling and tumbling across the stone.

He doesn't follow up the attack.

"That was early, wasn't it?" he says. "You weren't ready. My apologies."

I dust myself off, a bit theatrically. Inside, I'm cursing. "Have to admit, I was hoping you'd let yourself get fat and slow, you know, being atop your order and all."

"One of many dangers in my position," he says, with a smile. He flows into a defensive stance from one of the kicking-focused arts: val knacht. The man's already taller than me. Anything that keeps me farther away gives him time to judge my abilities.

I don't salute. Durzo would beat me if I treated this fight the way the blues do, all respect and ritual and tradition. He liked to say, 'The only fighting tradition I value is my tradition of winning fights.'

With a smile at that memory, I go at the grandmaster, answering his long straight powerful lines with the circles of chimorru.

Kick to stop kick, crescent kick absorbed on one thigh before it reaches full speed, dodge back.

I don't even penetrate his preferred distance.

"You haven't even used your Talent yet," I say.

"I assumed you were waiting for that."

"Well...yes?"

Fighting with the Talent isn't a simple matter of being faster and stronger. Let's say I throw a punch and aid it with magic so I'm throwing a punch with force equal to what a blacksmith three times my weight could throw. First, I have to make sure I have enough of a base to throw that punch without my feet sliding out from under me. Second, if I connect, I've got to make sure I strengthen my bones and joints. If I don't, I may break my own fist to pieces.

Against Grandmaster Vitruvius, I'm more likely to have to worry about the third thing: What if I miss?

On a miss, I have to deal with having thrown three times my own body weight into a strike. If you've never tried that, it feels like sprinting full speed and trying to stop in a single step. Even if you don't fall on your own face, it takes time to recover.

Martial artists don't give you time. Speed is all about collapsing your enemy's options.

We close again. He moves seamlessly from straightforward kicks to the sweeps and strikes of reck'sta. Within moments, he nearly closes a grapple hold on me, flipping me over one hip with a classic maich wan throw.

I fling myself out of his grip with my Talent, my tunic ripping in his hands. I tumble and roll, coming back to my feet.

He merely looks at me curiously, tossing half my sleeve away.

I shuck off the rest of my tunic.

"We'd leave the tunic on," he says.

The man hasn't used his Talent at all yet.

"Too easy to grab," I reply.

"Better an opponent grabs one's clothes than one's body."

And now I remember Durzo saying that exact thing once. Another lesson I didn't absorb. Another failure. "I didn't spend that much time on this sort of thing," I admit.

"I'd imagine Durzo Blint expected you to deal with your problems lethally rather than engaging in this kind of fight."

It's not the first time he's mentioned Durzo. What else does this man know about me?

We close again. I've got enough disadvantages without him figuring out my main problem here.

He's fast, and he's experienced. He's got an edge on me in that he's been training against other elite fighters daily. I haven't been able to do that since Durzo left.

Soon, I'm absorbing blows. Legs, hips, stomach. I get a wicked scratch down one arm when I pull out of another grapple by the narrowest of margins.

He breaks away, and I let him go.

He smiles as if he's enjoying this. "Ah, Kylar, if you'd train with us even for one year, I could turn you into—"

"I'm sure you'd turn me into something really special. Not interested. I like to think I'm already special, thanks."

"You *like to* think that?" Vitruvius asks, amused.

"In truth, I know it."

"A terrible burden indeed."

I stare at him, unwavering. "I've had a master already. I don't need another one. I've also had enough riddles for one life."

~Or more than one life?~

You're not helping.

"No riddles. That's not my style. You're making assumptions, Kylar, and you're not doing it well. I was going to say I could turn you into something very common."

"Excuse me?" I ask.

"I think we've warmed up now. Ready?" he says.

"Not quite. Since I'm so terrible at making assumptions, maybe..." With my Talent copying what I've seen at Tover, I throw out a dusting of glowing particles. The wind pulls them into him before he can move. They cling to him, glimmering, winking in the rising light.

A cloud of possibilities blooms around him, before him.

He looks down at them for a moment, curious, then appreciative. Then he attacks.

I fight completely on the defensive, dodging, circling, watching to see how the preceptions I've attached to him work.

Then he begins tapping his Talent, and oddly, the preceptions sharpen, become more accurate, more helpful.

Unfortunately, seeing a blow coming isn't as much help as you'd think if you're not fast enough to stop it.

Durzo told me once that there was a world of skills he wouldn't even be able to *start* teaching me until I could use my Talent. My childhood block is showing its true costs now.

I take a glancing blow to the jaw. Retreat, block block block, take a shot to a knee that I'm not able to fully soften. Bring up a block too slow to a side kick.

I go flying, tumbling, and he's on top of me, raining in blows as I struggle to stand. My nose explodes in blood.

A foot I hadn't expected catches me in a kidney.

As I blink against the pain, a blow I don't even see coming launches me out flat on my back. I lie gasping.

I pop to my feet and he's there, wrenching me into another throw.

Again I land flat on my back, breath whooshing out, shoulder shrieking.

I roll to my feet from ingrained instinct alone, but I can't see anything. I'm blinking against black spots. My shoulder—oh hells. It's out of joint.

With my Talent, even as I stagger backward, unseeing, I grab my own elbow and pull it away from me.

The sickening, familiar crunch of a joint popping back into place fills my ears under the howl of the wind. It hurts so much I retch.

Grandmaster Vitruvius hasn't followed up his attack. He stares at me.

"You didn't copy preception after seeing it once," he says.

"Technically," I grunt out, "I saw it twice."

"Ah, what a relief," he says flatly. "What parameters did you put into it?"

"Huh?"

"The possibles for my movements. Your guesses aren't ridiculous, but they're a lot better than I can do. I've been overestimated before, but the *ways* you're wrong suggest..."

I'm happy to talk about whatever he wants to talk about. I need to catch my breath. Need to see what Healing I can do.

But then I hit it. The blank. At Black Barrow, I was nearly killed—and with what Durzo'd taught me that very day, I Healed myself in maybe a minute. This is a broken nose and strengthening a shoulder so it doesn't dislocate again. It should be easy.

I know I know the magic, but it's not there. It's one of the things that Black Barrow scoured from my mind. One of the things that's so basic, I've been sure it'll come back.

It's not coming back.

"You put in *Durzo's* parameters for me, didn't you?" he asks, stunned. He swears softly. "He's that good?"

Ignoring his question, still grimacing against the pain, I point to where his cloud of possibilities frays like smoke at its greatest distance from him. "That's the part that intrigues me."

Is the blood streaming from my nose into my mouth and down my chin slowing?

He looks at me sharply with his gray owl-eyes. "You and the philosophers both," he says.

"What's that mean?" My nose stops bleeding. Thank the gods! But *I* didn't do it consciously. This is beyond natural, but it's nowhere near the miraculous Healing I've come to expect.

Will my body fix the bruising slowing me in the muscles of my right leg? Will it work on the nerve damage in my shoulder from the dislocation?

If I could direct the magic, I could make choices. Prioritize what should be Healed first. Instead, I have to wait. Hope.

The grandmaster says, "If there is a Creator and I ever meet Him, I'll ask Him two questions: 'Why light?' and 'Why turbulence?' I believe He'll have an answer for the first question."

"Turbulence? Like, what? Like where a waterfall pours into a lake?" I ask.

"You ever see the shadow of a flame flickering in a windless room? Same thing. That is the same thing that causes the blurring and flickering in the pre-ceptions. It's why meaningful prophecy is impossible."

"Yet I've seen prophecies come true," I say.

"Deceptions, guesses, parlor games and the confidence tricks of charlatans."

"Charlatan is a mantle that rests uncomfortably on Dorian Ursuul's shoulders."

His breath catches. "You do know Dorian, then. Quite the friends you keep."

"Not a friend. Not that," I say, remembering our last interaction.

"But you don't deny knowing him."

I feel like I've walked into a trap, but I can't see how it matters. "Does anyone *know* Dorian?"

"Did he send you here?"

"No." I don't think he did. But we spoke, and here I am. "Why?"

"Because Dorian Ursuul is the most dangerous man in the world."

"You said that. And maybe it was true once. But not anymore he's not," I say. "He's a chastened man, now. A harmless mad prophet."

"True prophecy is impossible; that's what I'm telling you. He's been right an extraordinary number of times, but that only makes him more dangerous. It doesn't mean he's got a real gift. He is very perceptive, Talented, and cunning enough to survive the regnal butcher's shop of the Khalidoran court. No doubt. But if someone bets the fate of the world on what Dorian says, our futures will be decided by a man lost in delusions."

My right arm is feeling a little better, but I'm unnerved by the grandmaster's owlish eyes watching me as if he sees exactly what I'm doing, as if he's learn-ing more about me even from this.

"I'm a very smart man," Vitruvius says, "and do you know what I've learned?"

"If you do say so yourself."

"Stop. That's beneath you. We don't have the time for false humility. What I've learned is that highly intelligent people are prone to a certain set of errors. Morally their world often constricts, rather than opening. They come to value intelligence above all else. They become invested in their own intelligence, and feel either threatened or awed by those more intelligent still. Instead of liberating them, this gift they did nothing to earn collapses their identity to a single facet. They become small. They value themselves and therefore others primarily according to their intelligence, and thus inescapably devalue those gifted less or differently.

"The same can happen with every great gift. Brilliance and focus should be rewarded in accord with their utility—esteemed, but not too highly. People who sacrifice their relationships, their families, and their health in pursuit of some ideal or dream are often useful to a community, but they are lopsided. The father who spends every waking hour with his research or his art or his reign may bless all the world, maybe, but he certainly brings untold misery to his spouse and his children—never asking if they wish to sacrifice their father for such long odds. He is a tyrant, a man collapsed into a single dimension, less a man than a beast, yet all too often, we praise him. We're so greedy for what geniuses may give us, so selfish for our own gain that we call them unselfish. We speak of *their* sacrifice. Could we be more blind?"

If Elene had lived, what kind of father would I have been to our child? "What's this got to do with me?" I ask. I shouldn't be trying to bring this to a point. I'm not all healed yet. But I can't help myself. Me and my stupid mouth.

"What could you be, Kylar, if you chose to be human first? If you chose to live that courageously? What could you become, if you chose to value the many parts of you that are common, rather than only those few parts of you that are so very special?"

"I'm not asking anyone to sacrifice for me."

"No, you're not *asking*; you're demanding it. By isolating yourself, thus shutting yourself away from those whom you would bless with your presence."

Right, my presence is such a blessing. "Maybe you haven't noticed," I say, "but there's a lot of work to do in this world. Someone has to do it. I've chosen to take up my burden."

"With as isolated as you are, who will tell you if it's the wrong burden? To whom would you listen?"

"Everyone I've listened to is wrong, or gone, or dead," I say bitterly.

It's not the time to think about Elene, but the sudden recollection of her cuts through me. I remember her spirit exactly, but her picture is getting blurry.

I'm forgetting her face.

I'm forgetting her. And I can't blame this on magic. This is just me, marooned far from her, the currents of time pulling her relentlessly away from me.

Life is the Great Storm, and with wings broken, I'm clinging to this rock as the wind rises, and rises, and I can't hold on much longer. Ruined, I can't fly, only fall.

What am I becoming without you, Elene?

Vi slammed the book shut. She jumped to her feet, breathing hard.

She shouldn't be seeing this. It was wrong. It was indecent. She blinked rapidly, pacing around the library. She wouldn't do it. She wouldn't. They couldn't make her look at him like this.

There was a lump in her throat making it hard to swallow. She rubbed at the corner of her eyes, grasping after the rage that was leaking away, leaving her alone with something far weaker.

Elene was dead. Her friend was dead, and though Vi had known she wasn't going to have an easy time of it when she read about Kylar's end, she somehow hadn't realized that she'd also have to suffer all the memories of Elene's death again.

You're stupid, Vi. She was his wife. Of course he's going to think about her!

Vi's grief over both of them intertwined, and her eyes felt hot with it.

She cursed Sister Ayayah out loud.

Only then did she look up and see Sister Ariel looking at her over her reading spectacles like an alarmed prairie dog standing at the edge of its hole.

"Is there something you'd like to talk about?" Sister Ariel asked.

"No!" Vi almost stomped her foot as she said it. "It's late. I'm going to bed."

"That may be for the best if you find your mental reserves depleted," Sister Ariel said. "Come back fresh in the—"

Vi slammed the door behind her, cutting off Sister Ariel's words.

She didn't sleep well, nor long, and the only dream she could remember seemed a vicious prank from some vengeful god. She dreamed of Kylar in her arms in that little cabin, the joy of his climax fading from his face, slowly replaced with limitless tenderness for her—but also grief, and perhaps regret. And all too soon, he pulled away.

And she ached. Ached. No matter how she wanted to hold him, he never stopped pulling away.

DAY THREE

Chapter Fifty-Four

The Dumbest Thing I've Done

Vi thunked the book on the desk. Her face was dry and cool, expressionless in the gray light before daybreak. She ran her fingers through her hair, absently readying the strands for tight braids. Then she remembered that those were forbidden her. She mouthed a curse, but stopped herself from voicing it. Curses were forbidden her, too.

Sister Ariel was already—or still—at her place at a corner table with many books. The woman weighed Vi for an instant, then returned to her own work without a word.

Vi—*Viridiana*, she reminded herself, again—appreciated her for that. Sister Ariel wasn't one of those women who poke and nudge and pry into your feelings.

It probably helped that she didn't have any of her own. The woman was all mind, a brain wearing an untidy gray bun.

Suppressing a small sigh, Vi arranged her lamp and inkpot and quills. She squared the book on the table and turned to her page. She could do this. She had to.

Today was day three. She had fourteen hours left.

"You were at Black Barrow, at the end," Grandmaster Vitruvius says. "Magic on that scale wrecks people. Changes everything."

"It wasn't the magic that wrecked me," I say. My voice comes out husky.

I don't want to talk about it.

"I'd wondered," he says. "We heard lots of stories, even in Tover. I'm sorry for all your losses, son."

I blink away the tears quickly, wind etching one across my cheek. "Are we going to do this?" I'm Healed now. Enough anyway. It'll hurt less to fight than to talk more.

"You returned the horse," Grandmaster Vitruvius says.

"So?" The horse? That seems out of nowhere.

"Why?"

"I don't know. I'm not a horse thief, I guess."

His face scrunches, confused, then amused. "You kill people for money, but you draw the line at stealing horses?"

"Maybe I like horses more than people."

"No, you don't."

"No. I don't," I admit. "But how'd you know?"

"The men at the stations said you weren't that great a rider."

"Really? Insults about my riding?"

"You asked!" He drops his hands in exasperation. "Tell me, Kylar, does it seem like I'm holding back?"

I think of saying *If this is you holding back, then you are terrifying.* But what I do say is "It doesn't seem like you are."

"I'm kicking your sorry, bedraggled butt. So if I'm not holding back, son, why *the hell* are you?"

I can't tell him the truth. That, for my purposes, he's an innocent and I can't kill an innocent without losing my last mooring to humanity. This is hard enough already. If I tell him that, he'll know he has every advantage over me.

"You belong to your brotherhood in a very real way, don't you?" I ask.

"Yes." He seems put off-balance by the question, though.

"So I always return horses to their owners."

"I get that, but—"

"Even when it's not the entire horse, just its hindquarters."

He laughs immediately.

Well, hell.

It's a little trick my master taught me. You can learn how smart a person is, not by what they laugh at, or by how hard they laugh, but by how quickly. Humor functions by surprise. To Durzo, the reason this mattered was that the speed at which a person reacts to the unexpected in peace tells you how fast they might react in war.

Grandmaster Vitruvius is, as he said, a very smart man indeed.

Worse luck for me.

I bow to him, Durzo be damned. I can't talk any more. I need the...what was the word Logan used for it? Nepenthe. I need the nepenthe of battle.

Vitruvius bows as well, and then, as the wind howls and the sun first touches the horizon, we fight.

It feels different now. I sink into my frame, shedding extraneities. Past and future. Thoughts of failure, success, grief, and longing—all thoughts, entirely. I shed them as a snake sloughs off its skin, momentarily smaller in order to grow. My very skin has become a sensory organ, feeling not only the cold of the wind but noting the rising of the light, judging the force put into a kick as I meet his blows, soft to hard, hard to soft. Dodge, strike, hesitate until he shifts his weight left expecting my next strike there, and then right, right, right. Speed feints and time feints. Reprise, remise, redouble. Attacks to counterattacks, counterattacks and counter time.

He breaks away. Smiles.

I barely register it.

His next kick flicks out unnaturally long, a magical line of force extending whiplike out from his leg.

I extend my block magically without even having to think. It's only action, reaction. Move, counter—and my own push kick stabs through his block into his lower abdomen.

He stumbles, then comes back with renewed intensity, now with magic aiding his every move and strike.

The whoreson. He *was* holding back.

I misjudge when he hits me with some kind of physical and magical multipronged attack I've never seen.

A part of it I miss catches me in the groin.

I stagger backward, then to the side. Even the pain of being kicked in the stones can be walled off with proper training, mostly, and now I've got an idea. I haven't used the wind yet. In my steps back, I make sure I'm upwind of Grandmaster Vitruvius. If I flare force out to either side of me, I'll block the wind we're both fighting against. If I do that at the right moment, he'll stagger at the very moment I can launch myself toward him—with my own movement aided by the wind.

Straightening up, with not-wholly-feigned pain on my face, I say, "Good shot."

"Wasn't aiming for your—"

But I don't hear the rest of his reply, because I glance toward the *Storm Racer.*

Everything snaps together. Vi being on the Special Problems Team. The Chantry's goals. Why they wanted to keep Vitruvius away. The Nemesis Compass. The kidnapping. Sister Ayayah's 'recovering' the child rather than rescuing him. Even Jenine's madness.

I hadn't asked the right questions, so I didn't even have a chance at finding the right answers. Logan would risk war with Alitaera to save his child. So would Jenine. So would Momma K. So would I. It's the right thing to do. He's a prince. He's the future. The hope of a huge swath of Midcyru. Of course all of us will risk everything to save him.

But that's moot. The right question is: Would the *Chantry* risk war with Alitaera to save Logan's child?

And that answer is no. The kidnapping of a child, even a royal child, is none of the Chantry's business.

Which would've prompted me to the next right question: Then why is the Chantry risking war to 'recover' this child?

Do you know what I really need after a kick in the balls?

My life: 'Another kick in the balls?'

My failure, already colossal, is suddenly total. "I thought the Chantry wanted concessions. I was wrong. And I was wrong when I thought your people had just heard rumors Momma K had planted here. Your people were right. There is an artifact here. But it's not a what," I say. My hands go to my head. "Jenine was at Black Barrow with us. In the middle of it all, at the end. She was pregnant, which means her sons were in the middle of all that magic, too. And you're right, magic like that changes everything."

"What are you...?" Grandmaster Vitruvius still has his hands up, on guard.

"It's not a what they want. It's a who!" I shout. "They want Logan's kids!"

"What?"

But I'm frantic now. "No, no, no. Not Logan's kids—not for the purposes of the magic. Jenine's and, and, and Dorian's! That explains it. My crazy dreams after I held him. Her madness. That's why Lord Repha'im kidnapped him. That's why the Chantry wants him. There *is* a magical artifact here. It's here, but isn't a thing. It's the *kid.*"

"What are you saying?" Vitruvius demands. He's stepped forward now, his guard lower, but he still eyes me warily, ready for an attack.

"I shouldn't have told you. Gods. But what's it matter now? Dorian directed all our magic in the last battle. Jenine was there, pregnant with his twins. The magic messed us all up in different ways, and I think one of the boys got Dorian's gift for prophecy. No, not got it exactly. His mother's gone nearly mad, and when I touched his skin, I felt—Holding the kid gives you dreams. Prophetic dreams. Maybe visions if you hold him long enough. I only held him briefly, and afterward...I had these intense dreams. Apocalyptic. I wouldn't have put it together, but..." I shake myself, look at Vitruvius. "I know you don't believe in prophecy, Grandmaster, but if that gift is real...if it's even halfway real, what would the Chantry do to get that kind of power?"

"An artifact that bestows the power of prophecy to others? That would be— I don't know—ten times more seductive than simply finding a new prophet. Anyone who doubted could be made a believer in one night. Even if it couldn't be controlled, how many people would be willing to pay a fortune to have their own prophetic dream? Not some charlatan telling you what you want to hear, but your own? And if it could be controlled, to any degree at all, either the content or duration or intensity of the dreams...Then it would be a terrifying power indeed." His guard drops altogether as he reels with the implications. "By the gods, even knowing that every dream that child confers must be false—*must be*—I'd give everything in our treasury to keep it out of others' hands, simply to stop the havoc it would wreak. Think of it! Everyone acting with certainty that they know the future, believing they're either protected from failure by fate or they must act swiftly to avert it! Kylar, you're talking about a gifting I've never heard of, but with the amount of power Dorian directed using Curoch and Iures together...No, I still don't believe it. But others would. Will. And... yes, such a gift *is* the kind of thing the Chantry would be willing to risk a war with Alitaera over. Magic like that could change balances of power throughout the whole continent and beyond." He shakes his head, aghast. "Gods save us. How old's the child?"

"What's that matter?" I ask.

"It doesn't. Unless he's under three or four months."

I hesitate. "Not yet three months. Why?"

He rubs his forehead. "Precocious Talents sometimes change or disappear. So if you're lucky, it may resolve itself. It may disappear altogether." Then, grudgingly, he adds, "Or you may have a problem."

"I'd noticed. More than one. But what's the new one?"

"In the Chantry's philosophy—oh!" But he sees the sudden look on my face and turns to look behind him.

Both of us watch a human figure in a wingsuit, rising kite-like in the wind with a rope tied to his chest. He lifts only slowly until he gets out of the wind-break that is the palace. As he rises to our level, suddenly the sky dancer is hit by sustained winds and shoots skyward. The rope drops away from him.

Red flares burst into life from his feet, trailing red smoke and sparks behind him. A sea of faces crowd the portholes and transparent walks of the *Storm Racer.*

"You know them well, Grandmaster, don't you? These Sisters."

"Most only by sight or dossier. Sister Ayayah Meganah is the only one I know personally. Let's say I'm not impressed."

"I thought you said they were the Chantry's best."

"I'm impressed by their abilities. Not by their morals. At least not hers."

Oh, that's lovely. The pit in my stomach grows larger still. "Grandmaster. If the Chantry can't steal the child themselves, what will they do to prevent such power falling into the wrong hands?"

"The wrong hands?" he scoffs. "The wrong hands are any hands other than their own."

"Including his parents'?" I ask.

His face hardens. It's answer enough.

"But they wouldn't...they wouldn't hurt a baby," I say at a sudden fear. I grew up among the worst of the worst.

A flicker of doubt, but then he says, "No, surely not. They might risk war, but not their own souls. The Chantry is arrogant, but they're not *evil.* I mean, they're humans. Some of them have been responsible for enormities in the past, but the Sisters as a whole treasure seeing themselves as working for the good of all nations, all people. Now, if this were an existential threat, then all bets would be off. But prophecy? It'd be a weapon, for sure. But it's a stretch. My men reported that Sister Ayayah's team lost their assassin in Elenea. Despite that, the team has continued on to this job without one, which means they considered an assassin useful but not key to their success on this job."

My stomach sinks lower still. "They might not be entirely without an assassin."

"But you said..."

"The new girl. She's a trainee. She has other gifts, they said. But she's got a history."

"A history?"

"In wet work."

"At her age? Ah. Well then. Most likely she's aimed at Repha'im. Does she have even a scrap of conscience?"

"Yes," I said. "Yes. More than a scrap."

"No woman with a conscience is going to hurt a baby, no matter what her philosophy tells her."

I stare at the *Storm Racer*. Eight other sky dancers have risen into the air now, burning different colors in beautiful tracks across the horizon. Vi is aboard that magic-and-metal monstrosity, aimed at the empress's new consort, a man protected in a hundred ways she must know and with powers she can't possibly understand. She misled me at the very least, and yet the thought of her heading into such danger makes me feel sick all over again.

And if, against all odds, she's successful? The Chantry steals Logan's son. They won't give him back. Not with his powers.

When Logan finds out, he'll go to war with the Chantry and damn the consequences. It will be the end of him.

I've failed, and now I learn that my failure is going to cost me at least one, but more likely both of my last friends in the world.

"I thought the imperials were going to be stupid enough to give you one last chance," Grandmaster Vitruvius says suddenly. He's moved closer now, but I sense no threat from him.

I don't care if he attacks me. I've no will to fight now.

I sink to my knees, barely hearing him.

"I thought they'd come after you up here," Vitruvius continues. "But it looks like they're too smart for that."

"What's it matter?" The question isn't even for Vitruvius, but he takes it as such.

"It matters for the same reason I threw away my suit. If you had wings, you could theoretically still make it to the *Storm Racer* before it disembarks."

I look at him scornfully. "Wings? That kind of body magic takes centuries to learn." I know, because Durzo told me I was too dumb to figure it out even if he'd been willing to teach me, which he wasn't.

"I didn't mean actual wings," he said. "That's not even possible, is it? Are you saying—? Never mind. I meant that you've been holding back, all this time."

"Huh?" I've only held back the black ka'kari, and what use would it be to beat up Grandmaster Vitruvius?

"We've got no rope, so you'd need to leap far enough out to catch the updraft that comes off that hill's wind ramp. See, there? They built it to help the sky dancers get aloft. But it's too far to jump, even with the Talent."

"I don't know what you're talking about."

"You'd need help."

"What?" I ask.

He looks at me with a strange intensity. "There are stories of you covering yourself with some sort of a black membrane. A second skin. My sources say you're able to form it into weapons as well, so it obviously has rigidity. Can you make a wingsuit of it?"

I'm a moron. It hadn't even occurred to me. I hadn't even thought to ask—

~I can do it.~

My heart practically stops. "How would I get inside the ship?"

"You see those lights by the wind scoops?"

Looking closely, I notice two bulbous open hemispheres at the back of the storm ship with lights halfway up a track next to them. Those must be the wind scoops. I nod.

"Those scoops are storing the power necessary to turn the storm ship out of the bay and past the rocks. When they have enough power, those scoops will close and the skin of the ship will be covered with another layer of seamless armor. You'd need to get inside before that happens. I'd say you've got... mmm, three or four minutes?"

I hadn't even noticed getting to my feet, the sudden energy of hope filling me. I watch the sky dancers with a critical eye, divining how they maneuver. Spread wings, go up. Tuck wings, go down. Lean left, go left. Wings spread wider to grab more wind, narrower for less. Seems easy enough.

Ha. Right.

"Why would you help me?" I ask.

"Other than to see what magic you've been holding back, you mean?"

"Yes." Though showing this particular man the black ka'kari is not high on the list of the best ideas I've ever had, I also don't have any other ideas at all.

"I could say because you didn't kill our mages at the waystation. But that might've been you simply being smart. You might've thought we'd give up chasing you so long as you didn't kill any of us. So the real answer? You returned the horse."

"It all comes back to the horse?" I ask, incredulous.

"It all comes back to the horse. Though not putting an arrow in my chest for my bracelet is a point in your favor, too. A small one."

I snort. Shake my head. "This could be a trap."

"And yet you're already gathering your magic," he says loudly, over the burgeoning wind. His face crooks a little smile.

"I never was too bright."

"It's not a matter of intelligence, Kylar."

"What is it, then? Fool trust?"

"Oh no. Naïve trust is nothing to praise. Mature trust, chosen while aware of the possibility of betrayal? Mature trust is an act of profound courage."

"How much of you is considering pushing me off-course?" I ask.

"As a proportion?" He pauses, mouth twisting as he thinks. "All of me."

"How much of you thinks that'd be a good idea?"

"Half? A touch less than half. It fluctuates."

"I'll take it," I say. "I trust any man who believes he's only a little more than halfway good."

He grins. "I fear instead I'm a little less than halfway wise."

"As long as you don't give me a halfway push."

"Oh no, Kylar. I'm like you in one way at least. Everything I do—even the wrong things—I do with all my might."

"Uh. Thank you?"

"Shut up and run."

I back up, leaning into the wind as I do so. It's gonna be an unbelievably long jump.

He waves his hands sharply. "No, no, no! We really need to bring you to Tover, don't we? You don't understand motion at all, do you? We're not going to try to throw you all the way to the ship. You wouldn't make it a quarter of the way! We have to throw you this way—into the wind. You get elevation first and then you *glide* to the ship." He says something quieter that I can't fully make out under the wind. Maybe something about 'if they don't knock you out of the sky'?

I look up as I move into the position he indicated.

"Kylar," he says, "something occurs to me."

"What's that?"

"Let's say you do this. You get past all of them—" He points up.

Oh, that's right; there are still the sky dancers up there. Enemies. Birds of prey who now seem very interested in what I'm doing.

Fantastic.

"Even if you somehow make it safely onto the storm ship, and somehow make it inside, there's no winning once you're there. Even if you get the child, there's no way for you to get away safely."

"Yes, there is," I say. "I just haven't found it yet. You ready?"

This has got to be the dumbest thing you've ever seen me do, huh?

~Oh, this one's in the top ten.~

"I'm ready," Vitruvius says, shaking his head. "And I'll be keeping you in my prayers, young man."

The ka'kari oozes from my skin and forms webs between my legs and between my arms and sides.

I don't want to give Grandmaster Vitruvius any longer to examine the ka'kari than necessary, so I run immediately, fully into the face of the roaring wind, only the force of my Talent keeping me on the ground and moving forward.

It occurs to me only as I reach full speed—which is barely as fast as an un-Talented sprinter because of the slowing force of the wind—that I am charging toward a precipice with very, very little idea of what's going to happen when I get to the edge. The last time we met, didn't Grandmaster Vitruvius say something about a precipice?

My gut muscles clamp down, my throat tightens, but I can't let Vitruvius see more of the black ka'kari, can't let him see me scared. There's no other way off this rock. If I stay there's only murder and death for me.

The fear passes in a single pump of my legs, *I can't do this* becoming, as it so often does, *Come hell or high winds, I* am *doing this.*

As I pass Grandmaster Vitruvius, a blue cloud extends from him, catches me from behind, and hurls me forward and up with immense force.

I throw my arms and legs wide and the ka'kari-black wings snap tight, straining the muscles of my chest and shoulders—and the buffeting wind flings me breathless into the sky.

Chapter Fifty-Five

Happy Landings, and Others

The force of the updraft nearly breaks me as it throws me up and up, wrenching my spread-eagled arms back and back.

But I hear myself laugh, fear left on the ground, far below, and more distant with every heartbeat. Joyfully, in the familiar paradox, my senses expand as my world contracts. Thought ceases and with it, every impediment to all thought's goals. I sense rather than think about where the wind snags at me as it blows past, and without having to order the ka'kari to smooth those snares, I simply adapt.

I am become a wing, not shaped through mimicry of the sky dancers, but molded in dialectic with the wind in order that we become perfect partners.

Catapulted toward great heights, the ground dwindling below, I am tempted again toward thought but cling to the moment, let it flow through me. To be a Night Angel, one's magic must live in the skin, I was once told. It is an animal thing, a kind of knowledge that doesn't emanate from brain or even heart, but from the blood. So now I don't know or even sense the edge of the weakening updraft; I *ken* it. The same instinctual knowing tells me that to make it to the storm ship, I shall have to change my very shape.

But the sky dancers don't wait for me to get my bearings. They attack.

My senses shout—too late.

One crashes into me from above, diving in so fast that my last-instant swerve can't make him miss, though he only strikes across my legs.

The hit sends me into a flipping spin.

Fear is back with a razorbeak glaive.

The wind is a roar in my ears, my eyes are tight slits, tears stream. Blinded, I flip and flip and flip out of the updraft.

I flare my arms and legs again, only to find that as my wings spread and slow my descent, I've rolled over onto my back and am staring up rather than down.

Another form plunges, smoking past, a striking hawk narrowly missing a fluttering dove.

I tuck my wings, roll, and flare, and another streaks by, barely missing me.

As I flail, desperate, trying to find where the next attack may come from, a body smashes into me from the side. I'm thrown into a free fall. But this one clings to me.

We plunge together, and I see the glitter of a knife. I smash my head into his, but he's wearing a helm. He slashes down with the knife in an amateur's overhand grip.

My block-twist-disarm-reverse-and-slash happens before he knows what I've done. Releasing the knife, I grab his helm and barely slow my sharp wrench to break his neck. I don't want to kill. I strike the side of his neck hard enough to stun him and launch away.

I flare my arms, and a moment later, below me, he does the same, and immediately veers to one side—his left wing slashed open to uselessness by the cut I made.

Two more sky dancers plunge past me to rescue their falling comrade. I'm already searching the skies for the others.

The sky dancers who tried to strike me and missed are now flaring back as much as they can, riding a narrow line: If they flare too much, they lose all speed and the wind no longer pushes them up; they simply fall. If they flare too little, they'll keep speed but still lose height compared to me.

The ground and sea are hurtling closer with every breath, and two sky dancers are still above me, each brandishing a dagger and—far more dangerous—their years of experience.

Flying looks easy enough, I'd thought, somehow forgetting how professionals always make things look easy. They look like they're planning to attack in tandem. Already, they're boxing me in, walling me away from the storm ship below.

The one thing they don't know is that though all of us can spread or angle our arms and legs to change the shape of our wings, I can also change the size of mine.

How strong are you?

~You'll break before I do.~ The ka'kari seems unconscionably happy about its reply.

We're right on the edge of the updraft, but the two sky dancers are experienced enough that even this doesn't faze them. One is in the updraft, the other outside it, but they compensate their glides perfectly to slide into position to bracket me from above. Veering into the updraft, I throw my wings wide and suddenly make them twice as large as before, my Talent surging in my arms—

The wind launches me skyward once more, but immediately, I pull my wings in tight, becoming a stone catapulted into the air between the two men, who each slash and miss.

I throw my wings wide once more and, stretching, enlarge them.

The sky dancers are all below me now, and I see them veering back toward the palace, where broad kites are flying.

The lowest sky dancer bumps against a kite, and somehow secures it to his chest. I watch as he's winched back in to safety. With the bleed-off of speed, he doesn't soar all the way in but drops the last bit into a large net set up for catching him.

Which makes me realize something, fully cerebral now, not at all in the beautiful instinctive flow I'd had before: At some point, I have to land.

I've never landed before. I don't know *how* to land.

The *Storm Racer* is far below and ahead of me, but I can see the light tracks on those great open wind scoops—doubtless put there so spectators from the palace can know when to stop partying and start watching the ship put out to sea. The light tracks are almost full.

Fantastic.

The rising light of dawn is strangely diffuse, the dust and dirt kicked up by the early winds of the Great Storm filling the sky with fine particles, dimming the scenery and painting it in deep reds. It's glorious. Beautiful. I wish I could stay aloft longer, and not solely because I'll probably die when I land.

The ship is fully loaded and ready now, all the gangplanks pulled back, all the doors closed and sealed flush against the wind. Though the windows are surely crowded with the thousands inside getting one last look at Castle Stormfast, there's no one in sight on the smooth back of the great beast. No one is fool enough to be caught outside in the coming storm.

Aside from the great shark-fin mast, the top deck of the storm ship is rounded, but of such size it's functionally flat and formless. At least it'll be a smooth place to crash on.

The scoops are at the rear of the ship, so I line myself up from the front, losing height and speed in some sort of arithmetical relationship that I have only a fuzzy understanding of, but which is becoming more and more important as I approach the iron deck.

If there were no wind, not even the best sky dancer could do what I'm about to attempt.

The framed pilot wings can soar, but the sky dancers' wingsuits allow at best something between a glide and a controlled fall. In order to maintain any lift, the wingsuits require incredible speeds.

There would be no landing safely if the wind were anything but strong and steady. A momentary gust or eddy would mean me shooting upward or dropping dozens of feet. But with the wind as fast and as constant as it is? I can be flying at incredible speed in relation to the wind while flying slowly in relation to the ground—and the deck.

So what I'm about to try is possible. Probably.

I hope.

For someone who knows what they're doing.

Which I don't.

But after one jumps from a cliff, not-falling is no longer an option. I can only choose where I land—and at these speeds, the white-capped water doesn't look much softer than the deck.

I line up, thinking I'll try to touch down on the front of the storm ship in case I—

I completely overshoot.

Oh hell, I'm going to miss the ship completely.

I dive, flare. Dive, flare. The shark-fin mast looms large before me.

Ah! I'm going to hit the—

I carom off the mast in a glancing blow, roll over, flare—and skid hard, skimming across the deck of the ship. My ka'kari-skin throws up a shrieking streak of sparks from the deck, but the smooth deck is too slick. It's not slowing me down. Battered, bouncing, tumbling head over heels, I glimpse the great humps of the scoops at the rear of the ship, first far off, and then all too soon, I skid partway up one, slip off its side, slam into the deck again, and keep sliding.

I feel the deck sloping. I'm heading for the water.

I throw my arms wide to the wind, meaning to dig my claws in, but my wings fill and flip me back up the deck, wrenching my arms nearly out of my sockets. I try to drop down to hug the deck but tumble over and over up it now—toward the great, roaring, open maw of the huge wind scoops, where I see flashing blades spinning, like the arms of a steel-edged windmill. Blurring with this much wind, they're effectively razor sharp.

I scrabble at the deck, dissolving my ka'kari-wings even as I'm blown into the leading edge of one scoop. I stab out claws from my fingers, but the magic protecting the steel hull is different from what protected the stone walls of Castle Stormfast, and my fingers slip.

The sound within the great scoop's throat suddenly changes, as of something under load shifting to spinning free, but the blades keep spinning at such speed they're a white and silver blur.

My claws stab into a seam, and I cling there with all my might, my feet not far from the blades.

But then the blades are slowing, slowing, and at last they stop.

Sucking in convulsive breaths, for a moment I can do nothing. With a ratcheting hum, the turbine blades twist from their wind-catching angle to be straight to the wind.

Through the now-stopped blades, I can see technicians armored and goggled against the wind, all tethered with harnesses and great ropes so as not to be blown away. I can't see their faces through their wind helms, but I see some stop, awed that anyone could be where I am.

The ship rumbles, and the entire scoop begins to lower into the body of the storm ship to come out of the wind. I get up to my knees, and the wind behind me nearly throws me bodily through the blades of the scoop. I stagger gracelessly, slip through the great blades still on my knees, and tumble to a walkway within.

Legs noodly, I stand, trembling, muscles twitching in my aching chest and arms. The technicians stand, staring at me, motionless.

Then the scoops rumble to a stop as they come fully into the body of the storm ship, and with a hiss, the decking above them seals shut.

The wind ceases.

I'm not only alive, I'm *in*.

I drop the ka'kari from my face where it had made a helm—I don't remember doing that. Maybe *I* didn't do it. Still wobbly but recovering, I walk to a desk shielded from the wind where I see a mug of wine. I toast the technicians, who are warily removing their own helms, staring at me agape, their tasks forgotten.

Even as I roll the shoulder I landed on, feeling it out for serious injury, my eyes flick around the room. I smile, friendly like. No weapons I can see, none of the telltales of incipient violence. These are technicians, tradesmen, not warriors. Thank the hundred gods and the One. My own body has a litany of complaints for me, but, it seems, no serious injuries.

"Bit brisk out there," I say. "Recommend you stay inside. Which...I guess we have to, seeing as there's no way out." I drink the wine from the mug I snatched and then say, "I'm glad we had this moment together."

Maybe it was his wine I drank, but incredibly enough, one of the technicians sees fit to reward my friendliness by sounding an alarm.

Chapter Fifty-Six

The Time and Place for Honor

The breath invading my lungs is an army pouring through a mountain pass, taking the strong points around my heart, putting every worry to flight. My body settles into ready position one, and my thoughts settle, emotions quiet, senses expand. There is a beauty in violence. All the ugliness is its aftermath. To do what I do is to be a whole, but to seem bifurcated. Half my face lit with hard unforgiving light, half-hidden in darkness, yet I am one man. If I am still a man, for when I enter the frenetic meditation, fate's dance, the first resort of fools and the last of the wise, I become something more.

Seventeen men, mostly technicians, are scattered throughout this large room with all its gears and wooden walkways on four levels and spinning iron axles disappearing into humming magical boxes.

I expel my breath and bow. It's only then I notice I'm half-naked. The ka'kari has retreated into my body, leaving me in my underwear. A half-naked man in a fight isn't formidable: He's either pathetic or terrifying.

I can work with that.

The ka'kari bubbles out of my eyes to cover my eye sockets in a blank black film. I smile to reveal black nothingness inside my mouth. With my breath, a blue iridescence flickers briefly.

I see eyes go wide.

These men are unarmed. They have no idea what they're facing in me. It wouldn't be honorable for me to pick up a weapon.

I slash a nearby handrail with the ka'kari bladed along my palm. The railing is lacquered wood over iron. I tear free a quarterstaff length. I believe there's a time and a place for honor; I just haven't figured out where yet.

Someone drops a tool.

With a howl, I charge.

They scatter. Except one guy. There's always the one guy. This one's got a fancy hat, like he's in charge, despite being young and at least as wide-eyed as half the people running away. He's holding an iron prybar with the air of a man who's only ever used it to pry things open.

I'm on him before he can react, swatting the prybar from his hand, grabbing his arm and yanking him into a choke hold trapped between my arm and staff, holding his other arm behind his back as he gasps.

"What's your name?" I demand, scanning the room for exits. Soldiers are pounding into the room from one of the lower forward exits now.

"Caravaldi. Hmmahcll Caravaldi," he says, choking on his first name as I squeeze.

"Your life could've ended here, Caravaldi," I tell him. "You're a brave man. Brave enough to do something better than this."

I grind the pressure points behind his ears to drop him, and then I run on toward the soldiers now pounding up the stairs with cudgels drawn.

Stairs in castles are designed to serve right-handed soldiers holding defensive positions on higher levels, and thus punish right-handed soldiers trying to come up. Clearly, these were built on the same design, though probably from convention, not because anyone foresaw the Night Angel needing to fend off seven—eight, now—soldiers galumphing up the stairs toward him.

I reach the top of the stairs before the first soldier does, and stab my staff, spearlike, right through his guard into the center of his gambeson-covered chest. I must have caught him midstep, because I easily launch him backward into his fellows.

Four of them go down, and it breaks the stride of the two following, who stop instead of advancing themselves.

It's so comically effective it throws me off. What kind of buffoons—

Ah, now I notice the fussy uniforms. These are not imperial soldiers. These are ship guards, trained in directing doddards to the latrines and dealing with drunk noblemen, not killing.

I pause for another moment, plotting my path, and then as soon as the men move, I dart forward again. They flinch hard as I come at them, but then I jump lightly up to the railing and leap down a level, roll as I hit the landing, and lightly swat the helmets of two reinforcements coming up with my handrail quarterstaff, left-right, then flip through the space between them.

Two technicians stand in front of the open double doors leading out of the large room. Each raises his hands in surrender and melts back to a wall.

Not hesitating, in case someone I haven't noticed has a bow, I slip between them and out into a hall, pulling the door shut behind me. The double door has looping handles, so I stab my length of handrail through it and use my Talent to bend it to lock the door shut.

My handrail-staff snaps in my hands, wood splintering and shards of steel exploding from it, peppering my forearm.

I curse. Steel. I thought it was iron.

But there's still enough length to it that I stab one end into the wood decking to anchor it in place while hooking both door handles. It'll slow them, but that's all.

I hear the pounding of feet down the hall and the unmistakable sound of an officer directing troops. Not ship guards now, but Alitaeran regulars coming to investigate the alarm. With the door behind me sealed, there are no exits in this long hallway except through a door directly toward them.

~Are you forgetting something?~

You know, if you want to be helpful instead of throwing asinine questions—

Oh. Right. You meant forgetting this.

I call the ka'kari to my skin and shimmer out of visibility a moment before a dozen soldiers burst through the door.

Chapter Fifty-Seven

Off the Rocks

*H*alt!" the officer bellows as he steps through the door—but he's not shouting at me, but to his men.

Somewhat less than instantly, his men obey, jostling each other, twelve of them in the hallway with me, and more visible stuck on the other side.

Officer's got good instincts, but his men aren't disciplined enough to be extensions of his will. If I wanted to spring an ambush, they've stopped right where I'd want them to.

~And you *don't* want to spring an ambush?~

My weight is already rocking toward my toes. I see the spear, loosely grasped in the hand of the man to the officer's left. A plan springs fully formed into my mind: side kick into the man's armpit to launch him into his fellows at the door, one hand on his spear, jerk its leaf-blade through the officer's neck, then—

But I don't want to kill. These men are doing nothing wrong. They're lawful imperial soldiers, investigating a mystery.

My delay is long enough for the officer to get two of his men to flank him and the rest to wait outside. He tasks his second-in-command with taking half of those to another entrance to the engine bay, then strides to the door I barred with the bent length of handrail.

"What's happened?" the officer shouts through the door.

There's no answer, so he directs his men to start wrestling with the bar, and shouts again.

"No time to answer!" comes a muffled voice. Maybe Caravaldi's. "If we don't"—he says some words I can't make out—"storm ship'll ram into the M—Rock in two minutes!"

I hear whirring deep in the belly of the storm ship, not a single tone, but several, some irritatingly high, and one deep at a level I feel in my diaphragm, the noises not quite synchronizing into a chord.

Or maybe it is a chord, just an awful one. What do I know about music?

This cacophony underfoot keeps shifting, its component noises all ascending in pitch, speeding up. At the same time, I feel a low, magical beat, as if I'm pressing my ear to a leviathan's chest and, as it wakens to life, hearing its heartbeat not only in my ear but throughout my whole body. And then another, and another, out of rhythm. *Whooommp...whomp...whomp whomp...whooommp.*

The deck shifts under our feet, and despite my wide stance, I almost fall.

I can't see the officer's face, but the soldiers clogging my exit are jostled around. They look worried.

Fantastic.

The officer's men get the door unbarred and throw the doors to the engine bay open with great vigor.

He looks left and right, left and right, surprised that everyone within seems to merely be doing their jobs. "What's the emergency?" he demands. He waves his hand, beckoning his men. I flatten myself against the wall.

The hallway isn't wide, and though most of the men are carrying their short spears in jogging order—choked up on the shaft, right hand, held at an angle so as not to jab the men running behind them—a few are holding their spears crossbody, point up and to the left, which means there is sharp steel jogging toward the space my head occupies. I duck and flatten myself, crouching as low as I can, but even as the men go jogging past, the mechanical whines come into a stable chord and the magical beats find a tempo.

Suddenly, the storm ship surges forward with power that shouldn't be possible for such a colossus—and not only forward, but into a turn, tilting the decks.

The turn throws the soldiers toward me—because *of course* it throws them toward me rather than away. That's my luck. If there's ever a one-in-two chance of the bad thing happening, it's gonna happen every time. I drop to the floor even as half a dozen men throw out hands to steady themselves against the wall where I'd been slinking an instant before.

One booted foot brushes my *nose* as a slender soldier staggers to the side. His hand slips off the wall and he's about to fall on me—but a younger man with blond hair and rounder features grabs him and hauls him upright a moment before he gets us all killed.

The younger soldier gives a big, infectious smile. "Why I gotta save ya every time?"

"Yeah, from certain doom," the other scoffs. "Mat, would you be this much of a pain in my ass if you weren't my brother?"

I lose the reply as they all push forward. Another soldier treads full on my fingers, grinds them unknowing, and then is gone.

The one who stepped on my hand throws a quick, disconcerted look backward, looking for what he stepped on. But his comrades push him forward to the engine room, where the officer is shouting, demanding answers. Caravaldi appears to be ignoring him, shouting his own orders at his own crew, getting the ship turning even more, the colossal chord of machinery and magics settling together in a triumphant crescendo.

I don't wait to see how it turns out. I already feel deafened both physically and magically. My Talent is so attuned to my environment that it makes me hypersensitive. This magic makes me feel like someone's been rubbing the same spot on my arm for half an hour.

Cradling my aching fingers, I'm already up and running silently out of the hallway and into a staircase. I head up, but at the mere act of climbing stairs, my body decides it's a good time to remind me how little I've slept and how much exertion I've put out.

Invisible, I reach the top of the steps. I catch a glimpse of alert imperial guards, and mages with single red stones on their chokers, and beyond them, nobles in conversation, turned toward a bank of narrow windows where they're watching the storm rise and the nearby passage of a jutting rock outcropping, blissfully unaware that less than a minute ago there was a real possibility we would hit it.

I see only solitary blue stones on the bracelets and solitary clear stones on their servants' bracelets; these are all minor nobles. I'm at the far rear of the boat. With how Alitaeran hierarchy works, I think it's a fair guess that everyone important will be all the way at the front.

Right now, I'm in no shape to handle mages and imperial guards. I head down the stairs, and down and down until I find a luggage room, the chests organized in such a way that I'm sure they're not meant to be accessed. I tuck myself into a tiny corner and pool the ka'kari onto its platinum bracelet, the black filling in the space around the silvery-white designs quite attractively. I usually keep it in my body when I'm in danger, but after a while, removing it completely feels as good as removing formfitting trousers at the end of a long day. No matter how good they feel in the morning, it's a relief to get them off.

I sleep like a normal person for the first time in I don't know how long.

It feels great. It feels restorative—despite the dreams.

When I wake, I bend my wrist so that my skin touches the ka'kari on its platinum bracelet. I can tell the bracelet was made specifically to allow such subtle contact. "Hey," I say quietly. I could merely think at it, but I have more control of what it hears when I make words. "I think it's about time you answered some questions."

Chapter Fifty-Eight

A Chat with an Ancient

I don't dream when I'm touching you, do I?"

~My magic is powered mainly from yours. I take excess from where you don't need it to use it where you do.~

"I don't need my dreams?" I ask.

~My creator didn't much like his dreams. He considered dreamless sleep a benefit.~

"So you've been eating dreams for centuries. You've gotta be some sort of dream expert by now, right?" I ask.

~How many times have you eaten wheat? That give you keen insights into farming? I don't devour dreams directly. I devour the energy spikes that attend them in highly Talented people.~

Directly was the key word there. It devours dreams, but not on purpose. What does it do to a person to be dreamless? I don't know if it's because I've been dreamless for so long that when my dreams came back, they returned extra weird, vivid, and portentous—clinging to the underside of a deck just above the water while some scaly monster swam below, seeking me; standing on a beach, squinting, scoured by sand flung by the Great Storm's winds; a boneless fall from a great height—you know, fun stuff like that. But I hope that's all it is. If my bad dreams are all aftershocks from one time holding Kiern, if Jenine has been dealing with nightmares every night for months—while also dealing with the stress of parenting two infants...

Then no wonder she cracked. Sleep deprivation, the strains of setting up a new court, the betrayal by and loss of one husband to madness, trying to learn to parent for the first time with twins, relational strains with her newly crowned, newly reunited first husband, and then on top of all that, bizarre and frightening dreams every time she slept? Or maybe all the ingredients of madness had been inside her already and the magic had merely stirred them together. Or maybe she would've broken down even without that push. I hear it happens to new moms sometimes.

Suddenly, in the storeroom's darkness, an image from my dreams rushes to my mind's eye with the speed of a shark emerging from the sea's murky depths, teeth wide: an unfamiliar dagger in my hand, circles of soldiers with steel bared, something warm in the nook of my elbow, wind and screams howling in my ears together in a chorus of desperation.

If dreams are the gods' messengers, I think the gods are telling me I feel trapped.

~You *are* trapped.~

Shows how useful dreams are, huh? And gods.

"You want to tell me anything useful? I could repeat everything I asked you a while back, but I think you remember the questions better than I do."

~Oh, I remember them. And I'll be happy to tell you something useful.~

"Really?"

It seems genuinely offended. Huffy teen boy? Maybe huffy teenage girl now. Put this as more evidence that it's not a real personality. It certainly doesn't have the maturity of someone who was supposedly ancient seven hundred years ago.

Oops. Sorry, meant to not be touching you while I thought that.

~Here's something useful for you, Stern. You should've picked this up already, but you obviously haven't: You can use me to solve your problems, but I'm not going to solve problems for you. If you die because you didn't think of an obvious application of my powers, so be it. That's outside my writ. I'm your tool, not your savior. So stop asking me to make your life easy for you. You're an orphan. Stop looking for Daddy to save you.~

I bend my wrist away to sever the connection.

~So. We have a little gap in our chronicle. You want to record what you've been doing in the last little while?~

Where you can hear and mock? I'll pass. If I ever get the chance to add to this after you've put it down on skin or parchment or whatever, maybe I'll do it then.

I'm scouting the next part of the ship.

Well, I'm not sure if it's scouting, but I'm calling it that in case I fail my infiltration of the next section of the ship. My nook here low in the rear of the storm ship...rear? Aft? I don't know anything about ships.

~Stern.~

Yeah? What?

~Not Kylar. Stern.~

What? I ask peevishly.

It doesn't answer.

Ah. Of the ship. The stern of the ship.

Anyway, my storeroom in the stern is safe. *Hey, I thought you didn't volunteer help.*

~That? That's not help. I'm smoothing out wording for clarity. An excellent tool sometimes makes its user look far more gifted than he has any right to look. Think of it as translating.~

From my native Stupid?

The ka'kari is silent rather than defensive. A human would say, *I didn't say that.* Not the ka'kari.

Hey, as you've been recording all this, how much have you been 'translating' everything else I've told you?

It doesn't answer.

When this is over, I'm going to have to look over everything it's done. Carefully. But now isn't the time. My nook in the storeroom is safe. But staying safe isn't what I'm here for. I need to push forward to the bow of the storm ship—and high up, most likely. These Alitaerans always want their physical placement to mimic their status. Higher up means higher up, even if in a ship in a storm they get a worse ride for it.

I checked my wounds before we left the storeroom. After my sleep, everything has healed nicely. I wonder sometimes what the limit is. I know that a bad wound will kill me like anyone, and then that triggers my immortality. When I come back from that, I wake up whole. But I've also been badly wounded, and found that where others would've been permanently crippled, I Healed. So there's a question mark around how much I can heal from—or Heal from—on this side of death. But then there's an equally big question on the other side. I know that Curoch—the now-hidden magical Sword of Power that Jorsin Alkestes made or bore or whatever—could kill me permanently. It was made to do that. But what if I get completely burned, or beheaded, or eaten? If I were cut perfectly in half, which half of me would come back? Both? Could I theoretically replicate myself?

That could be handy.

It's a silly thought to have, but only because it all scares me. What if I lose some body part and it never comes back? What if I'm condemned to live forever without my legs or something?

Durzo has disappeared; the only way I might find my limits is by testing them.

Testing them has real downsides.

~And you didn't have anything to do with why he left, did you?~

"Hey, shut it. Cut that part out. Where were we? Oh yeah, so you really can't tell me anything else about the Night Angels, about my powers, or even about Durzo?"

~Part of my design is learning whether you're a person who respects others' boundaries. If you're not, it'll take a lot longer for me to tell you things. My maker believed that the kind of people who won't respect boundaries in the first place are the people who will abuse your secrets after you tell them.~

"You're telling me if I want to go fast, I'd better go?"

~Ah, see? You're not as dull as Blint worried.~

That chafes. *So what you're saying is, 'If you want your questions answered, don't ask them'?* Ridiculous. It puts me completely at the ka'kari's mercy.

Oops. I didn't mean it to hear that last part. *He did not worry I'm dull*, I think, to change the subject.

Silence.

He didn't, did he?

The halls in this section of the ship have been suspiciously empty. I don't know what defenses they have in store for me. My sleep healed me, and it put me in a much better frame of mind, where I can make better decisions faster, thus making me a better fighter—but the hours have also given my enemies time to prepare defenses. They know there's an intruder on the ship.

If I were trying to stop a stealthy infiltrator, I would put my defenses in all the weird places where infiltrators wouldn't look for defenses, but military people tend to think in military terms. They think of controlling intersections, lines of fire, high ground. I've been checking every intersection before I approach it, and finally my work pays off—

Chapter Fifty-Nine

Shepherds and Scholars

*V*iridiana set the book down. She rubbed her temples. "Am I not supposed to talk to you?" she asked Sister Ariel.

"Have you been commanded not to?" Sister Ariel said, not looking up from her reading. The woman read at an absolutely infuriating pace. If Viridiana had been able to read that fast, she would've already been done with this wretched assignment.

"No."

"Then talk away. I will note, incidentally, that *I* have been commanded not to speak *to you*."

"You have? By who?" Viridiana asked.

"It doesn't matter. I have no intention of obeying."

Vi permitted herself a smile. Under her drab, mousy exterior, Sister Ariel could be a quiet firebrand. There was a tiny creak outside the door. A bolt shot through Vi and she flinched hard as the gut-twisting fear of exposure, of discovery, coursed through her. Her jaw locked, eyes fixed unseeing on the book in front of her, even before the door of the library opened a crack.

She willed herself to relax. *He's dead*, she told herself. *Hu Gibbet is dead.*

When she was a child, training under Hu to become a wetboy, several times he'd set her to tasks and forgotten her. Once she'd been copying his ten most-used potion recipes and their preparations for hours, fighting to keep her attention from wandering, telling herself she'd get a beating if she stopped, but eventually, she tried making one of the potions. He'd come in, not quite silent, the floorboard making one tiny creak.

When he was sober, he was utterly silent. She'd instantly known then the depth of her mistake.

After she'd healed from the beating, as punishment, he leased her out to work off her 'debt' for the ingredients she'd ruined. The *work* he'd sold her into was exactly the awfulness that Momma K had forbidden the Sa'kagé to send children into. In her Chantry entrance interviews, where she'd had to answer questions about such things, Viridiana maintained that it hadn't bothered her because by that time she'd already learned to wall off her mind from what happened to her body. It was the *injustice* that had infuriated her—she hadn't ruined those ingredients; she'd made that potion perfectly, and Hu must have known it, because he ended up using the potion she'd brewed.

She'd *helped* him, and he'd punished her for it. But Hu didn't care. In those early days, he hadn't been interested in having an apprentice; he wanted a slave. It was only when he saw the reputational benefits others accrued for having competent apprentices that Hu got serious about training her.

All that rushed into Vi's mind in an instant, the mental pathways of that old panic well-trod. The door opened.

This wasn't Hu Gibbet, she told the knotted muscles in her throat and under her diaphragm. This was just Sister Ayayah Meganah, the hag. Viridiana's muscles relaxed and she smiled. "Big Sister," she said easily.

"How's the work proceeding?" Sister Ayayah asked.

"Well enough," Vi said. She counted it a success that she made her tone pleasant.

"But not well?"

"Well enough," Vi said, more strained, trying to give a fake Chantry smile and doing a poor job of it.

"That worries the Sisterhood. Time is limited. You're to finish as soon as possible, not sit around and gossip with some old bird. If need be, I'll come back to supervise you myself. Any questions?"

Vi's fake smile dropped. "Just one," she said. Out of the corner of her eye, she saw Sister Ariel sit up straight, saw the older woman's hand waving her off, signaling Vi to stop, stop, don't do it. "Why do you have to be such a bitch?" Vi said.

Sister Ariel's hand froze in place, then fell, defeated.

Sister Ayayah's nostrils flared. Her neck went tight. "You know, I don't know if it was ever possible for me to have liked you. You're simply on the wrong side of too many divides. But you do make it so easy to hate you."

"I'm not on the side of anything," Vi said. "I'm not political at all."

"See. That's what I mean. You honestly believe that. And that makes you one of them."

"You've been looking for an excuse to hate me since you first laid eyes on me and realized I'm everything you're not."

"I said you're easy to hate, Viridiana, not that I do. A person has to have a certain stature for one to hate her. You? You're barely sludge in the bottom of the barrel of my contempt. And you've only earned that because your pretty face has fooled a few people who should know better into taking you seriously. They'll learn soon enough, and you'll be discarded without another thought, like every other broken tool in their merciless hands. I would pity you, if your overweening arrogance didn't make me despise you instead. You are the dung smeared on one's boot: a foul odor, bothersome, but forgotten as soon as one wipes it away." She turned from Vi as if she'd forgotten her already. "Sister Ariel, your intransigence has been noted."

Sister Ariel looked at Sister Ayayah over her reading glasses. She gestured to the veritable buffet of open books in front of her. "Do I look like I'm busy speaking to the girl, or just busy? Would you like to check the output of my research over the last two days for the one who holds your leash? Hmm? You think I don't know you spy on your own Sisters? You think I don't know who you report to? That I don't care doesn't mean I don't notice, Sister. And that notice could be relayed to those who do care. And it shall, if you slow my work any further. This is a library, a place for silence and, in case you have forgotten, *study*. Our little sister here has found no difficulty adhering to those traditions and working with full diligence and honor. You might learn something from her."

Then Sister Ariel turned back to her books.

Sister Ayayah gaped at her. Her eyes flashed and her mouth worked through a dozen expressions before compressing into a tight line. She sneered and jabbed a finger at Vi. Then she left. Silently.

Two minutes later, Sister Ariel lifted her pen. "Odd girl," she said. "Always has been cowed by my intellect ever since she challenged me in a class about this obscure little weave Ogogian shepherds were purported to use when treating wool before shearing. I'd shown mathematically how it was indeed possible for there to be seventy-three variations to the tonal incantations necessary. She challenged me to show how one could actually do that in practice, so I showed her."

"You showed her? So... you'd memorized seventy-three variations of... wool magic?"

"Don't be ridiculous. I'm not a Maker, and haven't the least interest in textiles. Moreover, I despise wool. I figured them out. But that's not the pivotal moment."

Viridiana cocked her head. The woman had figured out seventy-three unique tonal variants of a spell—on the spot?

"Ayayah—she wasn't yet a Sister, obviously—dug her heels in, feeling she'd lost face. From time to time, we all run into arrogant students who don't realize how stupid it makes them look when they approach scholarship as a contest with sides, and thus with winners and losers. If I put forth hypotheses that stimulate later scholars to study more deeply and thus they find something true that I've missed, then I've played an irreplaceable part in uncovering that truth. I've pushed forward all of human knowledge. I've been integrally important. Students such as she was, and the kind of scholars they too often later become, wish only to be the truth uncoverer whose name is remembered. It leads them to bastardize knowledge and even to sabotage those who would build on their work. They become dams in the streams of knowledge, fearful, jealous for their fame, believing their legacy can grow only if they stop others' learning. Pure stupid arrogant foolishness and a sin against knowledge. But for us, that's a tangent.

"Ayayah insisted that though there might be seventy-three variations of tone, what she'd *obviously* meant was that those couldn't produce seventy-three variations in the outcome of the spell. With that triumphant little smirk of hers, she said she bet that I would come back in two weeks with some obscure text claiming that a bunch of textiles that were all clearly the same were somehow different—but that we all knew the truth.

"Thus, in only a few sentences, she herself had moved the posts—horse racing analogy, you know this one? Yes? Good—and also insinuated that I would try to win the dispute with an appeal to authority. This exasperated me. First, the underlying accusation that I was trying to *win*—that I was playing knowledge as a game the same way she did. Second, I have to admit, the smirk as she said it, secure in her arrogance, vexed me. Third, she alleged that I was so dishonest that I would use a fallacy against her in the very breath in which she'd used one herself. So I took her bet.

"My sister Istariel says it was rash of me, but I was honestly hoping not only to save the entire classroom by inculcating a bit of humility in them, but also Ayayah herself, who has since proven to have all the flaws we Sisters are prone to, all those proud weeds whose roots grow in the soil of ability."

With a shrug and a glance at her ink-stained fingers, she picked up her quill and turned back to her work.

Viridiana stared at her. "You can't stop the story there. What'd you do?"

"Oh! Oh yes, I forgot to... Well, I made some guesses and I performed seventy-three variants. Thirteen of them were almost certainly not variants the Ogogian shepherds used because of the differences between wool and human hair, of course, but the fact that there *were* appreciable differences—if not necessarily useful ones—between the seventy-three different samples was enough for the class to adjudge that I was correct. Ayayah was so embarrassed and so furious that rather than wear it for a week as our bet had been, she shaved all her hair off."

"Wait. Wait," Vi said. "You performed the spells on her *hair*?"

"Oh, did I leave that part out? Yes. She had this beautiful halo of hair she combed out meticulously. She was very proud of her hair, and rightly so. Our bet was that should she lose, she would have to wear her hair with the variations in it for a week, and if I were to lose, she could do whatever she wished to do to my hair instead. She wouldn't back down. Too proud. She's never grown out her hair since.

"You know, it occurs to me now that because she immediately shaved her hair rather than wear it, she never did come to me to undo the magics I'd used on her. Some of those variants might have affected her hair follicles for months, if not years. Perhaps even—no, surely not to the present day. Huh."

"And you wonder why she hates you," Vi muttered.

"Oh no, I don't wonder at all," Sister Ariel said. "We Sisters are each of us special. When you fully accept that you are one in a thousand, if that matters to you above everything else, the hardest thing is not to meet a person whose gifts make them one in a million—those women are as goddesses to everyone. The hardest thing is to meet those who are one in ten thousand. Those people who are enough like you that you feel their presence pushes you further down some hierarchy."

"And you think you're one in ten thousand."

"Yes," Sister Ariel said with a puzzled sincerity, as if it were patently obvious, and thus the question must be aimed at something else.

"I think maybe you're being modest," Vi said, chuckling.

"No, no I'm not. I'm quite intelligent, and more than usually gifted, but I'm not a generational talent. I've come to believe that the main thing that makes me unusual in this Sisterhood isn't my intelligence at all; it's that I'm able to accept my limitations without rancor."

Vi didn't know what rancor was. With Sister Ariel, she constantly had to make guesses at what any number of words meant. "If you say so. I dunno. You're so many leagues above me I can't tell the difference."

Sister Ariel set her quill down. "No, Viridiana. Don't do that, please. I'm smarter than you'll ever be. That's true. Though I think you're more intelligent than you believe. You still believe the lies your master told you about you, don't you?"

"No!" Vi said scornfully. "What lies?" she asked, her throat unexpectedly tight. But even as the denial came out reflexively, she guessed what Sister Ariel was talking about. She could see the sneer on Hu's face as he called her a dumb cunt when she messed up setting a snare for the fifth time, fingers trembling under his gaze. 'What did I expect from a girl as stupid as you? All teats, no brain. Go to the bedroom and wait for me. I'll finish this and you can do the only thing you're good for.'

Sister Ariel sighed. "Do you think I've not had this conversation before with others? Do you think you're the first woman to feel intimidated or even stupid here? I know better than to try to argue women out of their pathologies. You're smarter than average. Unfortunately the women who are Talented and not at all smart don't make it at the Chantry. There's too much abstraction necessary in our work. Only Sisters who are smarter than average advance, so very few full Sisters aren't intelligent women. That means the average Sister is quite an intelligent woman out in the rest of the world. Here, if you're merely smart, you'll feel dumber than the women around you half the time, and you'll be right to feel that way.

"The thing is, for you, that's all utterly beside the point. All that matters for you, Viridiana, is that you are intelligent enough to do almost anything you want to do. Some things will take you longer than they will take others. Sure. But what you have, Viridiana, is pure strength. To make an analogy, if presented with the same problem, you and I will solve it different ways. Say— no, too complicated." Her eyes flicked up and to the side for a moment. "Say we come across a large stone, and we need to lift it onto a wagon. With your magical strength, you'll pick it up and put it on the wagon. Me? I'd figure out a ramp or a pulley or some such device. We each solve the problem."

"But a pulley could solve the problem a thousand times. I'd get tired."

"Precisely. The drawback for my approach is that I'll need to have materials for the pulley or the ramp, and it takes more time and materials, but the same job can be done. But now imagine I'm in the middle of a battle, and all that's available is the same stone. I know how to build a catapult that can send that stone a thousand paces, but if the problem is that an enemy horseman is about to ride me down, I'm lost. A strong woman like you will pick up the stone and throw it herself. Her excellence is fit for that situation. Put her in a library to translate texts, and it'll take her years. If the translations are time sensitive, she's lost. We are each of us special in our own way, and we are none of us special in every way. In the wide world, everyone understands that and accepts it, except for intellectuals, when it comes to intellect."

"No, fighters do it, too, when it comes to fighting. No one wants to think that no matter how hard they work, for how many years, that someone who works less than they do could be better than they are at the thing that matters most to them—or that someone who works exactly the same amount can end up far, far better than they are."

"Aha, there you have it. Yet another reason why I love the Chantry," Sister Ariel said. "I bring a specific truth to you, and you help me realize a general truth instead. Lovely. Now, if that revelation is also helpful to your reading, you'll have the perfect moment of academic serendipity."

Vi stared down at her book, twisting her lips to the side. Where had she even been? Oh, Kylar talking to the ka'kari.

When she looked back up, Sister Ariel was looking at her expectantly.

"Um...no?"

"Ah, well. We shouldn't appreciate perfection so much if its appearances were more frequent, I suppose."

"What do we know about the ka'kari?" Vi asked.

Sister Ariel's eyebrows rose. "Jumping straight to the dangerous questions, are we? I've always liked that about you, Viridiana, though I do worry it will get you killed. We *know* far less than most Sisters think we do, for they confuse what we suspect and what's been hinted to us by interested parties and what we want to be true and what we really know. Up until the last fight on the storm ship, the Sisterhood *knew* that there were six ka'kari, all created by a millennially talented and intelligent mage named Ezra, later Ezra the Mad, who was a confidant of Emperor Jorsin Alkestes seven centuries ago. We now 'know' that Ezra's six ka'kari were based upon another, older one. A black one sometimes referred to as the Devourer.

"To most of the Sisters who are aware of them, the reason the ka'kari are important is because we believe that some or all of them grant lesser immortality. You're aware of the traditional classifications of immortality?"

"Um...yeah." She wouldn't have been, before, but Kylar had written about that, hadn't he? On the page he tried to strike out. "Total invulnerability to time and the sword like maybe the One God would have if It exists. But for humans there's invulnerability to time but not the sword, and...no, I missed something, didn't I? The Strangers are in between, right?"

Sister Ariel looked impressed that Vi knew anything at all about it. "The in-between is controversial. Some claim that there are powerful creatures who can travel between the Thousand Worlds, taking on a mortal body as they wish, but if that mortal body is killed, or perhaps killed in certain ways, they themselves are not exactly *killed* but are permanently banished from their bodily incarnation in that world. Such creatures sound frighteningly powerful, don't they?"

"I, I suppose they do."

"Amusingly, some scholars posit that *humans* are just such creatures—that we are in our essences immortal, and that our death here is not a final death, though it does banish us from this realm. Personally, I find that such writings verge on the unfalsifiable and thus are not very interesting. It's a realm of speculation and religion, not scholarship."

"But we saw the Strangers at Black Barrow."

"Some did. Or thought they did. And I for one will not say that all who saw them are liars. Yet you yourself have wielded significant deception magics. Does it mean anything that a dozen mages saw something on a day when so much magic was in the air? It's evidence, I don't deny that, but is it *compelling* evidence? Maybe if you were the one who saw the things.

"Anyway, what Kylar dangles before the Chantry is the possibility of a lesser immortality: in which the ravages of aging are either stopped entirely or slowed to a crawl. The lesser immortal may still be killed. It either works—if there is such a thing—by freezing the normal processes by which a body learns it is aging, or it may work by aggressively Healing a body from the ravages of time.

"Sisters have been researching and experimenting for centuries on both fronts, without the benefit of the ka'kari. Their findings are why those of us who care to do so have greatly increased life spans. But our Healers and the leading scholars believe we've only picked the low-hanging fruit of life extension. No Sister has verifiably lived past two hundred years by using our methods, and most are so frail after a hundred fifty years that they choose to forgo more treatments. In contrast, the ka'kari seem to halt aging altogether or perhaps even reverse it."

"But Kylar—"

Sister Ariel hissed, and Vi stopped. Sister Ariel gave a significant glance around, seeming to say, even if she was almost certain they weren't being overheard, that there were simply things too dangerous to say aloud here.

Kylar had said he himself was proof that the Chantry was completely wrong—because Kylar came back from death. And Sister Ariel had seen that with her own eyes, had seen Kylar's body wick in magic and life, had seen him unbreathing and then saw him sit up and gasp.

"Kylar never spoke of such things," Vi finished, as if that had been what she was going to say.

"Nor would he. Nor would anyone his age. He was in the flower of his youth. How long would it take him to realize he wasn't growing old? He'd never been old before. He had no idea what it was like to wake with a knee throbbing that hadn't hurt the day before, or back pain that didn't get better in a day or two. It occurs to me that in a funny way, the reason young adults feel immortal is because in certain respects, they are. Their bodies are what we hope immortal bodies would be: ever vigorous, ever healing, perpetually full of vitality. Huh!

"Anyway, that's what everyone wants. True godhood would be nice. Behind that, perpetual youth would be lovely. Behind that, halted aging would suffice. A new consensus has been built in the last several months. Most Sisters now believe that permanently halted aging is within our grasp—if we can find a ka'kari, any ka'kari. But they've also convinced themselves that if they can find the black ka'kari, we could have perpetual youth—a far more tempting prize, when you're a hundred and thirty years old, having suffered decades of chronic pain and are now exhibiting the first signs of dementia. Or say if you're merely sixty years old, but you've got tumors growing in your guts. Such is a prize that would change every individual Sister's life, and all the Chantry, forever. And thence, the world."

Vi realized that never once had she looked at Kylar's powers and wished she could steal them. It came crashing over her like a wave that this might be far from everyone's reaction. To them, Kylar wasn't the young man she'd met in Cenaria—had he even carried the ka'kari then? To them, Kylar was a threatening figure who'd humiliated the Speaker, who'd happened to fight on the same side against Khalidor, who caused the Sisterhood limitless headaches and now kept perpetual youth out of their hands. Kylar wasn't merely an obstacle to what every last Sister wanted; by not giving the Sisters his secrets, he was condemning all of them to death. It was an affront, an insult. Unbearable. He was practically murdering all of them himself with his—what word had Sister Ayayah used? His intransigence.

The special teams had been away from the Chantry while this consensus had built. Otherwise, they would surely have turned all their energies on capturing Kylar.

But that shined new light on the pressure they were putting on Vi.

"So if I can figure out where Kylar's body is, and thus where the ka'kari is . . ."

"You'll change everything. Everything."

Vi took a deep breath. "Sister? If I tell you something, will you betray me?"

"It depends," Sister Ariel said.

Vi's chin pulled in.

"My highest loyalty is not to you, and I won't make it such simply because you ask it of me. If you require something that doesn't involve me betraying higher loyalties, though, I will never betray you regardless of the cost."

Vi took a deep breath.

"No, stop," Sister Ariel said. "I'm telling you. If you find anything pertaining to Kylar or the ka'kari's whereabouts, don't tell me. You don't tell *anyone*. You don't sell it cheaply, do you understand? Such information is of nearly infinite worth—and I'm afraid you're going to need it."

Chapter Sixty

The Opposite of Helpful

*N*ine soldiers. Three facing the hallway to port, three facing starboard, and three facing aft. Normal soldiers, not a mage among them, at least so far as I can see. So usually this wouldn't be a problem. After all, I don't have to kill them. I only have to get past them.

But we're not in the wide hallways of Castle Stormfast now. These halls are narrow enough that one man spreading his arms might brush both walls with his fingers. Three men standing shoulder to shoulder fully choke the hall.

Foolishly so, too. They're armed with spears taller than they are. Three men, side by side, trying to use polearms in a space this tight? They've sent the worst of the worst against me, apparently.

Well, they're soldiers, not ship guards, so the worst of the second worst. But still.

They're not the worst men necessarily, but they are men led by the worst officers. Sometimes the low ranks of a military are studded with remarkably competent fighters who never rise because they simply cannot keep their mouths shut about the stupidity of their officers, and whatever officer did this must be a prime example of—

Yep. There he is, sitting in a chair, a round shield on his lap functioning as a platter holding a tankard and a plate piled with food while he says around a mouthful, "You lot'll eat when your shift is done, you lazy—" He goes on to curse them half-heartedly while they stare in stony silence, inured to it.

I pull my head back from my own intersection. Risk and reward. Climbing on the ceiling above the soldiers? There's barely any space, and if they notice me, I'd be so close to the tips of their spears they'd skewer me before

I could react. Killing them all means, well, killing nine innocents. Maybe. It also means sending a message to those in charge that their unknown stowaway is someone who can kill nine soldiers.

King Repha'im will know instantly that it's me. Right now, a dubious story about some half-naked man slipping past some civilians and a few of the lowest guards? That story might not make it to the king for a while, if ever.

If it had made it to him already, I might not be facing mere soldiers here.

I peek out from around my corner and watch. The soldiers are chatting, bored, messing about as much as they think they can get away with under the baleful eye of their young officer, who yells at them intermittently but without much fervor. He's one of those idiots who thinks it's part of his job to yell at people to keep them in their place.

Why does every military in the world pick such men to be officers?

As I watch, a servant comes into view, stepping between them. He must have come from—uh, what's the opposite of aft? Abaft?

~No.~

The front of the ship—the bow, so abow? I mean, that's got to be it, right? Aboard, abaft, astern, aport, aweather, alee, adrift, aground, so…*abow*, right?—anyway, he must've come from the bow because I didn't see him come down either of the halls. Unfortunately, he doesn't turn my way, but instead heads aft. Minutes later, he comes back. He mutters some password my straining ears can't catch and is allowed through, carrying a sack of foodstuffs over each shoulder.

Wearing the ka'kari like a second skin, I go invisible, then sneak closer. From their eyes, the three men facing my way aren't precisely innocents; there's some degree of darkness in each of them: presumed superiority, hatred, greed, and vanity, but no murders, no rapes, no torture, no habitual cruelty that promises to grow in time. It's odd. I usually don't see so clearly, though sometimes I see more clearly even than this.

But it's the opposite of helpful. These are normal men. If I were to stand as judge and not only executioner—as I do—I'd not sentence any of these three to death.

One of the men shivers as if he can feel my presence.

I retreat as he mumbles to his comrades. "…notice something?" They shake their heads.

At the corner, under a lantern, I notice the niche cut into the wall. A bucket sits there. Under the various garbage discarded into the bucket—a brown apple core, chewing tobacco spit, and a lone stocking—I see that it's at least half-full of sand. A glance down the halls confirms that there's a similar niche and bucket under each glass oil lantern, tucked out of the way for aesthetic reasons.

Ah, sand buckets. For fighting fire.

It's always struck me as an irony that the greatest threat to vessels that sail into the middle of literal oceans is often fire.

I dig through the sand, seeing if there's anything I might use.

All I confirm is that there is, somewhere on this boat, a cat. Lovely.

I resolve, if given the chance, to throw it overboard.

Examining the lantern closely confirms that it's bolted tightly to a narrow decorative arm that is itself bolted tightly to the wall. I examine the small oil reservoir that makes it more of a pain to refill but less of a fire hazard. I study the placement of the wick, abandoning half a dozen plans as I do so.

There are lanterns like this at every intersection, sometimes several. I put my head against the wall, looking at the decorative arm in profile.

Double-checking my hall, I call the ka'kari to my fingers and touch it to that metal.

Got the taste of it?

~Mmm-hmm.~

Hey, tool.

~Yes, O Wise User of Said Tool and Coiner of Words?~

I shake my head ruefully.

I've called you back to my hand from a distance before. How far away can I do that?

~I don't know.~

Why not? How far could Durzo call you from?

~That's irrelevant. Calling me to your hand is a function of your magic, not mine. The intensity and sensitivity of your body magic comes at the cost that, unlike a mage, you absolutely believe that your magic must extend from your body out into the world. You can do magic at a distance, but it always originates from your body. Many mages believe and find it to be true that anywhere they can fully place their mind, they can also place their magic. That means line of sight for most of them, but for some, with some kinds of magic, it means any place they know with total familiarity. Though then their magic often doesn't work if that place has changed since they left, or if they misremember even the slightest detail.~

Fascinating. Also, not terribly helpful. Can you be silent when you land and roll across wood?

~Silent, no. Quiet, yes.~

There's nothing for it but to practice, so I find an empty hallway and throw the ka'kari.

Two minutes later, the ka'kari slaps back into my palm.

I grimace suddenly. *Wait. You didn't write down any of the stuff I was just narrating, did you?*

~Have we not covered this? I can't record things you think when I'm not with you.~

You have a gift for making me sound stupid, you know that?

It doesn't answer. It knows. Thinking it would do that on purpose suggests it has more personality than I know it does, but thinking it doesn't do this on purpose but it just happens suggests I'm stupider than I'd like to admit.

Well, I'm not going to repeat all the stuff I was just apparently *not*-narrating about magic and attack distances and all that. I guess if it's important, I'll repeat it later. Only thing that matters now is that the ka'kari *will* come back, and relatively quietly and relatively invisibly, but at the distances I need to put it out there, it may take an hour to make it back to me.

An hour where I don't merely feel naked, I'll *be* naked. Powerless.

But it's that or kill nine men.

I'm a good throw. Always have been. And the ka'kari can be formed into the perfect throwing shape. But because I can't both hold the ka'kari and throw it, I'll have to throw from this corner—with my body mostly hidden—not to the intersection the soldiers are blocking, but past the spears of the guards in my hall, past the lantern, past the spears of the guards down the next hall, and into the support arm of the lantern at the *next* intersection. If I can clip that arm, the lantern drops, and maybe shatters and spreads oil everywhere, maybe lights a fire. Even if it doesn't, it will still draw some of the soldiers down that hall to check out what happened.

If it works, I get past the guards with them none the wiser. If it doesn't, I have to fight nine men, while naked, and without the ka'kari.

I limber up my arm. It's not a good plan, but also not my worst ever.

I hold for a moment, trying to think of something better. But I'm overwhelmed by the feeling that the days are short, that I'm not the only player making moves, and that if I don't keep forward momentum, I might lose everything. I have to assume that with every passing minute, the ship will only get locked down tighter, and that my enemy will know more and more. I've already taken the enormous gamble of sleeping last night.

I know I'm simply bracing myself for the task. But I need to do this right. I don't like getting hurt. I hate dying. I haven't fought without the ka'kari in... in too long. Maybe I've become too dependent on it. I have to gamble with this. Staying put, or pulling back and checking some other intersection and having to start the examination of weaknesses all over again, those are gambles too, where the ante is hours of my time.

Sometimes the worst plans succeed because of sheer audacity.

I only wish this didn't feel so much like a worst plan.

Screw it. I test the ka'kari's weight in my hand. Shift its displacement a bit, making it a close replica to a stone from zuba I'd played in the street a thousand times as a kid. In the street, we used whatever we could for stones and goals; we always had to adjust to different stones' differing weights. I was little, so I generally had to throw from farther away than anyone. The wagers would cover dues or food for days, so I got good at throwing.

Using my own magic to pull thick, inelegant shadows around my head to hide me from the three guards facing me, I peek around the corner, chart out the ka'kari's path. It'll have to pass within a breath of the ear hole of the middle guard on my side, thread past the spearhead of the left guard on the other side, then begin to break right even as it snips the lantern support arm so that it hits the intersection wall beyond square with its backspin intact, and rolls back toward me, rather than rolling down one of the side halls that will take it out of the reach of my magic.

Doable. Totally doable.

For Durzo Blint.

I swear to myself. I don't have time for a crisis of confidence.

Here we go. Backing into the hallway just around the corner, I heft the ka'kari-zuba stone to my ear, lean around the corner, and hurl it.

Chapter Sixty-One

The Black Wave

~I see you found clothes. And what's that?~

A map. Diagram of the ship.

~Any trouble getting all that without my help?~

I handled it.

~Want to recap for your future audience?~

Ha. No. Not really. Not right now anyway.

~So things went poorly.~

Things went so well that there's nothing for me to tell.

~Hold up a moment. We seem to have lost something in our time apart.~

No, we didn't.

Fine. What? What'd we lose?

~Your pledge of honesty.~

Caught up short, I sigh.

What's it matter? No one's going to read this. My honesty or lies don't matter. My attempts at any morality in this are feeble and pointless and doomed. I daintily strain gnats from wine, then guzzle blood. We're not getting off this ship. This isn't a job that's impossible for others. It's an impossible job, full stop. I can't do it. And this time there's no Durzo Blint to come bail me out at the last moment.

Truth is, I could barely get clothes and a map without you. After all my training, after a lifetime of work, it's still not me who's exceptional; it's you. The only reason I'm special is because I've got you. Which means I'm not special at all. If someone snatches you from me and hurls you into the sea, I'm lost.

The ka'kari says nothing. Not in its instructions how to deal with its holder having a breakdown, I suppose.

People treat their dogs or horses as if they're human. They talk to them all the time. Hell, people treat their sword or spear the same way. Who hasn't seen a man kick a 'stupid' bucket as if the bucket had moved itself to trip him? So I suppose it shouldn't surprise me that I keep slipping into thinking of the ka'kari as a person.

But I do. I keep slipping.

My isolation may have something to do with that, sure. No one else to talk to, and I'm pouring out my whole story here. It's natural.

There's probably some danger in it, though, some point where I'll expect something of my new *friend*, and it will react instead as the tool it is. A superlative tool, to be sure, but a tool only.

Durzo would think of all this as weakness. He'd think I wasn't strong enough for the loneliness of this life—the crippling loneliness he warned me against from the very first. He told me.

Yet I swore I could do this.

Now here I am. I'm glad he can't see me. How could I not be a disappointment to him? I'm a disappointment to myself.

Hey, do you have as much personality as a dog?

~No.~

Uh…does that mean you have more, or less?

~Different.~

That was really helpful. Thanks.

I pull out the map I stole. Procuring it wasn't, sad to say, the fruit of some brilliant act of derring-do. These maps are posted in the halls so that lost nobles don't get more lost.

That means this map doesn't show service corridors, servants' quarters, or meaningful differentiations in places like the crew areas. Those would be handy. But that's not what I've got. This map gives me only the broad outlines of where I need to head, and possibly not even to scale.

Which means this map tells me only a little more than I already know. Surprise, surprise, I'll need to head forward and up. The royal suites encompass the entire top two decks, conceding only a bit of those decks to the bridge.

My job is the same as it ever was, but now I'll have to handle it differently. Rescuing Logan's son won't be enough; I need to have an exit strategy. At every moment, I can hear and feel the raging storm outside the ship's hull. Even this deep in the ship's guts, its rumbles and whines and the irregular shuddering of the floors and walls are a constant reminder of the noisy, watery death held at bay with creaky, flimsy wood and, one hopes, powerful magic.

There's no way I can hop out into the tempest and row myself to shore. I can swim, but even if I were a champion swimmer, it wouldn't matter. I have to get to shore *with an infant*.

Which means I need to work my way forward undetected. Then I need to scout my targets and come up with a plan. There are ways to fail here even in succeeding.

If I take the child too early, I could be trapped for a week, fighting every defender, alone, with a child in my arms. An infant is not a creature of stealth. They cry when they're cold. They cry when they're hungry. They cry when they're bored. They cry when they're wet. Or dirty. Or hot. Or for no reason at all. A baby is the space between a mouth and an anus, with no responsibility for either.

So unless there are any stops on the way—and scouring my memory, I can't recall having heard of any—I'll have to snatch him as close as possible to the moment we leave the track of the storm and enter Borami Bay. Then what? Steal a boat and row like hell?

I can probably row faster than anyone they've got, given my Talent. But that alone isn't going to be enough—they've got mages. I have to bet they'll be faster than I am. So I'll need to steal a boat secretly and escape without being noticed. Then I'll need to land somewhere, find help, and flee across the entire Alitaeran empire, with all the might of that empire hunting me. While I carry a baby.

This is insanity, a little voice in my head says.

I look at my terrible map. The child will be held somewhere close to King Repha'im. That means I need to make it to the grand stairs, which will take me up through successive layers of luxury almost to the top decks. Then I'll have to make my way forward to the private royal stairs or to the bridge access— each doubtless heavily guarded.

Those approaches have *Death Trap* written all over them.

I find the boring, undifferentiated block on my map: *Crew Quarters*. In front of that is *Staff Quarters*. I assume this means all the passengers' servants.

I still don't know much about ships, but I know a lot about egos, and if this is like everywhere else in the world, there's going to be someone who's very important on land—a chamberlain or secretary or some equivalent—who thinks he or she should also be very important at sea. Then there'll be someone on the crew who disagrees, because this is her turf.

The Alitaerans have had many years to figure this out, so maybe things work smoothly and everyone accepts who's in charge of what and when and where. But like trees leveled by a forest fire, pride is remarkably hardy and, as long as there's the least bit of soil for it, bounces back faster than you'd believe.

Staff Quarters it is. I'm looking for a big room in the block on my map, but nearest to the nobles. Important person who doesn't make this ship her home? She'll have the kind of map I need, if not for her own use, then to direct her underlings.

In minutes, invisibly, I come to a low-ceilinged, large room with dozens of tables and scores of chairs. Mess hall.

And a mess is exactly what it is. From the cups and plates left piled on tables, there must be kitchen slaves to clean it all up. Wait, not kitchen slaves. On a ship the kitchen is the galley. Galley slaves?

That can't be right. That's a ship thing, too, but it means something totally different.

I hate ships. But that's like the tenth time I've said that, isn't it? If you ever have someone write down everything you say, you'll be surprised by how many times you repeat yourself. Anyway, sorry to bore you.

~No problem.~

I wasn't apologizing to you.

~I know. I meant that it's not a problem for me to scrub all the previous references.~

Oh, you can? Thank you . . . I think.

Not sure how I feel about having my text scrubbed, but it's not like I have a whole lot of other options when it comes to scribes, and I have other things to worry about.

Not least among them, the nineteen men and women in the mess, seated in six different clumps—all on the far side of the room or I wouldn't have been wasting time wondering what to call the galley's, um, forced servants. I chart a path through the maze of pulled-out chairs and gesticulating sailors, most of them seated, though others are standing around or walking from group to group, making themselves roving hazards.

No obvious mages, but even if any are here, they shouldn't be a problem. Mages looking in the magical spectrum is like squinting your eyes as hard as you can: You *might* do it at any moment, but how many times a day do most people squint really hard?

As I move, again the joy of it steals over me. There are illicit and even tawdry pleasures enabled by my talents, but this isn't one of those. When I moved for the first time through a crowd invisibly, I was shocked by how social human movement is, how much of our animal minds are attuned to the other human animals around us.

Your own nose is constantly in the line of your vision, and yet without telling your mind to do so, you screen it out. Ever visible, it becomes invisible. So are other humans to us.

Move through a crowd and notice how each stranger you pass makes way, or adjusts to your unseen brushing past without complaint, usually without conscious notice. Now brush past the same person in the same way in an empty room. Very different response.

The human beast is social from soul to skin. Even amid the jostling of a crowd, it is attuned to touch. One out of place jangles, like a discordant voice in a choir. Moving through a crowd invisibly ought to be easy, but the animal part of us reacts viscerally; the unexpected touch may be the predator's touch.

Humans make allowances even for the stranger. But I stand outside even that.

So this is the joy edged in obsidian-leaf pain finer than any steel blade. For one heartbeat, I ache; in the next, when I step up onto the table itself, all my awareness will sink fully into my body. Conscious thought will cease in the stream of sensate, directed reactivity.

It is a game, though a deadly one. A contest where the first loss condition is that my opponents become aware we're playing at all.

My happy arrogance is tempered by the stakes and by the knowledge that I'm cheating at every moment by having the ka'kari covering my skin—and yet the joy remains, abundant, bubbling, bountiful.

Joy, as I step lightly over a woman's spoon rising to her lips, as another man's hand sweeps forward toward his cup and I have to step quickly over it.

Joy, as a man leans suddenly forward, intent on some point of gossip, throwing me off-balance as I bend my knees, arching my back, looking down over my shoulder to see if he'll straighten up before I topple over. Looks...like...not!

Wait for...Now!

I launch myself into a backflip just as he bobs his head with an exclamation. I land on the ground behind him. He doesn't break his stream of words, so he didn't notice the air I displaced as my feet cut the quick arc of my flip.

Magic could silence my landing, if I weren't such a poor hand at dampening sound. But they don't hear.

It takes another moment for me to regain my balance as I duck beneath the sweeping arm of a man bringing a bowl of broth to the table, and then I dart back as he throws a leg over one of the bolted-down benches to sit beside his friends.

The sharper edge of my joy scrapes me again as I make it past that knot of comrades—soldiers and staff affably giving each other hell, inside jokes bantered, rueful grins and guffaws—I'm victorious over them, and alone.

Then I see two familiar men coming toward me, their arms laden with food. It takes me only a moment to place them: They're the brothers from the hallway who almost stepped on me, Mat and something. At the same moment, they both catch sight of an attractive young engineer who's just sat down by herself, looking uncertain. They pause, cocking their heads at exactly the same time, same angle, as if they're twins, not merely brothers, and as they look at each other, a lifelong scroll of happy fraternal rivalry unfurls in an instant and demands a new chapter. And as they go sit on either side of the young engineer who smiles up at them, shyly, gratefully—from out of nowhere, my joy is unexpectedly tainted as if a bucket of blood plopped into the clean, clear water of my bath.

It's *rage.*

My focus blown, I stumble to a wall. Lean against it, trembling.

What is *that* about? What's wrong with me?

It takes me three deep breaths, and when the answer comes, I want the earth to open and cover me. It's brotherhood. It's belonging. It's seeing all the things that are denied me. Some black, ugly part of me envies that the brothers have all that.

Some even blacker, even uglier part of me resents it. Sneers that they have all that only because I didn't kill them in that hallway—and I could've.

Some gross part of me wants them to be thankful to me that I didn't murder them.

Some worse part wishes I had.

Maybe that part is the real me. Maybe, at my core, that's who I really am. Everything else pretense, fooling myself, trying to fool everyone else.

I take a breath and push all that down. I can't lose it like this. I'm better than this. Cry alone at night in bed, Kylar. Be a whiny little female dog when it won't get you—and them—killed.

You edited out 'female dog'?

~*Too much?*~

Three more knots of sailors, but I'll only have to go through one of those. I can already see down the long hallway ahead. The hall announces itself as being part of the nobles' areas by its gleaming red hardwood and the steady light that comes from magical lanterns rather than mundane ones.

I'm weighing my paths. The perimeter of the room has too many people leaning against the walls. The knot in the middle only has four men, but that one is jumpy, a wild gesticulator. The man here looks drunk but sedate, and those two women, despite the space between them, are giving each a glance that might mean they're about to hold hands, blocking my path—and that's when I feel something's wrong.

I rush through my scan for threats, first moving quickly to one side in case what my senses registered was a ranged weapon attack, then cycling through near, middle, and far, sides and behind me, then in front, then above and even below.

In the hallway ahead, a third magical lantern winks out before I focus in on what bothered me.

Then a fourth lantern goes dark, closer but still some hundred paces down the hall. A fifth, sixth, seventh—a wave of blackness is rolling down the hallway toward me.

I have the sense that the darkness is more than some magical lanterns losing connection to their power source. It feels *immense*, and it's rushing toward me in a wave, gaining speed.

I gather my feet under me to leap—I don't know where—but the black wave breaks over me.

I staggered, limbs robbed of Talent-strength. The darkness poured through the open door as if it were a tide, weightless and invisible to the naked eye, but swirling around tables, thrown briefly into eddies before filling the room entirely and then pressing on.

Though the un-Talented in the room couldn't have seen it, everyone was instantly aware something big had happened. I was as baffled by its nature as they were. I saw them looking to each other, looking around like people certain that at the edge of their hearing, some terrible alarm had sounded. In their slack faces and sudden silence, I saw they knew something was terribly wrong.

But of everyone in the room, I was the only one who felt as if I'd been hung up and flayed, a forest of stripped nerves exposed to the cruel elements as the ka'kari was torn roughly from my skin.

I heard a plate clatter on the wood floor. I turned to see the sailor gawping nearby. Still gasping in pain, it was only a moment after I met his eyes that I realized the obvious: His eyes *met* mine.

I was visible. The ka'kari was draped over me in a loose second skin, but it wasn't hearing me, wasn't responding magically or otherwise.

I reached out for it.

~Here!~

We fit together smoothly, a bloodied hand sliding into a worn gauntlet. But even as the ka'kari races to hug my skin once more, a sudden change in the air paralyzes me. The low, constant hum of the great engines propelling the storm ship suddenly drops in pitch, and then stops altogether.

It's like standing on a wagon as someone throws the brake. Without whatever it was the engines did to push the great ship forward, splitting the seas, without propulsion, the seas themselves become a brake.

I have only a moment to curse the Chantry's witches for whatever the hell they'd done to cause this, then I and everyone else in the ship's mess, and surely the entire ship, went flying forward as the great ship noses down into the ocean waves and, shuddering, stops.

The storm ship loses all its momentum in an instant. The rest of us don't.

I only have time to flip onto my back as the protruding edge of one bolted-down table slashes at my legs.

Half-flying, half-skidding, I skim over the tabletop. I barely have the wherewithal to push off to avoid the limbs of those who'd been seated and now were getting tangled with everyone else between the bolted-down table and bolted-down benches and stools.

I crash into some unfortunates who'd tumbled onto the floor before me, and I'm up before they can react. I'm invisible once more by the time I get to my feet, and mere steps from the forward hallway.

Amid cries and groans and odd shudderings and judderings that might be some of the smaller masts tearing away above us, I make it into the hall. An alarm bell begins clanging, and then another, and another, each crying their distress in a growing chorus.

My plan is a shambles. I've been seen. The other alarms will slow any response to what these sailors report, but that doesn't stop the inevitable, only delays it.

The hypothetical chamberlain I was looking to rob will certainly not be in her room now, and that halves my chances of getting her map. If she's carrying it, now it'll be unreachable. She'll be wherever the chaos and concentration of soldiers and mages and staff is greatest.

After a terrifying magical attack like whatever it is we've just experienced, every mage on the ship will be checking their magical sight constantly, shaving my odds of staying unseen down to a tiny fraction of what they were before.

But whatever else I need to do, I know this much: The sailors behind me will soon add my own unique alarm to the cacophony. I need to move, fast.

So I move.

Chapter Sixty-Two

An Unavoidable Spill

I sprint down a hall that dodges left or right every so often, switching decors, breaking up the visual monotony of what is essentially one long hall the entire length of the ship. Soon, though, I have to slow as staff pour into the hall, pounding this way and that to take their emergency stations.

Having so recently lost contact with the ka'kari, it's harder than it ought to be to summon the willpower to drop my invisibility. My throat convulses at the thought that I might not get it back, but I'll move faster and avoid causing panic when I inevitably jostle people if they can see me.

But I can't simply drop the invisibility in the middle of the hall. People tend to notice when a person emerges suddenly from empty air. I haven't practiced in front of a looking glass to even know how it looks when I emerge, and regardless, there are too many people in the halls for me to be able to guess when I might do it with no one looking.

So I grab door handles as I pass, testing each. Finally I find a room that's not locked. I duck inside, and drop my invisibility—

Right in front of a dozen nobles' guards passing out weapons from a closet in an officers' mess.

They've all seen me by the time I notice them. Mouths agape or foreheads lined with disbelief, we're frozen together in a surreal tableau. They have numbers. I have me. I know what they can do, but they have no idea what the recently invisible guy can do. And being nobles' guards rather than simple soldiers, maybe they're smart enough to understand how dangerous that might make me. Every last person in the room knows that any move will precipitate violence.

"Oww!" a guy yelps as the short guy in the back passing out the weapons drops a warhammer on his boot.

Fine, not every last person.

"What'd you do that for?" he demands.

"Whaddaya mean? Why don'tcha take it! Whatchu all doing?" a guy blocked from view in the corner yells.

The soldiers staring at me glance back. Apparently the yeller is their officer. Crap.

What did Phaena say, something about how I need to learn that not every problem calls for violence?

~A knife in the neck, if you want to be—~

"We don't have to do this," I say reasonably. "How about—?"

They attack.

I tear into them with gusto. *I hope you'll forgive that here, I've come back to expand on some things. This fight, which I'd thought a mere distraction, turned out to have more significance than I'd thought, so I'm adding whatever other details I remember, to see if I can figure out why things happened the way they did.*

When facing long odds, ferocity is required. *Durzo taught me that men fight differently when confident than when terrified—they fight better. One must strip confidence away from them immediately.*

But as the first men go spinning down before my hands, I feel more than a professional's determination. *I didn't wrench this arm; I snapped it. I didn't throw this man to slide across the floor; I took a split second longer to throw him so that he slapped against the wall, breaking ribs. I thought it normal ferocity for effect.*

It's more. *I was angry. No, beyond that. Furious.*

They attack with a shallow stupidity, barely spreading out to make things more difficult for me, not trying to coordinate their attacks.

I understand that there are different types of people in the world. I understand that some men care nothing for their work, and feel they've won if, for their day's labors, they give the least effort possible for the most reward. Perhaps if I were an abused servant or a slave of any type, I'd do the same and attempt to return some bit of my pain to my master.

But how can one invest so little effort in one's work when one's trade is violence? Who are you cheating when you cheat at the drills that will keep you alive? How can you be lazy when laziness today can easily mean death tomorrow? The margins in this work are so thin that the difference between parrying a strike one thousand times in practice and ten thousand times is only the tiniest difference in attitude, but on the field that extra practice can easily result in the difference between a lifetime without a scratch or a lifetime as a cripple.

I'm barely in my early twenties. I haven't yet matured into my full adult strength and speed. Yet I've done more purposeful work than any man twice my age here. Maybe ten times as much.

And it shows.

In a purely physical fight, one man should never hope to prevail against eight, much less twelve. And yet in an instant, I have more than a hope I'll prevail, I'm certain of it.

The first six are unarmed. The next two give me blades with which I can parry and block the blows of those who've gained their weapons already, as my feet and fists carefully demolish the others, leaving some broken, but none dead.

Even in my rage, I was careful—I swear I was. So here I'm reading my words again and again, wondering if they read true or if I wanted what happened next.

Had I grown so tired of my moral fetters that I cheated to free myself of them?

Was it fate?

Or was it nothing more than that I gambled too many times?

Then it happens. A heel block and a hard shove sends Nameless Guard Number Twelve careening back toward his friends, arms windmilling to regain his doomed balance. You can't incapacitate as many people as possible as quickly as possible and not have it happen eventually, I suppose.

Instead of catching him and taking themselves out of the fight for a few more heartbeats, his friends dodge his off-balance body, moving forward as he falls back, jostling past him, pushing him at an angle from where I'd directed him.

Yes, this is true! I pushed him to land between *the tables. I couldn't have foreseen...*

Couldn't have foreseen it? Of course I could have foreseen it.

His helmet, improperly secured, falls over his forehead at the whiplash from my shove, leaving his neck bare as he falls.

The base of his skull lands solidly on the chunky claw foot of a table.

His body goes slack, boneless as a rag poppet.

He could be merely unconscious, but I know he's not.

The fight didn't pause to honor the enormity of the moment. No one else even seemed to realize I'd just killed an innocent man.

I wish the world worked that way—handing us notes to tell us something momentous has happened, giving us two breaths to consider if damnation is really the course we wish to follow.

Those breaths would be more valuable to these guards than to me.

I've been fighting so carefully. First, I don't ever want to kill anyone innocent. But there's innocence and innocence, and fighting the imperials, I have a practical reason to avoid bloodshed, a solitary thread of hope: If I don't kill any of her men, maybe, maybe, I could earn the empress's forgiveness and bring disgrace to Repha'im, rather than bringing war to the realms.

That hope is now as dead as Nameless Guard Number Twelve.

And I feel a strange emotion surging up in me. *This was what I'd done everything in my power to avoid. You'd think I'd be dismayed.*

What would Durzo think of me in this moment?

Because do you know what I felt surging up in me as I imagined that man's soul leaping from his body?

Not remorse, nor sorrow, nor regret, nor any emotion humane or admirable or human. I felt exultation. *The exultation of freedom.*

Now, now I can *fight*.

Chapter Sixty-Three

Hierarchies of Loyalty

I should've been there with you," Viridiana told the book. It was all too late. Too late for anything she did now to matter. She couldn't read more right now.

"I need your help," Viridiana said, louder. "You're smarter than me. I need you to help me figure something out." Only as she finished did she look over at Sister Ariel.

Sister Ariel hadn't looked up from where she was apparently copying a quote from one scroll to her notes. "Uh-huh."

"I think I've figured out my problem," Viridiana said.

"Just the one?" Sister Ariel asked, mouth twitching a smile as she finished her sentence and finally looked up.

"Loyalty," Vi said. "Or loyalties, I guess. I spent my time on the storm ship crashing from one to another, ruining everything. You're smarter than me, and you said something about your highest loyalty, a while back. How do you decide what that is? How do you pick between loyalties?"

"Someday, Viridiana, we need to talk about this smart thing. I have issues with your conception of intelligence. But not today." Sister Ariel stretched and rubbed her low back. "The way I do it is, I suppose, the logical way. It's not the only way, but it works for me." Sister Ariel hesitated, thinking. "Actually, it should work for you, too. It's a flexible rubric that can accept varying inputs, even emotion- or tradition-derived ones. Yes." She stopped speaking and stared into space.

"Uh . . . was that it? I didn't . . ."

"No, no, you were making me revisit my own choices. I was checking if I'd slid into hypocrisy, but I haven't. What you need, Viridiana, is a hierarchy of loyalties. So, for example . . ."

Sister Ariel cleaned the ink from her quill against the side of her inkpot. She set the quill down in its rest. "My loyalty is to the truth above all, which is intermingled with but distinct from my own sacred honor. I mention it first because my understanding of what is true is the one thing that might shift my understanding of what it is to act with honor. Below that, my highest loyalty is to humanity itself. Given my own giftings and my placement in this world, that loyalty is expressed by helping the Chantry live up to what I have seen it be when it is at its best: the ideal Chantry—no, that's not quite it—the Chantry when it's being consistent with its ideals, yes. My loyalty to the Chantry as it *is* follows that, though sometimes my loyalty to my own scholarship of the moment blurs higher or lower depending on how much I believe it to be serving the ideal Chantry. Below those, though I wish they were lower still, are my loyalties to myself and my own comforts in being allowed to pursue the above without interference. Below that are my loyalties to things like my family, my own desires for fame and recognition, my nation and the like: the trivialities."

"You've . . . put a lot of thought into that," Viridiana said carefully. She wasn't sure how much of it she'd followed. Or how helpful it was for her.

"Doesn't everyone? Issues of ultimate moment deserve ultimate attention. I've found the initial investment richly repaid. A rubric clarifies and speeds decision making at every intersection."

"Too true, too true . . ." said Vi, nodding along. She could tell that Sister Ariel was using some of those words in ways she'd never heard before. Sometimes it wasn't the words Vi didn't know that tripped her up when she talked with Sister Ariel. It was the words that she knew being used in ways she definitely didn't— ultimate moment?—those halted her mind's progress like a low-axled oxcart getting high-centered in deep ruts. With a few tries, she could guess what a rubric was—nothing to do with rue, nothing to do with bricks—something like a sieve to sort decisions, maybe?

In a vague and unformed way, Vi had an intuition that Sister Ariel had just handed Vi the key to manipulating her. All Vi had to do was figure out how to package whatever she needed from the older Sister as aligning with Sister Ariel's own loyalties, and Vi could get anything she wanted from her.

But Vi couldn't do that on the fly. Or maybe at all. She wasn't clever enough.

And she wasn't sure how the hell she was supposed to build her own rubric.

"So if I ask you if I can trust you, what are you gonna say?" Vi asked.

"You already asked that. Hours ago."

"Oh, right. But I didn't... Can you repeat your answer for me, in different words maybe?" And Sister Ariel wondered why Vi felt stupid around her.

Sister Ariel interlaced her fingers, seemed concerned that Vi wasn't following her. "You can trust me to act in accord with the principles I've elucidated. Ergo, if you ask me to keep a secret and it turns out that secret will harm the Chantry, in almost all cases, I will reveal your secret to the proper authorities. Because of my own affections for you, I will do that with as much sensitivity as I can, but I will do it. Now, I'm generally wise enough to avoid giving my word in situations that would force me to become a liar, which I find reprehensible, which is why I told you 'No, I won't keep your secret' before you told me any such thing. But if it came to it, I'd do what I have to in order to abide by my own values, painful as that might be. Thinking through your values beforehand doesn't make choices easy; it merely makes them simple. You understand?"

"What I understand is that the people who are most likely to lie to you are the people who assure you of their honesty. I understand that the people who will be the first to betray you are the ones who swear they never will. So, I think you're either trustworthy or so clever I don't stand a chance."

"I never asked you to trust me," Sister Ariel said. "Quite the contrary; if you were paying attention, I think you'll notice I've all but counseled you not to."

"I want to be loyal to the Chantry, too," Vi said. "The Sisterhood isn't quite what I hoped, but... I don't think I could make it out there alone, like Kylar was doing. I think I have to choose loyalty. I've got nothing left, right? I dunno, does declaring loyalty count when you don't have any other option?"

"Oh, child. Did you learn nothing on that ship? When you lift yourself from the forge fires, glowing hot like hammered iron, the one thing you can know is that a plunge into cold water is coming, and it will either shatter your steel or temper it to new strength."

Chapter Sixty-Four

Developing Subtlety

Visible, I step out of the officers' mess, quickly closing the door on the moaning, injured men inside. I won't have long until one recovers enough to summon help. I've abandoned my shackles of fighting explicitly not to maim or kill, but I'm not willing to murder a dozen incapacitated men. I'm not that inhuman.

Not yet.

Standing in the hall waiting to join the press of people going to and fro, part of me thinks, *Right, but how much of that is because it would take too long?*

I reach down to adjust a boot and drop a piece of metal; it's the head of a war hammer trimmed by the ka'kari down to a triangular doorstop. I slap it under the door. Standing, I kick it hard with a heel to wedge it home.

Wearing the clothes I've stolen, blending into the crowd now should be easy. No one knows my face here. The staff is temporary and drawn from all over the empire, so strangers are the norm. So there should be no problem—but there is a problem. I feel air through my sleeves, over one thigh. Gods know where else I have holes. Maybe I don't want to know.

You devoured holes in my clothes?

~Needed to renew magic I spent trying to reestablish our bond.~

Its answer is brief, as it tries to keep things during emergencies. So for the moment I simply walk with my arms crossed to cover several holes, eyes fixed forward, trying not to draw attention to myself.

Peeved, I say, *So you devoured my clothes.* Again. *And now I need new clothes. Again.*

~Would you prefer I take magic directly from your glore vyrden?~

I hadn't thought of that. In other words, in an emergency, would I rather find some part of my clothes missing, or my reservoir of magic empty at a moment I might need to tap it?

I try another way. *Can you, I dunno, not refill your magic right away, and maybe ask me later how I'd like you to do it?*

~Yes. But there are caveats——~

Do that next time, okay?

~Your access to that circle of my operating directives won't be unlocked for another 2,904 days.~

That's odd. The ka'kari's voice seems to have a more mechanical tone than I'm accustomed to. Maybe this is its original tone. Maybe this is the response its creator designed, ordering it exactly what to say to users under certain conditions?

It's not really the time to think about this, but I can't help myself. I'm always doing this. Always thinking about the wrong things.

~Roughly eight years from now, if you prefer.~ Now its voice is in the conversational tone I know well.

I want to ask more, but I really need to not be doing that right now.

I just left a room with all those soldiers. I could've stolen clothes from them, if I'd known I needed to. But now I need the laundry, yet as soon as I think that, I remember that on my map, the laundry area is in the opposite direction. I'm not doubling back. I pass another set of double doors, then stop.

Barracks. Second-best place to find lots of clothes. A distant second best, however, given what else one tends to find in barracks.

Through the crack, I see one man standing inside. There are a lot of people out here, passing constantly. I'll have to go invisible at the exact moment no one happens to be looking my way. It's gonna be tight—but as soon as I push the door open, the man or men inside are immediately going to look to see who's coming in. I'll have to be invisible first, and swing the door open, step inside, and hope that they'll think some passing person bumped it open accidentally.

It's doable, but risky. And how am I going to open people's trunks while one or more sailors are still inside the room?

'You're more than your greatest strength, you know,' Grandmaster Vitruvius said to me once, and the words suddenly echo in my head.

Is there some way I can do this without relying on the ka'kari?

Maybe not. One way to find out. Probably shouldn't do this off the cuff, but I've got an idea.

I bang open the door before I can think to stop myself.

It isn't one man inside, but two, standing, alert but not alarmed by my intrusion.

"Hey," I say quickly, "can you direct me to Hassen's bunk?" I mumble my way through the name.

"Whose?" the nearer one asks. He's a tall man with a birthmark up his neck.

"Hassen? Hanson maybe?" I say, hoping I picked a common enough name. "Honestly, everyone was yelling. Hampton?"

"You mean Bronmer Haslin? Little guy, dark skin?"

You can't answer these questions directly. Too many specifics means if it's a trap, you're truly buggered if you answer wrong. "Look," I say, "I didn't see him. Someone yelled it down the line. Hell, maybe that *was* it. Dunno. *Everyone* was yelling. You know, the big emergency. Can you hurry up?"

The big one points to a trunk nearby, which I tear open and start searching. To burn time so I don't have to make up more lies, I say, "What are you two doing in here when all that's going on out there?"

"What happened to Haslin?" the other one asks even as the first says, "This is our station. Supposed to stay here in case—"

A new clanging goes off.

They both stop, look at each other, their faces falling.

"In case of *that*," the tall one says. "Come on, Gehm."

"Hey, wait!" I say. It turns out Bronmer Haslin isn't little, he's *tiny*. I can't possibly fit into any of his clothes. "I don't want to take anyone's stuff without permission—but, look, does Haslin have any friends who wouldn't mind if I take a spare tunic? They said he was bleedin' bad. And, uh, I don't think I'll be giving it back."

The regular one purses his lips. He curses and gestures to a chest nearby. "That one's mine. Take anything in there you need."

"And what's your name?" I ask.

"Why?" he demands suspiciously. "Look, we gotta go!"

"If someone comes in while I'm going through your stuff, they're gonna think I'm stealing."

"Gillson Jass, second galley."

I bob my chin at him and go toward his bunk. The two of them are gone before I throw his chest open.

~Be a real pity if someone thought you were stealing his stuff.~

I'll take that to mean Congratulations! Well done, Kylar. You have skills I didn't even guess at, Kylar. Truly a wonder you are, Kylar.

Somehow I can hear the ka'kari laughing. Not precisely *with* me, either.

I peel off my clothes and am dressed in short order as Sgt. Gillson Jass, either of the second galley, or the second sergeant of the galley. Hell if I know which, or what it entitles me to, but I doubt it's going to get me all the way to the king. It might get me up a couple floors, though.

Maybe I'm better at this than I thought. Maybe impossible isn't quite impossible, for me.

I take a few breaths, plotting out my next steps. Then I recall something. *Hey, I wanted to write down my immediate impressions. I better do that now.*

~Writing down what happened when we were separated, you mean?~

Exactly. The black wave thing. I'll want to go over that later. Best put down what I remember now before it gets any murkier.

So we take a minute to do that as I let my racing heart slow, and I realize I didn't come out too badly in a pretty dire situation. In fact, all things considered, things are going pretty well.

With a smile on my face, I exit the barracks into the hallway on the opposite side from where I entered—

Just in time to hear someone mere paces away scream, "Intruder!"

Dozens of soldiers are running my way, pushing people aside, bowling people over. I freeze, my smile stuck—and they run right past, one snarling, "Out of the way!"

A woman in the hall picks up the hat the shoving soldiers knocked off her head. She looks at me, then after the men who pushed her, and compares them to the end of an equine alimentary canal.

"Most of them are," I say. "Not all of them."

"No. Some are even worse," she says. She smiles at me. "Where you headed?"

She's cute in a spunky kind of way. I smile back.

Chapter Sixty-Five

A Soldier's Attention

*S*o I got caught up in things a bit and forgot to narrate for a few hazy, sunsplashed minutes there. Durzo didn't really teach me seduction as part of my portfolio of skills, and in my youthful idealism I resisted learning it all the times Momma K brought it up, thinking it would entail me somehow being unfaithful to the girl and then woman I was infatuated with. And then—

Long story short, I have no excuse why I didn't learn seduction techniques when I had one of the most skilled seductresses in the world willing to teach me, and now I'm trapped because it'd be too embarrassing to reveal to Momma K the depths of my seductionary incompetence.

~I don't believe that's a word.~

Well, it's a little hard to think right now, okay?

Short story long, all that is why I don't know precisely how I ended up in this alcove, kissing a woman with the most wonderful lips in the world. Her lips, not mine. I'm not kissing her with the most wonderful lips in the world—you, you get it.

Now, I'm not stupid. It's not like I don't realize that if a beautiful woman suddenly wants to get me alone, she may be setting me up. I mean, that's the oldest trick in the book. I'm not dumb enough to fall for—

~Isn't that how you met Vi?~

Sorry, spaced out there a bit. Arguing with you seemed like the worst of all the things I could pay attention to.

Oh my. The breath in the ear. That does things to me. Wow has it been a while.

She's doing this thing with her hands, clawing gently at my back and sides as she kisses me and undulates her body into mine.

If I want not to go to her room as I told her firmly a few minutes ago...

Why did I not want to go to her...?

Oh, yeah, it's aft. That's the wrong direction. And, yeah, there *is* the whole possibility of ambush and murder thing, that's right. Her room is a bad idea. Terrible idea.

Terribly appealing.

Horrid. Bad. Unlike her...

What was I saying? Oh right, if I don't—I kiss below her ear to give myself a moment to recover my wits—if I don't want to go to her room, I appear to be making a series of decisions not particularly well aligned with that goal. She stretches her neck for more—this is idiotic, I don't even know her *name*—she moans low in her throat and moves her hips in a little circle against my leg, which she's trapped between her legs.

It's an odd thing about being a man, how bringing pleasure to a woman is somehow even better than her bringing pleasure to you.

~I'm not sure that's even close to a universally held sentiment.~

I mean slightly better.

~You should ask Momma K how many men are like that, Kylar.~

Oh, come on, that's Momma K. A professional like her is gonna run into a different kind of man. But you know what I mean. I mean—I suppose maybe you don't, actually, huh? You're metal and magic, not flesh and bone.

I do a gently teasing thing that used to absolutely melt Elene, but I'm suddenly feeling deeply uncomfortable about having a conversation that—even though it's in my own head—is more like the bragging about conquests I used to hear on the streets. Even overhearing those kinds of conversations doesn't exactly leave you feeling like an upstanding human. Saying that stuff myself?

I really ought to not have physical contact with the ka'kari while I'm—

I start to remove it from my body and send it onto the platinum bracelet so I won't have the hanger-on eavesdropping on my thoughts.

~I was trying to get you to *think*, you microcephalic monkey.~

Meanwhile, I've distractedly continued to kiss and tease, noticing this comely stranger's deepening breath, the flush at her throat. Instead of turning to a puddle at my teasing touches, she turns fierce instead, suddenly grabbing at me through my trousers and hissing in my ear, "You are coming to my room. Now!"

"I, uh..." I want to. And what's the harm?

~You mean what's the harm if she doesn't kill you?~

Right. Obviously.

Sure, it's the wrong direction, but maybe going with her will give time for the alarms and whatnot to cool down out here. Already I can hear that the sounds of the engine have picked back up. The storm ship is once again plowing through the sea's heavy waves. Whatever repairs might have been required after that black wave seem not to be serious—but the news of my presence is surely spreading panic, or already has. Maybe I could use some time away to make up a new strategy about how to get to the front of the ship.

You know, afterward.

Or maybe she could help me get to the front of the ship, you know, if I gave her sufficient incentive to *want* to help me.

It'd be good practice for all those seduction lessons I missed out on.

"You're coming to my room or I will pull your trousers down right here where anyone in the hall might see. And I do not want to give Baradrick an excuse to get me defrocked."

That sounds important, but I'm already thinking something else.

Practice.

I can't even blame this on the ka'kari, though maybe I can blame it on Durzo, who apparently formed so much of the ka'kari's synthetic personality.

'Do you know what you need for practice?' Durzo once said. 'An environment where repeated attempts can be made and failure is clear but not catastrophic.'

Messing up a seduction when you're a fugitive—*and* a fugitive being actively hunted—*and* being actively hunted in the confines of a ship—*and* a ship that must remain at sea for a week where you have no way of escape . . . ?

"I can't," I say mournfully. The more I think about it, the more I realize this is literally true, at least if I want to stay alive.

Her eyes light defiantly, and she tugs on me down below, taking my breath. "This says you can."

"I need to get to the bow. I have duties. I really need to go. I'm sorry. Sorry."

Her mouth purses. She has not released her grip on me through my trousers. "What's your name, beautiful?"

Beautiful? Me? "Kylar."

I wince.

She laughs and finally lets me go. "You married, Kylar?"

"Not anymore. Why?"

"You flinched like a man who didn't mean to give his real name. And nothing *at all* like a lowly sergeant. Which tells me you're a noble dressed up in order to get into some mischief. Not that I'm judging. Because you know what? I'm about to be unattached myself, as soon as I can get off this cursed boat. I'm looking to make some mischief myself."

"Baradrick?" I ask.

"You know, there's things I'd rather you do with those sweet lips than say that cheating swine's name. But tell you what, Kylar—say, what's your surname?"

It's only now that I take her in more fully, my brain humming to life more slowly than the ship's engines did. Though casual, her clothing is so exquisitely fitted that she's either a seamstress or a noblewoman, and a seamstress wouldn't have the sheer bad sense to go among the rough men working in the bowels of a ship without any obvious insignia to warn them to treat her well. Only a noble does that. A noble who's going slumming, looking for a likely fellow to bed immediately in the heat of her desire—and not her desire for me, nor for any person particularly. Her desire is for retaliation against her philandering husband.

Her philandering *noble* of a husband.

Ah, fantastic. There's no way this can go wrong.

"Sergeant Gillson Kylar Jass at your service, milady. Second mess officer."

She laughs. "All that work, getting the clothes and everything, and you went for Gillson, instead of Hubert, huh? 'But Hu to my friends.'"

"I don't follow." Hu Kylar Jass? I can tell she's making a joke, but I don't get it and I'm not in the mood.

~From one who's inside your body, it sure seems like you're in the mood to me.~

"I can spot a noble, Kylar, but I don't know you—and I would if you were from Western Alitaeran anywhere—or if you were raised in any of the cities of the east. Maybe a foreigner? No, not gonna budge? Fine, it's on your head. My husband—sorry, my soon-to-be-ex-husband is Lord of the High Marches, Varisova, and Cawloon." She searches my face, which I'm keeping expressionless, though the fire in my blood suddenly cools. I don't know him, but though one title can mean anything, I've noticed that the more grandiose it sounds, the less likely it is to signal real wealth and power.

But three, used casually? That means he's the real thing.

"You don't know of him," she says. "Good. Either a foreigner or someone from the far reaches of the empire, but either way, not someone afraid of him. I'll make you a deal, *Sergeant*."

"A deal?" I ask, as if pretending disinterest, but I look at her lips, glance quickly at her low neckline.

I'm playing the part, I tell myself, the fool who can't suppress his interest. Not that it's an objectionable part to have to play.

"You're stuck back here, aren't you? I'd like to know why, but it doesn't really matter. You help me and I can—"

"I got robbed." I pretend it's an admission, an embarrassing one at that. "My brother owes a great deal of money to a certain lender of low moral character. Someone was supposed to sell me some leverage that we could trade for the debt instead of paying it. Instead, that someone robbed me. Took everything, even my clothes. I think he was going to kill me, but then all ... this emergency happened and I got away. I'd just stolen these clothes when you, well, when you came along."

She smiles devilishly. "That explains one mystery, then."

"What's that?" I ask, wondering if I'd made some terrible mistake in my cover story.

"I wondered why a sergeant was, uh, letting his soldier swing free."

For the second time in a short conversation, I don't understand. Then it dawns on me that she's noticed my lack of underclothes. I know, I know, I'm inconsistently squeamish—but is it so weird that I didn't want to put on another man's used undergarments?

To cover my sudden—and infuriating!—blush, I say, "I might note that for a soldier who wasn't expecting a surprise inspection, he's been standing at attention for quite some time."

She throws back her head and laughs toothily. Puts her hand on my shoulder. I don't think I was that funny, but I'm glad she does. I swallow. I swear I can feel myself getting dumber. Is there anything more intoxicating than a pretty woman's regard?

"So you'll help me?" she says, looking up at me with her big green eyes.

I manage something far less brainless than I feel as I say, "What exactly am I getting myself into?"

Chapter Sixty-Six

The Easy Way

I have no intention of going through with it, so stop it.

~Did I say anything?~

Your silences can be positively thunderous.

The ka'kari is silent. This time on purpose, even if it wasn't before. I can just tell. I'm walking half a step behind Lady Ysmaena Mulkin, soon to be Lady Ysmaena Isicleia again, as soon as she divorces Earl Baradrick Mulkin. I think she's a priestess of some kind, too. She didn't tell me all her titles, though, only her plan.

As I won't go back to her room and sleep with her (I won't? Oh yeah, I won't), she wants us to post ourselves in a little nook outside a little solarium that her husband and his friends frequent. Allegedly, he takes coffees there with his new paramour. As soon as we get word he's about to exit the establishment, we'll begin kissing and groping each other there.

When he sees us, Lady Ysmaena says, I can make myself scarce while she has the blazing row she wants so badly.

Sounds like the kind of thing that doesn't end well for the other man, huh? And that's the job I'm volunteering for—minus the most common benefit of being the other man.

"Can you tell him that we haven't slept together and that I didn't know you were married?" I say.

"Not a problem! First thing!" she says, leading us through a salon where musicians are playing a familiar tune while several day-drunk noblemen play dice and past another checkpoint. She seems really sincere, so I believe her.

~You do?~

No! What do I look like, a fool?

As Ysmaena takes my hand, the guards at the next checkpoint simply melt away.

Which means she's powerful enough that they know her by face. Oh boy.

I mean, I know what this all looks like, but really, I'm not an idiot. This is all part of my cunning plan. I'm not going to stick around to get myself killed. I don't want anyone paying the least bit of attention to me, so before we get to the big confrontation she hopes to have, I'll bail out, turn invisible.

You see, the solarium Ysmaena's husband frequents is one staircase away from the royal apartments at the very front of the ship—and she's walking me through every defense on the way there.

I can leave at any time, and I know it's better to leave too early than too late, but watching these well-nigh impassable checkpoints simply fade by without the least effort on my part is addictive. We've got to be in the front third of the ship already, and there are now not only long-tuniced imperial mages at every checkpoint, but increasingly more of them, and if my guess from their increasing age and the increasing richness of the embroidery at the hems and necklines of their tunics is correct, increasingly senior mages.

Finally, a mage with his hair shaved to his scalp on the left side displaying a jagged bear tattoo stops Lady Ysmaena. My heart stops too. My co-conspirator produces a bracelet with three glowing sapphires from a small bag. It seems the rules for bracelets and chokers are more lax aboard the ship than they were at the castle, but security tightens near the front. At the sight of it, the mage visibly deflates, but he then turns defiantly to me. "And you, where is—"

"This is my friend," Lady Ysmaena says. "My very dear friend." She takes my hand and kisses it in a coy challenge. My guts turn to water.

"Of course, Lady," the mage says, chagrined. He steps back.

As I step past him into a hall that's all blue velvet wall panels and bright woods, he mutters to me, "Hope it's been worth it."

I force a smile, guessing I'm maybe not the first servant he's seen involved with one of the noblewomen on the ship. Hell, maybe I'm not the first he's seen with Lady Ysmaena. She does seem to know all the kissing nooks on the ship, and come to think of it, she does have the attitude of one who cheats prolifically and then is outraged when someone dares to cheat on her.

I'm starting to think I may not be on the righteous side of this confrontation she's seeking.

Come to think of it, what do I really know about her... other than the obvious? Maybe I'm not so lucky after all. Just a moment ago, I was thinking how out of all the aggrieved spouses who got cheated on last night, I happened to run into one who not only took a liking to me but also happens to be able to move me a great distance toward my target.

That's awfully convenient, isn't it?

On the other hand, if she weren't able to help me, I wouldn't have come with her at all, and I did plan to leave her when she tried to take me back to her room farther back in the ship.

So maybe it's not *that* big a coincidence. Maybe I'm better at seduction than I thought. Huh! Me, the seducer, approaching a noblewoman and getting whatever I want from her through the sheer force of my good looks and charm and kissing abilities. Me, waltzing past all these checkpoints, with a near stranger doing my bidding because after being kissed by me, how could she not? Maybe I didn't need lessons from Momma K. Maybe I'm kind of a natural at—

"His men!" she hisses, ducking her head suddenly. "That's my husband's captain!"

I look forward and see two soldiers in conversation with the mages at the next red-velvet-walled checkpoint. They're turned sideways, so I can't tell if they're coming or going or just having a friendly chat.

They haven't seen us yet.

Ysmaena's like a squirrel stuck halfway between two trees that's just seen a cat. "This way!" she says.

She pulls me into a nook before wide double doors leading to an auditorium or ballroom. She tries the doors. Locked. She curses quietly. "If we could only get through here, we could get to the hall on the other side and past them."

She peeks her head out.

I test the doors myself, seeing if extra force will do it. I don't want to break anything, though, so I don't put my Talent into the push.

The doors hold firm.

She's still peeking out. "Maybe they're going forward. Oh no...I think they're..."

I feed the ka'kari into the lock, test the tumblers with a few shakes, making the liquid metal find the appropriate shape. Click.

"They're coming!" she hisses.

"Door! I got it," I say. "Just needed a little force!"

I pull her into the auditorium with me, leading her in the pitch-black darkness.

Striding behind the rows of benches with Ysmaena stumbling fearfully behind me, I'm halfway across the rear of the ballroom when I realize we're not alone. With my darkness-piercing eyes, hidden behind stacked benches and decorative pillars, I can see the curve of a shoulder here, a bit of exposed helm there.

It's an ambush.

Vi threw down her quill. "What. The. Hell!" She pushed her chair away from the table. She threw her hands up, then crossed her arms over her chest and slouched back in her chair.

Across the room, Sister Ariel sighed and set down her own quill. "Yes, child?"

"How can men be so brilliant sometimes, and then—and then—agh!"

"Given the degree of emotion you're showing, I assume *men* is here a synecdoche for Kylar?"

"A what—? Yes, *Kylar*! The big idiot. This is the bit where he met—"

"Tsst!" Sister Ariel said, cutting her off.

All the blood drained from Vi's face. She'd almost said it out loud. Here. Where the walls had ears. And those ears would have a very strong reaction to what she'd almost said.

And she thought *Kylar* was an idiot?

"What?" Viridiana asked for their eavesdroppers' benefit, as if irked. "He met a bunch of soldiers and did a...a stupid, stupid thing. You know, like he does. Totally unnecessarily."

"Indeed?" Sister Ariel said, who seemed to understand perfectly. "You know, sometimes I think precisely what makes Kylar most frightening is his frailties, among them his callowness. Which alone would be harmless, perhaps. Another young man among men. But when paired with his enormous strengths? Terrifying.

"So often he doesn't know that he can't do something that he obviously can't do, so he goes and tries to do it—to disastrous effect much of the time, because he's attempting feats that are so difficult most people know better than to even try them. But conversely, sometimes he tries those things and *succeeds*, much to everyone's vexation. It makes him very hard to predict, and even harder to control. So, I agree, yes, so brilliant and so…*agh*." She said the last with a flat affect, but a grin hid at the corner of her mouth. Then, as if that were a full day's worth of conversation, she picked up her pen and turned back to her papers, muttering, "The same could be said for someone else."

Someone…?

"Oh, shut up," Vi murmured to her notes. But she instantly forgot about Sister Ariel, and she almost forgot her anger at Kylar falling into such an obvious trap, because even though she knew very well what happened next because she'd been there, she didn't know how *Kylar* felt about it.

Her stomach twisted. No, that wasn't quite right. She wasn't curious about how he felt about most of it. What mattered was how Kylar felt about what she'd done at the very end.

Chapter Sixty-Seven

A Dark Performance

"This way," I say, pulling Ysmaena toward a large statue thing in the middle of the room.

"The door's straight across," she says. But she's behind me, and I'm moving faster than she is. If there lived any doubt in my mind that she was leading me into this, that kills it.

My choices have collapsed. I don't know who my ambushers are or what they know about me. All I know is that every moment that passes as I think through the possibilities is a moment the snare tightens.

Durzo once said, 'Possibility is danger: A thousand doors are a thousand murderholes. But the lack of possibilities is death. The blind alley is always a trap. The way of life lies in walking the shadow's edge, the path between danger and death. There is no other.'

The ceiling above me here is relatively low, with the theater holding multiple levels, but out at the middle it opens up three or four stories high. Out there will be more possibilities, more lines of fire, but I'll also have more options. Vertical options.

My vision snaps side to side, scanning, eschewing all the details that don't matter to see what does. I don't see royal green upholstery embroidered with electrum thread, I see cover. The half-hidden enemies I see not as people but by capabilities: spearman, spearman, officer, archer, a mage subtly spinning her hands around a secret ball she's about to call into light and death, confusing cover and concealment in the curtain she's behind.

From their sloppiness, they either don't know or don't take seriously that I can see in the dark.

All this I figure out by the time we're barely five steps into the room. Still my eyes are straining. How many more are there?

Ysmaena pulls hard against me, trying to stop me. She says something, but I'm not hearing her. Her words are details I don't need to know. She's already shown me all I need to know of her part in this. But with Ysmaena pulling against me now, my options regarding her collapse as well: kill, incapacitate, take hostage, or release.

Release? You don't release someone trying to kill you, especially not someone with a knife at her belt.

Beneath her raised voice, I've heard the scrape of wood on iron from the door we entered—a bar being set in place on the doors, trapping us.

From the corner of my eye, I sense a mage rising to call the ambush.

I snap Ysmaena toward me so hard it tears her arm out of its socket, snatch the knife from her belt, and hurl it at the woman standing up, even as the maga cries, "Now!"

The blade is no throwing knife and I misjudge it, but it nails the woman sideways across her face. She staggers backward, trips, and the magical light she'd been gathering to illuminate the room for the ambushers splutters out.

With the room pitch dark, I will the ka'kari to hide me from magical sight as I dive.

At the same time, I do this little pulse of light illusion I've figured out—as I gather my muscles, I stretch the ka'kari out away from me in the opposite direction I intend to leap. Then I pulse the lights first where I am and then farther away from me, one, two, then snap the ka'kari back to me as I leap. If my practice pays off, it looks as if a glowing *something* is jumping in the opposite direction I actually jump.

I hear arrows cutting the air. Ysmaena is screaming in pain. Cries of confusion and orders ring out an instant later. I land behind the mage and off to one side. Her face is bleeding from a shallow cut. She's being helped to her feet by a big bodyguard as two other spearmen slap tall shields together in front of her, both squinting into the darkness far away.

The knife I threw is on the ground beneath her. Too far away.

For an instant, I despair—how can I fight all these people and not kill anyone?

Then I remember. I'm past all that now. A strange glee surges up in me.

You want to fight? Let's fight.

As fast as a count, one, two, three, I seize a short sword from the nearest guard's belt, one, and—without the slightest hesitation, for I fight now unencumbered by ethical hindrances—two, I bury its point in his armpit, and twist it as I remove it, three. I stab forward again, on the fourth beat—but miss the mage's throat by a breath as I step on some unseen piece of clothing on the floor.

Overextended with the missed lunge, I break time, miss a full beat, defenseless, extended—I slap the blade weakly at her neck, and then roll.

Spinning low in case of some unseen attack, I hamstring the nearer spearman, my blade catching the backs of both of his legs though I was only aiming for one.

I'm tempted to attack the last man while he's confused, but speed is the imperative. I dive, roll—for nothing, so far as I can tell as I come up, but damn if you can always guess when dodging will be unnecessary.

An archer has the bad luck to be nearby. He's turning his grossly broad shoulders perpendicular to the sound of the men's dying grunts, arrow lifting, squinting into the darkness, but I rush past, slashing blade through bowstring and into his face. He goes down, disarmed and eyeless if not dead.

My first targets are the mages—but it's not a mage who brings forth the first torch. A plucky young officer decides to retire early by doing the right thing at the right time with the wrong enemy. His chubby, sweating, pale face gleams in the red light of the torch he raises. I sprint, Long Tail, measuring steps to the pivot. His mouth is open, shouting orders, when by some sixth sense at the last moment, he tries to duck.

Instead of hitting the soft tissues of his neck to take off his head, my blade hits him above the eyes, popping the top third of his skull spinning into the air even as it wrenches my stolen sword from my hand.

He drops the torch, his body staggering around obscenely, clinging to life when it should know better.

But now other lights are blooming, up in the circle of the balconies. I spot a mage up there, working at a spotlight that flares into a sharp bar of light cutting the darkness.

I dodge a spear thrust, grabbing the spear in one hand to pull the spearman in and punching him in the neck as I pass, the ka'kari becoming spiked knuckles an instant before contact. A spinning hook kick bats another man's heavy shield, which stops my momentum enough for me to flick a weak roundhouse to the man's face. He flinches backward far enough to avoid my foot but not the ka'kari-blade protruding scythe-like an extra handsbreadth from my sweeping kick. He spins bloodily to the ground.

But before I can move away, two men with shields interlocked charge into me. I'm carried by the force of their rush toward a nearby wall. I'll be crushed. Heads down, shields up, they roar.

With the wall looming, instead of fighting them, I collapse, reach for the bottom of their shields and heave myself down.

They trample past me, one actually stomping on my stomach—and smash into the wall themselves, their shields before them, but without me to absorb the force of their charge.

The ka'kari flicks into my hand as a stiletto and I slam each man three times in the kidneys before hopping away and disappearing from mundane sight.

As I dash along the tops of benches and tables, I take down two more men in passing, slashing cuts from an unseen wind, rapidly changing direction from moment to moment, but moving in, in toward the great statue at the center of the room.

The spotlight stabs down toward me. The speed at which it attempts to follow me tells me that not only is the light magical, but so too is the tracking mechanism, moving nearly as fast as a man can shift his gaze.

Damn the Alitaerans and their limitless gold. The mage using it seems to be able to see me in the magical spectrum, so I shift the ka'kari's powers to shield me from her.

I scramble up the shadowed side of the statue as fast I can, tearing bits and chunks of wood and paint from the gaudy figure of some old emperor before I vault off his head, the spotlight briefly illuminating my arc through the air, until I land a dozen paces from the mage. She panics.

Her lone bodyguard holds, attempting to cover her retreat, even though she's abandoned him.

Why do men with courage have to die for cowards? The mage has a hundred more weapons against me than he does.

He bites on my feint and, binding his spear as he thrusts, I leap past him, tumbling through, avoiding his counter as he aims the butt of his spear at my face, the ka'kari opening his left side from belly to back.

I catch up with the mage as she reaches the stairs down in heedless flight.

The magical spotlight winks out as the mage's body goes crashing wetly down the steps, her head bouncing separately behind and then over her.

In the darkness and sudden quiet, I keep moving—because you never stay put when you don't know what dangers are out there—but I move silently, senses keyed, padding carefully down wet, slick stairs.

Muffled yells sound outside, and I can hear them louder as I get downstairs. Men are banging on the doors ineffectually. Apparently the doors are barred both on the outside *and* the inside.

Someone out there is shouting something about the king and is demanding to be let in.

I can't see anyone still trying to fight me. I come to the spot where I left Ysmaena.

She's gone.

I need to get out of here. And quickly. I head for a door on the opposite side from where I entered.

The soldiers at the door I entered can't get inside, but they have or soon will send others to check the other doors before they start breaking doors down.

It's the beauty of working against old entrenched power structures: Men on the ground usually don't have the authority to use their own judgment. If you have to worry more about how much trouble you'll get into for breaking down a door than you do about how much trouble you'll get into for not getting to a fight on time, you'll not get to the fight on time.

Unfortunately, if I take too long, they're going to have a chance to try all the doors. And if they find that all of them are locked, I have to bet they'll break one down.

Just as I'm reaching my hands to lift the bar away from the door in front of me, soldiers begin pounding on the opposite side. And I hear others pounding on the other doors that go to the same hallway.

I have to guess there might be a dozen men out there, but there may be twice that. A dozen soldiers, in a single, well-lit hallway? How many mages might be among them? This close to the front of the ship . . . ? I don't know. Maybe lots.

I run for the doors at the front of the ballroom.

But before I get halfway there, I hear men yelling outside those as well.

There are soldiers outside every door. They may spend ten minutes out there arguing over what they're allowed to do and coordinating back and forth between the groups at each door. Or they may break down a door at any moment.

No, wait. I haven't checked every door, only every door on this level. This is a ship. Even if the designers wanted most people to enter through the main doors, surely one of the balconies—

With a distant bang, light pours in from a door at the far back of the topmost balcony. Soldiers with torches begin rushing in.

My heart leaps to my throat. Where did Ysmaena go? Would I have noticed a stab of light from the hall lanterns into the darkness of the theater if she'd slipped out? All the doors I checked on this level were still barred from the inside, though.

I rush to the stage area in the darkness as the soldiers above reach the first set of stairs, some of them fanning out to search that level. I scan the backstage area, hoping to see some small side door out to a hallway somewhere, anywhere.

None.

But there is a tiny hatch in the floor, a stage trapdoor. It's closed, but the handle ring is standing up as if it's recently been used. Standing to one side, hoping I'm out of the way of any attack, I pull it open. A stairway that's so close to vertical it's half ladder is there. Circling warily, I see the telltale signs of a dressing room below. Beneath the stage. Makes sense.

But I don't like it. It's a blind entrance. I can't see what's down there, and I won't be able to defend myself until I'm all the way down the steep steps.

If this one entrance is here, then there's surely another. Performers love to have some kind of a cunningly hidden lift to the stage so they can make surprise entrances for shows.

But I don't see one. Problem with hidden lifts: They're hidden.

I hear a yell, and the large door to my left suddenly lurches as men ram something into it. And the soldiers pouring down the stairs from the highest balcony have reached the lowest one.

"Again!" an officer outside yells.

They ram the door again, and wood splinters around the latch.

Suddenly, from below, I hear the unmistakable sounds of a fight. A yelp of surprise. A woman's voice cursing.

A thud of flesh, the *thwap-thunk* of a crossbow bolt being discharged and immediately hitting wood, and the ring of steel on steel—just once.

"Sister! What are you doing here?" a voice calls out. It sounds like Ysmaena's voice.

Hoping they're distracted by whatever's happening down there, I leap down the ladder-stairs.

In the small room, I see four dead or dying: Two bodies are still, two writh-ing. Stenches of burnt clothing and burnt human flesh. Curl of black smoke. Discharged magic. Ysmaena, sitting in a far corner, facing my stairs, is cra-dling a discharged crossbow over her knee, but one of her arms is injured, useless—dislocated from my yank on it. A bolt is stuck in the wall near me, but she's not looking my way.

Ysmaena's staring at the red-haired woman standing over the dead and dying, bared bloody steel in one hand and a writhing ball of fire in the other. Vi!

Vi lights up at the sight of me. I hadn't switched from magical invisibility to mundane invisibility: my mistake on charging into the light, but not a lethal mistake, this time.

Ysmaena sees me at the same moment. "Kill him!" she tells Vi.

"No," Vi says.

"Sister, that's an order!"

"No."

"My team outranks yours. You know that," Ysmaena says. "You have no idea how dangerous this man is. We need to get—"

"Don't you draw magic on me," Vi interrupts her, warning. "You know how that'll go for you."

Vi's still wearing her red jeweled anti-magic choker, but there's something slightly different about the quality of its glow. It hasn't noticeably tightened despite the fireball in her hand, so I guess it's disabled, which means she has full access to her considerable powers. The other woman's choker has the same quality, and I guess that all the Sisters have disabled their chokers. Security isn't as tight on the ship as it was at the party.

The sound of a doorframe splintering open upstairs takes our attention for a moment. Ysmaena's eyes light up and she opens her mouth to shout or throw a spell.

Vi's short sword flashes through her neck, ending Ysmaena's attempt at a yell in grotesque burbles. Ysmaena looks up at Vi in utter shock, horror. She tries to take a deep breath to shout in defiance of her now-inevitable death—

And sucks blood deep into her lungs, which goes about how any swimmer could tell you.

She coughs noisily, gagging, spraying out a vermilion cloud. Which misses Vi, who'd pulled back in anticipation of it, like the veteran killer she is.

Cursing, face set, Vi glides forward in the next instant and sends her blade down in a purposeful stab deep through the V of Ysmaena's collarbones to her heart. A sharp professional twist as she wrenches the blade free and dodges back once more to avoid possible blood spray. Ysmaena goes limp.

Face a mask, Vi tosses me a blade angrily.

"Make yourself useful," she barks, gesturing to the two downed soldiers on my side of the room who are still moving. "My cover's no good if word gets out I helped you."

As I close the trapdoor above us first, she stabs each of the men on her side of the room in turn, twisting her blade in already-still hearts. I'm not so lucky.

Twice I get to glimpse eyes widen, though I move on before they dim. I'm fast, but not fast enough to avoid what I see in those eyes.

Vi scans the room once and examines her dress. She killed four men and a Sister of the Chantry in a dress—a *white* dress—and didn't get a drop of blood on it! She notes with another muttered curse that she's torn the seam under her armpit.

She pauses at the open door, turns to me. "I don't have to tell you that you need to do exactly what I say or this is gonna get ugly, right?"

I push Ysmaena's bowed head back to rest against the wall. The full lips that I so enjoyed mere minutes ago are limned with blood, a red stream down her chin and into her neckline. I close her unseeing eyes. "Right. Hate for this to get ugly."

Chapter Sixty-Eight

A Thousand Cuts

$\mathcal{W}$hy do they make it so hard?" Vi asked.

"You mean by interjecting non sequiturs?" Sister Ariel asked, her quill pausing midscritch.

"Huh?"

"Forgive me. Go ahead. What do they make hard and who does so?"

"The Sisters. Being loyal."

Sister Ariel set down her quill. She held up one finger for silence, stood, and picked up her shawl. Then she led Vi through the hidden room to its exit, which was around a corner from the main library exit and therefore blocked from the door guards' sight.

Soon, they stood on an empty balcony in the morning sun as it cleared the mountains, setting aglow the mists rising from the lake below them.

Vi had been prepared to tell Sister Ariel everything, but the few minutes' break had given her a chance to regroup. Sister Ariel might care about her— she acted like she did, sometimes, anyway—but the Chantry was Sister Ariel's whole life. If Vi confessed that she'd killed a fellow Sister, Ariel would probably report her immediately.

Which meant Vi needed to come up with some other reason being loyal was so hard, other than that one of the Sisters had tried to murder Kylar right in front of her.

"So," Sister Ariel prompted, hugging her shawl tight. "Go on."

"Everything felt so amazing when I first got here," Viridiana said. "Teaching and learning and sweating together on the practice fields, sharing new techniques we'd discovered or old ones we'd rediscovered. It felt so good being part of a team with women I knew would give their lives for me, and who knew the same of me. I guess I thought that same feeling was there for the whole Chantry. That we really were Sisters, you know?"

"But things changed after the Battle of Black Barrow?" Sister Ariel asked.

Vi nodded. When they'd come back and Sister Ariel had disappeared into her own studies, everything else had seemed to fall apart.

"Do you remember what you asked for when you came back as a war hero?" Sister Ariel said.

"I wasn't a war hero—"

"Never mind that. What'd you ask for?"

"I asked to be allowed to keep working with the corps."

"Your corps of war magae, our total abrogation of the Alitaeran Accords. But I don't mean that. You demanded that the Chantry leave Kylar alone. The Speaker said yes, and made it quite clear that you'd expended all the goodwill you'd earned by asking that favor. You came in as a veritable stranger to most of us, and your first demand was to constrain our power—for a man most saw as a threat, a man who had embarrassed us. Do you see how that made enemies, Viridiana?"

"It's not like he's just *some man*. It's Kylar, and after all he did at Black Barrow he deserved our thanks, not—"

"Doesn't matter. And what you intended doesn't matter either. How could rivals and enemies use it against you? That's what matters."

"Is that why everything's been so hard?" The beauty of the morning seemed a mockery.

"Viridiana, you have to understand. You came out of nowhere. Practically a born war mage, which at first seemed like a horrible problem and then when the Khalidoran threat emerged, turned out to be the perfect thing. That catapulted you into prominence. A young war hero who also happens to be hugely Talented, a stranger to our ways and norms, well-liked by many in the lower classes and among the Chattel, and quite stunning. There are dozens of insiders who've worked and waited in line for power for decades. You show up from nowhere and, as they saw it, jumped the queue ahead of them. Were you really surprised to find knives in your back the instant you landed?"

"I thought this place was going to be the opposite of the slums and the Sa'kagé. I just wanted to be left alone to train and learn with my friends. Instead..."

"Let me guess. First, they had some excellent reason to relocate you and your warriors to different training grounds, somewhere farther away and less convenient. That meant some women couldn't come train and still attend their lectures, jobs, or apprenticeships. Then some of your key lieutenants were lured away with plum appointments that were either far away or that demanded so much time they couldn't keep training with you. Then your food got worse or disappeared. Gear went missing so sometimes you couldn't train at all. Feeling it was too much effort or even a waste of their time, more women quit. Duties called you away often—you had meetings you couldn't miss that oddly always were scheduled during your training times. Whenever you demanded redress or changes from the Chantry leadership, your demands were filtered to the appropriate channels to be addressed but only after an uncomfortably long time. The fixes were then often delayed further, or found to have been sent to the wrong office after all. By the time you ever got a hearing, someone else had a new claim to whatever resource you needed, and you were told they couldn't simply be uprooted, not just now. By the time you could force an issue like securing the training area for your women's use, someone would point out that now the facts on the ground had changed: You no longer had two hundred women to train, so surely you didn't need such a large space? And so on. Am I close?"

Vi's mouth hung open. "So you've been following everything they did to me?"

"Not at all. Every bureaucracy has its knife fighters, Viridiana, and the Chantry has more than most. If I had to guess further, I'd guess that every time you fought back, you were told you were being unreasonable, that if you kept pushing, you'd make enemies of Sisters who could be your friends if you weren't so pushy, that you just didn't know how things were done around here."

Feeling sick, Vi nodded.

"That last is obviously true, if not the way you thought. So that brings us to Sister Ayayah's special team. They insisted that if you wanted to go with them, you'd have to take all their orders, et cetera. As if your presence were a big imposition and they were doing you a favor to allow you to come along. In reality, with your background and skills, you should've been *leading* the team. At the least, co-leading it."

Vi was aghast. "I . . . I never even thought of demanding to lead."

"You're how old, child? No, don't tell me. You make me feel I've got one foot in the grave already. At your age, you're accustomed to taking orders. They took advantage of that. In a way, your position on the team didn't matter at all to most of your enemies here. What was important was that you would be away, and while you were away, they could dismantle every remaining support you still had here."

Vi blew out a breath, sinking into herself. "And if I didn't come back at all, so much the better."

"I suppose so, yes. See? Now you're thinking like they do. Keep doing that and—no, never mind, I was going to say you'll do fine. But that's obviously untrue. It's too late for you. Too bad." Sister Ariel turned to go back inside.

"Too bad? Too bad?!"

Sister Ariel paused awkwardly. Though it wasn't that cold, she hunched tighter in her shawl. "I seem to have spoken an awkward truth again. As I do. I'm not sure what I'm supposed to say now."

"Well ... if this all so obvious to you, why didn't you tell me?" Vi demanded. "You didn't ask."

"I didn't—! You're the one who brought me here! You should've been looking out for me!"

Sister Ariel's chin lowered and tucked toward her neck. Then she opened her mouth. Closed it. Her eyebrows lifted. "Do you know, you make a compelling case. You're right. I should have. Huh! I hadn't thought of that at all."

Seeing that the younger woman didn't look remotely consoled by this, Sister Ariel frowned. "Viridiana, for all my life—minus the increasingly slender fraction in which I wasn't a Sister—I've always considered politics to be destructive when it isn't ephemeral. One party does this thing here, the other parties push back; today's gains are wiped out by tomorrow's losses. A woman labors for years for some coveted appointment and the moment she gets it, her kingdom is invaded and it's all for naught. So I've always sought to add something permanent—however small—to humanity's stores of knowledge. The discovery of one cure to a common minor ailment might alleviate suffering for tens of thousands of humans now and yet unborn. Most of it's not so grand, naturally, especially for a scholar as limited as I, but—well, I'm digressing—I love my books, my studies. When we came back from Black Barrow, I was happy to dive back into them. You seemed content with your warriors, so I left you to it. I see now I was wrong in that. I apologize."

"They're going to crucify me, aren't they?"

"No, no. If the Chantry were to execute you, the most common method is called denial of light: Your magical powers are stripped from you at the root in a way that usually causes massive brain trauma, and if you survive the initial..."

Vi had gone white.

"This is not a helpful line of exposition, is it? Oh, you meant metaphorically! Then, yes."

"They're not going to...kill me, are they?"

"No. Of course not. You've made a lot of enemies, but you've also got unique skills—skills forbidden by the Alitaeran Accords, granted, but that's not your fault and the Speaker already knew about those. Istariel is not one to discard a fellow Sister lightly, if at all. Especially not a war hero. Well, maybe not *especially* not a war hero—in fact, the war hero bit might make you marginally more likely to be a threat and therefore more likely to—but that's beside the point, I think. None of us wants to throw away a Sister. It's a last resort for the gravest offenses: things like treason against the Chantry or murdering a fellow Sister. And as you told Ayayah, you didn't kill anyone. She's so angry and eager to pin the blame for the debacle on the storm ship on someone else that if either special team even suspected you'd killed imperial soldiers, you'd be in a dungeon right now, not a library."

Vi winced.

"So I think the worst you have to worry about is..." Sister Ariel trailed off. "Viridiana, you *didn't* kill anyone, did you?"

Vi avoided eye contact.

"Child, you do understand that at some point before the Council ends, they will be hearing the full reports from our embassy in Borami? Those Sisters will have spoken extensively with eyewitnesses. If there's any evidence that you took part in violence on the storm ship, you are going to be in a completely different level of trouble. Doubly so if you've lied about it."

Sister Ariel removed her reading glasses and began cleaning a lens with a corner of her shawl. Vi felt paralyzed. The wind blew pleasantly; the sun shone brightly and reflected orange on the still morning waters of Lake Vestacchi. The small Sister undoubtedly cared about her more than anyone had cared for Vi for the first half of her life. Everything here was open and free and beautiful.

She'd never felt more trapped.

"Viridiana. Is there anything you need to tell me?"

Chapter Sixty-Nine

New Lies, Old Loves

*J*acket, off. Closet," Vi whispers.

She's rummaging in a bag near the door of the dressing room. I strip off my sergeant's jacket and throw it in one of the performers' closets. She holds open a replacement coat: red with gold embroidery, expensive, exactly my size. We pull it on me. She throws a wig over my dark hair. I must've lost the one I was wearing earlier in the fight.

Then we head into the hall from the performers' door. Vi leads me with deceptive speed, jogging at times when there are no eyes on us, cutting sideways through adjoining halls.

"No tails," I tell her.

Her eyes flash. Anger always did come quickly to Vi. She uses anger to cover all sorts of feelings. Right now, probably guilt at killing Ysmaena.

Vi drags me along as if ignoring me for another few minutes. We climb two levels and finally divert into one of the private cabins. Vi's, unless I miss my guess.

"You have questions. I have lies," Vi says. "But quickly."

"Excuse me?"

"I don't have all day, Kylar. I've got a few minutes only, then I gotta go establish an alibi. What's the bare minimum you need to know in order to still be here when I come back?"

I blink stupidly. This is going too fast.

"Let's get the obvious ones out of the way first, shall we?" she asks.

"Let's," I say. I'm not sure what the obvious questions are, but I'm always happy for someone to think I'm smarter than I am. Especially while I catch my breath, literally, and also from the mental sprints I'm trying to make here.

"The Chantry didn't send my team only to help Logan get through the meeting with the empress."

"I figured that much out. What *are* you doing?"

"I'm trying to tell you, if you'd shut your mouth," she snaps.

"You already said you were going to lie to me!"

"I didn't mean it like that! I meant I'm ready to tell you about the lies I let you believe before now."

"That makes me feel so much better," I say. But then I shut my mouth. Momma K would've made some point about learning better with one's ears open, rather than one's mouth. "Go ahead."

"As you probably guessed, we're here to get Logan's kid."

"Which one?" I ask, immediately forgetting to keep my mouth shut.

"The one that matters." She starts taking off her dress.

I look at her blankly. She turns her back to me.

"Help me with the buttons, would you?"

I unbutton some buttons, having no idea why.

"Needle and thread, that box," she says, pointing.

I rummage through a drawer, finding the needle and pulling out white thread to match the dress, happy finally to have my brain working again. She's repairing the torn seam in the dress's armpit: A good disguise requires as much care as good armor and can as easily save your life.

She's standing in a shift that must have been specially sewn for the dress to maximally show off her chest.

I've heard rumors of magic that's very painful and usually doesn't work but sometimes permanently alters a person's figure. I don't know if Hu Gibbet forced Vi to go through that—he was the kind of person who would—or if Vi is one of those rare women who can be very fit, very lean, and yet still somehow busty. It's not really the kind of question you can ask someone, is it? *Hey, nice boobs. Nature, or torture?*

It took me a long time knowing Vi to not glance at her chest every few seconds.

~Every few *seconds*?~

Not literally. *I was exaggerating for effect.*

Right now, I don't know if it's the being single or the being celibate or just being away from her for a long time, but I seem to have regressed. Her shift has some sort of boning built in and is otherwise open to the belly button, and like a horny teenager, I keep glancing at her cleavage, despite everything else going on.

For her part, Vi is looking over every part of her dress, looking for blood spatter. "White dress?" I ask. "In our line of work?"

She curses floridly but dispassionately, then pauses, not meeting my eyes. "It's a season for colors. White in a sea of strong colors and patterns makes me pop." She gestures to her cleavage, as if, versed in wet work as I am, I should obviously understand these are her tools.

I understand what she means completely at the same time that I don't understand it at all. Yes, yes, I understand we go way back, and that your breasts are not being displayed for sexual purposes at the moment.

But still... breasts.

"I should probably say thanks for saving my life back there," I say, turning to the side.

"Don't," she says. "I probably... Gods, I don't want to think about it. Hey, you just gonna sit there? You're a better hand with needle and thread than I am. Can you...?"

How does she remember that? I mean, we did sort of live together for a while, Elene and her and me, while I was married to Elene and magically bonded to Vi and telling the Chantry she and I were married—what a disaster that was!—but I can't remember ever sewing.

"You stitch. I'll talk," she says, an apologetic note creeping into her voice.

I start stitching, glad to have something to occupy my eyes.

She says, "After Black Barrow, the first Healers noticed that everyone had been affected by our huge pulse of magic. Iures and Curoch held together and used together by the twelve of us? Nothing like that has happened in centuries. Maybe many centuries. Four of the women will probably never use magic again. On the other hand, one of the weakest of the Twelve is now one of the strongest Sisters living. Two can still work weaves but feel incredible pain every time they do. Our Healers soon came to fear the effect of the magic on the unborn. Rightly, it turns out."

"Logan's boys," I say. So I was right.

"Right. We had to see if anything had happened to them."

"What about you?" I ask. "Anything happen other than the hair?" I gesture to the streak in her hair, which rather than Vi's natural red is now black and orange and red and yellow as if flames were alive within it.

She checks the mirror and flinches. She mutters a spell and the hair goes a muddled color as if she'd poured red paint into the colors already there. She expels a breath between her teeth and mutters again. The streak goes pure white, and then it goes a red that matches her natural color.

She says, "Now's not the time to go into all that. The Gandians—the best Healers in the world, some say better even than the Chantry—have this belief that infants' souls don't fully anchor in their bodies until the third or fourth month after birth. They call it the fourth trimester. You've been around babies, right? You know how after a few months you'll sort of see babies kind of, I dunno, wake up? Apparently it's a thing magically, too."

"But magical Talents don't show up until puberty."

"Right, mostly. Unless you're freakishly strong, and most the time not even then. I guess, hell, it's chaotic. Maybe I just don't understand it right myself. But apparently, for some children their Talent will show up and stay, which is why once in a while you have stories of four-year-olds causing absolute havoc."

"I haven't ever heard stories like that."

"You haven't studied at the Chantry for the last six months. Anyway, magical tantrums, stuff like that. And if you think teens can be frightening with sudden, vast magical powers, consider how literal children do. It doesn't happen often enough for us to understand the rules, but apparently, they'll usually show their future abilities briefly, and then those will fade to nothing until puberty, when they come back. But sometimes they end up having totally different abilities as adults. We don't know for sure what course Caedan's abilities will take, but he's got 'em, and what he's got is terrifying to the Chantry and to every magic-user in the world."

"Caedan's the one on the ship, then?" Kiern's the one I held, isn't he?

"You didn't even know *that*?" Vi asked. "Then why'd you come after him rather than his brother?"

"I thought they were together. Anyway, this was my only lead." Should I tell her I'm working for Momma K? Should I tell her about the Nemesis Compass? Hell, I don't even know if there *is* such a thing now. If it isn't even real, I'll look like a fool, and if it is, I'll be bringing it to the Chantry's attention, so I decide to keep my mouth shut about that.

"Oh, this just gets better and better," Vi says. She looks like she wants to say more, but doesn't. It looks like she's holding things back too.

I keep my mouth shut and eyes down and keep stitching the armpit seam.

"I'm not supposed to tell you any of this, Kylar."

"You just killed one of the Sisters. If you're worried about making them mad, you're drawing the line in a strange place."

Vi steps close to look at my handiwork. It presses her body distractingly against me. "Watch it with the boobs," I grumble.

"Easy," she snaps, but she steps away.

Then she softens as I finish tying off my stitches. "Why do we always go wrong, Kylar?"

"Huh?"

"It's so good to see you. I wish it weren't *here*, and I wish I hadn't had to... do what I did back there. But it's good to see you. Really good."

I look up into her big eyes, then away. I hand her the dress. "You too, Vi. Viridiana," I correct myself quickly.

She steps into the dress and shimmies it up her hips. "So how'd you get on the ship?" she asks.

"You didn't hear?" I ask.

"Would I ask if I already knew?"

"I guess I kind of, jumped on?"

"From the castle," she says flatly.

"Yep. Glided over. Wingsuit. Real fun. Don't recommend it."

"Why are you such an ass?" she says, shaking her head in disgust. "It was a simple question. If you don't want to answer it to protect your new girlfriend or whatever, you can just say so."

"My new *girlfriend*?"

"It's none of my business. She make it on the ship, too?"

"I don't know yet. I was planning on looking for her once I get a minute to breathe. But she's not my girlfriend. I'm not even sure if she's a friend. She's, uh, someone I work with."

"Someone you work with?"

"We both..." I trail off. "Who's asking? Viridiana or the Chantry?"

"You're worried I'm going to tell them about your nursemaid?" Viridiana asks.

"Wouldn't you?"

"Yes!"

"Well!"

Her color is high. We're standing close. I see her glance quickly at my lips.

I brush them, wondering if I've got food on them or something. "Why are we yelling?" I ask.

"I wish she was your friend," Viridiana says, taking a half step back, looking away. She reaches behind her back to start doing up her buttons. I don't offer to help.

"What's that mean?"

"The Chantry has this rule: no loners. They won't let you advance if you can't maintain friendships. It's one of the things every Sister I've talked to about has said makes us superior to magi. They say talented loners are always a disaster incubating."

"Incubating?"

"Their word, not mine. Picture the lone genius in your mind."

"What?"

"Just do it, would you? It's an exercise they showed me. Got it?"

"Give me half a—sure. Got it."

"What's she look like?" Vi asks.

"She?"

"You pictured a man, didn't you?"

"Yeah. Dorian."

"Right, well, he fits, I guess. I think you were supposed to go abstract. So maybe that messes things up. But the Chantry would say you pictured a man because the lone genius mythos is a male archetype. And also a lie. I did the same thing, by the way, even though I know Momma K better, and she's at least as smart as Dorian, clearly more competent, and, you know, sane. I skipped right over Sister Ariel, too, you remember her?"

"Sure do. But what does this all have to do—"

"A real friend will keep you from making huge mistakes, Kylar, if you listen to them."

"You've gotta have friends first," I say.

"Maybe you'd find friends closer than you think, if you'd look," she says.

"What's that supposed to mean? That I don't listen, and I don't look? Need anything else to cut me down with? You sound like Durzo on a bad day."

"How is he?" she asks, chagrined.

"I dunno. He left to go do better things, I guess. Just like every other friend I've had."

I can tell that strikes home. I hadn't meant it as a shot at her. Hadn't realized I felt anything but good that she was doing well and moving on, until I said it.

"I shouldn't have—I didn't mean—" I begin.

"Whenever they talk about the dangers of isolation, I think about you, Kylar. I worry about you."

She worries about me? I don't know what to say to that. "I'm not isolated," I say.

Viridiana couldn't have looked more baffled if I'd suddenly turned into a talking honey cake. "I don't—I don't have time for this right now," she says, not angry, but almost begging. She doesn't want to fight.

But I'm thinking about something Dorian said when he visited me. 'Do you know what happens to a man too long isolated? I do.'

I'd misunderstood him. He didn't mean he did know what happens; he meant himself. He happens. What happened to him is what happens. I don't know the full chain of events that led Dorian to his madness, but maybe I know enough. He charged off into a perilous situation, alone, made terrible choices that seemed like the right thing at the time, and reaped madness and deceit and death. Maybe he meant all that wouldn't have happened if he hadn't been so isolated. Like I am.

That's a cheery thought. I say, "So, uh, I woulda thought Kiern was the important brother."

"Why?"

"The prophetic dreams?"

"Dreams?" But suddenly her mouth drops open. "Prophetic dreams? Is that what they ... ?" She sits down abruptly, her dress gaping open. Vi has amazing awareness of her body in physical space, paired with an utter lack of awareness of her body in social space.

I step behind her and start doing up the little pearl buttons.

"They, the team doesn't tell me anything they don't think I need to know, Kylar. But they had a big argument. Kiern gives whoever is holding him weird dreams. The Healers were trying to figure out if they were just hallucinatary ... ? What's the word? Hallucinations, anyway. But it happened to every one of the Sisters who held him. Anyone who had even a whisper of Talent is affected, they think. So Logan could hold the boy without any trouble, but Jenine has some latent potential in her, as many women do."

Feeling that I've finished with the buttons, she stands and shifts the dress around, then ties the last laces in the front.

"Oh gods," I say. "That explains everything, then! What did Logan and Jenine say when the Sisters told them? Because when I talked to Logan, he was still thinking she was craz..."

She winces. My mouth falls open.

"You *didn't* tell them," I say. "You didn't *tell* them?"

"Not me! I didn't know either while I was there. All I knew was that I was forbidden to hold either of the boys."

"Those *bitches*." It was so like the Chantry. They came in offering to help, took their time finding the source of the problems, and then decided not to tell the new king and queen what was happening with their infants—all while the queen was regularly hallucinating and everyone including her husband thought she was losing her mind.

"Easy!" Viridiana says.

"Wait," I say, ignoring her, "so if Kiern gives people dreams that tell the future, what could Caedan possibly do that makes him more important than that?"

"No one said he's more important."

"You don't have to *say* it, you're *here*. Or is he the only one you have a lead on?" Because she'd ridiculed that before, and now I don't know how much I should trust what she says.

"Well, no."

"Then the Chantry thinks he is more important."

"We have a team going after Kiern, too."

"But you're on this team, and this is the best team. You said so yourself. What does he do, Vi?"

She throws her hands up. "Isn't it obvious?"

"No."

"All the alarms, Kylar? They're all because of him. I mean, other than the one that was because of you."

"Huh?"

"The boys are almost three months old now, Kylar. His soul is attaching to his body. The shutdown? The boys' Talents are manifesting. His was more subtle than his brother's. At first, the Healers didn't think Caedan had a Talent at all. Certainly not anything spectacular like Kiern's dream-giving. If anything, holding Caedan settled Jenine down. But then...I need to go, Kylar. Can we—?"

"But then what?" I demand.

"Caedan seemed healthy, so the Healers mostly left him alone. But then one noticed that sometimes she couldn't use magic while holding him. More experiments confirmed it. First it was only while holding him. Then it was for a few minutes afterward. Soon, it was for a full day afterward. Then the Healers got too scared to keep experimenting, fearing they'd lose their Talents forever if they were in too much contact with him. And now...That was him. The null wave. He knocked out the magic on the entire storm ship."

"An infant? I don't believe it."

"*That's* why we're here. His Talent could fade, but instead it's getting stronger. The Sisters fear that when he grows up, if he isn't taught to control his powers, he might nullify magic. Not just around him. Everywhere. That's why he's more important than his brother to us. With Kiern, an enemy might gain visions of the future. But with *Caedan* in enemy hands, the Chantry may end. And not only the Chantry. Kings and empresses and chieftains everywhere in the world have used magic to prop up their regimes in ways subtle and complex. What happens to the world if all that disappears overnight?"

"He's a *baby*."

"You think I don't know that? I vowed to keep those boys safe, and I will!"

"You also vowed to obey the Chantry." I shouldn't have said it, but it's out of my mouth before I can help myself.

"And who's dead back there, Kylar?" she snaps. "You son of a bitch! How dare you question my loyalty? Do you know what that might cost me? What it *is* costing me? I did that for *you*! I'm already regretting it." She swears again and rubs her forehead, looks away.

"You need to stay here," she says, "and I need to go be seen. I may have waited too long for a solid alibi already. I'll be back in an hour. Bucket's there. Food's in the pantry. Please be here when I get back."

She doesn't wait for me to answer. She leaves.

I don't know if I should stay. I don't know if I should trust her, not for sure. On the other hand, she did kill four men and one of her own Sisters to save me from an ambush, so I don't know what else I could ask of her to prove herself.

Maybe I just feel too vulnerable right now.

It's not like I have many options.

I decide to lie down for a minute and think things through.

At some point in the night, I become aware of Vi returning. She closes the door quietly, locks it, and then undresses, hanging up her dress in the darkness. She pulls out a men's tunic that she pulls over her head to be a nightdress. With my vision, of course, I can see everything she does perfectly, but it's a testament to my newfound maturity that I don't watch. Or maybe my exhaustion.

But I'm going with maturity.

"Move over," she says either a few seconds or years later.

"Hmm?" I ask.

She pushes on me and I scoot over.

When I wake, one of my arms is trapped and feeling dead under Vi's head as her pillow. My other hand is holding a pillow that is unquestionably not mine, and not a pillow.

I suppose I should be embarrassed, if not at the placement of my hand, then at my body's stirring in response to it. This is the second time in as many weeks I've woken cupping a woman's breast without intending to.

But that's not the feeling that comes rushing up in me.

I apologize quietly and take my hand from Vi's breast, extricate my arm from under her head, and sit up. She mumbles but doesn't seem to wake.

Pulling my knees up to my face, I try to slam the feelings down *down* lest I wake her. But it's like holding back a tide with my fingers. Though my extended hands say stop, the tide boils through every digit in an instant and overwhelms me. The woman who fills my mind isn't Phaena, but Elene.

How many times had I held her like that before she'd died?

I'd dreamed it was her, dreamed that I was going to wake and make love to my beautiful wife, that it was her body curved small against me, that she would welcome me to her in all the ways, holding my face in her hands, her eyes holding all my frailties with love, a perfect acceptance that flared to desire as she pulled my hips to hers.

Elene could cycle from tenderness to hot desire to luxuriating in a caress to playful nipping to laughing and back to any point, and with her, stumblingly, I could do the same, slowly, slowly, slowly believing in her love for me, slowly, slowly stopping trying to earn it, slowly letting my many fears find an answer that wasn't an answer but simply her presence. In her I'd found a fragile peace. Her arms were a tiny haven and a world entire. She created a world for me in her love, and welcomed me in, told me to be at my ease, told me it was my home.

Now it's gone forever. There will be nothing so good for me, not ever again.

My weeping is shaking the bed, despite my best efforts to hold still.

From her breathing, I can tell Vi is only feigning sleep now. I'm probably scaring the hell out of her.

"I'll be fine," I say, shaming myself by letting my voice quaver. "I'll be fine."

But of course it's a lie. Even if I live seven centuries, I'll never be *fine* again. And I know this unending earthly solitary confinement is only a fair punishment for my sins. I had my chance at grace undeserved, and I lost her.

Chapter Seventy

A Killer Wardrobe

$\mathcal{G}$ood morning," I say, falsely chipper. "I'd have woken you with breakfast, but I'm told that might get us killed."

Vi mumbles something, rolling over, long lean legs scissoring as she stretches, her crimson hair tumbling over her face so that she looks half artist's model and half mop. "Stop laughing," she mumbles again. "The door. Check outside the door. Food."

As she sits up and fights with her hair, trying to regain her vision, I check outside the door and find a tray piled with covered serving dishes. Careful to keep myself out of sight, I pull it inside and close the door. "Are you kidding? They bring our food to us up here? Clearly I booked my passage in the wrong section."

"You're a stowaway," she grumbles. "Which means that's not our food. It's *my* food. Don't you dare touch it."

I hand her one of the plates at random and take another for myself, grinning as I ignore her. It's quail eggs or something. I couldn't care less. It all looks like energy to me. She sets her plate in her lap and binds back her hair, almost sighing with pleasure at having her typical tight ponytail securely in place.

Vi's always had something strange going on with her hair.

"I'm sorry about last night," I say, without really meaning to. Vi's been through a lot with me.

"About playing with my nipples or the other?"

I'm thunderstruck. "I—I did what? I, I mean I did mean the other, but if I— oh gods, Vi, I didn't mean to—"

"Don't worry about it. It's like it didn't happen," she says.

I put my hands over my face. "Oh . . . Vi, I am so—"

" 'Cause it didn't," she says, stealing some egg off my plate.

"—sorry that I . . . What?"

She grins around a mouthful of egg with a childlike joy I haven't seen in ages.

"Wh—I didn't?"

"Kylar, come on! You were asleep in my little bunk. I crawled in later. You touched my boob in your sleep. Don't make such a big deal out of it."

"Well, I wasn't making a—until you said—gah!"

She laughs and my emotions jump twelve times before she's done. She's like your best friend's kid sister one moment, an accomplice in your pranks, and then she's one of the boys, and then she's the sexy tomboy, dressed in a man's tunic and nothing else and aware of her body and your glances at her, and then she's a woman of her own, self-possessed, outside all the diminutives of what she is to you, she is her self, her own universe, and she is the familiar and the mysterious together, the comfortingly close and the endlessly fascinating— and then, in a collision, she is your wife's best friend. The tantalizingly close snatched suddenly, jarringly far away.

And all the rest comes crashing down: the simple joys of friendship and the more complicated joys of friendship admixed with flashes of desire and more than flashes, and the brief wicked thoughts of pleasures possible, and the longer considerations of relational possibilities beyond the merely temporary, the merely bodily.

And by the time she's stopped laughing, my own smile is strained. It feels unfair to smile as if I'm still in the moment with her, and it feels unfair not to smile, to have left that innocent moment already, when she did nothing to deserve me abandoning her alone there.

"I meant sorry about the other," I say quietly, sorrow edging in despite my best attempts. "I'm sorry about the other." A lump in my throat, I stand up abruptly and go to her closet so she can't see my face. "Can I, uh, sew anything else while I'm here?"

She doesn't answer for a moment, but I keep my back turned. I can't look at her, not now. "You could help me figure out my wardrobe for today," she offers. "You know, if you're going to block my closet."

I smile and grab some familiar things. "How about these?" I ask, pulling out her wetboy grays. "I can't believe they let you bring these along!"

"You want to know what I had to do to get them to let me bring those?" she asks.

"Yeah. What?"

"Check the next shelf. I had to convince them to let me bring all sorts of exotic things in order to hide the one thing I wanted."

I rummage through the most impractical and expensive clothes I've ever seen. I pick up something that appears to be little more than several strands of jewels.

"Why don't you wear this tod—?" I turn to hand them to her. She's completely naked.

I turn back around, blushing. "That was . . . completely foreseeable. Sorry." I sigh. "Am I ever gonna get not awkward with you?"

"I hope not," she whispers in my ear, giving me a quick hug from behind. A quick and very naked hug. "It's endearing. You're like my friend's little brother sometimes. And . . . I am definitely not wearing those, so put them down unless you're planning to wear them yourself."

Blushing again, I pull something else out.

She sighs. "Excellent choice. I love how that fits. But it's an evening gown. As in . . . an *evening* gown."

Muttering, I go back to looking.

"Oh, I meant to ask earlier. When'd you start wearing a cuff?" she asks.

I look at her blankly, and then see she's looking at my platinum bracelet. Guess maybe it's technically called a cuff? "I end up naked a lot. Figured I should carry something to trade for clothes."

"Mmm-hmm," she says, amused. "I wasn't meaning to pry. I meant it looks nice."

"Oh." I feel awkward again, and no platinum cuff is going to buy me out of it. "It was a gift. From Durzo. Not magical, unfortunately."

She doesn't ask more, and soon I find clothes for her, better suited to the day, plainer but made for good free movement, with practical underthings and matching shoes. Then add a contrasting sash and bag. Then earrings. Then a necklace.

At each addition, she cocks her head further until I'm impressed by the owlish flexibility of her neck. "You are way better at this than I thought you'd be," she says.

"Thank you," I say, "for having low expectations." I almost said *a low opinion of me* but saved it at the last second.

Wow, my emotions are still all over the place.

I fold the clothes she rejected and put them away, then lean against the closet with my back turned as she dresses, as carelessly unembarrassed and non-awkward as can be.

Suddenly, in the darkness behind my lowered eyelids, I can't move. Just being here is unbearable.

I adore Vi. I mean, I really like her. She's fun and she's funny, sometimes intentionally, sometimes not, and she's as awkward as I am, and as lopsided a human from her early training with Hu as I am from my early training with Durzo. Sometimes she can be unbelievably callous and awful and other times she's more sweetly human than you would think any killer could be. She's seen more of the world than many women three times her age, and seen more ugliness than most veterans of war, and maybe for me it will always be impossible to be with her and not think constantly about Elene.

And that's not fair, but there it is. When I'm with Vi, my dead wife is always in the room with us.

"I miss her too," Vi says quietly, coming up close. How does she know I was thinking about her?

"Yeah," I manage to choke out. "Thanks." I can't turn.

She puts a hand on my back. Doesn't try to turn me, merely rests it there. It's a comfort, but a comfort that makes everything ache more. Grief is a knife stuck in my frozen back, and as she warms my flesh, it makes me feel the wound.

She stands there, being with me, demanding nothing for what is at least a full minute but feels an eternity.

I'm too much. I know she's going to tire of waiting and leave, but she doesn't, and slowly, slowly the pain recedes. Finally, I take a deep breath, and only then does she lift her hand away.

I turn, not sure how to put my thanks into words, but she just gives me a tentative smile, then with regret says, "I gotta go report in. I'm late. It'll take an hour or two. Be here when I get back?"

She's late already. That means she stood with me and stayed, patiently, stayed even when she knew she had to be elsewhere. What's that mean?

A worried look flashes over her face at my hesitation. "You can trust me, Kylar."

I nod, a wash of warm feelings welling up in me. I know I can.

She goes.

*   *   *

Vi jumped up and dashed outside, snorting and choking weirdly. It was almost noon, and the Alabaster Seraph was bathed in light, though the library's balcony was in a fold of the great statue's sleeve and thus small and shadowed.

She stared over Lake Vestacchi and all the hustle of the small, lake-borne city that served the Chantry. Its streets were watercourses, with magical currents to propel the myriad little boats. She saw none of it, shoulders trembling, tears coursing down her cheeks.

A minute later, the door behind her opened. "You seem distressed," Sister Ariel said to her turned back. "Do you, um, need anything?"

"No," Vi said.

Sister Ariel left.

A few minutes later, Vi threw the door to the library open with a bang. The older woman looked up in alarm from her usual table, quill frozen in hand.

"What are you doing?" Vi demanded. "When someone's crying and they say they want to be left alone, you don't *believe* them! Even *I* know that. How is it that you're even worse at this than I am?"

"You didn't say you wanted to be left alone . . . Oh, so . . . You *do* need something?" Sister Ariel asked.

"No!" Vi said, slamming the door behind her as she left.

Half a minute later, the older woman came out. She came to stand beside Viridiana at the rail. Viridiana said nothing. Haltingly, Sister Ariel said, "Emotions exhaust me. They're confusing. Even when I solve them, they . . . they don't stay solved."

"See? You understand perfectly!" Viridiana said.

"I do?"

For a minute, they shared the day and the breeze. When Viridiana cleared the tears from her cheeks, no new ones spilled down to replace them.

"Is, uh, is there anything you want to tell me?" Sister Ariel asked.

"No, no, it's okay. I'm fine now."

"Am I—? Am I supposed to believe you this time?"

"I don't know," Vi said.

She could tell that Sister Ariel was on the verge of leaving, so she blurted out, "I tried to seduce my best friend's husband."

"Oh?" Sister Ariel asked carefully. "And how did that go for you?"

"Not well."

"Huh."

"Well, don't make it sound like it was stupid!" Vi said. "I mean, it was after she was dead."

"You're not—oh, you *are* talking about him," Sister Ariel said.

"I...I slept with a lot of men before I joined the Chantry. I mean, a lot. For work, you know. And it never...I swore I wasn't going to do that ever again when I joined up."

"We spoke about that, but I hadn't realized you swore yourself to chastity."

"No, not that! I swore I wouldn't make myself a tool, that I wouldn't f— adulterate?—that I wouldn't adulterate for gain, to hurt others, or at the direction of some mistress or master. Hu would—oh, what does it matter now? I mean, what's my problem, Sister? I decide I can't live with no morals, so then I pick out a few to hold on to so I can respect myself a little bit...and then I violate them immediately? Is that what you meant by the tempering-the-steel thing? It is, isn't it? Except I failed. Did you already know that, too? Or just know me well enough to guess?" Viridiana sank into herself, miserable.

"Sister Ayayah ordered you to seduce Kylar?"

"After I reported that he'd found me, they...I told myself it was okay, this one time, because I already...I already cared for him. And if by sleeping with him I could save so much, for all of us? I mean, what was the harm?"

Chapter Seventy-One

Scouting Paradise

$\mathcal{N}$ow that it's too late to ask, I suddenly have a lot of highly relevant questions for Vi. Where did the clothes she gave me come from? Were they stolen from anyone I may run into? Will the bracelet pass only visual scrutiny or magical scrutiny as well?

Did the Sisters prepare this for me because they expect me to join them in their plan? Or are they trying to get rid of me? What *is* their plan?

What's *my* plan?

I need to find Phaena. I need to get to wherever Caedan's being held—which is surely at the front of the ship, near King Repha'im. After I find the kid, I'll be able to plan how to grab him and how to get both of us out of here. But for now I don't even know what I'm facing.

Ergo, scouting.

The hallway outside Vi's room intersects another that, from the spacing of the doors, seems to house larger apartments. I find a stairway—steeper-than-usual stairs to save space even this far forward in the storm ship, but not the almost-ladders that one finds on other ships. I'm on the second or third level of the ship, far forward, which means that below me are the most privileged servants' bunkrooms, various workspaces, and a section of the hold.

Above me, in increasing order of importance as they get nearer the empress, will be quarters for the most powerful nobles and the ship's officers. The rest of the front third of the massive ship is split between the empress's apartments and sundry of her workspaces—including council chambers and small audience chambers and the like—and luxury dining and entertainment spaces for all the rest of the nobles, including an entire faux-city-neighborhood called Elysion.

Under the gaze of imperial guards, I step through a horseshoe-arch doorway into Elysion along with many others. The sight takes my breath; it is as if I've left the ship and stepped into the richest merchant's quarter of the empire. At least four stories here have been opened up, with a glass ceiling above, to mimic being outside. Buildings stand free, covered with vines. A waterfall pours over rocks to a pool four stories below. A stream crossed by lovely bridges meanders through faux city streets.

It is as if the prospect of being inside a ship for a whole ten days was so dreadful that the empire has spent a huge chunk of its limitless wealth and magic to replicate a delightful neighborhood inside the ship itself.

I walk perfectly cobbled streets, trying not to gawk and make myself conspicuous, though after a few minutes I realize that quite a few people are gawking. The lords and ladies who walk these streets are immaculately dressed—though not, as Viridiana pointed out, in evening gowns. I see men and women with what appear to be living tattoos, with glowing hair, with inhuman eye colors. Everyone seems to have flawless teeth, whiter than possible. On men who can't have worked a day in their lives, I see more muscles than you would in a blacksmiths' guildhall. A woman goes by with silvery metallic skin anchored with gold dust at her wrists and collarbones. I assume most or all of the oddities are illusions, but I don't take the time to investigate.

I pass lounges catering to specific tastes from every corner of the empire, complete with the appropriate decorations and garb on the servants. Musicians play songs familiar and strange, the latter sometimes on instruments I can't even name. It gives me a happy nostalgia despite myself. The bounty of the entire world is served here, scents and smells and foods and even peoples from regions throughout the empire and far beyond. Parlors, taverns, dance halls, even shops with luxury goods crowd the area. Gambling dens, opium holes, fighting pits, brothels, and other establishments serving the nobles' vices and addictions are all on a level below this one, well ventilated and accessible through several innocuous shops and discreet stairs, each with some version of a winking figure or a shushing man in heavy cosmetics or a shushing, blushing maid as if to say *What happens down below is our secret.*

Belying the illusion of a real neighborhood is that there is no dirt. There are koi floating in the stream and ponds, but no trash. And certainly there are no poor, nor even tradespeople walking about. There aren't even servants dipping their toes in the water for a few minutes while they rest from their labors. Everything is polished, pristine, and effortless-looking.

As I explore, it comes to me that this is how the disgustingly wealthy wish all of life were. That the Alitaerans can maintain such an illusion at all is impressive. That they can afford to do so inside this floating palace? Pure opulence.

If I correctly recall Momma K's politics lectures from when I was a child, Alitaera began as a trading kingdom that expanded into banking, became fabulously wealthy, was attacked by several of their jealous and indebted neighbors, barely survived, took over every kingdom that had attacked them, and then seemingly reverted to preferring peace. Now with vast natural resources, great harbors, excellent roads, protection for all traders, and strong guilds, there's no other kingdom like it in Midcyru.

For a few of the nobles, this level of luxury may be normal. I suppose this is how a few dozen actually live, every day. But far more of those currently wandering this hedonic paradise will go home to govern corners of the empire choked in dust, territories that can be crossed in a single day. What is a governor of a fractious people to think of his chances leading a rebellion when he returns from seeing *this*? When he considers that what is to him the ruinous cost of feeding and arming a thousand men for a month is less than the cost of a single one of the empress's outfits, of which she might wear three in a single day and never wear more than once, how is he to press forward in his dreamt-of rebellion and expect success?

When ambassadors from other lands attend the journey, how can they not feel overawed by all this? How will it affect how they open any trade negotiation or lodge any complaint?

In most ways, this display of wealth is an immoral waste, indefensible. In other ways, wasting so much wealth might mean there is less need for literal defenses, for there is no cheaper way to defeat a rebellion than to discourage it before it begins. It means better terms are offered by friends and foes alike, whether in trade or in war.

I have no idea if that was in mind when the Alitaerans opened their purses for this storm ship, or if its builders were merely recklessly extravagant, but having heard that the empress tries to bring as many visiting nobles on this journey as possible, and tries to include many who haven't made the passage before, I see now that she has taken this fixed expense—for surely an empress can't cut back on luxuries without seeming poorer and thus weaker than her predecessors—and turned it into a tool: wealth as weapon, profligacy as poniard.

Despite myself, my respect for her grows.

I spend the whole day exploring. During the nobles' mealtimes, a veritable horde of servants descend on Elysion. All are examined thoroughly before entering, though. There are no children anywhere. Like so many parents', it seems the nobles' conception of paradise has no space for children.

Which makes me think of Caedan again. And Phaena. But I find no hint of either.

There are incongruities. A ring around the pond's shore shows that the water level is down more than a handspan from usual. One bridge is roped off, with cracks showing in the mortar between bricks. Scaffolding shrouds one of the buildings.

It's only as I look at the repairs that I notice that, hanging in the open sky, there is a glassed-in walkway circling the whole of the little artificial neighborhood. Surely that's for the empress to observe her subjects at play—with several open stages at various heights so that she may address them.

There are workers toiling on the glassine walkway right now, including several who must be mages from the lights blooming from their hands. In the flaring of light and shadow of the magic, one looks quite like a squashed frog, neckless, with a huge mouth. It puts me in mind of Sister Ayayah Meganah. How would my mother have put it? 'That poor thing, she tumbled out the ugly tree, and got slapped by mos' every branch on the way down.'

I hear some musicians setting up in one of the park pavilions festooned with herms, and smile for the first time in what feels like years. I head toward the sound, avoiding the back street where butchers are cutting up a manatee and make my way toward a faux town square.

There are some fire-breathers practicing for the night's parade after the nobles' dinners, so I fall in behind them, juggling a few daggers to fit in. I can only do four, far short of what a professional can do, but I was never daring enough to risk the cuts on those days when Durzo chained me in. Juggling daggers seemed dangerous enough. But today I'm feeling good.

I try five. The gleaming, spinning steel is a joy to behold. Five, then six. I get to seven before I run out of knives and luck both. I've turned the corner to the park where the musicians are warming up when I drop all the knives as I see a big man.

Not the most subtle thing I've ever done, dropping seven knives on the cobblestones, and the big man turns and sees me.

King Repha'im, not ten paces away, is flanked by monstrously huge imperial bodyguards. He doesn't look happy to see me, perhaps because he's currently encumbered with that vituperative slattern Sister Ayayah Meganah, and she's got her tongue in his mouth, her hand down his trousers.

Nope, nope, on second glance, it's not her. This woman looks similar, but as she turns, I see that this woman is actually pretty.

"What's the meaning of this?" the woman demands.

I'm frozen, horrified.

"There's only one way you can answer for this offense," King Repha'im growls. "Only one way for us to settle all this once and for all!"

I know it, too. It was always going to come down to this, in the end. I adjust my belt and take a wider stance as he does the same.

He points at the band, and we both shout, "Dance off!"

And then the music starts, and the battle is on, and this is what you get for reading over someone's shoulder, you malevolent hag. Yes, I mean you, Sister Ayayah Meganah, with your saggy dugs and your expression of permanent constipation.

What the hell? Viridiana stopped reading, confused, and looked up. At a slight sound, she turned and looked behind her.

Not far away, Sister Ayayah Meganah was standing on a chair, with a telescope in hand, reading literally over Vi's shoulder. The woman was flushed purple, trembling.

Trying to regain some dignity, she stepped down from the chair but stumbled.

Vi couldn't help herself. She snorted.

She was always doing that, cracking a laugh when she absolutely positively shouldn't.

The look she got from the older Sister was pure poison. She stormed past Vi, huffing. "You won't get away with this. I don't know how you did that, but I won't be mocked. You, you . . . you ignorant little bitch!"

"I—I didn't do any—"

"Don't you lie to me! This isn't over!"

And then Sister Ayayah left, slamming the door behind her.

Vi turned to Sister Ariel, still at her own desk. "Did you know she was doing that?"

"I don't know how many times I can plausibly clear my throat in a few minutes," Sister Ariel said. "You did not appear to hear me."

Vi pressed her lips into a thin line. "Well, you do clear your throat remarkably often. I try to ignore it."

"I do?" Sister Ariel asked. "You do?"

"Yes!"

"Huh. That seems unbefitting behavior for a library. I shall endeavor to stop. Regardless, I couldn't do more. I've been forbidden to interfere with any of their investigations. I'm pressing my luck simply being here. Plus, I figured the spells on that book were good enough to make her reading fruitless at worst, and at best possibly entertaining."

"Ooooh," said Vi, feeling very, very stupid. "So the book made up all that stuff? Just off-the-cuff?"

"Off-the-margin, you mean?"

"Huh?"

"Never you mind. You said when you flip ahead the pages are blank?"

Vi nodded.

"The magic on the book senses who's reading it; that's why only *you* can read it. It wants to only be read by you, so when anyone else tries, there's some kind of trap triggered. The Sisters are lucky it didn't go up in flames. I've encountered such spells before on particularly dangerous books."

"I'd say *I'm* lucky it didn't do that, too," Vi said, for the first time thinking of her own proximity to a highly magical book as being in proximity to something highly magical *and possibly dangerous.*

"Who knows? Maybe it will change its mind and decide to kill you at the end," Sister Ariel said.

Then, at the stricken look on Vi's face, Ariel pursed her thin lips, sighed. "A jest. That was a jest."

"So ... uh, what do I do now?" Vi asked.

"The magic should've made some sign that it recognized it was being read illicitly. Probably something you would've known? Not that such signs are a necessary component of the magic. I've encountered a general encryption a few times, but I've only read about personally attuned encryptions, and only one volume that mentioned mockery as a possible outcome. I'm so pleased the mage who prepared your book must've read the same tome! What did it say to Sister Ayayah?"

"I...I probably should finish reading it before I go into all that. I'm already behind."

"Oh yes, yes, of course, and I do have some rather preposterous Pellestian interpolations I need to fix before dinner. Give me a good copyist over a bad translator any day, that's what I always say!"

Vi frowned. Then she turned back to the book, flipped back a page.

Everything still looked the same. What was she supposed to do?

She reread it. "Ah, this?" she asked, putting her finger on the part about Kylar's mother. Kylar was an orphan. She knew he was an orphan. She'd always known he was an orphan. The magic had even inserted Sister Ayayah's name into those first lines. It had all but waved its hands and jumped up and down to get her attention, and now that she looked at it, it was pretty much impossible to miss. Yet she had.

That's me! I do the impossible for breakfast. The impossibly dumb.

She went back to reading, skimming back through the bits about his scouting, which all seemed unchanged, but now, after the explanation of walkways, the text changed in midparagraph, without her eyes being able to even notice the shift. All the text about Sister Ayayah Meganah simply was gone: the insults, the manatee, the band, the dance battle. There was now new text—the real text—in its place.

Or what Viridiana assumed was the real text. That the words could change so easily and by someone's magic made her uneasy. Was it not *Kylar's* magic doing this? If he'd worked with a mage to do it, how could she tell whose words she had been reading when the magic had addressed Sister Ayayah?

Had Kylar's hired mage changed anything else? How many times had he done so already if he had? How could she tell? What if she couldn't?

But she had no answers, and no way of finding them except by going on.

There are workers toiling away on the glassine walkway right now, including several who must be mages from the lights blooming from their hands.

I take a seat on a little bench to watch. It is not an insignificant height, but then, I'm a good climber. From this distance, I have no idea what the magic does—though the mere fact that they're using magic is dispiriting. I assume it strengthens the tube at the very least, but other defensive magics are also possible.

I do have the black ka'kari, devourer of magic, so perhaps I've just found my way in. Wherever the empress goes, surely King Repha'im goes at least sometimes, and taking a social stroll to watch her subjects seems a likely activity for them to share some evening.

How much trouble might I save the world by assassinating King Repha'im?

He's not my deader. He's not even a target for what I need to do—but he could take me to my target, and he's the threat to my target, after all.

I look to the wall, to the placement of lights. There are huge reinforced glass panels overhead that are cracked open to refresh the air within. At night I'd guess those will be pulled fully shut.

I note where the ribs of the ship supporting the roof will give me deep shadow and where it appears that lookouts can be stationed, though the spaces are oddly empty now. If mages are often standing watch in those...

After a few minutes of scoping out the likely problems and threats of various approaches, I decide I've sat long enough that sitting longer may arouse suspicion, so I move on, building a mental map of the ship's interior spaces and how the decks align.

Taking my time, I scope out the servants' passages and explore a few of them invisibly. These are guarded only on one end or the other, but all are guarded, and I have to suppose with mages who are taking great care at their work.

As I head back, I see overseers with whips in hand guiding chained lines of male and female slaves downstairs to the vice rooms, all of them dripping wet, half-naked, bathed and scrubbed for the nobles' later use.

Servants with mops follow behind, wiping the wet cobbles dry, closing and padlocking the door downstairs where the wretches disappeared, erasing all evidence of the human cost of those noble bastards' pleasures, as if it's that easy.

For a moment, I consider going below. But what's the point? If I go down there, I'm going to kill people. I won't be able to help it—and for what? Those slaves aren't finding freedom no matter what I do. There's no way off this ship, no way out of this life for them.

Momma K was right. I'm very good at a very few things. None of them will help most of the people on this ship, no matter how much they need help.

On revisiting this later, I should point out that I was mistaken. The 'slaves' here were indentured servants. That seems very important to everyone—not only to the Alitaeran nobles who are far too moral and dignified to have any

part in slavery, but also, oddly enough, to the indentured servants themselves.
They shorten their indentures by serving this way, they say. They can leave if
they want to—that is, if they're willing to add extra time to their term of inden-
ture for breaking the subcontract. This isn't slavery; it merely looks like it,
smells like, and feels like it. But it's totally different.

Totally different.

I scout the rest of Elysion, at least the parts dedicated to the harmless vices.
After dinner, the nobles will flood into the faux neighborhood, which means
they'll vacate the areas I need to scout next. I'm making a lot of assumptions,
but I've already seen a cultural—or the empress's personal—aversion to having children underfoot. I'm guessing the same has got to occur with infants,
such as the young prince I'm attempting to rescue.

Infants are loud and demanding, and even when they're not being either of
those things, they still soak up all the attention of women nearby, which is
not an ideal situation for a man actively attempting to—how would Logan put
it?—*inveigle* one of those women into the act by which infants are made.

That is exactly what I assume King Repha'im is hoping to be doing on this
trip. Once the storm ship docks in Borami, the empress will have ten thousand
duties waiting for her from the half of her empire that hasn't seen her for six
months. Maybe she'll let Repha'im share her bed while she attends to those.

But he'd be a fool to bet on it.

That means the child, precious though it is to him, will likely not be in the
imperial chambers. It will be nearby, somewhere easily accessed and safe,
some servants' quarters or barracks. Maybe the brig if safety is of the greatest
import.

That wouldn't be a good look, though; I can't imagine the empress being
pleased with her new king if the first thing she saw of his character was him
imprisoning infants. Plus it would make him look scared. I don't believe he'd
let anyone think that.

But I can't *know*. Not yet.

Speaking of dangers, if Viridiana's right about Caedan and the null wave,
why the hell did Repha'im bring a child with magic-negating powers onto a
ship held together with magic? Does he not know what Caedan does?

On the one hand, it took some of the best Healers in the world from the
Chantry a long time to figure out what Caedan does, so there's no reason
Repha'im would necessarily figure it out immediately.

But it does seem like atrocious luck for him. Unfortunately, though, not for him alone. I had to go jump on the ship myself, didn't I?

What's his plan for the child, anyway? If he doesn't know about the null magic, is he assuming that the kid is going to inherit his father's abilities? As far as I know, children evincing Talent is more common among those with Talented parents, but it's far from a sure thing. But maybe that's one of the things Repha'im can see with his strange eyes. Maybe he can see that the kid's Talented.

And then I feel a chill. When I demanded to know where the boys were, I thought he was ignoring me as he'd gone on about how to make the perfect weapon, how you break someone, deform them to a singular purpose, leaving only enough humanity to be able to manipulate them. Is that what he means to do to this child?

But if there are any answers to that, I can't know those, either.

I find my feet taking me back to Viridiana's room. My heart's in turmoil. I *miss* her. What's that about? I was just with her! But mixed with my eagerness, I feel something akin to dread. I'm gonna mess it up. Any time things are going too well, I know not to trust it.

Besides, she's reported in to the Sisters. Who's to say what orders they've given her about me? She's one of them now. Even if I don't mess things up, the odds of us getting out of this and even being friends on the other side are slim at best. The Sisters who don't want vengeance for my harmless little prank with the Speaker last year want to capture me and dissect me—some metaphorically, but some literally.

A Sister of the Chantry can't be my friend. There's certainly no way she can be more.

I stop in the hallway outside her room. I should walk on by. There's nothing for me here. If I go inside, I either mess things up, or things will mess me up. Like Grandmaster Vitruvius told me, there's no winning for me on this ship.

Will you please tell me to walk on by the door?

~Kylar, keep walking.~

Thank you. You're right.

That decided, I feel better immediately. Then I open the door and step inside.

Chapter Seventy-Two

The Dagger and the Bed

"There's been a change of plans," Vi says, closing the door of her room and throwing home the bolt. She carries a stack of clothes over to a table, doesn't turn around. "Buttons," she says.

It's practically an order this time, and it irks me, but I can tell something is wrong, so I move close and undo the buttons. She strips as if she were alone, checks the dress, then carefully hangs it up. She peels off her shift and underwear, puts them nonchalantly in a laundry bag, then goes to her mirror and removes her cosmetics, utterly nude and unself-conscious.

When she does this, I can't tell what's going on. Is this a remnant of how messed up her upbringing was or is she doing this on purpose? Is she so disconnected from her body that she doesn't think anything of stripping naked in front of someone? Does she have no sense that her body might attract the interest of the young man standing right next to her bed? Does she think that her body is only attractive when she wants it to be?

No, surely not that. She has to have been harassed by strangers far too many times to believe that. So, then does she consider me to be sexless, the friend-therefore-eunuch?

I consider the alternative: that this is a seduction. She's craning her neck now, muscling the skin of her chest around so she can pluck an ingrown hair out of her armpit.

It'd be one hell of a clumsy seduction.

"What's wrong with you?" I demand. Why am I so angry? Why am I angry at all?

"What?" she says, continuing to worry at the hair. That's when I know she's doing this on purpose. Not why, though. Nor what *this* is.

"Trying to infuriate me, then, huh?"

"Not everything's about you, Kylar."

"This is."

She looks at me with pure contempt, but as I hold her gaze, level, she cracks and looks away, ashamed.

In a few years' time, I know, she'll be able to hold such looks. She almost broke me with it, damn her. It inflames me. I say, "What in that portable hell you call your brain are you doing? Do you want me to leave? You want me to beat you, call you all the things Hu did? Because I will. Leave, I mean. But if you want beatings and humiliation, you'll have to find someone else."

I stand and call the ka'kari to my palm.

"No, Kylar! Wait!"

She grabs for my hand and then drops to her knees and hugs my legs. And if I was pretty certain before that what she was doing wasn't a seduction, now I'm just as certain this is. A naked woman, clinging to you, cheek pressed against your groin, pleading? We're only one mood swing from here to the bed two feet away.

And my moods are swinging like a drunken pendulum.

What kind of man am I that this is stirring me? A woman feigning helplessness?

But maybe it's not the helplessness. Maybe it's just Vi. Her nearness, her availability. *She* is stirring me. Gods help me, she always stirs me. Always has.

"Get away!" I push at her face, at her shoulder, trying to get her away from me without hurting her.

But she holds on tight, turning her head to make my hand slide off, and she's suddenly kissing my groin. "Just let me. Just let me," she says in between kisses, one hand still wrapped around my back to keep me from pulling away, the other moving to my belt.

She's turning my body against me. I'm responding, responding as I don't want to.

My mind flashes to the last time I made love with Elene, and if some part of your heart could be strangled of blood in the same way a foot falls asleep, I feel the same pain at its awakening as feeling floods back into that long-denied part of me. With Elene, I made love whole, heart and mind and soul aligned, assenting, connecting fearlessly.

I feel like a moneychanger being offered a handful of counterfeit coins. I've handled the real thing. I don't need scales and weights to judge these.

But part of me whispers, *This is all you can get. Elene's gone. Take what you can.*

I don't know why Vi's doing this. It doesn't feel as if she even *wants* to do what she's doing.

She has my belt open. If I hesitate any longer, my body will make the decision for me.

I want her so badly I ache, but I don't want her like this. Not like this!

I grab a fistful of her hair and pull her head back. There's a *shunk*ing sound as the ka'kari leaps sharp into my hand, and she's forced to stare up the length of the ka'kari as a black punch-dagger.

"Enough," I say hoarsely, shaking.

She drops to the floor and starts weeping. Steeling myself against any sympathy, I go over to her drawers, find a nightshirt, and throw it at her.

"Put that on. Talk," I say. "What the hell is wrong with you?"

I turn my back on her, too furious to even watch. Part of me thinks that scorning a dangerous woman's advances and then turning my back on her may be the dumbest thing I've done in a month with many contenders for that title.

I half expect steel to cut a hot line into my back, but I don't want her to see what's on my face. I'm not sure what it will be myself. Disgust? Anger? Lust? Self-disgust at how I wanted to take her despite the fact that I could tell she wanted only to use me to blot out something dark going on inside her? Anger that I know my friend was acting against her own best interests?

That she would use me to act out a part in whatever drama she's reenacting in her head infuriates me again. I don't have many friends. Maybe any, if I think about it too hard. It's not easy to keep a friend in our world, in our work, and she almost took that away from us.

"They…" Her voice is ragged. "I got away with it, Kylar. Killing her. You know, they don't suspect a thing. But I didn't get away with it. Not really. Maybe we never get away with anything."

I look back and see that she hasn't moved from the floor other than to pull the nightshirt over her head. Her long red hair is still trapped beneath the cloth at her neck. She doesn't pull it free. Her eyes are downcast.

"What do you mean?" I ask.

"I told them…I told them when I joined the Sisterhood that there were two things I'd never do again, not for them, not for anyone. Sister Ariel said that was fine. That there were many, many positions in the Chantry that would never dream of asking such things, and none that would ever require either."

"Let me guess," I say. "They want you to do both."

She swallows, gaze downcast. Nods.

I curse the Chantry.

Viridiana scoots to sit with her back to the wall, hugging her knees. "There were two Special Tactics Teams. My team was supposed to recover Caedan. Ysmaena's team was attempting to infiltrate the new king's inner circle. She decided her way in was by serving him your head on a platter."

"That's what that ambush was about?" I ask. "But they don't know why it didn't work?"

"They know it had to be you that killed her. They don't know if you suspect the Sisterhood itself was behind the ambush, though. They don't think Ysmaena would've let that slip. She was too smart and too loyal to the Chantry."

"How do they know it was me?" I ask, though I realize as I say it that it's a dumb question.

"Kylar, who else could've done what you did in that room? Someone walked into an ambush planned for you and all the ambushers ended up dead. Some members of the team weren't at the Chantry when you pulled your little stunt or at Black Barrow. They didn't believe the stories about the Night Angel. Especially after they met you. They do now."

"Especially after they met me?"

"I meant you're younger than they expected," she says awkwardly. Sometimes she's a terrible liar.

Sure. But why do I care what they think about me?

Vi says, "Do you have any idea what it's like out in the ship right now?"

"Sure, I was just scouting out Elysion." Maybe I shouldn't have told her that.

"Elysion and farther forward in the ship they're doing their best to pretend everything is normal. And they have enough mages to pull it off. For the rest of the ship, though? Do you remember when one of the apartment buildings in the Warrens would catch fire? Hu had me watch once when he burned one down, killing forty-seven people in order to fulfill a contract on one. When the fire started, before the people even knew what was going on, there was this sudden flood of rats out into the street, a squirming carpet of filthy gray-brown fur.

"It's like that, Kylar. First it was every room in the back half of the ship and all the lower decks were being turned upside down by imperials looking for you. People lined up and checked one by one. Every deck scoured simultaneously in columns so no one could slip by. We were spared most of that up here because they were so certain you couldn't have made it through some of the defenses to get this far. Defenses the Sisters had to go and quickly reassemble, I'll have you know. I mean, not *me*—I'm not good enough for that work—but the others had to. But with what you did in the ballroom, they have to know you've made it up here. Probably the only reason they haven't found us already is that null wave. The ship's nearly falling apart in a dozen places. Some decks flooded near the back."

"What's the job?" I ask. "What do they want you to do?"

"With Ysmaena dead, I have to take her place. They say there's no one else who can do what she did."

"Take her place? You mean, work your way into Repha'im's inner circle? What about Melena? She seems like she could weasel her way in anywhere."

"She's not his type, I guess. She's working a different angle. Maybe the truth is that she refused to whore herself and she's got seniority so she gets to do that. Doesn't matter. To them, it's simple. I'd already caught Repha'im's eye. They want me to join his circle and stay there, maybe for six months, maybe longer, spying for the Chantry and waiting for further orders now that there's been so much havoc and chaos."

"And you need to be willing to share his bed or murder him, or the bed first and then the dagger. Your two Nevers, right?"

She looks up at me, but she seems absent from herself somehow. "It requires more than being willing. You know how I had a bit of a Talent for glamours?"

"You think I could forget how we met? I think you congratulated me for not actually drooling." I force a smile. On another day, it might be a funny memory for us to share: her barely failed attempt at seducing me.

It's not so funny now.

"My new team only needs me to be willing to do it. But now the old team needs me to get it done before we reach Cloud Point. Which means by dawn the day after tomorrow."

"Why?"

"Glamours are a kind of illusion magic."

"I know what a glamour is."

"Can you shut up, Kylar? I've been learning from the Chantry, and I've learned that some of the stuff I 'learned' growing up was wrong, so I don't know how many of the things you think you know are wrong, too. Takes two seconds, all right?"

You had Hu Gibbet for a master. I had Durzo Blint. I don't think I'm likely to be as wrong about magic as you were.

But I only think these things. I say, "By all means, then."

"So there's two ways to do illusions, at least that I've been taught. One is to make a somewhat physical construct of the thing you're imitating. Which has serious limitations."

I nod. "That's how I can craft new faces with my Talent. It takes forever, the masks are fragile, and the range of uses is severely limited, especially if you want it to move correctly."

"Right. A glamour is the other type. It directly impacts a target's senses. So I didn't realize it back in the bad old days, at least consciously, but my glamours were significantly stronger when I could engage a target's senses—if you smelled me, if I was touching you, if you were hearing my voice, and for them to work at all, you had to be seeing me."

I sit down on the stool where she does her cosmetics. "I'll admit I didn't actually know that."

"Thank you. Where was I? So a subjective illusion has different trade-offs than the objective type, but it's more effective for certain things. If I were to try to seduce a man with a strong preference for buxom brunettes, I wouldn't need to know that about him. With a glamour, his own mind would fill in his own preferences. The man standing beside him might imagine me as a tiny blonde if that's what he liked better. But regardless, when I'd leave, most men would have a sense that something wrong had happened. And the stronger the glamour, the stronger that feeling of wrongness."

"Lemme guess, the Chantry's figured out some way past such petty limitations."

"It's not like the Chantry made these things up, Kylar! Did you never listen to Momma K? Sex magic is the oldest magic. If anything, the Chantry has served the world by locking such techniques away, quashing their use wherever they could, and keeping them out of people's hands, where they could do untold damage."

"Uh-huh. With the totally unforeseen bonus that when the Chantry uses those kinds of magic, no one suspects it. It's real big of them to think of the world's welfare that way. You realize that if everyone knew to be on guard against that kind of magic, there'd probably be simple counters to glamours—but then the Chantry's games would be harder, wouldn't they? And everyone would suspect all Sisters of doing . . . Well, the things they are doing!"

Her eyes flashed. "Please, go on. I feel oh so convicted by the moral indignation of a professional murderer."

My jaw twitches. "I guess that's why we're friends, isn't it? I'm the killer;

you're the whore. I mean, I guess you're a whore *and* a killer, so maybe if we're going to stay friends I better take my game to new heights, but then, I thought you were planning to stop being both of those things."

Her face falls and her fire gutters out. "I thought so too."

"So what do you need to do for them?" I ask, quieter. I can't believe I just called her a whore. It's too late to call the words back, but I need to apologize right away. "Viridiana, I can't believe I said—I'm s—"

"I can't do the magic required on my own," she says, cutting me off. "I'm not good enough yet, not by a long shot. But they can help me do all the stuff I can't. And it's, it's weird magic for the Chantry. You know how most of our magic is mental, called into being through the voice and rhythms? This is different. Because this magic's got all these hooks to the senses, it needs hooks to the body. They've already used a weave to capture the sound of Repha'im's voice. Now I need to gather everything else I can from him—scrapings of his skin, his fingernails, his hair, his blood, his spit, his..."

"His semen?" I guess. It's not much of a guess.

She nods but looks away quickly. "I mean, I need to get his *urine* if I can. The more connections I have to him, the finer, stronger, and more subtle the glamour's weaves can be. More durable. The more we get, the more the Sisters can do with it. The most important thing all those things will do, though, is give him a deep attraction to me, an attraction that will last and should escape any magical examination."

"Which will make him keep you close, and make him trust you. Both things that will make you an excellent asset for the Chantry."

"And for my original team's mission, it gives them the possibility of making an illusory construct the other way—you know, an illusion, a physical thing—and make it far, far more compelling to him."

"What kind of construct are you thinking?"

"Not me, it's not my plan, but... The illusion will be of baby Caedan still asleep in his crib, so that after the Sisters snatch him, if anyone checks, especially King Repha'im, they'll see the baby's still there, sleeping quietly. The timing will have to be perfect, because, for example, no matter how good the illusion, they can't make a construct-baby draw milk from a nursemaid's breast. We'll have to learn the baby's routines, and I don't know if you know this, but babies' routines change *constantly.* But it should give us—them, I should say—hours of a head start. Hours will be all they need. At Cloud Point, at dawn the day after tomorrow, the *Storm*

Racer will pass through a lull as it starts north. The Painted Hills come to a headland there that briefly blocks the wind. A boat will be sent out to meet us there. One of the Sisters on the boat is a weather mage, but the timing's tight."

"I feel like you're getting way ahead of me. I was—oh yeah. Repha'im. What do you know about him?"

"Alitaeran noble from the hinterlands beyond the Ash Forest, has some properties and businesses in Cenaria, Waeddryn, Modai, and Elenea. Probably titles in all of them. He's one of these vultures looking for opportunity wherever he can find it."

"Yeah, I didn't mean that part."

"Then what'd you mean?" Viridiana asks.

"He said something about teaching the Chantry a lesson. Uh..." Then I realize I don't have to try to recall an approximation of his words.

What was it again? I ask the ka'kari.

~'Even though they suspect what I am, they still think they can pull one over on me. On me! And you people have such respect for the Chantry's long memory. But then, every so often they do need to be taught a lesson. Like a dog that nips your heels, a good cudgel across the eyes teaches more than a thousand sharp words. I'll be teaching them soon and bluntly.' That bit?~

You are useful!

~You always act so surprised.~

"He said that the Chantry suspects what he is, and thought it was funny that people have such respect for the Chantry's long memory. Said they needed to be taught a lesson, and that he planned to do it, soon."

"What's he mean about the Chantry's memory?" Viridiana asks.

"Like...knowledge that Sisters pass down to each other over time, I guess. Point is, he spoke as if he's ancient. As if he's"—I look at her carefully to judge her reaction—"not exactly human."

Her eyebrows climb. "We saw some crazy stuff at Black Barrow, Kylar, so I'm open to there being things out there I don't understand."

"But?" I ask.

"We've got papers about this guy, a whole history. That seems like the sort of thing the Chantry would note in big letters, doesn't it?"

"I saw his eyes. They...rotated."

"They what?"

"They weren't human."

"You saw this with one of your Talents?" she asks. And I see what she's thinking.

"I know lots of nobles use illusions here, but I don't think ..." *Was* it an illusion? Was he merely messing with me? But it seemed so real. "No, not with my Talent. There's something really off about him. If the Chantry can dig deep to find out more, they better."

"And how are we going to do that out here, Kylar? We have to act. We have a limited window of opportunity. If we wait until Borami, we lose every advantage we have. So, I dunno, is that everything?" Vi moves to stand, as if we're finished talking. At some other point in my life, I would have let it go, let the awkwardness retreat rather than confront it.

"Hold on, not so fast," I say, and I see guilt flash over her face. Funny how both of us can face death but not embarrassment. She's so like me sometimes. "So what was *this* about?"

"This?" she says, but the lie is as obvious as the red flush on her ears.

"A few minutes ago, you had your face in my crotch and were trying to pull my trousers off."

"Oh. That." Her hands fall into her lap. Her shoulders sag. "Kylar, I know you. I know once I go back to ... all that, that life ... you'll be done with me. I'd be done with me, too. I said I was getting out of it, and here I am, going back. So I thought if we were ever going to ... I don't know, I thought sometimes that maybe someday we—it's ... whatever."

" 'It's ... whatever'?" I repeat, as if our relationship can be discarded so casually.

She turns her glistening eyes away. "Maybe I wanted it to be my choice. My choice, one last time, or maybe for a first time. It's always been at someone's bidding before. Always for work. For Hu, and now the Chantry ..."

"So you just wanted to bed someone, and there was someone already conveniently in your bedroom, so why not him?" It's not what she's saying, but I'm so angry everything's threatening to explode.

"Maybe so," she says, a note of defiance creeping into her voice.

"Do you know how many friends I have, Vi?"

"Viridiana," she says sharply.

"Right, 'cause you're so different from the old Vi."

She starts as if I slapped her.

"Not many," I say.

"Not many?"

"Friends."

"Small wonder."

But I push past that like a charger breaking enemy lines. "Maybe none if I really think about it. I'm gonna lose Logan's friendship over this. You know, losing his kids because I was more interested in chatting with you? So that leaves you. And you know what burns me?"

She crosses her arms. "Pray tell."

"It burns me that you'd throw away our friendship because you've got an itch in your crotch. I mean, I think our friendship could've survived you being a hypocrite and going right back to all the things you swore you'd leave. Like you said, who am I to judge that? Totally fair. The Sisterhood means everything to you, and you're backed into a corner. I mean, sure, it's incredibly obvious that when they tell you they need you to seduce and murder just this one time that what they really mean is *just this one time this month*, and next month there'll be a new and equally important job for someone with your *unique skills*. That's how these people operate. They need tools for their dirty work, and that's what you're agreeing to be. So sure, that's obvious to me, and it should be to you, but maybe it's not. Maybe I'm even wrong. Maybe you do need to do this one thing, and after this you really will be done. One last job, right? We all fall for that one. But maybe you think, 'Better I do this than someone else dirties their soul with it,' right? Sure, you're a fool if you believe that, but I get it. I've been a fool myself. I could've understood all that.

"But you were planning to seduce *me*? Just to have some fun before you go upstairs and spread your legs for Repha'im an hour from now? You'd do that? You'd do that to us?

"Maybe it says more about me than it does about you, that I'd choose as my one friend someone who would treat me this way. You want to know something pathetic? I haven't been with a woman since Elene died. Since I killed her, I guess I should say. Since we're being all honest here. And I'm embarrassed to admit that even when she was alive I always had this funny thought about how you're everything she wasn't, Vi. *Viridiana*, sorry. You know, when I'd get frustrated that she was too uptight or too modest or whatever stupid thing I was mad about. But I never did her the justice of realizing what else that meant."

Vi is shaking her head, *no, no.* Her lip is literally quivering. But I can't stop myself.

"See, Elene was everything that you're not, too. Kind, thoughtful, putting other people's needs above her own whims, unfailingly acting with integrity regardless of what it cost her. I mean, I get it! I know how we grew up, you and me, our training was different, and the lessons I took away from my training were messed up, maybe especially about sex. Maybe I should treat it more casually than I do. Probably. But you know me. You *know* that I don't, so when you try to pull me into your bed, it's not sex you're treating casually—it's *me*. I can't believe with how well we know each other that you'd be so callous. You had to know—if you thought about it for even two seconds!—that I couldn't sleep with you and have it mean nothing. That it would kill me to find out you went from our bed to his. You had to know that I would think it meant something if we made love. That I would think *I* meant something to you."

And now *I'm* tearing up, damn it all. "I know I'm a mess, Vi, and maybe I shouldn't be this way, but that's not who I am. Damn you for this. Damn you for treating me like an afternoon's entertainment."

"Kylar…" Tears are streaming down her face. "I killed one of my Sisters for you. How could you think I don't care—?"

"Your *Sisters*, who were trying to hand me over to Repha'im. Who they know is evil. And why? For what I'd done? No. I hadn't done anything to them at that point. They were going to give me to him because they're afraid of me. Of what I might do. That's your Sisterhood. *That's* who you've pledged yourself to. People who would murder your friend so they can have more power."

"Kylar, you can't judge the whole Sisterhood by what one rogue team does."

"Well, then I'm sure the Chantry as a whole won't judge *me* when I kill that rogue team, then. Right? Probably thank me for getting rid of the rogues, huh? I'll be saving them from everyone else mistakenly thinking that those bad apples represent the Chantry!" I sneer. "You think that's how it'll go? Or do you think that if they learn that I killed one of their own, the Chantry will hunt me to the ends of the earth?"

"Kylar…"

"What else do they have to do to prove what they really are to you, Viridiana? They try to murder me, they force you back into sex slavery—and you still think they're the good guys?"

"They're not all like this. They're terrified, Kylar. You have no idea what you're talking about. It's not like this is normal for them!"

"Vi. Come on. There's always an excuse. 'This time' is always the exception. 'Just this once' is the same thing for an organization like the Chantry that 'one more job' is to people like us. I know you're young, but how the hell can you be this naïve?"

"We're talking about the end of magic, Kylar. Of all of it. And do you know whose fault it is? Ours. Yours and mine. Oh, sure, it's Durzo's and Dorian's and all the rest too, but of the twelve of us who were there, only you and I are *here*. We did something at Black Barrow that messed up centuries of balance, and the Chantry is the only group of people who have a prayer of putting things right again."

"Ah, 'we're the only ones who can fix this big thing, so you'll need to forgive us for doing all this little stuff'? Another one of the classics. 'Gotta break a few eggs to make an omelet'? Where's the omelet?"

Her brows draw down, her mouth pinches. "You're a real piece of work, Kylar."

"We're done here. I can see whose side you've chosen. Thanks for saving my life, Viridiana. I'm sorry for making you blur those very clear lines you've drawn. Next time I'll let your new friends kill me. I do hope they return your loyalty. I'm leaving." I pause at the door. "Oh. Should I send in the first man I find so you can scratch that itch?"

I step out, certain—even as I close the door gently—that I'm slamming the door on my last hope.

For some reason, Viridiana was acutely aware of the air crossing her tongue, brushing her throat, filling her lungs with cool air.

Sister Ariel looked up at her suspiciously. "Do you need a word?" the older woman asked. She looked like she was trying to be patient but really wanted to finish her paragraph.

"No," Viridiana said with a wan smile. "It's funny, I...I thought that of all the places where he might exaggerate or lie about what happened, this would be the one. But, uh, he told it straight. Didn't spare himself."

"He was an admirable man in many ways. I feel great regret to have been deprived of the chance for more conversations with him."

Sister Ariel looked at Vi's frozen social smile for a moment longer, then, appearing to think she'd done what was required, turned back to her work.

"Didn't spare me either," Viridiana said quietly. "Not that I would have it any other way."

Perhaps it was the truth itself that didn't spare her.

What would have happened if I'd gone after him then? If I'd told him all the truth?

Not this. Not this.

Chapter Seventy-Three

A Mad Queen's Wrath

*H*ave you ever messed up huge and known it immediately? Have you stood outside a door, knowing you should go back in right away, limbs heavy as if pride and anger and self-justification had tied down your every better instinct? Have you stood mere feet away, already replaying what you said and what they said, not sure if you should weep or scream or go beg forgiveness? Have you stood on the edge of that pool of weakness that's so deep that if you take one step into it, you'll drown?

I haven't. I'm a super assassin. I'm standing outside Vi's room calmly plotting my next steps. Emotions are baggage. Slow you down. So I leave them behind. I'm just taking a little rest here. Totally cerebral. Breathing is a little challenging. Not sure what that's about. It doesn't matter.

I'm hungry. That's it. Haven't eaten since breakfast.

With effort, I push away from the wall. The first steps away are like trudging out of a swamp—which proves how much I need to get away from here. Vi's presence makes me weak. I'll avoid her in the future.

Maybe Durzo was right after all. Emotions are baggage, he said. Relationships are ropes, he said. Love is...Well, this isn't love, so that part doesn't matter.

Practically starving, I end up going back around Elysion toward one of the nobles' lounges, high on the ship, with windows from floor to ceiling bathing the room in the surreal orange hue of a poison dart frog, the sunset colored fierce by the dust the Great Storm has carried out to sea.

Barely one step into the grand salon, though, I hear a voice that stops me in my tracks.

"I can't stop you. I know that now," a woman says. I feel as if someone's stacked stones on my chest. I turn, hoping I'm mistaken, hoping the face won't match the voice. But it does. Queen Jenine Gyre, Logan's wife, is sitting at a table set for two. She gestures to the empty seat, as if she's been saving it for me for some time. Her eyes are dying coals smothering in a cold visage.

There's not one chance in a thousand this will work, but I make my voice huskier and say, "Milady, I'm afraid you've mistaken me for—"

Those dying coal eyes go live and hot in an instant, but her voice stays level. "Kylar. Come speak with me. I insist."

From one huge mistake to another.

Hey, I've come up with a title for my story! The Kylar Stern Saga: From One Huge Mistake to Another. Real fans call it TKSS:FOHMTA, pronounced Tuh Kss Foam Tuh. What do you think?

The ka'kari doesn't answer.

Personally, I'm pretty impressed I was able to come up with the acronym.

A glance confirms that, yes, indeed, there are still mages and guards at each of the six exits of the grand salon. Otherwise, the room is uncrowded, with some nobles drinking and talking noisily, others grabbing a meal. I wet my lips, put a tight smile on my face, and sit.

The table is small. When I scoot in, my knees almost brush Jenine's slender, crossed legs. I'm careful not to touch her, uncertain what explosion might result.

She gestures to a plate with some canapés. "The crab is lovely. Very fresh. Help yourself."

I take one. If she's going to do violence to me, she's got faster ways to kill me than poison. I chew.

Swallow.

Her large hazel eyes study me minutely, and I wonder if the feeling sticking in my throat is evidence that she has poisoned me after all. Maybe she'd rather watch me writhe in agony than let a swift spear put an end to me.

Despite all she's been through, she's young. Her forehead is smooth and flawless. No lines adorn the corners of her eyes. Yet nothing of youth lives inside those eyes. This is a woman who walks among dragons.

I am in deep, deep trouble.

Did you edit that one? 'Trouble'?

~Yes.~

I finish the toasted bread with its bit of creamy crab and herbs.

"Wine?" She gestures to the second goblet on the table.

"Uh, no thanks. I'm..."

"Working? But of course you are. Please, lay down your labors a moment. Drink. I insist." Her eyes catch the orange of the sunset as she says this, and I see a flash of pleasure. Maybe the poison is in my goblet.

I drink, a real drink, not a tiny sip. I won't give her the pleasure of seeing my fear.

Besides, if I were going to poison someone who might suspect it, I'd certainly use a poison powerful enough that even the smallest sip would kill.

"Very good. How do they manage to serve it cold?" I ask.

"Magic. Woven into the goblets themselves, they say. Can you imagine?"

"Price is no object with the Alitaerans. They're making a point."

"Oh, certainly. More than one, and yet, even though you know what they're doing, it *still* works. Isn't that funny?"

It's as if I swallowed an eel, how my stomach churns. This woman is so poised, so far from the sobbing mess I've seen recently that I feel sweat in the small of my back.

"The Alitaerans are masters of this sort of thing, it seems," I say.

"*Masters*, yes!" she says quietly but with a sudden heat and intensity, as if I pumped the bellows of a forge on the embers in her eyes.

I swallow. Take another drink of the wine.

That heat down my throat is only the alcohol, isn't it?

I haven't seen her give any signal, but I hear footsteps behind me. My muscles tense for the attack, though I'm careful not to give any indication I hear the ambush coming.

I wait.

Wait.

And then, on hearing the scuff of the feet and the ease of their breath, realize it's men bringing our entrées. I force myself to relax as they take one plate away and set food before us.

The servant announces what our dishes are, but I don't hear him. Jenine is eyeing me, eyes disconcerting as they intermittently reflect the surreal sunset. I'm caught in some kind of game where I don't know the rules.

The last time we met, Jenine tried to get me killed. It almost worked, too. And now she's here. She should be halfway home with Logan. What the hell is she doing *here*? And why is she smiling?

"Do you recognize it?" she asks. "Seafood is so hard to get back home that I couldn't help myself."

She has fried red snapper on her plate, the whole fish—far too much for her to eat, but the Alitaerans do love their wasteful displays. On my plate, with its bones arrayed artfully to make it obvious what the creature was before being prepared, is a blowfish.

I smile indulgently. It's her first misfire. She's not on the level of Momma K yet.

Her own smile fades. "What?" she demands.

"Thing about veiled threats? They work best when they're veiled. You give a man in my line of work *fugu*? It's too much. If you're gonna serve that to someone like me, don't draw attention to it. It's like explaining a punch line to a court jester." I pop a bite in my mouth. "Just a tip from someone who's seen a lot of death threats."

Her eyes have gone hard. I should not have done that. But then, I've never responded well to threats.

"Mmm, my lips are tingling," I say. That your lips go numb is one of the myths about this fish. In truth, with fugu poison, you're either safe or you're dead.

Why am I mocking her?

I am in very deep trouble. Why is it when the waters come up to my neck, I push out deeper still, every time?

But her face has shifted from anger to something else I can't read. And now I notice what I should've noticed first by its absence. She seems exactly like the queen she is, neither disheveled nor overwrought, but rather prim and commanding. I should think this is a wonderful change, but the steel in her has me on guard.

How thin, how fragile is it?

"Why are you here?" I ask. "Where's Logan?"

"Logan's on his way home. I decided I had other business to attend to, here. Not that anyone wanted me here. But you see, it's very hard to deny a queen something she's set her mind on."

"Is Logan all right with you being h—"

"Logan is my husband, not my owner," she snaps.

I take a breath, then let it go without saying anything. There's no winning here.

Moving on, she says, "Is it wrong, do you think, to hate someone for something they'll never do—but the only reason they won't do it is because they won't have the opportunity?"

I stroke my chin. "I, uh, do think it's wrong to hate people for things they haven't done, yes. But maybe it's fair to realize that the reason most people don't do more wrong things is because they lack the opportunities to do them."

She leans forward. "Do you believe it's wrong to hate someone for what they *are* going to do but haven't done yet?"

"That's not really the kind of ethical question that makes sense. We don't get to know what people are going to do. We can guess, but people surprise us, don't they?"

"Ha!" she says, and her face betrays a deep bitterness, but I can't tell at whom. Perhaps herself. "Do you know, despite all the ways he hurt me, in these last months I've come to have a new compassion for Dorian."

"For Dorian?" I say carefully. If there's a list of things that might set Jenine off, discussing the man who deceived her into bigamy and fathered her twins has got to be near the top.

She'd had a distant look in her eyes, but now she snaps back to the present. "Logan was going to do something unforgivable. He won't do it, because of you."

"Because of me? That sounds good...?"

"He won't have to. Because you'll do something worse. So should I forgive Logan for what he won't have the opportunity to do? Should I think less of him because he would fail a test that most men would fail? How do I ever trust my husband again, knowing his limits?"

I want specifics—what *won't* Logan do that's so awful?—but I can tell I won't get them by asking directly. If she thinks I want something, she won't give it to me. "I think you trust your husband all the more, precisely because you know his limits."

"Ah, that's right." She gestures with her small seafood fork. "People surprise us indeed. I forgot your loyalty to him. Kylar, the ultimate partisan—at least when it comes to my first and third husband." She smiles wryly, but I see the acid in it.

"If you let that bitterness eat you up, you'll lose everything in yourself you love and respect. I'm worried that rather than abandon you, Logan will follow you into that abyss because of his love for you."

Her wine hesitates a moment on its way to her lips. "Ah, I . . . Yes." She sets down the wine and grabs my arm across the table, as if we're dear friends. "You know, I've a sudden idea! Would you like to come to court, Kylar? Be my jester?"

"Because no one else will dare tell you the truth? Is that the kind of queen you intend to be?" I look down at her hand on my arm. She removes it. "I see I've lost whatever chance I had with you, though I've done nothing to deserve it. I'm sorry to—"

"Don't you say sorry to me! Don't you dare!" Her voice rises enough that I see numerous imperials look our way. She seems not to notice, her burning eyes never lifting from me.

"Then I'll say only good day, Your Highness." I start to rise.

"Sit." She hisses the word, sibilant, not raising her voice, but there's something reckless under her cool demeanor. She doesn't know how it will end if she calls the imperials on me. She must realize it could go badly for her. As if I'd allow harm to come to her! But if she thinks about it at all, she simply doesn't care.

I sit.

"I've tried to stop you," Jenine says. "I told people where you'd be. Either they didn't believe me—because I'm a hysterical woman, don't you know? Or they tried to stop you, and they couldn't. So I want you to know something about what's coming, something that I've figured out from my sleepless nights as much as from the nights of unending nightmares.

"Fate isn't a kidnapper who tosses you over his saddle and races to a precipice to throw you to your doom. Fate is your own character, digging its heels in to that horse, whipping it, and pulling its head back toward the precipice, never letting it turn aside. I've seen something of the future, yes, maybe, but I know it could all be a delusion. I asked Dorian about it, do you know that? He said he and I see little more than any wise person might readily know simply by looking at the players. So, when you do it, I want you to know, no one is forcing your hand. If someone were, perhaps you might complain, perhaps you could think yourself guiltless. Perhaps you might not be damned. But you can't say that. And you will be damned. I'll have no apologies from you, and you will have no forgiveness."

"What are you talking about? What is it you think I'm going to do?" I ask. I know she's damaged. I know this isn't her fault, but my face is hot.

"You say that as if you want to know, but I know what this is. It's a trap. You're going to try to make me look insane again. Because if—" Her lip quivers between a grimace and tears. "If I say it aloud, I'll break down again. And then you'll escape. Again."

Escape again?

Whatever else that means, it confirms what I suspected: There's a trap waiting at the end of this conversation. She has no intention of letting me leave here.

I should go now. I should run. She'll shout, I'm sure, but waiting only plays into her hands. I extend my senses, glance at the reflection in a spoon for anyone approaching from behind.

I take a moment to scan the room again. There have been no signs of an incoming attack. I would've noticed the servants clearing out the room, the way the guards might do before they try to take me down. It hasn't happened. At least, until now.

On the far side of the grand salon, a knot of women stands up, more or less at the same time. Seated as they were, before now I hadn't been able to see them given the tables and plants and statuary adorning this space, but their moving together alerts me. Three of the women are dressed similarly in white with red crossed lapels, one adding red embroidery on her shoulders to that. Two military men accompany them.

I recognize one of those men—Ishael, one of Repha'im's bodyguards! I lean to my left so that Jenine's head will be between me and him. Ishael knows me by sight.

Jenine doesn't seem to notice anything amiss, but even as I focus my attention back on her to make sure that my momentary distraction appears to be the normal roving of eyes, it occurs to me that I've seen that white garb with crossed red lapels before. Phaena was wearing clothes like that!

The women are far away and leaving through a door toward the higher-security bow of the ship. Even though they surely entered from there mere minutes ago, the guards are checking them out again. I can't see them well, but I'm sure that two of them aren't Phaena.

"Did you speak to the Healers, at the funeral?" Jenine asks.

"Excuse me?" I say politely, wondering if I'm missing some cue, if she said something earlier that I didn't hear while I was looking at Ishael. But no, I'm sure she didn't say anything. I didn't miss anything. Maybe this is a part of her madness, the more cruel because it isn't obvious. Her illness isn't Dorian's mindless gibbering. It's this loose hold on reality instead, where sense comes and goes without announcing its departures, along with violent paranoia. "Which funeral?" I ask, pleasantly.

A woman turns from the group at the exit and takes a quick jog back toward the table they had left, saying something over her shoulder to the others. It's Phaena.

She hasn't seen me. I want to stand up and wave my arms and shout—but Ishael and his partner are right there with her, to say nothing of whatever trap Jenine intends to spring any moment. If I get Phaena's attention, I'll only be dooming her. But at least now I know where she is.

But what is she doing?

"One of the Chantry's younger helpers let something slip at the funeral. I suppose they hadn't been told what lies to tell me yet," Jenine says. "Can you believe that they didn't mean to let me know at all?"

Across the room, Phaena leans over the table and snatches up a white shawl. For an instant, she looks up and catches my eye. But she doesn't stop moving, doesn't hold my gaze, shows nothing to betray surprise at seeing me. With one hand in front of her shawl, as if to make sure I can see it and her guard cannot, she makes a motion as if she's drumming her fingers even as she turns away, the whole thing so fluid that even if Ishael watched her the entire time, he'd not have seen anything amiss.

Then she joins her compatriots as they leave. I don't watch. I don't dare.

"*Snakes*," Jenine says, quietly, but with such vehemence she literally shakes.

It takes me a moment to jettison the shock of Phaena and the mystery of what she was trying to signal me and to settle back here with Jenine, who suddenly looks fully capable of murder.

A helper from the Chantry was doing what? Oh, she's talking about the Chantry's Healers, when they came to help her. They kept secrets from her. I hadn't seen the fissure between Jenine and the Chantry before, but what is she talking about?

Apparently, befuddlement doesn't seem to be the wrong reaction. Jenine watches my face as intently as a viper inching closer to its prey. Except she's not so cold. She seems eager, brimming with malevolence.

"Elene wasn't pregnant," Jenine says. "The Healers examined the bodies minutely after Black Barrow, fearful of what all that magic might have done to us. The dead couldn't object, and the rest of us were too busy with other concerns to stop them."

A bolt shoots through me. She's talking about *Elene's* funeral. The Chantry used magic on Elene's body?

Without asking *anyone*? Without asking *me*?

I shake my head, guts clenching. I have no interest in talking about this. "It was early in the pregnancy. Some Chantry tyro missed it. Elene told me about her pregnancy herself. She wouldn't have said anything until she was sure, and she wouldn't have lied to me."

For a brief moment, I was going to be a father. I had that snatched away from me by cruel reality; I don't need it done again by cruel madness.

"I had it confirmed later, by others," Jenine says, coolly, still staring at me with such intensity it's unnerving. The sun has gone down now, but the sky is a deep red and so are her eyes. "Not by the Chantry. Dorian's meisters were killed in the battle, but among the wise women of the north, not everyone used tainted magic. I found my own midwives, women who'd treated me...before Logan's return."

"I don't follow."

"I was early in my pregnancy too. Maybe the very same number of weeks."

"So..." I'm trying to pay attention still to my surroundings, but I feel snared by her words. If this is madness, it's madness perfectly crafted to keep me rooted to the spot. "So what?"

"Do you know where Dorian trained early in his life, after he left Khalidor?"

"Now we're back to Dorian?" I ask, bewildered. "He trained all over the continent."

"And beyond! He was great, at everything, wasn't he? You went to Tover and found out about his time with the Blues, didn't you?"

I nod, uneasily. How does she know that?

"He spent time with the Reds, too. But first, after leaving Khalidor, he went to Horachi to study with the Hoth'salar."

"Where he became the foremost of the green mages. Yes, yes, I know all this. He was trying to learn to Heal his own oncoming madness."

"While he was there, he was renowned for doing what no one else could," Jenine says, and her eyes seem now full of light. "And all those incredible Healings? He did them without wielding Iures and Curoch at the same time. Imagine what he could do *with* them."

"He didn't have time for Healing, at the end. He was busy destroying an army of monsters." Dorian had been the director of all our magical efforts. He, the greatest of us at seeing all the grand design, had pooled our strengths, and wove them into his masterwork.

"And building a city," Jenine said. "Why didn't he save Elene, if he had time for all that? Surely, he could have left some mere construction for later, and saved your wife."

"Certain things can't be Healed. Like madness. Death. She was killed with Curoch. What Curoch does cannot be undone by other magic. Can't be undone at all. That was part of why it was made." Curoch was created so that even a creature like me could be killed. Indeed, perhaps singularly made so that *I* could be killed. If it kills me, I won't come back.

"But you admit he had time for other magic."

"So?"

"There was still a spark of life within Elene."

I don't want to think about this. I know there was a spark still. Elene's intent had survived into the magic making the city. Logan had honored her sacrifice, her saving all of us, by naming the whole city after her. Enough of her had lived on in the magic long enough to give the city those red springtime tulips. Those were her gift, and though the beauty was shared by everyone in the city, its message was for me alone. I'd tried to keep the last tulip alive until Momma K had come to visit me in my apartments.

"I don't mean that metaphorically, Kylar," Jenine says, her voice suddenly hard. "He'd done such magic before."

"Done what?" I say, my mind still desperately clinging to Elene's arms, our final, ugly embrace. "What magic?"

Jenine's eyes are bright, intense. I can place that eagerness now. It's the eagerness to hurt me. "When I say there was a spark of life in Elene after you stabbed her, I don't mean *hers*. The morning of that battle, I was pregnant, but not with twins. When they buried Elene, she wasn't pregnant at all."

My mouth feels dry. Whatever she's implying, it's refusing to coalesce.

She goes on, "The Chantry thinks I'm stupid, or insane, or a child. They still haven't told me how my children's magic works. As if I can't figure anything out. Dorian can see into the future. When I hold Kiern, at times I have dreams of the future. When I hold Caedan, he gives me peace. He gave me calm from the madness, I thought. First I thought him un-Talented, then I thought him a Healer, like his father Dorian. But he's not a Healer. He's a dampener. His gift counters magic. How very strange, don't you think? Children sometimes inherit their parents' gifts, and Dorian has many, many magical gifts, but none like that. And I have no magical gifts at all. Quite the puzzle. Can you think of anyone at Black Barrow who had magic-negating magic?"

Chest tight, I can't speak, feelings of revulsion and hope twinned and rising inside me.

"Dorian intended it for good, Kylar. He meant to help you. Your wife was dying, but he could save the child. How fitting that you should find out, as I did, that Dorian's kindnesses are always overtaken by his cruelties. Me? He made a fool. I joined a corrupt marriage and believed I was doing good by being Dorian's queen. I was saving a whole country, redeeming a culture from its dark history! I was fed the fruit of deceit, and I happily took my deceiver to my bed. My heart swelled with love and my belly with his seed. No one gave me the honor of letting me decide, Kylar, so though you won't thank me for it, I'm telling you the truth.

"I may not be able to stop you, but I can make sure you know exactly what you're doing. Don't mistake me: This isn't mercy. You deserve none. I'm telling you this to take away your only defense. You will never say you didn't know what you were doing. You know. Now you know. I can't stop you, but when you do it, know this: Caedan isn't Dorian's son. He's yours."

"What do you think I'm going to do?" I hiss, trying not to raise my voice. "The whole reason I've come all this way is to save your—excuse me? What?"

One part of me is unmoored, a ship's wheel spinning unmanned in the storm. Some part of me is saying *Don't make a scene; don't break your disguise*. And some part of me is casting back.

Hadn't Grandmaster Vitruvius said something about Dorian's time with the greens? I'll have to go back and find it. Good thing I've been recording all this. I can do that. Because, you know, otherwise all this could be a mistake.

~Are you asking to hear it in earnest? I can't tell.~

I don't know. I'm struggling to breathe. My eyelids are fluttering as if my eyelashes can bat away what I've heard.

~Grandmaster Vitruvius said, 'A newly pregnant woman with terminal lungworm came in begging not for her own life, but for her child's. They say he moved the fetus to her sister's womb...'~

I hadn't even paid attention to that story when Vitruvius told it. Hadn't thought for a moment...

A *son*?

Chin high, cold, Jenine says, "To my eye, Caedan doesn't look much like you. But his power makes it unmistakable, doesn't it?"

I don't know what he looks like. I didn't even *look* at Caedan. I'd barely looked at Kiern, and I'd been holding him. *What are babies to me?* I'd thought.

I feel like I'm floating a handbreadth outside my own body. This can't be happening.

She excuses herself to go use the ladies', but I scarcely notice her go. My mind is a twisting maelstrom, the facts dragging me down, down:

The black ka'kari can devour magic.

Caedan's gift devours magic.

She was pregnant. But not with twins.

Elene, buried with an empty womb.

Dorian, the Healer. Wielding Curoch and Iures both.

I'm staring blindly at my gold-plated fork when I hear a voice behind me. "Sir?" a young man says. The server again.

"Yes?" I look up, too late.

There are half a dozen imperial soldiers in a semicircle around me, all with crossbows leveled. Three mages stand behind them, keeping lines of attack clear. Beyond them, hushed nobles are being led out of the room, out of the reach of the violence they expect here.

"Come with us, please," the server says. He holds the crossbow as if he knows how to use it.

Beyond the first circle of imperials, there is another, larger.

Jenine has sprung the trap I knew was coming and somehow still didn't see.

What are my chances against so many? One in a hundred?

~On a good day.~

Today's not a good day. Brainpan cratered by a mace of shock. Guts ripped out by the billhook of surprise. Limbs clumsy, heavy, hemorrhaging hope. My battle's done.

I raise my hands, and men with truncheons rising and falling like black wings descend on me, a cawing murder to a battlefield ripe with carrion.

Chapter Seventy-Four

A Shadow Caged

$\mathcal{M}$y body shuffles forward as directed, but if there is some essential *I* that endures this minute, this hour, he is somewhere lost within me, somewhere deep in the unlit, nitred cellars of my mind, where he fled the trenchant horrors of daylight for the muddy gloom behind casks of old joys now turned to vinegar. When the monster you flee is yourself, there is no escape in escape.

I don't count the guards. I don't judge who seems competent with the weapons they carry, or which work seamlessly with the others, or who bungled the passphrases to see who's either new or stupid and thus a weak link. The gently humming activity of engaged perception that has become instinctive over the past decade is now eerily muted.

From the cellars of my mind, I see a sudden vision of Elene, radiant in white, holding a bundle in her arms, gaze cast down, smiling fit to burst. She's dandling the babe, and gets caught up in the moment, and begins dancing.

Waves of nausea slosh in my guts. Hot, acrid bile sears the back of my throat.

As she comes out of a spin, skirts twirling, she catches sight of me and flushes, momentarily embarrassed, then laughs and waves to me to hurry over. The smell of her eucalyptus soap and her gentle breath wafts over me as she tilts the bundle up. 'Look! He's smiling. Your son is smiling for his daddy.'

As she lifts the bundle, I see the gaping wound where I stabbed her.

Her voice grows indistinct as my mind veers away, runs from those razor-eyed phantoms deeper again into the catacombs of my mind. But their fingers have sunk into my brain as deep as the unique blend of her scents, which I'll never smell again.

Don't throw up. Don't throw up.

Darkness closes around me. Time passes. Awareness is pain.

A voice in the distance. ~Kylar?~

I attempt to open my eyes; one's swollen half-shut. The aches from the beating are nothing compared to the sucking chest wound left by Queen Jenine Gyre's words.

I close my eyes again. Retreat.

~Kylar. You're not finished yet.~

I come to some time later in a cell, facedown, bile pooled under my cheek. I spit, trying to clear my throat of the vomit taste. There's not enough spit in the world.

Breathing hurts. I can feel my ribs knitting together, know somehow that I need to take an agonizingly deep breath in order to properly align some of them so they'll heal correctly.

I can't.

A son. I've seen too many impossibilities come to life to disbelieve it simply because it shouldn't be possible. I was there at Black Barrow. I was part of it all. The least part of it, perhaps, but I lent my strength to Dorian's magical explosion. I gave him my will to direct as he pleased, as did we all. He did what couldn't be done. Who am I to say he didn't also do what shouldn't?

I'm not fit to be a father. I'm barely more than a child myself. But I can't abandon the boy. I was an orphan, and I wouldn't allow a life on the street for an enemy's child, much less my own. I can't let the world tear him apart and leave him maimed like it did to me.

But what's happening now? Was Jenine hinting that his adoptive father doesn't want him returned? The child's absence solves problems for Logan. In adopting the twins, despite only the best intentions, Logan invited civil war into his own family. Will he even take the child back?

Surely my friend couldn't fail so spectacularly.

And yet...Who am I to guess where other men will fail?

Oh, I'm the Night Angel? Do I weigh souls on the scales of justice so perfectly?

When was the last time I looked into Logan's eyes to weigh his soul? Ever? Or have I been too afraid to see my friend stripped naked before the judge's bench?

Even if I should see him, how do I know my own powers of judgment are perfect? Doesn't every man tilt the scales toward himself, most of us without realizing it? Who's to say that I don't do the same?

I take a deep breath to weep, and my ribs seize the moment, bone grinds on bone, sharp ends of rib snap off and the pieces set together.

I gasp, unable to breathe, retching on the floor, awakening a thousand other pains, twisting in agony.

Sometime later, I hold still, taking fast, shallow breaths like an animal, injured, lying on the stone floor, only iron bars in focus before me, my hands bound behind me.

A son. A son means some piece of Elene is still alive.

And here lies the unworthy father. The father who failed, who let that son be stolen away from a good life, perhaps already irreparably so.

"Welcome back." A chair creaks as a big man leans forward.

I close my eyes and take a deep breath. King Repha'im is sitting on the other side of the bars in this tiny, crowded room, as if he let me sleep for a time.

By old instinct, I note the mages with him. Six of them, packed shoulder to shoulder in the room, with two bodyguards whose necks are thicker than my waist. All of them are intent on me, as if a broken man behind bars in front of them is an imminent threat.

"I don't know if you're going to believe this, Kylar Stern, but I underestimated you—and I've never been happier to be wrong. Can you believe that I tried to kill you?"

"I was there," I croak. "I believe it."

"Stop making this all about you. What I meant was, can you believe that *I* tried to kill you? I, who am so good at seeing potential. I nearly cast you aside!"

Sitting up, back aching, I put my back against the wall, which isn't far away. The smells of old piss and body odor join the cutting stench of my vomit. Apparently Alitaeran fastidiousness doesn't extend to their brigs.

Repha'im says, "Bring in the mage."

One of the soldiers throws open a door in the flooring, revealing a stair down to the next deck, and disappears. From the sour sewage smell that escapes, it's an even lower and worse level of the brig. Nice to know they're going easy on me.

"So this is you not throwing me away?" I ask.

"Patience. You'll see. We have all the time in the world."

Maybe he does, but I don't. I want nothing more than to be left alone in my despair. It annoys me that part of my mind is already searching for ways to escape.

What do I care for escape? There's nothing for me out there.

Except a baby. But it's too late for that.

King Repha'im spends the time studying me.

"What's with the eyes?" I ask.

"Not in front of the children, dear," he says, with a little grin.

My heart sinks. That's not what he would say if what I saw earlier had been mere illusions. I turn to the guards. "How do you like the new boss? The one who calls you children? Feel good to think of dying for him?"

A spear butt flashes through the bars before I can react and jabs my belly. I fall, groaning.

Blue mage, then, I think into the floor. Speed like that can only be kineturgic. I look up. Not the butt of a spear. The butt of a trident.

By the time I stand, heavily, slowly, they've been joined by a balding prisoner from down below in grubby, stained silks. Around his neck is an ironwood collar with three blue lights at the front and four wide wedge-shaped blades blooming in a circle from it. It's a guillotine collar.

"This is—well, his name doesn't matter. He *forgot* to register as a mage. Funny how that happens. Can't have folks running around doing unauthorized magic on a ship held together with magic, endangering us all, can we?"

He looks at me like I'm supposed to assent. I hold his gaze unblinking.

He sighs and speaks to the striking bodyguard in cerulean blue who'd jabbed my stomach with her trident. "Kynígi. Hand. Make it visible."

The woman wears black leather boots laced to the thigh. She steps forward, muttering to activate a blue fire in her palm, which she offers Repha'im.

"Less. Just a glow," Repha'im says, taking her wrist. As he turns back to me, the flames cool and become a low glow.

I look her over as she does the same to me, with her cold dead eyes. Flamboyance isn't a trait the Chantry encourages, but this woman's wardrobe displays it, if not her personality. Blonde hair with a side-sweeping braid, interwoven with blue and gold streaks. Behind her head is a cowl with segments of steel—a retractable helm? Her left sleeve is thicker and longer and less flexible than her right, as if it's a light or partly magical version of a retiarius's manica, the whole arm used as a shield. Aquiline nose. Figure as lean as the trident she carries. It has a narrow head for such a weapon, with nasty barbs. Her corset is black leather with blue panels to match her hair and her magic but is mostly covered with a loaded weapons harness rather than a pretty jacket.

Repha'im snaps his fingers. "Kylar. Kylar. Good boy. Eyes here."

I look over at him, still somehow distant from my own body. In the few moments—or has it been more than a few?—that I've been studying Kynígi, the prisoner's face has become drenched in sweat. Why?

Oh, the magic.

"I get it," I say. I spit to try to clear the lingering vomit taste. "If he uses magic, the blades snap shut. You don't need to kill him to prove what a badass you are."

Gratitude washes over the collared man's face as he looks at me.

Repha'im points a finger at me. "Now this. This is good to know. You're *not* dumb. Not...consistently anyway. We'll see soon enough. But you're wrong about my motivations. I wasn't trying to intimidate you. Death threats? On you? No, I simply wanted to make sure you were clear about how it works."

The man wearing the collar takes what looks like his first full breath in minutes.

Then, as Repha'im brings Kynígi's glowing hand toward the prisoner's chest, the murder collar sounds a warning tone. *Doot.* One of the three blue lights on the front of the collar has turned red.

Four wooden handles rotate outward, and the four blades spin to point inward, a little razor flower tucking its buds away. Each wedged blade will nestle perfectly against the other blades if it snaps shut.

Repha'im sets Kynígi's hand on the man's chest, and the pitch rises. *Deet.*

Four pins I hadn't seen—blade stops I presume—fall out from the underside of the murder collar. A second blue light has turned red.

The prisoner's face contorts, and his chin retracts into his neck but that makes him brush one of the points of the blades. Blood trickles down his neck as the apple of his throat bobs. He breathes in rapid little gasps. He pulls away from the eager bodyguard, but his back hits the wall. The guards on either side of him tighten their grips on his arms and turn their faces away. There's nowhere for him to go.

Repha'im nods and Kynígi brings her glowing hand closer to the collar.

Deet! The last light burns red. He claws at the collar, but there's no space for his fingers. Kynígi's eyes widen in anticipation.

Click. With a wet, meaty *ka-chunk* of the four blades slapping together, the prisoner's head pops off.

The spray of blood hits an invisible wall of force Kynígi threw in place, and not a drop gets on King Repha'im. She snags the collar off the corpse as it falls. Two guards guide the body to the floor in the crowded room.

The body lies against the bars of my cell, blood draining from the empty neck.

"Every year," Repha'im says, "the governors are allowed to bring a small number of prisoners to the empress for particular adjudication, which is Alitaeran bureaucratese for us disappearing them. There were a lot more this year than usual. We ran out of collars. So. Now you know how it works." He turns. "Wurrick, please go to the Modaini ambassador and tell her what happened to her man."

One of the bodyguards moves as if to go, stops. "Uh...that he attempted to escape, Your Highness?"

"No. Tell her the truth. We ran out of collars, and we needed it for someone more important." He holds up a finger. "No, you're right. This requires some delicacy. Tell her...Tell her it was nothing personal, merely an oversight of how many collars we would require, as we know it was nothing personal for her when she neglected to register her spy, merely her oversight of what was required. The spy's personal effects will be brought to her, but he will be buried at sea."

I feel curiously disengaged through all this. Even my hatred at this pointless murder is muted. When hatred is hopeless, apathy is comfort.

~Kylar. You know what's coming next. Why aren't you asking me if the collar will sense me?~

It doesn't matter.

~Then I'll tell you, I don't know if the collar will sense me or not. I'll see what I can figure out. It may be a time before you hear from me. Don't call me forth, understand? If the magic triggers those blades before I can adjust to whatever metal they're made of, I'll be devouring them only after you're dead...~

Kynígi wrenches back each of the collar's handles in turn, drawing them as one draws a crossbow against the great forces that will propel them into my neck. She loosens the inner ring so my head will fit through the collar, then extends it to me. "Put it on."

I hesitate.

Her voice is crushed velvet. "Put it on or we beat you, then put it on yourselves. With your broken bones, you'll gain the satisfaction that you resisted us to the last, but nothing else."

I put the gory collar on. It's wet and still warm. The stench of blood and body odor and the fear-sweat of the dead man wafts to my nose. Kynígi moves forward to cinch it tight, and I hear two tones in rapid succession—*doot, deet*—and feel something flipping around at my neck, the blades snapping around to face inward. Kynígi freezes.

We both look down to see one of the drawn blades rocking back and forth against its stop, about to release.

Then we both look at her hand, which is still faintly glowing blue. "Forgot about that," she says. "Embarrassing."

She doesn't sound embarrassed, and her smile at nearly accidentally killing me is big and friendly. Seems like she's the Hu Gibbet type. She waves to another bodyguard, who quickly resets and then tightens the collar on my neck.

They lead me downstairs, my hands still bound behind my back, hobbles allowing me to walk but not run, and of course, a collar bristling with spring-loaded death.

King Repha'im, wearing a high-necked purple cloak over a pale blue tunic with thick platinum chains everywhere and many rings, follows me into a deeper level of the brig and pauses outside an open cell that isn't even a full pace across and only comes halfway up his chest. A cell like this is itself meant as torture. It's too short to stand upright, and too narrow to lie down in.

But he doesn't signal for me to go inside. "In the days to come, Kylar, some of your religions will preach that you tampered with magics that mankind was always told not to touch, and that in so doing, you've freed Outsiders who now will wreak destruction upon Midcyru." He raises his eyebrows. "Those prohibitions from using such magic were wise, and they really were given to mankind. But the priests were themselves told half-truths at best, because peasants couldn't understand all the truth, weren't ready for it.

"The Khalidorans wakened things at Black Barrow. That's true. Upset balances. The Vürdmeister awakened things on the earth and in the earth. Old things—but in the main, terrestrial things. Those threats had roamed before and could be laid to rest again with the powers that were available to you. But do you know why Black Barrow was a dome? Because when Jorsin Alkestes wielded many of the same magics centuries ago that you all did there, he knew to build an energy cage first—*before* destroying all the enemies inside it. He contained not only monsters but also his own magics.

"But you? To burn up your enemies, you fool savages lit them on fire. You set a fire on a hill. Wielding tools far beyond your wisdom, you sent a vast pulse of magic out into the universe. It continues in a wave to this very day, racing outward in every direction, even now reaching more and more of a thousand worlds.

"Most beings out there will be insensate to the light. Some will see it, but only as your peoples see a new star in the heavens. Others have so much magic themselves, they'll have no interest. Others will have interest, but no means to travel here. But others ... Are you starting to see the picture now? With so much raw and unguarded magic, you not only affected the magical creatures on this continent and around and under your world, you signaled parasites from afar that here they will find easy food. You didn't destroy your enemies. You rang a dinner bell for a ravenous universe."

The man's a liar, I tell myself. But the description chills me to the bone. Liars often salt their lies with some truth to make them more palatable. Maybe he's simply using my anxieties about what we did at Black Barrow. Maybe I'm one of those ignorant peasants who worry that we touched magics we should've left alone.

But I can't help thinking, what if he's telling the truth?

Aware that he's studying me for a reaction, I do my best to keep my face still.

He shrugs, as if unconcerned whether I believe him now.

That makes it feel more real. Liars care if you believe their lies; they want to know if they succeeded in fooling you. Truth-tellers know they're telling the truth whether you accept it or not. Especially hard truths.

He looks at the tiny cell, then at me, and seems to make up his mind. He closes the cell and walks to an exit, fitted with many locks. These he undoes himself, and as he does so, he says, "I'm afraid you're going to think this next part wasteful. In the years to come, you'll see that though the price was high, it was not only necessary but made necessary by your own stubbornness. So please, don't abort the lesson unless and until you're fully convinced of my point. If it doesn't take root, it'll have to be repeated later at even higher cost. Come."

He makes it sound like I've got an option.

Chapter Seventy-Five

The Mathematics of Murder

You're going to love this," Repha'im says over his shoulder, as if he's giving me a tour. "Hidden jewel of the ship. Unpolished as yet, but still!"

We're deep in the ship now, having passed through the luxe halls for the wealthy and into raw workers' passages.

He emerges ahead of me into an open space, still speaking. "Next year, this will be much more comfortable. Hardwoods, carpets, braziers to ward off the chill, thrones, boxes of seats over here, and the eyesores there and there either taken away or camouflaged."

My first view as we come out onto a large open deck is of the sky, oddly visible here at the midships as if through glass. Above the waves, I see weirdly bright mist, illuminating everything strangely, perhaps from the dirt and water in the sky from the storm, too bright to be early-morning or late-evening light, but too diffuse and too orange to be anything else. The light's so thin I can't tell if it's morning or noon or afternoon, but between the beating and my, uh, reveries, it looks like I've been out of it through the night and some of the next day.

As we get farther out onto the open deck, I see that one wall is the port side hull, and here by some magic the hull is as translucent as glass, many paces wide and giving a view that stretches from the keel to the clouds. I can see vast breaking waves tossed by the gale outside right beside us, many times the height of a man, taller than any normal ship. Below us, I can see into the rushing waters, hissing beneath the ship. It's unnerving, all the crushing power of the sea so near at hand.

I can see both above and below because instead of the ship here being divided into decks as it is elsewhere, in this huge chamber, we stand on a promontory of wood and iron. Across from us, flexing, disconcertingly asynchronous with our own movement, is another promontory: the next segment of the ship. Thick metal chains and girders of iron and magic crisscross the space, keeping the ship together but allowing whatever flexion is needed as the prow of the ship slams through waves taller than castles.

"Can you hear it?" he asks eagerly. "Step forward."

I wonder if this is where he throws me off the promontory to my death. Not that there's much I can do to stop him. I can hear the wind and the waves, muted by the hull, and I hear the groaning of timbers and strained joints. I hear a distant whisper of music, and a lady laughing shrilly as some door somewhere opens and then closes. But then I follow his look down, and I hear a frothing hissing noise coming from below, and when I step up to the edge of the abyssal height, I see that a bit of the hull is open into the waters below us.

Carefully mantled so that the jets of water rushing beneath aren't sent into the ship, the rear edge of the opening is reinforced with much-dented iron, stripped of its fresh paint. A mist rises from the opening regardless. Across from us, on a lower level of the sharp drop there, I see the use for the hole. Men are emptying buckets and barrels of the ship's trash into the sea through that little hole. Some detritus bounces briefly off the water jetting beneath the hull but is soon sucked under by its immense forces.

"A hole. In the hull," I say.

"I know. You'd think water would come in and we'd sink, wouldn't you?"

"What makes it work?" I ask.

"Magic, maybe? They tell me air pressure—you notice the seals on the doors? But I can't make heads or tails of that. Doesn't really matter to me as long as it looks like this. It looks open, and it acts open, and that's enough. The starboard side has the same layout, but takes care of the ship's sewage, so that side's a bit fragrant for the delicate lords and ladies." He smiles, and he's so handsome that his smile is disconcertingly pleasant.

He looks beyond me. "Are my guests ready?"

A man and a woman emerge from behind a screen of the royal guards in the hall that led here. They're not in chains, but there's something about them that screams fugitives. Their eyes shoot side to side as if looking for dangers, or escape. Their clothes are poor and dirty. Both are middle-aged, or come from such poverty that they look older than their years.

"These are some of the inconvenient prisoners I told you about," Repha'im says to me. "Come, come. By me," he says to them kindly. "Introduce yourselves."

The man looks behind him. The menacing looks on the guards' faces encourage him to go, *now*. The woman's jaw is quivering, but she makes no sound nor does she hesitate. She walks forward.

"Dorinda Cartwright, Your Majesty," she says. She curtsies. Pretty well, considering. The first time most people meet royalty they don't do half so well.

"Landin Cartwright, Majesty," he says. He swallows and bows, showing a ridiculous dollop of hair on his otherwise bald head.

"Ah, you're family?" Repha'im says.

"Yes, Your Majesty, he's my—"

"Brother," Landin breaks in. But flustered, she continues through his words, "—husband."

They look at each other, recriminating.

"Ah," Repha'im says, amused. "One of *those* families."

Dorinda winces. Clearly, they'd made some plan and she cocked it up. She says, "I mean, my brother's very dear to me since my husband passed."

Repha'im waves it away; their relationship doesn't matter to him; their games mean nothing. "I need your help, Dorinda, Landin. Will you help me?"

They look at each other.

But it's no real question. Repha'im goes on, "Kylar here is the kind of man who wears those manacles as a mere accessory. Despite all my efforts, I have little doubt he could be out of them in an instant. As a king, there is a category of problems I will face that I can only solve by sending ten or twenty thousand soldiers—or one man who has the skills that Kylar does.

"You see, Dorinda, there's a war coming, a war of the kind that Black Barrow gave us only a small glimpse of. To win that war, Kylar and his friends—yes, did you know Kylar here was one of the Twelve?"

The two of them seem not to have even heard of the Twelve.

Disappointed, Repha'im goes on, "Anyway, Kylar and his friends used magics forbidden to man." He shoots me a conspiratorial look. "Such things as even Jorsin Alkestes hadn't roused now turn over in their slumber and threaten to wake. Lesser nightmares were in fact released and are roaming even now, though the wider world hasn't yet heard of them. It will. The truth is, humanity will be paying a steep price for Kylar's easy victory for decades to come—or centuries, if we react wrongly. And that's enough for you to know."

He looks over to me as if to say *But you and I know the whole story, don't we?*

"Understand me, Dorinda, Landin. I know kings exaggerate all too often.

We like to speak of the fate of the world. Or the fate of all civilization. Useful stuff for rallying the troops, for convincing people to die for the cause. Me? I'm not saying we're fighting for the fate of the world. The world will go on. It will simply be a far more hostile place to human flourishing, one where human life is notable for its brutality and brevity."

"And what about you?" I ask suddenly, finding a spark of defiance. "You one of those nightmares?"

He stares at me, all signs of forbearance gone. "Yes, Kylar. At least those who imprisoned me thought so. I was swept up with all my kin, all of us punished equally for the outrages—which were real and grievous—of a few. Mankind has always excelled at collective punishment. Justice, not so much.

"Me, I tell you what I am. I tell the truth. It is my strength and my weakness. Do you think all the other nightmares will be so easy to recognize? Do you think all will give you such an easy glimpse of their true nature as I did? You think I did that by mistake? That I slipped?" He shakes his head, as if at my naïveté. "You carry a relic from my time. Do you think you can trust it? Do you think you can trust the Wolf?"

My throat constricts. How does he know about that? How *much* does he know? How much do I?

"Can you trust yourself, Night Angel? With your bloodstained hands, are you really the righteous arbiter you think you are? Are you really fit to separate saints and sinners? You blindly follow your friend Logan, as if he too were faultless, blameless, perfect in his judgments, wise beyond measure in his decrees. You think yourself incorruptible? You are as partisan as any good soldier. You call it loyalty; you try to believe it's one of your virtues. And yet you know—you can no longer deny—that you are too great to be any king's lapdog. You have ascended beyond that. You are greater than mortal kings, and your calling is to be who you are. It is a calling you have been too great a coward to follow. I am here to give you one last chance to flourish. But like the petty snake you are, first you must shed the skin that has grown too small for you." He sighs. "Kylar, you've been stupidly reckless, so let me ask you a question. Landin, turn around."

Landin looks at him and goes white, but whatever he sees in Repha'im makes him turn around and face the terrifying fall in front of him. I can see sweat beaded on the back of his bald head.

Repha'im puts a big hand on Landin's shoulder. "Kylar, when a man self-slaughters, when he decides to embrace the abyss in a more than metaphorical way, does it only affect him?" He pushes the dirty stowaway so that he's dangling at the edge, only just held by Repha'im's grip on his shoulder.

"Milord!" Landin says. "Please! I didn't mean to offend! I only—"

"Landin. Be silent. You're here to help me. If you interfere with that rather than assist in it, I'll drop you. Understood?"

Landin babbles momentarily, and then goes as quiet as he can through strangled sobs.

"Kylar," Repha'im says. "Do I need to repeat the question?"

"No," I say, feeling my stomach turn. "Of course it affects others."

"Exactly," Repha'im says, pulling Landin back from the edge. "Now let's take another case. How about a soldier who sacrifices himself for his squad?"

"He saves lives. It's kind of baked into the recipe that he affects those he saves, isn't it?"

"So he only sacrifices himself?"

My brows draw down. "Uh...yes?"

"Congratulations," Repha'im says. "You've managed to disappoint. Again. You're seeing only what every person sees. The trivial. The man who dies for his squad chooses his own sacrifice, but he also chooses his family's. Does not his wife, his daughter, his father, his mother, and his friends pay for his noble choice every day of their lives? Did he ask their permission first? Does his death not affect as many people as a suicide's death does? Unless you wish to posit a hypothetical man who has no one who loves him—and it would be very rare for a man who is the type of person whom no one loves to also be the kind of person who'd die for others—so the man who sacrifices himself trades one set of sacrifices for another. There is no price that can only be borne by the self."

"So?" I ask.

"So this is a fact. It's morally neutral: We all make choices for other people. This is not a problem reserved for kings and commanders. If a pregnant woman chooses to sacrifice her life for her husband, is she only choosing for herself?"

"Please find a different example," I whisper.

He looks at me with his piercing eyes and nods.

I hate that I feel grateful for it.

"Let's pivot, then," he says. "Let us speak in the language of the heart, not the head. You're not a contemplative, but a man of action. So let's act." He turns to Dorinda and Landin. "Pick one. The other dies."

"What?"

With a startling, savage movement, Repha'im kicks Dorinda, effortlessly planting his big foot square in the middle of her chest and launching her off the promontory and out into space.

He must have knocked the wind from her. She makes no sound. I see a flash of eyes wide, mouth open in an O, arms windmilling.

So great is the force of his kick that she touches nothing on her way down, the arc of her flailing body turned to a parabola, passing deck after deck with increasing speed. She lands squarely in the jetting waters of the gap in the hull and is simply gone, the sound I expected of her flat-backed collision with the ocean swallowed as fully as her corpse. The mists rising from that hissing, open mouth don't even turn momentarily pink.

Nothing marks her passing from this world except the horror on Landin's face.

He drops to his knees, blubbering.

"Silence," Repha'im says. As the man struggles to comply, Repha'im says, "Be silent or be silenced, your choice."

Landin's cheeks bulge grotesquely as he tries to suppress his sobs, his face pink then red from the effort, sweat on his forehead, tears on his cheeks.

Oddly, I feel little. Surely it would move my heart. If I had one.

"In choosing not to choose, you make a choice," Repha'im says.

"I don't know what you think you're proving, but you're failing. I didn't even know what you were doing."

"True. But now you do, and you know I'm serious, so we've gained two things." He waves a hand. Another man is marched out to stand next to Landin. The man—handsome, well-dressed, and smiling—seems not to have seen any of what went on before he was brought out. His smile dims as he sees Landin's terror, and he too drops to his knees begging silently for clemency.

"Choose one. Or both die," Repha'im says.

"I'm not playing your sick little game," I say.

Repha'im doesn't try to convince me he'll really do it. He simply kicks Landin's chest, and then the other man's. The handsome man flinches away from the kick and teeters on the edge. "What are you doing? What are you doing?"

Repha'im kicks him again, and he falls from sight. I hear a splatter from below, the shattering melon sound of a skull meeting something harder than a skull at great speed.

Somehow, despite all I've seen in this life, all I know of the kind of men who live in the shadows of this world, I'm dismayed by the unhesitating brutality. But I don't look away.

I watch Repha'im the whole time.

He watches them fall, then turns to me, unsmiling. He waves a hand, putting up three fingers.

"We all make choices for others, Kylar. Some of us make more choices for more people, simply by virtue of the positions we hold. This holds no intrinsic value but can be used for good or ill. Actually, both, always." He gives a regretful little smile. "In this life, some of us are the man giving his life for his squad and choosing to make his wife a widow, his children destitute, his parents bereaved. Some of us are the general who sent that squad to hold a gate, willing that not only that one man but possibly his entire squad or his entire platoon die to save a city from being overrun. Lives weighed against lives, miseries against miseries.

"Kylar, it is a very kind war if it lets you choose whom you save."

"I'm not playing your game," I repeat.

"If you choose to save nothing, you're making the pacifist's choice. A legitimate option, to be sure, but an odd one for you of all people to make. Personally, I find pacifists abhorrent. Can you imagine calling it moral to place the cleanness of your own hands above the lives of others? Such a convenient screen for cowardice and selfishness, too. 'Oh, I couldn't possibly go to war. It would be morally wrong...not to mention dirty, inconvenient, riddled with discomforts, superiors bossing me around, the possibility of being maimed or killed...'

"But choose as you will, Kylar. Or don't choose. We have three this time. Two on one side and one on the other. Do you wish to select who's in each group?"

Without meaning to, I look at them before I answer. They're kneeling at the edge of the pit, looking bewildered. They didn't see what happened to the others. Two young women about my age, and an older man. What did they do to end up here?

Tapping a finger on his lips, Repha'im deliberates for a while with himself, then says, "Kynígi, how many do we have left?"

"After these three, eight more," she says, smiling. She enjoys this.

"Ah, plenty, then. So many! We should ask their stories. But that would only confuse the point, wouldn't it? And it doesn't matter, does it? Every life is equally precious, is it not?"

He directs Kynígi to put the old man to one side, and the two girls to another. One is pretty, the other homely to the point of ugliness.

It's horrible to think of them that way as they face death, isn't it? But both are young, both brunette, dressed similarly, and I know nothing else about them.

"Choose whom you will save, Kylar," he says. "Or none, as you will. To make it abundantly clear, refusing to choose means choosing to save none of them."

The stowaways' eyes go wide as they realize what's happening.

One of the girls starts crying. The other seems petrified in denial. The old man merely sighs, defeated, and looks down at the floor. He thinks the choice is obvious.

The choice *is* obvious. Damn me. But it shouldn't also be a relief.

I say, "This has nothing to do with pacificism or bravery or cowardice—this isn't war. This is murder, and it's all on you. None of what you're doing here is on me."

"Kylar. Please. 'This isn't war'? Is the maneuvering of troops before the first battle of a war not part of the war? This here, what I'm doing today, is an early action that can change the shape of the war to come. And I agree. None of this is on you, unless you choose not to save lives. It costs you nothing more than a word. Time," Repha'im says, moving forward.

Time? What?

He's approaching the girls. "The two! The two!" I say. "I save the two."

He stops, and nods, suppressing a smile. "Very well."

For some reason, I feel as if I've lost everything.

The old man says, "Please, Your Highness. Mercy." He's got a white beard, and a regal manner, and though he doesn't want to die, there's no fear in his bearing.

Repha'im lays a hand on his forehead, as if blessing him. "I want you to know," Repha'im says, "that this is likely the most important thing you will do in your entire life."

And then, almost lovingly, he pushes him off. The man tries to grab Repha'im's hand, but he snatches it out of the way.

The plainer girl watches the man fall, then shrieks and scrambles on all fours to her feet and tries to run.

The butt of Kynígi's trident catches her across the neck, and the girl goes down in a squall of snot and petticoats.

"Stop it," I say. "Stop it! Why are you doing all this?"

"Because I believe in you, Kylar. You're worth this. Now, where were we?" He rubs his hands together. "Ah, yes. Choose one of them, now."

I saw it coming, but it still hits hard. My first instinct is as wrong as it is clear. I want to save the pretty one. It's not even close. She's not braver or stronger or better in any way that I know. Indeed, she may be less worthy—the other girl at least had the guts to try to run.

I'm this shallow.

But what then? Choose the plain one, simply because my first instinct was to choose the pretty one and I feel guilty about it? Is that any better? Make her die in order to punish myself for my shallowness? In effect, punish her with death for being pretty?

The plainer girl starts blubbering, "Please, sir, please!" she says—not to Repha'im, but *to me*.

I want to scream. This stupid cow is putting this *on me*?

It only then occurs to me to View these girls and see who's more deserving of life or death than the other.

But maybe that's what all this is about. Repha'im already knows too much about me. He's keeping me standing where he can see my face. Is this all a setup for him to see my powers? How will that help him?

Besides, can I even View them without triggering the collar?

"I thought this would be the easy one," he says, irritated. "Or are you trying to find a third way?"

"Choose crowns or castles," I tell the girls. "I don't have a coin on me, but I've decided in my head. I won't change it, I promise. You choose your own fate."

But I spoke as soon as I had the thought. I hadn't yet decided. It'll be crowns. No, castles. Screw crowns and those who wear them, like Repha'im.

"A coin flip?" Repha'im says. "Well!"

As one of the girls moves to speak, he moves faster and grabs her chin in his big hand. He growls, "Not a word. Or you fly."

He turns back to me, abruptly at his ease again, stately.

"Now you've told me quite something about yourself, Kylar. See? This *was* valuable! Now I know why you want to serve Logan. You don't want to serve *Logan* per se. You want to *serve*. You want someone else to have to make the hard decisions.

"But Kylar, Kylar, don't you see? You're choosing to be weak! I understand. I can work with that attitude in you, for a time, but you'll never be as great as you could be while you follow a path of less resistance. Think of it. This is how Logan uses you. He's a coward who will only use his words to kill. He soothes his conscience by avoiding shedding the blood himself. You soothe yours by denying culpability for the blood you shed. Between you, you diffuse the blame, shedding the moral weight as easily as you shed blood. You can both sleep at night. Logan's irritant still ends up dead, and you still end up *small*. Such a waste for a man of your potential."

"I haven't killed anyone for Logan that I wouldn't have gladly killed without his asking it."

"Really? For what services exactly was he trying to bring you back to his court? He wanted you there. Why? Your fine mind for administration? Your sparkling wit?"

"He's my friend. He knew I lost Elene. He was trying to help me."

"It was all merely his kindness? Having a legendary assassin at his right hand probably wouldn't do anything to ease any tough negotiations he was facing, would it?"

"It wasn't like that. Anyway, I've killed those he didn't want me to as well. When he told you I killed Lady Trudana Jadwin on his orders, that was a lie. He was protecting me."

"Oh, he lied about it. We agree on that. But why are you so sure he lied to me and the rest of the court, and not to you?"

I know it's not smart to look at my gaoler as if he's the stupidest person I've ever met, but I can't help myself. "Uh, because I was there?"

"How did you find yourself at my estate, Kylar?"

"I..." The obvious and snarky reply—*I rode and walked*—is obviously trite, too. That's not what he's talking about.

"How did you learn where to find Trudana Jadwin?" Repha'im asks.

"One of my sources. End of story."

"A source you recruited yourself?"

No, a source I got through Momma K...who is Logan's right hand. But Momma K said...

Yeah, and Momma K would never manipulate her friends, would she?

After all was said and done, I ended up doing exactly what Logan needed. Everything he said in his speech to the court was true.

The grief, the quick wounded feeling of having been betrayed is wrong—isn't it?—but it shoots strongly through me nonetheless.

No. It isn't that he wasn't saving me by bringing me into his fold. He was. Surely, it was the first thought in his mind—that I needed to do something after Elene's death or I was going to destroy myself. But he also had a thousand problems that I wasn't helping him with, and could.

He helps me, and he helps me help him. He draws me back into his circle, where I can heal and maybe even flourish, and I dissuade his *problems* from becoming crises. He may not have even intended to ever use me to kill for him.

But he did use me.

Logan is a king now, not the idealistic boy whose naïveté so irked me when we were kids.

Maybe I shouldn't, but suddenly, I miss that boy.

All these thoughts take only moments, like a plunge into a mountain lake from some paltry height, but as I emerge from the waters, the world is a sharper, colder place.

Repha'im doesn't rub it in, though I'm certain he sees his triumph in my slumped shoulders. Maybe he thinks it says something worse about Logan than I do.

It's not a betrayal. Hell, I didn't even give Logan the chance to ask me to do the Jadwin job. I avoided him entirely for months. Maybe he would've spelled out all his plans for me if I'd not been such a terrible friend.

But he did use me. I forgive him for it, but it changes things between us somehow, and that changes my whole world.

"I can help you, Kylar. Sometimes I will be able to help you on the hard path to becoming," Repha'im says. "Like now."

He pushes the plain girl off the ledge.

She screams. Briefly. I flinch as I hear the *thunk* of her hitting the metal edge of the hole below.

"See?" he says.

I close my eyes.

Breaths come. Breaths go. I don't even think. I'm feeling too wounded, too shocked. Imprisoned in a world where foes use me and friends do too. Do I have any real friends, or are there only people who wish to use me for whatever their idea is of a greater good?

I'm the sacrifice everyone is willing to make.

*   *   *

A tear dropped on the page.

Viridiana wiped it away before it could smudge the ink. "Oh, Kylar, I'm so sorry. I'm so sorry. Gods forgive me, I did it too."

"But not always," Repha'im says.

"Huh?" I ask, opening my eyes to whatever fresh nightmare awaits me. All the ragtag stowaways have been brought out, but not lined up on the edge.

"I won't always be able to help you as I just did. We both need to know something about you before we go any further." The swirling winds from below push a lock of his dark hair over his eyes. He brushes it back.

"*We* are only going as far as we happen to get before I kill you," I say. Do I smell blood on that wind? It's too far away. I must be imagining it.

Raising his voice, Repha'im says, "Final test! Who will you save, this lovely young woman?" He strokes her cheek gently with an open hand as she shies away from him, trying not to cry. "Or all of them?" He points a dagger at the other eight prisoners still alive.

I look at the girl. She meets my eyes through her tears. "I—I don't blame you, sir. If it saves all them, then I guess that's some good, huh?" She swallows hard and then I see her shoulders draw back, her chin lift.

"Do you understand yet, Kylar?" Repha'im asks quietly.

"I understand you're sick."

"You're a man of violence, Kylar. How do you decide when it's right to kill? I'm giving you a way to know, *to know*, that what you're doing is right."

"By throwing people to their deaths?" I explode.

"It's a harsh way to teach, sure. But you're a singularly intractable pupil. Sitting there in your clouds of self-pity. We haven't weeks to talk every day. We decide where things stand between us now."

A royal guard I hadn't seen before comes to Repha'im and whispers in his ear.

Repha'im purses his lips. "She can wait."

Then he scrubs a hand through his long hair as the guard heads out.

"No, stop. Tell her I will attend her presently, after I deal with a minor security concern."

The man hurries away, and Repha'im turns to me once more.

"Kylar. The difference between us is that you're making up your approach as you go. You have no foundation. You're constantly snared between what you think and what you feel. True philosophy is not nebulous, nor subject to interpretation, nor shifting and reversible as the tides, nor meaningless when stripped of context. Philosophy is firm, and certain, and true. True philosophy is not poetry; it is mathematics.

"You think I'm stacking the deck against you? Let's stack the deck *for* you. Think of all the people you love in the world. Now add in all those whom you like. Add in all those you like even a little. What's that number? Two hundred, maybe? Maybe half that, maybe double. Doesn't matter.

"You know some arithmetic, yes? For recipes? Measuring out ratios for your potions and the like? Yes, good. The number of your friends, take that number as your numerator. Your importance to everyone else in the world is the denominator. Now divide. For most people, the resulting number is one. They are important to exactly as many people as are important to them. If every human intrinsically has equal value, then if an action demands a greater cost than it benefits, it's wrong.

"But let's stack the deck for you further. Let's agree that your friends are special! Forget that everyone else would claim the same thing of their friends. Let's say that purely as a result of being known by the amazing Kylar Stern, every person you love and even like becomes more valuable than any ten normal people. The arithmetic still remains.

"As the denominator approaches infinity, the numerator's importance—no matter how large—approaches zero. One over infinity is functionally zero. A thousand over infinity is functionally zero. This isn't personal. This is the brutal mathematics of truth. This is the clockwork of the universe stripped bare. Others are too weak to stare at it unblinking. Weakness didn't get you out of the Warrens. Weakness didn't help you crawl out of hell. You never chose weakness in the past, Kylar. Don't start now.

"You look at this girl, and you know it's wrong for eight people to die that she might live. It's simple. But you? You're worth a hundred of these prisoners, a thousand, ten thousand! That's why I'm willing to sacrifice them to save you. That's why it's *right* for me to do so. Not laudable perhaps, maybe even regrettable, but not wrong to do so, not when the prize is so, so large.

"You know you're that important, Kylar. Key. You're special. That frightens you. It needn't. I am asking you to step into your strength. I am daring to tell you the truth, knowing you'll hate it, knowing you'll think it's ugly, knowing you will rebel and reject it at first, knowing you will hate me. At least for a time. How many other people in your life now will do that for you, tell you the truth? In time, you will come to see that even ugly truths have an ineluctable beauty."

"You mean…all this murder…all this is…You're trying to *recruit* me?!" My stomach churns and I taste acrid bile in the back of my throat.

"Of course I am! Why would I wish to fight one who—if he survives so long—will realize someday that every way we are different stems from your failures to understand what's at stake? I'm not claiming we're not different. We are. You have chosen uselessness and hand-wringing, leaving the terrible choices all in my hands. Enemies are coming. Enemies so terrifying that the mere sight of them could leave you gibbering with madness. Right now, you are fighting against the only one setting up defenses. If you want this world to be recognizable in twenty years, join me in this unpleasant work. Take up this uneasy yoke with me and pull."

"No," I say. But there's no defiance in my voice, and it comes out a whisper.

"Look at them, Kylar. This time, I'm not going to ask you whom you wish to save. I ask you whom you wish to kill. If you don't choose, you kill them all."

I've already lost. Maybe I lost a long time ago. There's no innocence for me, no moral high ground anywhere within my reach. "The girl," I say, holding her eyes as I say it. I swallow. The rising wind gusts cold, chills me.

"Right answer," he says. "Now do it."

"Huh?"

"Free his hands," Repha'im says to his bodyguards.

They do. I should be using the time to plan, to find some way out, but I'm frozen.

Are you there? I ask the ka'kari. *Help me!*

But there's no answer. Whatever magic is in this collar, the ka'kari is keeping quiet to avoid triggering it and making the collar lop my head off.

My arms drop free from my bonds. The royal soldiers all have their hard eyes fixed on me, weapons in hand, ready. I'm still wearing hobbles on my feet. The ka'kari won't answer. Hell, I don't even know if it's been hearing my words all this time.

"Kylar, your wife died in order to save thousands. Tens of thousands. She didn't ask your permission, did she? Yet she held your suffering worth it to save all those people—knowing that you, Kylar, would suffer for it. And that you will continue to suffer for a very, very long time. She made the choice for your unborn child, too. Not an easy choice, to kill a child in order to save the world, but the right choice. She was a great woman. Are you brave enough to follow her lead?"

"Don't…please…"

"What I'm asking you to see, Kylar, is exactly what Elene saw. The sufferings of those we require nearest us may be sad. May be tragic. But at some point, they become irrelevant compared to the good we might do for many thousands of others.

"This girl dies either way," Repha'im says. "If you won't do it, I will…and I'll push all of them, too."

He cocks his head, and oddly, I see the last thing in his eyes that I expected. I see *compassion*. "I know this is hard, Kylar. I know it feels different to bloody your own hands. But I need you to understand who you are. What you do here changes everything—for both of us, and for the world." He smacks his lips suddenly, shoots a look over to the exit. "But much as I'm sure you'd like to luxuriate in your wretchedness and waffle in your pain here, I need to leave, right now. You've made your choice. You've got five seconds to show me you can act on it."

You know how I said I'd let you look away, if it got too awful?

"Four."

The girl sees the look on my face, and all her gathered courage fails her. She keens.

I don't need the ka'kari to write down what happens next. You don't need to hear it, and I'll never have to remind myself what happened here. I'll remember. Like so many things in my life, my shame is writ across the pages of my life in indelible fire.

"Three."

Friend, it's time to look away.

Chapter Seventy-Six

Not a Good Man

$\mathcal{A}$s it turns out, there are more offensive things you can do than murdering innocents. Say, wallowing in self-pity about it. I dictated page after page of some really heart-rending woe-is-me soliloquies—turns out the ka'kari has been able to hear me, so one cheer for that.

Minus the harp and the talent, I felt like the second coming of Everard Ffanerund, leaving men weeping and maids fainting. You ever go to that place where melancholy feels *good*? Where you feel you've attained some sort of purity of suffering, a blackness of mood so deep and unrelieved that it's aesthetically pleasing? Where your self-punishment becomes self-abuse?

And yes, I intend the pun.

That's where I was. Prodded to confront the smallness of myself, instead I could only see the largeness of my own suffering. Perhaps suffering can be purgative, even ennobling, but it wasn't for me. Not today. Maybe you have to start with a better human for that to work. Me? I felt unique in my despondency, as if in all history, no one could possibly have felt so devoid of any redeeming value. In all the history of human pain, no one could match my sense of desolation, my hopelessness.

Gross, huh? Stupid and self-indulgent and self-centered and gross.

Then, suddenly, I imagined that dead girl stepping into my cell with an empathetic expression on her face, hair and clothes wet as if she'd just climbed out of the sea, blood dribbling out of her ears still, pelvis crushed from where she clipped the metal edge of the hole. She read over my shoulder, and said with all soft sweetness, "Oh, poor Kylar. Your life really is unfair, isn't it?"

I don't know how I imagined that. In how I should have imagined it, she'd have said the same words, but with all the mockery in her tone that I deserved. In this vision, she wasn't mocking at all.

Her sweetness instead was sharper than a sword.

"I tricked you," I told her ghost.

"But you didn't do it to be cruel, did you? Did I really have a chance to get away?"

"One in a million. I thought maybe that was better than no chance at all. It's how I'd want to die, not waiting for the end, but fighting it. Even if it was inevitable. But it wasn't about you. I'm sorry, but it wasn't a kindness. I wasn't trying to trick you, not really. I was trying to trick myself."

"Yourself?"

"I'm more hot-blooded than cold. You running away let me tap the predator's instinct. I made you make it easier for me."

"Sounds cold-blooded to me. But with extra steps," she said.

"I have to work pretty hard to fool myself sometimes. I don't always know what's right, but I do always know what's wrong."

"Would you have killed me if I'd stayed? If I'd held on to your knees and begged?"

"I didn't think so at the time. But now I know better. Yes, I would've. It was just easier for me this way."

She patted my hand, this phantom woman who wasn't really there, and still looked at me without rancor. "You're not a good man, Kylar, but I'm still sorry for you."

And then I imagined her no more. I had nothing more to say.

So. That put an end to my self-pity.

It didn't end my self-reflection in the dark hours that followed—but you don't need to hear a whole lot more about all that. I'll sum it up for you. I went from 'boo-hoo, woe is me' to 'boo-hoo, I'm terrible' to 'boo-hoo, I'm stuck.'

Yes, getting that far took me several hours.

They call me quick. Physically. Not so much any other way.

I'm not skipping dictating all that stuff merely because it's boring. Turns out there are things it's impossible to be honest about. Even if every word I said was unsparing of myself and unflinchingly true, it would still somehow be a lie because my words couldn't help but focus on me. In dwelling on my own pain, I would be pulling you along with me in skipping past the pain I've caused so many others.

How much suffering have I inflicted? How many have I killed or likely killed—even only counting the time I've kept this journal?

~Twenty-eight.~

That wasn't a real question. You have any way to get this collar off yet?

It's only the second thing it's said to me since they put the murder collar on me. The first was a somehow whispered ~I can hear you. I'm working on it.~

At the time, I was too myopic to ask it more.

The ka'kari doesn't answer me now. I guess that's answer enough.

When Repha'im brought me back here to this cell, he was actually apologetic for locking me up, saying, "You've now killed the innocent to save the innocent. I feel we're close to working together—but I have yet to convince you of the most important thing."

I grunted. He took it as a question.

"I have to convince you that I'm on the right side. That the enormity of the threat facing the world justifies even this monstrous and regrettable demonstration, not to mention all the distasteful tasks we have before us. Until I convince you that what we're doing is necessary, I must seem a madman. But I can't accomplish that alone, and I can't accomplish it now. I am required elsewhere. So do forgive me. Oh! One last thing. We are so close, you and me, to saving ever so much. Please don't escape."

I rattled my chains and stretched my neck to show off the murder collar, then said dryly, "As you've asked so nicely, I'll be sure to take your request under advisement."

He made to go.

"Wait," I said. "If you can't convince me by yourself, who can?"

He grinned. "The child."

That grin haunts me. How much does Repha'im know? And how does he know it?

What are the extent of the child's powers anyway?

My child's powers.

But I don't want to think about that right now. Put it aside.

What if Repha'im's right? What if he's justified? I mean, he could be wrong in killing all those people but still be right to recruit me. You can be awful and still be on the right side; I'm proof of that.

~I can't do it.~

Excuse me?

~Can't spring you. The collar is at the neck for a reason. It has fragile magical fields in overlapping bubbles all the way around your neck, and all the way through it. If one is broken, you'll hear the first warning tone, because apparently every mage tries to fiddle with the collars. Everyone thinks if they're subtle enough, they might be able to pick the magical lock, as it were. The tone tells you it isn't working. If you back off, there's no second tone. If you push through, you get the others. Push faster, they go faster. If you destroy any of the fields rather than simply disrupting them, nothing will stop the countdown.~

So there's no hope. Not even for you?

~I've managed to stay undetected, which is better than most mages do. If I'd gone up into your head when they put the collar on you instead of down into your body, I might've had a chance to devour the steel that releases the spring-blades before the magic could be tripped. But I went into your body. Despite the jokes I'd like to make, in truth there's not enough empty space inside your cranium for a ka'kari to reside without giving you permanent brain damage. Except maybe in your nasal passages—but you'd feel like you were drowning and you'd be unable to swallow, and I didn't think you'd be able to handle that without giving us away. Regardless, I might've disrupted the fields even if I'd stayed under the skin of the top of your scalp.~

That's all... very unfortunate. What am I supposed to do now?

~As your master told his apprentice once, 'When you can't act now, make plans for how you will once you can.'~

That makes sense. But... I don't think Durzo ever told me that.

~I didn't say you were the apprentice in question.~

For a long moment, I'm stunned speechless. Or thoughtless, I guess.

Are you telling me Durzo had an apprentice before *me? He hated the very idea of an apprentice!*

~That's why. It didn't turn out well. Is this really what you need to be thinking about now?~

So I examine my surroundings carefully, scout my possibilities, and make my plans and backup plans.

Sounds like a fancy way of saying I sit here and hope someone opens the door to my cell, doesn't it?

Honestly, I can't *do* anything. There are six guards, all staring at me. Kynígi is gone with Repha'im, though, which is really too bad; she was my favorite. The guards are irritatingly disciplined types. They haven't let up eyeing me as if I'm an imminent threat. I'm not.

I can't use my Talent.

I can't use the ka'kari.

I have no weapons.

Maybe Repha'im's got a point about me.

Why didn't I want to join Logan's court? I love Logan. I want to be small. Want to be directed. Want to shed culpability. Want to avoid responsibility. So why didn't I submit my will to Logan's? If I wouldn't serve him, I won't serve anyone. So why didn't I jump at the chance?

Maybe it's time to stop dodging. Maybe it's time to take on the thing I fear most, and maybe what I fear most is having to take full responsibility for these powers I have.

I've been willing to suffer, but I've never wanted to let anyone else do so. I've been small because I've never been willing to fix my eyes on a goal and tell others, *Take that hill, and if you die trying, so be it. It's worth it.*

Who would listen to me if I said such a thing? Those who trust me most, and love me best.

And maybe that's what I actually fear more than anything: not that those I love will go and die for an appropriately big and noble purpose—Elene did that—but that they'll die and they'll leave me alone, forever. Elene did that, too.

In the past, when I've been crushed, I've looked inside and found some small part of myself that refused to yield, that compacted and hardened in life's crucibles but didn't shatter. Something endured.

Where is it now?

Why is it that now I look inside and see wasteland? The choking hot dust of red desert and on the wind the swirling promise of endless drought. The bleached skeletons of desiccated hopes, too parched to even stink, too dry to rot, but also thereby preserved forever—as I am. I am Death walking, but I am no better than the dead myself. I too a soulless husk, moved only by the spirits of greater men and women, whose wills push me to and fro.

I keep thinking I'm special. But what makes me special other than holding the ka'kari? On purpose or not, Durzo learned how to break the bond. He lost it and was still just as special afterward.

Me?

A sudden feeling sticks in my throat.

Oh, another fear. Fantastic!

What if I'm nothing? What if I'm simply lucky that I grabbed a ka'kari that happened to be looking for a new master? I'm not chosen. I'm certainly not

Chosen. I'm just a kid who grabbed a ball in an alley and thinks he scored a goal.

I think of that idiot kid, back at Repha'im's estate, kicking that stupid ball against the wall, having no idea it was imbued with potent magic, wanting to hold on to it because he thought it was neat.

A little fool, playing a game inside a game with players larger and more deadly than he could possibly imagine.

That's me. I'm that kid.

Without the ka'kari, what am I? Which of these powers are even mine? Without the ka'kari, I'm barely a bad mage. I have a bit of body magic but can't do magic at a distance at all.

The only thing special about me is that I come back when I die. And that only works as long as I have people who love me enough to trade their lives for mine. I don't even know if they have the option to *not* die for me. I suspect not.

I am a horror.

I murder those who love me for power. When I die, I live again by sucking the life out of the people closest to me.

What kind of person am I to even allow that?

I can't even die to stop it, for the only sure way to sever my connection with the ka'kari would be to find Curoch, the Sword of Power, once more—now, as far as I know, hidden and guarded by the Hunter in Ezra's Wood. Even if I could find it and fend off the Hunter long enough to kill myself with it, in addition to killing me permanently, it might kill everyone connected to me. Might not, too, but the only way to find out would be to try it. So my only solution is no solution at all.

Durzo's is the only other way out, and I don't know how long he took to alienate the ka'kari until his bond eroded and broke. It may take me centuries, too.

I'm marooned in life. Life alone, life where any friendship I start will likely end in death for the person I'm befriending, *because* they became my friend. Who can do that? Who can do that and not be a monster? The purest expression of my love for anyone else would be to make sure they don't love me back.

And I'm supposed to be a father?

Maybe Elene wasn't only saving the world by abandoning me. Maybe she saw that I could never be a father, that I was destined to kill my own child, no matter what I did.

I'm certainly not a man who could raise a kid. What do I know about fatherhood?

I had no father of my own. Can you teach what you didn't have out of the void of longing inside you? Maybe others can, if they've become a reasonably healthy adult, if they've filled in the gaps in their own humanity. Me? What do I know about kids? For that matter, what do I know about being a man?

The best thing I can do for this kid—for my *son*, let's not spare my feelings under euphemisms here—the best thing I can do for my son is to abandon him. As my father abandoned me.

But not abandon. I can't leave him with just anyone. My father did that. I know I can't leave him with Repha'im. I can't leave him where he might become like that monster.

If I'd been taken in by Neph Dada instead of Durzo Blint, what could I have become? I'm bad enough as is. Repha'im hinted that he'd make my son a weapon. Take a warrior and break off all the inefficient human bits, leaving only enough to keep him loyal. The streets made me bury my humanity deep, and they made me sacrifice too much of it. But even at the worst moments, I had people who had a scrap of decency around me: Momma K, and Durzo, and then those with more than a scrap, Count Drake and his wife and Ilena and Serah and Mags. What would I have become without them?

What might my son become, surrounded by people who will beat and starve and torture him, who will kill him if he doesn't turn out as hard as they want?

I won't let it happen. I'll do anything to stop that.

Anything.

You know what'd be helpful? If only I had someone here who could tell me how all this magic works. Especially my ka'kari bond, how it chooses who dies, if the person could say no, if it applies to children ...

I wait.

Ahem.

You know what'd be helpful? If only I had someone who could tell me how all this—

~Heard you the first time. I'm not allowed to tell you how it works. Not for a long time yet.~

Figured. *'Not for a long time'? My ass. We both know you and I aren't going to get a long time. This partnership was never going to work long term.*

~Be that as it may. I have rules.~

Yeah. So you say. Maybe I need some of those.

It's a thought for later. For now, I need to get my son away from these people.

Later, I'll get him away from me, too. Lest I endanger him in all the ways I would, simply by being there.

I'll make Logan take him back. I'll do whatever it takes. But for now, I've gotta get him away from Repha'im.

But how?

Just like that, as if it were waiting for me, I suddenly have a plan. Not a *good* plan, mind you.

Repha'im's right about one thing, to do anything good, I have to be willing to put those I love in mortal danger. To save my son, I'm gonna have to use him.

And that's when I see something wrong. One of my guards nearest the door disappears through the crack as if snatched away by a giant hand. A new guard steps inside, and the big, squeaky door closes, noiselessly, as if by magic.

Or maybe omit the 'as if.'

Because I recognize the new guard. He's dressed like the others. But the new guard is Jasmine Jakweth, the Special Problems Team's muscle.

It only takes me a moment to recognize him and then to move my eyes on, lest I give him away, but that moment is enough for him to look unhappy that I looked at him at all.

The other guards are all completely focused on me, still, as if I'm still a threat.

There's only one reason the Chantry team would be here now—to save me.

No, that's not true. They could be here to kill me, if they're afraid I'll talk.

Either way, I don't want them here now. I don't want to be rescued. It goes against my plan.

Granted, my awful plan, which I came up with moments ago.

But suddenly, it seems the choice is being taken out of my hands. One of the guards looks at Jasmine's boots, which are a bit different from the rest of the squad's. He scans up the big man's uniform, curiously, maybe not even realizing yet he's looking for other flaws.

What happens when he finds them?

"Hey," I say to a different guard off to the side. "No. Not you. The ugly one."

One of them coughs into his hand to cover his snort. I have everyone's attention, so I go on quickly. "Go get your boss. Tell him I have some secrets to divulge, but only if he comes right now. Yes, I'm serious. It's the kind of intel that won't be valuable in an hour. Believe me, if you don't get him quick, he's gonna be furious."

Repha'im might be about to be furious, but Jasmine Jakweth already is. He seems to have missed the part where I saved his life by distracting the guard about to discover him.

"Merk," the officer says to a slight soldier. "You're fastest. And His Majesty hasn't torn you a new one in a while. It's your turn."

Merk purses his lips, then nods, salutes, and is gone in a flash.

I can only hope that he's given a bit of a shock to the Chantry witches outside. And also that Vi isn't one of them.

There are no yells, so it appears they've hidden themselves and the now-presumably-unconscious guard successfully.

I start eyeing each guard in order, judging height, stance, musculature, and presumable facility with their various arms, but it's all an excuse for me to finally look at Jakweth to see if I can figure out what he's doing.

But before I can reach him, I see him from the corner of my eye taking several deep breaths, as if readying himself for something. He settles his cloak back behind his shoulders where it won't get in the way, loosens his sword in its scabbard, and checks his grip on his infantry spear.

Surely he's not planning to take on the entire room?

The door behind him opens just a crack.

Then, in response to some signal I don't see or hear, his eyes go wide and rather than attack, he suddenly shrinks into himself and pulls back to the side, drawing his cloak around himself.

The door is flung open, and a hooded woman in a cloak steps inside, flanked by enormous men also in plain clothes, but whose very stature and bearing shout that they can't possibly be anything except what they are—the empress's praetorian guards.

The empress pulls back her hood. Every guard in the room snaps to attention. "Kylar Stern," she says. "I have need of you."

Chapter Seventy-Seven

A Gentleman Never Tells

$\mathcal{M}$y only consolation as my thoughts scatter to the four winds is that Repha'im's royal guards seem even more baffled and on the verge of panic. Without Repha'im here to order them otherwise, though, they obey quickly—if not as quickly as the empress would like.

In less than a minute, I'm following her down private halls with only her two monstrous praetorians attending us.

I'm still wearing the murder collar, unfortunately.

"'Case you get any ideas," one of them says in a basso profundo, "we're both magi. That collar will put a rather more final end to any nonsense you might try than any of us might like. So don't try anything stupid. Got it?"

His voice alone would probably have been enough to stop me. But a response seems required, so I nod as vigorously as I can while wearing a thick collar with spring-loaded guillotines embedded in it. If they throw magic at me, they could trigger the collar, even if they miss.

"You seem nice. What's your name? I'm Kylar. But my friends call me Kylar. You can call me Kylar."

He looks at me with a hooded gaze, then sighs, as if deciding the fastest way to shut me up is to respond. "They call me the Ibex. Or just Ibex. And you can shut the hell up."

"Ibex? We didn't have those in Cenaria. Mountain dwellers, aren't they?" It's only then that I notice that this monster-sized fighting mage only has one hand. His left arm ends in a stub. He doesn't hide it, so I'm able to get a good look, and I can tell it's not a battle wound, but a birth defect.

I look at him with fresh respect, and now understand why the empress feels safe having only two guards. If a man is formidable enough to prove every doubter wrong, and rise through the ranks all the way to becoming the empress's guard while having only a single hand, then he possesses a level of martial prowess I really, really don't want to test.

The other man, olive-skinned with perfect hair, is shockingly handsome. Him I don't fear as much. Everyone serves life on a silver platter to the really good-looking bastards.

I'm trying to think why arguably the most powerful woman in the world would want to interrogate me privately. So I might tell her something about King Repha'im? To ask me to assassinate someone? To assassinate *Repha'im*?

That would seem abrupt, but then, I've heard that Alitaeran politics is full of fast rises and faster falls, many of them fatal, with the only constant power being the empress herself.

How much do I want to tell her in what few moments she may give me leave to speak? How much will she believe?

Anything I say that's not calibrated to get me out of the immediate peril could get me killed.

I wonder again, if my head gets cut off, will I come back? What happens if my body is completely destroyed, say in fire?

There's one way to find out!

~You're not...~

No, no. I meant I should ask you. Not kill myself. That would be stupid.

~Far be it from me to cudgel you with a litany of your mistakes, but...~

You can just stop there.

Miraculously, the ka'kari does stop. Perhaps because we do, too. The empress leads us past another two giant praetorians into what can only be her personal stateroom.

Or maybe imperial apartments is more like it, I see as soon as I step inside, for her chambers are enormous: the luxury of a wasteful use of space, here emphasized by such repetitive splendor that it's as if its occupant circumnavigated the globe looking for ostentatious displays, got lost on the way home, and marooned herself on the shores of a poor person's idea of what rich people like. Gold? On everything. Exotic woods? Every kind, in every tone and color, none matching. Jewels? Gleaming from every surface, in every color, every cut. Ivory? On every surface possible, even the floor and ceiling. Art? Wall-to-wall, with only a little (bejeweled) space between each piece, and no apparent continuity in theme or color or even origin.

The unifying theme, it occurs to me, is merely that all of them are eye-wateringly expensive.

Animal skins? From exotic animals, naturally.

Fancy candelabra? Need you ask?

Soaring roof? An improbably large bathtub? A writing desk larger than some cities?

"Wow!" I say before I can stop myself. "So this is where Taste came to die."

The empress flashes me a look of surprise, but turns away and continues toward her titanic desk.

Magical decorations? Naturally! Every step we take lights up the floor with little personalized flashes of color—the empress's white shimmering out to iridescence below her, the guards' a matching blue, and mine a crimson red. The trailing corners of the empress's cloak are spread as if by invisible maidservants for best effect. Wandering little orbs of light float into the air.

"Can you keep the magic floaties away from the deathbox on my neck?" I ask my new friend the Ibex.

"Huh? Oh." He waves a hand and all the orbs retreat a few paces.

The empress sits at her desk, then turns to regard the wall behind it. With a magical shuffling of furniture and art, a coruscation of colors parts like a curtain, leaving a window out to the Great Storm the length and height of her entire wall.

The weather outside is bizarre. Heavy low mists hug the waters below us, driven about by wind that should be howling but in this special cabin are utterly silent. From this angle and with the smoothness of the ride, if I hadn't seen them myself from lower in the ship, I'd have no idea how far away and thus how large the waves are as they sometimes peek above the mists. In this cabin, the storm ship seems to cruise over them without the least disturbance. No groaning timbers or complaining metal is heard or even felt through the floor. At this height, the imperial apartments are more than simply insulated from the sound and fury of the wind and the waves. They're above the storm itself, basking in bright sunshine, looking down on the storm and all the world below as if the empress is a god on a mountaintop, ensconced in her power far above the concerns of humanity. The sun is at an angle—whether midmorning or midafternoon I can't tell; I lost track in my cell—but even with the sun high, the water and dirt in the air outside make the light strange, and with all the world below us stretching like a sea of clouds in every direction, I can't help but feel detached, a broken halyard, snapping in the wind.

The empress doesn't turn to me as she speaks. "It's taken me almost twenty years to thin this room of Hadrissan's trash even this much. It'll be twenty more before I can decorate it to my liking. The ship of state, Kylar Stern, is even more unwieldy, takes longer to redirect, and may take everyone even farther than this poor physical analog. Hadrissan was a peacock. Kept peacocks, too, live ones, as a matter of fact, literally in this room. Defecating everywhere. Made a fashion for rich households to keep menageries throughout the entire empire. Those may last for another hundred years. Other things will change faster."

Caelestia finally turns from her viewing of the ocean. She smiles indulgently. "For your honesty and courage in telling us what you really think, we grant you leave to insult our things once in this conversation without repercussion. You have now exhausted this indulgence."

"If you're hoping I'll do something for you, the fastest way to get what you want may be to ask," I say.

"I do not ask, uncouth little man. I *tell*."

Uncouth? Uncouth! How dare she be so—

Right.

There's an art to courtly speech. It is its own language, with its own conventions. The empress isn't hearing me and she likely won't, unless I speak her native tongue.

You mocked me before, but now I need your help. You were right. Every time I try to be fancy, I overthink it. Will you help me?

~Of *course* I will.~

I freeze up. I don't have the time to explain everything I want to say to the ka'kari.

~Durzo spent a few decades as a bard. I know you, and I know empresses. Repeat after me.~

So, like a parrot or a marionette, I say what I'm told.

Tenting my manacled hands and touching my lips with steepled fingers over my collar, I repeat, "I forgot my manners. By your leave, Supreme Highness, let me try again: As to a comet hurtling through the empty spaces, unmoored by the silvery leashes of obedience and patronage that spin these noble planets in their stolid spheres around you, I sail, tumble, fly at velocities undreamt, aimless—aye, but also free—until across your orbit I speed, O Empress, thus far slipping through the whirling circles of these your lesser lights without incident toward you, and a near miss now will leave us both breathless with wonder and awe at it and at what might have been, but a collision is well possible still, with consequences dire for us both."

"Are you…threatening me?" She seems baffled but also somewhat delighted, as if the incongruity of the spectacle of this helpless insect issuing veiled threats in a high court dialect delights her.

Am I threatening her? I ask the ka'kari.

~Yes, obliquely. Now this——~

I go on, "This poor rustic is but a simple simian, attempting to ape the language you speak so mellifluously. I'm far from the slums where I was born, though it seems to me the value of human life is similar in both places."

"About that," she says. "Is it true King Repha'im was throwing prisoners into the sea for your amusement?"

"No—"

"Good. I'd hoped—"

"He was doing it to prove—"

"Do not interrupt me," she hisses.

I swallow. This part I'd done without the ka'kari's prompting.

But she pauses, intrigued. "Go on."

"A point," I say. "He was attempting to recruit me. Trying to show me how we all kill people ruthlessly in pursuit of our ideals. It was all very high on noble sentiment and body count."

She looks troubled but only for a moment. I can't tell if she believes me. That seems less troubling than that she is ready to mentally move on from so many innocents being murdered. Maybe she's one of these nobles who think the lives of smallfolk and criminals don't really count as humans. She says, "I hear you're pretty high on body count yourself."

"A gentleman never tells," I say, repeating the ka'kari's words.

She looks confused.

"Oh, you mean literal body count," I say.

~I'd thought the teller of bawdy jokes would appreciate hearing one. Ah well.~

She doesn't look amused. The kind of woman who likes telling dirty jokes but not hearing them, perhaps. Or perhaps she is one of those for whom even humor is important only insofar as it is an expression of power.

"I think you can guess the real reason you're here," she says.

I nod. She's gone behind 'King' Repha'im's back, which means she thinks she has good reason to mistrust him. She knows Repha'im is interested in me, so she needs to hear what I know about it.

"Then stop wasting my time," she says. "What can you tell me about them?"

My brow furrows. "You mean 'him'?"

"What?"

"I think I misheard you. Did you ask what I can tell you about him?"

"Don't be coy with me, Stern."

"I assure you that my coyness is even shorter-lived than your patience. Who do you mean by 'them'?"

"If there is one of us in this room who might have an excuse to have forgotten a spouse, that one is not you, Kylar Stern."

"A . . . spouse?" The words are out of my mouth before I can stop them. What can Elene possibly have to do with her? Was there some magic at Black Barrow that affects the Alitaerans? Why would she think Elene would be especially notable out of all the mages who actually were there. Oh—

~She doesn't mean Elene. She means Viridiana.~

"Ah. You have spies at the Chantry," I say. "Of course you do. But no, I'm sorry. The information they've given you is not only old, but it was wrong in the first place."

"Oh, it's all coming back to you now?" she asks. "I've certainly had a few lovers I'd like to forget, but I haven't managed to do so. Pray tell how it's done."

But even while she's being full-on snotty with me, I'm finally catching up. By 'them' she means the Chantry. Maybe she means one of the Chantry's Special Problems and Tactics Teams.

They're certainly becoming a special problem for me now. How much do I owe the Chantry, anyway?

How much should I protect the secrets of those who were willing to sell me to Repha'im?

How much am I willing to let Viridiana's team suffer for what the other team tried to do? How much am I willing to let the entire Chantry suffer for what that one team tried to do to me?

I was also saved by a member of one of those teams. But that was Vi, and she was acting against her own team.

But if I sell out her team, I'm selling her out, too.

"I was fooling the Chantry," I say. "Got tied up in one of their internal political disputes regarding the so-called Chattel with a friend, who was a novice and didn't get any choice in the matter either. We were ordered to pose as husband and wife, but I wasn't ever married to her."

The empress sorts through some parchments on her desk, lifts a scroll, and produces several pages with sketches of six different noblewomen. One is recognizably Viridiana; two are others I recognize from her team. "Which of these were you 'not ever married to'?"

~Careful, Kylar.~

But the ka'kari doesn't tell me what to say. My lips feel suddenly dry. "If I say, technically, I wasn't ever married to *any* of them, that's not going to go well for me, is it?"

The empress's hazel eyes lose all sense of humor. She picks up a faintly glowing paperweight from her desk and brings it close until my murder collar starts vibrating, though not close enough to set off the tone.

Ah, you see, Jenine? This is how you convey a threat. Subtle while being not at all subtle.

I tap Viridiana's picture, wondering if I'm giving the empress any new information, wondering if I've consigned Viridiana to death.

"So it is. Not a liar on trivial matters at least," the empress says.

I feel oddly relieved. I'm still in it deep, but at least I didn't sell out Viridiana without *thinking* about it. Unfortunately, I think I'm about to be given more chances to decide my loyalties.

"Which of these other women do you recognize?"

Again, the ka'kari doesn't tell me what to say. It's a tool that can help me in how I work out what I decide, but it can't make the decisions for me. And if I take too long to decide, it can't help me even in that.

I say, "I'm sorry, I'm not going to tell you that unless—"

"Unless?" she snaps, interrupting. "You dare presume to issue ultimatums? To me? It seems you don't only forget your wife, sir, you also forget yourself."

"No ultimatums. Not at all. I am fully in your power. I understand the depth of my prostration. The only power I have is whether I cooperate with you. For me to decide that, I need to know why you seek these women. I'm not much enamored with the Chantry. They've done me little good, and sought to do me much harm. But not all of them have done so. I won't casually consign innocent women to death merely to spare my own life."

This time, the speech is all me. It feels like I've done pretty well matching the courtly tone, but the words are barely out of my mouth before a word flashes through my mind: *hypocrite, hypocrite, hypocrite.*

But doing this feels right. It feels like me. I'm the one who can suffer for others.

I smile.

"There's something very wrong inside your head," the empress says.

You have no idea, lady. She's right, but this is the first thing I've done in days that feels right.

She goes on, "It's been known for many years that the Chantry has certain elite teams that go to countries in covert fashion and make sure their will is done. This...doesn't please me, but neither does it trouble me overmuch. Everyone does this, quietly. They're better at it than most. But under the guise of it being necessary—this Battle of Black Barrow—they've moved to overt actions. Training magae for war. Dropping their ban on Sisters marrying, which makes me suspect they've secretly reinstituted the breeding programs they had of old, trying for super mages again."

"Again?" I ask. I wince. "If you pardon my asking."

"It's been done before. The fruits were some few wonders, and far greater disasters. The Sarasenn Sea incident? The Hrothan Sinkhole? The Abraxian Massacre? The Tolvaren Civil Wars? Possibly even the Great Storm itself."

I've only even heard of two of those, so I keep my mouth shut.

She goes on, "The whole world has benefited from the work my predecessors did in establishing the Alitaeran Accords. The Chantry is flouting these now, under color of *necessity.* There's always a necessity, Stern. Magic is always looked at as the panacea. Magic is the ultimate wish fulfillment for weak minds: wave your hand, problems disappear." She waves her hand with the paperweight, and my murder collar vibrates again: I'm a problem she can make disappear. She smiles derisively. "The Chantry knows this isn't true, and in many ways, no one benefits from the Accords more than they do. We allow them a monopoly on magic. We send our Talented young women to them and no one else for training. We Alitaerans established that precedent. We made it so that everyone else in other nations does it too. We have kept our politics out of the Chantry—despite grave temptations to flex our muscles there. We've played a long game. And so have they. Until now. I need to know why I'm looking at a newly militant Sisterhood."

"The team wouldn't know if their masters were newly militant or militant at all. It's classic information isolation: If you're on an elite team, you only know your own orders. Anything more you know may be tortured out of you."

"Or tricked out of you," she says with a selachian smile. "So there is a team here."

I blanch but don't want to acknowledge my blunder. I try to take it back: "You were the one who spoke of hypothetical covert teams, not I."

I don't think it works. It occurs to me that even as I've trained many years to angle my body and others' bodies into exactly the paths I want, no matter what resistance I encounter, she's trained equally long to angle conversations into the paths she wants, with similarly high stakes. It seems she has a similar gift for her art as I have for mine. I'd love to get her and Momma K in a room together. A woman like Phaena could probably sit in court and watch the empress talk all day and learn as much as I learned by watching the Storm Hands training with preception.

Unfortunately, they're not here. I am. And I'm alone. And I'm unarmed, literally and metaphorically.

Eyes narrowed, she chews at one lacquered nail, each dotted with a single cat's-eye gemstone. "What do you want, Kylar Stern?"

I raise an eyebrow. "Is this a trick question? My head. Attached still. Along with my body. No foreign bits of steel sticking through it. Or, for that matter, iron or bamboo or other materials. Hands unmanacled. As a matter of fact, it suddenly seems my list of desires is quite long. A nice meal? A kiss from those supple lips?"

She rolls her eyes and I stop.

~Kylar. You didn't.~

Well, obviously I did. And my charm is demonstrating its inconsistency.

"I meant," she says, "that you clearly want something because you went to a lot of effort to get on this ship. Why?"

"Fastest way to Borami," I say immediately.

She looks to her one-fisted giant. "Take him back to his cell. Beat him for his impertinence. Level two, as my new king may have some use planned for him yet."

The Ibex grabs me by the neck, just under the murder collar, which is never a pleasant experience when a man has a hand so large it literally wraps all the way around your neck, but this time is made even worse because the magic latent in his flesh makes the blades wiggle against their stops as if about to turn.

"Easy! Easy! Collar! Magic!" I say to him.

He shifts his hand away from the collar and to my tunic but marches me to the door. There's no resisting him. I can only hope she calls me back.

She doesn't. It's not a bluff.

Or if it is, it's one she can afford to play out.

I can't.

We're approaching the door.

Don't do it, Kylar.

We're through the door. But it hasn't closed behind us yet.

Don't say anything. It'd be a mistake. Don't—

My mouth ignores my better judgment. "He has my son!" I shout.

The door snaps shut.

"Who does?" the Ibex asks me, stopping for a moment, and turning me. In his grip, I feel like a kitten lifted by the scruff of my neck.

"King Repha'im. He kidnapped my baby for some magic he thinks the child has," I say miserably.

"Huh. That's too bad," Ibex says. I can tell he means it, too. But it doesn't stop him from marching me down the hall.

The door opens and I hear a silky voice say, "Athanasio? Turn him."

The empress is standing between the two praetorians at the door who are like vast mismatched obelisks, one a sapphire-eyed, black-haired Khalidoran highlander with skin white as the snowy mountain peaks of his homeland, the other a scarified, barrel-chested Friakian larger than the ponies of his native steppes.

She doesn't beckon me to come back, nor does she walk toward me. If it's a bluff, and she needs me as much as I need her, she's playing her bluff very well.

So quietly I can barely hear her, she asks, "Repha'im has your son?"

I can't speak. I nod.

Her eyes intense, weighing me, she asks, "What would you do to get him back?"

I take a breath. My shoulders slump.

Chapter Seventy-Eight

Things You'd Never Do

*E*ver been in the kind of fight where you threw punch after punch, hitting nothing, looking like a greater fool with every effort, while your opponent took pieces out of you with the bored dispassion of a butcher on a slow day? Have you ever experienced the verbal equivalent to being taken out behind the woodshed and getting your backside beat until you couldn't walk?

That's how it went, negotiating with Empress Caelestia. I'm not gonna repeat the whole conversation here because, to be frank, it'd make me look even worse than me just telling you it was bad. Really bad.

If I were a bigger man, I'd dictate it so I could go back and see how she did it all to me. Study it, you know, so as to not let it happen again.

But that'd require me to watch it play out...over and over again. I don't have that kind of fortitude.

Long and short of it is that out of all the terrible stuff I've done in my life with my own bare hands, this felt somehow worse. Cleaner.

The cleanliness is a lie, and I, who deal in lies, have a gag reflex that keeps me from swallowing the things people use to make evil palatable.

I went in thinking I'd only name one of them: Sister Ayayah Meganah has no claims to my loyalty, right? She *told* me she wanted me dead. Seems fair I return the favor. She declared war on me first, right?

When it became clear pretty much immediately that I was in way over my head, I only swerved a little. I gave her up, and I gave up Petaria Feu, the unpleasant little thief who'd been so eager to see me dead. The empress didn't seem like she would believe that the first person I gave up was the leader of the team, so I said Petaria was the leader. It's not a lie that will hold for half a minute if the empress ever meets Petaria, but I was trying to salvage some sense of dignity by lying at least a little.

Within a minute, I'd agreed to hunt down Petaria myself—a kill to show the empress I'm trustworthy.

That wouldn't have been so terrible by itself. I know Petaria's done enough evil that I can find a way to sleep at night. And if I murder her quickly, the empress will never meet her, and my lie that Petaria is the team leader will hold. So maybe I should count myself lucky. I lied and got the means to cover up my lie within a minute.

Granted, at the cost of agreeing to commit murder.

And yes, that's what I'm calling a win today. That's how low the bar is.

Then I got bullied into giving up the names of everyone else on the Special Problems and Tactics Team.

And I somehow let slip that there are two teams.

Honestly, the whole interview was a compilation of moments that were each not my finest.

The empress had this way of interrogating me where she remembered everything I'd said, and made me repeat my own lies a dozen different ways, and somehow picked apart chronological inconsistencies at every turn. I barely had time to consult with the ka'kari, because she took every pause as evidence I was planning to lie.

Which I was.

Even when I was telling the truth she didn't always believe me—like that Logan wasn't more involved with the Chantry's plans.

Or maybe she feigned her disbelief to get me to tell her more.

I did manage not to mention Vi.

Heroic, huh?

Now that I'm describing it all at such length, you probably wish I'd narrated as it happened, huh?

Well, tough. This is my story, and you only get what I'm willing to give you. You don't like it, you know what you can do.

But you're not gonna leave the story at this point, are you?

You've heard what happened at the end. That's why you're here, isn't it? You want to see a man fully debased, don't you? You want to know how I could do it, so you can tell yourself how different you are. How you're better than me.

Maybe you are.

                          *   *   *

I leave the empress's rooms shaken and probably damned—but with no collar on my neck.

Did that mage do anything to me when he took off the collar?

~Scanned you. No residue.~

Did he notice...?

~As far as I can tell, I was not detected.~

Where'd he put the spell to track me?

~In your hair.~ The ka'kari seems amused.

What's that about?

~You *are* learning. It's nice to see.~

I grunt. *Is the tracking spell devourable? Preferably without killing me?*

~Easily. Say the word.~

I think about it as I walk. I need to get out of this area quickly lest I run into King Repha'im or Ishael or anyone else who might recognize and want to kill me, but I don't know where to go first.

You know what would be handy? Running into Phaena right now. If she just so happened to be around the next corner, say. With keys. And a plan. A plan would be good.

I come around the corner.

Go on, guess if Phaena is standing there.

Of course she is. That's how it goes in stories, right? You need something to happen, and it happens. It doesn't matter how improbable it is. It happens because otherwise the story can't go on. I mean, when you get to that part in the Alkestia Cycle, where Princess Bel Ishta flees to Trayethell and Gol Gannu goes after her? You know, she's disguised as a commoner in one of the largest cities of the ancient world, and how long does it take him to find her? Immediately, right?

Whereas you or I might live in the same city as one of our friends and never see them for years.

I guess I should probably say *you* might live in the same city as a friend of yours. I'm getting low on the friend count.

Anyway, conveniently, Phaena is standing there when I round the corner.

Except she's not. I come around the corner to two imperial guards flanking the hallway. One says, "Hey! Stop it!"

I miss a step—but he's not talking to me.

"You mess with the red and whites," he tells the other guard, "and you're gonna lose a body part you're rather fond of."

"I wasn't messing with her. It was a little appreciation is all!" the other complains, and from the words and a glimpse of a woman in white disappearing down the corridor, I surmise that he made some advance or some crass comment to her.

"Show some appreciation for your own tiny—'lo, milord," the first says, seeing me. He shoots a warning glance at the younger guard as I go past.

I breathe again. Nearly gave me a heart attack. His 'milord' is generous, probably more offered because I'm in this part of the ship than that I look the part—because after my beating and barfing, I'm not looking my best. But they let me pass without another word, more worried about their own poor behavior than mine. It's still just me and my thoughts about the magical tracker the empress has on me.

The instant I destroy the tracker, I'll be declaring myself the empress's enemy. Letting her track me was never mentioned as part of our deal, but I've seen how the empress operates. She'll treat any move I make to get away from her as a move against her.

Only when I turn a corner into yet another hardwood and marble hallway do I think about what they were saying. What are red and whites? From how the man said it, I assumed they were talking about women, and that one of them had made some unwanted advance. I've seen women in red and white—with Phaena.

I'm glad to hear that the women are protected, whatever it is they do. I've seen other servants in specific uniforms showing whom they serve and their level of access. Given her talking with Repha'im back at the dock and being accompanied with the others by Ishael in the salon, I have to guess she's embedded among his household servants. It's good luck coming to Repha'im as he became king—the man surely had to expand his staff quickly to meet the demands of his new station.

What she does exactly doesn't matter too much. It tells me she's been working on infiltrating his defenses. I can't know how far she's gotten, but it doesn't matter until I can find her.

And I can't do that now. Certainly not while I have a tracker on me. And I can't get rid of the tracker until I've done the job with Petaria.

In my work, the first and foundational part of any hit is defining the problems. What is the range of acceptable solutions?

There are times when simply putting on some dingy clothes and walking up to a deader and knifing him half a dozen times while pretending to try to rob him is not merely acceptable but the best course. You'd think people like me wouldn't get hired for jobs like that. You know, why would anyone pay the prices a professional commands for jobs any thug ought to be able to do?

But you'd be surprised. Most of the people contracting wet work are repeat customers. They're the kind of people who need people killed on a somewhat regular basis.

People like that have usually tried solving the problem the cheap way. What happens? He pays some idiot basher to kill a woman who's become more trouble alive than she will be dead, and half the time, your basher gets soused or blonkered to get his courage up and flubs an easy job that could've been done right on the street with a knife and ten seconds of sharp motions. Once the basher fails, then the target knows she's a target. She holes up somewhere. Maybe she starts plotting payback.

Now the target's graduated from problem to headache. She might end up killing some of his people. His attempt to remove a source of discomfort has increased his discomfort instead. After wasting time and money, now he has to hire someone like me anyway, and I charge by the difficulty of the job, which the amateurs have made much more difficult.

I take care of that job handily, despite the hurdles.

The next time, he comes to me first, even for the easy problems, because then he can be sure they don't become difficult problems.

Those jobs are the bread and butter for rising wetboys. Durzo Blint was an outlier among outliers. Other wetboys would send him the jobs they didn't want to touch—though only after checking out the clients they were sending to him. You didn't want to be the person who sent Durzo a royal plant.

Regardless of the money, Durzo would regularly turn down work that didn't interest him. He might only do a few jobs a year, usually ones that caught his fancy or were favors for Momma K.

But I've left that world behind.

Maybe not all the way behind.

In this job, the problem is a little more complicated. A mugging gone bad? Not credible on a ship where everyone's rich or a trusted servant of the rich. No one's going to kill someone here for the amount of coin they happen to have in their purse at the moment.

A robbery of Petaria's stateroom gone bad? One could imagine a burglar targeting the greater riches in a noble's stateroom, getting interrupted, and resorting to violence.

A lovers' spat that got out of hand? It's corrosive work, this murder business. It forces you to think of these things constantly, like how many women are murdered by men they love. That number is certainly high enough for wetboys to work with: Break in, drug the man, beat the woman to death, trash the place, shout loudly to summon the neighbors, and leave.

The neighbors find the man smeared with blood, drunk or hungover after what looks like a terrible fight, and they pin her death on him. Half the time, the man gets a trip to the gallows and you kill two for one, clean.

By certain definitions of *clean*, that is.

But I don't know if Petaria's got a lover, and I'm not killing two people regardless, so that's out.

I don't need to make Petaria's body disappear; in fact, I can't. If I do that, the empress might not believe I did kill her. So that gives my problem one bookend. Need body. Need it to be found by the empress's people.

So no pushing her out of a window—porthole? whatever. That's too bad. No one's swimming to shore in a storm like this, so a push overboard has got to be the easiest way to kill someone on a ship.

She's a mage, so the kill will have to be a surprise and fast. I can't give her a chance to defend herself or to signal the team.

The team is a real problem. Obviously, this murder can't point them to me. Together, they could well take me down, but even if they can't, if they have a chance to send a message about what I've done to the rest of the Chantry, then I'll have vengeful, magic-using women spread around all of Midcyru, with vast networks of spies, power, and riches, who will keep coming after me in waves for as long as the Chantry exists. I'm immortal, but in a very real way, the Chantry is too.

You know, it's starting to look like I didn't think this hit all the way through.

Why am I always pushing future me deeper in the pit just to give present-day me a bit of breathing room?

When I was starving on the streets as a kid, sometimes we'd stalk rich merchants, hoping we might have a chance to cut a purse or knock them down and steal something. Half the time, it seemed like these finely dressed fools would be complaining about their money problems.

Money problems? we'd think. *You have warm clothes, a safe place to sleep, and you ate a meal today!*

I couldn't believe back then that those merchants did have problems or that those problems were real, despite all their obvious wealth.

Now here I am, ludicrously powerful, highly skilled, the owner of a magical item of unbelievable potency, and yet somehow still utterly and completely buggered.

It's almost as if the problem isn't in my circumstances, but in me.

What am I saying? Of course it's the circumstances.

~Excuse me. Did you call yourself my 'owner'?~

Yes . . . ? Wait, are you offended? Seriously?

~Why don't you call yourself my 'master' and be done with it?~

Done. I'm your master. I was confused about our relationship.

It huffs.

What do you want then? Am I your 'wielder'?

~Wielder! As if I'm a *knife*?~

You have, uh, actually been a knife for me before. Pretty good one, too. Love how you do that little stiletto thing. Very handy. But you're right. Master it is. Glad we cleared that up.

~I wasn't being—Oh. This is your attempt a sense of humor. How droll. I am so glad the malnutrition at critical phases of your youth didn't result in all forms of retardation.~

Merely social, moral, and mental, I agree.

It hates it when I do that.

~You know I can hear these asides, right? You are narrating *to me*.~

And you're making me look good, aren't you? Editing out the um*s and ah*s, *that sort of thing?*

~You're commanding me to go back now and take out the *um*s and *ah*s?~

Yes!

The ka'kari sighs. Still don't know how it does that, silently, without lungs. One of those tricks I'll probably unlock at some later date.

In fact, I have another command: Make me look good in this story, would you?

~My most abject apologies, *Master*, but you have now given me two contradictory commands.~

I have? I don't know why I ask the question. I can feel I've stepped in a trap already.

~Do you wish me to take down your words, or to make you look good?~

I wince. This has got to be a new low, even for me—losing a battle of wits to an inanimate object.

This is not my week. Ambushed by Jenine, ambushed by her goons, beaten, captured, locked up, threatened, lost every argument I've had, and now doing dirty work the empress could've had any of a thousand people do simply because I . . .

I stop in the middle of a hallway.

That's not actually true, is it? It seems the empress could have her soldiers simply arrest the Chantry team on any pretext she likes. But for some reason, she isn't doing that.

I'm not doing a job she thinks she could have anyone do. She and the Chantry are right on the brink of a full diplomatic disaster, maybe even war.

The empress can't risk starting a war over a death or two.

There's a funny thing that happens when great powers are poised at the edge of open war, at least if they're being led by basically sane people who realize they have more to lose than to gain by a war: The brink is much more stable than most people assume. Durzo taught me this because it's a great time to find assassination work, some of it even moral.

When a leader sees their side's possibilities as ranging between vast expense and little gain as the best case and total ruin as the worst case, they'll ignore far greater offenses than they would in normal times.

Say an ally's diplomat gets in a duel and kills the queen's nephew. That diplomat in normal times might go home in a box. But put the two powers a handsbreadth from war, and many times that diplomat will be sent home with nothing more than a sternly worded letter.

The stakes become so high that no one wants to risk the usual responses, lest it push everyone off the cliff. When everyone thinks war is close, that, paradoxically, can be a time you can get away with almost anything.

Which gives me . . . well, not quite a plan, but the beginnings of one.

I head straight for the nearest imperial guard. "Hey, I've been looking everywhere for Athanasio. He's not on duty, or at any of his usual meal places."

"Who?" the man asks.

"You know, the Ibex. Praetorian. After all this time, now I realize I don't actually know where his room is. You help me out? Can't be far, right? Can you just walk me there?"

Please say no, please say no.

"I—well, no, can't leave my post here. But it's real easy to find."

I smile. "Great, thanks."

Chapter Seventy-Nine

The Way of Blood

The Ibex is a trusting soul. His room isn't locked. I step inside. It's small, but it's a measure of how exalted the imperial bodyguards are that it is a single room. Maybe he trusts that no one would be stupid enough to steal from *him*.

Well, I sometimes surprise even myself.

I find a spare tunic in a drawer, neatly folded, exactly as I was sure it would be. I examine it closely, then keep looking until I find another, with gold buttons. Then I look around. He's got all sorts of gear in here that could be helpful, but I only take a waxed bag. I don't want to keep any of the stolen goods on me.

My eyes fall on a distinctive halberd, seven feet tall, its blade and butt spike golden. I kneel and scratch at the butt spike. Some gold paint flecks off. I smile.

Finally, something not done with magic. It is possible to harden gold with magic, but perhaps even the seemingly inexhaustible riches of magic of the Alitaeran empire do have some end after all. Or perhaps crusty old veterans simply like to do things the hard way sometimes.

I take a few breaths, consciously donning one of my favorite disguises: the harried, mildly incompetent servant. I push my noble's bracelet up my arm and out of sight, ruffle my hair, check my reflection in his tiny looking glass for crusted blood or vomit, then slouch my shoulders, tuck the folded tunic into my belt, and grab the halberd in two hands as if it were a live serpent.

Carrying it through the hall as if I'm scared of scratching it or of accidentally impaling the few groups of nobles and other servants I pass, I make it to the room where the empress told me Petaria Feu is staying.

All the consolations of a life in blood are partial and incomplete. One of the sweeter ones, though, is this: In every life, glittering moments arrive that change everything thereafter, where you hoist your courage high and act, not knowing what will happen, only knowing that this matters, that you are about to do something that will mean either delight or ruin for you or others. How many moments like that does a normal man have in his life? Half a dozen?

If that. Maybe he finally asks a longtime friend to see him as a love instead. Maybe he volunteers for a war. Maybe he balls his fists, stands, and faces the bully. Maybe he quits the secure job he hates. Maybe he finally tells his wife what he's always thought of her grandmother's-family-secret-recipe lentil stew.

In contrast, the Way of Blood is drenched slick with moments like that, common as rain in the coastal mountains. If the burden of most men's lives is knowing that nothing they do today really matters, the benefit—I won't call it the blessing—the benefit of our way is that what we do *always* matters.

With uncanny calm in my heart, I knock on Petaria's door, knowing that what happens next means heaven or hell or both.

There's no one coming in the hall, but I crane my neck back and forth, back and forth—an act for Petaria's benefit, in case she's got a peephole mundane or magical. I drum my fingers, twitch, mutter to myself.

The door opens a crack. Petaria is standing with only head and shoulders exposed, craned around the way someone does if they're keeping a foot wedged so you can't push the door open.

"Thank the gods," I blurt out before she can say anything. "Take this, take this before the imperials see it!" I push the tip of the long polearm up through the open door, trying to hand it to her.

She takes it, flustered. "What the hell is this—?" She steps back as the seven-foot-long halberd clatters against the door.

"It belongs to the praetorian they call the Ibex, you know the one? Gigantic— well, they're all gigantic—by the gods, it just occurred to me. He's only got the one hand. How the hell does he use a *halberd* with one hand?"

Funny thing about weapons: Many people understandably freeze up when they see a man carrying one coming toward them, but when *handed* a weapon, the set of questions they have shifts so suddenly it leaves people off-balance. From being a mortal threat, it becomes at most a social threat: Why did you hand this to me? Where did you get it? What am *I* supposed to do with it?

We expect someone who hands us a weapon to explain. Enemies don't hand us weapons.

"What're you carrying all that for?" Petaria says, stepping back, looking at the praetorian tunic tucked into my belt. "You'd better start explaining yourself."

"Oh, this? I—" Shoving the door shut with one foot behind me, pretending to pull the tunic out of my belt, I reach underneath it, whip out the belt knife it concealed, and ram it into her chest.

Running forward with her as she lurches backward, halberd still in her hands, I twist the blade hard to open the wound, pull it out fast, punch her hard in the nose to stun her, aiming low in case she ducks instinctively, and then stepping forward as she staggers back, I grab a handful of her hair and wrench her head back. Her arms dart to the usual inverted V as her hands reach up to her broken nose, which gives me the narrow open window to bury the blade again, this time in her voice box.

I hold it there.

A man or woman with a perforated heart is doomed—but it can take up to a count of ten to lose consciousness. When killing a maga who could shred you with magic in a count of three, this is important. Magae generally need to speak to do magic. Thus, for a count to ten, you need to make sure your dying mage isn't going to speak death for you.

Her eyes fill with tears as I hold her. It's a mistake to think she's crying for grief or fear at her impending death. You get punched in the nose, your eyes water. Besides, with great enough shocks to the body, the mind doesn't have time for profound thoughts.

Her lips move, but no sound comes out. I can't tell if she's trying to speak or curse me or cast a spell.

The secondary surprise, that look of *Oh, hell, I'm dying, aren't I?* is only just rushing to her face when the slack darkness closes in.

I've forgotten to start counting ten, but with the light faded from her eyes, I don't have to, which is good, because time dilation is a thing in moments like this. I can never tell how long it's been.

But—well, this is gross, but hey, you wanted a glimpse into this life, right?—Petaria lets me know when she's truly dead by releasing her bladder. I hold her up a couple moments longer to be certain, then let her fall, concerned only about not getting blood on me and catching the halberd that was trapped between us lest it clatter to the floor.

She collapses dead into her own blood and urine, and for a moment, I simply study her dispassionately.

This is my future. Becoming a corpse, lying graceless and stinking in my own fluids.

It's yours, too, so don't feel too superior, huh?

In one form or another, it's everyone's destiny: relaxed bowels and blood and slumping to a floor in adignant repose.

I pull my blade carefully from her throat and clean it thoroughly on her clothing. There's a temptation to judge a person by how they die, as if the last moments before death grant us some unique insight into a life as a whole. It's true often enough to seduce us to misunderstanding.

If a soldier who's shown heroism a dozen times finds one day that he can't run into the face of certain death, we see it as proof that he's not insensate to danger. He's not a madman or a moron, and thus we know that he is *truly* brave. Paradoxically, a moment's cowardice lifts all his previous courage to a higher plane, for we see that he acted heroically all those times before—though he's made of the same stuff we are, he is regularly able to act in ways we only hope we would. And we rightly expect that tomorrow, he will be able to brave death once more, for the arc of his life has shown that the bravery is part of his essence, the fear a passing affliction.

In the same way, if a man of faith suffers doubt on a normal day, we take it as evidence he's not an unthinking zealot.

But then like dishonest merchants, we swap the scales by which we judge that man if he suffers a doubt on his dying day. We take it as proof that his faith was a lie and he a charlatan.

Or if, weakened and tormented by a long illness, a stern matriarch cannot rally courage for her last agonies, we sigh, disappointed that she was revealed at the last to have secretly been a coward all along.

If you think that way, if you judge by such measures, go ahead and hold on to that smugly superior attitude until your own last moments. We'll see how you do.

Here's how I look at it. In this world, getting really good at any skill—whether it's streetball or juggling or abstract philosophizing—requires practice: attempts, failure, correction, and thoughtful repetition.

Even a veteran of a thousand fights can have a day on the battlefield where his legs won't carry him forward, where he finds yesterday's heroism out of his reach. You ever stumble walking down the stairs? If we can louse up easy things, then certainly each of us can louse up something difficult, even if we've done it a thousand times. We can have a bad day. How many of us do something difficult perfectly the first time we try it?

Durzo told me that you're bound to screw up your first time doing anything. Guess what? Most people die only once.

So be slow to cast aspersions on the bravery of a sick woman in a fight to the death, carrying the burden of knowing she'll lose. Every man of faith has moments of doubt. Why is it so shocking that in the worst moment of his life, he might have another? Why are we so quick to believe that one moment of weakness casts a fatal shadow over an entire life?

If, without any practice, you can manage mediocrity at some new task, consider it a victory, especially if it's something as difficult as dying well.

With the blood now having pooled sufficiently below her throat, I squat down and lay the halberd's smaller spike (opposite its ax blade front) in the pool. I stand, hold the halberd high, spin it fast—and stop it hard.

Flecks of blood rainbow out onto the walls and ceiling. No gush, but that's not what I want. I'm trying to leave subtle evidence for the Sisters to put together to paint the perfect wrong picture. They need to believe that they—superior as they love to believe they are—have found signs of a murder happening in this room that sloppy soldiers will miss.

Next I examine the baseboard trim around the room, then play out a possible quick fight, at one point spinning the Ibex's halberd's gold-painted buttspike and scoring the trim with it, scuffing off some gold paint in a place where soldiers in haste might not see it.

I roll her over full on her back—*it*, I mean, not *her*. The corpse. The meat.

It's hard not to slip and get caught in the fuzzy emotionalism, even for me. And for me, it's important not to. I'm not desecrating a body here. I'm setting a scene, dispassionately, so that as few people die as possible.

Right.

I ram the spearpoint of the halberd through the corpse's throat, precisely where I'd stabbed her before. Then I remove it. Wipe the blade clean with a rag. Stuff the rag into the wound to keep it from seeping. Then I stab the buttspike through her ribs where I'd knifed her perfectly in the heart.

There are ways the very experienced can tell if a wound happened before death or at death or after, so maybe Durzo would've used the halberd to kill Petaria in the first place to be that extra bit more convincing. Me? I was more worried about making sure she couldn't kill me back, which is also a thing

Durzo taught me. Some wet workers are artists, some mere tradesmen, I suppose.

I pull the buttspike out of the corpse's chest, clean it, and stuff that wound with the bloody rags as well.

I tear one of the gold buttons from the Ibex's tunic that I stole. I scrub the button with a cloth, in case they have some magic that could detect who last touched it. I tighten the corpse's fist around it. Then, grabbing its wrist, I catapult the button against a wall. It lands at the edge of a clothes pile, shiny side up. Too visible.

I roll it over with a boot, tuck it out of sight in the clothes pile.

Then I frown down at the corpse. She must have been dehydrated when she pissed herself; the urine stench from her releasing her bladder is acrid and potent. I'm caught in a crux between speed and subtlety.

Sighing, I strip the corpse of its underclothes, clean its skin, squeeze out the urine and the water I used to mop it up into the chamber pot, fold the urine-damp garments tight, and then conceal them within the waxed sack I brought from the Ibex's room.

I truss up the body quickly, binding it for easy carrying, paying particular attention to securing the bandages over its wounds. It's no good concealing a body to carry as an innocuous package if it's going to dribble a blood trail behind you.

After throwing several loops of rope to make myself a harness, I go into Petaria's closet, grab several dresses and her cloak, and do my best at folding them.

When I'm done, the body is bound in as tight a package as I can manage, its knees to its chest, arms tight around knees. Petaria was a small woman, which is all that makes this possible. But I'm not a large man, so this is far more difficult than it would be if I were the Ibex's size.

As is, with dresses beneath, a cloak overhanging, and the Ibex's own cloak over the top, I hope I look as if I'm carrying a thick bundle of clothing: just another overburdened servant in a world where servants are invisible.

Even with the hidden straps, the weight of a body wouldn't be something I could carry easily in such a position, especially not as easily as I need to appear to be carrying my bundle. But that's where my Talent comes in. Magic doesn't solve as many problems as you'd think, but the problems it does solve it solves wonderfully.

Petaria's room is a mess, which has been a boon for finding rags. Now I kick her clothes around a bit, trampling them as soldiers might.

Then I go over and blow out the lanterns, replacing the glass chimneys as the wicks smoke.

I tuck my little note for the empress under the edge of one of the lanterns.

Ready? Kill the tracker.

I scrub a hand through my hair, and the ka'kari makes my fingers tingle as it devours the tracker the empress's mage put there.

Squatting low, I throw the coils of rope over my shoulders, then struggle to put on a jacket to hide them, and lift the bundle of clothes and corpse.

I'm reaching for the handle of the door when there's a knock on the other side.

"Petaria!" a woman's voice calls. "You're late."

I look at the latch, which I never locked. Turning my back, I push myself hard into the closet, nearly tripping as I try to push out of view of the door.

The door opens. "Petaria? It's lunchtime. Please tell me you aren't still in bed."

From an angle in the darkness, I see Melena's head poke through the door. I press myself back hard, trying to hold the bundle of clothes utterly still.

I hear Melena sniff. I freeze up. Is she smelling the smoke of the extinguished lanterns?

"Ugh, girl, you are such a pig. You have *got* to put this outside."

She steps into the room in the darkness and picks up the chamber pot gingerly.

I hold my breath. I don't want to kill Melena. Hells, encumbered as I am, I might not be *able* to kill her.

She turns around—the other way, turning her back toward me instead of her face—and walks out of the room, chamber pot extended, making a snort of disgust. I am suddenly unspeakably grateful I squeezed the wet pee rags out into that pot. If I hadn't, the chamber pot would've been empty and she would've known the smell must be coming from elsewhere.

Going into the hall, she calls out to someone, "Don't know why I clean up after her. Worse than my little sister." She closes the door behind her, and I finally breathe once more.

I can't wait long; the empress's people will be coming soon to see why my tracker disappeared. I carry my stack of clothes and the body hidden within it to the door.

I open it a crack. Nothing obvious in the hall.

Not that an ambush would be obvious.

Now is when I find out how lucky I am.

Durzo would beat me for moving forward after thinking such a thing. 'If you need luck for a plan,' he'd say, 'you need a better plan.'

But I don't have a better plan.

Throat constricted, I walk into the hall, using my Talent to make it seem that my bundle is light, the Ibex's halberd held deliberately awkwardly against my chest.

I make it out of the hall and round the corner just as I hear jogging footsteps from the far hallway—soldiers sent to check why my tracker has disappeared?

Throat tight, I walk quickly down to the midships flexion zone King Repha'im showed me.

My luck holds. I see no one here.

The sound of my heart pounds in my ears. I wrap the Ibex's cloak around his halberd and hurl them together into the hissing waves far below. The ocean accepts my gift without comment. I untie the straps binding me to the body and hide the corpse in a nook near where King Repha'im threatened me. I spread the clothes over the body. It's not well hidden, but it's not meant to be.

I turn, certain I've taken too long, certain that imperial guards will be blocking the exit, springing an ambush.

There's no one there.

I sheathe myself in the ka'kari for the first time in what feels forever and shimmer out of sight. It shouldn't be long until the imperials come bursting in here, having found my note in Petaria's room:

Your Imperial Majesty, I've upheld my side of our deal. You'll find the proof in a nook opposite where King Repha'im likes to dispose of his trash. I trust after verification of the deed, this will make your men's own discreet disposal work easier. While working, I discovered that one of your mages mistakenly put a tracker on me. Its presence could've easily been spotted by our opposition. Not only did it endanger me unnecessarily, it also could've tied you to certain activities you wish not to be associated with. Thus, I've removed it for both our sakes. Faithfully yours.

I hadn't signed the note. Not that holding back my signature will keep me anonymous from the people who are the most dangerous to me. But it seemed like a sloppy risk to announce my name in writing, so I didn't.

I move invisibly down the corridor, where I can watch to make sure that no random servant stumbles across the body.

Luckily—again! how much luck can one man expect?—no servants go there. After a few minutes, I see several of the massive praetorian guards come from the direction of Petaria's room and head toward the disposal area.

I don't need to see any more. I leave.

And as easy as that, I began—and I hope I've concluded—my career as an imperial assassin. With all my old highly refined skills and a disconcerting amount of luck, it seems it went really well.

Now all I have to do is all the stuff I'm terrible at against the people who may be the best in the world at such things and therefore the most likely to notice an amateur flopping about like a fish trying to teach hummingbirds to fly: With her blood yet warm on my hands, I need to deceive Petaria's friends, insinuate myself into one of the best covert action teams in the world, and use (and, in so doing, destroy) my last friendship.

All in all, sounds easy enough . . . at least the friendship destruction part.

Chapter Eighty

A Handkerchief and Wine

I feel ill," Viridiana said, pushing back from the table as Sister Ariel came into the library. "I'm finished."

"You've reached the end, then?" Sister Ariel asked. Her head tilted. "I expected rather more tears." She looked down at the handkerchief she was holding in one hand and the wine jug in the other uncertainly.

"No, not finished reading the book. Just finished. With reading this book." Viridiana's stomach churned. This had been bad enough. How could she face the end?

"We need to work on your communication skills, don't we?" Sister Ariel asked.

"Huh?"

Viridiana hadn't known that Kylar had killed Sister Petaria.

That made everything worse: for the Special Problems and Tactics Team, for Viridiana, for the hope of peace with Alitaera, and . . . well, things couldn't get worse for Kylar, could they?

She hadn't even suspected Kylar! Which made sense. If you wanted someone murdered in a horrific way to send a message, you hired Hu Gibbet. If you wanted someone artfully or silently *removed*, you contacted Durzo Blint. Kylar took after his old master.

At a sudden thought, Viridiana looked at the handkerchief and wine jug. "You're hoping to get through my messy emotional stuff quickly—not hinting that I'm out of time, right?"

Sister Ariel wrinkled her brow.

"Tell me I have time," Viridiana said.

"You have time."

"Are you lying to me?"

"As requested," Sister Ariel said without hesitation.

"What about all that 'loyalty to the truth' stuff?"

"I didn't think you'd *believe* me."

Vi was taken aback. Was Sister Ariel…teasing? "What's going on?" Vi asked. "You're not like this."

Sister Ariel shifted from one foot to the other. She set down the tumbler from its upside-down perch over the wine jug's mouth. Filled the tumbler and picked it up, but didn't drink it. "I'm wrapping up my failed commentary, so I've been listening to some of the speeches through the spy hole as I've been rather laboriously sifting my research to see if any of it has the least value beyond confirmation of what other, better experts have said more eloquently, and, well, the parliamentarian read out a revised schedule. You're not on it anymore." She said the last part in a rush, as if trying to get terrible news out of the way.

"I'm not?" Viridiana asked. "Does that mean I have as much time to finish reading as I nee—?"

"But what is on the schedule is a vote."

"How can they have a vote if I haven't testified? I thought they were going to vote what to do with me."

"It's a vote whether we declare war on Alitaera."

"*What?*" Viridiana sat upright, ready to jump to her feet. But there was nowhere to go.

"It seemed to me that they're doing things in the wrong order, so I asked my sister what was happening. Istariel says it's quite the coup by the old guard. Not a literal coup, nor a literal old guard, come to think of it. A clever move. She says assemblies have to work themselves up for war the way young men work themselves up for a fight. If they wanted war, we'd never vote on war first thing. They would arrange it so we would first vote on some trivial punishment for you as if that were an isolated matter. Then that matter would be considered closed. Then we'd vote to either overturn the Alitaeran Accords or, less aggressively, to set a commission to study how we can exit them. If the Alitaerans responded by sending soldiers, we'd be merely defending ourselves from that point. They would be the aggressors.

"On the other hand, a vote declaring war, without lining up any excuses first? This vote will undoubtably be lost. No one wants war, and almost everyone opposes a war of aggression where we're clearly at fault. By getting the Chantry to vote against war first, the old guard sets the terms of the debate. With war out of the question, the debate focuses on what price we're willing to pay for peace."

"I don't understand," Vi said. "This sounds like telling a bully that you aren't going to hit them no matter what they do to you."

"I didn't either understand either—Well, my goodness. I think you may have it. I asked her and she said if the Council began by voting whether we hand over a Sister to a foreign power, no one would vote for that. It's unthinkable. But putting it in the context of the price of avoiding a war and saving many other lives, the unthinkable becomes suddenly unavoidable. 'We've ruled out thing one, thus we must do thing two.'"

"The Alitaerans are seriously asking for a prisoner?" Viridiana asked. "I knew Sister Ayayah was going to be in deep trouble, but..." Viridiana swallowed as she saw Sister Ariel wince. *"Sister...?"*

"If the old guard were planning to hand over Sister Ayayah, you'd still be on the list to testify. There would be leading questions about who was in charge of the Special Problems and Tactics Team, who gave the orders, what it means to have authority over those teams, how culpability has been determined in other cases. They'd ask if Sister Ayayah ever temporarily handed over the leadership of the team or if she was the leader the whole time, if she ever asked you to do things against the Chantry's charter and values... that sort of thing. Again, not my analysis. This is all from Istariel."

"But if Sister Ayayah isn't going to be handed over, then who—? Oh..." Viridiana sat back in her chair. "Oh."

"That's their plan," Sister Ariel said. She looked at the cup of wine she'd poured and drank it down in one gulp. "It doesn't mean things can't go wrong for them. Though it doesn't look like the vote is going to be particularly close. But..."

"But what?"

"There's still a way out, a way that doesn't involve you being handed over to Alitaera."

"Well, what is it? I'm open to suggestions!" Viridiana said, fears snapping eagerly to anger.

"Finish the book. Find out if his body can be recovered. Make yourself so valuable to us we can't hand you over to them. It's a slim chance, Viridiana. I know. But..." She shrugged awkwardly.

"It's the only chance," Viridiana said.

"In the meantime, I'll go and see if there's anything I can do." With that, Sister Ariel stomped off toward her exit.

"Hey!" Viridiana called.

"What?" Sister Ariel didn't turn, obviously peeved.

"Leave the wine?"

Sister Ariel snorted. She didn't leave the wine.

Chapter Eighty-One

The Impertinence of Old Flames

The problem was so daunting that I decided to tackle it immediately. Which means, naturally, that I do no such thing. Why is it that the more urgent the main thing is, the more alluring all the side things become?

As I walk through the crowded hall, I see a man with a hat tucked into his belt. I turn my head over my shoulder and nod as if agreeing to someone behind me, and graze his arm, snatching the hat and mumbling an apology as if for jostling him.

I could simply go to the empress, right? I've accomplished the job she contracted me for. Why worry about the Chantry at all? If there's any group that's likely to see through my lies, it's them.

The Special Problems and Tactics Team has, frankly, nothing I want. Yet. The empress has everything. Maybe this next part could be easy. Maybe I'm taking something that could be easy and making it complicated. Maybe *I'm* making things hard with my own suspicious nature.

It's happened to those smarter and more devious than me.

But I haven't stayed alive this long by being trusting.

~Technically, you *haven't* stayed alive this long.~

I don't need to have that argument right now. I need to concentrate on the empress.

Stepping into a nook with a looking glass, I pull the stolen yellow feathered hat on my head and tuck as much of my hair into it as possible, and then slip out into the crowds of people walking by, chattering. No one takes any notice of me.

I've seen what power does to people. I've seen how people make their peace with extreme power: either reveling in it or trying to avoid becoming twisted by it as they use it. This empress keeps everyone guessing, which doesn't tell me how she operates. If only. But it *does* tell me how she doesn't operate.

The empress isn't *handled* by all the people around her who make it their whole occupation to handle her.

If she always did what seemed most convenient, least likely to cause immediate trouble, then her courtiers would easily have her dancing to their tune. Such people sniff out weakness instinctively, use people's failings against them, use lies and threats and intimations of dire consequences with the same facility with which I use knives and spears and swords. So she's no slave to ease and convenience.

If she always did what she thought was right—as Logan tries to do—she might be as easily swayed. For doves, wisdom lies in fleeing the company of serpents, which means most doves are not wise to serpents' ways.

But this doesn't always hold. And regardless, she's no dove.

Some rulers are truly chaotic, or present themselves as such, understanding that their courtiers are playing a game, and determined to win that game, even if it costs them the greater games of ruling effectively.

Other rulers are truly stable, with a clarity of vision and firmness of purpose that the double-minded can't believe an intelligent ruler would hold—and thus, with simplicity they confound the wise.

Other monarchs see a distinction between their private honor and the necessities of the state, being at once capable of humbling themselves profusely and living their private lives with profound integrity, while baffling their enemies by simultaneously acting with the utmost in cunning and even deceit in matters of state.

I don't know in which camp she falls.

And yes, this is procrastination. I feel like a knife juggler who's reached the limits of his abilities, panicked, and has thrown all the knives as high in the air as he could. Now I'm huddled on the floor waiting for them to land.

With the knives falling, I'm in exactly the wrong place.

The praetorian guard is too small and tight a group for me to infiltrate, so I don't bother trying to disguise myself as one of them. A mage, that's what I need. The empire needs lots of mages. Some of the younger ones—which is to say the ones who are my age—won't be familiar to all the courtiers and the imperial guards and praetorians. Disguising myself as a mage will also give me an excuse to not hide that I'm Talented from those who can sense such things.

It takes some searching, which means sometimes ducking my head and walking past people, and other times going invisible waiting for them to pass. For whatever reason, though there are similar numbers of mages as soldiers, there isn't a barracks for the imperial mages. Which doesn't mean the mages live in luxury. They each have their own tiny room, so tiny that they'd be better off in barracks. I'm guessing that's a pride thing.

Mages will tolerate discomfort, as long as it makes them look like they're more important than mere soldiers. The ship's designers, on the other hand, clearly only cared that they weren't going to give the mages more deck space than necessary.

I break into four of the tiny cabins reserved for mages without finding any clothing remotely my size. What is it with mages being either tiny or incredibly fat?

Looking for another bank of cabins, I slow down before I reach the common area. With little warning, because they're all sitting or standing so quietly, I've stumbled upon a group of almost fifty imperial mages.

Despite the proximity of their own cabins, half of them appear to be asleep—right here, in chairs or right on the floor. The others are concentrating intently, all facing the windows to the outside. They stand or sit in a variety of poses, some even moving formally as if they are martial artists. Almost everyone who's awake is doing magic.

I smelled the sweat before I stepped into the chamber. I'm surprised I didn't feel the magic. But it's all so tightly focused toward the windows, so disciplined, it's baffling. Most of the women are murmuring, barely above a whisper, the minimum they need to bind mind and magic with their words, but some women appear silent, and some men too are murmuring. Whatever they're doing, I'd guess they've been doing it for hours.

They have the air of soldiers digging trenches preparing for a siege: After the first hours, there are no wasted words, no wasted movements.

An older man and woman sit nearby, their backs to me. Gray-faced, he takes off his scrimshawed ivory spectacles and rubs his temples and his eyes, his back slumped. She sits straight as a queen but is as drawn as he. Both have more insignia on their uniforms than anyone else I can see.

"We'll lose a few of the youngest and the oldest ones, but we can keep it together," he says. "She shouldn't leave. If she does, they may panic. And the mages she'll take with her may cause the very disaster—"

"We'll do our duty," the woman says. Gray-haired, sharp-featured, she's got a surprisingly deep voice. "No. Don't say it again. I happen to agree with you. But we can't gamble with the empress."

Gamble with the empress? Does that mean gamble *against* the empress, or does it mean put the empress at risk?

I look over the assembled mages, trying to figure out their uniforms so that when I steal one I don't botch it. Militaries always have status clues embedded in their uniforms, but quasi-military institutions can be the worst, because they have either far more freedom or far more formalism, or some weird combination of the two.

All the Alitaeran mages, male and female, wear a long, long tunic, past the knee. They seem to allow a variety of tones from white to gray or silver to black. The hems and necklines are embroidered, either in gray or yellow for the lower-status mages or silver and gold thread for the higher-status ones. Or maybe simply the richer ones, though it all too often goes hand in hand, doesn't it? The tunics are high-slit on the sides, and the mages wear trousers beneath them, sometimes in the same color, but often contrasting or even in bright colors. The choice of shoes or boots also seems idiosyncratic.

Higher-ranking mages clearly have more flexibility in their dress, as do women. Or perhaps the women simply have more imagination: Their necklines are often rounded or square rather than the simple notch or V the men wear, frequently with runic embroidery at the neckline to match the hem. The women also wear necklaces, earrings, and bracelets, while the men sometimes wear torcs. The women have no dominant hairstyle, but many of the men have short-cropped or even shaven hair on the left side of their head. Some display tattoos or scarification on their bared scalps.

The overt and standard signs of office seem to be in the reinforced fabric of the shoulders down to the chest, which bears colored pins on the left side. The right seems blank, until I bring the ka'kari briefly to my eyes.

Oh, there's a whole invisible magical symbology on the right side of their chests purely for other mages to see. Fantastic.

"Not even if her leaving means we lose the whole ship?" the man says.

That makes my ears prick up. I'd thought this was merely the usual stuff: people griping about the boss. I hadn't even really paid attention to what they said before.

~Which is why you're relating all this to me, remember?~

Hey, you're right!

Amazing. I *am* smart.

The ka'kari gives me the little huff that would be the equivalent of rolling his cute little eyes. If he had eyes.

The woman has been silent. Now she says, "Better we lose the whole ship and everyone in it, including us, than lose the empress."

The man nods as if that goes without saying.

You know what? I'm gonna have to disagree.

But what is she talking about?

Then the woman says, "If she chooses to disembark, I'll make sure you are assigned to go with her, Intan."

"I'm not asking for that!" he says sharply. "I take my oaths ser—"

"I wasn't impugning your honor or your bravery," she snaps. "I'll send you with her because yours was the voice that told her to stay. If the rest of us all die because she left, you will be a constant reminder to her not to throw our lives away again so carelessly. Plus, those who take a stand when it's unpopular should see some benefit for doing so, if they're right. It's good for the corps because it encourages similar bravery in the young."

"That is . . . very kind, Agatta. Especially given our past. But all things considered, we should send Mircelle and Havdan. Those two will be the corps's heart and soul in the future, and a greater loss than me at least. You, naturally, being an incalculable loss."

She snorts, as if too exhausted to hold to any pretenses. "This. This is half of why I don't like you, Intan. I speak the truth, and you think it a compliment-debt to be repaid. But you make a good point. If we must choose . . ."

The conversation continues into further bickering and talk about the organization, plans for the future, but my mind drifts, pretty sure that the relevant bits are finished, and still uncertain what they mean by the empress 'disembarking.' I mean, I know what the word means, but I don't know why they're using it. I'll have to review it later.

"It's odd," Intan says. "But these nullification waves. Something about them reminds me a bit of the myth about Forethought and the accursed gift from the king of the gods."

"Which version do you mean?" Agatta asks. "Thesiod's?"

"No, the Schylius. You know, the bit where—"

"Uh-huh. I see it now. That's a bit grim, don't you think?"

"Coincidental, I'm sure," Intan says. He shifts uneasily. "But if one were to worry about the Jordanic Circularity Hypothesis . . ."

"I was afraid you were going to go there. Even if you didn't go that far, and merely approached it with Temisic Iteratives, it's a bleak trajectory. I had trouble sleeping before, you know. Now I'll have nightmares about the gods taking away..."

Naturally, she mumbles the last word and I can't see her lips to guess at it. Whatever they're talking about, though, no matter how important it is, they're speaking about it in the shorthand that two people in the same line of work so often speak. Part of me wants to stay to see if I can puzzle it out, but I've been here too long already.

Plus, there's now a maga scowling at me. She seems to have finished her shift at the window.

"Mircelle!" Agatta says as the woman heads toward me. "Join us. We were just speaking of you."

Mircelle turns to them, and I take the opportunity to move on, quickly.

In the next bank of rooms—unlocked!—I finally find a fitting change of clothes. It takes me only a few minutes to make my way from there back to the empress's staterooms.

This shouldn't be frustrating—but one of the most frustrating things about wet work is that sometimes you plan for every eventuality, spending weeks or months on a job, only to have some problem you'd never even considered pop up at the last moment and wreck everything.

That part doesn't surprise me. That's simply the nature of the work, evidence that you didn't think of everything, that you still need to grow, get better. But then other times, you make all your preparations and plans and fallback plans—and then you get to walk right in. Guards whom you *know* will give you a full pat-down simply wave you through. Areas with overlapping patrols suddenly have none. A passphrase that you spent a fortune procuring won't even be asked of you.

Those times infuriate me more than anything. When you do all the work to do a job that no one else could do, and then the job becomes something anyone could do?

I know. I know! I should take it as a gift. I know you can't plan for those things, and having all the contingencies and not having to use them is better than not having them and needing them. I know all that.

I don't care. It *irks* me.

Today? Today is that day. There are no guards in one of the places on the stairs where I was sure there used to be guards. People are distracted and barely glance at me.

Sure, sure, you can say that I walk past the praetorian guards without a care in the world and that very fact makes them not stop me, because such confidence can't be faked. But it can. I do it all the time.

Truth is, any time I have good luck too many times in a row, I hate it. I *know* that dice don't have memory, but it *feels* like they do, doesn't it? Like I'm stockpiling a store of bad luck to hit me all at once. And I've had a lot of good luck recently. It's adding, bit by bit, to the ball of dread growing in my gut.

Anyway, I could keep going. In fact, I'm just barely getting started with all the things I hate about things being too easy—but I don't have time for that, because I'm already abruptly through almost every possible impediment between me and meeting the empress.

Here I am, facing the door into the empress's chambers. There's only one praetorian between me and her room.

"Business?" the praetorian with a forked beard half dyed blue asks. His eyes are different colors, too, one brown and one blue.

"Message from High Thaumaturge Intan," I say. "Not urgent."

"Ha. That's a first. Might want to hang back a bit," the mountainous praetorian says. "Suspect you'll be waiting a while."

I nod in thanks and step inside the empress's chambers quietly. As I close the door softly behind me, I hear why. There's a man's voice ringing out on the other side of the big room. A familiar voice. And a heated conversation.

Neither of them looks at me. Neither has even noticed me yet.

I look around quickly, don't see anyone else, though there are privacy screens on the sides that might be concealing others. For the moment, that doesn't matter: I'm also screened from them.

"I'm not threatening you!" King Repha'im says. Calmer, he says, "And I won't. Ever! Caelestia! Why would I wish to take things away from you? Anyone can take away. That *assassin* Stern can take a woman's life." He waves a hand vaguely toward the door—which happens to be right where I'm standing.

My pent-up bad luck flips over in my stomach. I slip to one side, keeping a pillar between me and the imperial couple.

"Killing takes nothing but hatred and a bit of steel. But me? I adore you. I want to *give* to you. I want to give you the world—all your heart's desires! And do you think I, I who see you better than all these petty lordlings—do you think I don't know your heart's desires?"

"Yes, you're exceptional," the empress says coolly. "I see it now. You're not like all the others." She yawns.

Repha'im pinches the bridge of his nose. Takes a breath. "Perhaps you're right. Perhaps everyone sees what you want as clearly as I do. After all, it takes no hidden powers. The caustic wit might simply come from the series of disappointing men you've dealt with. Perhaps from the fact that none of them, still, has been able to compete with lowly Arevy Tilsin—"

"Excuse me!" Her face is instantly flushed, jaw rigid. "How do you know that name?"

"—who himself disappointed you by marrying that charming little countess before you could raise him to a rank where he might marry you instead without outraging all the empire's peers. Then he had the temerity to spawn a half-dozen sons and three daughters in . . . what is it? Twelve years. *Nine* children in twelve years? And by all accounts Lord and Lady Tilsin are deliriously happy, well beloved by their tenants, adored by their neighbors, respected by their peers, though not, it is true, particularly well off. It's said Lord Tilsin turns down any lucrative business dealings that would require him to travel too far or too often, and he's certainly not had any time for political machinations, though one hears he is a stalwart empress's man and will brook no critical talk whatsoever of your person."

"That's *enough.*" I can't see her now with the pillar between us, but the empress sounds livid.

"I wonder, which offends you more, their happiness or their fruitfulness?"

"Watch yourself, Rabisu."

"You let everyone think that you've been putting all the lords off, either not sleeping with them at all or choosing not to conceive through magic when you do. You've even orchestrated leaks to that effect, but you know you can't keep up the charade for much longer. You're, ahem, thirty-eight years old. Everyone thinks this means surely in the next year or three you'll decide to have children at last and turn the next consort into an emperor. They don't know that you *have* been trying. As far as I can tell, for four years at least—you've tried with the last three kings, not to mention with numerous lovers. Your Healers can't find anything wrong. You've employed wise women, magae, zhuzhin casters, torphalines, cha-ryen manipulators, and even a few charlatans. Some made you sick. Some helped in tangential ways. None has enabled you to conceive an heir."

Her voice is as unaffected as if she were discussing the price of imported cloth. "If you've kept such a close eye on me, then you should know my health issues are something I've explored simply as part of being a dutiful sovereign. I don't feel any lack, personally. Have no wish for the burdens of pregnancy, and no desire to disfigure myself by bearing a child."

"Odd then that you told your dear friend Caranna Darivar two months ago that you felt as if there were 'an abyss growing black in my belly where a babe should be.' In future, you might remember that when revealing one's secrets it's best not to do so with a memorable turn of phrase. Too tempting for a confidante to slip up and share, even only with her husband, who himself is also the soul of discretion. Unfortunately, the walls of their solar are rather thin."

As I take a peek around the pillar, I see the empress's thin lips tighten. "When the time comes to secure a succession, I will either promote one family to the fore above all others, or if it's necessary, I'll simply adopt a child from a leading family. Perhaps even skip messy childhood and adopt an adult ally directly. If you think I don't know a hundred ways to secure my reign—"

"Of course you do, and you know that all of them come with significant dangers. Every one of which breaks two hundred years of precedent. Adopt too early and you'll be pressured to step down in your ally's favor, and risk being assassinated if you resist. Adopt too late, and the losers will contend you weren't in your right mind or were exploited in your poor health. For an empire with a barren empress, many are the roads to civil war. The greater problem is, you may even make a perfect plan, but as you won't be alive to see that everyone else follows their part, the empire may be doomed no matter what you do. Your infertility threatens not only your own family and your legacy but thousands of other lives—and more dangerously, thousands of other ambitions.

"If you deal with this challenge correctly, it will be no more than a footnote to your reign. All your other accomplishments will be given the weight they deserve. But if you fail in this, those accomplishments will be mentioned in passing if at all: 'She did some great things, but...' and then the downfall of this empire will be laid at your feet, for the only thing worse than leaving an heir poorly suited for the throne is leaving none."

"Do you think me remotely unaware of any of this?" the empress snaps.

"I know that one of the reasons you like me is that I tell you the truth. So I will: I don't know. I can't tell what you're aware of by your actions thus far. I see you insulated from your people by lickspittles and leeches and fawning flatterers, the whole constellation of simpering sycophants—all of them keeping you from being the ruler you can be."

Her voice is so quiet I can barely hear it. "How dare you."

"How dare I what? Speak the truth? You need more such daring in your court."

"Get out! Get out before I decide to have you thrown off this ship for the merriment of those *sycophants*."

"Of course, my liege. But one last thing." I can't see his face now, but from his voice, he doesn't sound like a man who's losing, who is being kicked out and probably about to lose his position and sooner or later his life. "The problem," he says, "isn't physical. Good day."

He starts walking toward the door, which means toward me—which means I'm going to have to choose in about a three count whether I move into the empress's line of sight or stay where I'll be in his.

Two. I can hear his footsteps.

I throw the ka'kari over myself and step into the empress's line of sight.

She doesn't have powers. At least, none I know of.

"What is it, then?" she calls out to his back. His back—because he'd turned his back on the empress, in violation of imperial etiquette, practically begging for punishment. The man's arrogant. I'll have to remember that.

He's also right on the opposite side of the pillar from me. If he moves quickly either way, I'll be exposed to—well, maybe to nothing. I don't know what powers he has. I don't know what he sees with those unsettling eyes of his. Maybe he can't see me as the empress can't.

As I hope the empress can't.

Not turning, Repha'im says, "Your infertility is the work of an outside spirit. A minor god, if you prefer. Possibly two in concert. I don't know which one or ones, yet. I will."

"Ah," she says, sneering, "let me guess. For a sizable donation to a certain priesthood you know—"

"None of that," he snaps. "You've not been listening to me at all, have you? I've not come to *take* anything from you, Caelestia. Riches? I don't need your gold. Power? I can find power other ways. Sex? I've no problem obtaining whatever I desire. I am here *to help you*. Very well, I can see you're not going to listen to me any other way. This isn't my forte, but..."

Even from the side, I can see his pupils suddenly stretch, giving him that stomach-turningly caprine look again, with subtle green filling the pupils instead of black, but then they go back to human proportions in an instant. "There," he says.

She must not have been able to see what his eyes did from her distance.

She seems confused. "What? There what?"

"You may feel it as warmth any moment now, with some radiating excitation of nearby nerves."

"I don't feel any—" The empress jerks bolt upright as if someone has poured ice water down her back. Or perhaps in her lap. She clamps her legs together with an involuntary yelp.

Her voice breathless, she struggles to keep her tone level. "What are you doing?"

"Doing? Nothing. It's done. It was too late for this cycle, but starting next month, you're fertile again—and will be so for years longer than other women your age. I may not have fully recovered all the years stolen from you, but I did my best." He cocks his head. "And still you don't believe. Hmm. Easy enough to test, though, isn't it? At the appropriate time of your cycle—I'm sure even your indoltened mages can help you figure out when that is, if you can't tell yourself—bed a man you know spills good seed, so you may wish to avoid your venereal-pox-ridden nobles. I don't know, maybe you could send for your old flame Lord Tilsin."

She's breathing heavily, as if the 'excitation of the nearby nerves' might have been a bit more intense than Repha'im intended. Trying to maintain composure, she smooths her skirts.

Or maybe it wasn't unintentional at all.

"You're...you're telling me you don't care who my heir is?" she says, disbelieving.

"You huma...You've not been listening. I'm not helping you so my own heir can sit her fat little bottom on your throne someday. I'm helping *you*. Sleep with whomever you want. Breed with whomever you like. It makes little difference to me."

"You're saying you don't want me?" She sounds offended.

"Yes, I want you! But I don't want any good thing for me to come at your expense. Or for you to think it does. I don't want you to believe that I'm here to use you for my gain."

"But you are here to use me," she says.

It takes me a moment to even follow what she means. What I think she's implying is that what he's saying may be technically true but is also misleading. She's used to such speech in her courts—or perhaps she's just that quick.

I'm certainly not.

"Of course I'm here for a reason," he says, exasperated, "else why should I have come at all?"

"And I'm asking you, if you're such a truth teller: What is it?" She balls her fists, annoyed, but also shifts her hips.

"I don't know if you'll believe me," he says. He sounds troubled or uncertain, but I don't know if I dare peeking too often.

"After this?" she says, pointing to her belly. "If you've really Healed me, I shall believe anything."

As I risk another quick look, he takes a breath, then nods to himself, as if making a decision. "The world is about to change, Caelestia, radically. Already has. Some suspect already, but most of the world will find out about it soon. In fifteen to twenty years, the kind of threats that emerge once a millennium will arrive. Except instead of a single millennial-sized threat, right now it appears there will be three of them, striking consecutively like hammerblows. After them, nothing will remain the same."

"What do you mean? What's at stake?" Even from here, the empress looks flushed.

"Consider this one: It sounds trivial yet will affect everything in time. You know how some argue that mankind is at core bad, corrupt, and needs to be hedged with institutions and laws to keep them from acting out all their terrible impulses, whereas others contend that humans are generally good but are corrupted by bad institutions, poor education, and ignorance about their own best interests. Yes?"

"I've heard such arguments. I've always thought—"

"This will end the arguments. What's at stake will be human nature itself. Not a full reforging of human identity but instead a small but significant push right at the beginning inside every child, inside every human will, forever, with each generation, for eternity. Little will change, at first, but over time? *Everything* will shift, forever, in a slowly gathering avalanche that will never stop. Compounding upon itself as wealth compounds in palaces and banks and debts compound in the slums, except for all of humanity, over all the world, for all time.

"I've come to *your* court because I believe you could be the best ally in all Midcyru for the coming battles." He smiles, but it is a smile over sadness. "Compared to that, what is everything else? I...I have enjoyed sharing your time and your bed more than words can say, but if having you trust me and join me in this long war means I need to sacrifice that companionship and deep pleasure? I will do so, and bear my grief behind a smiling façade, should my silent suffering over the next decades make your life easier to the smallest degree."

She looks troubled, and then I lose my view of her as she comes closer to him. "I...I don't think anyone's ever said anything so romantic to me in my entire life."

Then she throws herself at him with such violence, I think momentarily that she's attacking him.

Which she is. Just not that way.

Though I move with some alacrity, they're making love before I can leave the room.

The praetorian bodyguard looks askance at me.

I say, "They're, uh—" A simultaneous squeak of delight and creak of furniture floats out of the room behind me.

Understanding floods his face. "Busy?" he says. "And you thought it best not to interrupt?"

"Exactly," I say, with a pained smile. "It can wait."

Chapter Eighty-Two

The Wrong Guest of Honor

*H*ow, uh, long might this, ahem, take?" I ask the big bodyguard.

He shakes his head. "Couple minutes, maybe."

"Oh, that's not so bad. I—"

"Or maybe two hours. Depends on the mood and the man."

"...Ah."

"Was there anyone else in there? She likes us to clear the room when she's ... you know. Sometimes courtiers think they'll just hang around, lest they lose their place in the queue. Which, truth to tell, definitely happens. Tough luck for you if it does."

He doesn't even know if there was anyone else inside! I could've been even more careless today. Surely this isn't normal. But things slip. Even with the best teams, things go wrong.

"No—well, I, I actually was rather focused on being terrified of their fighting, and then that rather abruptly changed to—" There's a sudden high-pitched giggling from within. We both pretend hard not to have heard it. "I was distracted," I finish lamely.

He grunts. "Guess I get to go check. But hey, you played straight with me," he says. "I'm on shift until nightfall. If you need to leave and come back, I'll put you to the front of the queue."

"Thank you! That's awfully kind of you," I say. "I've been holding my bladder since before I came up here! Can you direct me...?"

He points. "Down those stairs, two lefts and behind the curtain. Set aside for praetorians' use, but not exactly forbidden for others." The big man sets his shoulders, turns, and grabs a hat from a pile of gear behind his station. He pulls it to a low angle, obviously to block his view of anything happening in the direction of the imperial bed. "Good l—" he starts to say, but then notices I'm gone.

Gone here only meaning gone invisible.

I'm not leaving. Not with the job undone. I always finish the job.

My bodyguard opens the door to the imperial bedchamber a crack (a wide crack, he's a huge man), and slips inside. I slip in after him, my breath held, so close I could be his shadow. I don't know if he's going to close the door behind himself.

But he doesn't. He takes a few steps in, checking the shadows of the room, then reverses the low side of his hat brim so he can check the other half of the room with his vision of the bed still blocked. I stay on the opposite side of some pillars farther into the room, not trusting my invisibility, not against a praetorian, not even on a day when they've made so many careless errors.

He goes, leaving me alone in the room with the gleefully copulating couple and my own malevolence.

I'm standing, unseen, in a lovemaking couple's bedchamber where they think they're alone. Is it a sign of how sick I am, or how far estranged from humanity that I don't feel any of the normal human emotions at being here? Embarrassment surely should be the guest of honor, Prurience would likely have a place set at the table, and Loneliness at my own isolation from such human companionship and acceptance might show up uninvited. But none of these feelings show up. Not even that garrulous neighbor, Self-Pity.

Instead I think, *I could kill both of them. I bet it would save all sorts of trouble later.*

It frightens me a little, because I don't know that I'm wrong, but I know it's alien to think so dispassionately about murder. That I think first: *This person might cause trouble someday. Better kill them while I have the chance.*

That can't be right, can it? Even if it's objectively true, what kind of person thinks like that? Is that what it is to be a Night Angel? Sometimes my humanity feels like a handful of sand and the air a storm, blasting that blinding grit in my face, an irritant best discarded.

But when my hands are finally empty, what will be left?

Where did I get this sense of shame at my shamelessness?

I move deeper into the room, checking the couple's distraction furtively, aiming for the screens and furniture off to the side of the room so that I'm not standing by the door, waiting to be seen.

The empress cries out, her splotchy-faced ascent to the carnal heavens bringing me down to earth. At that moment, in Repha'im's face, I see not joy nor pleasure nor pride at his own potency, but as her head turns skyward and away from him, without ceasing his athletic motions, he turns to a looking glass.

He admires himself. Then he picks at something between his teeth, examines it.

In the instant she turns back to him, he is staring at her once more, his face all rapt attention.

He is alien, too. Though by his sudden grunts and paroxysms he hides it well. Or perhaps his own body is under his command even in such things.

Then he is atop her, face-to-face, grinning fit to split the heavens with his smile. He searches her face—not with the ardor or the joy that a man might bring to the sacred bed—but searching for what will enmesh her further. Chuckling, he rolls over, holding her so she lies atop his big chest. She rests her head on his chest, spent, fingertips caressing his defined muscles.

"Kylar killed the witch," she says.

"Really? Already?"

"It's why I wanted us to be quick. I figured there were about even odds that he'd be pounding on the door any moment demanding more payment."

"You put a tracker on him, surely?"

"Of course," the empress says, with only the tiniest hesitation. If I hadn't been looking for that hesitation—that possible crack between her and Repha'im—I wouldn't have seen it.

"How'd you manage to place a tracker on him without triggering the collar?" Repha'im asks, playing idly with her hair, but I see tension in his stomach muscles.

"I took his collar off."

"You what?" His fingers freeze, strands of her hair between them.

"So he could do the work," she says. She sits up, troubled. "You have a look on your face that I don't appreciate," she says sharply.

For a moment, I marvel at her. She doesn't cover herself. Alone with a much larger man, most people would feel terrifically vulnerable in a sudden conflict.

"Does my look tell you that you've been very, very stupid?" Repha'im asks. "Because that's what your own good sense might've told you, if you had any."

"Excuse me?"

"Tell me you at least tripled the guard on this room," he says as he gets out of bed and pulls on his trousers.

She stands quickly and slaps him. "Know your place!"

His muscles taut and his form huge, jaw clenched, he takes a breath, then says, "You're right. Please forgive me." He kneels, then lies prostrate.

Her eyes flash, still hot, but there's a brief twist to her lips as she regards his humbled form. "Then I guess there's just one thing to decide. Would you like your punishment to be public or private?"

He looks up at her, and there is no weakness in his eyes, nor in his voice. "I trust you to make the best choice."

"Give me your belt," she says as she pulls on her shift.

He gets up to his knees, expressionless, removes the belt, and hands it to her. She's barely taller, standing, than he is on his knees. "Shall I lie down once more, Your Eminence?" he asks.

I don't detect any petulance or defiance in his tone. He honestly doesn't seem to care.

"No," she says, doubling the belt in her hand. "I give you mercy instead."

Sounding chastened, he says, "I shall reward it."

"Kylar removed the tracker," she says, watching him closely.

His lips go briefly white, the muscles on his neck stick out, then he says, "I see."

"It reported nothing beforehand. He didn't use his Talent until after it was gone. He must have known it was there all along. Meaning he was happy to kill a mage without having his powers available—on the chance we might record what he did. Or how." She tosses his belt back to him and snarls, "Get up. Get dressed."

"He's dangerous," Repha'im says. "I would never pretend otherwise. Taming him will be like taming a wolf: fraught, but attended by so much payoff for generations that the attempt is eminently worthwhile."

"So long as he doesn't kill us, you mean?" she asks lightly, pulling her hair free of the neckline of her shift. She rings a bell to summon her servants.

I duck low, squatting behind a regal chair in the sitting area on my side of the room, invisible from mundane sight still.

"Precisely," he says. Then, as a team of servants bustle in from a door near me, he says, "Your Highness, given this new danger, will you move forward with my Cloud Point suggestion?"

She sighs, spreading her arms for the attendants to be able to reach all of her, but otherwise ignoring them. "Fleeing would hurt me with my people. You know that. They'll say I abandoned them in the face of danger."

"I know," he says simply. "But it will remind them of their relative value to the realms. And after all, what does one heap up a good reputation for, if not to spend it when necessary?"

Reluctantly, she says, "You still wish to stay behind?"

"Wish it? I would much rather go with you. But it will remind them of *my* relative value to the realms, too."

She shakes her head ruefully. "You mean it will allow you to be seen to be in charge in my absence. You do like to assert a masterful presence quickly, don't you?"

"You see right through me, Your Eminence. I admit it did occur to me that a small but early sign of your trust would help an outsider like me a lot with all the nobles in Borami and beyond. Plus, I'd be merely nominally in charge of a ship with a single destination and skilled pilots at the helm...How much can I louse up?" He smiles rakishly at her.

She smiles, charmed. "Oh, very well. I'll give the orders for my disembarkation. But I warn you, I will expect a very enthusiastic greeting at the palace."

"Very," he says, looking at her with undisguised hunger. Then, when she turns to her servants, he adds, carefully, "And the praetorians?"

"What about them?"

"Doubling or trebling the number protecting you?"

"Don't be ridiculous. Stern's no threat to me. I need my praetorians to be sharp later."

He moves to object but stops himself, apparently seeing it's not a good time to press his luck.

"You may go," the empress says sharply to him, and Repha'im goes, quickly.

But as he reaches the door, the empress raises her voice. "Kylar said something...troubling. He said the child is his son."

I feel as if a trapdoor has just swung open inside my guts.

I can't see Repha'im from here, and I dare not look lest he see me. There's a tiny hesitation, and then his voice is edged very lightly with derision. He says, "And you believed him?"

Without waiting for further leave, he closes the door behind himself.

These people lie constantly. There is no truth in them.

I should get out of here. What am I going to do? Bargain with this woman? What could I offer her? Threaten her? How?

Whatever I'm going to do, I better do it fast. A ruler's time is not her own. As soon as she's dressed, she'll surely be accosted by someone with a list of things for her to do.

She didn't promise to give me my son in return for killing Petaria. She only promised my freedom. And that was before I cut her magical leash.

I hear her make an exasperated noise from her dressers—three women and one painfully skinny man who stands contrapposto with feathers pasted to his eyelashes. "No," she says, "we can redo the cosmetics as I talk to my secretary."

This is not going to go well.

With a scraping slam, I bar the side door. Disengage the bypasses. I dash to the main door and do the same.

Everyone stops, standing up, heads prairie-dogging from one sound to the next, baffled at the exits locking themselves. The effeminate dresser waves his hands in fear, but the empress puts out her own hand, motioning him to settle down.

Do you know what happens when you take people who spend a lot of time and money to feel safe and rob them of their feeling of safety? Me neither. But I'm about the find out.

"Your Imperial Highness," I say, appearing in the middle of the room with a scintillant flourish and a bow. "I finished the job, as agreed. I'd like to talk about the next."

"You dare!" she says, rising. From the uneven color in her face, her dressers have gotten as far as removing her cosmetics.

"Yes," I say carefully. Didn't she just say that same thing to Repha'im?

"Get out!" she bellows.

I look left, then right, where I hear someone fidgeting with the locks. "Mmm, no."

"Get out!" she shouts again, with the outrage of one who rarely has to repeat herself.

"Highness," I say. "You asked what I would do to get my son back. The answer is everything. But the boy isn't only my son. High King Logan Gyre adopted him. He's Jenine and Logan's child, too, and you risk war if he isn't returned to me. All I ask is that you give him to me—or to any of Logan's representatives. Jenine Gyre is on the ship; she will be overjoyed to be reunited with her child. What you do with Repha'im for his kidnapping and the murders he's committed is up to you. At a word, you can come out of this a hero to the people of Logan's new empire."

"A hero?" she says, as if I'm stupid.

"And more besides. I know you didn't have anything to do with his kidnapping, but now that you know he exists, I'm sure there's some temptation for you to simply take him from Repha'im and use him as a bargaining chip. But I can offer you far more."

She raises a calming hand to her dressers again, seeming suddenly almost charmed at my gall. "How could you?"

It won't be right, what I offer her. It will prove some of the worst things Repha'im said about me. But I'll do anything to spare my son the hell Repha'im has planned for him.

"Your Highness, I offer you my services. My fealty. I took care of Petaria for you in a single hour. I infiltrated your own apartments easily. You've seen that my skills are unrivaled. No one can stop me. I can be yours. Your knife in the shadows. No enemy, no rival, will ever be safe from you. I can kill and make the evidence point to any killer you wish, or to no one at all. I trained under the legendary Durzo Blint. I can make it appear that an enemy grew despondent and killed himself and have his own family cover up the circumstances of the death, proving to everyone who looks that it was a suicide. Accidents, poisonings, disappearances. I can do them all, at a level of proficiency even you wouldn't believe."

"What happened to 'I'll be damned if I work for you'?" she asks.

"Oh, I fully expect damnation. My son's worth my soul."

She barks a laugh. It's an ugly sound. "You'll have to look for your damnation elsewhere. I don't need your services. You may go. And you will thank me for my mercy in overlooking this...very serious error." She waves a finger around at the locked doors.

If she's afraid of me, she shows not the slightest hint of it.

She doesn't understand. How can she not understand? "Your Highness... *he's my son.*"

Her eyebrows draw down, then twitch up. "No. He's mine now. Not my son. But *mine.*"

"Your Highness, you have no idea what you're doing."

She shoots a quick look at her dressers, puts out a hand, again seeming to signal them not to take any action. Then she turns to me, indulgent. "*I* have no idea? Speaking of no idea, do you know why, out of all the contenders, I elevated Repha'im to be my King in the West?"

"Uh..." I'd assumed he'd worked his wiles on her, but now I have a sick intuition.

"Because he brought me that child, Kylar. A boy who at the least is a hostage to guarantee the good behavior of Logan's rising empire, and at the best may give me a way to negate the growing threat of a newly militant Chantry. I have all that in my hands, and in trade, you offer me the services of...an assassin. And you think *I* have no idea what *I'm* doing?"

It's all so obvious now. To me, the kidnapping was a travesty. To her, it's politics. It may even have been her idea from the beginning.

"He's...he's my son," I stammer.

"Was," she corrects. "He was."

"Let me...let me raise him. I'll still serve you. I'll teach him whatever—"

"Out of the question," she interrupts.

"You can't trust Repha'im! He'll turn the boy against you, against everyone!"

"A problem for tomorrow. You're my problem today." She nods to her effeminate dresser. The man clenches a fist and all the doors pop open—including one I hadn't even seen concealed in a wall.

Her dresser, with his lacquered fingernails and feathers woven in his hair and his cowardly persona, is a mage. I'd thought him panicking. He wasn't panicking, he was instantly ready to use his spells—and she stopped him. I can't believe I overlooked him. Overlooked the professionalism of the Alitaerans. Foolish of me to think they would leave the empress defenseless even for a moment.

Two dozen enormous praetorian guards stream in and take up positions surrounding me but don't advance.

The empress looks down at her feet and moves a bit to her left, then looks up at me. "Kill him," she says. *Shunk.*

The floor drops out from under her, and she disappears from view. A second *shunk* follows a moment later as the trapdoor snaps closed, walling her off from me.

"Hey," I say, backing up to the wall, looking at the daunting forms of two dozen of the empire's most formidable warrior-mages, including the Ibex, who looks more than a little annoyed about his missing spear. "Gentlemen. I'm not *completely* sure about this, but I'm pretty convinced she was kidding. As we say back on the farm, *That empress, she shore is a joker.* But before we get into this, I do think it's only fair that I warn you—"

They don't let me finish the punch line. They attack.

Chapter Eighty-Three

Dido Discovers Diuretics

There's an ancient technique taught by the old masters on how to take on many armed men at the same time: So difficult that few will even attempt it, it requires discipline, timing, dexterity, willpower, and luck. In short, for you to have any hope of success, you need the entire skill set of an elite warrior in his prime.

Like many of the best techniques, it's been discovered and rediscovered by all the great fighting traditions, so I've heard it referred to by many names. Eyvar's Implacable Itch. The Egret's Egress. Dido Discovers Diuretics. Durzo hated cute fancy names for combos and only shared them with me so that if I trained with others, I wouldn't make him look bad by not knowing what they were talking about. He taught me this advanced technique in his inimitable style: 'Someday, you'll face too many fighters. As you get better, the number will change. But you'll know when there's unquestionably too many. When that happens, there's one and only one way to win: Run away.'

Dumb kid that I was, after a few seconds of waiting for him to tell me he was joking, I said, 'That's not winning.'

'In some games, there's no winning. Don't play those games. But sometimes, you'll start playing because you didn't realize it's that kind of game. When you do, change the game if you can. Cheat if you can. If you can't cheat it or change it, change your definition of winning. Sometimes winning means getting the best outcome possible from the place you're in. Even if it's a place you shouldn't have gotten yourself into.'

Then he'd done that thing to me that he sometimes did. He got this look on his face as if he were hearing the words coming out of his own mouth for the first time. I didn't see it then, but now I think he was realizing that his words applied to himself.

A haunted look came over his face, and then anger, and he said, brusquely, 'Surviving an encounter that should kill you *is* a win. Sometimes the only win possible.' Then he'd stormed off, as he had so many times in my youth.

Which is sort of too much thinking for me to think as I'm backing up toward the wall with far too many elite, well-armed warrior-mages closing in on me, but I can be pretty quick-thinking, especially when all that speed of thought is taking my mind in a direction that isn't helpful.

As the Ibex leaps forward to attack me, first of all his peers, I throw myself forward and to one side, diving and dodging into the little open space still left me.

Or at least, an illusory image of me does, giving me a couple more heart-beats for the ka'kari coating my back to complete devouring the bulkhead behind me.

Could you be *any slower?*

~You have no idea how many layers of steel and magic there are!~

I throw out another illusion, hurtling up to cling to the ceiling as I go invisible. But that illusion is cut to odd shimmering tatters before it even reaches the ceiling, and fully half of the praetorians, with their eyes glowing with magic, don't even turn their gaze to follow it.

The praetorians move forward with terrifying coordination: The circle flexes to accommodate my illusory movement. At the same moment that some are moving forward to attack with spear and halberd and chain, others draw back to protect the gaps left in their line. On some tempo I don't know, every praetorian's eyes shift to the magical spectrum where they glitter, or from the magical back to the visible spectrum. Those with glittering eyes shout at what they're seeing as the others shatter the illusion I threw before me.

But the shouts are unheeded, unnecessary, for at that very moment, the ka'kari cuts through the last layers of the hull.

~Now! Done! Go!~

For one moment, wind whips into the empress's stateroom with a snarl—

And then the snarl becomes all-encompassing as the storm's claws snatch me out of the ship with the horrifying ease of a grizzly ripping grubs out of a rotten log.

The roar of wind and its raking claws along the length of my body blot out all sense for a moment, a moment out of time.

Then the ka'kari encases my skin fully, and I can breathe and see again.

Which is wonderful. Rather than simply feeling myself slide helplessly along the slippery, featureless side of the ship, I get to see it, too. As ever, the wind is blowing from directly behind the ship, shooting it through the massive waves, but also blasting me horizontally toward the front of the ship, which isn't far.

I'm sliding down and forward across the hull's featureless armored skin, slipping from outside the empress's chambers near the peak of the ship's closed hull toward the great storm ship's widest point.

Already too far forward to hit the wings of the storm ship that arch out to its pontoons, if I slide off the waist, there's nothing for me but wind and waves and death in the churning waters.

I roll onto my belly and the wind almost plucks me from the ship to send me airborne, but the storm ship bucks as a massive wave lifts the prow high, and the hull rises to slam me from below with such force I bounce.

I stab clawlike fingers into the hull. The ka'kari reacts as if it's part of me—it knows the magic protecting the hull now, and knows the perfect counter to it. My fingers dig in, sparks of magic and metal flaring bright—and my slide stops.

Turning my head over my shoulder, I look to see how close I was to shooting off the hull to my death.

Actually, I'm not that close to the edge. Huh. If I were telling the story down at a local watering hole, I'd say I only stopped myself when both my legs were dangling over the abyss. Oh, and that I was holding on by one hand.

Probably then I'd do something to showcase my jaunty, fearless attitude.

Come to think of it...*Hey, if we live through this, remind me to come back and embellish this a—*

Without warning, a greater gust of wind within the tempest suddenly plucks my legs from the hull and shakes my whole body like a barman snapping dust out of a floor mat. My hands maintain their clawed grip for the first snap, then slip, and then, as I focus all my Talent, hold.

Just as suddenly, the wind relents and drops me back onto the hull once more. I'm left trembling and gasping, my face turned away from the wind, cheek against the cold, slick hull as I recover.

Then I send the ka'kari down to my feet to make hooked claws there, too.

I mean, um...How about this?

After I'm able to get my second hand back to the hull, with magnificent effort, I pull myself away from the edge where I'm dangling, and heroically, where other men would crumble in fear, I climb hand over hand until I'm able to send the ka'kari to my feet to make hooked claws there, too.

Then I dig in at all four points—Nah, forget that—I stab the ka'kari out of my waist too, and cling, tick-like, to the hull.

What do you think? Too much?

~Kylar. Rule of thumb. When you wonder if it's too much, it's way, way too much.~

Yeah, maybe so. What do you think about—?

Another gust hits me, even greater than the earlier one, and threatens to tear me from the hull.

I don't know why this time it triggers a memory. One of my earliest. I was a little in our street guild, and I hadn't brought back my coin for dues. It was the first time I was expected to contribute, and I didn't understand it, I think. Ja'laliel was yelling at me, cursing me out publicly. I remember cowering as the words passed over me like a storm.

He didn't hit me. Ja'laliel wasn't cruel. Scratch that. He wasn't *more* cruel than he thought he had to be to survive. Maybe I should say he was brutal, not cruel. He didn't take delight in disciplining us—but he sure did it. For littles as young as I was, that meant a big had to stand in as my whipping boy.

Funny thing, they called 'em that whether they were boys or girls, and it usually wasn't a whipping. In my case, a big who barely even knew me volunteered. Gritch.

I haven't thought of Gritch in years. Gritch took Ja'laliel's punch to the gut and two slaps like it was nothing. But Ja'laliel was wearing a ring we'd filched, and one of the slaps cut Gritch's cheek. Nothing serious, we all thought. But it got infected. Two days later he was feverish. Sleepless. Moaning. We couldn't afford a poultice from the Healers. We'd been robbed recently by one of the biggest guilds, so it wasn't even a possibility. Two days later, Gritch was dead.

He'd stood up for me, stood in for me, and he'd died for it. For me. He died because I loused up, because I didn't understand how things worked on the street. Because I was too slow and stupid. Because I failed.

Maybe the cursing-out I'm remembering was the one Ja'laliel gave me after Gritch died, telling me all those things. Blaming me through his angry, guilty eyes. I dunno, those two memories have run together, mingling like the streams of sewage and swampwater in the Warrens' sloppy streets.

Memory's funny that way.

I have to move. Have to get back inside. Which means I have to think, have to work, have to put aside all feeling and act. Searching the featureless side of the storm ship, I try to visualize where I am. If I'm going to have to try to dig all the way through the hull, I want to do it somewhere thin, and preferably somewhere safe.

The hole I came out of has been sealed back up with magic, which, all things told, is a lot better than the bodyguards sending someone out after me. I can only hope they think I'm dead.

~Well, you must be. There's no way they would have been able to see you, what with you dangling off the ship *by one hand*, right?~

All right, all right, it was too much. Let it go, would you?

I turn back to my decision. Turns out I'm not particularly good at remembering vast parts of the ship's interior that I have never visited. Finally, I decide to just dig through the hull and deal with what I find once I get in.

Then a pinprick of golden light astern from me seizes my attention. The hull is bulging there. And then a moment later, the bulge tears, shooting a flare of golden light out as a hole appears in the hull.

No! They're coming after me.

The sudden twist of fear—where can I go? how can I possibly fight them from here?—unknots all at once as I recognize the back of a red-haired head.

Then she turns. Vi looks up and down, searching, and finally, as her eyes find me, her whole face lights up. The joy on her face tells me all is forgiven and everything is going to be all right. Then she disappears. A moment later, her hand appears, holding a coil of rope. Her head follows, and she attempts to toss it to me.

The wind snatches it away, pulling it nearly horizontal. I watch her face wrinkle in consternation, then she looks back at me, and I can't help but laugh.

I'm not going to release the hull to hold on to a rope anyway.

She shouts something, but I can't hear a word of it over the wind. She realizes it, makes hand signs to me—but again, I only know the basics of signing, and I miss whatever she's saying.

More slowly than either of us would like, I crawl to her, making as low a profile against the greedy, snatching wind as I can.

In minutes, though, she pulls me inside. As I tumble in, the ka'kari-helmet receding into me, taking her to the ground with me in my eagerness to get away from the winds out there, I can't help but laugh, relieved.

She stares up into my eyes as I finally suck the ka'kari back in, and there is much there I can't read, but even I can't miss the tenderness and joy in her gaze.

Leaving me on the floor, she stands and, muttering, seals the hull, leaving us alone in a closet now lit only by her softly glowing hands.

My heart trips over itself as I look at her in that golden light. I stare at her, arrested. I can hear my heart pounding. As the storm is sealed away, the world seems suddenly very quiet.

I don't know if you've ever had your life saved by your favorite beautiful woman in the world, but if you haven't, I highly recommend it.

His favorite...?

Viridiana rubbed the bridge of her nose. She remembered that look in his eyes in that little room. She'd caught it, then told herself it wasn't what she thought it was. Not from Kylar. Kylar, enraptured? No, not him.

Something felt like it was blocking her from swallowing. Her eyes felt damp.

But for the first time since she'd started reading the account, there was something in her besides grief at the coming debacle. For the first time, she felt eager to read the next section. It was the voyeuristic thrill. *I know how I felt, I know what I saw, I feel like I remember every detail—but what did he feel, what did he see when we were together? What details were important to him? What hadn't mattered at all?*

Viridiana looked at the empty cup that Sister Ariel had left—she hadn't even given her a single glass of wine to steady her nerves. It was past lunchtime, but there was no way Viridiana was going to leave now.

With a deep breath, she leaned over the book.

And there was a knock on the door.

"Oh, come on!" Viridiana punctuated the sentence with a curse—Sister Ariel wasn't here to reprove her, and sometimes cursing is required.

There was a question from the other side of the door. Whoever was there had overheard her.

"I said come in!" Viridiana said loudly. "It's not my chambers, just a library, after...oh."

The door opened and, preceded by a tray with fruit and a covered bowl and a tiny bundle of flowers, a girl came in. Maybe thirteen years old, she was dressed in novitiate's robes that were a bit too short at the hem, as if she was in a growth spurt. She had a bad haircut that Viridiana now suspected her superiors had done deliberately and was gangly and awkward-looking in a way that gave few hints that her mother had been renowned as the greatest courtesan of her era. Viridiana wasn't good at this sort of thing, but she didn't see much of Ulyssandra's mother or father in her features. For Uly, though she hadn't known it for the first twelve years of her life, was Durzo and Momma K's daughter.

As Uly approached, the book went blank once again. The girl set the tray down on Viridiana's table, grabbed Vi's empty cup, put the flowers in it, and used the skin she'd brought slung around her neck to squirt water into it.

"No wine, huh?" Viridiana asked.

"They're still not big fans of novices taking entire wineskins from the kitchens, oddly enough. Especially given what happened last time."

"That was not my fault."

"It was totally your fault!" Uly said.

They laughed.

After a moment, Uly said, "So, are they going to kill you or what?"

"How'd you hear about that?"

"Is that yes?"

"Yes."

"Guess it saves me copying all my lecture notes for you."

"Hey! But seriously."

"I've been skipping lectures to bring refreshments to Sisters on the Council floor for two days. Hasn't turned out to be the best way to spy, but it was all I could think of." She worried at the flowers, arranging and re-arranging them. "It's not really going to happen, though, is it?"

"No?" Viridiana said, pained.

"You're lying?"

"Yes."

"I could help you get away. I know all the secret tunnels and stuff."

"All the Sisters were novices once, too, you know. They all know the secret tunnels and stuff, too."

"You think?"

"Adults aren't as dumb as they seem."

"Some of them are," Uly said.

"Uly. You know I'd rather joke and gossip with you than anything. But I have to do this thing."

"What thing?"

Kylar and Elene had taken Uly with them to safety when Cenaria had fallen to Khalidor's invasion. For a time, Kylar had been something between a big brother and a father for the girl. "I can't tell you that," Viridiana said.

"Is that Kylar's diary? Why's it blank?"

"How—how do you know that?"

"I told you I've been eavesdropping. Can I read it?"

"It's magic. It only lets me read it. If it weren't, you think the Sisters would trust me with it?"

Uly's mask of cool detachment cracked. "Will you read it out loud to me, then?" she asked plaintively.

Viridiana looked down at the pages. She knew what was coming next in the pages, but she had no way to know how much detail Kylar had gone into. "Uh..."

"Why are you blushing?" Uly asked.

"I'm not blushing."

"Why are you lying again?"

"Uly! Out! I've got to read this. I, I can't—You're distracting me. Please, go now? Thanks for the food."

Uly looked crestfallen. She turned to the door, stopped, and rushed back, giving Viridiana a crushing hug.

For a moment, Viridiana didn't know what to do, and then she hugged Uly back, hard. It felt both good and somehow so raw and tender that she could hardly stand it.

"Don't let them kill you, okay?" Uly said into Viridiana's shoulder.

She couldn't answer; she only hugged the child harder.

Chapter Eighty-Four

Out of the Frying Pan...

*I*n the fading golden light of Vi's magic, I climb to my feet, heart pounding. The room feels suddenly, intensely quiet, the sound of my breath harsh. The smallness of the room forces us so close I can smell her. Her breath, her hair, a trace of fading perfume, rose water and fresh sweat as if she ran to get here. I drink her in as if parched, wide-eyed, noting the casual blue noblewoman's dress she wears, but with attention only for her face, cosmetics done in that barely there style that is the height of the art: *Cosmetics? No, I simply happen to have naturally flawless skin, large, luminous eyes, and the faint flush of romantic interest in you.*

Her emerald eyes narrow with concern. "Kylar?" she repeats. I think it's a repeat. Missed it the first time, staring at her.

"Know what I am?" I say, feeling somehow disconnected from my body. "I'm a super assassin. Walk through walls and everything! Hahaha."

Without magic coursing through my veins, my muscles suddenly remember that I was recently clinging for life to the side of the storm ship. I weave suddenly—

And Vi catches me as I nearly topple. "Easy there," she says in my ear. "Easy."

I hold on to her, trembling, and the feel of her arms around me, skin to skin, is like a dagger cutting a merchant's stuffed coin purse, all my feelings rushing to spill on the floor. Her smell fills my nostrils. Her neck is close. I wet my lips to kiss it.

She pulls back. I stare down into her eyes. "I like your freckles," I say. "I don't think you should hide them."

I see a blush rising in her cheeks. She tucks back an errant lock of hair, which is an odd streak of gold amid the red. "Kylar. You know you're naked, right?" Vi asks.

"I'm what?"

"Naked," she says.

I look down. It turns out she does indeed know what that word means.

The hell is this?

~You want them to know as little as possible about me, right?~

Oh, that's right. She's one of *them* now. A Sister. I keep forgetting.

That explains why you're not covering me. It doesn't explain where my clothes went. Was the wind really that bad?

~It might not have been the wind alone.~

Oh. The ka'kari had devoured parts of my clothing—enough, apparently, to make it easier for the wind to tear the rest away.

"I brought you clothes," she says, gently.

"Clothes?"

She smiles as if I'm hapless but adorable. "A fresh disguise. You keep forgetting; I do know you."

"When did you see me as the Night—? Oh, at Black Barrow at some point, huh?" I say.

"Feels like a long time ago, doesn't it?" she says, handing me the clothes.

"Forever," I say, starting to get dressed. "In some ways." I pull on the tunic of pale blue. "So how'd you...? This fits perfectly. Thank you. How'd you find me?"

"I put a tracker on you."

"A tracker? How'd I miss that?"

That should've been a question for you. How'd you miss that?

~I don't know.~ It sounds troubled.

"I put it in your ear," she says. "Your suit thing usually doesn't fully cover the ears. I figured you might miss it there."

~Huh! Isn't this the girl who thinks she's dumb? It's not there now. Must have blown off in the storm winds.~

"Is it still on me?" I ask, not able to stop from touching my ears.

"No. I came running when I felt you suddenly fall down five decks in a place I knew there weren't any stairs. Then when I felt you get blown off the ship and the weave break up when it hit the water, I thought..."

She stops. The tracker fell off me and into the sea. I can guess what she thought. Her mouth twitches up in a forced smile. "Well, I was wrong, wasn't I?"

"Did I say thank you for saving me?" I ask, feeling suddenly awkward, and not sure why. "Thank you for saving me."

She smiles for real now. "Yeah, I got it, Kylar. We should get moving, though. I used a lot of magic to punch that hole in the hull. Someone will have noticed."

I turn and see that she did indeed *punch* the hole. Splintered wood and deformed metal still show on this side of the magic she's used to patch the hull. I try to whistle, but I'm so exhausted my lips are too clumsy to make the sound. "Is that why your hair's got that streak in it? The magic reactive thing?"

"Oh, I always forget!" she says, chagrined. She closes her eyes and mutters and the streak shimmers in a wave from her scalp out, going back to her natural red. "Good?" she asks.

I nod. "Me?"

She fixes my belt to make it hang right. It's one of those silver-inlaid ones where the loose end dangles annoyingly all the way to your hip. Decoratively, I guess. I hate belts like that. But I decide not to complain about it.

"You know, you don't look half-bad when you're dressed right," she says.

"Uh…thanks," I say, moving a hand to smooth my hair.

"Don't touch your hair! That look's in fashion right now."

She pokes her head out of the room. Moments later, we're walking down corridors.

"So," I say, "now we have our answer."

"What's that?" she asks.

"Didn't you say once, 'Kylar, it wouldn't kill you to try to look fashionable once in a while, would it?' Now we know."

She doesn't even crack a smile, though. "I didn't say that."

~She's right. She said——~

Right. Never mind. Remind me to make that funnier when we come back to this, would you?

~Sure thing, boss.~

"Yeah, let's talk about how you got out there, and why," Vi says. "In a bit, though."

Crap. Probably shouldn't have brought that up.

Luckily, the wind blew me forward, so we don't have to pass any checkpoints—the only ones of those I'd have to worry about are those directly above us, near the empress's chambers, which are of exactly zero interest to me right now.

I'm not in any shape to do anything about her, and I really need to have a plan next time if I hope to do any better.

I follow Viridiana without question. I can't focus at the moment.

"You know I have questions, right?" I ask.

"I know," she says, distracted, leading us on past a queue of two-jewel nobles. Though she has us cut across that queue, I do get a glimpse of it, and it goes as far in either direction as I can see.

I don't ask any questions, though, because we're passing people constantly. We go up a deck and around, and soon, by their bracelets and by the richness of the clothing, everyone is either high nobility, their servants, or the highest-ranking diplomats. Imperial guards are a constant, but we see no mages.

In minutes, we emerge onto a wide, glassed-in deck high up at the prow of the ship. There are dozens of chairs set up. I've been pushing forward in this ship all this time, and now I've gone as far as I can go.

"It's the Fresh Air Deck," Vi says.

"Just what I've been missing," I say. "Fresh air."

"Haha," Vi says, unamused. When she's all business, she's all business.

"Where's the fresh air?" I ask.

"Kylar," she says. "Focus. When we reach Cloud Point tomorrow morning and the wind is blocked, this dome will retract. These areas below, where all the people are already queued up? They're for the lower nobility. The upper nobility have reserved places up there. There will be entertainments, fire-juggling mages and the like."

"Fascinating."

"It is, for the people who've been locked inside in windowless, crowded, cramped quarters."

When I seem insufficiently interested, she says quietly, "Look around a bit. Think tactically."

"Got it. Done," I say.

"Already?" she says.

"Uh-huh," I say.

This is the second or third time I've heard the name Cloud Point. With the wind blocked and this deck open, this must be a possible exit point for the Sisters.

It doesn't seem like a good exit to me, given how far above the waves it is, but we can save those judgments for when I know the rest of the plan.

"Is there another?" I ask.

"You've barely...all right. Yes. This way."

She takes me toward midships, taking a circuitous route. Eventually, she stops outside a staff door. "If you go straight through this door, one hallway and three rooms deep, this hallway connects," she says.

"To?" I ask. I've a strong inkling, but she's enjoying herself, so I don't want to take it away from her.

"You'll see," she says.

She takes me up several levels, then aft.

"We're not technically supposed to go to the area through this door," she says, "but nobles break the rule so often I've heard that next year they're going to remodel it."

"That's on the port side, though," I say absently.

I know where we are now. I follow her into the midships flexion area— though we're on the starboard side; this is the same area where King Repha'im took me to show me the disposal of the ship's garbage, and his disposal of innocent civilians.

Vi walks me out to the edge of the precipice and lifts her chin subtly to point down. "That's where that staff-only door I showed you earlier connects."

Numerous decks below us, at the level of the water, there's a door. I'd guessed correctly earlier about how they connected.

That's fine, but it doesn't answer why it matters.

Unlike the port side where Repha'im took me, rather than having the magically reinforced windows from the sky to the deeps, the starboard hull has a huge section that's opaque metal, just above the waterline. No wonder they want to use the other side for the proposed nobles' viewing platform. Not only does it stink here from any sewage that hits the sides of the hole, but the metal spoils the view of the waves.

I look at it, confused about its purpose. The whole metal section has huge hinges.

"For loading and unloading?" I guess. "That must only open when the ship docks in Borami, right?"

"And also at Cloud Point," Vi says. "There have been emergencies on the ship before. Like I said, at Cloud Point the ship is blocked briefly from the storm winds, but there's no place for a ship this size to dock. In fact, that whole mess down there flips out and becomes a dock so other ships dock on us.

Anyway, if the ship has problems, they have to solve them there before they head back into the storm. The ship only stays in the storm shadow of the mountain for a few hours."

"I think it's time for you to tell me the job, Vi."

"I will," she says. "But right now I have a meeting."

"Not with...not with *him*." The idea of her going to Repha'im's bed rouses black feelings so suddenly it shocks me, and so strong I can't even name them.

She shakes her head. "Planning. I mean, the planning's done. It's a last check that everything's on track before..." She makes a face and looks around, as if someone might be overhearing us, or reading her lips. Before the kidnapping, she means. "I really have to go right now. You know your way back to my room?"

I have to think, and there isn't any time for thinking. Anything I do or don't do here could be a fatal mistake.

"I have to go with you to see the Sisters."

"That's a bad idea," she says. "You're not currently the most popular—"

"Oh, believe me, I know." I have to leap without looking, and I'm overdue for the long drop with a sudden stop. Though I can't see anyone else in the huge chamber at the moment, I cover my mouth as I say, "They need to know Petaria is in serious danger. She may be dead already."

Vi looks stricken, horrified.

And with that, I've settled on my play. "Unless they already tried and Petaria got away. But *she*"—I gesture with my head to indicate the empress—"sent the kind of men after her who would give even you and me trouble, Vi. I don't think Petaria will be able to take out a couple of praetorians if they ambush her."

"She? Who do you mean? Who sent...?" Vi asks.

I pause to let her think about who is able to order praetorians to assassinate a guest.

"You don't mean..."

"I do," I say.

She expels a breath. "I guess that decides that. You're definitely coming with me."

It's what I wanted. So why do I feel like a man given a sponge bath with raw steaks jumping into a shark pool?

Chapter Eighty-Five

...To the Backup Plan

*S*omeday, I will get old enough that terror about my own likely death will be sufficient to stop me from thinking about sex. Today is not that day.

"I better take the lead," Viridiana said a minute ago. "If they see me first, I should be able to keep them from attacking you on sight."

So there she is, in the lead, giving me an excellent opportunity to plan my lies, my evasions, and even how much truth I'm going to reveal to a team of women who know I killed one Sister and who by now may suspect I recently murdered another.

In my defense, Vi *is* dressed to seduce—sure, not to seduce *me*—but it is a task for which she has been amply equipped. I know fashions come and go, and that different cultures value certain body types over others, but whether or not Viridiana's specific body type puts her at the height of Alitaeran beauty standards, I'm pretty sure a balanced hourglass figure with a narrow waist is sneered at precisely nowhere.

And yet I can't help but smile. She walks with her shoulders squared, jaw set, an athlete deciding whether to blast you out of the way or to run right over you, not a dancer who will flow around you like water. Her steps are broad, giving her a solid center of gravity from which to attack.

She looks back at me. "What are you smiling about? Why are you doing that?"

"Doing what?" I ask innocently.

Honestly, I love this about her. The more things change, the more they stay the same.

Then she stops and I nearly run into her. "Gah! I keep forgetting!" She looks up at the ceiling and mutters to herself in a thick accent, "...is no walk like angry bean farmer."

She straightens and makes a motion above her head as if lifting herself by a string attached there. Did I mention her hair is perfectly coiffed? Magic. Everyone uses magic for every annoying chore around here.

Except me—me, I just hang outside the ship and let the wind style my hair. You know, as nature intended.

Come to think of it, that's also me using magic to style my hair, so maybe I can't criticize.

Settling into her role, Viridiana turns to me and winks. "Watch. Tell me if you notice any difference."

Then she walks, tall, head up, neck straight, leaning slightly back to take long steps, feet crossing the center line at each step to add hip movement. She moves with the—

~Don't say the grace of a dancer. I refuse to put that down.~

I wasn't going to!

~Liar.~

Ahem. As I was planning to say, she moves with the proprioception of the elite martial artist she is.

~*Proprioception*, that's a Logan word.~

Psh! Proprioception *is totally within my active vocabulary. Use it all the time. I mean, when I'm around people who I know have sufficient linguistical chops to comprehend my effortless sesquipedalia. I don't like to show off. You know, I try to dumb things down when I'm talking to those who can't understand. The senile. The simple. The senescent. Children. Ka'kari.*

I feel something like approval radiating from the ka'kari. Might be the first time I've felt that from it.

~Sometimes you do surprise, Kylar Stern. Let's hope you do it again with the Sisters.~

That brings me right down.

Not that all of me was off in the land of repartee. Not with Vi sashaying in front of me. It's not just me. Everyone we pass notices her, too. I can tell even from behind her that she's throwing around social cues at those we pass: length of eye contact before looking away, degree and timing of a coy smile, the interplay of bold and shy.

If I weren't a little distracted, I'd be laughing outright. Not a few men fully stop and turn to gape at her after she's passed. I see a man with his wife, and he's almost sweating trying not to turn around and stare after Vi, he's so aware of his wife's eyes on him, as if she's daring him to look and promising retribution if he does.

And then the wife looks first, and he does too, like a hound loosed for the chase, quickly snapping his eyes back front and muttering something to his wife, who didn't catch him looking. His relief is palpable.

We pass through the last of a crowd, and a few steps later, she turns and smiles at me playfully. I barely snap my eyes up as she turns.

In her eyes, I see old, joyful Vi, her expression saying *See that fun thing I learned? Isn't it great?!*

I smile back, hollowly, and feel relief when she turns back to keep leading us on. Her conspiratorial joy tears me in half.

She expects me to be with her, finding it hilarious how well this new skill she's learned works.

But it works on me, too.

Is this a glamour? I don't think so, even though I feel shot through with unwelcome feelings. Not trivially, desire, like every other lusting stranger we've passed. But I also feel grief. My old friend who, though beautiful, walked like—ha, like an angry bean farmer—is changing. Not merely randomly changing, she's being changed by the Sisters.

Do I feel threatened by that? That she's coming into her own, discovering how to wield social powers more fluently than she did before?

That'd be pretty small, petty, and gross of me.

Maybe it's less that she's changing and become more than she was, and more that this is one more sign of the chasm opening between us. The Sisterhood is taking the friend I knew away from me. That she could be beautiful and awkward at the same time was a thing I loved about her. I thought it was charming, cute. And now they're making her beautiful and at ease, sophisticated.

Good for her. I guess.

But I can't help but feel I'm losing her.

And I definitely shouldn't be worrying about this *right now.*

It's just a body, Kylar. You're being ridiculous.

Before the last hall, she stops and says, "So? What'd you think?"

"Uh, I kept waiting. Did you—did you do something different?" I ask.

She opens her mouth to protest, but then my smile gets away from me.

"Not bad," I admit. "Some of the weaker-willed men were incapable of keeping their eyes off you."

"Some of the weaker-willed men?" she repeats.

Stiffening my joints and immobilizing my face as if I'm a marionette, I widen my eyes, and with my movements confined to one axis at a time, woodenly swivel my gaze over and then down to her chest.

She smacks my shoulder. "Kylar!"

I smile but I feel suddenly sick to my stomach. I like this woman, a lot.

What the hell am I doing?

Then, caught by her own thought, Vi's face falls. "You ready for this?"

"No. But here we are."

She doesn't hesitate. Say this about Vi, she's no coward.

When we step into the meeting room the Sisters have reserved, none of them kill me, so apparently my big sacrifice of walking behind Vi was worthwhile.

At the sight of me, Sister Ayayah Meganah gets a look on her face like she's enjoying her first bite of lemon. "He stays out. You watch him," she orders Jasmine Jakweth.

The double doors close, and I hear her through the wood saying, "Seal the room."

A small crackle sounds from within. Then—I assume by magic—I can hear no more of what they say.

Jasmine watches me idly, but not idly. He's got the coiled-serpent look that the untrained could mistake for rest.

"Kind of thought they'd be eager to talk to me," I say.

"Mm," he grunts.

Minutes pass.

"Mind if I call you Jasmine?"

"Mm."

"You have any hobbies, Jasmine?"

"Mm."

"Grunting! Really? That's my hobby too! Lot more can be said with a grunt than people realize, don't you think?"

He gives me a side-eye. "Mm."

"Why, Jasmine, I'm shocked," I say, putting a delicate hand to my chest as if he's just said something inappropriate.

Involuntarily, he shakes his head and cracks a grin.

If things go bad, we're probably going to have to kill each other, but that doesn't mean I have to dislike him—and I don't. Quite the contrary. "So how'd you end up at the Chantry?" I ask him.

He doesn't grunt, but he doesn't answer right away.

Finally, my stunning charm wins out, or maybe his boredom. "That's a deep question."

"In my defense, I meant it in the most shallow way possible."

"By horse."

"A bit deeper than that."

"Then I'll tell you it was really the only place for me."

I purse my lips. "Maybe a *smidge* deeper than that too."

Jasmine flashes a regretful smile at some memory. "People get their ideas set pretty firmly sometimes. Everyone does. The Chantry too. In my case, I was at Sho'cendi when I realized I'm something they think doesn't exist. Or maybe shouldn't exist. There were some tutors who were very sympathetic with my plight, but fighting all the time with the others about it got too taxing."

"Uh . . . what about you doesn't exist?" I ask.

"Oh," he says, surprised. "Thought you knew. I use magic the same way women do. See auras like women do. Have to speak to form the weaves. The whole thing."

"Huh. Any idea how that happens?"

"Yeah, sometimes when you have twins in the womb, one dies and the other sort of subsumes some of the other sibling. Turns out I should've had a sister."

"Should've?" I say, shocked.

"Still feel guilty about it sometimes, but yeah, apparently as a fetus I devoured my sister and took her magic."

"Whoa! Really?"

"No."

"Huh?" From his self-satisfied look, I finally get it. He got me. "You get that question a lot, huh?"

He nods. "I try to give a different answer every time. Makes things more amusing." He shrugs. "We have no idea how it happens. Truth is, magic is weird. It has laws, but the laws have exceptions and special cases, and we don't really know what half of them are in the first place."

"Huh," I say.

"You've got a look on your face. Go on, ask."

"A look?" I say. I have no idea what he's talking about.

"You want to know if I'm homosexual?"

I don't and I wasn't thinking that, but he seems convinced I do and was.

"Be tragic if I were," he says.

"Why tragic?"

"To waste so much attention. Handsome man like me, surrounded by thousands of lonely young women, far from their homes? Lonely older ones, too. With all those magics women 'really need to try out to see if it'll work in the real world'? You know, magics that can really only work *on a man*. That they need to 'practice.'" He looks into space as if reliving pleasant memories.

I grunt. Now I do want to kill him. Braggart. Amusing one, though, and he's probably just tugging my reins again.

He grunts, too, pleased with himself.

I look askance at him and grunt back.

He grunts back.

Then we notice that the door is open behind us. Sister Ayayah Meganah is looking at us grunting back and forth as if we're morons.

The woman clearly doesn't have a refined sense of humor.

She sneers as she says, "Come inside." Then to the others, she says, "Reminder, operational names only in front of our guest."

When I get into the room, I'm not surprised to see that Melena and mousy Aashvi are there with Viridiana and Ayayah Meganah, but I am surprised that there are six other women in the room. I can't recognize any of them, because each has dense clouds magically swirling around her face. Obviously, they're meant to hide their identities from me.

These must be the members of the other Special Problems and Tactics Team—Ysmaena's team. The team that already thought killing me was a good idea, back when I hadn't done anything to them.

"Oh, hullo," I say. "No one's tried to seize me, so I take it no one's dying in the next minute or two?"

"Don't be a nitwit," Sister Ayayah says. "The Chantry's covenant with Viridiana Sovari holds. We all have disavowed Sister Ysmaena's ill-considered actions and have agreed"—she stares around at them, as if challenging them to defy her—"*have agreed* to hold you blameless in that matter."

From the rigidity in their bodies, I can tell I'm on the knife edge here. These women are holding their magic, and some are hoping I'll make the wrong move.

I decide not to antagonize them. "I really liked Ysmaena. She seemed really nice," I say. I purse my lips. *Don't say it, Kylar.* "Right up to when she led me into an ambush to murder me for an evil madman."

Oops.

They bristle, and one leans to another, muttering something.

"Kylar!" Vi hisses. "Can you not?"

"So if you all want to kill me—and I get it, but the feeling's not mutual, in case you were worried. You acted like murderous traitors and got what was coming to you—but if you all want me dead, why'd you make Ysmaena take me on alone—?"

"Kylar!" Vi says, gritting her teeth.

"Fine, fine," I say, but in a loud whisper, I go on, "But seriously, Viridiana, why weren't the rest of them there? Even one more of the Chantry's best would've guaranteed she lived, while—"

Vi speaks very quietly. "They're all in deep cover, Kylar. Separately. Communication on the ship takes time. Ysmaena was—"

A portly woman in a slashed gray overdress with many gold laces over a red chemise with a face of swirling storm clouds says, "In addition to being a wonderful friend, a wit, and diligent to a fault, Ysmaena was also a rash glory hound. Marvelous when she plowed her own fields, but prone to wandering into her neighbors'. Hers is a lesson the rest of us would do well to remember. You may call me Sister Prudence."

"Ah, so you're in charge. Only of your team or both?" I ask.

"Enough with the pleasantries," Sister Ayayah says in a voice that tells me I've hit a point of contention. She walks over toward the large table in the center of the room, where a series of illusions lay out maps of the ship, a door with a central engraving with a number of runes on it highlighted with glowing magic, colored paths presumably for each Sister's exit, and several others. "Let's go over the plan one last time, shall we?"

My heart leaps. Finally!

"No," says Sister Prudence. "Not with our guest present."

There's some sighs and muttering—but then as she waves her hand, the illusions all crumble, shocking everyone.

"What the hell!" Melena says, furious. "Aashvi and I worked three miserable hours to make those!"

"You can tell that monster his part," Prudence says, pointing at me. "He needn't know what any of the rest of us are doing. Just in case."

"Just in case?" Vi demands. "I vouched for him! He's not going to betray us. Kylar has no reason—"

"Not on purpose. I accept that," Prudence says blandly from within her now-placid clouds. "But I'd hate for him to *accidentally* let something slip to one of his friends."

"Friends?" Vi asks, missing the sarcasm. "He doesn't have any friends on this ship. For that matter, he doesn't have that many friends off the ship, either."

Ouch. "She meant torturers, if I get caught," I say. "But I appreciate your honest assessment of my personal life."

Viridiana cringes. "I didn't mean . . ." But she trails off because of course she did mean it.

"We have to go with the backup plan anyway," Sister Prudence says. "Or is it the backup to the backup plan now? What with Sister Petaria so mysteriously dead at the hand of some unknown martial professional."

But despite her sharp look at me, there's part of me that's a tiny bit delighted. The teams are so much at each other's throats that so far this is going much better than I'd feared.

"So they got her?" I ask.

"Much to your obvious dismay, yes," Sister Ayayah says, turning her fury on me.

Yep, should've kept my mouth shut.

"She took a hating to me," I admit. "Which I didn't really return, but you're right. She wasn't my favorite person. However, I do see her as an ally. And all of you as allies now. We have to work together if we hope to rescue the child from these people. So, tell me what Petaria was slated to do. Maybe we don't have to throw away the old plan. Maybe I can fill in for her?"

I can see heads shaking around the table.

"Can you pick pockets?" Sister Ayayah asks.

"It's been a few years, but I have pretty good hands. And I'm not bad at being sneaky."

~Admirable understatement.~

"Don't the targets know him on sight? That makes it a different matter altogether," Melena says.

"Depends on the targets," I say. "Who are they?"

"King Repha'im and the empress," Vi says.

"Silence, little sister. You forget your place," Sister Ayayah says.

Mumbling an apology, Vi looks at the floor, chastened. Apparently, she's not supposed to speak at all.

I like these ladies less and less. And I didn't like them much to start.

"They both know you by face," Sister Ayayah says, but there's a bit of a question in her voice. Maybe she's hoping to catch me in a lie. If I say that I haven't spoken with the empress, it would mean I was lying about coming to warn them Petaria was in danger.

"They know what I look like, and I'd venture to opine that they're not going to be easy to fool." 'Opine'? Something about the Sisters and their hierarchical everything makes me talk as snooty as they do.

"Could you lift a key off her and a small pocket ledger off him?" Sister Prudence asks.

I look from Sister to Sister. "Yes, but no. The trouble isn't the lift. It's getting close enough to attempt it with the praetorians around. Did Petaria say she could do that? Was she that good?"

Sister Ayayah says, "The question is, are you?"

"Not even close." I don't even have to think about it. I mean, I could've stolen whatever I wanted while Repha'im and the empress were making love and their clothes were on the floor—but there's no way I'm getting an opportunity like that again.

There's a ripple of disappointment around the table. Melena says, "Back to the backup plan of the backup plan, then?"

"Sisters," a woman shrouded and masked with red sunset clouds says. "Won't anyone admit the obvious? We need to call this off. The entire operation. Your team should go back to the Chantry and tell them in person what we've learned. The rest of us will continue on to Borami and work to win our ways into the various circles there, keep an eye on things, and wait for a better opportunity."

Sister Ayayah says, "In Borami there are entrenched spy networks from every country in the civilized world and beyond. Not to mention all the empire's spy defenses, physical defenses, magical defenses, and probably a half-dozen other kinds. If a heist is going to have any chance of success, it's now."

"Oh, give it a rest, Ayayah," Sister Prudence says, crossing her arms. "This isn't about our opportunity being better now than it will be later. It's about you returning to the Chantry with a loss on your perfect record. It's about your ambition."

"It's doesn't matter why she wants to do it," another of the shrouded women says. "It's moot. We can't get it done. We're not looking at the differences between two difficult jobs. We're looking at one impossible job and one question mark. This one is the impossibility."

Not impossible for *me*, I think immediately.

"One moment," I interrupt before Sister Ayayah can retort. "You called this a heist. Either you're using the term wrong, or you're telling me more than you think. I grew up in the Sa'kagé, and I know a bit about heists. Ran lookout for a few. Had conversations with old legends. A heist has a couple defining characters. If you choose them poorly, everything falls apart. You've got your teams and your skill sets and that's great, but every heist needs its Lamb—its *paccio*, the gull, the rickie, the dupe, the mark, right?"

"We call it the Fool," Vi said quietly.

"Right, your Fool. Without a Fool, a heist is a plain old theft. You grab something when no one's looking and run away with it. That's safer, smarter, better. You only do a heist if you have to. Because with a heist, your Fool watches the whole thing unfold right in front of his eyes, and he sees everything. All the pieces are there, but he puts them together wrong. Then he does what you know he'll do with that wrong information and, say, open the door for you to walk right into his treasure room, right? Because you're the ones dressed as the treasury guards.

"The second-worst thing you can do with a heist is to pick the wrong Fool." I speak slowly so that I don't start calling them all the names they deserve. "And you're picking *Repha'im* as your Fool? You think you're going pull off this job right under the nose of a creature who sees *everything*? He has been ahead of me and you every step of—"

I stop. I can see I've offended them. I go cool once more. "But that's only the second-worst thing you can do. You've had a view of the worst thing already. You're seeing the warning signs: You're *already* trying to make your backup plans work. That's telling you something. Can you hear it?"

They've gone quiet. Some of them clearly don't like what I've said, and I suspect they won't like the rest of what I've got to say, but they're listening. I go on before they can change their minds: "I worked with the best of the Sa'kagé baggers and spooks and griffs and all the rest. I heard a lot of stories. The Sa'kagé has an institutional memory for crime like the Chantry does for magic. They've tried everything and failed at all of it at least once. And where they learned slowly, they failed again and again, losing people every time until they figured some things out.

"So please take this with all due respect. I know you all have excellent skills. But the truth about heists is that they almost never work. And when heists get complicated, they always fail.

"Lots of people think that's because their crew wasn't good enough. They think it doesn't apply to the best teams. They're wrong. It doesn't have to do with your skills. It has to do with too many moving parts. Complicated heists always fail because you can't foresee all the players in the game. That's because anyone, and I mean *anyone*, can suddenly become a player. Some random steward breaks off a key in a door you need to go through—not to vex you, but by accident—or maybe a civilian decides to play the hero, or a road or hallway gets blocked because two drunk noblemen get in a fight, or Lady Fainting Spells decides she hasn't had enough attention for a while, or someone spills juice on the stairs! If a problem only has a thousand-in-one chance of happening at the exact moment it will hurt a plan, we all take our chances. We figure that thing won't happen today. But for even the simplest heist, there are a million things that can go wrong, and for each complication, add a hundred thousand. Most of them won't happen, but enough always do.

"They say a battle plan never survives contact with the enemy. You think you're going to go into battle with twelve plans and they're all going to go flawlessly? How many of you can fail your tasks and have your plan still work? Half of you?" I look around, try to read their faces or stances. "*All* your plans have to work?" I try not to make it sound like I think they're idiots. I'm not sure I succeed.

"Enough," says Sister Prudence sharply.

But I go on. "Have your teams worked together before? Do you trust the other team as much as your own? If someone's late and it's putting your life in danger, will you wait as long for her as you would for your own teammate? This is not about competence. It's about complexity. It's a question of wisdom—or dare I say, of prudence?" I turn to Sister Prudence.

She holds up one finger.

Gradually, everyone goes silent, expectant. And that's when I know she is in charge. Maybe not by position, but by personality.

"Thank you for offering your thoughts and the weight of your experience. However, I think we need to figure something else out first," Sister Prudence says quietly. Then she waits again. "Something about you and us, Kylar Stern."

I spread my hands, hoping I look merely curious, rather than guilty, my heart thudding *I did it, I did it.*

"There are many questions I should like to ask you," she says. "And many questions I should like to ask you while you hold the scales of truth. There are many ways I should like to examine you, some of them not possible while you are alive."

"That is remarkably"—at the last moment, I veer like a drunken horseman around the word *bloodthirsty*—"honest," I say.

Sister Prudence's storm clouds bob. I think she must've nodded. "I have suspicions about you, and what you've done," she continues. "But those can wait. We have need of you." Sister Ayayah moves to interrupt. "At the very least," Sister Prudence hurries to say, "we need you not to come into our plans with the subtlety of a stampeding iron bull. At best, we think that your ability to extemporize may be helpful. The question is if we can trust you at all."

Here Viridiana moves to speak, but Sister Prudence puts out a hand, staying her.

"You know where I grew up," I say. "So I know better than to try to convince you to trust me with mere words. Instead, trust me to do what you know I need to do. I need to get that child away from Repha'im, who's told me how he'll destroy that boy. I need to save Caedan for his parents, or I'll never be able to look myself in the mirror again. I failed my friend Logan once. That's why I'm here. Saving that boy is my only chance at redemption."

The cone of cloud tilts to one side. Finally, Sister Prudence says, "I believe you. Shall we agree to a truce, then?"

"A truce is a long way from an alliance," I say.

"Yes. It is."

"And why should I trust you?" I ask.

The other Sisters bristle, but I don't even glance at them. Sister Prudence strikes me as the kind of leader who plays it straight even when she pays a price for it. I hear her take a breath, and she reaches up to her neck, her hand disappearing into the clouds.

"Sister Prudence!" Sister Ayayah protests.

But a moment later, the clouds unroll into nothingness with a blue shimmer from her neck to the peak above her head. The clouds also unroll downward, which surprises me.

In the place of the portly woman in a gray-slashed robe with a mask of clouds is a petite, middle-aged woman with wavy dark hair and olive skin a bit darker than Phaena's, but with striking light green eyes. "My real name is Sister Prospaya Beteh," she says. "I know that showing you my face and telling you my name is but a small token of goodwill. But I would like to remind you that though one of our number tried to hand you over to the king, before that we saved your life when you were going to attempt entry to the empress's party with a bracelet that was known to be stolen. Though I don't think we can be friends or even allies today, and maybe not for a long time, we're not enemies, young Master Stern. We're here to save lives, and for now, I believe you are, too. So, do we have a truce?" She extends her hand.

"Until when?" I ask.

"When would you like?" she asks, keeping her hand out, and again I see that Sister Ayayah is furious about this—which strangely makes me trust the Sisters more. If she's furious, it's because a truce holds real weight.

"How about until we leave Alitaera—?"

~Don't forget Alitaeran territorial waters.~

"And Alitaeran territorial waters and ships and properties," I say. "As in, from *now* until we get the boy safely out of Alitaera. Do I need to hedge more than that?"

The other Sisters clearly want to confer, looking at each other. Only Melena and Viridiana quietly study me.

"No hedging required," Sister Prospaya says, not even looking at the others. I see flashes of their displeasure.

I take her hand, and though her hand is small, her grip is firm.

"You can make it stick?" I ask, releasing her hand but not her gaze.

"And I will," she says, her face growing grim.

"Well, then," I say, "I overheard the empress say something when she didn't know I was in the room that may change your calculations."

"Are you sure she didn't know you were in the room? Maybe she was trying to manipulate you," Melena says.

It's not the first question I would have come up with, but then, these people think differently.

"No," I say. "She didn't know I was there."

"How can you be sure of that?" Sister Ayayah asks.

"Because it was her bedchamber, and she was, uh, busy bedding someone. King Repha'im. If you want more details about what they were doing... I can tell you, but I'm not sure they're relevant."

They look at each other.

Sister Prospaya says, "No, that's quite enough. What did she say?"

"I didn't realize what Repha'im was talking about at the time, but they're worried enough about the ship breaking apart that he convinced her to get off the ship. At Cloud Point. She thought leaving would hurt her standing with her nobles, but it seemed he convinced her to do it anyway."

Again they look at each other. In the cloud-masked Sisters' stances, I read uncertainty, surprise.

"That changes nothing," one of the still-shrouded Sisters says.

"Not true," Sister Ayayah says. "It changes everything! Sister Prospaya, surely you see that?"

Sister Prospaya holds up a hand. "Maybe," she says.

"We must discuss this," Sister Ayayah says, "but not in front of the murderer."

I'm about to point out how it wasn't murder when I killed Sister Ysmaena, but technically they didn't say I murdered *her*. They called me a murderer. Which I am.

Quibbling will only draw more attention to the point, so I keep silent.

"Kylar, would you be willing...?" Melena says, gesturing me toward the door. She's a consummate peacemaker, sounding regretful, trying to mollify both sides.

"Of course," I say. "You've been such gracious hosts. I'd hate to overstay my welcome. But about the job. If you're going to do it despite all I said, you should be leaning on me to help plan it." I look at them and see there's no way they're going to trust me that much. "Fine. I'll go. And I'll do what you ask me to do, quickly and without question. But I have a condition. I go where the kid goes. Let me be your ally in this. I want to help you. I think you'll find my help..."

Quick, gimme a word! I can't say they'll find my help helpful. I've said 'help' like twelve times.

~Indispensable.~

"...indispensable," I say, as if deliberately settling on a nonthreatening term. "But if you cross me, it will go poorly for all of us. As your leader Sister Prospaya said so wisely, there's no reason for us to be enemies. I don't think any of us can afford that right now. So let me make this clear. One way or another, I swear by all the gods of the seas and the underworld, the kid leaves with me. That's the only way this goes. Got it?"

They take a moment to absorb this. Some seem nonplussed, others unsurprised. Sister Ayayah bristles at the 'leader Sister Prospaya' part, which I enjoy immensely.

"Sister...Justice," Sister Prospaya says, nodding toward a woman whose real name is obviously not Justice, "ask your people whether Repha'im is also disembarking at Cloud Point. Sister Charity, check if the porters are packing any of the empress's belongings in ways suggesting a quick departure."

The two women nod low enough for their storm clouds to show the movement but say nothing—perhaps to keep from me hearing their voices.

"Sister Viridiana, take Kylar to your room to await our plan," Sister Ayayah says.

I head to the door and hear Sister Prospaya say, "I don't suppose you can quickly reconstitute that map for us, could you, Sister Aashvi?"

As I step outside where Jasmine Jakweth is standing, I realize the meeting went pretty well. The Sisters were so consumed by their rivalries and by needing to figure out what to do next that they didn't interrogate me nearly as well as they might have. On the other hand, I still have no idea what their plan is, nor any way to get it out of them early. I think I bluffed my way into helping them—and they don't seem to be trying to kill me.

Is that a win? Today I'm calling it a win.

Jakweth closes the door behind us and takes up watch outside again, apparently content not to be part of the planning discussion. He nods to me. "You ain't smart, Kylar, but you got balls. Watch yourself 'round here, though, or you'll get 'em torn off."

Chapter Eighty-Six

The Last Rule to Break

I had some food sent up. Why don't you come with me, Kylar? We can't do anything here," Vi says.

"I can't believe they don't even want my help planning—"

"Kylar. Not even talk. We can't even *talk* here." Vi looks at a blank section of paneled wall significantly, as if there may be spies behind it. I sigh. I'm so tired. I'm gonna make mistakes if I don't get some sleep soon, but I'm also worried that I'm so tired I'm gonna feel wretched if I do sleep. The mention of food hits me like a punch. I've been ignoring my needs for a long time.

"We'll talk," Vi promises. "Come on, you've been through it. Let me take care of you a bit."

That lands funny. Someone take care of *me*?

With where we left things? I look at her skeptically.

She reaches out a hand with a tiny smile, as if coaxing a skittish wild animal. "Come on."

I take her hand and let her pull me into a walk, and I'm glad she's a step ahead of me, that she can't see me, because something about human contact absolutely tears me open.

And then I remember the last time I held Vi's hand.

At Elene's funeral.

Elene. *Gods, Elene, I love you, but I wish I could forget you. And I wish that for every detail of you that fades from my memory and for every hour that passes and I don't think of you I didn't feel like I'm betraying you, like if I'm forgetting you, then it proves you never really mattered to me at all.*

Vi must feel something in how I hold her hand, for she releases it now, with a quick glance back at me.

I don't know if I compose my features fast enough to hide what I'm feeling. I'm just tired. Edgy. My whiny-little-snot side comes out when I'm too tired. Gods, I'm gonna embarrass myself.

We get to her cabin door without speaking. A covered tray sits in a nook nearby, the tray itself hot to the touch. Magic everywhere with these people. Magic to keep food warm! What would the kids of my old guild think, seizing the leavings from the gutters nearest the taverns and trying to judge the safety of eating this bit of scraped-off fish skin that was next to—but maybe not *in*—the sewer water?

The lowest scullery mage on this ship could've fed my whole guild for a month with a single day's wages.

I wish that made me less hungry. But it didn't then, and it doesn't now. As I so often do, I push the rage at how things are and my inability to change anything meaningful and my own constant, ceaseless woundedness down, down.

"This is great," I mumble, devouring something. It has delicate flavors beneath complex aromas. It's merely kindling for the fire to me. Fuel.

What did I say I was, a super assassin? More like a supper assassin.

But my own attempt at humor fails to raise my spirits.

Couldn't I eat something one-tenth this fancy, one-tenth this expensive, and give the difference to kids out there who need the money?

But the world doesn't work like that.

Viridiana has been watching me. Probably judging me for eating like a barbarian, though her gaze on me is soft. Softer than I expect. Softer than I deserve. "They'll give you some simple part in the job," she says. "They won't trust you with more, and keeping you busy with something small will keep you from messing up anything big. Or so they hope. They need you, though, and they fear you."

"So with our deal, do you think they'll wait to betray me until we get the child to shore, or until we actually leave Alitaera?" I ask.

She winces. "I'm sure they're debating that now," she says. "I...tried with them, Kylar. But they think I'm...compromised where it comes to you."

And are you? I think, but I manage not to say it aloud.

"I said some things, earlier—" I begin.

"Let's not!" she says quickly. "Let's...not revisit that. There's nothing for us to do until an hour or so before dawn. Whatever tasks they give us will be simple. You need to sleep. I know I do."

"Is it safe here?"

She snorts. "Safe?"

"You know what I mean."

She shrugs. "If anyone tries to come in here to hurt you, I'll kill them."

She is such a badass as she says it that my heart feels oddly warmed.

Then she looks up at me, and then quickly away, as if embarrassed. "Kylar..." Then she seems to change her mind. "Lie down, facedown. Looked like you probably tore some muscles in your back out there."

"How did you—"

"I'm good at a thing or two. Give me a break. Lie down."

I lie down, reluctantly. "Vi, my magic—it'll all heal anyway. There's no need to—oh hell!"

Somehow her hands found exactly the most painful spot right beneath my shoulder blade. I'm momentarily breathless with the pain as she pushes way too hard on it.

This woman has no idea what she's doing.

"Oh," I say. "Oh. All right. That was different."

She curses under her breath. "Now I see why Sister Ariel wants to get her hands on you."

"What do you—ow, ow, ow ow ow—oh." Now she's found, hurt, and Healed a completely different spot low in my back.

"You have these layers," she says. "Part of you is trying to immobilize these areas, these hurts, some of them old, and at the same time a deeper magic is trying to Heal them, but you're so strong that you're cutting off your own magic from doing what it needs to do. So if I—"

"That's fascinating, but—" I cut off with a yelp. It trails off to an embarrassing moan.

Viridiana ignores it. She says, "Do you know, when I was a kid, my mother had this one boyfriend, early on. I liked him a lot. He'd lost his wife and daughter in a fire. Slum apartments, you know? He'd been a smith, but he lost his forge after they died because he couldn't pull himself together to work for a long time, so when he was with my mother, he was working as a stone cutter, trying to save up to buy tools again, but he kept getting drunk every so often and losing everything. My mother would give him massages like this when he'd come back from the quarry.

"He talked about being my new dad and asked if I'd like that once, but he

was drunk then." There's a different kind of pain in Vi's voice here, and I wish I could see her face.

Part of me wants to stop her. Vi's suffered so much violence at the hands of men—especially her mother's boyfriends—that there's a dread rising in me. It's making me sick to think where this story is probably going, how he probably beat her, and maybe worse. Worse still, she doesn't seem angry at him for it.

"He seemed mortified the next day, which confused me. Did he not want me?" Vi says.

I have nothing to say.

She runs a hand through her hair as if to pull it into those tight ponytails she prefers, but she stops herself, tucks a red wave behind her ear instead. "Anyway, I saw my mother, well, do a lot of things with a lot of different men in our one-room place in the years after that. But that was later. I, I remember her making him a meal and easing his hurt body when he'd come back from the quarry, and it felt wholesome, you know? Like maybe we could be a normal family. One day, he asked me her favorite color, and whether she liked lace."

Oh gods, please don't let this veer into something sick.

"I found out he was saving up to buy her a nice dress, like she'd not had in years. A dress for a wedding. He was going to surprise her."

She goes quiet, her hands still finding my old wounds, hurting them, and making them slowly feel better, as if guided by an intuition wedded to instinct. The wounded know wounds.

"What happened?" I finally ask. I don't know if I want to know, but I want her to know I care to hear her.

"I don't know exactly. My mother loused it up. One day he stopped coming around. She accused him of stealing her money—she didn't work then, so really it was *his* money. She said he was sleeping with this older woman. Said she'd followed him. It was the dressmaker.

"She demanded he show her 'this supposed dress' to prove himself. He refused to show it to her, said if she wouldn't trust him then they couldn't be together. Then he made some comparison to how different she was from his old wife. My mother lost it. Said he was obviously lying. There was no dress. Said other, vile things. He left and never came back.

"I visited him two years later. Alone, halfway to dead from drink, still waiting for my mother to come walking through that door. He had the dress, Kylar.

Still had it. He'd always had it. He'd never cheated on her. They were this close to a whole different life. We all were. But he was just too broken."

"So was your mother, huh?"

Vi's hands stop on my back. "Yeah. But her I blame." She withdraws her hands. "Sorry. Didn't mean to . . . This just reminded me of the last time I saw— I guess it reminded me that touch can be healing. That we can use our hands to serve each other, not just hurt or use each other."

"Thank you," I say. *"Thank you."* I sit up and face her. "For the talk and the touch. It feels like . . ." My mind veers around a number of unacceptable words, words that are too close to the heart, that carry promises. "Like trust."

She smiles, but there's an ocean of pain in her eyes, the memories gasping in the open air like dying fish on the shore, wanting only to return to quiet of the waters.

My throat goes suddenly tight. "Viridiana? Why does this feel like goodbye?"

She takes a few moments to reply. "This job is doomed, isn't it? Not just hard. But like . . . like we've got no chance at all."

"I don't know," I say. "I've defied the odds before. Right? We'll find a way. I always do."

"Just like that?" she asks, but there's something sad in her words.

"We have to," I say. "I can't let him go."

"You mean Logan's kid?"

"When I was really young, I made an enemy of one of the older kids in my guild. I took my eye off one of my best friends for a few minutes. And that was when he was taken, hurt. And then I sank into myself, ignored the warnings, and I left Elene exposed. And when I lost her too, I lost something of myself."

I see Vi swallow. "That friend? That was Jarl?"

"Yes," I say. But I don't want to go into all that history. Not mine. Not hers. "Caedan's this close, Viridiana. I can't lose him now or I know—I know! I'll lose him forever. I can't do that. I can never abandon someone to a monster's grasp again. Some of those Sisters want us to wait until after we get to Borami and someday, maybe, we get another chance to save Caedan? I've seen how fast destruction can happen. How fast a life can be ruined, a *child* can be ruined.

"If you take a kid's foot and smash it with a hammer, the pain will fade, the crying will stop, but he'll never walk right. He can learn to limp. With time and work he can become very adept with a crutch. But he can't be made unbroken. I learned on the streets that you can break a child's soul, too."

"I know," Vi says quietly. "It happened to me."

"Me, too," I say, bitterly, looking away. "Repha'im looks at me and he doesn't see a broken human; he sees a weapon with all the unnecessary pieces trimmed off. And I think maybe he's right about me. I don't have the hindrances of family or clan or even loyalty to a country. I kill without hesitation, and usually without remorse. I can be pointed in a direction and loosed like a hunting hound or an arrow to kill. And he wants that. But he knows I won't be that for him, so he wants to make Caedan that. The slums broke me, but that just sort of happened, you know? I made my choices and they carried me here.

"I won't let him do that on purpose to a kid. It's too late for me, but I'll save that kid. I swear I will. I'd do it even if he wasn't my..." For some reason, I can't finish the sentence. My throat is blocked, and my eyes are filling. "...you know," I manage, blinking rapidly. Vi's pretty blind to stuff like this. Maybe she'll miss it.

"Your son," she whispers.

I try to talk again, to play it off. Can't manage it. Nod quickly, clear my throat.

"Anyway, I feel good about this," I say.

"You—you what?" she says, eyebrows shooting up.

"This job. It'll be fine."

"What? Were you not just in—? What are you talking about?" Vi asks.

"Well, I don't know how to say it without sounding arrogant."

"You're the Night Angel. I don't think you're gonna sound arrogant."

A brief smile sneaks up on my lips. I'm the Night Angel.

Right. But what does that really mean? I push the thought away. "What I mean is that I, I always find the third way. Not that I seek out impossible situations, not on purpose, but when I get into them, I don't stop fighting. Not ever. And it usually doesn't go well, but somehow I always fight my way through."

"I don't know how you got here from there, but..." Vi lowers her voice to a whisper. "But that's exactly what I told the Sisters."

She knows me. She knows me and yet she believes in me.

My heart leaps through a dozen flaming hoops, and turns half from stone to something softer, and the cool beauty of her face suddenly warms to something both less threatening and far, far scarier, something as entrancing as music and deeper than an abyss and somehow maybe possibly an answer to all the yearnings I've been trying to smother since Elene died that keep fighting their way out of every prison and to the surface of every lake in which I try to drown them, and she is herself, the woman I know so well, and she is an avatar for some goddess, some energy ancient and entwining and stronger than stone. I reach my hand reverently to touch her face.

And, miraculously, she accepts my touch. She pulls my rough hand to her soft cheek and closes her eyes as we connect, and she steps in toward my body as if my touch were drawing her in, as if she wants to be pulled into me.

What are you doing? some part of me whispers. *You can't have this. You'll ruin everything.*

She's hugging my hand to her face, her eyes closed, and now she's releasing it, her hand trailing down my forearm, setting my skin tingling, and her eyes open to mine, tentative, vulnerable.

I don't know if I lift her face with the lightest pressure toward mine or if my fingers merely rise with her movement, but her lips rise.

The shock of our lips meeting is like the first lightning strike of a sudden summer storm, the thunder crashing a moment later, obliterating all else in the world, as fear and hesitancies and guilt and even time itself are forced to stand outside the door, as the chattering voices in my own mind cease for once—for once!—in the sweet strong haven of her.

I have not the words to describe what Vi was to me in that little room, how she knew me, how she pulled me away from every poisonous thought with her eyes, her lips, her touches, back into the beautiful now by some magic deeper than magic.

How she was with me, how she read me, perhaps only a poet could express. I felt her reaching into the depths of me, finding frayed bits of my soul I'd thought forever lost, and knitting them back together, stitching me back to a world I thought I hated and didn't need but secretly loved and missed so terribly I couldn't bear it. She saw me—not the me I saw and hated, but a me somehow brightened, the shadows and darknesses yielding to her eyes, eyes that saw my brokenness and hated me not.

I looked away from her eyes. Had to, the intensity of it too much to take.

I become once more aware of the room. Our clothing askew or cast away, I lie atop her, she beneath me, ready. If we do this, nothing can ever be the same. Maybe if I stop now, years hence we might say, *Remember that one time we almost…?*

But I know better. There's no future for us. I'm only asking for pain here.

I look once more to her eyes and see my own longing mirrored there, and a ghost of my own fear.

"This doesn't mean anything," I say.

"This doesn't change anything," she agrees, immediately, and I know I'm right. She's thinking the same thoughts, and cares as little.

Looking deep in her eyes, I settle into her body and the embracing circle of her arms as if stepping into a strange house and finding it unexpectedly my own home—a home I'd never known, a homecoming I'd never thought possible.

Overwhelmed, fighting even to breathe, I say, "I don't love you."

Her eyes are fierce, unflinching. "I don't love you either," she says, pulling me in, in, in, and I believe her exactly as much as she believes me.

Vi slid out of her seat. Tears were hot on her cheeks, and an abyss of weakness and despair was yawning wide for her.

Jumping back to her feet as if motion itself might help her escape paralysis, she shouted in a rage, "No. No. No!"

As she slammed a fist on the table, some fragment of her rage slipped the leash and escaped into magic like a hound bolting through a carelessly cracked door.

A shock wave rushed out, fast as thought. All the windows of the little library blasted out at once, and the bookshelves were surrounded in a sudden protective glow.

"Ah," the glowing, shielded form of Sister Ariel said. "I forgot the windows. Alas."

Huffing, shocked, and noticing that all the desks were glowing as well with the same protective wards, Vi released her magic as quickly as she could.

"So you've reached the end, then?" Sister Ariel asked. "Good. Then we've things to—"

"No. Not yet. Not far now," Vi said.

"Then..." Sister Ariel looked off-balance. "Dare I ask what that was for?"

Vi wished she could vomit, but the churning wasn't in her stomach. "It was good, Sister." She shook her head, eyes unfocused, for one instant reliving the comfort and closeness of Kylar's embrace. "It was so..." She trailed off. Words always failed her. *Pure? Good?* She'd already said that. She felt like she'd walked hesitantly into a temple, enjoyed the rites, and connected in prayer for the first time to something greater than herself.

And then, having been renewed and changed, having touched the holy with trembling fingers, on her way out she emptied a bag of shit on the altar.

"It was so good I forgot what I'd been ordered to do. I—" She opened her eyes and saw Sister Ariel, the last person in the world who would be able to understand this.

"So, yeah, to cut to the chase, when I woke up and realized I hadn't done what I'd been ordered to . . ." A sob started low in her belly, rising like a swimmer desperate to breathe, but she grabbed it by the hair, shoved it down hard as she'd learned to do with every admission. That belonged to some other body, a weakling, a victim. She was practiced. She knew how to do this.

When her voice emerged, it was quiet, calm, lifeless. "When I woke and realized I hadn't accomplished my mission, I did as I'd been ordered."

Sister Ariel looked baffled. "And what was that?"

Vi snorted, her voice sounding sneering and cold and somehow thin to her own ears. She whispered, "I raped him."

"Excuse me?" Sister Ariel asked.

But Vi couldn't say it again. Not even from this distance.

For a time, the confession hung in the air, naked and shameful. Sister Ariel said, "You . . . ? Oh, you used a glamour."

"He didn't even . . ." She couldn't get the words out. Kylar hadn't even thought that she might use such magic on him. She'd fooled him, and she was ashamed. Ashamed *of him* that he'd been fooled.

How sick was that? That she'd be embarrassed that he'd been fooled more than that she be ashamed of herself?

The parts of her she'd split wanted to unite once more, but she couldn't allow it. She'd heard of bones healing badly and needing to be rebroken to set properly, but she was too broken to fix. Why rebreak a bone if it could never heal right? She was going to be a cripple regardless.

"He didn't notice?" Sister Ariel supplied, unhelpfully. "Yes, glamours are morally ambiguous at the best of times. Some—and I count myself among the number—think we ought to ban them outright. It's why we have so many rules limiting—"

"Rules I was ordered to break!" Viridiana snarled.

Sister Ariel made a small motion of surrender.

"When'd you get back anyway? Never mind. Get out of my face," Vi said. "I have to finish reading. I dug this hole. You understand? Not Kylar. I dug straight to hell. Now I have to see how deep it goes."

Chapter Eighty-Seven

The Final Plan

*A*fter we'd made lo—no, not that.

Strike that, would you?

After we'd satisfied each other amply, as I was dozing off, Vi eventually pulled away from where she was snuggled into me, and rolled over, putting her back to me.

I become dimly aware that she's shaking. Crying.

My eyes snap open. I reach a hand out but don't roll toward her, don't crowd her in case what she's rejecting is me. "Viridiana? Are you all right?"

She flinches. Then she rolls over quickly, as if I'd caught her doing something wrong, and gives me a red-eyed fake smile. "I'm fine. Really."

"What's going on?" I ask, propping myself up on an elbow. That reactive streak of her hair has a swirl of colors in it. It must be from her earlier magic, Healing me. I reach to touch it, but stop, remembering how she is about her hair. "Can I—"

"Just all the pressure," she says quickly. "It's nothing. You're sweet for asking."

She leans over and gives me a peck on the lips, then pauses as she's pulling away, as if that was much nicer than she'd expected. She kisses me again, more than a peck. Then, with a sound low in her throat, she melts into me, molding her body to mine.

We kiss, but I pull away. There's something off. "Viridiana, is something wr—?"

"Vi. Call me Vi. At least when we're alone."

"I don't understand." She'd made such a big deal about how she was different than before. She'd been mad every time I'd called her Vi.

"I like how you say it. I like that you knew me before, and, and you like me now anyway." I can't read her eyes as she says this. It feels like it's partly a lie. But I'm not sure I'm reading her right. She seems confused herself, and now uncertain as I hesitate.

That uncertainty kills me.

"You think I *like* you now? Huh. Seems pretty presumptuous, don't you think?" I lean close and kiss her neck. "You have any evidence for that?"

She makes a little moue and stretches her neck. The hydra rises in me. I need this woman. The whole room seems to dim, leaving her alone luminous, my attention riveted to her. She entwines her legs in mine and pulls my hand on her breast.

There's some part of me that thinks what Vi needs right now isn't more love-making; it's connection. We've changed things between us. Maybe destroyed things. We need to talk, to figure out what we've done, what we do from here. We need to figure out if we're going to be all right.

"Vi, no, stop. I think..."

But I lose track of my train of thought at the sight of her, her smell, the sound of her voice, the warmth of her breath in my ear making me drunk.

"I don't know," I say, my resolve crumbling. But I'm not sure what I don't know. I'm feeling like this is all a mistake, like we should talk. But I've already screwed up everything. We can't be friends after this. It's all already lost. It's too late already. Might as well take all the pleasure this one night affords us, right?

But that doesn't feel right. Feels selfish. Regretfully, I pull back away from her.

But she doesn't let me go. "Kylar, I'm gonna mess things up if we talk too much. Can we just have tonight? I need you." Her voice trails down to a whisper, and there is only the feel of her body against mine, the golden shimmer of her hair, the smell of her filling my whole head, and the roar of my desire drowning out the whisper of my objections.

And then she does things that make me forget all about speech. I know I shouldn't yield—but I yield. Fully. Joyously.

But unlike earlier, for some reason I don't understand, this time leaves me feeling worse, as if I let her get away with silencing the real Vi, as if I joined her in it. And, now, afterward, I realize it all felt somehow impersonal, as if she were sinking back into an old rut, as if even as we connected sexually, she was disconnecting from herself.

Did I do something wrong? Like, did I say Elene's name while we...?

~No. You didn't.~

Ew. I did not want the reminder that you were here the whole time.

Maybe she just didn't want to talk. Didn't want to answer my questions. Or maybe she thought she had to trade me sex to get what she needed.

It makes me feel sick and somehow betrayed. What did I do to deserve her treating me like that? Why would she have such a low opinion of me that she would think she couldn't just say, *I don't want to talk right now? Can we just cuddle?*

But regardless of this new ache, I'm exhausted, and despite everything, I sleep.

When I wake, she's not in bed with me. Still lying in bed, I stretch, hearing a dim chatter of voices from the hall. Two women, one of them Vi.

"Hsst!" Vi says. "Quieter. He's still in there."

A murmur of something, but it ends on an up tone, asking a question.

"Yes, I'm sure. He hadn't slept well in days. Or at all. He..." There's more I can't make out, and I'm tempted to rise from the bed.

A sharp note from the other voice.

A question from Vi, maybe ending with "...really? Sure I'll check."

The door opens on silent hinges. I close my eyes and make sure my breathing is slow and even.

Vi must be studying me for a while. I wonder if there's magic they can use to see if someone is merely feigning sleep.

But then she closes the door quietly.

I rise and pad shamelessly to the door to eavesdrop.

The other voice is Sister Ayayah Meganah's. "...terrified," she's saying. "We were right. The child's soul will fully attach to his body within the week. When that happens, there will be another surge of magic-negating power. At the very least it will be as bad as the last time, but we expect numerous null waves, each much larger than that last one."

"That sounds... scary," Vi says.

"...an understatement. If it happens while the child is aboard, the magic holding the ship together will fail. The imperial magi are already fighting to hold it together as is. They can't hope to succeed against another null wave. Not even a small one."

"But that means..." Vi says, horrified.

"Yes. It means the ship will break up. Everyone will die. That is, unless they get off the ship before that happens—or better yet, the child gets off the ship. Soon. Which we've learned is exactly what the empress intends. So it turns out Kylar gave us information we would've learned two hours later regardless. And for *that* he bought our cooperation." She gives what may be a grunt of disgust.

"But the deal with him holds," Vi says, warning the other Sister. It's a relief to hear her take my part.

"Of course it does. The Chantry is this close to having a war with the Alitaerans on our hands. You think we can afford having a magic-impervious assassin hunting us, too? Kylar will answer for his crimes at some later date, after things settle down with Alitaera."

This is a greater relief.

Though, on second thought, they could be lying to Vi, too.

"Who's giving us our assignments? Where do we go to get those?" Vi sounds relieved that our truce is, apparently, going to hold. The job is going to be hard enough.

"Others are already in place, doing their parts now. You and Kylar read this, and then burn it."

"There are no labels on this map," Vi says. She must be looking at the paper the Sister gave her.

"That's right," Sister Ayayah snaps. "Because we're not idiots. It's…" She lowers her voice and I can't hear for sure what she says. 'Deck four,' maybe? She continues, "All you need to do is take the packages. You'll get them over *here* from Sister Hretta Ferrule at first light. After what your murderer friend said, we made some fallback plans in case not all of us succeed in our tasks. So if Sister Hretta doesn't show up by sunrise, you get here as fast as possible and pray your new contact is already there. She'll be in servants' white with red stripes on the shoulder and front with the crossed lapels of the imperial nurse-maids; she'll say, 'Hell of a night.' You reply, 'Better one bad night than many bad days.' You take the two packages—carefully!—to the escape boat, here. You must make it to the dock by the time the sun's fully risen."

"You're telling me I have to make it from here to the docks in two or three minutes?"

"That's why it's the backup plan, little sister. We'll hold for you as long as we can, but the margins are tight. Hopefully, Sister Hretta will do her part and this will be moot. Regardless of when you get the packages, remember, no violence if at all possible. If you must hurt anyone, raise no alarms and leave no evidence. If necessary, though, you have full license for this. Please don't, though."

"Anyone?" Vi asks. "I mean the empress—?"

"*Please* don't. But yes. Including her. The weight of the packages should be identical. There should be no sound from either. There's a lot of careful magic involved. Understand, if you mix up the numbers—everyone on the ship dies. So please don't mess with the numbers."

"You mean the packages are—?"

"Don't say it out loud!" Sister Ayayah interrupts.

The child is in one of the packages, I realize. Are they doing something involving switching bassinets?

"If you're able to keep your identity secret, and possibly even if you can't, you will stay on the storm ship for your other mission," Sister Ayayah says.

With Repha'im, she means.

"And Kylar?" Vi asks.

"He'll come with us, as promised. We assume he'll try to double-cross us once we get to shore, but that's a problem for another day."

"What's the rest of the plan?" Vi asks, and I could just kiss her.

"You don't need to know that."

"Hell I don't! Plans go wrong. If I need to improvise, I need to make sure I don't mess anything up that you're trying to do."

There was a long silence.

"Fine," Sister Ayayah says. "No details for all the obvious reasons, but the other team is attempting to influence the empress not to leave the storm ship. At the same time, they'll be placing agents to delay and divert her ship should she disembark anyway. That'll give us a head start getting home safely. If she's kept on the storm ship past Cloud Point, she won't be able to disembark until you reach Borami, or even pass messages for six or seven days. On the other hand, if she does abandon the storm ship and her vessel lands at the same time we do, it could turn into a horrible race to the Chantry against her most elite fighters. That'll mean war for sure, and maybe death for us, too. As for the rest, you already know what our team is doing to get the ch—the package."

"Got it," Vi says. "If you end up in that race, Kylar would be very helpful. I know you weren't there, but surely you've seen the reports of what he did at Black Barrow."

I can't hear whatever Sister Ayayah grunts in response.

I appreciate Vi trying to stick up for me, though I have no idea how much good it will do. And right now, I'm more focused on wishing they would spell out what each team is doing in more detail.

"Why are you looking at me like that?" Vi asks.

"There's something else," the older woman says. There's a silence.

"What's this?" Vi asks.

Is Sister Ayayah showing Vi something? "There's a reason you've been chosen to stay on the ship, Viridiana."

"To infiltrate Repha'im's court, I know," Vi says.

"Not that. Beyond that, I mean. If things go wrong."

Silence.

"What?" Vi asks angrily. "What is *this*?"

I really wish I could see them now, but the door has no cracks, the cabin no windows. As is, I'm going to have to dive back into bed on a moment's notice lest Vi realize I've been eavesdropping, and part of me thinks I should do that now—but I can't.

"The work you used to do," Sister Ayayah says.

"What about it?" Vi demands in the same outraged tone.

"Repha'im is rumored to have strange magics. Forbidden things. He's been seen, by sources we trust, to perform incredible acts of Healing. Even in cases where death seemed a foregone conclusion."

"I don't understand. What does that matter? Good for him," Vi says.

I expect a rebuke for her attitude, but Sister Ayayah accepts it without complaint. "Good for him. Not so good for us. Or the world. Maybe."

"What are you *saying*?" Vi says.

"Quiet, not so loud! You'll wake him," Sister Ayayah hisses. Then, after a moment more of silence—argh! I need to see their faces!—she says, "If *everything* goes wrong . . . You're a killer, Vi."

"Viridiana!" She keeps her voice low, but it's fierce.

"Take it. It's specially hardened against the null waves. If we can't get the child off the ship at Cloud Point, you do what needs to be done."

"No no no no," Vi says. "No. You do not get to talk around this with me. Not for this. You say it, damn you."

My heart is sinking.

"Listen to me, whore," Sister Ayayah snaps. "If the package stays on the ship, everyone on here dies with the next null wave—including you! But you know who might *not* die? With his powers? Repha'im. In our nightmare scenarios, everyone dies except the two of them. Maybe Repha'im somehow uses his strange magic to save the two of them, and then there's nothing and no one to stop him. If that happens, we lose everything. Our lives, the Chantry, and more. We know that null wave is coming. We know it's coming soon. So if we fail to get the package off the ship, you kill it. Kill it with this. That will guarantee it's beyond even Repha'im's magics."

Her voice softens, but is still tense. "It's not going to happen. But if it does, with one kill, of a body whose soul hasn't even yet attached to it—a mere body, an animal yet!—you will save a thousand lives and the entire Chantry. Not to mention your own life. Those are the stakes, Viridiana. And that isn't our fault; it wasn't the Chantry's powers at Black Barrow that caused all this—it's *his*, in there. Your *friend*. If you want to see who's at fault for the deaths of three Sisters already and who's putting all of us at risk—and this whole ship!—you can go back in there and drop your robe again and climb straight onto his—"

There's the unmistakable sound of a slap.

"Burn in hell!" Vi says.

"One more thing," Sister Ayayah says in an icy tone, as if she hadn't just been clobbered. "If you have to do it, after you've killed it with that, toss the bassinet overboard. Even if the king can't Heal it—which he won't be able to do—he still might learn something by studying the body. Don't let him have it."

"If we fail, and I have to do that...alone, that's a suicide mission," Vi says, so quietly I can't make out all the words.

"Yes, it is," Sister Ayayah says. "And if your suicide mission fails, there are a dozen Sisters in Borami who will launch a suicide mission of their own as the storm ship docks, forfeiting their lives and undoubtedly sparking war with Alitaera in an attempt to save us all.

"It's that serious, Viridiana. That child, in Repha'im's hands, is the end of all of us. Do what you have to do. As for me, I've got someplace to be and something to do right now so that you don't *need* to die. Something that puts my own life in danger, by the way. And I'll do it, even if it does cost me my life. I'll do my job, Viridiana, because even though I despise you, you're my Sister, and loyalty means something to me. Now take the goddam knife."

Chapter Eighty-Eight

Preparations

$\mathcal{N}$early leaping to the bed, I lie down as fast as possible, arranging the covers and rolling onto my side, trying to slow my breathing and appear innocent. But I needn't have rushed. It's a long while after the echoes of Sister Ayayah Meganah's stompy footsteps fade before the door opens.

Looking at Vi blearily—my heart is pounding too hard for me to feign sleep—I say, "Heard raised voices. Something happen?"

She rallies from a defeated look.

"Oh! Just our galley steward. She forgot to bring the meal I ordered us, and then took an attitude with me for asking about it. How are you?"

I sit up. "By that do you mean how are we?" I ask.

Her face is blank. As if we didn't just make love.

I hate that phrase, but I hate all the other euphemisms more. What is it about sex that does that? They range from too cute to too clever to too agricultural, too vulgar to too clinical. You know, *coitus*. Who says that? But what's better? Rolling in the hay? Making the beast with two backs? Buffing the scabbard? Humping? Plowing the furrow? Or maybe worst, a *tumble*—as if we tripped, clothes went flying, and oops! she made an unlucky landing on my coincidental erection.

If I'm being honest, wasn't lovemaking what it was?

For *me* it was, but maybe only for me, I think as the blank look on her face continues. "I meant, uh..." she says. "I meant did you sleep well?"

I'd partly asked my own question to direct her away from any suspicion she might have that I'd been eavesdropping, but she's not following me at all.

It didn't mean the slightest to her. Just an itch to be scratched, not even worth mentioning.

I feel suddenly exposed, mortified.

Damn it. Damn me. I *knew* this was going to happen.

And why am I even thinking about this? Right now? With what I've just learned—I'm thinking about whether I regret sleeping with a girl?

See? I always do this! I always worry about the wrong things. What's wrong with me?

In one way, this is the right thing to do. If I dwell on what I just heard from the hall, there's no way I could keep the shocked rage about their plan to kill a child off my face. Better to be trivially mad at Vi for her treating me casually. There! That's it! She'll understand that. If any of my rage at the other leaks through, she can think it's just the old argument coming back.

"I was that forgettable, huh?" I say.

This isn't part of my cunning master plan, though. It just sneaks out.

"Huh? Oh! That *us*! How are *we*," Vi says, aghast. "We're fine! I mean, I'm fine. Are you fine? Not fine. I'm good. Better than good. How are you? How are we?"

There are empires at risk here, maybe the end of the entire Chantry. All that's obviously more important than this, isn't it?

Why can't I swallow?

I swing my feet out of bed and onto the floor. "I guess we've got a lot on our minds, huh?" I say, as if I can breathe. "So when do we start?"

I try to give a breezy smile, but I don't think it fools even Vi, who can be as bad at picking up other people's emotions as she is at hiding her own.

"Kylar, I didn't..." Her icily beautiful face has turned almost green.

"What?" I ask, as if asking directions to the nearest inn. "Didn't what?"

A profound sadness washes over her face. "I wish we could bottle up today and keep it forever."

Like, in a memory? *That is what memories do!* I shout at her—but I manage to only think it, not let it past my clenched, smiling teeth.

A moment later the lying rictus fades enough for me to say, "We're doomed, aren't we?"

She reaches out and takes my limp hand. Squeezes. "Don't hate me, Kylar? Please?"

I smile at her, about to tell her I could never hate her, but instead, without meaning to, I say, "Did earlier mean to you what it meant to me?"

Why did I ask that? I know the answer.

"Yes." But her head is softly moving no.

"I shouldn't have asked that. That wasn't fair."

She bites her lip, eyes filling with tears. "Kylar..."

I shake my head, look away. Smirk reflexively. "It's not your fault. It's me. I'm too broken, I guess. Got all messed up about women. I knew how this was going to go, and I—I'm sorry." I shake my head again, smile again, stuck with the same inadequate expressions, gruesome—because what the hell am I going to do? Cry? And look even more pathetic?

"Kylar..." She sounds so sad. I can't look at her now. She's the empty ache, the Tlaxini Maelstrom around which all my life swirls. All the acceptance I thought I'd felt from her earlier was just me reading everything wrong.

She was tired and horny and I was available and most men are able to disentangle their bodies and their feelings better than I can.

I met a woman who could understand me once in my life. How dare I expect that again?

Like I'm such a prize anyway.

"Let's, let's get ready, huh?" I say.

"Kylar, I, I didn't mean—"

"You don't have to say anything." I'm so embarrassing. Gods, I've got to pull myself together. "You're a great friend, Vi. And I hope I didn't mess that up for us. Our friendship, I mean. We'll get it back. Someday. Maybe with a little embarrassment, right? It was just a little tumble. We'll joke about it someday." The pain of holding my smile gets to be too much. I try to start over. "Say, earlier did I see you'd snuck a punch-dagger onboard? Can I borrow that?"

I turn my back quickly, and start prepping my gear. 'We'll joke about this,' I'd said.

I'll never joke about this.

"Punch-dagger's in the thing," she says weakly. "False bottom in the cabinet. Help yourself. Here's our orders." She hands me a note.

I read it in an instant. "Is it really that simple, or is that just how they say things? Pick up a couple of chests and move them from point A to point B? Are they expecting us to be attacked?"

"You never know."

"No, I guess you don't." I'm reduced to being a courier? Maybe after everything, I deserve a simple job. I like to be the linchpin of every plan, but that's not going to happen with these women.

I grab a few weapons, and then I'm abruptly finished. The ka'kari ends up doing pretty much everything for me that once would have needed layers of clothes and weapons harnesses.

She's laid out all her things on the bed, arranged by the layers she'll wear for the tasks we may face: battle, and stealth, and disguise on top of it all.

She undresses and dresses. Leaning against the cabinet, I watch her with an altogether different longing than filled me before.

Before, with the erotic filling the air around her like the smoke of a nearby forest fire, washing hot over my skin, stinging my eyes, shortening my every breath, filling my nostrils, changing even the sunlight to red embers, it overwhelmed all my senses to deprive me of all sense.

The erotic element hasn't now vanished like an illusion popped; instead, like copal incense wafting in lazy curls in your lover's chamber, it adds a pleasing sight and smell and aura, enhancing, not blotting out, everything else.

Odd how heartbreak can clarify things. Or perhaps it's not odd. Isn't the whole point of tears to clear our eyes?

Maybe everyone does this to everyone, or maybe young men are worst of all—or maybe I shouldn't speak for anyone else but simply confess that *I* often see others as what they are, and not as who.

I see her more now, appreciate the dedication it took to carve the muscles in her legs, the strength in her back and shoulders. I note the professionalism of how she checks each buckle and blade and tool, examining the integrity of the long splice of her grapnel rope, checking not only the sharpness of every blade but also of her muscle memory to snatch each out of its hiding place in a blink.

I feel as if I finally see Viridiana—not yet in full but more fully than I ever have before—and seeing her now, I feel like a condemned man watching his last sunset, knowing it must fade, that it is changing even as he watches, and not daring to blink lest what little he has left be stolen.

She's obviously been aware of me watching her. It didn't seem to bother her, or I would've stopped. But now she looks up at me, troubled.

"Kylar, are . . . are you—?"

"Ready?" I interrupt. "Yeah. Whenever you are." I stop leaning on the cabinet, showing I'm ready to walk.

She raises her eyebrows. "Do I look ready, Kylar?"

From her tone, the answer is obviously no, so I look her up and down, wondering what I've missed.

"The *hair*, Kylar," she says.

"Oh. Oh."

Though she's fixed its color, our earlier activities have flattened her hair. "Are we doing one of these girly things, really?" I ask.

She expels a breath. "I didn't expect you to understand."

I can't believe she's worrying about fashion right now. "Pull it into one of those tails you like. Looks great."

"I'm not worried about how it looks, Kylar!"

"Then . . . ?" I raise my hands palms up, mystified.

"It's forbidden."

"Forbidden? A ponytail?" I ask.

"Yes."

"I saw like two of the others with—"

"For me, they're forbidden, all right? As is a simple braid. Or matching tails."

"Why are—?"

"I don't want to talk about why, all right?" she snaps.

"Then . . . magic it into how it looked earlier. The Alitaerans use magic for their hair and cosmetics and all that. Surely the Chantry—"

"We do. *I* don't. I mean, I can. But that's forbidden too. Except for the color thing. And yes, just for me. Don't ask, all right?"

I have many questions, but I swallow them. I don't want my last interactions with Vi today to be fighting over Chantry idiocy. "So what are the requirements of the job, then, and how long do we have? Maybe we can take on this contract together."

She smiles at that, me talking about a haircut like it's a hit. "Has to be appropriate to a lady of my supposed rank. Needs to take less than ten minutes. And I'd like it to stay out of my way if . . . well, if things don't go well."

"If things don't go well, we might be out twisting in the breeze. Literally. They're really going to keep some stupid rule about your hair while allegedly the whole future of the Chantry's at stake?"

"Where'd you hear that?" she says sharply, and I wonder if I've just revealed my eavesdropping.

"From listening to the empress and Repha'im," I say. "And obviously the Chantry concurs—because you're all here."

"Oh," she says. "Well, I could petition for a rule suspension, but you don't know how Sister Ayayah loves to hold that sort of thing over your head."

"What's the deal with that, anyway?"

"With what?"

"With Sister Ayayah."

"She's a bitch."

"I'm well aware. I mean, what's with all the rules? You said not to ask, but I'm asking."

She sighs. "Forget it," she says. Turns toward the mirror. Picks up a brush.

"Gimme that," I say. "I've got an idea."

She hands over the brush, dubious.

"You really don't know any other styles?" I ask. "Thought Momma K always had the girls learn a bunch of looks that would look good even after vigorous, ahem, exercise."

"I didn't want anyone to touch my hair," Vi says.

"Oh. Right." I'm touching her hair right now. I've found a balm that gives the hair a bit more grip, and I begin working it through her hair. Her eyelids flutter as I rub her scalp.

Then she opens her eyes suddenly, as if getting control of herself. "The rules are a test. Supposed to make us humble. To see if they can, I guess. A rogue mage can cause nightmares for everyone, so the Chantry tries to weed out anyone who's going to become dangerous. Even if it means they lose out on some highly Talented magae."

"Makes sense," I admit. Elene showed me how to do this style for Uly, back when we were fostering her. She called it two-minute hair.

It never took me less than five. Doing it now makes me wonder how Uly's doing. I know she's safe at the Chantry, and that it's the best place for her, but I suddenly miss her.

Vi is continuing, though, so I refocus on her. "More rules for those who aren't far in the training. More rules still for those who are highly Talented, and the most rules of all for those who come to the Chantry late, as if we need to catch up on all the rule-following we missed in the years we weren't there."

"So you get all the rules, pretty much," I guess. Her red hair is a lot thicker than Uly's brunette hair or Elene's blonde.

"Most of them aren't a big deal. Like, if you break them you have to do chores."

I know that. I was there, but maybe she's forgotten.

"But..." She swallows.

"But?" I ask.

"If you really mess up, it's not just chores. I want you to know, Kylar, it's usually not like this. I mean, these teams? This is so much not normal. Back at the Chantry, I have friends. Sweet girls who are smarter than me and barely know a quarter of what I do about the world. Good people."

"Yeah?" I say. I'm trying to remember this braid. Do I bring in new hair to the braid every fourth twist? 'Two-minute hairstyle' my ass.

"For some violations, they'll burn out your Talent. For others, you get shunning. Some people say the shunning is worse. If you get shunned, you carry a mark visible to all magae. They won't speak to you, and usually, they'll work to block you from everything. Jobs. Promotions. Access. Sisters will be disciplined if they do any sort of work with you at all. They can even have *their* Talent burned out if they dare to teach you."

"The Sisterhood has a lot of power," I say, neutrally.

"And I know you don't see it, but they use it for good, Kylar. They really do. Almost always. But they have to be tough to keep people in line."

I don't answer. I twist the last strands of her hair sunwise and then twist them around each other the opposite way. I bind the ends, then pull on each part of the braid to give her hair body. It's an excuse to give me time to think.

No; it's more than that. Taking care of Vi's hair feels like my last chance to take care of her at all. To use my hands to serve her. It's goodbye.

I clear my throat at the sudden rush of heat to my eyes, glad that I'm behind her, where she can't see me.

Viridiana has hated this job all along, but she loves the Chantry. She loves the Sisterhood. She's part of something she believes in—despite all this.

If she doesn't obey their rules, they can take away everything. Her new life, her new friends, her hope. If they take her Talent, Viridiana won't even be able to go back to the miserable life of killing for hire. Without the Chantry—and I'm sure this didn't happen by accident—she'll have nothing and be nothing.

Finally settled enough, I check the braid from the front. I pull a few strands loose to frame her face and soften the look. It looks really, really good.

Shocking how on a beautiful woman even a mediocre hairstyle looks good, huh?

She nervously turns to check herself in the looking glass for the first time. She gasps audibly. "Kylar, this is—this is . . ." Her chin rises and she says coolly, "Acceptable. I suppose."

But then she grins.

My heart lurches. "Well, my customer was acceptable, too. I suppose."

She laughs joyously, and it's a stab of light against the darkness. I'm lost.

But then like frost blowing in and killing a budding flower, her smile freezes. "We need to go," she says. She strides over to the cabinet and reaches into a drawer, where she grabs something I can't see, keeping her body between me and it, and tucks it out of sight. It can only be Sister Ayayah's knife. I note which pocket she puts it in.

Then she faces me at the door. "Kylar, I can be...slow about some things sometimes. I don't have words for things sometimes. Freeze up." Her brow furrows. "You asked me a question earlier, and I think maybe I messed up. I think maybe...it *was* the same for me."

Her eyes search my face, but I've gone cold. She leans in and kisses my lips, but I can only return her kiss in the most perfunctory way, and that much only because it will forestall the conversation we might have to have if I don't return the kiss at all.

She kisses me with a tenderness and surrender I've never felt—while she carries a knife to kill my child.

For one candlelit hour, this cabin was wholeness in a shattered world. For a brief moment, in our brokenness I felt whole; in my loneliness connected. I felt a hope as golden, soft, and flickering as that candlelight on our skin.

She finally notices how much I'm not returning her kisses. She looks like she's about to ask about it.

"Let's go," I say. "No big thing, right? Grab a couple packages and take them to the boat. Easy."

"We've still got a few minutes," Vi says.

I feel the deck beneath our feet shift suddenly and the storm ship creaks as old familiar sounds suddenly cease, and the complaints of straining wood echo through the new quiet. "Was that a knock at the door?" I ask.

"I don't think so. I think we've entered the lull."

"So we should probably get moving, huh? There's not all that much time to get off the ship, right?"

"Not just off the ship. We have to get all the way to shore. But, Kylar—"

"I really think that was a knock," I lie. "One moment."

As I open the door, a young woman sags into my arms, nearly unconscious, her clothes drenched red. With her hair matted dark with blood, for a frozen moment I don't recognize her. Then I wish I couldn't.

It's Queen Jenine Gyre.

Chapter Eighty-Nine

A Bang-up Beginning

The questions why and how can wait. There's a gravely injured woman here, maybe dying.

I snatch Jenine up and carry her back into Viridiana's room, heedless of the blood she's smearing all over me.

Vi steps out into the hall to look for attackers, muttering, a low hum of magic emanating from both of her hands.

Setting Jenine on the bed, I grab a tunic from Vi's closet, rip off one sleeve, and dunk the rest into the washbasin. I have to find the young woman's wounds as quickly as possible. My gut tells me the blood's not all hers or she'd be dead already. There are bits of brain splashed over her shoulder and face.

Bringing the ka'kari as a blade to one finger, I slit away her clothes from one shoulder to see blood pumping rhythmically from a stab wound.

"Need you in here!" I shout.

But Vi's already coming back into the room—and she has both of the packages we were supposed to get in her hands. They both have blood-smeared handles. Small, with stamped leather in geometric designs, they don't look like cradleboards or bassinets. They're fully enclosed and squared off with numerous handles, as if they were any other luggage good for stacking.

"She was carrying these," Vi says, putting them down and grabbing the bandage I've just cut. She puts it to the wound on Jenine's shoulder.

Slicing the sleeve into strips, I say, "She wasn't your contact, was she?"

"No!" Vi says. With her free hand, she grabs at each piece of clothing in turn to help me put the cloth under tension so I can grab it with one hand and slice it away from Jenine's body with the other.

Then I wring out the remains of the tunic I'd plunged into the washbasin and hand it to Vi. She begins sponging blood off Jenine's body in long strokes, looking for any other wounds.

There's a slash on her leg that any other time we'd think was pretty serious, but right now, it's not life-threatening, so it's not important.

It takes longer than expected to get to her torso. She'd been wearing some sort of magically hardened base layer beneath her dress. Armor.

Then we find it. Despite the armor that may have turned lesser blows, there's a stab wound off-center in her belly.

Vi puts pressure on that one, too, eliciting a cry of pain from Jenine, who seems to have regained consciousness once more. I check her legs again, groin, and scalp. Then we roll her over to check her back, making her whimper.

There are no other wounds. Not that it matters.

As I set to work securing the bandages in place, Vi says, "Kylar, she needs magical Healing. We need to take her to the Sisters. Now."

"The Sisters?" Jenine hisses through her pain. "Your Sisters are who gave me these!"

I stop midway through tying a bandage.

Vi shakes her head. "No. They would never—"

"Why would they do this?" I ask Jenine.

"Tried to stop them. Don't know if they knew who I was. My visions told me where they'd be. Visions told me I couldn't stop them too."

"Did they tell you you'd get stabbed for your trouble?" I demand.

"Yes," she says.

Looking her in her eyes—pupils same size, no obvious head trauma—I believe her. Thus the armor under her dress. Which didn't stop the blade but may have saved her life.

"Had to try," she says, weakening. "Convinced a few imperials to humor me, and we . . . tried to stop you all. Now here I am anyway. Nothing I do matters."

"Are any of the Sisters Healers?" I ask Vi.

"Several are pretty good at it," she says defensively.

"If you had this wound and had other options, would you go to them first?"

She hesitates. It's answer enough.

"The imperial mages," I say. "While we're in the lull, they won't all be holding the ship together. There'll be a dozen first-rate Healers in the empress's entourage. I'll take her to them."

"Kylar, you can't!" Vi says.

"Look at her," I say. Her head is lolling, eyes blinking. She's fighting to keep conscious. Depending on the angle and depth of whatever stabbed her, she's either not got long to get help or she's not got long, full stop. From what I can see, I think she could pull through fine, but only with competent help—and I could be wrong. I'm very good at ending life, not at all at sustaining it.

In my professional opinion, if she were my deader, I'd stab her again to make sure. I wouldn't leave her as is and expect to collect my pay, not for sure.

Makes me sick that I see this bleeding young woman and think of it in those terms, but that's been my life.

All this takes only a couple moments.

"Kylar, everyone's looking for you. The Alitaerans will kill you as soon as they see you."

"I can probably escape," I say. "They'll be paying attention to her, right?"

"No, no, no," Vi says. She takes a breath. "I'll take her. It's gotta be me."

I don't want to admit that my heart leaps at this. It makes sense. Gods know I don't want to have to kill any more innocent soldiers or mages to escape. I don't even know if I'd be able to. Regardless of if I could get away, what might happen to Jenine in such a melee?

How many people will die if Logan thinks the Chantry killed his wife?

How many will die if he thinks the Alitaerans did it?

There aren't enough curses in the world.

"I got it," Vi says. "I can do this and still continue on to Borami. You take the . . . the chests. It's not too late yet."

Her continuing on to Borami means her continuing her mission to seduce Repha'im and embed herself in his court. It means losing her forever.

But then, I knew I was saying goodbye to her either way.

"Please, open it?" Jenine says, breaking in. "Let me see my son one last time?" There's a hysterical edge to her voice.

"I can't do that," I say. "It'll break the magic, and then none of this will—"

"Please! Please!"

"I have to get him off the ship. Have to, or he'll die—and everyone else onboard will too," I say, feeling unbearably cruel. "I—I can't do anything that will make that mission harder than it already is."

Her face goes deathly pale, and it's not a good tone to see on someone who's lost so much blood. "Then the visions were true," she says. "All of them. They got fuzzy, farther out. I hoped..."

"Take her," I tell Vi. "The packages—how much care do I need to use handling them?"

She knows what I'm asking: *Can I fight?*

"They're stabilized somewhat. He should stay asleep. But... we never could test it."

I swear under my breath. Vi comes over, but Jenine holds up a hand. "Wait, one word. Let me have one word with Kylar. Please. Privately." Her voice fades quieter even as she speaks.

I lean close, picking her up so I can hand her over to Vi, and Jenine whispers in my ear.

I won't share what she said. It's no one's business but hers and mine, and I don't need to put it on these pages to remember it.

I won't forget what she said if I live to be twice Durzo's age.

Then, as she finishes, leaving me blanched and shaking my head, she lunges—and tries to sink her teeth into my neck.

But my reflexes are too good, and having missed her chance at surprise, she's far too weak to press an attack. I stop her easily.

As I hand her over to Vi, leaning close and stumbling a bit, Jenine says, "I had to... try." Gods, but the woman's ferocious. Fully believing she was doomed and that nothing she did could change it, she's fought on every step of the way.

She hated me for no good reason. She tried to hurt me, and yet I can't help but be moved by her courage. If you came to this tale looking for real heroism, this is it.

She loses consciousness.

"Kylar..." Vi says from the door.

But she can't find any more words. Words never were her strength.

I wonder if I'll ever see her again. I wonder what kind of person she'll be when I do.

"Kylar, I lied," she says.

I blink, distracted by what's in my hand. "Which time?"

Her expression goes black. "Go to hell. Just go to hell."

Then she leaves.

I look down in my hand at the small, enameled-blue knife Sister Ayayah gave Viridiana and that I just pickpocketed off her. There's no sign of the magics I know must be swimming within it. I tuck it away and pick up the two chests. The weight of each is exactly the same. Nor does the weight shift within the one and not the other. There's no sign at all of which holds a child in a magically induced slumber and which a dead weight. Each has a different small rune on the underside, but as I don't know which means what, I don't bother with them.

The Sisters had studiously kept me ignorant of their plan, but obviously, at some point they'd intended to switch the two chests to deceive the empress and King Repha'im. Originally, from where Vi and I had received the two packages, the plan had been for Vi to carry one and me the other. Feeling distrustful, I'd planned to swap which one I took in case she'd been ordered to betray me by disappearing with the other.

Now I have both. Their heist has fallen apart in more than one way.

I don't know how much else has gone awry with the plan, or what the imperials now know. At this point, I'd guess the intended switch may well already be moot—but it may not be, too. If I break into one of these chests, I'll wake the child within. That will make life much, much harder. There's nothing for it but for me to take both and get moving.

It's only after I step into the hall that it occurs to me what Vi was probably talking about—when she confessed that she'd lied.

Heart seizing up, I stare after her—but she's gone. It's too late. Maybe it always was. My path leads the other direction, relentlessly away.

After a single pained breath, I go.

Chapter Ninety

When Your Boat Comes In

I've done a few stupid things in my time. I'm not sure any can rival heading into battle with a sleeping child in my arms—well, a sleeping child in a box in my arms.

A jolt goes through me. Hold on, the kid's *in a box*! Can he breathe in there?

As I keep striding through the mahogany halls I search the side of the boxes for breathing holes. There aren't many people in the halls before dawn. It seems to be mostly servants, old people who barely sleep at all, and a few nobles in casual clothing out for their morning constitutional. I smile weakly at an older lady who looks askance at me, dressed like a noble, but carrying boxes like a servant, and angling them around like a lunatic. But no one calls an alarm, and that's all that matters to me now.

Surely, surely the Sisters who'd spent so much energy on this plan, preparing the weight of the boxes, even figuring out how to keep the kid asleep, wouldn't have overlooked his need to breathe! Would they? Even street kids like me who captured a frog had known to put holes in the box.

But I can't see any of the Sisters handling frogs as children. Nor are any of them exactly the motherly types.

Minus Melena. But then, her entire personality could be veneer. You can never tell what's under the skin with those women.

I mean—oh, thank the gods, there are a few holes, along the seams. Doesn't seem like enough to me, but who knows how much fresh air a sleeping baby needs? I sure don't.

I've already figured out what I'll do if we get into a fight: Set the boxes down, go invisible, and hope I can take out any opposition fast.

Great plan, huh? But can you think of a better one?

~Are you asking me?~

Not really. Was more thinking of my hypothetical future—yes! Do *you have any great ideas?*

~Avoid situations like this in the future?~

That is *a great idea. And I wonder why don't I ask for your help more often?*

~I'll shut up now.~

Even better!

I approach a noblewoman who's dressed down and her handmaiden happily chatting in the hallway as they walk. No weapons I can see. I feel taut as a bow-string as they go past, though.

They don't attack. Of course. I glance back at them after they've passed, to see if they look back to note which way I turn, as spies would.

The handmaiden glances back, sees me looking, then says, not quietly, "Mistress, I do believe he's staring at your bottom!"

"Ada, hush!" the woman says, staring back at me, clearly excited.

I nod and fake a smile, not slowing. She looks disappointed.

~Oh, one suggestion.~

Are you serious? Now?

~How about one of those illusory masks Durzo taught you?~

That's your great idea?

Actually, that *is* a great idea.

I glance back. The noblewoman is gone. When it feels like everyone's out to kill you, it's good to remember that not everyone's out to kill you.

At the next intersection, there's a looking glass. I stop in front of it. There's no time to anchor the illusory face properly to my own so that its expressions shift with mine, and sometimes, a bad mask can attract more attention than simply throwing a hood over your head. There's something deeply disquieting about a human face that isn't quite right.

But... I'm a wanted man. A mask like this won't bear scrutiny from up close, but at least I can put something on that holds up from a distance.

Blond hair, yes, definitely different hair. Long beard, for sure. That'll cover the mouth so I don't have to worry as much about expressions, but nicely trimmed. I'm among nobles here; even the servants are well-kempt. Nose longer than mine, slightly hooked.

Need to keep my own eyes, though. Unmoving illusory eyes look dead.

It'll have to do.

I look up. Ten steps away are two noblewomen, gaping at me. One is holding the other's arm, maybe in fright. Of course they're standing down the hallway where I need to go.

"Neat, huh?" I ask them. "Makes every ball a masked ball if you want it to. Just imagine the uses!" I wink at them. "I'm the empress's man. Sensitive mission." Keeping my gestures small so as not to alarm them, I point past them to let them know I'm heading their direction.

If they bolt and scream for help, I'm doomed.

Is that fear in their eyes?

"You can get a charm that'll do it once," I say. "Surely you've seen a lady at a party before and thought she looked a little too good, haven't you? Could be one of these. Could be something else, naturally. Cost you a fortune, though."

"Really?" one of them asks, fear turning to consternation. "Ria, wasn't I just saying that Lady Kellanah was..."

It's a good sign. It means her brain is working.

Another part of me is screaming inside that I'm wasting too much time here, talking.

Next they're going to ask me where they can get one. I can't afford small talk. Any misstep may cost me everything.

I realize I need some specifics to sell this. So I bluff. "You know the goldsmith's area? Big shop there, you know, the one with the annoying woman who runs it?"

"Alexias? I always thought she was very nice!" the clutchy one says. She's relaxed her grip. I've got her calm, too.

"Oh, to your set I'm sure she is. Anyway, head down the alley from there, little place, black door, ask for Fergund. Not precisely legal, so you'll have to talk a bit carefully until he trusts you."

They suddenly get very excited about the prospect. It sounds like an adventure to them. They've heard of such charms before, but something about mine seems different. As they chatter, I'm able to walk forward, but they watch me like hawks.

One reaches out a hand toward my face. "No no no," I say, then try to soften. "The mask'll break apart with the lightest touch. Not like the most expensive ones. Can't even go out in the rain with it, and still ridiculous so it's not worth the price unless you're filthy rich. I shouldn't have said anything. Anyway, need to go. Lovely to meet you."

They move to let me pass, and I feel a small surge of satisfaction. Phaena would be proud of me. I've solved what could have become a huge problem without stabbing anyone in the neck. Which makes me think—

"One moment," one of them says, stopping me. "What's your name?"

I wag my finger at her playfully. "You know I can't say."

She folds her arms, pouting. "Well, if you're ever in the neighborhood—"

"Oh no, my lady," I say, cutting her off. "You don't know the reason I get picked for mask duty."

"And why's that?"

I wave toward my face. "Under this? *Hideous.*"

They laugh.

But they also let me slide past, and I hear the pouty one say, "Oh, Alona, I simply must have one."

"Indeed," the other says, voice throaty.

"And one of those masks, too," the first says, and then I hear them laughing.

I won't be approaching the staff area from the side that Vi originally showed me, but I have enough of a sense of the boat now that I think I can find where I'm going.

Sure enough, soon I come to a door with a little sign that denotes it's only for staff members. Balancing my two boxes, I try it.

Locked. And in trying to balance the boxes, one brushed my face and popped my illusion mask.

Looks like all that good luck I had earlier is running out.

Not a pleasant thought to have. Wish I hadn't had it.

I feed the ka'kari into the keyhole. Sometimes this works perfectly as a mobile, faster-than-fast lockpick.

The lock hisses.

Sighing, I pull the ka'kari back into my skin as the door swings open, its guts utterly devoured.

Just had to, didn't you?

~Oops.~

Glancing behind me, I see no one. I pick up my baby-in-a-box and the decoy. It really would be handy to know which was which, in case someone starts throwing fire at us or something.

Holding the boxes up to partially screen my face, I step through the ruined door like a man who knows where he's going.

Stepping around the corner into the hull-side hallway, notable by its not-quite-rectangular shape and its frequent iron supports, I come upon a group of stewards chuckling and sharing riot weed. I glance significantly at the tobacco-leaf-wrapped scrag. Their laughter stops and the woman holding it hides it quickly behind her back, with all the nonstealth of someone a bit too intoxicated to care as much as they know they should about the trouble they're about to be in.

In my best nobleman's voice, I say, "Carry on, carry on. Puff away. If you're dealing with my lot all day, I'm sure you need it. Most days, I think I need it myself, dealing with my lot all day." I wink.

With the gusto and glassy eyes of the pharmacologically gleeful, they laugh and let me through.

Thank the gods. No killing innocent stewards and staff today.

Hey, I'm getting good at this not-killing stuff. If you've never tried it before, I'd highly recommend it!

From here, it's a straight shot to the great open area where the sections of the ship attach and where Vi told me the dock opens to the sea. Not far now to the Sisters—and maybe, safety. Shifting my hands on the boxes, I wipe each sweaty palm on my tunic.

I step through a set of double doors into the bottom level of the huge open room that is the midships flexion area. Iron girders imbued with magic criss-cross the space above me, but their complaints are muted now as the storm ship cuts cheerily through the quieter seas here in the lee of whatever tall headland shields this area from the wind. Cloud Point, I guess. Through an open door in the hull, not much above the level of the waters, I catch my first view of the sea itself. It is as glassy blue calm as my heart is a whitewater churn.

On either side of the exit stand two imperial guards with polearms. Next to one of them, casually chatting as if she hasn't a care in the world, I see Sister Melena.

She sees me instantly and immediately steps closer to the guard, who turns fully to look at her. With one hand down by her hip, shielded from his view, she flattens out her palm toward me. Stop.

I veer down the first and only passage, off to the right, taking a few steps so I can get out of the guards' view. I set the boxes down and pull a scrap of parchment out of a pocket, as if examining instructions. I don't think anyone can see me here, but looking like you're doing something is less suspicious than standing and staring.

Not half a minute later, the guard she was chatting with goes trotting past me, happy to do Melena some favor she'd asked of him.

Wow. She is really, really good.

I take a step back into view, my head down looking at my parchment as if I'm confused.

Despite the other guard standing next to her, Melena gives a swift little wave forward with her hand.

I go back, pick up the boxes, and hope to hell I can trust her. If the Sisters have a betrayal coming for me, this might be the time for it.

Not like I've got a choice. I start into the large open area, the hiss of the water in the misty disposal hole complementing the gentle groaning of the decks. There are Sisters standing outside on a dock that's unfolded from within the storm ship. Otherwise, miraculously—or through the Sisters' cunning—there is no one else in sight, not on this deck or on any of the overlooking decks.

It's disconcerting walking past the glass-and-magic section of the hull. It looks fragile. The sun is barely touching the horizon, so the water is dark through the glass, but I think I see the flash of large fish on the other side of the hull. Sharks, maybe. My throat goes tight. Maybe it's just my imagination.

I hadn't been aware I was scared of the water before now.

Walking toward the guard, I keep the boxes high to shield everything below my eyes but smile tightly as his attention turns toward me. I see several Sisters step into view behind him.

I'm only steps away when he jerks. The head of a crossbow bolt juts out of the center of his chest.

In a sudden flurry of motion, a garrote is looped over his head and with a single, bloody half-cough, he's yanked backward through the double doors outside onto the dock by three women. Melena snatches the polearm from his hand and passes it to another Sister, then comes to me and grabs my elbow.

"Quickly now, quickly!" Melena says, staring past me.

I follow her motion. There are laborers I hadn't seen before working on the far side of the open area, greasing gears and checking joints. They all have their backs to us at the moment, but if any had seen . . .

"Are you all insane?" I hiss at her.

"No, we're Sisters, trying to prevent a calamity," Melena says. But her eyes are only on the boxes. "How'd you find—we thought that—no, never mind. You can tell us later. Those look intact. Is he safe? Never mind, come, come."

By the first part—'We're Sisters'—I can only hope that they did some-thing magical to shield their murder from the workers. At least, that's how

I'm choosing to interpret it. If she merely means that they're determined to do whatever it takes, then they're more fanatical than I'd thought.

The worst kind of person is one who has something they value so much that threatening it will shut off their reason and turn them into a fanatic.

~If you find their something, every person is that kind of person.~

I know.

In a moment, I've been ushered up a few steps through the double-doored opening in the glass-and-magic hull and out onto a retractable flying dock suspended above the water, supported with chains like a drawbridge. At either end there are berths for smaller boats with space for a larger boat to dock parallel to the storm ship.

It's a relief to step out into the light of the sun as it clears the horizon. I hadn't been aware of how caged I felt until I came outside. It smells free. The sunlight is still tinged a deep red by the Great Storm's dust, but out here it feels beautiful, not menacing, and sunlight on my skin has always felt good to me. I know that's partly attached to my magic as the sun fills my glore vyrden, but that seems too trivial an explanation. Surely everyone revels in the soft kiss of sun on their skin? But my reverie is as short-lived as it was sweet.

There's no boat waiting for us. Nor is that the only dismaying sight.

"I'll take those," Sister Prospaya says.

"What are we supposed to do, swim?" I ask, not handing over the chests.

"You should find that even less enjoyable than you think." Her voice sharpens. "The chests? Please?"

"No. And I wasn't thinking it would be enjoy—why wouldn't I?" I think suddenly of the things I imagined swimming in the waters, and my chest tightens. What if I didn't imagine them?

She waves at the sky, and then the sea. "Those up there plus all the magic brings those down there."

As I step past her, with her hands still outstretched to take the chests away from me—which I ignore—I turn back to my second source of discomfort out here. The sunlight I'm basking in, that's filling me with power, is filtered through a haze of clouds.

But they aren't clouds. Countless seabirds fill the sky, perhaps tens of thousands, and as many more are taking their rest on the waves, bobbing up and down with the swells in this oddly protected area out of the Great Storm.

I'm about to sarcastically ask why seabirds would make a swim so terrible when I see numerous splashes, both near at hand and far away. Within a few moments, I see more. But with the speed of them and the splashing water, I can't tell exactly what I'm seeing.

Sister Prospaya says, "The birds come from everywhere for refuge from the winds of the Great Storm. The sharks come to eat the birds when they tire and rest, it seems. Perhaps other reasons as well. We don't understand what happens under the waves during the storms. Regardless, the *lotai* come too. Perhaps because of the sharks, or the other carrion, or maybe they're drawn by magic."

"The, the what?" I ask.

"The lotai. It's said they can smell blood from a league away, and fear from two, but the real—actually, just watch. They're less tentative than sharks."

Sharks, tentative?

At the end of our dock, with obvious reluctance, the Sisters dump the dead guard's body into the waves. Almost the moment he hits the water, the waves start churning. But my eyes aren't on the body. They go instead to Jasmine Jakweth and a burly Sister from the other Special Problems and Tactics Team who take up defensive positions above where the guard was dumped, their spears lowered to cover the water.

What's in the water that they have to—?

Something leaps from the waves toward them, and Jasmine spears it in midair with practiced ease. A fish of some kind, easily the length and width of one of Jasmine's massive legs, wriggles on the big man's spearpoint.

He swings it in to the dock where he stomps on it, yanks his spear clear, stabs it again and twists to make sure it's dead, and then settles back into his defensive stance covering the waves, one foot still holding the thrashing, dying thing in place.

But now the ship's progress has carried the guard's body far enough away that there seems to be no more immediate danger to us.

"Nearly as ugly as you, eh?" he says, grinning at me.

"I was thinking I wish I looked that good," I say, staring with mixed awe and horror at the fish. It's not a fish. It's a spiny, bony half-dragon-looking thing with a tall blade of a tail like a thresher shark and a disturbingly humanlike face spoiled by a jaw that unhinges wide to show a nightmare of razor teeth. Between the bone ridges of its body and stubby wings, its skin glows a sickly green, a green that reminds me of the moon dragon that once attacked me and Logan.

"Never seen 'em this big," he says. "Largest one I ever saw before would fit in my hand. I wonder if—nah, probably it's just a different breed way over here."

"Or maybe the magical balances we upset at Black Barrow have changed them, too?" I ask.

He stares hard at me. With his spear, he flips the dead thing overboard. "I hope not. That battle was far, far away. If it changed things all the way out here this much . . . I'm afraid worse is coming."

'Worse is coming' is the story of my life.

"All right. Fantastic. That's great. Just great," I say, my stomach twisting. Now I get to feel both immediate impending doom and, um, intermediate impending doom together. I'm not sure if I'm using the right words to describe it, but it's a great feeling. If you've never had it, I recommend you check it out. It's almost as good as not killing people. "Where's our boat?"

"Should be here soon," Sister Prospaya says, her voice falsely bright.

"Should be here already," Sister Ayayah says dourly.

"Kylar, you need to *not* be here when the other guard gets back," Sister Prospaya says. "Which could be any moment."

"She doesn't mean you need to leave. She means you need to not be seen," Sister Melena says.

All the Sisters turn to look at me. Too many of them. This is where I hand over the chests—or don't. Does their whole plan hinge on this moment?

Of course they want me to hand over the kid. But why? So they can betray me?

Surely flinging magic at me while I'm holding the child is too dangerous. And though I know they'll kill the kid if they have to, they're not going to risk it when it's so close at hand, right?

"If they were going to betray you," Melena says hurriedly, "they wouldn't do it now. We can't afford to fight before we all get away. Not that anyone intends to betray you! But I can see you're worried—"

"Then why are you all staring at me?" I ask, hating that she read my hesitation so easily.

"Because we've lost so much to save that child," Melena says. "Because we don't trust you. Because most of us are afraid of you." She shrugs. "And because all of us want to see what happens when you embrace the shadows."

Embrace the shadows? How do they even know that term for me going invisible?

Oh, Vi. Right. Loyal-to-the-Chantry Viridiana.

Or, it occurs to me, they may have known that term for a hundred years. The Chantry never forgets. They're always adding to their institutional stores of knowledge and power and magic. I should know by now that they will always have four things they want from any one interaction with me.

"I'm sad that most of you are afraid of me," I say, slowly setting the chests down amid the piles of their own luggage, many of them matching the kid's chests in color and style. Only the size of the child's chests distinguishes them from the Sisters'.

Smart. They want all the chests to look like their own luggage, but they only want to confuse others, not themselves. Two identical chests is confusing enough; if there were a dozen, if things went to hell, they themselves wouldn't know which chests to protect.

"May I examine them?" Sister Prospaya says, tense.

"She won't take them away," Melena adds quickly. "She only needs to see the runes on the underside. Hurry, Sister."

I grab the top chest and gently—mindful there may be a sleeping child secured inside—tilt it up. She kneels to look for the rune.

Part of me shouts, *Kill her! You can't trust these witches!*

No, trust them or not, they're my only way off the ship.

"That's the one," she says. "Praise the Seraph."

I set the box back down as Sister Prospaya rises. Her proximity puts me on edge, and I'm ready to kill if she makes any move to attack.

"Should we open it? Make sure the kid's safe?" I ask.

"Yes, we should," Sister Prospaya says, "after we push off. Not until then."

"Why not now?" I demand.

"Perhaps as a bachelor you are unaware that crying children draw attention. It's the whole reason they cry. And attention is not what—"

"Yeah, I get it," I say. "But if we don't check, we don't know if we have two empty boxes here, right?"

They look at each other, and I see that this is something they've thought of but hoped I wouldn't. I wish Vi were here. Hell, I wish Phaena were here. She wouldn't let us get pushed around by these old cows.

"The weight of the empty one would be wrong," Sister Prospaya says, "and if our enemies knew enough to fix that, it's already too late. We have to leave regardless. To stay on this ship is death."

It's the right call, I know, but I don't like it.

"I've got to check the hall," Melena says. "Watch for my sign."

As she leaves, Sister Ayayah says, "Where's the boat, Prospaya? You promised us it would—"

Sister Prospaya's glare is enough to stop Sister Ayayah midsentence. "And nothing *your* team has done has gone awry on this mission? Why don't you sit there and quietly figure out how to stab me in the back while I try to figure a way out of this mess for all of us?"

"Boat!" Jasmine Jakweth says. "It's our boat!"

"Not a moment too soon," Sister Prospaya breathes, relieved.

"And maybe not soon enough," Sister Ayayah says. "If we don't get off this ship immediately, we might not make it to shore before—"

"Oh, would you shut up!" Sister Prospaya says. "One worry at a time."

Just then, in the hall, Melena claps her hands together like an excited little girl without a thought in her head.

I don't have to have been briefed on their signals to understand immediately—the other guard's back.

I'm struck with a sudden, inappropriate desire to laugh at the way the Sisters' heads all swivel in unison toward Melena, and then back to me.

"Kylar, if you're gonna disappear," Jasmine says. "Now would be a good time."

But I ignore him and point over to a spot on the white handrail not far behind Melena. "Hey, amateurs," I say, "you think maybe you might want to clean up the blood spatter from the guard you murdered? It's gonna be right in his line of sight."

Sister Ayayah gasps. "How'd it get so far?"

But others are already moving their feet rather than their lips, darting to stand between the guard and any incriminating evidence.

I take the moment to send the ka'kari rushing over my skin and go invisible. Only Jasmine Jakweth is still staring at me, his eyes glittering with magic so he can still make me out.

"You know he's going to switch his vision as he looks for his friend, right?" Jasmine says. The Chantry knows about *that*, too?

~You ought to have them brief you on your own powers. Might be enlightening.~

If only someone else I know would brief me on my powers!

~You know I can't do that.~

If you won't help, be a friend and shut up, would you?

I nudge one of the Sisters' large chests so it moves a bit. "If you had to lose a chest, which one would be okay?" I ask.

He furrows his brow, and we both watch as Melena embraces the guard, who's just handed her some knickknack or other. She kisses him sweetly on both cheeks, embarrassing him. The Sisters behind her take advantage of the distraction to wipe up blood.

One sweeps the white railing with a handkerchief and then moves her body between it and the guard, muttering. The handkerchief shoots from her hand deep into the waves, obviously propelled by magic.

Another simply steps onto a spot where there must have been drops of blood on the dock.

But the guard freezes in flushed midsentence. Asks a question. He points at the railing, then disencumbers himself from Melena's embrace and tries to push through the Sisters, heading at an angle away from me.

"Jasmine," I hiss.

"The one on the left," he says. "No, my left!"

But I'm already tossing the one on my left high into the air.

I dive after it, but not to catch it. I skid on my belly across the wood slats and off the dock and then pike my torso down hard as I go over the edge, snatching the crisscrossing metal supports underneath.

As I flip upside down, swinging, I pull my knees up to keep from slapping noisily into the waves. Then one of my hands slips off the wet metal of the support.

With my Talent coursing through my arms, I manage to keep my grip one-handed, but my body twists uncontrollably, spinning me as my momentum carries me back up toward horizontal, crunching into the metal support beams before swinging vertical once more.

Above me, Jasmine Jakweth is covering whatever noise I've made by cursing loudly about the loss of the chest.

I hear rapid footsteps on the wood slats above me as the guard comes toward us. "What is it? What was that? What happened?" the man demands.

"See? See it there?" Jasmine says. "Our luggage! That idiot must've balanced it wrong. Do you have a pole? Anything we can snag it with? Quick! It fell overboard."

Back at the double doors, I see Melena quickly swipe at a spot on the railing with her hand. I think she's wiping up a spot of blood.

She looks around for someplace to clean her hand, her usually universally pleasant expression for the first time sharp and worried. She's wearing light colors and must not have a handkerchief. The others are too far away.

"It's already gone," the guard says. "Sorry."

With a grimace, Melena puts her fingers in her mouth to lick them clean. And none too soon.

"Who stacked these?" Jasmine says loudly.

"Not me," Melena says cheerily. "I was out in the hall talking with my friend Sehravein, who—did you all see?—brought me my favorite comb!"

Her attitude edges into the borderlands of brainless vanity without overplaying it. I'd have to appreciate it more if I weren't trying to find a place to brace my feet to help me cling to the underside of the dock.

"Oh no," Jasmine says suddenly, too quietly for the guard to hear. I hear the guard go thumping back toward Melena, walking right above me. The planks of the deck have only small gaps between them—enough so I can see the shadows of those who pass above even as I hear them. I'm not sure how I appear to mages when they look at me in the magical ranges of vision. Do I *glow*? A glowing person would be visible right through the gaps. Why didn't I ask Vi about that when I had the chance? With the darkness of the sea below me, I'll be hard to see in mundane sight. But there are a lot more people who can see normally than magically.

Torn, I don't switch invisibilities yet, but I don't feel good about it.

I find a place to loop my feet over a narrow iron support and can finally relax my use of the Talent. What's Jasmine worrying about?

With a note of despair in his voice, Jasmine says, "I was wrong. That's not our boat."

Oh gods. Can things possibly get worse?

I barely have time to remember one of Durzo's old rules—or maybe it was one of mine: Never ask if things can get worse. If you can still ask, the answer is yes.

"Those are imperial colors," Jasmine says. "That's the empress's boat."

Chapter Ninety-One

Not a Surprise

I try to breathe. All right. This is not a total surprise, right? I knew the empress was getting on a boat to disembark from the *Storm Racer*. Granted, we wanted our boat to come first. And, granted, ours is overdue. But that she should have a boat coming is not a surprise.

Feeling a prickle on the back of my neck, I turn my head toward the deep blue chasm of the waters beneath me. Suspended in the expansive sea like a cloud high in the pitiless sky, there's a lotai swimming directly beneath me.

Clinging to the dock above me, I freeze up for a moment—I, the Night Angel! I, the one who knows best to attack first, and ask questions never. But by sheer dumb luck, freezing is the right thing.

You're invisible, idiot, I think.

I watch the lotai coursing through the waves, its body pulsating in the gaps between its bony armor with a magical green. It's beautiful in the primeval way a shark is beautiful, moving effortlessly at great speed with casual flicks of its tail.

It rolls onto its side under the waves, keeping pace with me, and I see the eye turned toward me pulse a deeper green as the lotai breaches the waves for an instant. Its pupil, veined in many colors, searches, shifts focus. I can't shake the sudden conviction that it's hunting me. It's a creature of magic itself; can it see magic?

It sinks into the waves, perhaps giving up, and disappears from where I can crane my neck far enough to see it.

Is it gone, or is it regrouping to attack from my blind side?

There are footsteps and voices directly above me; I can't focus on them. I have to flip over. I can't have my back to the waves, not when those things are down there.

"Is the empress coming to dock here?" Jasmine Jakweth says. He doesn't manage to sound as casual as he's trying for.

"Empress, here? Nah, she's got her own dock up there, don't she?" the guard says.

Wedging my foot deeper and sideways into the space between a girder and the dock, I loosen my other foot to prepare to flip over and start walking my hands over each other. Strength is nothing without balance.

Sounds like a thing Durzo would say, but I don't think he ever did. Anyway, it's probably about time I start stealing his phrases without crediting him. Bastard probably stole them himself. Bastard should be here helping me. Stealing his aphorisms is the only revenge I have available.

"Oh, sure, sure, there it is up there now," Jasmine says. "Pretty amazing how these flying docks fold out from the side of the storm ship, how all the little panels go flush."

"Huh?" the guard says.

Taking a deep breath, I drop one of my hands off the girder I'm holding and twist my body as far as I can to look behind me in the waves.

Oh, hell, there it is.

The lotai is far enough back that I wouldn't be able to see it through the undulating looking glass of the sea's surface if not for the fact that its bony blade-edged tail is protruding from the waves.

"Yeah, haven't you noticed how practically any section of the hull has little panels that look flush, but if you press on them, they pop open with a handhold? Guess it must be for the workers to check on things," Jasmine says. "Thought that was pretty amazing."

"I guess," the guard says, sounding puzzled at why Jasmine is saying this. "Say, I need you to do me a favor."

In long, lazy S-curves, the lotai is catching up, that wicked tail scraping gently across the girders supporting the dock as if it's groping blindly for me. Even though the creature is going to pass to one side of me, the quiet, menacing sound of edged bone sliding and then clicking across iron slats cuts straight to my spine.

Srrrrr-ick.

Srrrrr-ick.

I realize too late that its S-curve this time is taking it on a sharper course than I'd guessed. It's not going to pass beneath me before that tail crosses my position—it's coming straight for the only hand I still have on the girder. But if I let go and so much as touch the waves, it'll sense me for sure. If I touch the water, I'm lost.

Srrrrr-ick.

I drop my hand out of the way of the bone blade at the last instant. My upper body sags toward the waves.

Crunching down and levering myself hard against my feet wedged deep in their own grips, I hang, suspended by my legs for a long moment as the bony tail cuts across the place my hand had been a moment before. Muscles rigid holding myself up and making myself small, I can't see it—but I hear it go past.

And then I feel one of my feet begin to slip. In preparing to flip over, I'd loosened its grip, and now—

Oh no!

My left foot shoots out from its place and my face droops toward the waves once more, twisting me as I've gone from four points of contact down to one.

If I hadn't sent a rush of magic down my leg, it would've snapped my shin or knee. My leg holds—but it still hurts like hell, the metal biting deep into skin.

A coming swell threatens to wash over me. Stifling a groan, I lean hard against that sole support, my body rising to hang sideways again, parallel to the waves. Pushing hard against my protesting leg and praying that my foot's grip holds, I strain to reach up—and snag my handhold once more.

The swell passes without touching me.

I gasp a huge lungful of air, and rather than go back to my old position with my back to the waves, blind, I now hang by four points inverted, belly down.

I feel terrifically exposed, but at least now I can look for the lotai.

But look where? Where did it go?

And what was it Jasmine was saying just moments ago? There was something weird about how he was talking, as if he wasn't talking to the guard, but to me. Something about handholds.

But now he's saying, "Favor?"

My arms are twitching with the strain of holding myself at this angle, and I'm sweating buckets. Where *is* it?

"I need you to open—"

"Hey, look! There's our boat!" Jasmine interrupts.

The lotai is gone. Maybe it's given up. It's only a dumb animal, after all. Plenty of humans don't have the attention span it already showed in hunting me.

Then I catch a glimpse of it, some twenty paces back, its tail cutting out of the water in slow arcs once more. Maybe this is a different one, though.

I scan the depths below me while I begin looking for the pop-out hand-holds Jasmine mentioned. Again, his words only slowly make their way into my mind: Our boat is coming.

The relief I should feel is blunted by my hanging helplessly over the lotai-infested waters, where a slip will mean a very short, very bloody swim.

"Good for you, good for you," the guard is saying. "Now, hate to say it, but I need you to open some of these chests."

His feet are still almost directly above me. I've found a circular seam on the skin of the folded-down section of hull that forms one of the supports above me. If I push or pull on it—whatever I need to do to open the thing—will it make noise? Will the guard hear it?

Truth is, I don't have many options. There are only a few metal support beams. If I want to move any farther, I'm going to have to find another way. That means either puncturing the hull with ka'kari claws—I've done that, and it means jets of incandescent magic at each point I do it, which is not exactly stealthy—or finding and opening the panels.

Above me, the Sisters have gathered around the guard. "Opening our chests?" Sister Ayayah Meganah says. "Outrageous. We're doubly indemnified from arbitrary searches, young man."

"Young man?" he says, annoyed. "We're on the empress's ship, and I am—"

Sister Ayayah cuts in. "What you are, is about to make a serious mistake by infringing on prerogatives of duly appointed and approved—by the empress herself, I might point out!—ambassadors from the Chantry. Every ambassador to Alitaera, whether from Modai or from the smallest chieftaincy of the least of the Ymmuri tribes, is afforded certain bare minimums of respect, not least of which is immunity to unreasonable searches and the detaining of their persons."

"Which search," Sister Prospaya says, butting in, "is doubly unreasonable given that all our luggage was already voluntarily submitted before embarkation to Lord Steward Havoylund."

Another Sister, whose voice I don't know well enough to guess, jumps in,

"Perhaps this young man wishes to suggest we've made off with some of the imperial silverware, as if the Chantry is a refuge for common thieves."

"I—I—I said nothing of the sort!" the guard stammers.

Their play is obvious to me now. I suspect that around the Sisters who are hounding the guard, some others are quickly restacking the luggage to make the child's chest more difficult to reach.

It's all stalling—but how long do they need to stall for the escape boat to arrive?

"Now, Sisters," Melena says, her voice coming from right beside the guard. "I don't think it's such an egregious request. My chest is here, and so long as Maniple Sehravein is careful not to let anything blow overboard, if he wishes to peruse my underthings, I'm not terribly—"

"Sister, I am sad to say that shocks me not in the least!" Sister Ayayah says, turning on her.

"What is that supposed to mean?" Melena asks sharply.

The guard says, "I wasn't trying to go through anyone's underth—"

"I mean that you haven't exactly been shy about who you show your underthings, have you?" Sister Ayayah says. "But as for the rest—"

I hear the hearty sound of a slap.

Then silence. Shocked silence, I'd guess. I know what they're doing, and *I'm* shocked.

In fact, it wouldn't surprise me in the least if Melena has been nursing spite for Sister Ayayah and was seizing this opportunity to slap her with gusto.

"There's a name for women like you," Melena says icily, "but a lady only uses it when speaking with the Master of the Kennels."

I wish I could see the looks on everyone's faces at that.

Instead, my guts go cold as I watch a shark twice as long as I am tall go gliding by beneath me.

I have to get out of here. My arms and legs and abs are burning at the effort of holding myself suspended. My foot has gone numb from how it's jammed into a corner, and a drop of sweat is stinging my eyes.

"Easy—easy!" the guard says, raising his voice.

"I suppose you and your new friend here have something in common," Sister Ayayah says. "Both of you are willing to put your hands where they don't belong, and both of you will face the fullest punishment possible!"

"*I* didn't do anything," the guard protests. "I was simply told to—"

"Told to what?" Sister Prospaya demands. "To violate the Alitaeran Accords

and try to spark a war between the Chantry and Alitaera? Do you have any idea
how your superiors will take that?"

"I, I..."

"If Melena wishes to show her underthings and share her chest with you,
that's all well and good, but—" Sister Ayayah says.

"Sister!" Sister Prospaya interrupts. "Sisters! That is quite enough!"

But Sister Ayayah bulls on ahead. "But if you wish to take the fate of empires
in your hands, you'd better have a writ from the empress herself, laying out the
reasons for this outrageous violation of diplomatic norms, else I think you may
find your head and shoulders parting company as she learns what you've risked
already."

"Maybe I...maybe I overstepped," the guard says. "Sisters. Sister Melena.
Look! Here's your boat now."

"Thank the One God," one of the Sisters closer to me mutters.

"Thank them all," another says.

I hang my head as some of the tension knotted up in me eases. From my
position, I'm able to see the hull of a small boat approaching. At last.

Now all I have to do is climb out from under here, get on the Sisters' boat,
and worry about them betraying me while we're either still out at sea or shortly
after we land. My bet is they'll wait until I sleep—which means I'm not going
to sleep well for a long, long time.

But still, at least on land I'll have access to a lot more of my own strengths.
Out here, I'm totally alone, totally exposed, outnumbered and overwhelmed—
and I sure as hell can't swim to shore. Not with those things in the water.

I've been on the lookout constantly while the Sisters argued with the guard,
but now I take a moment to scan the sea more fully.

The seas still splash from time to time, mostly far away, as sharks or lotai
snatch the seabirds resting on the waves, but near me, I can't see any lotai. Nor
off in front of us. Nor off to either side. A ways back, I do still see a tail break
the surface momentarily, but that could be coincidence.

It's probably paranoia to think that the one lotai that nearly snagged me is
back there, waiting for me to make a mistake, right?

Some people say it's not paranoia if they really are out to get you. Durzo said
it's not paranoia if it keeps you alive.

Of course, Durzo had a lifetime of making powerful enemies. A very, very
long lifetime.

My arm trembles, and I balance on the other to shake the blood back into it.

Annoyingly, my guard friend hasn't left to go stand back at his post inside. One of the Sisters must have the same thought I do, because she asks him a question I can't hear. His tone is chastened. "Thought I'd help get your boat docked and all. Make up for the earlier, uh, misunderstanding," he says cheerfully. It's the cheerfulness of a man who hopes his empress doesn't lop off his head for nearly causing an international incident.

Go away, I think.

But whatever kind of magic I have, it's not the kind that works that way.

In fact, if there's something good that has an even chance of happening, I have the kind of magic where the other thing happens every time.

I scan the waves once more and see that now the lotai—if it's the same one—is only five paces back.

While I'm staring at it, suddenly the Chantry's boat thuds hard into the dock, jarring us.

The force of the collision nearly throws me into the water, wrenching my leg, scraping my ankle, and making me smack my head against the support, dazing me.

Voices call out above me as the boat is secured, but that's mere noise to me as I blink my eyes and shake my head, trying to recover. The lotai is closer now.

My eyes sting with sweat, but I latch back on, holding myself firm—and then, as I watch with horror, a drop of sweat rolls off my nose and drops toward the waves.

Flashing one hand out wildly, I catch my drop of sweat before it can touch the waves.

And then I breathe again. Maybe all that stuff about smelling the scent of fear at two leagues is simply lies and legends—but I don't want to find out the hard way.

"Thank you so much for your help, Maniple Sehravein," Melena says above me.

"I'll be happy to help load your things," the guard says nervously.

"No, no. Some of my Sisters...it'd just be an irritant to them. You do *not* want to give them any excuse to cause more trouble, believe me. They'll say you did something wrong if you don't go."

"Um," he says, then hesitates. "So, do you think I could ever see you again?"

She laughs, but sweetly. "Oh, believe me, if I can ever make the trip to Borami, I'll look you up. Promise."

"If you want to find me, you can—"

"Oh, I'll know how to find you," she says, lightly teasing.

"You will?" he asks, brightening.

"I'm a Sister of the Chantry," she says. "I have my ways."

I can't see if she kisses him, but the outline of her form leans close to his, and finally—finally!—he starts walking away.

That's when I see a single tiny ring of waves on the surface of the greater swells below and behind me.

What the—I'm not dripping sweat from my leg!

But then I see it isn't sweat. When the boat colliding with the dock made me scrape my ankle, I must've gotten a shallow cut.

I crane my head in time to see another drop of my blood hit the waves.

Swimming five paces back, as it reaches the spot where the first blood drop hit the waves, the lotai quivers as if hit by lightning.

Chapter Ninety-Two

An Amateur Pyrotechnician

I knew the lotai could move fast. I had no idea.

As I struggle to free my bloodied ankle, the creature disappears under the waves with the speed of an arrow leaping from a bowstring.

I catch the briefest glimpse of it streaking up through the haze of deep water before it shoots out of the waves at the very instant I throw my leg to one side.

The lotai thuds into the decking so hard it shakes the dock.

For a moment, there's total silence. I'm scanning the waves, hoping the beast's killed itself or knocked itself senseless—and scanning the dock above for handholds.

I've got to get out of here.

As the guard's voice above says, "What was that?" I see the lotai below me, shaking itself, coming out of a stupor.

Bringing the ka'kari to my hands and feet, I push on the circles in the skin of the hull that Jasmine Jakweth had tried to get me to see earlier.

They open quietly but not silently—not that I care now.

If the Sisters above are lying to cover for me, I don't hear it.

The lotai streaks upward again, breaking the waves at the spot where I was before, not jumping as high, snapping its oversized jaws in hungry circles, seeking. It snags teeth briefly on a girder. It tears the metal loose as its weight falls back into the waves.

It bounces out of the water again immediately, this time twisting in the air and stabbing little claws into the deck.

A part of me is shouting disbelief—it has little arms and legs that I never noticed? Its claws can pierce the deck that easily?

The rest of me is already fleeing. I've flipped over from my stomach-down position in order to better hold to the grips above me, and after the first two folded-open grips, I abandon all hopes of stealth and punch ka'kari claws through the skin of the hull above me.

With each puncture, magic flares weird orange and green around my hand.

I'm almost to the edge of the dock and its momentary safety when I feel the vast pressure of jaws crunching down on my foot, the lotai taking my whole foot into its throat.

The weight of the lotai almost tears me off the deck and into the waves. In the next moment, with my Talent surging through me, I throw all of the ka'kari that I can spare from the claws down into my leg. I pop it out in all directions—like armor, like a spiky exoskeleton.

"Oh, look there! What's that light?" I hear one of the Sisters say above me. "By the empress's boat!"

"What?!" the guard says. "Who cares? The hell is going on right—?"

Bellowing, I kick my foot up, lifting the lotai and impaling it against the underside of the dock. It's hissing and snarling like a dog savaging a bone, except the bone is my leg.

I shift and lengthen the spikes and kick again, and again, making the spikes into long blades. The lotai spatters wetly against the deck above us, red blood and green ichor hitting the waves in little fans beneath us. I kick it one more time and will the ka'kari to slide up the length of my leg—and thus the length of its open jaws—like a filleting knife.

The lotai's halves split and it falls off my leg into the waves, where immediately I hear thrashing and fighting.

I reach the edge of the deck and heave myself up, landing bloody face-to-face with the startled Maniple Sehravein.

He must have been lowering himself to his knees to see what was happening under the dock, because he's trying to rise, pushing against his planted spear for leverage to stand.

I slap a hand out, sweeping the butt of his spear off the dock.

Thrown off-balance, he staggers, steps to catch himself—but I lock one of his boots in place. Unable to take a step, he falls toward the dock. A quick kick with my healthy foot redirects him into the water.

Splashes of light hit my face as I sag onto my back. Pyrotechnics are bursting in the air—pyrotechnics that seem vaguely familiar.

I'm seized by many hands as the Sisters descend on me and pull me into their ranks. Their voices are down, but they're berating me, calling me every variety of fool and dolt and moron.

"Stay behind us!" Sister Prospaya whispers fiercely. "You may have gotten us all killed. Jakweth, is the man surfacing? Don't let him scream!"

I'm lying on the deck still—I don't know if I can stand—and despite all the Sisters talking, I can hear the sounds of water being threshed to foam and many lotai fighting over meat.

"He, uh, he won't be screaming," Jasmine says.

And then all sound fades from the water.

"Sister Viridiana may have saved us all," Sister Prospaya says.

"But she only meant to save *him*," Sister Ayayah says bitterly.

"Oh, you can read minds now?" Sister Prospaya snaps. "You grow more impressive by the minute, Sister. The rest of you, load our things! No, you four, you stay to shield Kylar."

"What'd she do?" I ask. I need to look at my foot, but it strikes me suddenly where I've seen those pyrotechnics before. Before the Battle of Black Barrow, Vi learned how to make bursting fireballs, which she taught some of the other Sisters.

She's using *those* as pyrotechnics? In front of the very empress whose Accords forbid war magic?

What the hell are you thinking, Vi?

Melena is one of the Sisters staying with me, and the only one even feigning a kind expression—maybe she isn't feigning it. Though I know I shouldn't trust her, she is the only one who keeps on showing me kindness. She says to me, "Viridiana's trying to distract everyone. People on the empress's dock were staring over here. Viridiana was with them. I think she saw Sehravein looking for you. She must've guessed you were about to do something dangerous."

"Something foolish," one of the others says.

"Foolish?" I ask. "Like I had any—"

"Like killing a guard in front of an audience, you damned brute," someone says. I don't know which one, but it doesn't matter. They all agree.

"Did it work, though? Why are we still here? Let's go!" I say. The Sisters' boat is docked. Almost all of their stuff is already on it, and tense faces I don't recognize have joined us.

"One of the storm ship's defenses against pirates and smugglers is to lock every boat that docks in place magically until it's cleared to leave," Sister Prospaya says, as the others grab the last few chests and pieces of luggage and take them aboard. "We're stuck, because only a guard can release us—you know, like the friendly guard you just *murdered*. Who had the key."

"So what about the other team's pickpocket?" I ask. "Surely she snagged it, right?"

"No, I didn't," a wide older brunette says, "because he was just about to use it to help us."

"So if the lock's magic," I say, "magic it."

They roll their eyes, as if I know nothing.

"We can do that," Melena says, "probably. If we can override any secondary defenses that may be in place to destroy us if we try such a thing. And even if we do that successfully, they'll know what we've done instantly, destroying any hope we had of leaving without pursuit. The whole point of the job was stealth, Kylar, something Viridiana said you knew something about."

"And it'll take time," says Jasmine Jakweth. He looks north. "Which we don't have much of. We're not far from the storm wall."

As the people on the empress's dock break into applause—Viridiana's light show is apparently finished—I follow Jasmine's gaze north. I'm not good at judging distances at sea, but not far away (a league? half that?), as abruptly as if someone had drawn a line in the sky, the clouds of flying birds simply end.

We're about to head back into the storm. The little escape boat we're boarding will have no chance out there.

"Get him aboard," Sister Prospaya says.

"Excuse me?" Sister Ayayah says.

"You heard me," Sister Prospaya says, staring hard at Sister Ayayah. Something about the way she says it tells me Sister Ayayah was hoping to abandon me here. "How badly are you injured, Kylar?"

Jasmine Jakweth curses. "You got bitten?" he asks. "How are you still talking? Those things have poison that can fell an iron bull. Least the little ones do. Maybe these big ones are different?"

"Now that you say it, I'm not feeling too great," I say.

"*Sister*," Sister Ayayah says to Prospaya, "this is our chance." To get rid of me, she all but says out loud.

"You should wait until my back is turned before you stab me in it," I say. "That's just plain common courtesy."

"Jasmine, carry him aboard. Sisters, screen him from sight," Constance says. "And clean his blood off the dock!"

"Jasmine, do not do any such thing," Sister Ayayah says.

"You know what you can kiss," Jasmine says to Sister Ayayah, and he puts his hands under my armpits and drags me onto the boat behind the screen of Sisters' bodies, so that no one from the empress's dock might see us.

It's only when I get aboard that I dare look at my foot.

"I'm a Healer. May I help you?" one of the Sisters asks. She's middle-aged, with short spiky hair, many facial piercings, and the reassuring air of a woman who's seen death and mayhem and stood unshaken.

"Not at first," I say. I look—

—and try to keep a straight face at the mess of blood and lacerated tendons and little bones of my foot sticking out as if to mimic a porcupine. A porcupine slathered with puke green poison.

"Ah, not so bad," I say.

"You just went white as death. So we both know that's bravado. If it helps your ego, consider me impressed. Will you let me help now?" the woman asks.

"Yes," I say. "Are you going to need to use any more magic today?"

"Quite a lot, I should think," she says. "All of it on you."

"But other than on me, I mean," I say. I'm feeling woozy, though I know my body is fighting off the lotai's poison on its own without any direction.

She answers, but I lose whatever it is she says.

I say, "Put whatever you're willing to use on me into a ball, hold it here. Don't form a direct connection to me or I might take too much and hurt you."

She responds with the admirable haste I've come to expect from experienced Healers and veteran soldiers. It's the obedience that says, 'I don't know why you need this, but I trust that you need it right now, so here it is.'

In an instant, the ka'kari sucks her magic into itself, and my body or the ka'kari or my magic or all of them together begin knitting me back together. What the Healer could offer wasn't much magic as I measure such things, so I don't blot out the pain—relying on my body's natural shock to shield me as my magic snaps bones back into place and stitches tendons back to the appropriate muscles and bones.

But the magic interferes with the shock, so I feel everything. I'm gasping and whimpering, nothing of bravado left.

The poison makes it feel as if I'm fighting something every step of the way.

In a few moments, I'm out of magic, having used all the Sister offered and as much of my own as I dare.

It's enough to knit the bones and sinews together, but not enough to regrow all the savaged skin. I didn't get to choose what was fixed; I'm at my body's and my magic's mercy. I can only hope it's done enough of the right things.

"Bandages, please," I croak.

The stunned Healer closes her mouth, slathers a salve on my leg, and quickly bandages my wound. She is barely finished when Jasmine bursts in. "Hide! Hide yourself, Kylar. They've sent a team to search the boat."

"The chest!" I say.

"Hidden. We had an exigency plan for just this. Don't worry. Can you keep yourself out of sight?"

I'm feeling depleted, but I nod. Standing slowly and then stepping gingerly on my imperfectly Healed foot, I draw the shadows about me in front of the again-baffled Healer, who pauses momentarily in her wiping up of my blood from the deck.

It's not a large boat. As I make my way from the cabin to the small hold, I see an officious-looking little man coming down the half flight of stairs. He looks around briefly and barks to the Healer, "What's this? Where'd this blood come from?"

I hear the Healer say dryly, "Bloody nose earlier. We didn't have any clean rags handy, so I used the Sisters' menstrual rags. You wish to inspect them?"

The official recoils with revulsion. "Just get out of the way!"

I move deeper into the little hold, perching by some cargo netting by one of its open portholes.

I'm surprised to see that the empress's boat hasn't cast off yet, either.

I hope that fact isn't connected to what's happening here. My throat suddenly feels dry.

The official comes in and pokes around, opening boxes here and there, but there's something false and perfunctory about his motions. I get a sick feeling in my stomach. This is not the random search of a port authority. Nor is it the determined, methodical search of someone certain we're hiding something but doesn't know where.

He pokes around a bit more, then goes to the farthest point forward in the hull, moves some boxes, and confronts the blank wall. Looking quickly over his shoulder as if to confirm no one is watching, he twists a cargo-net hook, digs under a board near his feet, and lifts it.

It clicks, and a section of the blank wall pops open.

A small white chest is in there.

He chuckles triumphantly, and my heart drops.

Still chuckling under his breath as if he's so, so clever, the officious little bastard carries the chest out of the hold. Do I kill him now?

Despairing, I shoot a glance out the porthole again. There's a man standing on the empress's dock, looking out this way as if waiting for a signal. Any violence I do will be seen. My mind spins.

It all *is* connected. The empress has a spy—either among the Sisters here or among those on land who sent the rescue boat to us. *Someone* told her people the location of that hidden compartment, and she's waiting to leave until she gets a signal from her official.

What can I do?

I follow, hobbling, shadowed, all my plans in shambles.

How many guards are with him? What happens if he doesn't give the right signal?

I come out toward the dock where the Sisters have gathered. Some are holding each other. Caught in the act of espionage, they'll lose their immunity and probably be executed—and they can only make things worse. If they attack, whether they escape or fail to, they'll have perpetrated an act of war.

Then I see that more defenses appeared from the hull of the storm ship. Two ballistae are aimed at the little boat, along with two smaller harpoon launchers with long coils of rope to haul us back if we get away. A dozen archers in imperial garb stand shielded at murder slits. Several mages back them up.

We've been set up. But how?

Maybe I can't know how—because the Sisters never let me know enough of their plan for me to know what its weaknesses were. I have no idea which parts of it failed.

It failed, and that's enough.

We should've known it failed as soon as Queen Gyre showed up at my room, but we pushed on anyway. This is on us.

As the self-satisfied little man sets the white chest on the dock, I stay back in the boat. Surely there must be a dozen mages covering the boat beyond what I've already seen. No one is going to try to stop all these Sisters without many magic-users of their own. If I go out there, whether visible or invisible, I'll be seen.

It's hard to breathe. Every plan I think up is more terrible than the last.

The moment I try any hostile action, this arrest will turn into a battle. And for all their excellence in covert actions, these Sisters aren't ready for that. They're not battle mages. That's the whole point of the Alitaeran Accords, and indeed, these women believe it's better for them to sacrifice their lives than to start a war.

Which means if things go sideways, they'll be no help to me.

More sideways, that is.

"Would one of you like to open these for me, or shall I smash them open?" the little cretin says. He's so oily in his triumph, I'd be happy to gut him without looking in his eyes to see if he deserves it.

He deserves it enough.

I see now—barely—that he has both of the small, matching chests on the dock in front of him. I wasn't paying enough attention to see which is which, but it's not going to matter. Sister Prospaya steps forward to open one, and everyone leans forward, blocking my view.

A moment later, everyone sinks back, disappointed.

"Now the other one," the official says, annoyed.

Again, everyone holds their breath and leans forward for a look, as if no one's seen a baby before.

But then a ripple passes through the Sisters and the soldiers facing them.

Everyone sinks back, not a few of them bewildered.

"Where is it?" I hear the man shout.

I see clothes fly into the air as he digs through the chest. He shakes it upside down, kicks at the clothes at his feet, roars—and throws the chest into the sea. Then he tears into the other one. He pulls out a dagger and attacks it, looking for a false bottom. He shakes this one upside down, too, shouting, and throws it into the sea as well.

The soldiers are stony-faced, as if by standing at attention, they might avoid his attention. The Sisters had all sunk back, certain of their doom.

Now some have recovered.

But I haven't. The baby. Where's the baby?

"Does milord wish to throw any more of our personal items into the sea?" Sister Prospaya says coolly. "Or may we go now?"

There's a shout from the empress's dock, a demand.

"A moment! A moment!" the official says. He shoves his way back onto the boat at a run, pushing past Sisters roughly. I barely dart out of the way in time,

I'm still so stunned. In a moment, I hear him slamming things around in the hold, now searching desperately.

But he comes out quickly, literally baring his teeth at the Sisters as if he might bite them. "You . . . you witches won't get away with this!"

He calms himself and straightens his flyaway hair before stepping out onto the dock. As if unperturbed, he raises his arms to the lookout on the empress's dock and crosses his arms: *nothing here.*

The lookout shouts a question I can't make out.

The official turns purple with fury and merely repeats his sign. He turns away. "Sisters. I see . . ." His face looks as if he's trying to swallow his hat. "I see that a tremendous mistake has been made. You will be given recompense for any of your belongings accidentally lost in this . . . in this perfectly legal and ordinary search of your vessel."

"Oh, we'll be in touch, I promise you that," Sister Prospaya says icily. "Now may we go? The storm is nearly upon us."

"Yes, yes, you're free to go."

The man gestures an angry dismissal to his people, and the guards rapidly melt back into the ship; the defensive engines are abandoned and quickly begin folding back flush into the hull. On the empress's dock, I see the lookout finishing a conversation with the dockmaster there, who signals his soldiers to throw off the mooring ropes. Soldiers and sailors and servants in white are scurrying around behind him, finishing the last-second preparations for the empress's emergency journey to land.

As the last of the soldiers leaves our dock, I hear a loud sigh of magic releasing our boat, and the unmistakable rock of separation, though there are still a few ropes holding us to the dock.

"Hold," Sister Prospaya says. All the Sisters are looking at her. All the soldiers are gone, and even I can't see any stragglers watching us secretly. "Excellent work, whoever did it. You can tell me *how* you did it later. But for now, Sisters, is the cargo safe?"

The Sisters all look at each other. Back and forth, as if mystified, but as if sure that one of their number is only pretending.

"Sisters, we have only moments," she says tensely. Her words come out clipped. *"Is the cargo safe?"*

No one answers.

"Sisters . . ." she says, her voice dipping dangerously. "Where is the child?"

Chapter Ninety-Three

These Leaps Go Well

I swear I did every part of my task flawlessly!" the pickpocket brunette from the other team says.

"As did I!" another I don't recognize says.

"And I!"

No one's to blame. No one ever is.

"The nursemaids wouldn't have dared betray us," Sister Melena says. "Bribed, and blackmailed, and offered immediate sanctuary the instant we—"

"Shut up! All of you shut up!" Sister Prospaya says. "I demand each of you—this moment!—look me in the eye and swear, swear on Seraph and all your loyalty to the Chantry you have no idea where the child is!"

"I do so swear," says Melena, without hesitation, looking her in the eye.

A chorus of the same words rises from the others. Every face has a meretrix's easy innocence. But Sister Prospaya is having none of it. She shushes them and points at each in turn, demanding they say it directly to her as she looks them in the eye.

Perhaps she realizes the same thing I did—there is some traitor here, or some spy who somehow revealed this boat's secret hiding place to the imperial forces, else how would that official know exactly where to look?

Or perhaps it's all mummery, a show for me alone. Maybe this is the betrayal.

My heart leaden, I turn away rather than watch every Sister's oath. Could I even tell if they lied? Maybe someday after I've held the ka'kari a few centuries, but not today.

I stare over to the empress's boat. On the dock, I see the back of a tall man's head. It could be King Repha'im.

How did you do it, you monster? How did you beat us?

Or was this not his work, but merely the Sisters' incompetence?

Then I see the empress herself step to the edge of the boat. Even from here, she's unmistakable. The man I guess is Repha'im steps forward and servants in white part for him, a rotund woman with red crisscrossing lapels moving gingerly past so as not to be knocked into the waves as the royals embrace—for it is Repha'im indeed, saying goodbye to his queen, his quarry, with a kiss.

He's beaten me. All the hate in my heart is impotent. I can do nothing. Unless...

I whirl, stepping back in among the Sisters before dropping my invisibility.

The babbling Sisters fall silent. "This was the plan all along, wasn't it?" I say, stepping toward Sister Ayayah. "This is where you betray me, isn't it?"

"Easy, Night Angel," Jasmine Jakweth says. He's holding a short blade but doesn't look like he wants to use it. Beside him is a similarly armed brick of a woman, who looks like she does. She must be the other team's muscle.

"Where's the bait?" I say. "What's the last-moment lead that gets me off this boat? What's the plan to get rid of me now? Misdirection first, murder as a last resort, am I right?"

"You're out of line, Kylar," Sister Ayayah says. "It was you who brought us empty chests. It was your failure—if not your betrayal of us."

"My betrayal?" I say. "What would *I* gain by getting off the storm ship without the child?"

"Kylar, Sisters," Melena says. "We approach the storm. We have to go. All of us, Kylar. There's no betrayal here. Only failure. It happens. Even to the best."

It seems to me we're yet minutes away from reentering the storm, but then, I don't know how much leeway we need to give the little boat to escape the currents and the seas on our way to shore.

"Kylar!" Sister Prospaya barks before Sister Ayayah can say anything else. "We have no quarrel with you. Something went wrong. Clearly Queen Gyre thought she was bringing you the child, but she was mistaken. We have no way of finding out *what* went wrong right now. I don't think you tried to mislead us—no, Sisters, he's right. It makes no sense. We've failed. All of us. Accept it and move on. We need to leave now or die. *We* are leaving now. You're welcome to come with us. You're welcome to stay, though I'm afraid every soul on the *Storm Racer* is now doomed. The child's Talents may awaken at any moment, and when it does..."

"Come or go, but move," Sister Ayayah snarls, and pushes past us to go belowdecks.

The rest of the Sisters begin to disperse. Jasmine goes to a mooring rope, shaking his head sadly at me.

Sister Melena stays. "Kylar," she says gently, "come with us. Perhaps this isn't the end, but it's the end here. We might get lucky. Maybe we're wrong and the child's Talent won't awaken until after they dock, and we'll be able to take up the chase in Borami. And if the worst happens to the *Storm Racer*, there's still the other child who needs to be saved. By the time we return, the Chantry will have turned up other leads."

"Oh, and I'm sure you'll share those with me, right?" I say bitterly.

"Of course I'll share—" She breaks off and looks at Sister Prospaya, who still stands nearby. She shakes her head. It seems the woman's honest.

"I'll share whatever I'm allowed to," Melena says sorrowfully. "But—but you have other friends, right? Other sources of information who can help you."

Sure, won't that be fantastic for the Chantry? I land on the southernmost point of the continent and have to travel all the way north before I can even get a new lead from Momma K, and then likely have to ride all the way back to Borami or Friaku or Ladesh or wherever the hell the second child has been taken. If we even know.

"It doesn't make sense that the empress outwitted us. Or even King Repha'im," I say. "Why send a man to search our boat if they already knew they had us beaten? Why give away that they have a spy in your ranks when there's no payoff?"

"They don't have a spy in—"

"Oh, come off it! Repha'im doesn't give something for nothing, and I don't think the empress does either. What's the play where what they just did makes sense?" I hesitate. I'm assuming they're perfectly united. With the empress disembarking and Repha'im staying, maybe they're working against each other. Not that it helps me.

"Kylar, we're casting off now," Jasmine Jakweth says. "You good?"

What am I going to tell Logan? What am I going to tell Momma K?

I feel the blood draining from my face.

Momma K.

What did I just see, moments ago, as the empress stepped to the edge of her boat?

Quick, quick! Tell me!

~'The man I guess is Repha'im steps forward and servants in white part for him, a rotund woman with red crisscrossing lapels moving gingerly past so as not to be knocked into the waves as the royals kiss...' That enough?~

'Red crisscrossing lapels'? Did I use that phrase before? Or hear it?

~No. You never used those words in that order any other time. 'Red' appears many times. 'Crisscrossing' only twice, and the other time referred to metal supports——~

Sister Ayayah! What'd she say about my contact for the job?

~'She'll be in servants' white with red stripes on the shoulder and front with the crossed lapels of the imperial nursemaids.'~

Why's a nursemaid getting *off* the empress's boat at the last moment?

You've got to be laughing at me as you're hearing this, huh?

I think I even said *What am I forgetting?* at one point. Right now, you're probably thinking, 'That moron. Is Kylar seriously asking who else might be on the storm ship trying to get the child? Is there *anyone else* out there who might have shown herself to be clever enough to get into places even Kylar couldn't? Someone in white with crossed red lapels, maybe? Ooh, tough one, I dunno...maybe the person Kylar started this whole job with? Maybe the person he traveled with? Surely Kylar won't forget *her*!'

But I did. *Phaena.*

That 'rotund' woman was Phaena. She didn't merely infiltrate Repha'im's staff; she infiltrated the *nursemaids.* She'd become part of the very group that the Sisters then tried to bribe and blackmail. Gods! While I fought and climbed and hid and snuck and deceived my way from the ass end of the ship one guard post at a time, Phaena had been with the child the whole time.

Had the Sisters' plot failed *because* Phaena was there?

The empress's boat pushes off from her dock, but a moment later, I hear someone over there shout.

We all look up, shot through with fear, but no one is looking our way. Their gazes are turned inward, toward the storm ship.

Lights flash on the empress's dock, and now the whole dock begins to rise to fold flush with the storm ship once more.

"What'd they shout?" I ask. "Did anyone catch it?"

"'Stop that...' I didn't catch the rest," a Sister says, shaking her head.

"Kylar, we have to go. Now!" Jasmine says.

"Was it 'Stop that woman'?" I ask, horrified.

"Yes, yes, I think that maybe was it. Why?"

Why would Phaena look fat? She's not fat. When I saw her at the grand salon, her disguise wasn't as a fat woman. And if she didn't want to leave with the empress, why would she get on the empress's boat only to get off at the very last moment?

Maybe she was helping them pack?

But then it hits me like a slap in the face, even as my own boat slips away from the dock, that the answer to all my questions is the same. Why would Phaena take such a huge risk? Why would she look *rotund*? My stomach drops. Why risk blowing her cover at exactly this moment? A hot-cold shiver crosses my skin.

Because she grabbed my son. She stole him at the last possible moment from the empress, hoping the empress's boat would depart without noticing that their second-most-precious cargo was no longer aboard. And she almost succeeded.

It's the worst thing in the world she could've done.

I leap from the deck of our boat onto the dock. Even as I land, lights begin to flash on our dock as they did on the empress's dock. In moments it will begin to rise and fold flush into the storm ship.

"Kylar, what are you doing?" Jasmine shouts.

"Kylar, come back!" Melena says.

Heists always fail, I'd told the Sisters, because you never foresee all the players. "Keep the boat here. I'll be back in a few minutes," I shout over my shoulder.

"What? Why?" Jasmine says.

"Keep it here!" I shoot a look at the storm looming ahead. "Give me three minutes!"

"We can't stay! We're leaving!" Sister Prospaya shouts, and indeed the boat is already farther away from the ship. As soon as the dock folds shut, there will be nowhere for them to dock even if they wanted to.

I don't waste the time answering. My decision's been made. I run inside.

Chapter Ninety-Four

To Stop a Scream

The hammerblows of my heart aren't enough to drown out my thoughts. My body may dodge around passengers unaware as I sprint through the passageways, but I can't dodge the truth. There is no world in which this ends well. I run toward doom.

There's no way off the storm ship. Even if I snatch up the child, I can't save him. Can't save Phaena. Can't save myself. How do I get away? *Swim?*

I've seen what's in the water. Those things would be death to me even if I were alone. Swimming with Phaena and a child?

No. I know how this goes now. Whether or not I can save Phaena or the child momentarily, the child's Talent will awaken, the storm ship's magic will fail, and everyone aboard will die. Including Vi. Including me.

Can the ka'kari bring me back from death if I've been devoured by a hundred fish?

~I can't answer that.~

I wasn't asking. I know there are ways even my immortality must fail. Beheading, or fire, or certain magical weapons—and I assume that being crapped out the back ends of several thousand fish will give even my magic some pause as to which bit of crap to start trying to rebuild me from.

I can't bear to think anymore. I need the clarity of a fight. The calm of chaos. The anti-introspective balm of battle.

My invisibility costs magic, so I drop it. I have little enough remaining. My body used most of my reserves in Healing my foot, and in the artificial indoor light, my glore vyrden will be slow to refill.

Reaching a locked staff door, I lash out, heel-kick right next to the knob.

Wood splinters, the metal latch tears free, and the door bursts open. But I stagger.

Like an idiot, I kicked the door with my recently mangled foot. I hobble, feeling fresh fire rush up my leg. I lean against a wall, pulling up the leg of my trousers and grabbing my ankle. No fresh breaks, but the skin is raw, every nerve angry. I turn my foot in pained circles. It hurts, but it still moves. There's nothing for it. I put my weight on it gingerly, and it supports me.

Walling off the pain as well as I can, I push on. Within a few steps, I start jogging, and then running again, roaring against the pain.

I run past a circle of cleaning staff, their mouths agape. None armed. I sprint through the next area before any of them even thinks to yell. In some sort of laundry, I leap over baskets, charge past the baffled faces. None a threat. A giant of a man, slack-jowled, stupid, stands in my path, hands stretched to stop me.

Arm, head, belly? Which do I slash? No no no.

Running straight at him without slowing, I wait for the flinch at the last moment to see which way he moves, then slide under his still-outstretched hands, the ka'kari turning into hard skids at the three points of contact with the floor, helping me slide. He lifts a foot so I don't sweep it out from under him, but I push his knee up even higher as I pass him, flinging him off-balance.

Then I plant my left foot—not my right this time—and skid up to my feet. I keep running.

Bursting out from the staff areas, I head up, and up, until I see an imperial soldier running ahead of me. Imperials will be the ones hunting Phaena. They'll be going the right way. Or at least they're more likely to know the right way than I currently do.

But the man I see turns up a stair guarded by two regulars, who see me a moment later. I recognize them—it's those brothers.

"Hey!" I say, as I jog toward them. "I know you two! You're brothers, right? Nice to see you, Mat." I mumble his name a bit, in case I've got it wrong.

"Don't think I recognize you," the slender one says, head tilting.

I'm in their kill zone now.

"No, no, I'm not surprised. I don't think you saw me at all. It was down by the engine room. Practically stepped on me. Anyway, thought you two seemed real close."

"Close?" Mat says with mock disgust. "With this guy?" He's clearly one of those guys who doesn't have a mean bone in his body.

"When did you say this was?" the first brother asks.

What am I doing? I need to kill these men. Incapacitate them at least. After I survived my brush with these men and their squad when I first got on this ship, I wanted to kill them for having something I'd never have—and now, with every excuse to do it, I won't?

"In the hall," I say, quieter. "You walked past me. I was glad not to kill you."

"Glad not to what?" Mat says, not even offended yet.

I tsk, as if remembering something. "Oh, right, you might not recognize me. Different outfit. I looked like this."

I go invisible.

The brothers look at each other. One's mouth drops open. The other's knuckles go white on his spear.

"Did...? We didn't just see that, did we?" the slender older brother asks.

There's a moment.

"See what?" Mat asks.

Carefully, I step between them and head up the stairs silently. Why'd I do that? Why did I waste the time being human?

I get up the stairs, go visible again to save magic, and make a guess at the direction: deeper in, farther forward, surely.

Two halls later, I see I guessed right.

I overtake an imperial and club him with a forearm as we pass nobles at gaming tables. The nobles gasp, but they're unarmed, frightened, don't matter. I've already caught sight of my next target, the next link in the chain of my victims.

None of them matter, I realize.

If I don't figure out a way to get the child and get him off this ship, literally everyone here is dead. I needn't hold back now. Anyone I kill is already dead.

Unless I figure a way out.

I'm Kylar Stern. I'm the Night Angel. I'm the one who finds the third way. I'll find the way out. I always have. It'll be hiding somewhere, but I'll find it.

The next knot of soldiers, six of them, lumbers along in two lines with all the care of stampeding water buffalo. They don't bother to watch their backs, so they don't see me. I think about drawing the blue dagger I pickpocketed from Vi, but I don't know what its magic does, so instead, drawing the ka'kari sharp along the blade of my hand, I chop a soldier's neck and snatch the short spear from his hand.

Lunging forward with that spear, I ram it through the man before him—and with a surge of Talent, lift him, skewered, into the next man in front of him.

That takes out all three men on the right, and my lunge pulls me past one man lined up on the left.

My slash misses his neck as he staggers aside at the sight, but I catch the neckline of his gambeson with my fingertips.

I fling him hard into the wall atop his dying comrades.

One of the last two tries to turn too fast and catches the butt of his short spear on the wall behind him.

Ruthless, relentless attack. Your enemies' fear will cover your mistakes.

I launch into the man, pinning him to the wall with a forearm strike to his neck. Knife hand spears his guts half a dozen times before he can cry out as I drop his still-dying carcass.

His friend, the last of them, flees.

I fling the blood from my hand as I withdraw the ka'kari. The point of the short spear sticks out of the chests of the two pinned soldiers to my right, the one in front still gasping for air. Faster to grab that one.

Seizing the skewer behind its head, I pull it all the way through his body, then hop a quick sideways step, and hurl the spear like a javelin.

A noblewoman steps into the hall between me and my target even as the bloody spear leaves my hand.

As the spear flies past, she startles backward, hands going up to her nose. Down the hall, the spear stabs into the fleeing soldier's butt. His leg gives out midstep and he careens into the wall. The woman starts keening.

I run past her. No threat. Her bloody hands hide how badly the spear injured her.

Doesn't matter. They're all dead anyway.

In an instant, I'm on top of the soldier. Good-looking kid. Imperial guard, at not yet twenty. Either he was connected or he was really good at his job.

"Where are you heading?" I ask. "You live if you tell me."

Propped against the wall, he half-swords to a Bastard Cross, a good choice given his wound. His hands tremble. He looks ashamed of his trembling and his earlier flight.

"The trembling's shock from your wound, not cowardice," I tell him. "No shame in it."

He doesn't answer me, fixated, either brave, or shocked, or stupid.

I have no time for any of them. A *figuri* disarm puts several of his fingers on the floor and his blade in my hands. I kill him with it.

A scream from behind me makes me spin on my heel. It's the woman I injured. A noblewoman, richly dressed. She's *rushing* me. Furious, screaming, blood pouring down from a light wound to her nose.

I strangle my immediate instinct to kill her. What am I?

But I can't let her grab me. Someone else might attack, and I can't afford an encumbrance.

Plus, gods is that scream annoying.

And she's slow.

She runs at me, arms flailing. I wait. Wait, and then I flick out a stop kick. Quick and light, with the ball of the foot, usually used to—well, obviously—stop other people's kicks, stopping their foot before they can raise it. But I stab my stop kick out and up, leaning my upper body way back, catching her in the center just below where her ribs come together as she runs into me.

I absorb most of the shock so as not to snap any bones, but still her breath whooshes out as she lifts into the air, forward momentum stopped as if running into a brick Night Angel.

She collapses, wind gone, choking fit to puke. She'll be gasping in a moment. But for now she's quiet, and no more threat. And though I'm sure she feels like she is, she's not dying.

At least, not any faster than the rest of us on this doomed ship.

Her friends appear back at the intersection where she appeared. Confused. Aghast. Useless people. When we die, the empire will be losing its richest people, but maybe not its brightest.

I'm already running. Reach another intersection, see a running imperial ahead of me, disappearing around another corner.

An intuition tickles my mind, and I pull the ka'kari to my skin, go invisible. I've always been a quiet runner, but I double my efforts, slow as I approach an atrium.

"Barzdun, take us a peek," a man whispers.

There's a pause as I draw closer.

"Barz, do it or I'll rip your sack off," he whispers.

An ambush. Naturally. There's no need for me to engage with it at all. I could walk right past. Which is what I'm going to—

A man pokes half his head around the corner, and his one exposed eye goes wide. Despite my invisibility, he sees me.

Because Barzdun's a mage.

A ka'kari punch-dagger to the forehead drops him, and then I tear through the three others. It's not a fair fight, but at least it's quick. None of them suffer.

Well. Except for Barzdun. He's still alive somehow.

The Devourer can be nearly frictionless as it cuts through flesh when it's hungry, and Barzdun fell off the punch-dagger blade before I could twist it around in his forehead and pith him.

He's twitching and foaming, and magic arcs around the wound in his forehead, as if he's hopelessly trying to Heal himself. I move to kill him.

Pause.

I dip the ka'kari into the magic sizzling around Barzdun's wound. It pulsates in many colors until it finds whatever it needs to home in on magic. And then it slurps it up, like a dog lapping up a pool of blood after a battle.

"Hurry up," I say. Barzdun is still twitching. Not the kind of twitching the dead sometimes do. He's doing the awful kind that means he's still alive. Poor bugger.

The ka'kari bleeds him dry of magic, and then I quickly open his carotid to bring the end. It still feels dirty, leaving a man writhing in pain to take his power. But I've done worse. Probably will again.

I hear a shout, first muffled by a door, and then louder. Going around the corner, I see the great double doors leading to Elysion. I had no idea I'd made it so far forward. Through it, I see soldiers mustering.

Instead of rushing right in—done enough of that today—I stop myself. I look back at the soldiers I've just killed. Then at their clothing.

~A disguise? What could possibly go wrong with that?~

You know, I hate it when you do that. Whenever you ask that question, we find out the answer.

Chapter Ninety-Five

The Eldest of Betrayers, Hope

Cut this.

~This? What do you mean?~

All this next part. Cut all of it. Skip ahead. It's all wrong. Everything I thought was wrong, and anyone who listens to it will think the wrong things too. It's all lies.

~I wasn't aware of you being dishonest here.~

You're a thing of magic. A subcreation. Your maker must not have taught you that lies can be told honestly, and yet be lies.

~That doesn't make sense.~

You can't understand? No, maybe you can't.

Look. When people learn what I do, they assume I have some peculiar wisdom. They think one who works with death must gain unique insight into the land beyond the veil. They don't know—they don't understand that I am the worst man to learn anything about death from. I am the least of beggars. I'm not Death's chamberlain, his confidant, or his counselor. I'm Death's usher, at best the keeper of the keys to his outermost gate.

I push men and women—yes, and children too!—through that gate, but then I leave. I leave! Worse, because I'm immortal, I know less of Death than any pimple-faced teen on the day he first awakens to the fact that someday he won't draw breath ever again, that his wife will awaken one day to his clammy cold corpse beside her. I know not the fear of the precipice when I stand at its edge. I know not the curse of time or shouting that the days are not enough for the path I finally know I wish to tread. I know not Death, and thus everything I once knew of humanity is fading from my mind with every passing day.

*So erase it all, I beg you. The pleasures of my strength are obscenities to me.
I killed and killed, and I loved it, and every detail in this record is only a further
lie. Please, skip all that. Give them a line or two of summary, and start the tale
again when I reached the foredeck. I don't have the strength to go through it
line by line myself. I can't bear to read my cursed words again. My folly.*

Cut from 'When I step onto the killing field' *to... where is it? Maybe to* 'I
don't want to fight Vi.'

~As you wish.~

Vi looked at the next lines, confused. She'd been reading intently, barely able
to catch her breath, for she knew nothing of what had happened in this part.
But here?

The next line did indeed start with 'When I step onto the killing field,' but
then the page continued on. There was no reference next to not wanting to fight
Vi or anything like that. What Kylar had ordered to be cut...hadn't been cut.

What did that mean?

First, she supposed, it meant Kylar's instructions to purge those lines were
from later—after the fight. Kylar must have come back at some point to edit
these words, if only briefly. Had he met his end before his commanded edits
could be finished, or did the ka'kari disobey him? Or had Kylar later still
changed his mind again and decided to leave it all in?

She looked out the window to the darkening sky, but she couldn't wrestle
with such questions now; her mind was firmly with Kylar, trapped on the *Storm
Racer.* She turned back to the book.

When I step onto the killing field, there's a wave of feelings that usually overtakes me: fear and excitement, a potent mixture of disgust at what is about to be
and secret eagerness for it. Perhaps that makes you think I'm sick, broken. I am
both those things, but not as much as you hope in this, I think. The eagerness
isn't—usually—an eagerness to spill blood. It isn't the eagerness to see fear or
to watch the horror in a man's face as he realizes he's dying, and sometimes
worse than dying, that he's dying as a coward, weeping, and not the hero he
always told himself he'd be.

For me, that part brings the revulsion. Usually. Though I confess I've killed men I was glad to see die badly, men who—to use a phrase one ought to use sparingly and with the greatest care—needed killing.

My eagerness comes instead from the chance to test myself: to see how my many hours and many years of practice align with reality. One may be felled in battle by a random arrow or a foolish ally accidentally riding over you. A thousand things can happen to blot out all the advantages of your superior skill. But superior skill still most often prevails. All the training is for something.

This is that something. The chest tightens, the heart pounds. At the prospect of death, I can't help but feel the sweetness of every moment. Usually.

But not today.

My heart is leaden. Wearing a stolen soldier's tunic, carrying a stolen spear, donning a stolen conical helm with a nosepiece, I jog into the faux neighborhood where so many other soldiers are gathering.

What does it matter if I stop them from finding Phaena? She's dead anyway. I'm dead.

There is no winning here. There's no slim chance at the one solution by which I walk out of here with everything I desire, victorious.

I move like a man in a fog, jogging because other soldiers are jogging to the opulent faux town square, where a commander on a third-floor balcony is assigning platoons to search grids. I should be focusing, but I feel in a daze. I said myself once that I'm immortal, not invincible. How could I forget it? A few improbable victories made me believe I was always going to be the man who found the third way? Did I really think that I could do any job at all, that the impossible isn't really impossible for me?

I'm just that special?

Yes. I think I did believe it: Things have to work out, because I'm me. How could I—coming from what I came from, learning everything from whom I learned it—how could *I* fall into such an obvious trap?

A thought strikes me though: It's true that there's no winning here, but there are worse ways to lose. Intolerable ways.

Which must mean there are better ways to lose, too, right?

Phaena deserves better than to get killed for trying to return that boy to Logan and Jenine, and if all I can do is delay her death by a few days, then that's what I'm going to do.

What's your plan, Phaena? You're smart. Surely you thought beyond *get the child*. How do I find you before all these men do? Where would you think you could hide a child until the ship docked in Borami? What did you hope would happen once it did?

Though now that I think of it, you probably didn't know that the empress had decided to get off the ship at Cloud Point. That must've scrambled all your plans. And then the Sisters tried to snatch the baby—or Jenine had. Or both had.

Strolling off the empress's boat with a baby strapped to your belly and hoping that no one would notice might seem foolhardy—but it surely wasn't Phaena's first plan, but one of the backups. Backup plans are by definition the worse plans or they'd be the first plan.

And throughout, she must've hoped that I would be showing up soon to help her. And I never had.

Are you cowering in a room somewhere, Phaena, all out of ideas?

I'm out of ideas too. We're doomed. We're going to lose. But if I'm going to lose, I'm going to lose fighting for the people I care about.

I move through the soldiers gathered in the square. They don't stand in ranks but rather in bunches: These aren't the elites.

If she's cowering somewhere, it's only a matter of time until they find her. She knows I'm on the ship, but will that change what she does?

Phaena's not the type of woman to wait for a rescue; I saw that from the first time we met. She's the type to try to defy the odds with desperate action rather than passively accept the brutality of bad men. I saw that the first time we met, too, and I've just seen it again.

I'd hoped all these soldiers would give me a clear direction. Maybe that it would then turn into a foot race between me and some ironfoot clods. Looking up at the bickering officers on the balcony above us, it seems clear to me instead that they have no idea where Phaena is, either. Which means their next step is a broad effort to search the entire ship—which they did so unsuccessfully for me.

A race against a thousand men I might win. A search against a thousand men? No chance.

Around the square, in the other buildings, I can see nobles gathering once more to their amusements: The soldiers milling about below them seem to be the best entertainment going. The officers have commandeered only this one building and the square; elsewhere nobles are standing at their own balconies being served food and drinks, even listening to chamber music.

If you can't do what you want to do, at least make sure your enemy can't do what he wants to do.

"'Ey," I say to a soldier near me. "Where's the second-in-command?"

"Up there, ain't 'e?" the man says, motioning to the balcony.

"And the third?"

"In command?"

"Am I using too many big words?" I snap.

"No needa get crinkled. They's all up there, what?"

"'Pologies," I say. "Hate waiting to see what piss comes down from on high and have 'em tell me it's rain, eh?"

"If that makes ya sore, you're in the wrong job, ain'tcha? They shore is high enough to make it, uh, *rain*, though, eh?" He grins a broken-toothed grin and slaps one of the great wooden stilts holding up the elaborate balconies above. I immediately like the man.

My own answering smile fades. I hope I don't have to kill him.

I head inside the building. The main floor is empty, but there are stairs leading down to the kitchens. Confusion's always helpful for an escape, so I poke my head down and say, "Hey, all you! Commander says you got one minute to get out. Out unless you wanta die."

The men there blanch, but before they can shoot questions at me, I say, "And go out the back!"

Returning to the main floor, I pause before I go up the stairs to where all the officers are.

I'd planned to go upstairs and kill them all. If I can't speed up my own search, at least I can slow down theirs. It's a rare opportunity that you can wipe out an entire officer corps.

But maybe I can do better than that.

I head back out front and lean against one of the great wooden stilts. I put my hand on it. Like everything else on this ship, the architecture is showing off. Here, these stilts support not only great overhanging balconies, but it seems, half of the building itself.

Can you devour this?

In response, a moment later I feel my hand sink into the wood. It's beautiful lumber, hedge apple, I think, taller and more radiant than any I've ever seen. It'll be a pity to destroy it. Going slowly, I push my ka'kari-black hand through the wood, leaving only a thumb's width at the front edge, which immediately crumples a bit under the load on it.

I breathe slowly, ready to bolt if it starts collapsing. Then, as it seems to hold, I move to the next stilt, humming a bit of the tune the chamber musicians were playing. This probably does not make me seem inconspicuous.

Again, the ka'kari sinks in, smoking slightly as it bites through the varnished outer bits but otherwise devouring the wood easily—if not quite as quickly as I'd like.

"'Ey, whatcha doin'?" the soldier I'd chatted with asks, walking over.

"Could you do me a favor?" I ask, keeping my eyes up, and hoping he does the same. The front edges of the pillars are intact, but any close inspection will certainly draw a shout. A shout here isn't what I want. "The captain said that all the cooks inside were supposed to go out back. Could you check that they've done it? Think they might've left out a bit of brandy that nobody'd miss."

I give him a wink at this last part.

Please go out the back. I'd really like it if you didn't die.

"Which captain?" he asks. Gods I hate it when people ask me specifics of my lies.

"Not one of ourn," I say. "Empress's praetorian. Reeve, I think his name was? Supposed to keep my eyes peeled for him here *and* check they're obeying down there. At the same time."

"Orficers," he says, shaking his head. "Same all over, ain't theh? I could stay here."

"You don't know what he looks like." I realize an empress's bodyguard wouldn't exactly be hard to identify, so I rush on. "And if I come out with a few skins of brandy, he'll smack me up the head, whereas if *you* did it . . . who's to say you're not acting on orders?"

"I like how ya think," he says, and then ducks inside.

As I stand by the third pillar, I start to rethink my exit strategy. Instead of sprinting to the side and then toward the back of the building as soon as I round the corner, if I cut this shallowly, then run inside and through the building, I can grab my new friend before the balcony comes down. Probably.

What am I saying? I'm going to jeopardize everything so I can save some stranger? While I'm trying to kill a score of other strangers?

The hell is wrong with me?

My hand passes through the third support.

The whole thing holds. Maybe I've left too much material. I wander over toward the fourth and last pillar. I swear several men are watching me now, wondering what I'm doing. I hum the tune again—and stop.

That tune. That's not just any tune.

Sweet but with strains of loneliness that later rally to playful before sinking ever darker. It's not merely a familiar tune. That's Phaena's tune, her Night Angel leitmotif. I think now of how when she saw me at the grand salon she seemed to drum her fingers for me to see. It hadn't meant anything to me.

She wasn't her drumming her fingers. She was miming playing notes on her lyre! She *did* leave me a message. I can only hope it isn't in the music itself but rather with the musicians.

I've got to go to them!

But...I've got to drop this balcony. I'm about to start total chaos precisely when I need everything to remain calm so I can get to those musicians. My chest goes tight.

"'Ey! Whatcher at there?" my new friend calls from the door. He's holding two skins of wine, and he's looking at the partial pillars between me and him, horrified.

"I'm about to drop this building on our heads," I say. "You should run."

Sometimes nothing stuns like the truth. I complete my broad cut of the last pillar, then flick my hand out. A ka'kari-blade springs out even as the wood groans.

I dash toward my new friend with the speed of my Talent, slashing the ka'kari through the thin points of each stubborn pillar.

He drops the wineskins, but they haven't even splashed on the ground before I reach him and dart past as he claws at his belt for a weapon. I grab the collar of his gambeson and snatch him off his feet, bringing him along with me and hurling him clear even as I turn the corner and call the ka'kari up over my skin.

As I disappear from view, I move sideways to dodge any incoming arrows and turn my gaze back to the square. Every eye that had been drawn by my blur of motion is now fixed on the looming edifice of the building. So many people gasp, it's an audible sound throughout the town square.

The four great wood pillars sag and drop from their bases, and then hold for a moment, falling forward together as if felled like the great trees they once were, tearing the front wall of the building off with them before snapping apart in midair with sharp reports that vie with the screams of the falling. The complex of wood and stone and humanity falls atop scores of massed soldiers in the town square.

Dust billows out in a great fan, and a rumble and then a roar overtakes the screams and cries and groans as the rest of the stone building, pulled off its moorings by having its front torn off, sags and collapses into its own footprint.

I hit the ground as shrapnel of dirt and stone and shattering metal blasts overhead.

It's so deafening that when I stand a few moments later, gasping through my cloak in the dust cloud, I can't hear my own coughing.

I stagger through the darkness over to my new friend, who's lying against the next building over where I threw him, trying to save his life.

Threw him too hard, I see.

His helmet is crushed in at the top where he collided with the wall. There's blood running freely from his eyes and ears, making red tracks across his dust-caked, unmoving face.

It's a punch in the gut, but it's followed immediately by others. Before I can take two steps, I see a man with one arm wandering disoriented through the clouds of dust, apparently unaware of the blood spurting from his stump in time with his heart. He stares at me blankly before pitching over sideways.

Another sits on the ground near the edge of the field of rubble. A section of stone façade the size of a horse is lying across his legs, but he's sitting upright. Seeing me, he says, "I think I'm all right. Good gods, I think I'm all right. Doesn't even hurt." His legs from midthigh down are trapped, crushed to goo thinner than my flat hand.

"You think you could help?" he asks me.

I flee. I did this.

The clouds hide a hellscape of pain and death. There are screams and moans and the sounds, muffled by the pall of dirt, of crowds running. I stumble over something soft and daren't look, knowing it must be some detached piece of what was a man a minute ago. I see a nobleman, clean, with a flagon of water and a tablecloth for bandages come rushing in, looking for victims to help. A hero. I wave him away from me, point to where some might be alive.

More nobles are running away: the usual stampede of fear and self-preservation.

In another minute, I reach the building where the musicians were playing. The stairs down from the balcony have become a bottleneck of terrified nobles and staff fighting to get out and away, shoving, screaming, calling for their servants, demanding where the soldiers are to help them.

I'm not getting in through that—but maybe it means the musicians haven't gotten out through it, either.

Outside the building once more, in the settling dust, I use my Talent to leap high and pull myself up onto the balcony. I feel a twinge from my ankle, and check it. It's whole now. The skin pale and hairless and baby fresh, but whole. After what I've done to maim so many, I'm Healed.

The world is absurd.

I go inside, checking for the musicians. There's almost no one on this second level, merely the clot of humans around the stairwell and those pushing down the stairs from the third. I scan the crowd for any people in musicians' colorful garb but see none.

Going back to the balcony, I leap again. Finding the space where the musicians had been performing, I grab an abandoned stack of parchments. Seeing a floppy hat on the floor, I snag it and tuck it into my belt.

The crowd here is thin, and I spy the musicians at the back of it, trying to shield their instruments and flee.

"Someone gave you a message," I say, wading into their midst. "A woman. She gave you that song."

Three of them give me blank looks. The last licks his lips. "No message," he says. "Well, not as such. She wrote it on our—"

I shove the parchments of music in his face.

"This isn't connected to any of what just happened..." He trails off as he sees the look on my face. "This one, this one here. This is it. See? Not a message, not really."

Amid the musical notation I could never have deciphered on my own, there's a number and a couple of letters. A room.

A few minutes later, I knock on a door, carefully standing in full view of the peephole, my hands spread to show I'm unarmed, the little blue dagger I stole from Vi still hidden in one sleeve—just in case.

The peephole goes dark, and a moment later the door is thrown open.

Phaena stands there, cradling a baby at her breast.

"Kylar," she breathes. "Thank the God. Maybe we have a chance after all."

Chapter Ninety-Six

The Storm and the Calm

$\mathcal{S}$he doesn't know.

"I'm glad we could be together. Here at the end," I say, closing the door behind me.

"I'm almost done feeding him," she says. "Then we can go. I'm glad you made it here first. I was going to head out with or without you. I can't believe our good fortune. Or maybe I shouldn't call it good fortune, huh?" Phaena smiles beatifically. "It must be the God himself intervening for us. Hurry up, little one," she says, stroking the baby's cheek. "No, no, no, no falling asleep just yet." She looks back up to me. "He'll be out for an hour at least. I've already got him changed and clean. You need anything?"

"Phaena..." I say. "The Sisters have left. We're back in the storm now. There's no way out."

"Don't be silly," she says. She bounces the child gently. Ordinarily, I'd probably be a bit more captivated by her bare breast. But oh, look, all that's needed to tamp down the libido is the prospect of sharing certain death with someone who's currently happy and hopeful and has no idea the awful news you're about to tell them.

"Phaena," I say firmly. "Do you not know about the child's magic? He's awakening. The Sisters and their Healers—who know more about this sort of thing than anyone in the world—are certain that his soul will fully attach to his body in the next few days, and that means huge surges of magic. Or in his case, magic that wipes out magic. That null wave earlier nearly sank the whole storm ship? That was him. The Sisters say the next one will be much stronger and more prolonged. No matter what else happens, the next null wave is going to come long before this ship reaches Borami. Phaena, it's over. We either die fighting or we die by drowning when the ship breaks apart and goes down. That's it. This is the end."

She takes the babe from her breast and puts a cloth over her shoulder, covers herself, and then begins burping him. "Lay out the swaddle on the bed, would you?"

I lay it out on the bed. As if that's the thing to do right now.

She's quietly talking to the baby, encouraging him to burp as she alternates patting his butt and rubbing his back.

"You're not taking this quite the way I expected," I say. "Do you not understand me?"

"Babies are sensitive, Kylar," she says, smiling. Though she can't have known the child for more than a few days, she smiles at him with obvious love. Is that a woman thing, a mother thing, or a Phaena thing?

Something in me envies those who can love so quickly, so easily. I think my own childhood on the streets broke that part in me. This is supposedly my kid. I'm supposed to have some mystical attachment to him or something, right? And I don't even feel curious about him.

She goes on, "All babies pick up on the emotions around them, and this one is more sensitive than any I've ever known."

"You're keeping up a good front for the kid," I say.

She takes a breath and rubs her cheek against the baby's. Then she goes back to burping him. "Kylar, who do I work for?"

"Momma K."

"And what does Momma K have?"

I can't think what Phaena's going for. "I don't know. She sort of has everything."

"Everything is right."

The baby burps, and Phaena breaks off to praise him, wipes his mouth, then brings him over to the swaddle and begins wrapping him up tightly with practiced, efficient movements.

Then she goes on, unperturbed, "And she gave me access to all of it for this job. She put all her resources at our disposal. We knew that getting the child before he was taken aboard this ship was our best chance. Obviously, you and I both know how that went. But..."

"'But'? Phaena, I know you're trying not to upset the baby, but if there was a time for a backup plan, that time is past. It's gone. We're in the storm again."

"I know," Phaena says, perfectly calmly. Perhaps that's for the baby's benefit, though she's now hoisting him into some kind of sling. "Which is why they won't be expecting us to leave now."

"Leave?"

"We hired smugglers, Kylar."

"Smugglers who took your money and ran, I'm sorry to tell you. Have you even looked to see what it's like out there? Smugglers are crazy as a rule, but they're not stupid. No smuggler's going to risk the Great Storm."

Phaena grabs a cloak off the bed, holding the baby tighter against her with one hand as she leans over. She flips the cloak inside out, from the dark brown I saw earlier to a pale blue. Her dress too has been turned inside out, its distinctive white and red now hidden fully by a plain blue hue. She buttons the front of her cloak and puts on a matching broad hat and suddenly looks like simply another heavy noblewoman rather than a slender nursemaid in official attire carrying a child.

"Smugglers might risk it," she says, "if offered a prince's ransom, and if they were accompanied by a couple of very good weather mages."

"Weather mages?"

"I know. They're not common. We don't need them in Cenaria, but every port has a few, especially on this sea. They're generally not as powerful as they pretend, but significantly calming heavy seas in a very small area is basically all they do. It's their whole specialty. Harbors use them to keep ships off the rocks. But all the best ones quietly work as smugglers, too."

Which means they all work for people Momma K knows.

I can't speak for a long moment. I was so certain we were going to die. I killed a lot of people to get here, thinking it didn't really matter, that we all were doomed anyway. I may have created some colossal problems for myself later.

But this means there will be a later.

Maybe.

As I feel the first thing like a smile on my face in a long time, I say, "Where do we need to go?"

Chapter Ninety-Seven

Long Live the Empress

*H*ey, you!" a captain leading half a dozen soldiers the opposite direction shouts to me. I'm walking rapidly, just in front of Phaena, and only as he shouts at me do I realize I'm still wearing the uniform I had in the square, and it and I are both liberally coated in dirt from the building I knocked down. "You're going the wrong way! Come with—"

"Sorry, sir, been ordered forward. Need to report to Commander Reeve."

"Why would you need to do that? Come with us!" he says.

"Sir, I got my orders."

"Orders from whom?"

"Are you joking?" I demand. "It's like hell back there. Everyone's coated in dirt and ash. I don't *know* who told me, but they did and they seemed in charge. Honestly, I think you'd better hurry back there too and start helping—"

But he's not having it. He's a small man, but he puffs his chest up big. "You'll come with us, or—"

I've gotta run into one of these guys? Now?

The ka'kari snaps out of my fist like a stiletto. Launching into him, I jab him through the eye and, as his head rocks back, slash deep through the throat. Push off, sending his body into the men he's leading.

They're all armed with spears, and in the tight confines of the hall, I'm already too close for them. I slash one below the ribs, cutting all the way through, and bring the ka'kari-blade back to hamstring him with my right hand even as I draw his dagger with my left. The next target isn't even looking at me yet, busy sharing some joke with the next soldier over.

My dagger blows past his relaxed grip on his spear and into the base of his throat. My momentum blasts me into him and him off his feet.

Ripping the blade to the side as it comes from his throat, I slash at the next soldier's shin.

The ka'kari cleaves cleanly through it, leaving a foot standing alone in the hall. I crush the remaining men all together against the wall, and as they fall, off-balance, tripping each other up, my blades blur like a tattooist's needle, decorating each body with the brutal art of fate.

Phaena tears her wide eyes from the sudden carnage and steps past them.

I notice that one isn't dead, and finish that.

I can hear distant alarms, or maybe I only notice them for the first time. Is that because of the mess I made in Elysion, or is something else happening too? It can't be another null wave. We'd be the first to know about that.

As I stand from dispatching the wounded soldier, I see a gray-bearded nobleman poking his head out into the hall, gawping at the dead.

"Traitors!" I shout at him. "Long live Empress Caelestia! Whose side are you on?"

"L-long live the empress," he says weakly, afraid to be put on the spot. He ducks back into his room.

I don't think he'll come out any time soon. You can't count on bystanders to be cowards if something awful is happening in front of them. Some will turn hero. But if you muddy the waters, confuse them, make them wonder if they won't be jumping in on the wrong side? People love being given an excuse to not get involved.

We move to a parallel passage and keep pushing forward.

"Kylar...?" Phaena says, worried. Though the child is completely hidden from view, she's bouncing it in a manner that could be pretty much nothing else.

"What are you doing?" I demand, taking her elbow.

"He's not sleeping," she says tensely. "He always falls asleep after a feeding, and now he's...not."

"He always does?"

"What do you think I've been doing since I got on the ship, Kylar? Anyway, maybe I didn't burp him well enough, or—"

"How far? How far do we have to get?" I ask her.

"There's a stairway after the nobles' courtyard and before the foredeck. Down that."

That can't be more than a hundred paces from here. We're already approaching the nobles' courtyard.

"Make way!" I hear a man shout up ahead. We push to one wall as another squad of soldiers comes pounding down the hall.

They run right past us. Only one of them gives me a curious look.

I'm grimy, and there's no way to get perfectly clean quickly. But this soldier disguise has outlived its usefulness. I shuck off the tunic.

I rip off the sleeve. "Arm," I say. She obeys immediately, and I wrap the sleeve around her arm in a very poor imitation of a bandage. "Favor this. You got injured back there in the collapse. I'm your man, taking you back to your apartments." I reach into my belt, pull out the floppy hat I took earlier, and pull it low over my face.

She chews her lower lip, and I can see her putting together her story. "Got it," she says before I can ask if she's got any better ideas.

I step into the nobles' courtyard leading her by the arm, and my heart immediately seizes up. The far side of the courtyard is clogged with hundreds of mages and imperial guards.

Why didn't I come scout this first? I should've had Phaena wait outside while I checked it. How could I make such a mista—?

"Sir? Milady?" a young man says politely.

I turn to him, heart in my throat.

"Courtyard's been commandeered for a bit," he says. "Staging area until we figure out what the emergency is. 'Fraid you'll have to come back later. Sorry for the inconvenience."

"I do hate to be a bother," Phaena says. She lifts her arm. "My room's on the port quarterdeck. 27Q? I know I could backtrack and find my way forward another way, but with all the crowds on the back stairs...I don't suppose you could let us duck through to the front stair? I don't want to get you in trouble, but it would be so very helpful..."

She gives him a pleading look with a tentative smile, and I see him waver. I mean, she doesn't literally bat her eyelashes, but some men can't think straight when a beautiful woman needs them.

"Sure thing," the young man says. "Just don't loiter. Chief's a hardass."

"Thank you!" Phaena says.

We start walking across the open space, trying to be both quick and discreet.

"Not sure crossing here is a great idea," I say under my breath as we go past row after row of empty tables.

"Kylar, look out the window," she whispers.

Outside, I catch sight of a distant catamaran cutting across the stormy seas toward us. It's hard to guess scale from this distance, but the waves look to be twenty paces high. I don't know what I expected when I heard *weather mages*, but it wasn't this brutal physicality.

One mage is lashed to the catamaran's deck near the prow. Carefully timing his blasts, he's literally tearing trenches into the faces of the towering waves before him, waiting until the moment his boat would be buried to hurl his magic forward, flinging geysers of water to either side.

The other weather mage is tied in not far from the captain at the wheel. He's got both hands ready, head on a swivel, force darting out from him repeatedly slapping aside torrents of water falling from overhead to keep the boat from being swamped. As I watch, an especially large wave picks up their boat, and the mage at the front blasts a hole through it, his body rocking as he does so as if there's a significant muscular element to his magic. I've seen a lot of impressive magic, but my jaw drops at the spectacle. I'd never be gutsy enough to pit my magic against the sea itself.

They're obviously strong mages to have made it this far, but I have to guess they can't keep up that kind of effort for long. With every wave, their bodies are bashed back and forth by the boat's motion, and hurling aside lakes of water, over and over?

With the ship under way and in the storm again, hardly anyone looks out the windows, and at the moment our smugglers are far enough away they might never be seen. But what happens if someone does? Will anyone aboard be so baffled they say nothing and merely watch, as I want to—or will they report it to Repha'im?

Phaena's right, we don't have the luxury of time. We have to risk the shortcut.

She's humming under her breath, a lullaby to the baby. But she's doing something else too. Something magical.

I see one of the many mages, an older woman, stiffen as if she's heard something.

"Phaena, whatever you're doing, stop," I breathe.

"If I stop, he's gonna cry," she says through gritted teeth. "Dammit, this'd be so much easier with my lyre."

I slow down a step to put my own body between Phaena and the mages. The mage turns, and I recognize her as one of the leaders I eavesdropped on earlier.

Agatta. She stares suspiciously at us. Should I tell Phaena to shut up and risk it for a few seconds? How long does it take for a baby to start crying, anyway?

I've had moments when my whole life changed right in front of me and I didn't have any clue how important that moment would turn out to be. This is not one of those times.

If we can make it ten more steps...

I nod tightly at Agatta from across the room, as if I'm a noble who recognizes her and whom she should recognize in turn. There are thirty imperial mages with her, give or take, and an equal number of soldiers. Then I turn away, so I won't see if she motions to me to stop.

As I turn, I belatedly notice that Phaena has stopped walking.

"Hold up," a man with a basso profundo voice says.

I narrowly stop myself from lifting my chin to meet his eyes: It's the Ibex. The enormous praetorian is *here*? I keep my head low. A hat is my only disguise?

How fast can I pull together an illusion mask? I glance toward Agatta, who's still looking at me. I can't risk using my Talent, not under her eye.

"Milady's room is just down the steps yonder, sir," I say, trying to mask my voice, "pardon our trespass. Got hurt back in the square, what?"

The Ibex shifts. He turns to Phaena, who's humming quietly. "Knock that off. What are you doing?"

"Just an old favorite tune," she says, with a frank look just this side of insouciance that perfectly apes the noblewoman she's pretending to be. Then she hums the line again and I see him visibly relax.

I feel myself relaxing as her voice washes over me, too. It takes me an extra moment to say, "We'll just get out of your way, sir."

Then I hear a voice that shatters my new calm. "Ibex! Hey, Ibex!"

From among the gathered guards and mages, a man is standing up—a man nearly as big as the imperial bodyguards, and even more imposing: King Repha'im, hidden until now, seated behind a screen of standing officers. He pauses in the act of waving to Ibex.

Despite the distance, I see a flash of color in his caprine eyes.

I duck my head quickly to hide my face behind the brim of my hat, and turn it into an awkward bow.

"Who's that?" I hear King Repha'im say suspiciously.

"A noblewoman, sir," Ibex rumbles beside us. "Injured in the attack."

"I can see that, churl. What's her *name*?"

My muscles tense, my mind blanks. I need to make up or think up a name before this all goes—

But Phaena makes a slight hand gesture to stop me from speaking and says easily, "I am Lady Istabelli Goulyrtte, of Hightree Park, originally of the Paxton Greenwoods, Your—"

Repha'im says immediately, "No, you're not. There's no one of that name on the manifest."

"I was a late embarkation, Your Majesty. Family emergency. I took my brother Magnos's place."

There's a hesitation. I daren't look up for fear that those searching eyes that once saw me out of a throng of hundreds despite even greater distance than this will see through me once more.

My fate is out of my hands. Out of every choice I made that brought me here, of everything I ever said and did where I shaped my own life, this, this is beyond my grasp. I am helpless, adrift rudderless on a sea of fate. All I can do by any action is make things worse.

The silence stretches. It can only be a few seconds, but it feels like millennia. Cannot one officer urge him to return to the pressing work at hand? Cannot one mage raise some urgent question?

Have you ever been the passenger in a wagon or a buggy as the driver veered at some danger, and in an instant you felt the depth of your own helplessness? No matter what you see, no matter what you know, your life is in other hands. This is why I always work alone.

"Come here," King Repha'im says, and it is a death sentence.

"Think he means you," I say under my breath to Ibex.

I know he doesn't, but if I can buy a few more seconds, that's a few seconds where one of those officers or mages might blunder into saving our lives with a single impatient question.

"Do I know you?" Ibex asks me.

"Nah, I got one of those faces," I say quietly, not raising my eyes to his. "But seriously, sir, don't think you should keep 'im waiting."

The Ibex steps forward just in front of me, and I motion to Phaena to go.

"No, not *you*, her!" King Repha'im says. *"Kylar?"*

We're lost.

Before Ibex can react, I slam a Talent-strengthened punch into his ribs and feel several crunch. I kick the back of one knee and snatch at his collar. As he stumbles backward, I pull him backward faster, putting his body between mine and the many mages and soldiers.

Ibex scrambles for a few steps, trying to keep his feet. Usually if you go down in a fight, you're finished. With his massive bulk levered in front of me, that makes him the perfect shield.

But then, just as a fiery dart streaks past our heads, he stops fighting the fall and drops.

I stoop, dragging him for a few steps, hitting him with blows to the neck to stun him and keep him from doing more—but I flick my eyes up.

Even as chaos is descending among the officer corps, I see King Repha'im, not screaming orders but speaking with one of the junior officers, calm. Two of them go, quickly. Then Repha'im leaves, too. Not toward me, but away. What's that mean?

He doesn't move with the air of a man unconcerned; he's moving with a purpose. But what purpose?

"Shoot, shoot!" Ibex shouts, gasping with agony in his broken ribs for having done so.

An arrow skips off Ibex's shoulder armor past my ear. They're not holding off to save him.

Snatching his sword from his scabbard, I drop him and turn, seeing Phaena already disappearing down the steps. I dive and roll as another half-dozen missiles in every color magical and mundane go streaking past.

I catch up with Phaena by the third floor of steps. She's holding her front tightly, shielding and steadying the child beneath her robes as she runs. She interrupts her humming to him to say, tensely, "Kylar, to keep this child asleep, I have to keep calm. Kylar, I'm not keeping calm."

A new alarm peals through the ship.

"Where do we have to go?" I shout to her back as she leaves the staircase and heads out into a large, open hold.

"Right . . . here," she says, stopping running without any warning.

With the Ibex's sword in hand, I nearly run into her back and skewer her. I barely keep from shouting a curse when I see the rest of the hold—and why she's slowed.

The storage area in this hold has been repurposed: the boxes and chests expertly stacked and pushed aside to clear a large area in the center. An area for warriors to train.

An area where warriors *are* training.

Or were, until the alarm sounded, until we ran in.

Not just warriors. Minus however many went with the empress herself, this appears to be the entire praetorian guard. Every last one of these warriors is also a mage.

"Viridiana, we need to go now."

"Not yet. Not yet! I'm almost finished."

"I fear it's too late for that," Sister Ariel said.

"What do you mean? Actually, don't tell me. I don't want to know. I can't stop now."

"If you don't, the issue may be decided for you."

"Go!" Viridiana said.

Chapter Ninety-Eight

Speak Friend

$\mathcal{T}$wo dozen of the world's best warriors are off to our left, staring at us. Opposite them to our right, ten paces away, is a small door set into the ship's hull. Through that many-latched door is where we're to meet our smugglers.

There's a moment of confusion among the praetorians as they stare at us, as they listen to the alarm blaring, a moment to slip a knife into.

I could attack first, and mow down a few of them. Would it matter? Maybe it would. Fear can turn even a veteran's guts to water.

But I've seen these men and women, seen their discipline. I know that at the first clash of arms, their training will take over.

I'm a great killer, that's not in doubt. But after everything that's happened, am I nothing more? The great masters always say that the pinnacle of the martial arts is to attain victory without striking a single blow.

"Friends, listen," I say, raising my voice not in a shout but in calm command, first lowering the Ibex's big saber to a loose Middle Iron Gate and then raising my right hand, the fulcrum, away from the grip as we walk into the hall, making our way slowly toward that small portal, toward the possibility of life. The stance is as casual as I dare to be against these warriors, and far more casual than I'd like. Loudly, I say, "I am the Night Angel, the most forlorn of Death's harvesters, first among the ushers to the great beyond. But I have no quarrel with you. Your lady's consort Repha'im has broken the laws of gods and men in kidnapping a child from his rightful, loving parents. I have come to take that child home. Nothing more. If you will stand by your own principles and be bold enough to stand aside, we all will live to fight other battles, battles we believe in. But if you stand instead for one who tears a family asunder, for one who longs for a war that will doom this continent to ceaseless bloodshed, then I am sorry but it will be your own families who will learn what it is to grieve a lost child. Would you choose to fight, knowing that you fight to keep a baby from his father? From his mother who wastes away, sick with worry? Friends in arms, in time Death will take us all, but Death need take no one today. Please, now, pardon our interruption and return to your training. We will be gone in a moment and never disturb you again."

I stop. I could tell them that the child is the source of the waves of anti-magic that threaten the whole ship, but they won't believe me. Better that I pit their decency against their orders. Warriors won't believe that a babe could threaten their very lives.

For a moment, no one moves. None of them wants to be the first to move. Phaena puts her head down and keeps walking, emerging from behind me. I can see it now—I only need one praetorian to pick up his practice sword and say to his comrade, "Shall we?" and continue training as if they'd seen nothing.

One only, and this nightmare may end happily.

But then I hear the clatter of armed men, confused, still flights above us on the stairs, but close enough now that they'll soon intrude. I flinch, and I'm not the only one.

At the sounds from above, the spell breaks. I see half a dozen of the praetorians nearest the stairs start guiltily—feeling guilt, of all things, over considering doing what is right.

Phaena dashes forward toward the door. There's no way she's going to make it. These aren't stupid ship guards.

"Stop!" someone shouts.

I see weapons coming up everywhere. I find the grip with my fulcrum hand.

They don't warn us more. Through the thicket of warrior-magi I see the characteristic motion of an archer acquiring his target. There is no pause, no hesitation. The arrow flies.

I lash out, knowing that the odds of knocking an arrow from the air are a thousand to one—

—and I miss, cutting not behind it, but in front of it.

The arrow hits Phaena in her belly.

No, not in her belly. It hits *the child*.

Then it skips off, and rattles against the bulkhead beyond.

Phaena stops, face painted with horror, a mere step from the door.

Off-balance from my lunge, I'm closer to the arrow than anyone. My eyes fix on it. It's a practice arrow, slowed in its flight by the bunting packed around the tip.

The child might be uninjured.

"Stop! Next arrow's real!" a man shouts.

Phaena has her hand on one of three large locks. She stops.

Everywhere blades are coming up, magic is alighting in hands, men and women are moving to surround us. There's no way I can fight so many on my own—and I need to protect Phaena and a child, too?

There's no way.

A feeling of utter despair floods through me and is only cut short by a sound—

A baby crying, the briefly delayed wail of startled pain from a child awakened by being struck in his sleep.

It stuns everyone, not to a stop—those in motion continue moving, but slower. Phaena lifts her robe over her head and flings it away from her, exposing the child wrapped tight to her chest. Quietly, shaking, she begins murmuring, trying to sing through her fear to soothe the child.

"Don't shoot! It's a baby!" one of the women among the praetorian guards shouts.

"The king's baby! That's the king's baby. *Hold!*" someone else yells.

It takes a moment for everyone to understand, and longer for the gravity of that news to hit them—they try to grapple with what that means even as they try to stop us.

When it does, I'm ready.

"Door!" I shout to Phaena, who's still trying to quiet the child. I lunge toward the nearest guard. Ibex's saber pokes a neat hole in the man's practice doublet before he even moves to parry me.

With less-skilled troops, I'd kill three or four before any reacted. Here, all those nearest seem to have recovered by the time I close the next line, guiding a blunted spear thrust past my ribs in the same action as I advance and bury saber in belly before shoving hard off to clear a man away and to change my own trajectory.

When outnumbered, you forfeit many of the helpful phases of a duel. Scouting shrinks to nil; covering your intentions, misleading the opponent, and preparing your own actions compress further the more people you have to fight.

All that remains is attempting to impose initiative and influencing the opponents' moves and intentions. Time is the enemy, so you must attack, which means savvy opponents know they must only defend.

Magic can overcome this, unless your opponents have magic of their own—mine do.

Ferocity can be countered with discipline—these have that.

Fear can be countered with experience—these have that too.

I cross my saber with the first sharp blade yet. She's in Rising Boar. My speed feint gets her to overcommit on a parry, and as she finds only air to block instead of steel, her sword goes wide enough that my saber dips deep into her armpit.

As we fall back, me to find my next target, and she to the ground to die, I throw out glittering dust motes of magic in a crescent to stick to every warrior before me. Those motes cling to the fighters and blossom into the ghostly outlines of every way each warrior might move, the potentialities of preception. It's a veritable wall of ghostly forms in various colors, a thicket of lethal possibilities shifting as each warrior moves, color bleeding to color, bouncing off each other in a dense cloud. And that's all I need.

I don't think I can take on so many fighters no matter what tricks I use; I don't intend to use preception as preception—I throw it only as a screen, a distraction to make everything hard to see. I dive in, attacking, cutting a leg here, a wrist here.

But even as the magic blurs, overwhelmed by the multiplicities of movements, the wall of potentialities recedes away from us, as everywhere the praetorians fall back into ranks. Soft in the middle, and iron-hard at each edge, so I can penetrate if I choose, and thus be surrounded.

I hold back, not willing to let them get between me and Phaena.

Then the glow of my preception dies, snuffed out by someone's magic.

Beyond it, visible again, are the praetorians. The glistering aureole of magic surrounds many.

"Kylar!" Phaena shouts. "I can't get the lock!"

It's death to retreat, but not all the warrior-mages have their eyes on me—some are training fire on Phaena, their eyes low, as if preparing to throw magic at her legs or feet, where they won't hit the baby.

The latches before Phaena are all open except one, which has a hasp of thick iron. The ka'kari can cut that. Nothing else will.

It takes me no more than a heartbeat to decide. I can't win. There are too many praetorians. They're too good. Outside that door is life—but not life for me.

Maybe I can defend Phaena and the child long enough so they can make it through the door. With my sword and my body as a shield, I might block the incoming fire for a few moments. A few moments may be enough for them to escape.

I rush for the door and my death.

The ka'kari comes to my hand to form a blade to shear the metal lock.

That's when it hits.

I feel like a farmer in late summer afternoon, foolishly wandering into a grain elevator with a lit torch. As I recoil, spun by the force of the concussion, I see volleys of magical missiles and darts streaking from dozens of praetorians' hands toward my turned back.

Every missile simply winks out of existence.

If last time, the infant had sent an implacable wave of anti-magic through the ship, this time the null wave hits with the force of a tsunami bursting every dike.

Every one of the praetorians using magic to power their movements is suddenly enervated—half of them fall. I stagger, too, catching myself against the bulkhead.

Having magic torn away is more profound than suddenly feeling faint where one expected to be strong. If you weren't holding your Talent when the first great null wave rolled through the ship, it felt like the momentary panic of waking to the feeling of a deadened arm. You look down, and the thing doesn't respond. It won't move. It tingles. It hurts. It seems alien, and fear shoots through you that something is deeply, deeply wrong.

But if you were holding your Talent, as all of us in this room were, it's worse. It's like when a hunter skins a rabbit. After the first careful slices, with a wet ripping sound, he yanks the skin clean off.

I'm the only one here who's experienced having his magic torn from him three times—for now I realize that this didn't only happen to me in the galley here on the ship. This is also what happened to me the night the twins were first kidnapped. It wasn't the poisoned wine that took my legs out from under me. It was Caedan's awakening power.

So maybe it's natural that I recover first, coming to my feet while numerous of the praetorians are still kneeling, unblinking, aghast.

The anti-magic explosion saved my life from all the killing arts the praetorians had aimed at my back. But as I stare at the lock, eager to use these few seconds to escape, I see that the null wave only saved me for the moment, and it's doomed us all. I tried to trade my life to get Phaena and Caedan out the door. Now none of us can leave.

The iron lock will only yield to magic.

I stare at the ka'kari, which lies as if dead in my palm.

Are you there?! Tell me you can hear me! I need you!

I know it can hear me, but the ka'kari doesn't respond. Can't.

Come on, come on. Come back to me!

My ears are ringing, I feel deaf. Phaena looks on the verge of vomiting—her Talent was torn from her, too—but she's making movements with her mouth as if she's talking to the baby, trying to comfort him.

There's a lull, a blossoming of hope on her face. The null wave ceases. There's a moment beyond the ringing of my ears perhaps of quiet, even silence, and then I see Phaena grimace, her mouth move. I think she's saying "No no no no!" to the baby, trying to settle it before it descends into pure meltdown.

And then a wave hits again. Praetorians who were starting to stand fall on their faces. Someone vomits.

The null waves before were waves. They passed.

This isn't passing. If this is a tsunami, it feels like it'll be a long time before the floodwaters depart.

But it doesn't feel like waters. It's a raging inferno, and I'm at its heart.

It feels like it's scouring magic away from my very soul. Have you ever seen a burn victim degloved? This is like having your mind degloved. My skin goes hot and cold in prickles as if I've been vomiting all night. I taste metal in my mouth, and colors flare weirdly in my vision.

I grab Phaena, haul her to her feet. It's harder than it ought to be. I realize I called on my Talent to do it, without even thinking. But my Talent isn't there now.

"Come on! We've gotta move!" I shout.

Pulling her away from the door, I hear the groaning of metal as the storm ship responds to its own loss of magical protection. I can hear again!

Though everyone's dazed by the sudden loss of their magic, not everyone is down.

Mentally quicker to recover than her compatriots, an archer turns her big war bow on us. She begins drawing an arrow with a practiced grace but then grunts, her fingers slipping off the string—without her Talent, the draw is unexpectedly heavy.

I turn, pulling Phaena along with me, but as we reach the stairs, she cries out—and falls. Wounded? Did the archer get a shot off? I catch her as she tries to shield the baby from her fall, twisting. We all go down.

As we hit the ground at the foot of the steps, startling the baby, the anti-magic storm abruptly ceases.

I can see the back of the null wave ripple outward, a weird distortion in the air like a mirage that's closer than any mirage could be. Already back on my feet, I pick up Phaena—without my Talent. Even without an active null storm, it's going to take time to reconnect with my magic.

If I ever do. What if it hurt me permanently?

But I can't think about that now. Lifting Phaena first by the armpits, and then scooping her into my arms, I carry her.

I only make it up one flight of stairs before I hear voices and the pounding of feet from above, coming down. Whatever made them hesitate before, they're coming now.

"This way!" Phaena says, pointing, her voice and face taut with pain.

I dodge through the next door, onto the second deck of the storm ship. Huffing, already tiring with the effort of carrying a woman and a still-crying baby, I barely half jog down the hall. "Next one's my room," Phaena says, pained. I lean against the door as she fumbles with the lock, and then we all fall in as the door opens.

Her cabin's mercifully empty. I kick the door shut with a heel, and it bangs, loudly. Maybe too loudly. I curse.

The clamor of soldiers pounding down the steps to hunt us floats through the door. Only their own noise and the shrieking of numerous alarms responding to the null wave covers the soft crying of the infant, and maybe my slamming of the door.

Its crying isn't causing new null waves now. I don't know why.

Even as I set them both down on the bed, Phaena's doing her best to soothe him. Her brow is sweaty and her breath ragged, but she's already settling her own fear, focusing on the baby. An arrow protrudes from the meaty part of her leg. I check the angle.

Keeping her voice light and cheery for the baby's benefit, she says, "From the look on your face, there's bad news, isn't there?"

"Don't pull this out," I tell her. "Don't even move. It may have clipped the artery. Pull it out without a Healer here, and you could die in less than a minute."

It's all true, but I regret saying it the instant I do. If I so much as move her again, I may kill her.

And I have to move.

"You have a plan?" she says. She seems oddly calmed by what I said. Or maybe she's in shock and doesn't understand what I said yet.

"If we can make it to the Fresh Air Deck at the bow, we can leap into the water. It's a long drop, but the monsters in the water may not get us before we reach the smugglers' boat."

But anyone bleeding copiously into the water won't have much of a chance. The lotai are fast.

"By 'we' you mean yourself and the baby," Phaena says. "Right?" She's already untying the knots of her sling.

The time for lies is past.

"I don't know if I'll be able to make it off the ship even if I were alone," I say. "The jump could kill me. Much less the swim. With the baby? Far less likely. With the baby and you, injured like this... ?"

"I'll delay them as much as I can," she says. "My lyre's there. Give it to me."

An old part of me that wants to rescue everyone rears up. I can't leave her here!

Ah, I recognize that voice. That's young me. The one who wanted to be a hero. The idealist. The one who loved the stories, even though I knew better. No man left behind! No damsel unrescued!

~If you don't leave her, everyone dies. Everyone.~

You're back!

~It was like before. I could hear you. But nothing else.~

They're both right. If I try to play the hero and I don't get the child off this ship, everyone dies—including Phaena.

And Vi.

The only thing that gives anyone a chance, slender as it is, is to take the child and go. Quickly.

Phaena's already tying the sling around my neck, cooing to the babe, soothing him.

"You won't be able to slow them," I say.

"Yes, I will. Grab me the lyre," she says.

"You can't fight them," I say, handing her the lyre. "A few will tear apart this room while the others go on. Don't die for nothing."

"Never said I'd fight," she says, tuning the lyre effortlessly, despite the pallor setting in on her face. Her shock is yielding to pain. Trying to smile, reaching a hand out to pat Caedan one last time, she says, "You can do this. Don't give up, Kylar."

"That's my curse," I say, mirroring her strained smile. "I don't know how."

With practiced efficiency, she secures the baby low against my chest. "With the swaddle, you shouldn't need to hold his head as you run," she says. "But when you jump into the water . . . well, I'll be praying for a miracle."

"Relax. I'm the Night Angel. I make my own miracles," I say, but my grin feels like a rictus of death.

It's time to go, but I'm struck by a sudden fear. "Phaena. The starboard side of the ship had magical defenses and ballistae and stuff. Do you know if the port side has those too?"

She manages a quick flash of a smile. "It *did*. Momma K's money took care of it."

That eases the tightness in my chest. A little. I still don't know if the smugglers got walloped by the null wave. What if they've already sunk? But I can't know that.

I need to go regardless, but I don't know how to say goodbye, don't know how to abandon Phaena without feeling like a traitor and a coward.

"Hey, I figured it out," she says. "Your motif. Needs to be in minor, doesn't it? Such a simple fix, when you know the . . ." She trails off.

"The ending?" I say.

She looks at me, eyes large, face pale. I wish I could read other expressions as well as I learned to read fear and anger, but I can't tell you what was in her eyes except that there was no anger there, nor fear. She begins playing, and something about the world changes. It's magical. I don't mean it's *magic* magical. Or maybe I do. I don't mean it's really good, though it's even better than that. In a world where all other music is prose, this is poetry.

Though all music can dredge emotions from the depths of a heart willing to attend to it, this music finds sympathetic harmonics over the very air, plucking emotions directly, transforming its listener from an observer to a participant and finally an instrument.

She smiles sadly. "Better, huh? It's you, isn't it?"

But I can't say a thing. She's stirred a sadness in me too deep for words.

"Go," she says. "Save us, Kylar. Save us all. Go!"

Chapter Ninety-Nine

The Way Out

In the hall, I see drops of Phaena's blood. I close the door to her room. I don't know if they'll see it, or not see it. I don't think it'll slow them much either way. They'll find her no matter what I do. I'll have to hope they don't attack her out of hand. If she lives through this, she'll be heading someplace very unpleasant: a gaol, if not directly to the headsman's block.

But there's nothing I can do about that.

My throat tightens again.

The storm ship has lost all forward momentum. It slews about, dead in the water, rocking so hard I have to push off the walls every few steps to keep going.

Holding the child but not looking down, I jog as quickly as possible. Heads are peeking out of a few of the rooms, but no one's interfering with me. Something we said earlier is tickling at the back of my mind. What is it?

I reach a stairway, but instead of my heart soaring that I've made it so far without being stopped, my dread only increases. Are they waiting for me?

No, they can't know where I'm going. *I* didn't know where I was going to go until a minute ago.

Where was King Repha'im headed? He's been ahead of me at every step. Where is he now?

I see a woman's head poking out of a room down the hall as I ascend the steps. Long red hair, bound back. I come to a full stop, but then she turns and looks my way. It's not Vi.

Vi. That's who I was thinking of. That's what was bothering me.

Where are you, Vi? I need your help!

I feel the blue knife at my belt, the knife I stole from her. Sister Ayayah bound Vi to use this knife, on this child, if their plan went awry.

I swallow.

It couldn't have gone more awry than it has. Now here I am. Of the Sisters, only Vi is left on the storm ship. I don't know where she is, but I know what her orders are and what she thinks the stakes are. The Sisters will have given her some signal when they departed, and with the Sisters' plans having failed, Vi thinks that if she doesn't kill this child, everyone on the ship dies.

Which isn't wrong.

That's why I've got to get us off this ship. I turn up another flight of stairs, pushing through crowds buzzing with curiosity but not yet fear about what's wrong. I can't stop the thoughts.

If Vi thinks we can't get the child off the ship, she's been ordered to kill him—even if it takes her own death to do it. Sister Ayayah thinks Repha'im might survive the null storm and save the child. Which is giving Repha'im too much credit. He's not going to survive the lotai any more than I would. But I see why she's worried, given the stakes. If he escapes and ends up raising the child, she thinks the Chantry will fall and all the world will suffer. Which probably isn't wrong either.

Vi thinks that if she fails, a dozen of her Sisters are going to give their lives to kill Repha'im and the child as soon as the ship docks in Borami. Whether those Sisters succeed or fail, an open attack like they plan will mean war between the largest empire in the world and the Chantry and whatever allies they can pull in.

No one's going to do well in a fight that size.

But the only reason I'm thinking about all this boils down to one question: If Vi shows up, is she going to help me, or is she going to try to save her Sisters, the ship, the Chantry, and the world? Is Vi going to listen to me, or attack first and ask questions later? Who's she going to be loyal to? Have I given her any reason for that to be me?

You're laughing at me because you think that's a lot more than one question, huh?

~I'm not laughing at you.~

Well, it really is only one question. Asked lots of ways, because I know the answer.

I know Vi, and I love her to death. Hell, maybe I love her, period. But she can get fixated on one course of action. She can act without thinking. Hell, she's often at her best when she acts without thinking.

But today?

Well, it's a big ship. I know she's in the front half of it, but she has no idea where *I* am. There's no reason she should show up—and now, opposite how I felt not even a full minute ago, I hope she *doesn't* show up.

I don't want to fight Vi.

For that matter, I don't know if I *can*. I glance down. I'm holding a child! I can't put the kid down to fight her fairly, because the kid is literally her target. There's no way I can win, not against Vi.

Except by getting off the ship.

"Let's do this, kid," I say, glancing down at him.

His eyes are open, and he's not crying now, soothed by my rapid walk, maybe. I think I've been avoiding looking at him. Haven't wanted to see him, haven't wanted to know who I might fail. Haven't wanted to think about who he really is.

He's cute, and cutely gnawing on one slobbery fist that he's somehow snaked out of his swaddle. He's got blue eyes. Like mine. But then, all babies have blue eyes, don't they? That's a thing, isn't it?

Gods, I don't know anything about children. Don't want to. I look quickly away.

I step into an intersection, and in my distraction, I haven't covered myself with the ka'kari—but then, I don't know if I can cover the child with the ka'kari. What would the confluence of their magics do? A praetorian guard and his partner aren't far. The farther-away one is checking rooms they're passing, but the one in front locks eyes with me immediately.

He's only steps away, and he's holding his sword higher than mine already, so I step into Full Iron Gate without thinking to invite his attack. Only as I settle into a very low guard do I notice how much having a baby strapped to my chest messes up my stance. Full Iron Gate to Peasant's Strike? Iron Gate? More like Butter Gate!

Seeing my momentary confusion, the praetorian takes the High Guard of the Lady, betting on his own speed, and as I close quickly, to not give him time to reconsider, he does the same to not give me time to change guards. He bites on my low guard and the closing distance with a strong overhead strike. Sidestepping, I parry lightly to let his power take him through, reversing with the Peasant's Strike as his momentum carries him through his strike. My blade cuts into the back of his shoulder and neck, and then I cover my own back against his counter. He spins, slowed with the realization that he's been wounded, and my lunge takes him through the chest. With my left hand, I catch his slowly rising blade, then close to slam my right elbow into his chin, sending him careening into the wall and then down.

His partner—a spearman—is nearly upon me as I snatch up my blade and take another low guard, this time the Boar's Tusk.

Spears, not my favorite.

Having learned from his partner's example, this big man makes a feint at my hands before striking at my groin. I bat it away, advancing—you have to close distance with a spearman; otherwise he can take a hundred stabs at you while you only defend, and eventually, a stab will get through. But he's ready, and despite his size, he retreats at a speed that seems magical.

Because it is.

Because he's a blue mage, and he knows what I need to do against a spear, and he knows how to use magic to aid his movement to help him do what he needs to do.

But I have a sudden dismaying insight. Again I think of Durzo telling me there were whole fields of martial training that he couldn't even begin to teach me until I could use my Talent. With Talent-strengthened muscles, a man can move faster, farther, stop more quickly, and reverse his movements, too—all of which destroys your preconceived notions of what a fighting man's killing range is, or what yours is. With those assumptions exploded, techniques that would ordinarily be simply too slow or too short to bother practicing come into play, and figuring out which ones are and aren't affected by one's opponent having magic is surely something that takes years to learn.

But what magic doesn't change is the speed a warrior makes decisions. It's why Lantano Garuwashi—un-Talented as he is—can be the best duelist in the world.

I charge in, rising to a Crown guard at the last second, daring him to strike my legs—which he does just as I stop. I fling my front leg high, barely clearing the point of his spear, then stomp down on it. His spearpoint hits the ground, and as he holds on to it, his own retreat is slowed. He tries to reverse tack too late. My swordpoint goes through his eye and out the back of his head. My lunge and his carry us into each other even as he goes boneless.

He crunches into the kid, and I shove him off my blade, careful to make sure he's as dead as I think.

There's no one else in the hall. I check the first praetorian's body, lest he rally to throw magic or a knife into my back.

The kid starts crying again. I pat his butt within the sling as I've seen other people do. Butt pats, they're what you do, right?

"Easy, buddy. Easy," I say.

Buddy?

This hallway is the wrong direction. Gods, how much time has passed? Is the smugglers' boat still waiting?

I run as fast as I can, first backtracking past the bodies, and then straight forward. Almost there.

The child keeps crying. Maybe I'm patting it wrong.

I see more nobles, but they do nothing to stop me, maybe at seeing the blood on my blade, maybe at seeing that I've got a child, maybe at seeing the look on my face.

And then I'm out onto the open deck at the prow of the ship, under the glass or glassine covering. The deck's empty now that there's nothing to look at, the glass canopy closed against the weather. One blessing, one curse.

Grabbing the nearest chair, I stuff it against the door to bar it shut as I look around for some kind of control or levers to open the glass canopy covering this wide area with its chairs and tables and lounges and open areas for music and dancing and juggling and all the other entertainments the obscenely rich and powerful enjoy. It's easier than I expected. I head into a little central closet, and there's an array of obviously magical reception panels—which I have no idea how to operate.

But I do know how the Alitaerans think, now. And in moments, I think I find what I'm looking for. There are half a dozen offset cranks of the kind sailors use to hoist sails or augers, moving their hands in rapid circles opposite each other. Hand cranks, here? Where there are no sails? It can only be one thing: The Alitaerans built in redundancies in case the magic for closing up their ship safely failed. Perfect!

Turns out there's a use for punctilious bureaucrats in this world after all.

I grab a hand crank and run back outside.

The kid is *still* crying. Gods, it's the worst sound in the world.

Now that I know what I'm looking for, I see holes immediately—not one hole for the whole canopy, apparently the canopy is broken into at least a dozen sections. That suits me. Easier to move one section quickly than try to crank open the whole thing.

Slamming the crank into the hole, it takes me a few tries to get it to sit in whatever mount is inside. It sticks for a moment, and then, as soon as I begin turning it, a new alarm begins ringing out, announcing what I'm doing to the whole ship, which—granted—is already vibrating with a cacophony of alarms and yells.

I didn't think to barricade all the doors. In truth, it wouldn't be worth the time. Mages aren't going to be stopped for long by a few pieces of wood. Speed is my only friend here. And I pour it all into turning the hand crank.

I'm not lucky enough for the lowest section of glass to *rise* so I can slip under it once there's a gap. No, no, instead, the glassine canopy has to *lower*—from halfway across the high dome above me to slide into its sheath in the gunwale itself. Mercifully, the mechanism is well-oiled and the gearing easy. The glass slides smoothly and relatively quickly down, aided by its tremendous weight.

"All right, kid," I say. "Looks like we're gonna do this. Maybe. I need you not to do your little trick again for a bit, all right? No anti-magic until I get you to shore, got it?"

He stops crying. I realize it's the first time I've talked to him as if he were more than an animate blob. Not that he can understand, right? I mean, the Sisters said his soul isn't even attached to his body yet. He's still nothing more than a tiny animal. A piece of wiggling meat, not a person. Alive, but not human. Just a mouth, a butt, and an appetite.

I want to look him in the eye, check him to see what's going on, but all that matters is getting the glass down. I move the hand crank to the next hole. Anything that slows me from that isn't worth it.

And it's not far now. Over the sound of the storm knifing in from opening the dome, I hear a rattle at the door I barred. See a face, but it disappears. I don't recognize the person, can't even see if it's a praetorian or a servant or engineer of some kind, coming to check on the alarm. It could be the latter, right? If I'm lucky.

The glass is down to a mere ten feet over my head now when I hear a voice.

"Kylar!" someone says; it seems far away.

I look around. Can't tell where it's coming from.

"Kylar, can you hear me?"

Through the storm winds, I realize the voice must be coming from below, on the port side where the smugglers' ship should be. Is it them?

"Who's there? Who are you?" I shout, not slowing. Eight feet above my head now. I glance at the doors, but no one's there. Can I make the jump while holding the kid at seven feet?

"It's me! Your friend!"

My heart sinks as I finally recognize the voice. King Repha'im.

"I got here a while ago and was going to do this without you, but now . . . I'll wait. I want you to see this," he says.

I don't know what he's talking about. He's somewhere below me, but it doesn't sound like he's as far away as the smugglers' boat or the door at the waterline Phaena and I were trying to open. So where is he? Can he throw his voice with magic, like Scarred Wrable can? I twist around, suddenly fearful of an attack from behind.

My hands have kept making progress even as my mind does not. The glass is fully down. I lean over the side rail to see if the smugglers' boat is still here and if so, where I am in relation to it.

My heart leaps. It's here! Floating in the lee created by the storm ship itself, the smugglers' boat is manfully fighting the waves, which are smaller in the lee but still large enough to swamp the small boat. The smugglers see me as I see them, and wave triumphantly.

But halfway down the side of the ship, invisible to their eyes as they look up, I see Lord Repha'im and a dozen others crouching low on an inset deck.

At their feet, I see several other men in imperial tabards, lying dead. Attached to the railing, I see the ballistae and other ship's defenses. It takes me only a moment. The dead men are either the original defenders of the ship, killed on Momma K's orders to make the smugglers' approach safe, or they might be the men she hired, killed by Repha'im. Either way, it means the same thing. We did have friends trying to help us escape—and they're not here anymore.

This is where Repha'im went when he left—to bring reinforcements to the ship's defenses.

Repha'im sees me, and a huge smile curves his lips.

"Kylar!" he shouts. It should be harder to hear him, but the wind is so unnaturally steady, I can make out his words clearly. "Don't go. I've got a deal for you to consider."

There's another rattle at the door I blocked, but I can't even look back. Despair is rising in my throat like vomit.

"But first . . ." Repha'im says. He waves a hand. "At will, men."

The reinforcements rise as one, levering the ballistae up into place, the mages with magic blooming in their hand.

The smugglers see it. One jumps to the rudder to cut away from the storm ship.

A ballista bolt hits him so hard that he disappears, the only evidence of him a shoe flipping ten paces through the air toward the waves. The water hisses where magic bolts in red and blue and purple dimple the water as they miss the little boat. But other arrows and magic hurtling through the air thunk into wood and flesh. A portion of the boat's deck is torn away by another weighty ballista shot.

Gutshot by several arrows, one of the weather mages sags against the ropes holding him to his boat, then he levers himself upright. Roaring defiance, he reaches two separate hands of magic up into the very clouds. As huge powers gather to him and rain starts falling in weird sheets in two spots on the waves, I see sparks arcing and dancing along the defensive deck where Repha'im stands, and I have an intuition that when the weather mage brings those two magics held in either hand together, something awe-inspiring is going to happen—and I'm not sure I want to be close enough to see it.

He's hit by more arrows, but more miss. Magic streaking toward him curves inexplicably away. He shouts—

Before the two poles in the clouds touch, I see Repha'im raise a hand sharply as if delivering an uppercut and clenching it into a fist. An instant later, the seas erupt beneath the smugglers' boat, water shooting every direction, but through the fans of spray, bits of the water turn white and grind together like ice in a frozen river. An enormous fist of churning ice snares the weather mage. The hand is so large only his head sticks out. Then the hand clenches hard.

The mage *pops* like a meat pimple.

Repha'im jerks his clenched fist diagonally down, and a moment later, the ice fist slams diagonally down into the water, crashing through the decks of the smugglers' ship, which was barely holding together.

The weirdly localized rain ceases immediately, and the energies the mage was gathering rebound into lightning illuminating the clouds above us, diffusing into unnatural red and purple tones but not reaching the ship or the seas.

Repha'im hasn't stopped, though. He raises his open hand once again, fingers wide this time, and then clenches tight. Waves swamp the broken ship, four on one side, one on the other, then those watery fingers and thumb turn to ice and grip the broken ship. Then Repha'im pulls his hand down.

Desperately sawing at the ropes lashing him in place, the captain of the smugglers' boat leaps overboard an instant before the hand yanks the ship under the waves. He swims as arrows and magic pierce the waves or sizzle out in them.

I can't tell if he's diving to get out of range or if the waves are burying him. Even here in the storm lee of the ship, the waves are at least the height of a man and often twice that.

Then I see light bloom under the waves. The smuggler's using magic down there. Suddenly, he shoots up to the surface and into the air, his movement clearly magic-aided, but he's screaming. There's two lotai with their jaws sunk into him. He falls back into the waves, which are quickly stained red. He stops thrashing—but the lotai don't.

So the lotai are here, too. We didn't leave them behind when we reentered the storm.

The smugglers' boat is gone, reduced to flotsam. The smugglers, dead.

I fall back from the railing. It's over. The impossible job was impossible after all. Even for me. There's no way out. I'm finished. We're all dead.

Chapter One Hundred

A Cold Courage

The familiar voice floats up from below. "Kylar?" It has an amused tone to it, as if Repha'im's coaxing a silly cow that's trying to head into the wrong pasture. "Kylar, I know you can hear me. I know you're listening." His voice cuts through the sound of the wind as easily as his ballista bolt cut through that smuggler's body. "Kylar, I want to offer you a new deal now that I've seen how formidable you are."

I hear him, but I can't answer, can't even think anything.

"Kylar, do you want to know the deal?"

He sounds so pleased with himself that a sudden stab of hatred breaks me out of my shock. "What is it?" I ask, surly.

I shouldn't let him know I'm still here. I shouldn't do exactly what an enemy wants me to do. Durzo would beat me for forgetting such an elementary lesson: Never give the enemy what they want unless it gives you something you want that's better.

"You give me the child, and I let you swim for it."

"Sounds like a great deal," I say.

"You understand, surely. You've killed far too many of the empress's people for me to offer better than that. You threatened us all."

"I'm trying to *save* you all," I say.

"Sure. Sure. My men are on their way, Kylar. This is your last chance."

"You're serious? That's the deal?"

"To be honest, it's a little worse than that," he admits. "It's too bad. I would've let you be my slave. After you proved yourself loyal and did things that would guarantee you could never go over to my enemies, I would've let you raise the boy for me. For a time. But I was always planning to raise him as my own son. Properly managed, sons are so loyal to their fathers, or even their father figures, aren't they? You're still loyal to Durzo, even after everything. And I'm very particular about loyalty. So the boy will grow up as my son. Of a sort. You recall what I was telling you about a perfect weapon?"

I should be using the time while Repha'im's talking to run away. To do something.

But there's nowhere to run. Nothing to do.

"It's simple, really," he says. "I leave him with a trainer who abuses him frightfully, taking him right to the edge of breaking. Then I swoop in and rescue him, before leaving him again with another trainer, who is even worse. Then I swoop in, in a fury and kill the trainer, pretending I've just discovered how the man was abusing my son whom I love so much, and on we go. Girls and women will be brought in to train and betray him in much the same way so he learns that I'm the only one who cares, that all the world is against us. If ever he's slow in his training, when I come to check on him, I tell him I can't save him until he learns the skills that trainer alone can teach him. He'll learn that he must earn my favor through excellence. We all so want to earn our father's favor, don't we? And thus, with only a few weeks' personal effort over the course of years, I'll forge my weapon. Perhaps I forge magical bonds on him as well, but I doubt I'll need them—other than the obviously necessary hidden ones so I can kill him if he ever rebels.

"He may break under the training. I know that. Most would. But it's a gamble I'll take. Given his patrimony, I think this child will be able to take quite a lot of torture, don't you? After all, he is my son."

My gut's twisted in circles. I can't help but think how, minus the willful nature of it, Repha'im's plan for my son does sound similar to my own upbringing. If Count Drake and Momma K—my outside trainers—had been cruel instead of as kind as they were, and if Durzo had saved me from them, how much more tightly would I have been bound to him? As it was, my constant fear of coming up short—and him being forced to kill me—had driven me to the edge, repeatedly. It had certainly driven me to excellence. My son will have that and worse.

The prospect of someone deliberately inflicting a childhood worse than my own on my son is too much to bear. I know King Repha'im is taunting me, but I don't think he's lying about his plan. It's too well thought out to be an invention on the spur of the moment.

He's taunting me, but more to the point right now, he's freezing me. What am I doing? I have to move!

But where can I go?

There's nowhere. I can't hide away with hundreds of soldiers looking for me while I hold a crying kid. Even if I could hide myself for days, I have no way to feed him. He'll die.

And that's moot anyway. He's going to take out this whole ship as soon as his Talent awakens again, which seems like it could happen at any moment. Everyone's dead here, even the kid, who'll surely drown or be devoured by sharks or sea monsters, along with everyone else. Which might be the good trade the Sisters think it is, if I could trust that King Repha'im would die too.

For me, it turns out magic doesn't solve everything. For the kid, it turns out nullifying magic doesn't either.

But I can't give up. I'm Kylar Stern. I'm the Night Angel!

I'll think of something. I'm the guy who thinks of the third way. I am the breaker of dichotomies. I am the one who stares down the horns of a dilemma and vaults over the charging bull's head. I'm special, unique. I'm the one who can do what others cannot. That's who I am!

I peek over the railing. The defenders down below, still on their ballistae, still with arrows and magic ready, are watching, ready for me, in case I jump into the water. Only King Repha'im is gone.

If I jump into the water, they'll eviscerate me. And if by some miracle they miss? There are those things in the water. Alone, I'd give myself one chance in a thousand to make the swim to shore. And no chance at all if swimming with the child, and the child less than none.

Jumping into the water is like assassinating the child myself, only with extra steps.

I feel the dagger, the Sisters' little blue dagger, at my belt—and I push the idea away violently, my stomach turning.

There's banging on the door I blockaded.

By all the gods, where's Vi? She's here somewhere! She's going to show up, right?

She's got to show up. Maybe—maybe she's learned weather magic! Maybe she can help.

It's too painful to think that it's far more likely she's sitting gambling at some *zardu* table somewhere, sipping summer wine, trying to insinuate her way into the right social circles.

I scope out the defensive possibilities of the top deck: the chairs, the tables, the locked closet, the glassed-in observation bubble at the front. None of it's good. None of it makes victory remotely possible.

Vi, come on!

The idea that someone could be nearby in this floating city and not even have any idea that my fate, and the child's, and theirs, and possibly the entire Alitaeran empire's is about to be decided seems somehow too awful for words. I know that's literally true for thousands of the souls on this ship. But how can it be true of Vi?

She should just *know* I need her. She should feel it, like she would have felt it back when we didn't love each other but merely shared an intractable magical bond.

She must be on her way. She's somewhere, doing something that will turn out to be the key to our escape. I know it. She's fighting her way here. That's it.

She's got some secret way out of this. I know it.

I just have to hold out until she gets here. Vi wouldn't turn against me. When it really comes down to it, she'll help.

That's what love is; love means showing up, even when you can't fix anything. It means being there. And she loves me, I know she does.

Outside the doors, I see what's taking them so long. The imperials are mustering at all the doors to coordinate their attacks. Every way out is blocked.

The warrior-mages arrayed against me are too competent and too many. There's nowhere to escape *to*, even if I could escape. This is it.

"Kid," I say aloud. "We're not gonna make it."

As I hear the words in my own ears, they are a revelation. The heat of denial dissipates in the cool flagellating winds; the dissonance of telling myself lies that I know to be lies is blown away like gauzy cloth in a gale. My eyes clear.

My heart settles, settles into the cold courage of despair.

The child and I will be killed, but before the end, King Repha'im will come here to oversee the work himself. And I will kill him then.

That, now, is all my goal. I have to hold out to fight against impossible odds, not for rescue, but for the chance to save the world from Repha'im.

Pulling back the sling, I stare down at the child. He's awake but doesn't seem to notice me looking. I brush his baby-fat cheek with a finger. His cheek is unbearably soft. "Sorry, kid. I'm sorry for all the things you'll never get to do. Sorry I . . . Sorry I failed you."

Sword in hand, I walk to one of the doors that I haven't barred.

Be nice if Durzo showed up right now. It's the kind of time he's showed up before. On the other hand, I'm glad he hasn't seen all the dumb decisions I've made to get here. Doesn't matter. He's not coming. Not this time.

As I reach the door, I hear the soldiers in front shouting for orders, panicked, but they get answered by officers immediately. Too bad.

I throw open the door, and rather than let me waltz in to take their choke point, they charge.

The first soldier through the door loses some fingers, then his throat. The second, stumbling over him, swallows steel and vomits blood. The third, shoving aside the second, can't get his guard in place and loses his sword hand but keeps his life as the next two come through simultaneously with spears in the overhead Iron Bull guard to drive me back.

A blast to the side of me tells me the barricaded door has been blown open. A rising flower catches the first two pushers in front of me as my feint raises their quick guards and I slash across their thighs as they can't evade with the pressure of the men behind them.

Falling, they're trampled by their own comrades as the enormous praetorians pour through the twin doors. They rush hard, each man focusing on defense and positioning so they can bring their superior numbers to bear. But their desire for position gives me something to deny, and I do.

The third man has one of their few shields, and in his haste to move forward, I'm able to hack at a briefly exposed foot before sliding my parry up his comrade's spear into the man's fingers. I press in, attacking the men behind those two, guiding aside a spear into the fingerless man's back. But then I have to retreat as I see that they're fanning into large and small circles, and the opposite side of the small circle is collapsing in on me to flank me.

I've never seen such discipline. They push hard to take up advantageous positions, ignoring losses to deploy their men into place. Their very orders are shouted in code so I can't gain the slightest advantage.

As the circle falls upon me, the world both fades and sharpens. Inessentials fall away. Buffeted backward by a battering blow barely blocked, I can't make out words—but I *can* hear a footfall on wood as I complete my backflipping roll over a table, body tucked around the child, launching with my Talent to kick a praetorian in the face while he's in mid-backswing. I do hear the hiss of expelled breath as a man behind me lunges. There is now only perception and proprioception: danger and my body in space evading it.

I don't see men or faces, but the turn of hips, telling me where weight is about to move; the landing of the front foot signaling a flèche; the pivot of an empty hand gathering magic.

The ka'kari is now armor, now a shield, now another set of limbs: a blade from my foot as I spin and slice through the leg of a pergola, and then as I evade a long thrust from a saber in Hanging Guard the ka'kari becomes a glove allowing me to snatch the blade with one hand as I perforate my attacker's chest with four quick stabs. I turn and the ka'kari blooms to a shield as a gout of flame hits it and mushrooms every direction.

As the pergola falls—it seems as if a minute has passed, though in truth it fell immediately—I cross-step behind my own leg and then kick the post again before it can crash to the ground, throwing the entire structure into a mass of soldiers, buying me time.

A detached part of me registers approval. I've never fought so well in my life. But that satisfaction is distant. What's immediate is the sheer pleasure of movement, paired with the joy of being confronted with test after test, some with simple answers—facing this, you must retreat. Retreating, what direction is most advantageous? When do you turn to a new opponent, and when do you double back? Other tests are more difficult: Having stepped here, with that incoming poleax, and these attacks possible from his compatriot with the hand and a half sword in that guard, do I grapple or bind?

The end of the test is inevitable. There are questions coming to which there are no right answers. They can make a hundred mistakes; I can't afford one.

But the end doesn't matter. Only now matters.

The battle becomes a moving meditation. I am the nexus of beauty and ugliness, the axis of life and death spinning off-kilter, destined to fall, held up only by the speed of its own motion. I hear, see, feel, know. Hear the tempo of a man's movement like the terrestrial echo of the music of the spheres. See in a glance how a man's musculature and training and the length of sword and arm and leg come together to determine how he is able to move, I can feel the possibilities of his attacks: Even if he moves at double time or in triplets, there are only a few speeds at which he can move, and thus can I ride his beat, waiting for his attack to commit him, counterattacking before his blow can land.

And finally I understand how Lantano Garuwashi, without the Talent, is the best duelist in the world. Along with his mastery of fighting styles and his many natural physical gifts and long training, he always feels these currents, rides them. He understands fighting intuitively. With long training, many people come to learn their own capabilities on an instinctive level. He knows himself and his opponent, not in the mind, but in the body, where knowledge becomes instinct, which is faster, more lethal.

It's how I know that no matter what, I'm doomed.

A head pops off after I crash into a spearman, a shield bearer, and a pure mage. I have no memory of sweeping it off, only the grapple to disarm, coming away with the spear in my left hand and sword in my right, spear's feint blocked high by the shield, stab through the shield bearer's shin, and then I kick the falling head through the twisting magics the retreating mage is gathering between his hands.

The collision or the mage flinging his hands wide as he falls backward throws fire into the men lined up around him. As they're distracted, I call the ka'kari into the form of a knife and punch it through the chest of the shield bearer who's writhing on the floor.

The mage's flames give me an opening. I hadn't seen the circles close around me, but now I see a gap in the circle, and I leap through.

My roll is thrown off as I realize belatedly I'd not thought of cushioning the child, but I make it back to my feet outside the closed circle, though not—unfortunately—on the side nearest the exit. Instead, I'm outside of the circles, but toward the front of the foredeck.

"Stop! Stop, you fools! Pull back!"

It's the only voice that could've broken my reverie. King Repha'im's.

"Fall back!" Repha'im commands, furious. "He's got my child! How dare you attack him this way! Nets and catchpoles, now!"

It takes a moment for the soldiers to disengage.

Maybe I should go after them, but as my concentration is broken, I'm suddenly aware of how exhausted I am. My breath is haggard, body shaking. They draw back in good order, too, covering each other as they grab those who are merely wounded, dragging them to safety, leaving behind the dead.

They don't leave the foredeck, though, and the retreat to regroup is the worst thing for me they could've done. Whatever I'm gaining by getting to rest, I'm losing by our separation, by their restoration of order. They have mages and will have bows momentarily: Bows are rarely carried within the tight confines of the ship, but I know they have them aboard, stowed somewhere. With the addition of more ranged attacks to the fight—even nonlethal ones—my position has gotten much, much worse. Before, I could keep close to the impe-rials and move quickly, frustrating any attempts at magical ranged attacks. No one wants to throw a fireball into his comrade's back.

"Kylar," Repha'im says loudly. "It's time for you to face reality." He doesn't come out of the ranks of his mages and bodyguards, doesn't put himself within a league of whatever danger I might pose to him.

"And what's that?" I shout. I've put a support beam between me and many of the troops and upended several tables to give me some concealment, if not cover, should they decide to light me up. I have no more plan than that. I could use the ka'kari to break a glassine window, but...to do what? Can't jump. Can't keep the kid safe and try to climb along the hull to some other part of the ship.

Even if we made it, *nowhere* is safe on this ship as long as he's on it. Repha'im killed us all the moment he brought a magic-negating child aboard a ship held together with magic.

"My deal!" Repha'im shouts. "You can't win. You know that. It was a val-iant last stand. You've proven your courage. If you don't surrender him now, things only get worse for everyone. Hand the child over, and you at least have the possibility of escape. It's hope, Kylar! Live to fight another day."

"Live, huh?"

"You're a good swimmer, I'm sure. Or you can stay. I'll take you alive. What happens afterward won't be pleasant. The empress is not forgiving."

"There is no afterward," I say. More men are arriving, handing out catch-poles and weighted nets. The longer this goes on, the more the noose tightens around my neck, and I still have no plan.

"We want at least one of the same things, Kylar. We want that boy not to be harmed. So let's put him aside."

"Fine," I shout, "a duel, then. You and me, winner keeps the boy and goes to shore."

"You're challenging me to a duel?" he asks, incredulous.

"What are you, a coward?" I say.

He laughs. "Not a coward, Kylar. But not a moron either. A duel!" He laughs with scorn.

Sitting with my back against a table, I scan the stormy skies.

You know, Durzo, you flying in out of nowhere right about now would be real nice.

But there's no Durzo. No Vi. No one's going to save me from the consequences of my own choices this time. If I drop the kid and jump, regardless of whether I make it to shore, Vi is going to die. Either with everyone else in the null storm, or in the suicide mission the Chantry has given her. If she succeeds, and if by some further miracle she survives the suicide mission...she'll have to live with having murdered a child.

It'll destroy her. For years, she's been trying so hard to escape the way of shadows. If she does something for the Chantry that's more awful than anything she ever did for the monster Hu Gibbet, it'll tear her soul to pieces. She'll never recover.

"I won't let you have him!" I shout.

"You will," King Repha'im says. "And I'll be a better father than you ever could be. Do you know why?"

"I don't want to hear this." I open the sling and look at the baby.

"Because you're you," King Repha'im says. "You're unfit to be a father and you know it. Rash, mercurial, gullible, inconstant. You're rootless, friendless, resourceless, and alone. No, not just alone. You will pass along to him that disease of loneliness Durzo bequeathed to you. That thing that keeps everyone at a distance, that makes you brittle and hollow and increasingly full of rage. That is all you own, all you are, Kylar, and that is the only legacy you have to pass down to any child. I, on the other hand, will give him the world. You've lost, Kylar. You've lost everything to me, and all you can do now is make it worse."

"You need to let us go," I say, looking at the child's tiny features. He grabs my finger. I can't even muster the will to look and check that their men haven't moved to threaten us from some new direction. The black tide of desolation rolls through me. "The boy's going to send out another null wave any moment now. One that'll knock out the magic on this ship permanently. It'll kill everyone. You've got to have an escape boat. Put us on it. Put me on it with a dozen of your mages. But get us off the ship, or everyone dies, Repha'im."

"Oh, you know this? How?"

"The Chantry's Healers—"

"The Chantry! And you believe them! How quaint. You think those witches know more than I do?"

"You..."

I'm about to say he has to believe me. But he doesn't. And he won't.

"No," I hear him say, obviously not to me, though. I peek my head over the table. He's chastising Intan, one of the head mages I eavesdropped on earlier. "No, I can't spare any mages now! They'll be down in due time. It'll be soon. Make do with the mages you have."

I notice only then that some of the alarms have stopped going off, and the storm ship is moving again, if still listing. The mages and technicians are making some progress combating whatever damage the last null storm did to the ship.

"All right, Kylar, then let's do this the hard way," Repha'im says.

I'm about to raise my voice to answer him when a gentle, icy wave laps through me. It's coming from the child.

I immediately feel weak. Like solid ice melting to slush and then to water, my Talent slips from my grasp, and then I can't even feel it.

Are you gone? I ask the ka'kari.

It doesn't answer.

It's like a kick in the stomach. I thought if I had to go out, at least I'd go out powerfully. I knew I'd tire eventually, misjudge a feint, not see an arrow—but Death would find me on my feet, roaring defiance. Strong.

Not like this.

Null waves are pulsing gently from the child, surrounding us in a nearly invisible bubble. From inside it, I can't see exactly how far it extends. But I have a guess.

I watch the imperial guards slowly fan out, with more shields now, and nets and catchpoles.

You can still hear me, right? Hate to be talking to myself, narrating my end to no one.

My end. The words rattle around my head like potsherds, jagged, scraping the inside of my skull. Truth is, it needs to be my end. It'll go even more disastrously for the world if I'm captured and studied than it would be for the child to be captured and studied.

Vi never showed up.

I suppose maybe if she had, she would've had to fight me—but still, it would've been nice to see her one last time.

They've spread out widely enough now that my cover is about to be totally ineffective. Standing, I shift my right hand low on the pommel and put my left hand onto the blade of my sword in a Short Serpent Guard.

Immediately, several of the warrior-mages pop out over the tower shields their comrades hold, shooting white balls of light toward me in a wide spray. I try to leap backward—but my Talent isn't there, and I don't move as fast or far as intended. I bring the sword to slap aside the bolts, but there are too many, too well placed.

But at four paces away from me, the white balls are torn asunder, the carefully gathered energies ripped and then devoured, with only a small splash of light before even that is devoured. Not one of them gets closer than three paces from me.

I see consternation sweep through their ranks. No one's ever seen anything like it.

Someone tries again, this time with a much larger white missile the shape of an arrow.

It gets no farther than the first did.

I take advantage of their confusion to run to the point farthest forward on the deck, dashing up a few stairs to the area that looks like a glass globe, protruding out from the prow like a figurehead, hanging over the very waves. The entrance is three paces wide, and the observation globe probably four or five. There's only one way in and out, no furniture, no cover except the doorposts. I've sacrificed all mobility to force them to attack through a bottleneck.

They close formation and advance without any hurry. Their ranks part enough that I see three men making their way to the front. Someone's dug through the baggage and found three sets of full harness: plate with maille beneath and full helms with magnificent plumage. It's showy stuff, appropriate for the empress's bodyguards: embossed and filigreed with unique designs for each of them. The one in the lead is unmistakable with his armor's long-curving horned ibex design, and his one arm. Helmed and visor lowered as he is, I can't read his expression, but I can tell exactly how happy he is to see me again. Immediately behind the front three praetorians' shieldwall is lean Kynígi, her cold dead eyes glittering beneath a helm like a howling mandrill, with her heavily plated left-arm manica enameled blue and her narrow-headed trident weaving, ready to stab for any opening.

My heart's in my throat.

No armor and no space to move and no Talent and holding a baby, against these fighters, armored? And then the forty beyond them? Even if I can kill these praetorians, as soon as their comrades coordinate the mundane missile weapons they're holding, I'm dead.

I look down at the child.

The three armored giants set foot on the stairs.

"Stop," I say.

I toss my sword to the deck and scoop the child out of the sling.

Packed tight in his swaddling except for one arm, he's easy to handle. His eyes are open and alert, but he's not crying.

If I ignore every one of my failures and all the folly that brought me here, if I simply run it by the numbers, this gets simple, doesn't it?

I can't give up. Giving up means letting everyone die. Repha'im isn't going to take the baby's powers seriously until the ship is going down, and even if he can get out of here himself, surely he won't have any better luck than I would trying to keep the child alive on a swim through these waters.

Maybe Repha'im's right: Make it a problem of arithmetic. Philosophy as arithmetic. Morality as mathematics.

Take the ship's total manifest and decide: From the total, is it better to subtract one soul, or every soul? Act now, or hope that some miracle saves me from having to act? If you want to call that a hope. I've been delaying. I've been hoping.

Hope has made me its fool long enough.

There is no good way out, there's no bad way out, there's no way out at all—but there is one solution that's slightly less intolerable than the others. I always said I was special. I always thought I was the one who could do the impossible.

Maybe I was right. Only it turns out the impossible thing I have to do isn't the impossible thing I thought I'd get to do.

I draw the blue dagger I stole from Vi. So this is what Jenine saw me doing. This is why she hates me. This is why she tried to stop me, even though she knew she couldn't.

I feel my mind splitting. I feel as if I'm watching myself from outside.

"Kylar!" Repha'im shouts. "Kylar, stop! What are you doing?"

I look into the child's eyes, and his eyes focus on mine. The Sisters say a child's soul doesn't attach to his body until around three months, that it's merely an animal until then. You can kill it and it's not murder. Unpleasant, but not murder.

Maybe they're right.

But even if they are, it's too late for this child. It's been three months. These eyes aren't vacant. This is no animal. This is a child.

My child. My *son*.

I haven't really, really looked at him until now. One glimpse of his blue eyes was all. I stopped. Why? What was I afraid of?

"Kylar…" King Repha'im is pushing through his men, now, coming up the steps. "Don't do it."

"If I don't, everyone dies. Even him."

"No, Kylar. Not everyone," Repha'im says, pitching his voice lower. He turns to the praetorians. "You three, back for a moment. Ishael, cover me."

His personal guard Ishael takes one of the tower shields and the praetorians pull back warily, and not far.

"There," Repha'im says. "Privacy. Look."

He pulls up his sleeve to show me something. There, filling the rune-grooves of a platinum bracelet that matches the one Momma K gave me to hold my ka'kari, is a deep blue stone. It's the blue ka'kari. In a flash, I remember someone said something about the Tlaxini Maelstrom closing and becoming a shipping lane. That's where the blue ka'kari was, absorbing and then exploding out water, over and over, for centuries. Now Repha'im has it. He says, "I've not mastered its powers yet, but I can save him."

The Sisterhood must've had some hint of it. It was exactly what they feared—Repha'im and the child alone escaping. I feel like he's hit me in the guts.

But that doesn't explain—

He answers the question before I can ask.

"Alitaera's too ossified, too stable to move as quickly as I need them to for the coming wars. The child solves that. Half the court gone so they can be replaced, by me," Repha'im says with a little glance back to be sure the praetorians are far enough away not to overhear him. "And the storm ship sinking? *Clearly* a magical attack by the Chantry, an attack demanding our vengeance, spurring Alitaera to turn all its might toward making war."

He smiles, a real smile that lights up his handsome features. "I have to admit it. I got lucky. It almost all went wrong for me. The Sisters tried to kidnap the boy. Can you believe it? But one of them told me everything. In return for letting them leave, I sent a man to collect the chest they'd concealed the child in. So imagine my surprise when I said my farewells to the empress on her dock and found out she'd gone behind my back and was snatching the child away herself, taking him with her to Cloud Point. I couldn't complain, not to my empress. I had to play it off as if I didn't care, as if I didn't feel betrayed, as if she weren't making everything ever so much harder with her silly little power play. And when it seemed nothing more could go wrong, that's when I saw Phaena, my newest nursemaid, dressed up looking fat as a heifer. Why would she look like that? I asked myself. There was only one answer.

"So I distracted the others to make sure Phaena made it off the empress's boat, and waited until it was too late for them to dock again before calling the alarm myself so the empress would know it wasn't my work to keep the child on the ship. We'll see if my luck holds. I hope the empress was deceived. I'll find out soon enough. For you're only half-right, Kylar. The blue ka'kari changes everything. Everyone else will die, but Caedan doesn't have to. Accept the loss, Kylar. Hold on to hope that you can find him some other day. But for now . . . give me my son."

It's a mockery. He can't help himself. But it doesn't move me, except to make me look down at my son.

I was never going to get to raise him. My life is too dangerous. Everything Repha'im said about me is true. I'd be a terrible father.

Repha'im waves to the praetorians to step forward once more.

"Stop," I say to Repha'im, bringing the knife close to my son's throat. Ishael angles his shield to block Repha'im, in case this is some trick. Repha'im stops in place.

I look at Ishael. He's no friend of mine, but I've got no reason to believe he's insane. "You heard what he said," I say. "He's planning to let everyone die. Including you."

"That's what he said," Ishael acknowledges. "If it's true, I'll die loyal."

I curse him, the death of my last hope hurting more than it should.

"Kylar," Repha'im says gently.

I look down at my son, stroke his baby-soft cheek with a thumb, and tears leaking from my eyes, I smile at him.

He smiles back. I've never seen him smile before.

I've never seen anything so beautiful.

A hum begins, so powerful it reverberates in my chest. It's emanating from my son, though he seems untroubled by it. I can feel vast energies gathering to him.

I glance at the Sisters' dagger. It's swimming with magics, still, hardened like they said against the anti-magic pulsing around us. I don't know what the

Chantry's magic does or why they thought it was so important Vi use it. But I've got no reason to trust them.

The humming is pitching higher.

Repha'im backs away, alarmed. He's looking at the blue ka'kari, scowling as if he's surprised that it's not obeying his commands. He hasn't had it long. Apparently he wasn't lying when he said he hasn't mastered it yet.

But it's too late. I can feel the null bubble pull back, power returning in to my son, not as if it's over—though the others seem to think so. No, this is like how the ocean recedes from the beaches right before the tsunami strikes, the waters drawing back into the mouth of the sea before they're spewed forth to race up and over the wall of the dikes and burst into the flatlands, obliterating all beyond.

Caedan's eyes scrunch in discomfort. He gathers himself, twisting, pained, as if preparing to wail.

Like the last time after the null wave, the black ka'kari has puddled into a ball from the null wave hitting it.

'There are no impossible jobs, only impossible prices,' Durzo once said.

I always thought he was talking about money.

There's only one way I can save Vi's life. And Phaena's. And Jenine's. And everyone else's.

I know what I need to do. What I need to obey now isn't hope, it's arithmetic.

I've never been more alone. This is why I serve in darkness.

Make the knife.

The ka'kari stays a ball, runes pulsing with cold incandescent blue fire, words burning, desperate, but illegible to me.

I know you can hear me. Become the knife!

The runes fade. The ka'kari sinks into my palm, silent, obedient.

Hey. Listener. You know our deal? How I promised I'd tell you when it was time to look away?

I lied. This time you don't get to look away. This time, you have to look.

Look, damn you! You wanted blood, didn't you? That's why you're here, isn't it? So I'm not going to let you turn away. You *fucking* look!

I hug my son to my heart. I know what I need to do. Repha'im's distracted by the blue ka'kari's refusal to do what he wants. Ishael's a stone, either not understanding or not caring what I'm about to do, but a look of confusion passes over the Ibex's face, then disbelief as he sees I really mean to do it. I look down.

My heart fails. I can't do it.

Do it.

Help me!

"*DO IT!*" I scream, weeping as powers gather, as the wave of power within my son crests, as he takes a breath to wail a cry that will destroy the ship and kill everyone aboard. And in that moment, as if I've waited until the very moment my enemy is committed to his attack to launch my counterattack, I hug Caedan's head tight against my cheek.

"Do it," I beg the ka'kari.

The ka'kari shoots out from my hand like a spring-loaded stiletto. It stabs into the base of my son's brain. I flinch, my training outrunning my horror as I twist the blade in the golden triangle by pure instinct before I pull it out.

My son goes limp, boy turned to body instantly, painlessly. A good kill. Dead before he can even tell anything's wrong. That everything's wrong.

I hug him convulsively against me. Someone is screaming. My throat hurts.

With Caedan's magic-dampening field gone, my Talent comes rushing back like a tide. The ka'kari's screams are suddenly as deafening inside my head as my own.

But I can't make out the words. As all my senses shriek, faces before me blurring, expressions twisting, magic roaring, somehow I'm splitting, somehow I can't hear.

All the gathered magical energy goes rushing back out and away from us in a vast concussion. It blows out all the hardened windows of the observation globe behind me, and all the windows of the foredeck, leaving me standing with nothing behind me but a few metal support beams, and the raging oceans beneath.

The three praetorian bodyguards have tackled and pulled back King Repha'im. He's shielded under their huge bodies, a bubble of magic surrounding him, protecting him already. Men are yelling, clambering back to their feet, confused, afraid, not yet comprehending.

I close my eyes. I'd be happy to let them kill me, but I can't let them get Caedan's body, can't let them run their damned experiments on my boy.

I have no heart to fight, but I can't throw him away into the sea like so much garbage, can't let him be meat to be devoured by the monsters there.

Far away, the doors to the foredeck blast off their hinges, magic and fire roaring out. Viridiana flings warrior-mages out of her way as if they're chaff.

She is wreathed in flames, her hair itself glowing as if afire. She is awesome and terrible and far, far too late.

"Kylar! No!" Vi shouts, seeing me. In a snapping inferno of gold and red, she blazes a path through the soldiers, most of them too stunned to resist, men tossed to either side by her glory. And as if it took no time at all, or maybe that's only because I can't think, can't act, she's before me. She scoops up the blue dagger where I must've dropped it. Tucks it in my belt. "Keep this. It'll keep you safe," she says. She scoops the child from my arms before I can react.

Only then does she look down.

My skin is awash with Vi's magic. Flares spark around her and me as soldiers' arrows are burned to ash by her whiplike defensive spells, the iron arrowheads snapped away, heated red-hot, ricocheting away. My eyes take in the threats, as they always have, reading the battlefield, but I can't read her lips, her expression.

But even I can read the confusion yielding to shock in her face as she sees what I've done. Even I can recognize the utter horror filling her eyes. Next she'll turn her eyes toward mine. She'll ask me what I've done.

I snatch the boy back with a howl like a madman, possessive, as if I can conceal what I've done now. It's too late to hide what I am. I flee from what I know I'll see in her eyes.

Retreating across the open metal supports, I hug my son to my chest, his soft cheek already cold against mine in the cruel lashing winds. There is nowhere else to run. I've reached the end. Hugging tight a treasure I've already lost, I lean back, back, and I fall, fall—plunging from the prow of the storm ship into the frigid embrace of a merciless sea.

Chapter One Hundred One

Poisoned Wine

*I*n the feeble light of the solitary candle, a teardrop glistened atop the word *merciless*. The ink didn't feather into the water, nor smear, nor spread. The lonely tear, shimmering with reflected candlelight, stood proud on the page.

Viridiana felt as if she were watching a curiosity from some great distance. A teardrop? Who was crying?

She wasn't sure how long she had sat, watching the teardrop soak into the parchment, not thinking, praying she could continue not to think, when a knock startled her. Little light filtered in through the fresh foxglass they'd used as a temporary repair for the windows she'd blown out earlier. The knock hadn't come from the door to the little library, though. It had come from where the hidden door opened.

Sister Ariel was still gone. She wouldn't have knocked regardless.

Viridiana stood uncertainly.

"Vi," a voice called from the hidden room. "Can you open up? I don't know how this thing works." It was Uly, her thirteen-year-old roommate.

Viridiana tilted the book on the shelf she'd seen Sister Ariel tilt before, noticing dimly that it was titled *There Are No Secrets: 400 Debunked Formulae on Properties of a Circle*. The door swung open, scraping the floor in its arc once again. Uly followed, looking tense.

"They voted for peace," Uly said without preamble.

"Oh? That's good," Viridiana said, still dazed.

"No, no it's not, Vi," Uly said. "It's a disaster. They're gonna murder you."

"Oh, that's too bad." Viridiana was trying to focus on Uly, on the present, but she felt far from her body. Nothing that happened here felt important.

"You finished your project?" Uly asked.

"Uh-huh."

Uly stared at the remaining pages. "You reached the end of the book? There's no more?"

"There's more. But I'm *finished*. I can't..." Vi trailed off. She was still in a fog, still seeing that forecastle deck, then the waves rushing up at her, her vision split between her own memory and Kylar's account. She should have more than one tear, shouldn't she? What was wrong with her?

"Did you find what they wanted?" Uly asked.

"What they—oh, no. No, I didn't. I found nothing but my own guilt," Vi said, and it felt like the first honest thing she'd said in months.

"Then...maybe you should finish reading?" Uly said. "Are you all right?"

"No. And no, I'm not," Viridiana said, hugging herself.

"Sister Ariel said you need to find it. That you can't stop. She got the kitchens to bring dessert up to all the councilors to stall them. They're still there, on the floor. She says if you can finish before too many leave, there will still be a quorum. It might not be too late."

"What do you mean too late?" Viridiana said, finally feeling like she was coming back to herself.

Uly looked around as if worried about eavesdroppers, then shrugged as if it didn't matter. She merely lowered her voice. "She said if you want them to vote for war, you need to trade them something worth the blood and treasure it'll cost. You need to tell them where the ka'kari is."

Viridiana pulled back. "I don't want them to vote for war."

"Yes, you do," Uly said.

"No, I don't."

"You're supposed to be the grown-up here, Vi!" Uly said. "No one wants war. But peace always comes at a price. The peace declaration empowered a small group of Sister Ayayah's friends to do what they must to secure the peace—and you're a war mage. And not one of those neutered blues the Alitaerans can control. You're the one whose very existence violates the Alitaeran Accords. You're the one who made it obvious what you could do on the storm ship. They say you scared the hell out of the Alitaerans. Sister Ariel says that means as soon as dessert is over, delegates will be voting to hand you over to Alitaera as a peace offering. It's all already decided. The Alitaerans will charge you with several dozen counts of murder."

"Several *dozen*? I didn't kill that many. Humiliated a few, sure—"

"Every one of Kylar's kills is to be laid on you."

After a moment of surprise, Vi smiled. For the first time in what felt like days, she smiled. "Oh. That's fair, then."

"Fair? Vi!" Uly said. "You have to stop this. You can't do this. Vi, I can't lose you too. I've already lost Elene, and then Kylar. I can't lose you too." She was trying to hold herself together, but Vi could see the emotions rising in her young friend like a tide.

"I know this is hard, Uly, but—"

"I know a way out!" Uly blurted, then flinched at the prospect of having been overheard.

"There's no way out," Viridiana said, patiently, sorrow welling up in her. She had never even thought of what this all would do to Uly.

"I mean an actual way. Of here. Of the Chantry. You can come with me. We'll escape together. Come on, Vi. You're my best friend. If a friend can't get you out of trouble, it's their holy duty to get into trouble with you. Isn't it?"

"Oh, sweet—"

"You can teach me everything I need to know about magic, and fighting, and . . . it'll be great. It'll be way better than here!"

"Oh, Uly."

"Don't 'oh, Uly' me!" Uly said, tears springing up in her eyes. "Don't you dare give up. Kylar never did. You have to keep fighting. For me. For you, too. He wouldn't have given up on you. How dare you! I can go get Gwaen and Sarren and, and Aeryx—all right, maybe not Aeryx. And we can—"

Vi took a deep breath. "I'm not giving up, Uly. Anyone who betrayed Kylar should die, don't you think?"

"Yes!"

"That's *me*. I betrayed him. I deserve whatever they do to me. If my death can buy life for many of my Sisters? Then maybe that'll be the best thing I've ever done."

"No, I don't believe you. You're just trying to get me to go away. You're protecting me, aren't you? You don't want me in danger. I can make the choice myself. This is what I want, Vi. I'm almost fourteen years old, and—"

"You barely turned thirteen a—"

"Same thing! You're lying!"

Viridiana didn't want to face all the truth, not with Uly, maybe not with anyone she loved, but maybe it had to come out. Maybe that was the price she had to pay. "You remember the story I told you about the rooftop, where Kylar and I got poisoned the night the twins were abducted?"

Uly said nothing, merely glared at her defiantly. She remembered.

"I poisoned the wine, Uly. I drank it myself first so he wouldn't suspect me. Worked better than I'd have believed. I mean, I read this"—Viridiana waved to the book open on the desk—"and he didn't even think *once* about me taking an antidote first. Which, given his training, he really should've."

"You poisoned Kylar?" Uly said, incredulous.

"I had to fight the team about it. I told them I was going to drink it first because I feared they'd use a lethal poison if I didn't. Reyhan—she was the team's assassin, she died later during the operation—didn't like that one bit, which made me think I was right and she'd been meaning to murder Kylar. But you see? I've been going back and forth on my loyalties from the beginning. I thought I could build peace on a foundation of lies. But peace built on anything but truth is a tower built on sand."

"Vi, please. Please. You have to come with me," Uly said, her face racked with confusion and denial.

"It's Viridiana now, little sister. And you're wrong. I have to stay. Please go now. I'd hate for you to get in trouble for nothing."

As Viridiana went to sit down again, sitting before the manuscript where the tear had finally soaked in, Uly shouted, "I thought you understood. I thought you were like me. You're nothing like me! I hate you!" and slammed the secret door as hard as she could, sending books tumbling off the shelves.

Viridiana stared unseeing at the manuscript until she heard the outer door of the hidden room slam too, telling her the young woman was safely away.

"See, Uly? Turns out we have something in common after all."

A few minutes later, the main door of the little library opened. Four Sisters that Viridiana had never met before came in, their hands up, Talents full to bursting, ready for a fight. Six guards followed them. The words on the page of the book disappeared.

"Sister Viridiana Sovari, you're under arrest," a square, freckled Sister said.

"It's kind of insulting that they only sent four of you," Viridiana said. She sighed. Moving slowly, she pulled the lever to seal the protective magic over the book and stood.

The guards, all of them big men who clearly thought they were tough, took offense. At least those who realized whom Viridiana was omitting from her count.

"Viridiana—" the freckled Sister began.

"Please don't tell me it'll go easier for me if I come quietly," Viridiana said.

The woman cut off, robbed of her words.

Viridiana put her hands out, and they slapped manacles on her, none too gently. "No gag, huh?" she asked. "For a Sister?"

One cringed. He'd forgotten. He dug in a pouch and belatedly produced a gag.

"Guess it was too much to hope," she said.

"You seem to know how this goes better than we do," the Sister said. "How many times have you been arrested anyway?"

"Depends how you count," Viridiana said. "Good news for both of us, though. Looks like this time'll be the last."

JUDGMENT DAY

Chapter One Hundred Two

A Self, Fragments

*V*omiting water and blood. Choking, coughing on sand and seawater. Collapse. Blackness again.

Sand beneath cheek. A flaying wind. Volleys of sand shot deep into my many wounds.

Bright sun but cold. Blood flowing up my arm, driven by the blast-furnace wind, studded with sand, drying in spiderweb lines.

I uncurl my body from around the small corpse. Wet.

Lost. Confused.

The flashes bring only pain as they pull mind and body back together.

I stand, leaning hard against the wind—

And fall again, skin cut as if by a thousand knives.

I lie there until dark comes and light comes again, fading in and out. When the light comes full, I feel new strength. My Talent.

I'd forgotten.

I pull the ka'kari to my skin, make an armor shell of it. Hold my son to my stomach and cover him too with ka'kari, as if bearing him in a womb. We share a skin.

He is dead inside me, and together we walk. Together, we rot.

We pass valleys. Those with streams feel unnatural, so thick are they with wildlife, all sheltering from the killing winds, as I've heard animals will do in forest fires. I drink and move on. Even though I'm wearing the ka'kari tight as a skin, the carrion eaters can smell the stench of death on me. There will be no rest under the hungry eyes of coyotes and buzzards and wolves.

I snatch up a cowering rabbit and keep walking.

Find a dead valley. No water. A few small animals. More of them dead. The sickly sweet smell of decaying flesh not blasted away as soon as one would like, here in the storm lee of some pitted boulders. A lone olive tree, its upper branches denuded by the storm, clings to life despite the winds.

Don't know how long I've been walking. I find a spot in the shade of the olive tree. Ka'kari coats my hands to make spades. Kneel on the earth. The work would be easier if I set the body to one side while I sweat and stoop. But I can't. Can't see him for so long, staring, judging.

So I dig.

Sun sets. Sun rises. I finish. I am as hollowed out as the earth at my feet.

I know death. Know what's coming, what's waiting as soon as I pull the ka'kari-skin back. Take a breath, hold it so as not to vomit.

Pull away the ka'kari-skin that was the last thing to bind us together.

He's so small!

I feel myself flying from my body, as if flung to a great height, away, away.

Against the howling wind, a man keens.

The figure far below me moves through actions I can't understand. Putting a bundle in a hole, climbing out, fingernails splitting on rock. I feel flashes between things too close and too far away.

Sudden panic. It scrambles away from the hole, vomits on nothing. Then I'm far away again, watching it push dirt into the hole, then stones, then more dirt. With a large rock, it pounds the dirt flat, scatters the extra dirt, one trip at a time.

No hurry. It takes hours. I feel burning in my chest, weakness in my limbs.

It notices a blue dagger, and it is a reminder of death. It sets the blade in the dirt to mark the spot, then reconsiders. The blade is hideous under its beauty; it was made to kill a child. The figure snatches it up and hurls it far out to sea.

Then it finishes, quietly stands over the grave, which it has carefully set vegetation and rocks on as if randomly. In a month or two, no one will know it's a grave at all.

I find myself falling back toward my body, though I don't want to go, don't want to lose this calm.

But the calm is here, too. I'm empty.

"I'm supposed to have words now. Give you that much, at least," a voice says. Mine.

I stand for minutes. Hands folded, half-naked, it seems a mockery. "I, uh, did my best to make it safe here. Neither animal nor man should bother you. Son, I wish..."

There's no way to end that sentence that isn't obscene. Nothing I could say that isn't an excuse for the inexcusable. No one else did this. I did it. I chose it.

I'm the Night Angel. I'm supposed to be the Avatar of Justice, and what have I done?

I stand there a long time.

Nothing comes to me. Neither solution nor solace.

Eventually, I walk. Without that weight at my belly, I feel grotesquely light. Empty.

I leave my heart in that hole, and walk north.

One day, the storm ends abruptly.

Two days later, I come across a herder with his flock at evening. As soon as I see him in the distance, I withdraw the ka'kari from my skin. He doesn't hail me as I approach. Seems suspicious, staff in hand. Seems to be waiting for me to talk.

I don't.

"Thought you were a night demon when I first saw ya," he says. He hands me a waterskin. His face is leathery, lined by sun and wind and dirt.

I drink. Hand it back.

"Eyes play tricks on ya out here, I guess," he says.

I have nothing to say to that.

"I should offer some victuals. You on the run from the law?"

I shake my head, then stop. "Maybe. But I think they think I'm dead. Don't mean to bring you trouble."

"Appreciate you tellin' me true." He offers the skin again.

I don't take it. "Nearest town?"

He points west. I nod my head to him, and keep walking north.

"Hey," he says, "you want food?"

"And claim guest right? No. Anyone asks, might be safer to say you haven't seen me. But you do what you like."

He says nothing until I'm some distance away. "That's not the way to town!"

I keep walking.

"Hey," he shouts a few moments later. "You want clothes?"

I stop. It hadn't occurred to me. My current state will cause me all kinds of trouble.

I go back. He takes me to his campsite, digs all the way to the bottom of a rucksack, and pulls out a tunic, trousers, belt. I see they're too small for him. Nearly perfect for me.

I don't have words to ask, but he sees the question in my eyes.

"Been meaning to get rid of these awhile," he says. He smiles, but it doesn't reach his eyes. "Never could."

There's deep pain in his words, and I can't hold any more pain, so I don't ask.

But I don't need to. "Those were my son's," he says gruffly as I get dressed. "He don't need 'em where he is now."

The wave of emotion hits me so fast I almost collapse. "Why?" I whisper. "Why help?"

He shakes his head, fending off sudden emotion. His voice hoarse, he says, "Seems like the thing ta do, don't it?"

I can't muster words to express a fraction of what his kindness means. Without clothes, I'd be chased off as a madman, seen as a threat, attacked. "You're ... you're too—"

"No need for that. I already finished my supper. What's in the tin there's my breakfast. You can eat half. Can see you need it."

I shake my head. "I couldn't bear to—"

"You can stay the night if you like. No matter how pretty starlight is, fire's warmer and brighter, too, my meemaw used to say."

"If I stay I might sleep—"

"Aye, that's the point, innit?" He's got an interrupting way about him, this grizzled, bearded old shepherd does. But I don't mind.

I finish quietly, "If I sleep, I might dream."

That catches him short. "Ah, so that's how it is. Then let me burden you a bit more before you go."

He rummages until he finds an old waterskin and a flint. He doesn't need to tell me they were his son's. He hands them to me, says, "Don't ask why. The desert fathers say, in this life we're all wanderers, and every trail's flooded out by tragedy from time to time, and our many paths all lead to death. It's right to share what you can."

"You've given me food and water and clothes and kindness. I've given you nothing. This is a debt I can never repay."

This time his smile creases old smile lines long dormant. "If you think of gifts as debts, you cheapen the gift and the giver and yourself. See the generosity in others and you might be able to find it in yourself. Man can summon hell to earth, and hell roars and kills and whispers lies strong as shackles. But it don't get the last word."

He's simple and surely deceived by his own desire for it all to somehow make sense, but he's a good man, and I won't start an argument with him that I don't want to win, so I accept his generosity and his directions. He points out a few landmarks, how to find watering holes and avoid towns.

He doesn't try to stop me when I go.

The rolling hills must be deceptive, or I lose track of time, because when I finally look back for the old shepherd and his flock, I can't see them anywhere.

Chapter One Hundred Three

The Politics of a Lifted Skirt

"This is an abomination," Speaker Istariel Wyant said as Vi was led into an enormous office in the bowels of the Alabaster Seraph the next morning. The room bore the signs of some eclectic Sister who must've had significant power to have been allowed such a large room. Skulls of creatures long dead and pieced together from fragments of bone floated in random places along the floor. A green stone larger than Viridiana was tall with red veins slowly pulsing in it lay to one side. Glowing orbs—the planets, maybe, but there were too many?—spun around each other by old magic. There were no books, but piles of parchments thick with dust lay on tables long enough that they must have been stolen from the dining halls.

"Get those off her, now. Ridiculous!" the Speaker told Vi's guards. The woman looked decades younger than her sister Ariel, her hair tumbling in a perfect golden waterfall, her neck as magically free of wrinkles as her figure was constrained by her corset. She looked every bit the hard-edged middle-aged queen. "Try not to touch anything, Viridiana. We don't know what half of these things do. When one of the archivists tried to move that, it bit her and she forgot her own name for a fortnight."

Happy to lose the manacles, Vi needed a moment to figure out what the Speaker was talking about, and then she looked up where the woman gestured.

Seeing the spider larger than a dog on the ceiling over her head, she leapt to one side, tripped over her long hem, and as she slid, scrambled at her belt for a weapon that wasn't there. Then she realized the spider wasn't moving. It appeared to be stuffed.

"Everyone does that—well, not the jumping part. But my apologies. Wrong way to warn you."

Vi stood slowly as her guards smirked at each other.

She looked around warily, wondering what this place was and why she was here. No one had told her where she was being taken this morning, and after her night in the dungeon, she'd guessed it would be somewhere worse than this gilded, gleaming hardwood cage.

The Speaker dismissed the guards. Then, turning her back to Vi, she stared at a beautiful painting on the wall. The weather in the landscape seemed to move.

After half a minute, she spoke. "The Battle of Black Barrow changed us. A brotherhood of mages tasting a miraculous victory in its first time at war would've been inflamed, their appetite for battle whetted. We've swung the opposite direction. Maybe too far. We saw magics there that dwarfed our abilities. In their secret fears, men would be drawn to develop such abilities themselves, throwing their treasures and energies into learning the bloody arts of war. Indeed, I believe that's what is happening among our scattered brothers even now. But we have recoiled from the destructive power we've witnessed. In their fear, our brothers wish to lash out. In ours, we run away.

"Not that we put it so indelicately," the Speaker continued, sardonic. " 'Now is the time to find allies,' our Sisters say. Which brings us to you—our own little weapon of war—you who outraged the empress of the greatest power on our continent, if not our world. 'We need allies, not a schismatic,' our timorous Sisters say."

"And what do you say?" Vi asked.

"I say that disarming unilaterally in order to prevent a war is an idea so absurd you'd have to be an intellectual to believe it."

"Or a politician?" Vi asked. She could see that the words stung. But this woman had been Speaker for years. She'd weaseled her way around the Accords even when they'd become ludicrous. She could have made a stand then. She hadn't. But maybe she would after Vi was gone. Vi said, "Allies want their allies to be powerful. If someone moves to make you weak, it means they've got plans for you once you can't stop them."

Speaker Istariel looked sharply at her, her long face appraising. "Oh, how I wish I could keep you without losing everything." She stared at Vi for long moments, and Vi guessed she was trying to think of some way to do just that.

Seeming to abandon the idea, the Speaker said, "I need you to tell me about the heist."

"Surely the others told you everything?" Vi asked.

"Indeed. And yet I want to hear about it from you."

"Is it gonna make any difference?"

"Not to what happens to you, if that's what you mean. But to what happens to the others? It might. Eventually. I believe in keeping the score, little sister. I know what they've told me, and if you tell me something different, I'll triangulate the truth and bring judgment if it's required. And when it's possible."

"Too late for me, though," Vi said. "And too late for Kylar."

"Justice is setting things right after they've gone wrong, not preventing every wrong. You may begin with the Greater Deception Spell. Did anyone tell you that I had given my permission for that spell to be used?"

"No. Why?"

"So you're not aware that such magic requires my personal authorization?"

"No. But then, you weren't around."

"Whose idea was it?"

"I don't remember. They all concurred by the time they brought me in."

"So it wasn't your idea?" Speaker Istariel asked.

"I didn't even know we could do stuff like that. I just gathered the...the components. The reagents, I guess. They said it was far too complicated for me, so I didn't touch either of them."

"Either of them?"

"Kylar's or Repha'im's. Repha'im's spell was anchored on a belt. Kylar's on the knife."

"Interesting. I was told there was only one. Who gathered the reagents for the other spell?"

"Someone on the other team infiltrated Repha'im's inner circle as his barber. She claimed to be able to get all the reagents without ever whoring herself like I did. You know, nicked his neck while shaving for the blood. Got fingernails and hair easily enough. Checking his sheets after he'd been with the empress for the...you know, checking the chamber pot for the other unmentionables. But she might've been lying. Regardless, I had far less time."

"You know that woman's name?"

"No. Some of the team let that stuff slip, but not her. She was Sister Verity or something for her cover."

"Sharp face, thin, buck teeth?" Speaker Istariel asked.

"That's right." Vi waited, then said, "Oh, you're not gonna tell me her real name in case it's tortured out of me."

"I'm glad to see you understand. Back to the job, though. You can guess what I really want to know."

"I've already told the others six times. And I haven't changed my story, as I'm sure you know. I've seen them checking the dictation from each interrogation."

"I need to see your face as you say it," the Speaker said. "What color was the dagger?"

"Orange," Vi said without hesitation. That wasn't a question they'd ever asked her before. "Hold on. No, that's not right. Kylar wrote that it was blue. More than once, I think. But I remember when they prepared it, it was undeniably orange. I saw that with my own eyes. I mean, most of it was steel, but there was orange enamel on the grip. I can't remember when I took it from Sister Ayayah what it was. I wasn't really looking at it. I think it was covered, wrapped up in the bundle. I was trying to remember my lines. You know, for Kylar to overhear as we'd planned. And then he and I argued, and then it was gone. He'd taken it. Like we figured he would. He always referred to it as blue in his diary, though. Weird."

"And he was supposed to take it? That was part of Ayayah's plan?" the Speaker asked.

"Either way. It didn't matter. I thought he might take it, because I know him. But if he hadn't, I was supposed to bring it to him at any point before or at the end. Which, naturally, was supposed to happen in private—at most in front of Repha'im, and definitely not in front of mages who would see through the Greater Deception Spells. Kylar had overheard how important it was to use that dagger, so at the end, either he'd use it, or if it looked like he wouldn't, I was supposed to. But now I'm confused. Does the color matter?"

"Yes, but not to you. Tell me, did you learn why the child wasn't in the chest when the Sisters escaped at Cloud Point?"

"Repha'im told Kylar the empress took the child behind his back, intending to take it with her when she disembarked. So I don't know what happened with Queen Gyre, but she got injured stealing two empty chests. But that's not the most important thing I learned from Kylar's diary. *Repha'im* was the one who sent the official to search the boat."

"The special teams thought that was just bad luck. Any ship leaving could legally be searched."

"Kylar watched the official search the hold, and he wrote that the man knew all its hiding places and secret compartments. Later, Repha'im said that he had someone on one of the Special Problems and Tactics Teams. Or...maybe on the boat? One or the other, though, because that's the only way they could've known that part of the plan. We've got a spy, a traitor. Going forward, you'll—"

"Stop!" Speaker Istariel's eyes had widened at the mention of a spy, but now they narrowed. "What *exactly* did Repha'im say when he allegedly told Kylar this?"

Vi thought how it'd be nice to have a ka'kari that could give her verbatim quotes. "I don't remember the exact wording," she admitted. "I could go back and see if I can find it. But it doesn't matter. Repha'im was bragging, not confessing before examiners tasked with getting every detail. He didn't give away who our traitor was."

"Traitor, hmm."

"What's that mean?"

"Queen Gyre somehow found out her son was supposed to be in one of those chests. We don't know what she did, but in the course of getting it, she was injured. One may fairly assume she was injured by those who were responsible for guarding the child. So Repha'im might have learned about our attempted rescue of the child from what Jenine did?"

"That we were attempting a rescue, sure. But not where the child would be taken. Even if he simply guessed that whoever was trying to leave the storm ship was probably the guilty party, that wouldn't have told his official exactly where to search on the escape boat."

"Ah, true." Sister Istariel deflated, as if she'd been holding on to a hope that no Sister would really betray the Chantry. "On the other hand, if that child had been found in one of those chests, *none* of the Sisters would've been allowed off the storm ship. Every Sister on each of the special teams knew that if they weren't able to get the child to shore, the storm ship was doomed. Any spy who helped keep the child onboard would've known she was condemning herself to death as well."

"Sister Ayayah was willing to die herself or to kill me to save the Chantry. It's not that much more fanatical to let the entire team die, if you think you're saving the whole Chantry and the world, is it?" But Vi didn't like to think of Sister Ayayah having even the smallest streak of heroism or selflessness. "Or maybe her boss did it, if Ayayah was reporting to someone. Who is her boss, anyway? I heard that she serves someone, but never who."

"You don't need to know that." But Speaker Istariel looked troubled. "I'd thought my adversaries liked to talk big about how boldly they would act if they were in power. Throwing away the lives of their own closest supporters, women they know well and seem to like...that's something else. It's a long way from proof, but it's helpful. Was there anything else you learned from Kylar's diary? Anything we didn't know?"

"Repha'im knew what keeping the boy on the ship would mean. He wanted the storm ship to sink, too."

This one caught Istariel up short. "While he was on it? That's preposterous."

"He claimed to have bonded the blue ka'kari. He believed he could get himself and the child back to land safely. The ship sinking would kill a lot of Alitaeran nobles, allowing him to put his own people in their places and goading all Alitaera to prepare for war. War with *us*. He was planning to blame us and our magic for the ship sinking."

For several long moments, Istariel didn't even breathe. "These are remarkable claims. The Council would require remarkable evidence to support them before they could possibly accept them. We have only Kylar's word?"

"And the book only allows me to read it, so...you have only my word about Kylar's word," Vi admitted.

"Did any of the other Sisters see Repha'im with this blue ka'kari?"

"No idea. I just read about it in the book. I didn't see it myself. No one here had said anything to me about it before that."

"Then that's that. Are you ready to tell me about the very end? You have to know that's why we're meeting."

"It's not right," Vi said. "The Alitaerans are calling him an assassin or a wetboy. He had multiple opportunities to assassinate the empress. He never even tried. They're calling him a madman, a butcher, a maniac. Everything they're saying about him is a lie. Kylar saved everyone on the storm ship, and by stopping Repha'im's plan, Kylar saved the Chantry, too. Again."

Istariel shook her head, as if it were hopeless. "It's too little and too late. He'll be known as a villain for fifty or a hundred years. After all the interested parties are dead, someday a historian will reexamine the evidence and publish a more balanced reading. Let it lie."

"I will not."

Istariel shrugged like Vi was being uselessly belligerent. "Tell me about the end, little sister."

"Is that really why you brought me down here?"

"You know we can't figure it out. What happened?"

"I've told you already. I don't understand either!" Vi said. "I was too late. I was supposed to be there by then, but I was trying not to fight anyone, trying to keep my cover, trying not to show that I was a war mage. So I got to the open deck where Kylar was fighting too late. I saw him stab the child. Not with our blue knife. Or whatever color if he wrote things wrong." She looked at the floor. "He had this look on his face. Have you ever seen anyone damn themselves? I—"

"I'm not interested in his feelings," Speaker Istariel snapped. "Did you find out where his body is?"

It was the question that had been looming the entire time Vi had been reading. How many of Kylar's greatest secrets would she give to the Chantry? How much more would she betray him?

She didn't hesitate. "He was bloody and exhausted and despairing, and he jumped into water teeming with sharks and lotai. Big ones. We all saw those lotai. I'm sure you heard the reports of how one attacked us on the dock? There were hundreds more. I watched Kylar jump from a ridiculous height into storm-tossed water filled with those things. I saw it with my own eyes, and I knew he was dead. There *is* no body."

Speaker Istariel studied Vi, who wrapped herself in her hot righteous rage to avoid showing her fear. There was one question the Speaker could ask that would end everything. Her sister Ariel would've asked it immediately. But the bit about seeing Kylar jump with her own eyes was perhaps the most inspired misleading truth of Vi's life.

Vi had watched him jump with her own eyes. She had been certain he was dead. It was only later she'd read about it through *his* eyes and learned he wasn't.

The Speaker sighed. "Then we're done here. The Council has decided to admit that we have indeed abrogated the Alitaeran Accords, and have housed and trained a war mage. Your Sisters have decided that your life is an acceptable price to pay for peace with Alitaera."

"That's a pretty shitty reward for loyal service," Vi said.

"I agree. And exemplary service it's been, minus the tantrum at the end on the storm ship. If you hadn't flung Alitaera's best about like poppets as only a full war mage could—and as we forbade you to do, I'll remind you—if you hadn't done that, I'd be able to save you."

"You've got me wrong. I'm not complaining. I'm merely holding up a mirror for you to see what the Chantry is. I deserve death—but not from my own Sisters, who are the reason I deserve it. What I meant is that when you reward loyal Sisters by handing them over to the enemy, it's going to get a lot harder to sign up new recruits. If you think the Sisterhood might need to go to war any time in the next generation, this is stupidity. You think that because you've scattered my closest lieutenants to the corners of Midcyru that you can control what people say about me? The opposite is true. You've scattered my friends like seeds, and now you're throwing *manure* on them." Vi felt a brief pleasure that she'd managed not to say *shit* again. "You think that's victory? It's fertilizer. In every part of Midcyru, they'll grow, and you'll reap a bitter harvest. I'm not a leader. I'd mess up any movement if I stayed around and tried to lead it. I'm more dangerous *dead.*"

For the first time, there was a flicker of fear in Istariel's eyes.

"Speaker, I've got a question for you. One I hope you've asked yourself: How many times can you do what's easy but wrong before you've betrayed the whole reason you sought power in the first place?"

The Speaker's back, already straight as a galley mast, stiffened. Her voice went quiet. "Are you quite finished, young lady?"

Vi took a breath. "Yes, I am."

As if Vi had said none of it, Speaker Istariel said, "Before you go, you'll be fitted with a mind wipe spell. It's made to react to tampering, but you'll also be told several other ways to trigger it in case…well, *in case.* I'm sure you can imagine several scenarios in which you might prefer no longer to be aware of what happens to you. We ask that you wait to trigger the spell until you're fully in Alitaeran custody. The mind wipe has to look like something you did, not that was done to you. We can't hand over a walking corpse and expect them to be satisfied. They will suspect us regardless, and may even foresee and attempt to forestall your use of such a spell. They have excellent mages, so do be careful. Triggering it too soon is better than too late."

"And if they don't torture me?" Vi asked.

"After what happened? Oh, they will."

"And if they don't? If they're unexpectedly merciful?"

Istariel hesitated.

"That spell will wipe me anyway, huh?" Vi asked.

Frown lines briefly appeared on the Speaker's regal face. "Some fear that you may be turned against us, not by force but by trickery. Charm."

Vi understood. "Really? *Turned?* After how good you've been to me?" So there was some kind of timer on the spell, as well. She had no hope whatsoever.

Istariel flushed, flustered for the first time. "It's meant to be a mercy, you know, to spare you the pain of torture and the horrors of public execution. Do you want to know the treatment you can expect given what you're to be convicted of? You humiliated dozens. Most of them men. Do you know what men do to assert their power over an enemy woman who's humiliated them?"

"Let's be clear what this is," Vi said. "You're not only handing someone who trusted you over to an enemy. You're murdering a Sister who's served you faithfully and at ruinous cost to herself. You're not killing me for anything I've done; you're killing me for something I've given no sign I would *ever* do. And to be honest, if you keep this up, you're going to hurt my feelings."

This, which Vi had thought would mark Speaker Istariel most deeply, instead seemed to touch her not at all. As easily as if she were ending a meeting so they could simply go eat, she said, "We're done here. Until they come get you this evening, I'm sending you back to Ariel's little library."

Surprised for the first time, Vi said, "You are?"

"I need you to do me a favor."

"A *favor*?" Vi couldn't believe the woman's presumption.

"With as much time as you have left, I need you to pore over Kylar's journal. Tell my sister whatever you learn. Answer whatever questions she has. Reread sections as necessary. I want to know if our acquisition of that book is a stroke of good fortune or something else. I need to know, for sure, that Kylar Stern is dead. And if I can't see his body with my own eyes, I'll need proof some other way."

Vi had thought she'd made it through the crucible. She'd thought the Speaker had missed the one question Vi had feared since she'd begun. But maybe the woman was simply attacking it from another direction. At the best, she was flinging Vi to Ariel—who certainly *would* ask it. For the question was simple, once you thought of it:

No matter how honest he is, there's one story no man may write about his life. That's the story of his death.

Even if the strange way Kylar had dictated his thoughts as he went along somehow meant he could tell his tale up until his very last moment, jumping into the sea with his journal meant the journal should still be in the sea. If Kylar had died in the water, as Vi had told the Speaker he did, how had he managed to send his journal, which included his very last moments, *here*? If he was dead, when did he find the mage to enchant it so only Vi could read it?

"Lift your skirts," Vi said coldly.

"Lift my—excuse me?"

"Lift your skirts, because you've got some balls, asking me for a favor after all you've done."

Then Speaker Istariel did the most shocking thing yet. She laughed. "I haven't been spoken to like that since... well, I see why Kylar liked you. And why Ariel does."

Vi was struck by a thought. "You seem awfully ready for me to report to her. Did you send her to spy on me in the first place?"

"Of course I did. Oh, don't look so scandalized. Ariel didn't realize it. I knew you two were friends, so I arranged to cross paths with her. I asked her about her current studies. As ever, she was happy to tell me about them at mind-numbing length. I asked if she needed any particular volumes. When she told me which ones, I mentioned I'd seen a couple of those in the library where I was planning to have you sequestered. Then I sent the Head Librarian to make sure those books were placed there immediately."

"You Sisters," Vi said, shaking her head, "you can never simply ask for what you want, can you?"

Her mouth twisting, Istariel turned to leave.

"Wait! I'll do it," Vi said. "If."

Speaker Istariel stopped but didn't turn around.

"If you'll tell me, honestly, what you're going to do. You know, with *him*," Vi said.

"And why would you believe what I tell you?" Istariel said.

"You're going to mind wipe me anyway. Right? You've got nothing to lose by telling me the truth. And I dare say I've earned it."

Istariel looked nonplussed. "You want to revisit your earlier answer, then? Excellent." She mumbled a word and a side door opened magically. She nodded to someone outside. Vi heard footsteps going away. The Speaker said, "You said you were on the front deck and that you had a good view of everything. You say that you saw baby Caedan stabbed. In the back of the neck."

A woman walked in, carrying a baby. She handed him to Speaker Istariel, who took him far more adeptly than Vi would've expected. Istariel held the baby's head in her left hand and cleared his hair out of the way.

"Where's the wound, Vi? And after everything everyone has ever said about him, why does this child show no sign of having any Talent whatsoever? What happened to it? Will his Talent come back?"

"I already told you, I don't know anything about any of that. But please, you have to tell me you're sending Caedan back to his parents. Kylar gave everything for this. I let Kylar think he killed this baby—"

And in an instant, once again, she was back on that accursed ship. She'd scooped up the knife with its Greater Deception Spell and put it on Kylar's belt, and as its magic swirled around him, triggered to make him not merely believe but experience whatever she commanded it, she'd snatched the child from him and had given him a bundle of tied clothes; he'd believed he still held the child. After Kylar had fallen off the prow of the storm ship, she'd leapt off the port side herself, using magic to cushion her collision with the waves. She'd barely surfaced when the Sisters' boat—which had hidden behind the storm ship waiting for her—had quickly scooped her and the child out of the water. The team who'd brought the boat from Cloud Point had four weather magae on it. Those women had brought them safely home. There had been no pursuit from there. Nor had Vi seen Kylar.

The deception spell used Kylar's own expectations for the weight of the child, its smell, and even how it looked for as long as Kylar and the bundle were within several paces of the knife. From Vi's reading, it had been long enough. It had lasted until Kylar buried the child and finally threw aside the dagger. The feelings of wrongness he should've felt in the aftermath of the deception spell, he'd interpreted as feeling wrong about what he'd done.

"In doing what you did," the speaker said, "you saved the child, from all his enemies. And you saved the Chantry, and perhaps magic itself, for which you have our eternal gratitude. I've made a note in my own diary—in code, I admit—noting the part you played, so that someday, history will celebrate you."

"I don't care about history! For all the gods' sakes, give the child back to his parents. You said it yourself. He's got no Talent. He's no threat to anyone."

"The High Council has decided that until we can be sure that his peculiar abilities don't come back, we can't risk giving the boy back to his parents. He's too dangerous."

"Until you can be *sure*? How long is that going to be? Until you run more tests?" At the stony look on Istariel's face, horrified, Vi said, "You're going to wait until his Talent would normally quicken? You're going to keep him here until after he goes through puberty?"

"The stakes are too high to do anything else. We don't think his powers will come back. But can you guarantee that? Can anyone? Quickening is mysterious. It's the only way to be sure. After that, we may be able to let him go. Or he may need to remain our guest for life."

"You can't..."

Istariel smiled as Caedan suddenly cooed. She rubbed her nose against his, as if she were a kind auntie, not a woman who was leaving his parents grieving and who was planning to let him grow up thinking himself an orphan. "If we're wrong, and his magic-negating powers come back and ripen to great power, this boy could be the death of us all. I want you to understand, Vi, I had to fight those who thought the job should be finished. You understand what I mean? But that's not who we are. I put a stop to that kind of talk." She smiled at Caedan again. "Didn't I?" she said, baby-talking. "And you are the best little baby, aren't you?"

"I can't believe you're doing this," Vi said quietly, aghast.

"We do what works for us, Viridiana. If you think you can get better results by asking women to show you their balls, you go right ahead."

Chapter One Hundred Four

The Impossible Price

$\mathcal{A}$ morning comes when I can see the sun. I ate last night. Built a fire. Slept.

I made a decision, and finally I know why I've been heading north all this time.

~You seem something like your old self again.~

It's the first time the ka'kari has spoken to me in ages.

I think about what it said as I walk. No. I'll never be my old self again. But I suppose I am functional now. I need to be.

I have a problem.

~Many. But I see now you have a plan.~

Several, but their order depends on Momma K. And I'll need your help.

~For the benefit of those who read or listen to this someday, you want to say what you're doing?~

Guess I've gotten out of the practice of narrating as I go, huh?

I nudge the trussed-up wet worker with my foot. It takes a few minutes to really tie up someone correctly, especially someone from my old line of work. You can't get sloppy with the rest of the ropes and make assumptions simply because it's a woman and you've got such a good gag on her that she won't be able to use her Talent. You've got to leverage the bonds such that even double or triple human strength simply doesn't help.

She's a dirty blonde, muscularly thick and pretty and wearing her hair loose and long enough to be impractical, which surprises me. Until I find her ear. Or lack of one, where it was messily cut off, years ago. She wears the hair long and swept over to cover that scar nub of an ear.

I don't recognize her, but from how she was acting, it's obvious she's a wetboy, a magically augmented and magically bound assassin trained by the Sa'kagé and working, ultimately, for Momma K. Here, she was on guard duty.

Like me, she wasn't very good at it.

"I figure it'll take you four hours to escape. What do you think?" I ask her. "I really only need one, but... well, losing has consequences, doesn't it? We both know I could make those much worse for you."

I remove a pane of glass from the skylight, set it aside, absorb the magical field on the other side with the ka'kari, and holding on to the frame by fingertips, lower myself into the chamber below.

Momma K has equipped the entire level with nightingale floors. At my suggestion (and surely Durzo's before me), she's set subtle magical traps at several of the places a highly skilled assassin would be tempted to place their feet as they tried to traverse such a floor silently.

So I skip the floor. The ceiling's smooth and lined with magic to keep any intruder from doing what I'm doing. But I have the black ka'kari. It makes certain things unconscionably easy.

I'll miss it.

~You'll... You'll *miss* me?~

See, I've figured out why Durzo left me the ka'kari-holding bracelet. I've been defaulting to letting the ka'kari hear all my thoughts. Durzo knew better, and tried to tell me as much. He gave me a way to keep it close enough to use if I needed it at a moment's notice without deluding myself into thinking it was my friend. I didn't understand.

Momma K is at work at her desk, as she so often is late at night. Today, she isn't wearing the scholar's spectacles I've gotten used to seeing her wear when she's alone. She looks good; there's something about her that doesn't let you ever forget that not all that long ago she was accounted the courtesan of the age. Somehow, what she has, even age cannot steal.

I drop to the floor in front of her desk silently.

She jumps—and then looks angry that she jumped. Angry at me. She turns her eyes back to her work.

Not needing to take a single step, I sit in the chair facing her.

She finishes working on whatever she's writing. Signs her name to it. Puts it in a stack of other letters. Probably orders for her many spies and agents. Then she looks at me, quill in hand, clearly trying to decide if she should address me now or pick up another parchment and continue working to vex me.

I sit, passive, patient.

"You're more like him every time I see you," she says finally, putting the quill in a rest.

I don't ask who she means. Durzo. For some reason, I don't want to say his name. It shouldn't, but it still feels like a betrayal that he didn't show up when I needed him. "Seen him around?" I ask, as if unconcerned.

"Not since before you left." She says this without any apparent emotion. But if she's lying, this is one area where I have no hope of penetrating her armor. I let it go.

She doesn't ask me where I've been or how the job went. She's very skilled with small talk, and with turning it in whatever direction she wants. But she also knows me, and clearly she doesn't want to play games.

"Kiern. Any leads?" I ask.

"Many. All leading ultimately to nothing. We've spent more treasure and spilled more blood and burned more relationships with powerful people than we can, perhaps, afford. And for nothing, except now we know who wants to help us, or used to, and who takes offense easily, and who the power players actually are in several realms throughout Midcyru. But in terms of helping us find the child? We've found nothing. Logan wishes to speak with you, you know."

I don't answer. I wasn't sure I would get here before the news from Borami about what happened on the storm ship arrived, but a source told me I got back first. It looks like it's true: Not even Momma K knows what happened yet.

I owe it to Logan to tell him everything, but I can't face him. Can't bear to lie to him. Can't possibly tell the truth. He'll demand it all, and he'll deserve it.

How did the simple job of protecting a couple of kids turn into this?

"Kylar..." Momma K asks softly, "something is really wrong, isn't it? I know you. What is it?"

"You knew too much, and I want to know how," I say, ignoring her. "You tried to send me to Stormfast before the abduction even happened. I don't think you were behind it. But I can't figure it out. How'd you know so much?"

Momma K sighs. "I wasn't her first choice. In fact, I might've been her last. But when no one else would listen to her, Jenine Gyre came to me. She was having dreams. The Healers asked her lots of questions, very specific ones, but they wouldn't tell her anything. Brushed aside her concerns, her suspicions.

They told Logan it was all a consequence of childbirth. I was the only one who pretended to believe her. Soon she opened her heart to me. Then I saw some of her dreams come true, and I came to believe her in truth, about everything. I believed that we couldn't stop the children from being taken. So I tried to get around that prophecy by sending you to where you could take one of the children back. But you wouldn't go."

"So the Nemesis Compass wasn't ever real? That was bait to get me moving the direction you wanted."

"Bait, yes. Merely bait?" She shakes her head. "Durzo gave me a list of the most dangerous artifacts he'd either seen personally or suspected had been used at the Fall of Trayethell centuries ago, when Jorsin Alkestes originally raised Black Barrow. Durzo suspected some of those artifacts might've survived. Of them, he thought the compass might be the most useful or the most dangerous, depending who held it. It was one of the things we quarreled about. When he left, I suspected he might have gone hunting it. His trail led toward Tover, which was I why I sent you there, out of all the places you might have been able to steal a bracelet for the empress's party. I had some foolish hope you might find and help each other, either him helping you or you him, depending whose hunt was going better."

"You were trying to play peacemaker?" I ask, skeptical.

She rubs a tiny scar on her arm, pensive. "I turned you against each other once. I figured I owed you both. Some silly old women matchmake young couples. Apparently I matchmake old masters and their apprentices. And a weak effort it was, wasn't it. Even if he'd still been in Tover, what were the odds of you running into each other?"

But I'm thinking of the arrow with the unsigned note that hit me there. That note saved Phaena's life. I'd later assumed it must've been shot by Vi, but with everything else going on, I'd forgotten to ask her. Could that have been *Durzo*?

It makes my heart ache with a different sort of longing. But it doesn't matter now.

"So Jenine's dreams. She told you all about them?"

"She's young, but she is a queen. Even in great anguish, she's not a fool, Kylar. She held back whatever details she thought necessary." Momma K pauses. "Ah, but you weren't speaking generally, were you? You mean, did she share any dreams she had about *you*?" For a moment she seems amused. "Hoping to know your future?" But then her amusement fades as another thought occurs to her. "Or are you wondering how much she found out about your past?"

Chest tight, I don't answer. Can't hold her gaze.

Momma K lets me off the hook. "She told me you would fail to stop the kidnapping. She knew we were close." She goes quiet; after a long moment, as if afraid how I'll answer, she says, "Kylar, do you have something you want to tell me?"

How long will it be until Jenine gets back? How long until Momma K finds out everything regardless? It'd be better for me to share it myself, to make sure she gets the full truth, not whatever hateful things Jenine will share.

But those words won't obey my call. "I'm going away for a while. A long while, I think."

"How will I reach you?" she asks.

"You won't." I feel myself falling away, deeper and deeper into myself. No Kiern and no leads to finding him means it's time for my *other* plan, sooner rather than later. That's just as well. Less helpful to Logan and the world perhaps, but equally necessary.

"Kylar, have you been by to see Count Drake?"

I don't see where she's going with this. "No reason to."

"Did you know he used to be a gambler?"

"A gambler? Doesn't seem like him. Thought he did the accounting for you, you know, way back when."

"I noticed that he played rarely, and rarely with the same people, but only ever for the highest stakes. Under some duress, he told me he'd developed a system. Everyone has a system, of course, so I pressed on the details. He'd taken scholarly works and converted them, charting out tables of probabilistics. He memorized those, and then by watching and remembering the hands that were played, he said—how did he put it?—that he could have a statistically significant advantage over time. I saw him sometimes lose big hands, but I never saw him push back from a table with less money than he'd had when he sat down."

"And you're telling me this why?" I ask.

"I asked him why he'd given up gambling. He had some religious reason, but when I pressed him for the real reason, he said he'd once made the biggest gamble of his life and won, against all probabilities. He figured he'd used all his luck."

"Good for him. Man deserves a win. World needs more rich men who—"

"He meant you," she interrupts quietly. "You should go see him."

It takes my breath away, and suddenly, I'm near weeping. I can't breathe.

She must've had that conversation a long time ago. Count Drake wouldn't say it after our fight. He wouldn't say it now.

No, he lost a big hand with me. Maybe Blue, the orphan girl I left with him, will be his real win. Maybe he'll be able to push back from the table with a win with her.

Momma K sees my shaking head. She says, still quietly, "Kylar, will you go see Logan?"

I don't answer. But my face must answer for me.

"Then Caedan is lost." She still does it, after all these years. Speaking her questions, yet somehow still demanding answers.

The words come out a low whisper. "More than lost."

"Dead?" Momma K puts a hand to her mouth in horror.

It's interesting, some detached part of me thinks. She's ordered so many kills in her time, you'd think she'd be immune to horror at death, but she always did have a weak spot for children.

I was one of those once. I wonder if she still sees me as something like her child, her wayward son, still in need of saving.

"Kylar," she says, and her voice is gentle, "I know you. I've known you since you were a child. I've seen how much decency there is in you, despite everything."

"You don't know me," I whisper. "If you knew me—"

"Tell me this, and I'll ask nothing else," she says, ignoring me, cutting me off. "What you did, did you have to do it?"

"I should've—"

"Did you have to do it?" she snaps.

"I...I couldn't think of any way out."

"Then rest content."

I scoff, bitterly. "Content?"

"Would you do it differently if you had to do it again?" she asks.

I look at her for a long time, this woman who has seen more than her share of terrible things, and done more than a few of them herself. "At the end?" I ask.

I shake my head. I don't know if it's a *no* or an *I don't know.*

"Then put it behind you," she says sharply. "Anything else will ruin you, and more than you."

I can't even breathe, I'm suddenly so afraid she's going to ask what I did.

"Kylar, whatever you did, you did it on my orders. You did it to save Logan and his whole kingdom. It's not your fault."

I feel myself going far away again. "You know, I believed that once."

Quietly, Momma K says, "What happened?"

She wasn't intending to ask. As an old friend from the Warrens, as a substitute mother at times, she wasn't going to ask. But she's asking. Which means she's asking as a vassal of the king, an embattled woman whose life and career depend on her service to him.

"Maybe I did what I had to do," I say, "but now because of what I did, I have to do something else."

"You're not making sense."

"Phaena was marvelous. Better than me. She's either dead or in a dungeon in Borami now. If you can, please, get her out? Here's the codes for my bankers and managers, as if you don't know them all already." I hand her a scroll. She makes no sign whether she knew or not. I don't care. "Use as much as you need. Use it all if you like. I know that if she's imprisoned, it's easier to have her silenced than rescued, but you'd be losing a great talent. She's smart, and loyal to you, and so competent that she nearly succeeded by herself. One more thing. Whether she made it or not, her family's in bad shape. If you'd put them up in decent housing and give them a good stipend from my rents, I'd appreciate it."

If I were a better man, I'd go find out if Phaena is alive myself, and rescue her if she is. But Borami is the most dangerous place in the world for me right now, and I'm in no shape to face any job, much less another one with hopeless odds.

"Consider it done," she says. She gives me a moment, reading my despair. "Kylar..."

"My full briefing's there, with the codes. Not that anyone else will believe it all. I wouldn't believe it myself, if I hadn't seen everything with my own eyes." The empress being behind the kidnapping all along? Repha'im being some kind of otherworldly or underworldly being? Sure. I don't have it in me to explain it even to Momma K, who knows I wouldn't lie about such things.

But she and Logan need to know what's coming.

"Durzo was right, you know. Almost always was," I say with nostalgia like a fallen autumn leaf edged in sharp crystals of ice. "He'd say, 'There are no impossible jobs, only impossible prices.' I thought he meant something cynical about making people pay us a lot for the difficult jobs. He meant that too. But I was wrong when I thought others pay the price. I did the job. Now I pay the price for what I did."

"Kylar, tell me. What's wrong?"

What's *not*?

In her face, I see she knows she's losing me.

But I say, "I need to kill someone, someone who deserves killing, but I can't do it."

"All my networks are at your disposal. How can I help?"

"It's not that kind of problem."

She gets quiet, and I'm stuck between unbearable lethargy and intolerable restlessness.

"Kylar, who? Who do you need to kill?"

I stand.

"Kylar, do you have any news about Jenine? Logan's sick with worry."

"Alive, last I saw. She'd been badly hurt attempting to rescue Caedan herself, but Vi was taking her to the empress's Healers."

Momma K takes this in without so much as a grimace, though it surely means an enormous amount of work coming for her. She doesn't ask more questions. I think she can tell I'm finished.

"Thanks for your help," I say.

"I should try to detain you. Logan ordered me to do so." She sighs.

"I'll go see Logan, don't worry. Your bodyguard already tried the detaining thing. Let's not do any more of that."

"Kylar, you didn't kill her, did you?"

"No, no. Almost, when I thought she was here to hurt you. I left her tied up. She should escape by dawn."

"Tell me you were gentle."

"I was gentle."

"Liar. Did you humiliate her? You know how important it is for a fighter to have self-confidence."

"It's more important to know there are always bastards out there tougher than you are."

"And you've become one of those, I see."

"And you always were one, Momma K. Goodbye."

I head to see Logan next.

I don't want to talk about it. It goes about how you'd imagine. He didn't kill me, torture me, or imprison me. That's the downside.

There is no upside.

Chapter One Hundred Five

The Coin We Pay

*W*hile Sister Ariel tinkered with the magic barring the door to the library, Vi read the last few pages of Kylar's book. It didn't take her long. She turned the last leaf and sat between desolation and confusion.

His voice had changed so much in those last sections as he approached the promontory. He'd been alienated not only from the ka'kari and everyone around him, but also from himself. He'd also been concealing things, obscuring his path, omitting details purposefully.

Vi spoke to Sister Ariel, though the woman seemed off in her own world. "Have you ever seen something that's total horse—um, I mean that's totally loused up—happen right in front of you, and for all your power, you can't do anything to stop it?"

Sister Ariel turned to regard Vi. Lifted her eyebrows. "I'm seeing it now."

"This?" Vi said, incredulous. "I'll die for the wrong crime, but, really? I'm not exactly undeserving of death. I was Hu Gibbet's apprentice. You don't know a quarter of the stuff I did for him. And then all this, with Kylar..."

"Don't take too much credit for that," Sister Ariel said.

"Too much credit? Have you not been listening—?"

"You've reached the end of the book. Did it tell you where his body is?" Sister Ariel asked.

"He concealed all the details. Very deliberately." She'd read it carefully, looking for things that might have tipped his hand. She hadn't seen anything that would narrow a search much.

"Then the ka'kari is lost. And so are we. Well, *you*."

Kylar hadn't given even the thinnest hint about the ka'kari's location anywhere in the whole book. Not that he would. Vi should've known better. He knew how powerful it was, what a catastrophe it would be if it fell into the wrong hands.

Sister Ariel had already switched to a different tack, as emotionlessly as usual. "I've been looking at this magic on the door, and it's not something we can defeat quickly, not even with your strength and my knowledge together. Which does mean there's no escape, as I'd guessed. So I suppose I should tell you."

"Tell me what?" Viridiana asked.

"I wasn't going to, when I thought the information could be tortured out of you. With the mind wipe, though, that won't be a problem. You were mumbling as you read the other day about overly complicated plans, and it got me thinking."

"I was?" Vi asked, thinking back. It must have been when she was reading about the heist. "It did?"

"I was wondering how such an experienced team could so thoroughly fail. I've read enough history to know that brilliant people make mistakes all the time. They'll be twelve steps down some perfect plan and never realize step two requires the opposition to do precisely the right thing or even a simple, rational thing or whatever. But! This wasn't a mistake."

"I'm not following," Vi said.

"I know the Chantry's most gifted Maker. I went and asked her about that knife. They hadn't contracted her for the job. So I went to the second best. They didn't use him either. But eventually I found the right woman, Savina. She was surprisingly willing to talk to someone who had even the smallest understanding of the difficulties of Making. First it was all very hypothetical; she'd say, 'If someone were to Make a tool that…' But that soon became, 'When I Made the knife…' I was careful never to give any physical details about it to her, but she described it exactly as you have, so I know we're talking about the same tool. She had no idea what they would ultimately use it for, but she knew how to harden it and reinforce it with anchor points for certain kinds of spells. Unusual spells. She got hypothetical for a while again when she talked about that part."

"Now I'm following you. I think," Viridiana said, troubled at where this was going.

"Savina builds safety protocols into her work, which is ingenious and should be more widely adopted—but that's neither here nor there. One of her safeties is making her creations change color according to which kind of spells are present. She deliberately codes it, so that Sisters in the know can tell at a glance which item is loaded with which spells. Three relevant points: One, a Greater Sensory Deception spell could indeed be anchored to that knife. Two, mind-affecting spells should turn the enamel orange. Three, blue enamel is the most severe warning Savina ever uses. She thought red would be too obvious. Regardless, a blue blade, when coming in contact with blood, will explode with significant violence."

Vi felt her throat tighten. "Explode? I—I don't understand."

"Understand Kylar's death is not your fault," Sister Ariel said.

"Not my fault? Every last part of this is my fault!"

Sister Ariel folded her hands as if ready to wait out a rant, but Vi didn't go on, so she spoke. "Viridiana, the blade was set to explode as soon as it touched blood, whether it was in your hand or Kylar's. As in, as soon as it stabbed someone. The explosion would've killed everyone in the vicinity."

Vi felt like she'd been punched in the gut.

"But who would do that? The team worked so hard! We all..."

"I don't think all of them were in on it. Savina said that when you all arrived back here after the mission, Jasmine Jakweth came and asked her all about the dagger's powers himself, asking some of the same questions I did. He then resigned from the Special Problems and Tactics Team. Melena Gerrick also resigned from the team as soon as she landed, though to my knowledge, she didn't visit Savina beforehand. I tried to find each of them but ran out of time. We'll have to guess they either didn't like what they did to Kylar or to you, or they were asked to do something worse but refused, or that they assumed they would be scapegoated for what happened and wished to flee before that could happen."

"What's that mean?"

"It means the special team's mission ceased being a rescue as soon as Caedan Gyre boarded the storm ship. From that moment, as far as Sister Ayayah was concerned, the mission was an assassination."

"No." Vi shook her head. Her mouth felt dry. Her mind cast about for evidence to show Sister Ariel she was wrong. "Everything we did was for a *rescue*. The plan was too complicated for an assassination. There was too much that could go wrong."

"What you call things going wrong was things going right. At least for Sister

Ayayah, and she thought, for the Chantry. Savina, the Maker, said that Sister Ayayah specifically asked if spells causing an explosion could be anchored to the dagger. Obviously, the answer was yes. And Ayayah asked if two spells could be placed on it at the same time, such as an explosion spell and a Greater Sensory Illusion—which is the polite name for a Greater Sensory Deception spell. Again the answer was yes. Savina told her the dagger would show blue to warn of the more dangerous of the spells on it.

"Think, Viridiana. What's the best way to safely get your Sisters off a ship while carrying contraband? By not carrying any contraband. It's entirely possible—and I believe—that Sister Ayayah herself leaked Caedan's whereabouts to Queen Jenine Gyre. Jenine would either rescue him and keep him somewhere far away—but somewhere on the storm ship—or, more likely, Jenine would fail to rescue him and get him locked down. Either way, the Sisters would be forced to leave without him."

"Instead, Jenine sort of succeeded, then came to me, thinking I'd help her," Vi said, sagging.

"By leaking Caedan's whereabouts, Sister Ayayah ensured that her entire team—well, the rest of the team minus you, Viridiana—would safely get off the ship. We know that *someone* leaked the plan deliberately. Sister Ayayah didn't see this as a betrayal, because for the Chantry, the best possible result—albeit a ruthless, immoral enormity of a result—would be for Caedan to *stay* on the storm ship and wipe out the ship's protective magics, causing it to sink. She had every reason to believe that if her team failed to rescue Caedan, that you, Kylar, King Repha'im, a child who might wipe out all magic, and maybe even the empress herself would all die. All the Chantry's Alitaeran problems would've been solved at once, without the Chantry appearing to have done anything at all."

"And what about the thousand innocent people she was condemning to death?"

"Oh, far more than a thousand. The empress dying without an heir would mean civil war in Alitaera, doubly so with many of her most powerful court officials perishing at the same time, sowing chaos in noble houses in every corner of the empire. But again, the relevant thing about an Alitaeran civil war, at least to a loyal but completely amoral Sister, is that no one is going to march soldiers out of their country to punish mages far away for violating some old treaty when they need every last soldier to stay in Alitaera to fight off all the other contenders for the throne."

"But surely Sister Ayayah wouldn't be willing to throw away so many lives just for—?"

"For power? For the entire Chantry's continued existence? None of the lives lost would've been Chantry lives. That's all she cares about. Except for your life. But you were trouble anyway. Obviously, her first plan failed. Her backup plan was that Kylar or you assassinate Caedan with that dagger, which would then explode. The explosion would take out the child and everyone nearby: ergo, the child, Kylar or you, and if she was lucky, maybe even King Repha'im or the empress. Maybe the explosion would damage the ship enough to sink it. If so, the storm itself would kill everyone else. Depending when you or Kylar used the dagger, anywhere from one to four major threats to the Chantry would be eliminated in one untraceable act."

"Look, I don't like Sister Ayayah and I didn't do a good job hiding it, but why would she kill me? I haven't *done* anything to her."

"Oh, I hope that you were the most lamentable of all the deaths for her. A Sister, even if she didn't like you. If they knew the plan, I expect that the others on the team fought to save you. But in the end, if things went badly wrong, they couldn't risk you being tortured into admitting that you were working for the Chantry. That might cause the very war they were trying to avert. If you were dead, even if it was discovered that you were behind an assassination, you could be easily disavowed as a rogue; they could point to all the ways they tried to get rid of you, admitting you were a war hero, but presenting that as a problem because they couldn't get rid of you overtly, even if you were generally hated by the Chantry's leadership. You see, they agreed with you that the actual job—the improbable heist-rescue they pitched to you—was impossible, Viridiana. A heist with so many moving parts is doomed."

Vi sat down, deflated, hopeless. "Unfortunately, impossible jobs are Kylar's specialty."

"No one wanted this to happen the way it did. Not the empress, not Repha'im, not you or Kylar or the team or Logan or Jenine Gyre or even Sister Ayayah. No one really wins here."

"No, but some of us lose everything," Vi said. "But if I was supposed to die, then why'd they stick around in the escape boat? Why pick me up out of the waves at all?"

"Basic decency? Maybe not everyone was in on the whole plan? Certainly it would've been valuable to find out what happened to the storm ship before anyone else did. To see if you'd armed them with a new weapon. To know if they had to flee Alitaera or if they could go directly on to other assignments. Regardless, if you haven't noticed, many of the Sisters who 'saved' you are the same ones who are voting to give you to the Alitaerans for torture and execution. You make a much better scapegoat by being alive—briefly. It shows how fully they disavow your actions. But do you know, I've been pleasantly surprised? If it were personal, I would've expected Sister Ayayah to come gloat."

"Oh, she's got time yet," Vi said. Vi suddenly imagined Sister Ayayah waiting outside the chamber where they were to fit Vi with the mind wipe spell. Sister Ayayah would approach, dabbing at her dry eyes with a handkerchief, and then she would lean close and hug Vi, and whisper some poison in her ear.

Vi put her head in her hands. It was one thing to go to her own death stoically. It felt a lot worse to face death knowing it would seal Sister Ayayah's victory and aid her rise to power.

"I'll have to study her in further depth," Sister Ariel said, pensive. "It seems to me that she's no mastermind, simply a survivor. Her plans didn't work flawlessly—perhaps because they involved people like Kylar and you doing what was expected and logical—yet somehow, she appears positioned to come out of a disastrous special operation she led without any negative consequences to her own career. That's surprising. I mean, she was willing to aid in the murder of eleven hundred eighty-four people immediately and far more later, but honestly? It was a good plan!" Sister Ariel saw Vi's look and added quickly, "I mean, if you're a soulless hag without a functioning moral compass or any decency."

But Vi's thoughts had turned inward. Her voice was barely over a whisper. "I thought I was saving them. I thought I was saving Kylar and Caedan both. You're telling me..." She could see it now, suddenly, starkly. "I thought it was *Kylar* we were playing, that he was secretly the Fool of our heist. He had to see everything and put it all together the wrong way so that he would do exactly the right wrong thing. But he wasn't alone. I was the Fool, too. They were playing *me*. They knew only I could deceive Kylar—that he wouldn't let his guard down for anyone else. Only I could betray him so completely. I did exactly what they wanted."

"Don't count that a flaw, child. You trusted your Sisters, who are sworn to look out for you. It doesn't make you a Fool to be fooled by family. It makes those who betray you traitors."

"Traitors who believed they were saving the Chantry," Vi said bitterly. Did that make them not traitors at all, but simply women who did what had to be done?

"Traitors who may indeed have saved the Chantry. Traitors regardless. They betrayed Kylar, they betrayed their oaths, and they betrayed you."

"And if we call the Sisterhood back to a new emergency convocation, and we tell them all the truth, what will they say? Will they denounce Ayayah and the special team, or will they say they did what they had to do? Will they turn their heads and say war is ugly and because it's so ugly, sacrificing a few lives is worthwhile to avoid it? They've already said as much, haven't they, by handing me over?"

Sister Ariel looked drawn and worn. "No one's at their best, here, Viridiana. It will be a vote that haunts many a Sister for the rest of her life."

"Is that the only difference between the Chantry and the streets, then?" Vi asked bitterly. "Everyone does what they must to protect themselves, but when the Sisters do it they feel bad? That's it? That's not good enough. I was ready to die for what I thought this Sisterhood was, but I'm not sure I want to die for what it actually is."

Sister Ariel heaved a deep sigh. Vi had the sense that the next words, chosen carefully, cost the woman dearly. "Maybe...maybe you shouldn't," she said. "Maybe sometimes we live to see institutions we've believed in for our whole lives become something else. When the price to save something good is to do something evil, it behooves one to ask whether one has saved goodness and stopped evil, or merely switched their places. The reason I serve the Chantry is that this Sisterhood overwhelmingly and consistently does good. If it ceases to overwhelmingly and consistently do good, I risk serving an institution unworthy of my devotion."

"Maybe they're not wrong," Vi said, empty. "I'm nothing. Compared to all the Chantry does all around the world, I'm an insignificant line in the ledger. One debit in a ledger with credit after credit. Too small to matter."

"Sister Ayayah believes so. Others may agree, reluctantly or otherwise. I do not. And I will stand up and say so, until they stop me."

"Until...? You don't—you don't think they'll try to kill you, too?" Vi said, stirring.

"I doubt they'll hand me over right away. Maybe they will. They might say I was your handler, the mastermind of the plot, and hope that the empress takes it as a gesture of good faith. They might be arguing about it right now. But even if they don't, they'll have to kill me sooner or later. They know I can't be controlled, and they know I won't keep my mouth shut. So I'll likely be joining you in the not-too-distant future."

Sister Ariel said this without emotion, too. As if her own continuing life were simply another problem for the Chantry—and a problem with an obvious solution.

But all Vi's sorrow was churning slowly into rage. "So Kylar saves thousands and damns himself in the process, and the woman who set him up gets a medal? Even though he stopped her from doing most of what she was trying to do, she *still* wins?"

"So it seems, does it not? The ancients said that she who does violence to others does equal violence to her own soul, and—"

"I don't care what they said!" Vi stood up angrily. "She did all this, and—what? Some of my 'big sisters' knew and didn't do anything to stop her? Helped her? Those absolute pieces of sh"—she bit it off—"trash."

"Viridiana," Sister Ariel said sharply, "a Sister learns to control her tongue."

"I *was* controlling my—Is this really the time?"

"Proper control dictates using accurate language—and those Sisters are pieces of *shit*."

Ariel cursed so rarely that Vi knew the Sister meant to show she was on her side. Vi flickered a smile. But the joy was a guttering flame.

"I wish I'd realized all this sooner," Sister Ariel said. "Maybe I could've helped you in time to save you—and stop them."

"They've had their vote. They've decided their course. You said you're loyal to the Sisterhood above all."

"Oh, but I am! I am." She seemed struck by a thought. "Who is more loyal, the one who stands by and cheers as her sisters happily tread the path to hell, or she who shouts *stop* and stands in their way, even if her sisters hate her and denounce her and trample her and continue on regardless? I think the latter shows the best form of loyalty. I think it shows love."

That last word cut through Viridiana with barbs. She pulled her ponytail tight. She didn't remember pulling her hair up in the first place, but at finding it already tight, she remembered once again that she wasn't allowed to have a ponytail.

She pulled it tighter. "I don't want to die," she said. "More than that, though, I don't want to let her win. Are you sure we can't break out of here?"

Sister Ariel looked wistful, as if she wished they could make the attempt. "The spell locking us in is a variation of the Athinnesian Prison Box. It's a cube, tied on the outside. Each wall, the ceiling, and the floor are protected, and magical attacks simply make it stronger, pull the knot tighter, as it were. In fifteen to twenty hours I could untie it. However, I can't imagine they'll give us that long. I'm not categorically against hopeless gestures, so if you wish me to begin an attempt, I am willing to do so."

Vi cursed and slammed the book shut.

Sister Ariel looked scandalized—not by her language, but at mistreating a book.

"I read this whole stupid thing! I went through hell to finish, trying to find one helpful thing—and does it help? Not in the least!"

"Maybe you weren't paying attention to the right th—"

The book popped back open.

Both women stopped. Looked at the open book.

Looked back at each other.

"Look! Are there words?" Sister Ariel asked, clearly wanting to step closer, but mindful that the book didn't let anyone else read it. "A message?"

On an otherwise blank page, there were two words, centered.

Vi said aloud, "It says, 'Take me.'

"Uh...I can't take you," she told the book. "The Sisters have cast spells making sure no one can remove you from this desk. Not that we have anywhere to go. Right?" She glanced at Sister Ariel.

"Yes—what's it writing now?"

Vi didn't read it aloud now, but the words didn't disappear as Sister Ariel came to read over her shoulder. The page read, *They put binding spells on the book.*

"That's what I said," Vi said, feeling strange to be talking aloud to a book.

As she watched, it wrote, *While Kylar yet lives there is much I cannot tell you, but it's better that you have me than that they do. Don't take the book.*

"What's it mean, 'Don't take the book'?" Vi asked, looking over at Sister Ariel, who seemed suddenly excited beyond words, her hands fluttering. Vi followed her gaze.

The ink on the page shimmered, then the words began deforming, sentences running together like rivulets of blood, black ink glomming together, thick, rising from the open page to quiver there in a black metallic ball.

The black ka'kari.

Vi picked it up, stunned. "You? You were here all the time?"

Bringing a lantern close, Sister Ariel flipped through the pages of the book—the blank book. On each page, there were tiny holes where the ka'kari had eaten through the parchment to write words on the next page, spelling out the story as Vi progressed. She hadn't been able to flip pages to read ahead because there was no text waiting there to be read. The ka'kari had been telling her the story all along.

A voice spoke in her head, shocking her.

~Now you have a decision to make. If you hand me over to the Sisters, it may be enough to buy your life and your freedom.~

The last vote had been late last night. Most of the Sisters were still in the Chantry. Even those who had left wouldn't have gone far. They could be recalled. Mistakes could be undone, new paths found, new votes taken, old votes overruled.

CAN YOU TAKE ME TO KYLAR? Vi thought hard at the ka'kari.

~No need to shout. You read the tale's end. You know he hid his location, even from me. I can only show you where to start.~

She felt a pang to the depths of her soul. Here at the Chantry was everything she'd wanted and had thought she'd lost forever: more than friendship—*sisterhood*, belonging, and being important to important people, power and community and a place to learn and grow among people who knew far, far more than she did.

So things were harder here than she'd thought? So what? Anything good is worth fighting for, isn't it? She'd let them give her their thousand cuts and she'd fought back with the wrong weapons before—but she could learn. She could do better. She could make them need to take her seriously. She could wipe the smirk off that damned Sister Ayayah's face.

If she gave the Sisterhood the ka'kari, she could have all her dreams back. In truth, she would become more prominent and powerful than ever, because if the Chantry didn't hand Vi over to the Alitaerans, it would mean war, and that would mean the Chantry was going to need war mages more than ever. And she was the best of those.

They would need to recall the women Vi had already trained—the women who were loyal to her.

She was spinning out strategies—did she tell them she had the black ka'kari, or should she simply use it to unweave the mind wipe spells and come back unexpectedly?—but she was getting ahead of herself. She stopped.

She looked down to the ka'kari, troubled.

So you're the answer to Speaker Istariel's question. And mine, on the ship, when I saw that Caedan was somehow still breathing.

~What question is that?~

How is the child alive? The answer is you...you're the Devourer. You devoured Caedan's Talent, didn't you? Instead of killing him, you destroyed his Talent right before he could unleash the null storm. It knocked him out. You saved everyone.

~You call what I did *salvation*?~

Did you see through our deceptions? Did you know about all our spells on the dagger?

~By the end, yes.~

All of them. Not just the deception spells, then, but also the spell that would've exploded, killing Kylar and the child both.

You saved Kylar. But, but he never realized it! You didn't tell him! I guess— I guess you couldn't at first, right? Because the null waves had interrupted your connection with him and he couldn't hear you. But why not afterward?

~He never asked.~

It said no more.

No, no, no! Don't give me that. I read this whole book. You volunteered information when you wanted to. Kylar might've believed that you're just a thing, but I know better. I saw how many times you helped him. You were his friend. How could you do that to him?

~His friend? Kylar asked me to kill a child. Demanded it. If I didn't, he would've picked up that dagger and they both would've died for nothing. Or everyone would've died. What friend does that? Afterward, if I'd told him as soon as I could what I'd done, Kylar would think he'd defied fate and the whole world again, that he'd found the third way, that he is just that special. You think that's justice? Kylar tried to murder a child. Justice is that he thinks he succeeded. If he lives a thousand years, he'll live knowing that's the kind of man he is.~

Vi put a hand to her mouth. Kylar would never be the same. Even if Vi found him someday and told him all the truth, the man she found might never be more than a shell.

Was it worth it, leaving everything, abandoning all her dreams, if that's what she found?

Then what's justice for me? she asked the ka'kari. *I'm the one who tricked him into doing everything he did!*

~You're not a Night Angel, so that's not my problem.~

Trembling, Vi looked at the paths before her, defying her yet again. Every time she thought she'd made a choice, the other choice tempted her once more. She might give up everything to save Kylar, and find there was nothing left of him to save. Besides, Kylar was gone! He didn't want to be found. He'd hidden himself, and he was uniquely suited to hiding himself very, very well. He was as good as dead.

"Are you talking to it?" Sister Ariel asked.

Vi looked over at her, startled out of her reverie.

"What is it saying? Is it offering you things? Trying to bribe you?" Sister Ariel asked. "The Chantry believes that the ka'kari hold the keys to higher forms of magic than anything we know. Immortality, imperviousness to the elements, limitless Healing, and more. For even the least of the ka'kari, the Chantry would gladly go to war with Alitaera. And the black is by no means the least of them. If you offer it to them, in return you can demand anything and everything you've ever dreamed of."

"Thank you, Sister Ariel, you've made things incredibly clear."

"I have?"

"I don't know a whole lot about making good choices, but I know all about bribes. So on one side, there's everything I could ever dream of, and on the other, sacrificing my position and every comfort with no guarantees it will ever amount to anything. The only thing extra I get down the terrible path is whatever tiny bit of self-respect I earn back along the way."

After watching someone else's tale scrawled before her eyes, Vi felt something changed about how she thought about her own. Life isn't a book where you can flip to the end to see if the tale ends happily enough to be worth pursuing. You can make goals, but you have to jot one page at a time, one paragraph, one line, one word, knowing every time you touch the quill to the page that some other character you have no control of may come crashing into the story to change everything.

But as much as it seemed that the choice of what she was going to do next was all about Kylar, in the most important way it wasn't about Kylar at all. He was merely the present iteration of a recurring question that Vi would have to answer in love and war and everything in between until her answer became part of her character: *What kind of woman am I?*

For Vi, for today at least, and for as long as she had the strength and the breath to keep it up, the answer was, *I'm the woman who makes the stupid choice that lets me sleep at night.*

It wasn't a great answer, but it fit her.

She smiled tentatively.

"Seems you've made your choice," Sister Ariel said. She smiled wistfully.

"I have. But you haven't made yours."

"What do you mean?"

There was something immensely gratifying in seeing the brilliant Sister with a puzzled look on her face. Vi said, "You wanna come along?"

Sister Ariel shook her head. "Me? Don't be ridic—" Then she stopped, her expression froze, and then expressions flitted over her face as quickly as a hummingbird's wings beat, ending in a slowly spreading smile. "Why, yes, I think I do. I think I very much do." She sounded surprised at herself. "Will you have me? You have to know I'll slow you down."

"No, you won't, because you're only bringing two books."

"Two?!" Ariel looked like a mother being asked to save only two of her many children.

"C'mon. You've already memorized all the good ones anyway, haven't you?" Vi said.

"Well, I—why are you saying this like it will be easy to get out? We're stuck, Viridiana."

"No, we're not. And call me Vi." Vi lifted her hand, and the black ka'kari pooled into it.

Sister Ariel's eyes widened with understanding, but she raised a finger.

"Viridi—Vi," Sister Ariel said. "Before you touch that door, you must know there will be guards outside. They will trigger alarms that will draw many, many more."

Without answering, Vi walked over and extended the ka'kari into the nexus of the magics holding the door locked. In moments, with a rushing sound, the weaves of the Athinnesian Prison Box were sucked into the ka'kari. Then Vi put the black ball into the heavy lock mechanism.

As the latch melted and voices rose in shock outside, Vi smiled at Sister Ariel, broadly now. "I think we can handle it."

Chapter One Hundred Six

Slouching Toward Justice

The kid is out late, first slumming around with three runty friends barely in their teens like he is. Then they leave one by one as the night falls, and only his little girlfriend still hangs around with him. They walk together shyly, not three sloppy Cenarian blocks from Lord Repha'im's estate where I first met the little streetballer, while I walk the rooftop above, rope in hand, watching like an unholy chaperone, patient for my moment.

They stop at the corner of my building, as far below me as my old idealism, my weakness. The ka'kari covers my face with the mask of Judgment. He turns to face her, takes both her hands tentatively in his, as if screwing up his courage for a first kiss.

I toss a stone into the street not far behind her. They both startle, releasing each other, and she turns as she should. It's not a safe neighborhood. Monsters love Mother Night, and I am her favorite son.

It isn't easy, tossing a lasso vertically, keeping the loop open on the right plane when it reaches your target, but I don't think even Durzo Blint could've done better. Even as the midnight silk rope spools out from my left hand, with my right, I throw another rock, farther away. I stop the unspooling and step left to make the rope below swing, and then I throw a quick whip-snap down the rope.

The noose slaps under his chin and the whip-snap yanks the knot tight behind his head an instant later. The rock I threw crashing into the alley covers whatever sound he makes as I lift his skinny ass off the ground. I swing him around the corner of the building, reeling him in as quickly as I dare without snapping his neck. Gotta be careful. In wet work, a mistake can mean a dead kid. If you can't deal with that, you're in the wrong line of work.

Truth is, it's the wrong line of work. For anyone.

With smooth movements, I lift him another few paces, then throw a quick loop over a protruding roof beam and step back to the corner to see the girl.

She's just turning. I see her flinch at the emptiness where she expected to find him. "Zeddick?" she says. "Zedd?! Where are you?"

I step back toward him, hoisting him higher. She'll check this alley any moment.

He's fighting now, hands dug into the rope at his neck. Couple ways this could've gone. Could've snapped his neck outright. Or a silk rope like this could easily cut off enough blood to make him pass out quick before he strangled slow. He took the least convenient path; choking with his fingers luckily wedged in the right spots to keep himself from going limp and silent. I pull him up to where he can barely reach a rock ledge with his feet.

At first, in blind panic, he does all the wrong things. All the noisy wrong things. Doesn't notice the ledge until I bounce him off it a few times. He considers taking a hand out to grab the ledge—and reconsiders quick. Finally plants his feet on it.

Before he can do anything more, I lift more, pulling him to his tiptoes, his weight leaning out to space.

"Zeddick? This isn't funny!" I hear the girl call, her voice louder as she dares a look down our alley.

Little Zeddick can't speak. I don't know if he hears her at all. She doesn't look up, though. Most people don't.

I toss another rock down where I'd tossed the earlier ones, and at the sound, she bolts.

Smart girl. Smarter than he ever was, that's for sure. Smarter than me, too. She knows her limitations.

I find a place to tie off the rope, moving slowly now, lethargic as a spider with its prey trussed and ready in its larder. His gasping annoys me. The dead are quieter.

Usually.

Finally, eyes burning with smoking blue fire, I step to the edge of the building and look down on him. His eyes go wide at the sight of me, all in black with lightly pulsing blue accents, and his knees buckle.

He spins away from the wall, retching, gargling. He kicks but can't reach the ledge.

I grab the taut rope and swing him back in.

When he's recovered enough to hear me, I say, "The last time we talked, I gave you a choice. You remember?"

Even as he fights for breath, he nods tightly, with all the intensity of the condemned.

"One chance for mercy, or ruthless justice with no more chances, I said. Threatened you. You chose to keep serving Lord Repha'im. People died because of your choice. A lot of people. Some of 'em innocent."

I trail off.

I should go. Just leave him here. Let him live, as all the rest of us do, tortured, for however many minutes he can hold himself upright against despair and death. Then die the moment he weakens, as all the rest of us do. Except me.

I say, "My master taught me a threat's a promise. On the street, it's the one promise you can't break. An empty threat makes you weak, invites attack. But instead of the death you deserve, I'm gonna give you a gift, kid. Don't get excited. It's not a very nice one.

"Someday I'll be back. Could be next year. Could be ten. Longer maybe. You've lived as if your choices don't matter. They do. The gift is that you get to live knowing you live in the shadow of judgment. I'll be back, and I will judge you. Live every day as if you feel the hot breath of justice on the back of your neck.

"But I've lied before, haven't I? I've made one empty threat. Maybe this is one, too. That's your gamble, kid. You decide."

I kick the kid in the face, and he goes spinning. His hands knocked loose from the knot at his neck, he's unconscious by the time I lower him to the ground.

When he wakes, facedown in the grime of the alley, he stares unseeing at my other gift. His streetball, perfect and priceless. The bauble he gave so much for.

As his eyes slowly focus on it, he recoils as if it were a serpent. Stares at it. Staggers to his feet, and flees. He doesn't take the ball.

I can't decide. Does that make him an ingrate, an idiot, or someone who's learned something?

"Back to our project," I tell the ka'kari.

It doesn't respond. Doesn't ask why I'm speaking aloud rather than thinking words at it. Doesn't ask why I've kept it in my saddlebags, only taking it out when we're inside a tent for this whole journey. These gaps and oddities in our conversations are one of the things that remind me it's not a person. It's magic imprinted with a certain amount of person-likeness that I sometimes mistake for personality. It serves me according to its creation. No more. It's been a good tool, but it's not a friend.

"We got to where I traveled south before, didn't we? Let's erase most of this part. No one cares about travel descriptions. It's boring."

~The boring part where you befriended a wolverine and fought razorbeaks?~

I can't tell if it's mocking me or merely being factual. Again, I'm probably projecting too much personality on the thing. "Mention those in passing, I guess; otherwise skip the rest. It doesn't have anything to do with the rest of the job."

And on we go. Erasing my tracks.

I can't fix everything. Or don't, anyway. Some sections I edited at two different times. Others I can't bear to relive even once. All that really matters is that you can't find me, Vi. Sorry. Is it Viridiana now?

I guess I don't know what to call you. I don't know who you are. You tried, at the end, I know. Tried to stop me. Your Sisters couldn't have liked that.

You didn't make it in time to stop me, but you tried. This story almost had a hero. Would've, if I'd hesitated. It would've been you.

I probably should've rewritten all the sections with you in them, now that I'm sending you this. But I'm too tired. I have no shame left.

"You know what the problem is, right?" I ask the ka'kari days later, as I continue to ride.

It doesn't respond. It's in a pocket so it can't tell where I'm going, and I merely lay a finger on it when I want to make sure it can hear me. I don't really know how much it absorbs about its surroundings even in the best of times, but for now, the less it knows the better.

"I'm the Avatar of Justice, but I've made justice impossible. I deserve death for what I've done, but if I give myself the death I deserve, someone else will die in my place, and I'll come back anyway."

I think about a few people it could be. I don't know the rules exactly, how it chooses who dies for me. The ka'kari won't tell me. But I know that the person who dies for me is someone bound to me by love. My love? Their love? Does it have to be both? I don't know. Regardless, if I die, someone I love dies, and I come back. I have no choice in the matter. Not after the first time, when I didn't know what I was choosing.

If I kill myself, who dies this time? Vi? Maybe Durzo, out there wherever he is, finally stripped of his own immortality. Maybe Count Drake or Ilena Drake. Haven't I cost them enough? Maybe Uly? Wonder how she is these days. I wonder if my killing curse would go further afield.

Does love bind me and Momma K? For that matter, when the bond is invoked, how does it work? Does the person have a chance to deny it? If they're a mage, could they stop it?

For now, it doesn't matter. It works. I've seen it kill. I can't allow that. Killing someone else for my crimes is the opposite of justice. Even risking it is intolerable.

But equally intolerable, equally unjust, is letting a murderer off without any punishment at all.

The last time she crossed my path on the storm ship, Queen Gyre whispered in my ear. Knowing what I was going to do, she said, "I know nothing can stop you. I know the world will need you again. But I don't care about the world. I know you'll torture yourself, but that's not enough. You won't die, and for what you've done and what you're going to do, I pray you suffer every torment. I only wish you could burn for eternity. Forever would be too short a time for you."

Dorian told me, back in Elenea. Told me he wasn't trying to change my path, that he knew he couldn't. He wanted me to know when I didn't change it would be because I'd chosen not to.

He asked me, 'Who judges the Night Angel?'

As the Night Angel, you'd think I'd know a lot about justice. I don't. Not really. But I know this. To the oppressed, justice is welcome. To the suffering innocent, justice is beautiful. To the rest of us, justice is terrifying. And I know what I deserve.

So I go now, toward my rough-hewn approximation of justice. I go toward hell.

It isn't as easy as you'd think. It takes a blacksmith and a stonemason and a skilled mage willing to enchant a book with no questions asked. A black ka'kari is quite a help, though, when you're preparing hell—in all the ways, come to think of it.

When we arrive at the place I've chosen, I leave the saddle on the horse, and his barding to protect him from the razorbeaks. They won't attack him here in the trees, but one or two might as the beast makes his way out. I put a heavy feed bag on him. The man I bought him from said the horse had a good sense of direction and would always wander home.

Shading my eyes, I look up at the cliff. I'm not going to describe it or I'll make it too easy to find, but it's beautiful out here. Feels surreal.

I pull out the ka'kari and cup my hand around it. I don't know how it senses things, but I need it to see as little as possible.

I show it the contents of the saddlebags, including the enchanted tome that's my diary, right on top. A flap covers the saddlebags. Once it's inside, the ka'kari won't know where the horse is going, so it won't be able to retrace its steps.

Slinging the ropes over my shoulder and taking my iron walking stick, I say, "Mark this place. You'll have to find your way to the saddlebags. You said you can do that, right?"

~I did. I can.~

I must be nervous, making it repeat itself. Now I tuck it away again.

I hike all day. I do things to make it harder for anyone to follow me. Again, pardon me for not telling more. I'm terrified, and I'm sure part of me is trying to hide clues to help me escape the sentence I've decreed for myself.

How do you pay for the inexcusable? With the unimaginable.

I have to fight off one of the razorbeaks when it tries to pluck me from the cliff face so it can eat my flesh after I fall to the rocks below. As the day passes, I'm forced away from the face of the mountain as it becomes too steep.

By nightfall, I reach the peak, set up my ropes and safety harness, lower myself, and take out the ka'kari once more, again shielding its view as much as I can. At my request, it bores a hole into the exposed cliff face.

Then I feed my metal 'walking stick' into the hole and, with a hammer and my Talent, pound it deep into the rock until its deepest part bends, mushrooming inside the cavity, holding it like a fishhook. There's only a small iron circle sticking out of the rock. I try to pull it out with all the force of my Talent, but it doesn't budge. I hammer on it some more to make sure. If I've done things right, though, I'm being overly careful, because I won't be able to get any leverage to pull it out. But I need to make sure.

My future opponent will be wily and desperate and strong.

I climb back up.

On the top, I sit on the bare, wind-scoured rock, smelling the trees far below on the wind, watching the stars turn in their courses, slowly fading as the east turns gray. There's almost no life here. A few splotches of lichen cling stubbornly to the rock. A tiny seedling is attempting to grow in one crack where some dirt has accumulated. I turn my eyes to the horizons, where I can see— well, never mind what, descriptions might make it possible for someone to find me. But what I see is glorious, in a way only muted by my own despair. I'll soon enjoy the sunrise, if enjoy is the right word.

I made choices all along the way. Choices that mattered. Choices where things would be different now if I'd chosen them instead. At the end, maybe I made the only choice I could. But I made it, no one else. And now it's time to pay.

Most people don't understand my work: They think murder is the hard part.

In the beginning, maybe. But even then the hard part wasn't the dying; the hard part is the living. I deserve to be condemned to death. Instead, I'm condemned to live. This will be torture. But I'll survive. Jenine told me as much. She didn't say it to comfort me. It doesn't, except that I know what I face here won't kill me, so it won't trigger the terrible power of my immortality and cause someone else's death.

Standing, I pour the last of my water out onto the tiny seedling, then toss the waterskin off the precipice. I fit the manacle to my forearm. I was worried that with a normal manacle, if I go out of my mind, I might simply tear off my thumb and little finger to slip out of the cuff, so I had this one custom-made to my arm, wide and tight, reinforced, hardened, unbreakable.

Sun's almost up. Time. I scatter my tools and weapons, flinging them as far as I can with my Talent. I set the ropes up again with a knot I'll be able to release from below.

I touch the ka'kari. Who am I without it?

I don't know. But I don't think much of the man I was with it.

"Hey," I say. "You're going to go through a few hands before you get to Vi, if you ever do. I did what we had time for, but if you do end up telling this story, could you...clean it up a bit?"

~I'll take out all the naughty words.~

That's not exactly what I meant.

~The rest doesn't need cleaning up.~

I breathe slowly. I see the silhouette of one of those hateful birds in the distance, winging this way. I wish I could...

Death always cuts off life midsentence. It's only right that this living death should plague me with guilt for things left undone.

"I guess we'll have to disagree about that. But you owe me nothing. Do as you see fit."

There are drawbacks to letting others tell your story. When I dictated this, I said it was for Count Drake at first, then myself, then Vi, but I always imagined some audience, didn't I? Said I'd let you get a peek at my life, but not too much. Made a deal with an audience that didn't even exist yet.

Why'd I do that? Who asked me for that deal? Sure, I tried to tell things straight, mostly. But when I decided not to tell about the look in that soldier's eyes when he tried to stab me but impaled his friend instead, did I skip that because it wasn't relevant to the outcome of the story or because I thought my listeners couldn't handle it—or was I hoping that by never describing it I could skip my nightmares about it, too? When I edited out so many horrors on their journey between my eyes and my mouth, was that to spare some stranger listening to this tale years from now? When I took all these steps to back away from my own story, was it really for you, or was that for me?

I said I went and confessed to Logan, Vi. I didn't.

I lied. I couldn't face him.

Do you see the extent of my failure now? Do you see what I am? Supposedly I'm the Avatar of Retribution, but this—*this*—is easier for me to face than Logan, my king and once my best friend.

I climb down the cliff face for the last time. I chain my manacle to the end of the spike protruding from the rock. The giant razorbeaks, birds the size of condors but far more intelligent, have seen me now. The villagers told me those birds never forget a human face and hold a grudge forever. When I came through last, in that section I mostly erased so no one would be able to find me, I killed some of them. They followed me for days, and attacked together, intelligently.

I expect they're going to feature prominently in my coming agonies.

Holding myself precariously by my free hand and my toes and leaning against the rope, I slowly work the knot above me free. As the rope drops, I lose my tenuous grip and am caught to swing painfully by the one arm chaining me to the precipice.

I'm still holding the end of the rope. It's my second-to-last hope.

I toss it away, watching it twist in the cold wind until it disappears from sight.

Then I take out the ka'kari. With it, I can escape even this.

I'll need to throw it so it lands in the tiny clearing near the horse. It'll glom onto the guide rope, climb it, and then devour it, freeing the horse, and then slip into the saddlebags. The ka'kari seems to stick to my hand as I empty my Talent into it to make sure it has whatever magic it needs.

~You don't need to do this.~

"Yes I do."

~There are other paths to redemption.~

"There isn't any path to redemption for me. That's not what this is about."

More and more razorbeaks are circling now. Their raucous caws are taunts. They're eager for revenge, eager for flesh. They'll soon have both. But my nerve is failing me. I hoist myself up on my manacled wrist so as not to louse up my throw. The birds seem now a gathering cloud, black and blinding as my sins. If I wait until the first beak or claw tears me, I'll never throw the ka'kari away.

I wanted to be stoic. Truth is, I'm a coward.

But you know what? You're a coward, too. Not Vi, I mean *you*. You're the one fascinated by killing, not me. I became a killer so I could survive. So I wouldn't be constantly afraid. You come to all this killing for entertainment. You ask others to do the violence you love. You're the one who sends your sons and daughters to patrol the darkness, to fight your wars. If they come back, you call them heroes. You know why you do that? It sets the ground rules. You're telling them what stories they can't share, what you refuse to hear. You send children into the werewolf night, then demand they come home tame, stubborn fur shaved down to baby-soft skin, claws trimmed to neat fingernails, clothes pressed, stories appropriate. And on those nights when the moon comes out for them, you demand they hide themselves away, so you can ignore the prices they pay, so you can tell yourself your hands are clean.

You think this story is only about me? Go to hell.

Or maybe I should say, come to hell. The werewolves and I are already here.

I wanted to face this bravely.

But now my chest is so tight I can barely inhale, breaths shallow, quick. I lower myself to the limit of my chain again, a deserter, fearful, weak. The world seems to be closing in.

Sobs rack me and I grip the ka'kari so tightly my arm shakes.

Do it, Kylar. Damn you. Do it!

I gauge the distance again, though I've got it locked in my mind. I was always a good throw. But I can't do it, can't throw away my last hope.

Then the image comes back, as vivid as madness, stern as justice: the *thunk* of a weapon slamming home. My son's wide, blue-blue eyes as their light guttered, snuffed out by the one who should love him most.

My hand loosens on the ka'kari, until my grip is as loose and careless as my grip on life itself. I hold here nothing of worth. To hold on to the ka'kari is to hold on to power, is to hold on to my way out, is to become a thing I despise even more than I already do.

I overflow with disdain for myself and for my hopes and for all my striving to save something I don't even want to keep. This isn't courage. Don't you dare admire me for this. Don't think I'm brave. The soldier who has a beloved wife and children awaiting his return and yet still charges the enemy lines? *He* is brave. A madman charging the lines hoping the enemy puts an end to his suffering is something else. It's not courage to risk losing something you hate.

Any more thinking now is mere delay, and the birds are swarming. They come to feed. There's no more thinking to do. There's a price to be paid. Only actions matter.

I hoist myself up, and throw

Acknowledgments

I've been wanting to write this book from the moment I sent in the galleys of *Beyond the Shadows* to my publisher and thought, *Now what?*

But I had a problem: My skills weren't up to the task I envisioned. I could write the story I had in mind, but could I do so masterfully? Writing a long series of long novels has a way of exposing one's weaknesses as a writer—and even as a human being. Thus, the Greek philosophers' injunction "Know Thyself" may warn a level-1 debut novelist armed with rusty pen and wearing a loincloth of reputation (−1) not to wander into the level-70 dungeon called "So You Think You Deserve an R. R.?"

I didn't feel ready yet, so I decided to power level by taking a brief writing detour. Sure, I'd been building Midcyru for eleven years at that point, but now I was a bona fide pro! I'd build a brand-new world, dash off three books in three years, and then I'd come back to Midcyru armed with new skills and fresh perspectives.

I have come back with new skills and fresh perspectives. But not in three years. Nor in three books. So my first thank-you has to go to you Night Angel fans who have been waiting nearly as long as I have to see more Midcyru.

My next thank-you has to go to John Scalzi, who made me the kind of friendly wager that Kit Marlowe and Will Shakespeare surely bandied back and forth. On hearing me say that after the massive tomes of Lightbringer, I was going to write a shorter book, John said, "Ha! You epic fantasy people couldn't write a short book if your life depended on it. How long's this 'short book' gonna be?"

Me, trapped: "Maybe 125,000 words?"

John: "You call that short? The average thriller is 80k! But fine. I'll bet you—" Here he tossed a brick of white powder onto the table. "Do you know what that is?"

"Cocaine?" I asked, looking for hotel security.

"We're in Michigan, not Miami. It's a kilo of confectioner's sugar. The good stuff. Translate that kilo into dollars and that, sir, is my bet that you can't write a book that's under 125k words."

I blanched. "John, that's gotta be, like, five dollars! You can't be serious."

"I see," John said. "You're scared."

So I've been on the hook since then. I've pared down this volume, cutting every extraneous adverb and excising each unnecessary "said" to starve it down to its current lean, veiny fighting weight of 315k.

The mathematically astute among you may have already realized that 315k is somewhat more than 125k. Now you understand why I need your help. Buy a second copy. Give it to a friend. John asked some gentlemen wearing fake Rolexes and tracksuits to collect my debt.

Do you remember how that friendly rivalry between Marlowe and Shakespeare ended? I'd forgotten, too. Turns out, one day Marlowe was knifed in a tavern over an unpaid debt.

This novel started as something simple, intended to showcase the strongest of my current skills. I planned to get in and get out. Easy. (With Scalzi's loss and cash sweetening my triumph.) Then the story insisted on becoming something far more ambitious. My agent, Donald Maass, was there all the way, encouraging me to dare the perilous road that tempts fate and failure, helping me dodge the lorries and leap over the speeding Maseratis. I'd planned to write a shorter book more quickly. I'm so happy I didn't. You've been a gift, Don. My thanks to the rest of the crew at DMLA, too, especially Katie Shea Boutillier.

In recent years, there's been a burgeoning movement of scholars and martial artists decoding and translating treatises by historical European duelists. Most of these treatises were selling something—often their authors' sometimes dubious skills as teachers. So a skeptical eye is required. Fiore dei Liberi was a fourteenth-century mercenary who became a fighting master and wrote an illustrated fighting manual called *The Flower of Battle*. (I mainly consulted the Richard Marsden and Benjamin Winnick version.) Many of the positions therein seem at first to be fanciful rather than practical. But Fiore dei Liberi, it turns out, was the real thing. I found the videos by Akademia Szermierzy (on YouTube and Patreon) wonderfully helpful in demonstrating how even the more outlandish positions actually do work. They're also a lot of fun to watch. Also check out Adorea's "longsword fight" on YouTube. It's far cooler than the usual Hollywood sword fights where even plate armor parts nicely if you slash it with appropriate conviction.

Bradley Englert, I've been so happy to have you as my editor. You've been a true partner in both art and business. On the page and off it, you've done a hundred things to make this book better for me and for readers and listeners for years to come. Thank you for pursuing excellence with me.

One of my favorite parts of the writing life is when I get to interact with amazingly skilled and invested people in adjacent fields. Seeing a pro do work that's close enough to mine that I can understand what they're doing (though I certainly can't do it myself) is a real joy. Managing Editor Bryn A. McDonald brings together a linguist's understanding with an artist's eye. Bryn jumped in to save me when a production thing went sideways—and then saved me from myself dozens of times throughout this book. A question from her might go like this: "The normal rule is X, but I see that you're breaking it because of Y. To be consistent, would you like to also do Y 600 pages later when Z?" Thank you, Bryn. You were far kinder to me than I deserve.

Simon Vance, it's a joy to witness how much your performances add to my words. After your work with Lightbringer, I knew the greatest gift I could give my audiobook listeners would be to beg you to bring your talents to Midcyru. I can't tell you how grateful I am that you made room in a very busy schedule to make it happen. (And a special thanks to Hachette Audio and to my editorial team for going above and beyond what is required of them to bring you in.)

Lauren Panepinto, you're brilliant. The task you took on this time around wasn't simply to make one book cover that looks amazing (though you certainly did that); you had to refresh a series whose original covers—that you also directed!—were groundbreaking when they came out but, through being copied, slowly lost their impact. Added to that, you and Alex Lencicki and Ellen Wright and Rachel Goldstein and Tim Holman and Bradley took on finding a new direction to bind the identities of my two very distinct series into one united identity. I never wanted to be a brand; I wanted readers to look to the *books*, not to the writer who made the books. But one can be too much a purist, and the Ka'kari Codex and the Lightbringer series do have one element in common: the author. You and your teams have been doing amazing work in managing that pivot. You all have gone the extra mile to make sure your teams are nailing it at every juncture—and you've been so kind to include me in discussions where I likely mostly functioned to slow down the pros' work. My thanks to Tim Paul for the beautiful maps and interior art, and to Will Staehle of Unusual Co. for the stunning covers. (He also did the reimagined covers for the entire Night Angel Trilogy.) Paola Crespo, Senior Marketing Manager; Natassja Haught, Channel Marketing Manager; and Stephanie A. Hess, Senior Designer, I'd say your work picks up right around the time mine slows down—but the truth is, you're always doing something to intrigue potential readers, to remind fans, and to make this work look as sleek and buttoned-up as possible. You're all immaculate professionals who by some dark arts have convinced the world I'm a professional, too. Thank you.

Melanie, you've been the one who picks up so many things I can't or don't want to do. One might say it's a thankless job, except that once every few years I say, "Thank you." Yes, that was it. But seriously, thank you for sailing the word seas as the Dread Pirate CAPSLOCK, for managing everything from the beta read to the webstore and tackling so many random things so I can have more time to write.

Any struggling writer has either had someone offer to read their book or has asked someone to do so. It rarely goes well. Eyes especially tend to glaze over when you can quote "Paperback Writer" by the Beatles and mean the words literally: "It's a thousand pages, give or take a few/I'll be writing more in a week or two…" So it's not fair that somehow I got Grace Bower, Ryan Bruckman, Kris DeAngelis, John DeBudge, Nick Freeman, Rob Goods, Craig Hanks, Heather Harney, Tim Harris, Oli Henderson, Drew LaMunyon, Sarah Lockwood O'Brien, Nick Pelto, Chris Ridenour, Elisa Roberts, Sophie Thornton, and Rob Verstegen to volunteer to be beta readers. And then when I decided to make some significant changes and asked if a few of you might be willing to relive the whole ordeal and read it all again—almost every one of you did. You caught continuity errors, you answered and asked delicate questions, and you picked up on foreshadowing with scary accuracy (especially on the second read-through). Some of you have an editorial eye as good as any professional editor I've worked with. You put an extraordinary amount of passion into a highly imperfect book. The final product is a…highly imperfect book. (But *less* imperfect, right?)

Dr. Jacob Klein, our long talks always give me plenty to think about. I really wanted to use that Glaucon quote. Hopefully by the time I do, I won't have forgotten I got that from you. Or maybe that true story about that guy's awesome speech as he was going to his execution? (Clearly, I need to shoehorn more executions into my next book.)

While signing many, many tip-in sheets for my last book, I discovered that fountain pens help me avoid carpal tunnel pain. I was already finicky about my pens, but Goulet Pens and Tomoe River FP paper and Galen Leather journals and Jacques Herbin sheening inks opened a whole portal of temptation for me. When I realized there's something about the physical movement of pen across paper that gets me unstuck when I'm stuck on-screen, I leapt through that portal wholeheartedly. Much of *Night Angel Nemesis* was drafted with a Visconti Homo Sapiens Bronze Age with a Cursive Italic nib ground by nibmeister Mark Bacas. Fountain pens are amazing, and I encourage every writer with a budget to avoid them.

The phrase "the cold courage of despair" was G. K. Chesterton's. He was referring to the Roman people's attitude about facing Hannibal's armies as they rampaged unstoppably through Italy, demolishing Roman legion after legion for *twenty years*. Elsewhere, I've quoted Aristotle and others, noting as I can that the words aren't mine: "As the Philosopher says…." Chesterton and Aristotle don't exist in Midcyru, but great lines deserve to be stolen, and stolen lines deserve to be credited.

There *is* an in-universe rationale for why certain bits of Earth wisdom and bons mots are present in Midcyru and also in the Seven Satrapies, but as none of my characters have yet had any excuse to find out why this happens (or even to know it's happening), I've chosen not to shoehorn in that bit of worldbuilding. The characters haven't needed to understand it yet for the novels to work, so the main reason for me to explain it in the text would be to show myself to be purposeful rather than haphazard. I've been waiting quite a few years for the right scene to present itself, however, and it still hasn't. I think I've got just the spot in the next book. And if not, the shoehorn beckons. Someday, little shoehorn, someday.

Kristi, when we got married, I said, "You know I hate repeating myself. So. I love you. If I change my mind, I'll let you know." You've been vital to every book I've written: my first reader and my sounding board, asking questions of such keen insight they make pieces fall into place, reminding me of truths of characters and myself—so there's no need for me to point out how profoundly you've done that again. You've always been as faithful as you are long-suffering, and as kind as you are wise, but you've also never liked being the center of attention, and I've never been one to express my gratitude in public at self-aggrandizing length, so I'm mentioning you briefly so no one thinks you're dead, but otherwise we'll skip all the saccharine and spare everyone the embarrassment.

My daughters. Oddly enough, I'm avoiding using your names here so that later in life you aren't known first as Brent Weeks's daughters, but as yourselves. You two have had a part in making this book, too. I know the cost a kid pays when they have a parent with a passion rather than simply a job. Your mother and I have tried to weigh carefully what it costs you when I travel or work late too many days in a row. I know that you have had to make sacrifices that you never volunteered for. Thank you for doing hard things.

Lastly, to my readers. In 2008, I asked you to take a leap of faith on this new writer. I said if you gave me a few pages, I'd do my best to take you on a helluva ride. In 2010, in the acknowledgments after *Black Prism*, I joked that on your way out, you should tell someone, "You gotta read this. No really. C'mon, there's a maa-aap!" More than a few of you did—and you recommending my books to people you thought would enjoy them has enabled me to keep doing the work I love. That surprise *extra* map when Kylar reaches Stormfast is my thanks to you.

Sincerely,
Brent R. R. Weeks